Th

Medici Queen

Book Three in the Medici Warrior Series

by Emily Bex

Foundations Publishing Company
Brandon, MS 39047
www.foundationsbooks.net

The Medici Queen
Book Three in the Medici Warrior Series
By: Emily Bex

Cover by Dawne Dominique
Edited by Laura Ranger

ISBN: 978-1-64583-033-7

Published in the United States of America

This is a work of fiction. Names, characters, businesses, places, events, and incidents are either the products of the author's imagination or used in a fictitious manner. Any resemblance to actual persons, living or dead, or actual events is purely coincidental.

The Medici Queen

Dedication

The Medici Warrior book series is dedicated to all the dreamers, the hopeless romantics, and to my partner in crime, Johanna Morisette.

Acknowledgements

This book could not have been written without the help of my collaborator, Johanna Morisette. She dragged me reluctantly into a world of vampires and inspired me to write. She had the initial vision for Shade and was instrumental in the development of his character. Throughout the seven years it took to write this series, she remained my sounding board for the development of the storyline. These characters, and this saga, would not exist if not for her constant support and input which kept me motivated to keep pushing forward.

Table of Reference

Italian to English Translator for Book Three....13
Recap of Book One and Two....15
1....17
2....21
3....35
4....45
5....48
6....52
7....61
8....70
9....77
10....80
11....89
12....95
13....104
14....109
15....112
16....116
17....120
18....127
19....130
20....134
21....140
22....144
23....149
24....156
25....158
26....165
27....169
28....173
29....176
30....179
31....181
32....191
33....203
34....206
35....214
36....221
37....223
38....227

39........229
40........232
41........238
42........242
43........244
44........246
45........250
46........254
47........259
48........261
49........268
50........274
51........276
52........283
53........289
54........292
55........295
56........299
57........317
58........322
59........327
60........333
61........341
62........353
63........357
64........360
65........366
66........373
67........379
68........385
69........389
70........392
71........398
72........407
73........411
74........415
75........421
76........423
77........426
78........430
79........436
80........439

81..443
82..448
83..457
84..461
85..466
86..469
87..472
88..477
89..480
90..484
91..492
92..495
93..498
94..502
95..506
96..510
97..520
98..524
99..529
100..534
101..541
102..544
103..547
104..549
105..552
106..560
107..564
108..567
109..572
110..580
111..583
112..590
113..593
114..596
115..601
116..604
117..606
118..609
119..611
120..615
121..618
122..621
123..625
124..629
125..633

126 637
127 639
128 641
129 648
130 652
131 659
132 663
133 666
134 669
135 672
136 682
137 686
138 695
139 697
141 705
143 710
144 712
145 715
146 718
147 722
148 727
About the Author 730
More From Foundations Book Publishing 733

Italian to English Translator for Book Three

Addio	Good-bye	***Alzati***	Stand-up
guerrieri	warriors	***Amica***	Friend
Amore	Love	***Bambino(s)***	Baby/babies
Bastardo	Bastard	***Bel***	Beautiful
Beleeza	Beauty	***Bellissimo***	Very beautiful
Bravado	Brave	***Buonasera***	Good evening
Cazzo	Fuck	***Ciao***	Hi/Hello
Dipendenzo	Addiction	***Dolce***	Sweet
Dormire	Sleeping	***guerrieri***	warrior
Familia	Family	***Figlia/Figlio***	Daughter/Son
Fino ad allora	Until then	***Fratello***	Brother
Grazie	Thanks	***Guerrieri***	Warriors
Impavido	Fearless	***Lei e il mio***	She is my
Vero amore	true love	***Madre***	Mother
Meile	Honey	***Mi/Mio/Mia***	My
Mio vampire	My courageous	***Coraggioso***	Courageous
Moltobella	Very beautiful	***Nostra Figlia***	Our Daughter
Padre	Father	***Per Favore***	Please
Per Sempre	Forever	***Rosso***	Red
Scusi	Excuse me	***Si***	Yes
Signorina	Young Lady	***Sorella***	Sister
Stupido	Stupid	***Ti Amo***	I Love You

Recap of Book One and Two: The Blood Covenant and The Turning

The Medici Warrior Series is a serial story told through a six-book series that must be read in sequence. The Medici Queen is book three of the series. If you have not yet read books one and two, *The Blood Covenant* and *The Turning*, stop reading now! Order and read books one and two before starting this book.

Re-cap of book one, *The Blood Covenant*, and book two, *The Turning.* (THIS RE-CAP CONTAINS SPOILERS)

In book one, Shade Medici, a vampire warrior king comes to the United States from his native Florence, Italy to provide protection services to another master vampire, Alec Canton and his mate, Larissa (Rissa). Alec and Rissa are both day-walkers and live freely among mortals. Alec has entered the world of mortal politics and holds a seat in the U.S. Senate with a goal of seeking the Presidency.

In the course of setting up protection for Alec, Shade meets and falls in love with a mortal woman, Kate Reese. Shade is royal blood and the sole surviving member of the Medici dynasty. He is expected to mate and produce an heir to maintain the longevity of the Medici coven. However, cross-species breeding is forbidden by the ruling Council of Vampires. Mortals are playthings, but they are frowned upon as mates. Shade ignores this directive as he pursues her, needing her to fall in love with him before she discovers he is a vampire. She gradually lets her defenses down, and succumbs to his charms. He convinces her to leave her home just outside Washington, D.C. and move with him to the estate in Virginia, which he named after his pet name for her, Bel Rosso.

Their relationship is a struggle as Kate tries to adapt to the changes of the vampire culture, and Shade tries hard to protect her from the more violent aspects of his world by keeping her secluded at Bel Rosso. Their world is shattered when one of Shade's ex-lover's, Sabine, shows up. Sabine sees this mortal female as someone underserving of the vampire king and tries to kill her.

Shade comes to realize that in order to protect her, he must take Kate deeper into his culture. She is introduced to the Medici warriors in Florence, where one warrior, Luca, is chosen to remain as her protector for life.

Kate becomes pregnant, presenting more complications as she is still mortal and their infant would be a half-breed, unable to inherit the Medici dynasty. Alec and Rissa see the pregnancy as an obstacle to their own goals as Shade's attention becomes solely focused on Kate. They devise a scheme that will kill the infant, and hopefully kill Kate at the same time. Their underhanded deception goes undiscovered...for now.

When Kate miscarries, the grief over the lost baby creates a divide between them and they both struggle to reconnect with each other. Shade takes his grief out in rage and anger as Kate retreats into a dark place. Luca acts as not only her protector, but as an intermediary, pulling the two of them back together. Seeking an outlet for her anger, book one ends as Kate is asking Luca if he will train her like a warrior. He reluctantly agrees as they both know this is a task that must be performed behind Shade's back, and without his approval.

In book two, the Aries coven continues to wreak havoc in Washington, D.C., keeping the mercenary warriors on their toes. The master of the Aries coven remains anonymous to both Shade and Alec, but is revealed to the reader as Max, a former lover of Rissa's, who has decided he wants her back in his life. His goal was to destroy Alec's ambitions, leaving him weak in Rissa's eyes, and win back her heart. Max seems to have forgotten Rissa has no heart for anyone except herself. However, Rissa being Rissa, she can't help but to play with fire and in her attempt to turn the tables on Max, she has an illicit affair with him, betraying Alec in the process.

Tomas, working as a mercenary for Alec, is actually an agent of Max's and helps Max set up a plan to destroy Shade by staging an ambush on the Bel Rosso estate and killing Kate. Without Shade, Alec is easy prey. And without Kate, Shade will crumble. The assassin Cuerpo is hired to take out Kate. While Shade and Luca are defending Bel Rosso against an attack from rogue vampires, Cuerpo has Kate isolated and alone inside the house. Cuerpo is expecting a fragile mortal, but what he encounters is a mortal trained by a Medici warrior who takes him out with a single kill shot from her crossbow.

Kate's skills are unexpectedly exposed, and Kate and Luca must come clean with Shade about Luca's efforts to train her. Although Kate is stronger since she has been feeding from Shade, Shade is more aware than ever that she will always be a target in his world, and he will have to make her immortal to protect her.

Shade and Kate return to Florence, where Kate is taken to the chambers below Castello for the turning where she will undergo the arduous process of becoming an immortal. When she emerges, she is officially mated to Shade, and royal blood, the new Queen of Medici.

1

Alec and Rissa arrived by private jet at the Firenze airport, where Alec had a private car waiting with Alto at the wheel. Rissa had packed half her closet for this trip. She had dozed on and off through the flight and slept now with her head on Alec's shoulder.

"Rissa, we're here, my darling. The car is waiting to take us to Shade's home."

This flight felt like it took forever, Rissa still had reservations about this trip, but she had no damn choice. Max could easily be here, or he could have sent someone here to come after her. She heard Alec's voice break through her light sleep as she sat up, looking out the jet window.

"Oh good, these long flights are ridiculous. Make sure they don't damage my luggage or leave anything behind. I need everything I've brought."

"Rissa, your luggage will be taken care of and delivered to the castle. Now come." Alec exited the plane with her, as Alto held the door open to the car. Alec allowed her to enter the car first, then slid into the seat next to her. "Refresh my memory. Have you been to Florence before?"

"Not Florence, Milan, of course. What fashion expert doesn't know Milan? Rome too, but Florence, no. Why do you ask? And how far is this drive?"

"Not too far. Alto has some Midnight for us. Would you like a drink? We'll drive through a little of Tuscany to get to Florence. The Medici Castello is on the far side of Florence. You'll see it as we approach. Just relax and enjoy the countryside. It's quite beautiful, if I do say so. This is all Shade's territory. Pretty much everything you'll see on this trip will be inside Shade's territory. It's been a while since the last time I was here."

She looked out the window and although the landscape was stunning, it did nothing for her, she was a city girl at heart. *He owns all of this? Damn, that bitch! She can't be happy enough with all his property, the bitch has to take my Paris house as well?*

"So, you were here before? I think you mentioned his home and visiting here."

"Yes, I've known Shade for centuries, my darling. Before I lived in the States and presented myself as American, I was British, lived in London mostly. That's where I first met Shade. I believe we met at a Gorean Cult orgy that was held in London." He laughed at the memories. "Let's just say we have found our association to be mutually beneficial through the years.

The castle is quite impressive, as I recall. Again, haven't been there in a few years. A little too opulent for my taste, but he inherited it from his father."

Rissa glanced over at him. "I knew you were British, but you've completely lost any accent, Alec. I was wondering, since we have a bit of a drive, are there things I should know before I get there about any protocol? I want to make sure I make no mistakes. I already know going into this I'm not well received by the masters."

He lit up a cigarette and cracked the window to release the smoke. "For our free time, there are no rules. We can do what we want. At the ceremony, you should only speak when spoken to. You shouldn't approach a master or his mate. Their mates will do the same. I may initiate a conversation with another master, or he with me. Other than that, I think you'll be fine. You've never seen a coronation, so I'd think you'll find it interesting."

"I'm sure I will since I've never had the pleasure, nor probably will again, unless, of course, they have brats." Sighing, she threw her head back on the seat. "All of this, she has all of this, and still she gets my damn Paris house. Seriously, Alec, there's something immensely wrong with that!" Leaning over, she kissed him on the cheek. "But I'm sure you'll find me an even better house in Paris. And besides, I get to spend the whole weekend alone with you, without Zena the bitch warrior."

Alec struggled to keep the annoyance out of his voice. "Rissa, first of all, it's my Paris house, not yours, but if it's important to you, although I can't imagine why because neither one of us ever takes vacation time, if you want a place in Paris, I'll find something. Now please, can we drop the subject? And that warrior bitch? She's there to keep you safe. What has you so disagreeable? Most women would be delighted to have this trip. Are you so jaded already, my darling? Eternity is a long time to be bored."

She laid her head back and looked out the window. "No, Alec. Point taken."

Watching as the Tuscan landscape slid by, she was lost in her thoughts. As they crested a hill, she saw they were approaching a huge estate and it was something to behold. She sat up straighter in her seat and cocked her head. "Is that it? Tell me, it can't be!"

Alec saw the castle ahead. "Hmm, I do believe it is. Welcome to Medici Castello, surrounded by formal gardens, and sitting on the banks of the Arno River."

Alto pulled up to the estate and stopped at the huge gates where he pressed the intercom button. Once he identified himself and provided the password, the gates were opened to him.

Rissa laughed, but an annoyed and jealous laugh. "Well, it's regal."

She watched as Alto pulled into the huge roundabout drive, the buildings and gardens went on forever. Several house staff came out to open doors and Alto held her hand as she exited the car. She remained quiet and waited for Alec to do whatever he needed to do to get them inside this palace. She intended to remain quiet or she'd never hear the end of it. This was important for him, and she wanted him to be proud of her and how she presented herself. The staff started removing the mountain of luggage from the trunk. Gi stood at the entrance, overseeing the activity. Alec led Rissa up the steps to the door where Gi bowed deeply.

"Master Alec. It has been too long. It is our pleasure to have you as our guest at Medici Castello once more. And Miss Benneteau, our warmest welcome to you on what I hope will be the first of many visits. My lady has requested we reserve the Gold Room for you. I think you will find it to your satisfaction. And this is Carlos. He will be your private butler for the duration of your stay. You will also have a personal maid, Miss Benneteau. Carlos will introduce her to you in your suite. I believe she is drawing a bath for you, so you may refresh after your long journey. Now please, come with me inside."

Alec took Rissa's arm and followed Gi into the grand foyer. *Ah yes, how could I have forgotten this?*

Rissa was already impressed with getting her own personal maid. She should have one of those at home. She made a mental note to work on that. As they were escorted in, she gasped. “My, this is impressive. It's gorgeous!” Her head appeared as on a spring, she couldn't take it all in.

Alec smirked, finally something had impressed her. He watched as she tried to take in the over-the-top opulence of this room with the gilded gold bannisters on the marble staircase, and the massive chandeliers.

Carlos stepped up to greet them and bowed deeply. “Master Alec? If you're ready, I can escort you to your room now. I or someone will be stationed at your door twenty-four hours a day. We've been informed you are both day-walkers. If there's anything you wish to see in Castello, please ask and you'll be escorted, otherwise, sir, I'm afraid you'd only get lost. Your car will be kept in the garage, and your driver has been provided with private quarters. You need only let us know if you wish to leave the premises and your car will be brought around. This way, please."

He led them up the massive staircase and down a long corridor of rooms, behind closed doors. When he reached their suite, he opened the door and stepped aside so they might enter. "If there's anything not to your liking, please let us know and we'll have it changed."

As Rissa walked into their room, she stood with her mouth open. *Is he joking? Not to my liking?*

“Alec, this place is immense. This is gold, real gold! Oh my god, look at these roses. There must be seventy roses in this bouquet. This is over the top. I can't imagine Kate living here, living like this, every single day. I'm jealous, I'm beyond jealous, I'm astounded. Now I do need a drink!" Turning to him, she wrapped her arms around him and kissed him on the cheek. "Thank you. Thank you for bringing me here, Alec."

Carlos bowed to her. "Miss Benneteau, my lady has requested you have fresh flowers every day of your stay. If you have a favorite, please let us know. Oh, and this is Rosa. She'll be your personal maid. Just ring and she'll respond, otherwise, you'll not see her."

Rosa curtsied. "Miss Benneteau, I've drawn a hot bath for you, and filled it with fresh rose petals, my lady's favorite. It's ready whenever you are. My lady requested you have silk robes to wear after your bath and when you're in your room. Please feel free to keep them as my lady's gift to you. Your toiletries have been laid out for you. Please let me know how I can be of service."

Nodding to Rosa, she perused the housemaid's outfit, the traditional black and white, and the Medici crest was everywhere she looked.

"I wish to bathe immediately, and you may assist me with my clothing. I also require all of my garments and shoes be unpacked and put into the wardrobes. Do you have rose-scented bath salts and oils since you have placed rose petals in my bath water?"

Turning to Alec, she smiled. "You won't mind if I smell like roses tonight, will you, Alec? Very romantic, don't you think?"

Alec dared not tell her roses were Kate's signature scent. "Of course, my darling, I'd find it quite romantic."

2

It had been two weeks since Kate stood in this master bedroom, preparing to go to the chamber for the turning. And now, she was here again, with Theresa preparing her for the Coronation Ceremony. Shade dressed in another room, assisted by Gi. He said he'd have Gi escort Shannon to the ceremony, since Luca must stand with all the other Medici warriors. Kate hadn't seen her mortal friend since the night of their food fight, before the turning. And now, tonight, she was to be presented to hundreds. She had paced until she had worn a path in the plush rugs that covered the marble floor. She stood at the window and watched as the people gathered, throngs of people, most of whom she didn't recognize. Her heart was pounding. She was more frightened of this ceremony than she had been of the turning. *What was Shade thinking? That I could be queen?*

Theresa spoke softly, "My lady, you should be putting on your gown now. We must stay on schedule."

Theresa removed the long white ball gown from the closet and laid it across the bed. The gown had an elaborately beaded and fitted bodice and a voluptuously full skirt, with layers upon layers of tulle. Theresa patiently waited for Kate as she stood at the window. "My lady?"

Kate turned to look at her. Theresa had been so helpful during this whole trip, she'd be sad to lose her when they returned to the States. She knew Shade had offered Theresa the opportunity to stay here in Florence with Marco, and Kate was happy for her. He said they'd bring Emma back to the States with them instead.

"You know, Theresa, we'll be returning to the States shortly after the ceremony. Shade is eager to get back to Virginia, to get the new warrior camp started. We won't have much more time together."

"I've decided not to stay in Florence, my lady. I wish to return to Virginia, if you'll have me."

Kate was startled by the news. "What? Is there a problem with you and Marco?"

"There's no problem, my lady, and I haven't yet told Marco, so I beg you to keep my confidence."

"Theresa, of course. But are you sure? You love him!"

"I do love him, my lady. But, with Marco, I'll always be second place. He's a warrior first. He's a man who prefers the camaraderie of men, and only seeks a woman when he needs comfort. It's not a complaint, it's an observation. He doesn't desire children, he doesn't desire to settle down, and he's always looking for the next battle. I know he loves me, he'll always love me, but a life here with Marco would be lonely. I've been with the Medici household for many centuries. I came as a housemaid when Queen Portia still ruled. And now, I'll be Lady in Waiting to the Queen. I'll be nanny to the children of my King. I'll have served three generations of Medici's, and it's an honor I could never have imagined for myself."

Once again, Kate was floored by the devotion the staff had to Shade, and through him, to her. "Theresa, it's I who is honored. And quite selfishly, I'm delighted to have you stay with us, but please, be sure. Talk to him. And if you change your mind, I'll understand."

Theresa straightened the skirt of the gown master had designed for her. A one of a kind dress that looked like it came from a fairy tale, designed by Valentino. "We will talk, my lady, but my mind is made up. I wish to serve my king and queen and will follow wherever that takes me."

Kate crossed the room to stand by the bed so Theresa could help her get into the long gown with the voluminous skirt. "How will I ever walk in this thing? Will you be at the ceremony, Theresa?"

"Yes, my lady. I have a small role to play." Theresa lifted the dress and Kate put her hands above her head, as Theresa slipped the gown over her.

From underneath the dress, Kate asked her, "Do you? Are you nervous?"

"No, my lady, I'm excited and proud to stand before the Medici household and all the warriors and invited guests as your Lady in Waiting."

Kate had a nervous laugh, as she let the dress fall around her. Theresa buttoned each tiny button up the back of the fitted bodice.

"I wish I could say the same. I'm beyond nervous."

Kate lifted the skirt as she slipped the white satin heels on her feet, then walked to the mirror, dropping the skirt to the floor and taking in the image before her. It was almost impossible to tell the difference between her white skin and the snow-white dress. What did Shade call her? His lily white? Her hair looked even redder by contrast, and fell around her shoulders, her eyes looked more amber than brown. She looked the same as when she was mortal, and yet not.

Theresa stepped up behind her. "Beautiful, my lady. You'll take his breath away."

Kate caught her eyes in the mirror. "Will I? I know there are people in the crowd tonight who don't approve. Who'll never approve of his choice of a mortal mate."

"Perhaps, but no one that resides in this household, my lady. I promise you. For all of us, we've watched our master grow from child to man, to take the reins of this dynasty at far too young an age, and bear that burden and responsibility for all in his coven. It hasn't been an easy road for him.

We watched his loneliness as a child, we watched as he sought for and never gained the approval he so desperately needed from his father, we watched as he battled for Tuscany and established his dominance here, providing security for all of us, and then built upon what his father started. We all waited for him to find his mate, his queen, to share in all he had achieved, but we had all grown to think his heart was hardened after losing his own parents so young. He courted many, to be sure, but none captured his heart. We'd never heard him laugh. Oh, he would smile, but it was a smile that never reached his eyes. There was always sadness behind those eyes, until you, my lady. And now we hear laughter, we see a light in his eyes, and we watch his joy in bringing you joy. We watch him play, and chase after you, and I can promise, that food fight in the kitchen will be talked about through the ages. There's no one under Medici rule who will question his choice or challenge your right to rule."

Kate laughed at the memory of that night. It seemed so long ago already, another lifetime, another girl. The last time she stared into this mirror, Portia appeared to her, to give her encouragement before the turning. **"Do you see me now, *Madre*?"**

Kate watched as Portia's image appeared faintly in the mirror, superimposed over her own. **"*Si, mia figlia*, I see you and I am with you always, just as I am with him. You are right, *mia figlia*, there will be those who doubt, there will always be doubters. But you are Medici now, you must walk with pride, and do not show them your fear. Tonight, my only son will place a crown on your head, claiming you as his queen, The Medici Queen. Hold your head high, *mia figlia*, walk with a regal bearing, and bow to no one except your own master and maker. You have made me proud."**

Kate watched as Portia's image faded and she reached out to touch the mirror, Portia's hand reaching back, touching her fingertips as she faded from view.

"And now your red robe, my lady." Theresa carried the red velvet robe across the room to Kate and slipped it over her shoulders, as she buttoned the single frog closure at the neck. Kate lifted the hood over her crimson hair, tucking the loose tendrils back and pulling the hood forward so her face was partially obscured. Theresa nodded. "There, you're ready, my lady."

***

Looking into the full-length mirror, Shade was wearing the newly designed ceremonial leathers from Cory, bearing the Medici crest on his chest. Closing his eyes, he let his hands drop to his sides, taking a deep breath to calm his nerves. She was his, but until Malachi drank her blood, claimed her immortal and gave the Councils' blessing of her entitlement to be Medici Queen, he wouldn't be completely satisfied.

Shade had no doubts she would rise to be a mighty queen, more so even than his *madre*, to show them all she was born to be his and rule as a Medici. He realized he'd lived his entire life for this night. To have his beloved *bel rosso* reign beside him. The ceremony wouldn't be long, but filled with great tradition, and he knew Kate would be fine. He had fed her this night, right before leaving her to begin her own preparations. Those he loved were all here, Gi, Theresa, Marco, Luca, Raven, Marcello and Fiamma, waiting for the ceremony to begin.

Gi stepped up behind him. "Master, the time has come for you to escort our Queen to the Throne Room. All has been arranged, everyone is waiting and in place. Malachi has not arrived, but I am sure he will make an appearance worthy of his high status."

Lifting the heavy red robe, Gi carefully placed it over Shade's broad shoulders and defined back. He lifted the hood over his head and glanced over Shade's shoulders as their eyes locked in the mirror. "*Si*, Master Shade, Christofano would approve. You befit your royal station, as does our queen. Hold your head up, show them who we honor as our master and king. Your *madre* and *padre* are among us this night. Neither would ever miss this event in your reign."

As Shade locked eyes with Gi, his words brought his chest up, his chin up, his eyes lit with pride. He stared at himself in the mirror and what he saw was what he had strived to become, a powerful master and king, in love and mated. Shade turned from the mirror, giving Gi a hug, which Gi returned in his fatherly fashion, but Shade's own *padre* didn't appear.

"I am sure he will be in his glory this night, Gi. He told me in the chambers he has accepted *bel* as my queen, just as *Madre* has as well. Thank you for all you have done to make this happen, make everyone comfortable here. I can never repay your dedication to me, my queen and my coven."

Gi could feel the truth of his love for her. He had watched as his master lost his way many times in his search for his mate. But Gi never doubted his choice of Kate, and the greatest reign of Medici lay in their future. He hoped he survived to see the next generation grow and prosper.

"There is one simple way to repay me, master. Walk out that door, claim your queen, and reign as only the Medici can."

As Gi gave him a smile, Shade spun on his heels and strolled to the door, walking proud and tall. Gi rushed out behind him to get to the Throne Room, making sure all the last-minute details were attended to, before the king and new queen arrived.

Theresa had just finished adjusting the red robe when there was a tap at the door. She moved to answer it and Kate turned, trying to manage the long skirt on the gown and the heavy velvet robe with the hood. Kate heard the door open and could feel him as he entered. She didn't have to look up to know it was Shade. Her head was bowed, and she saw his black boots, and a hint of the ceremonial leathers on his legs, and he too wore a long red robe. She raised her eyes to his and locked into that icy blue gaze. He gave her a soft smile as he walked to her and extended his hand. Kate placed her hand in his palm, and watched as he ran his thumb over the back of her hand. His dark olive colored skin was such a contrast to her lily white. Her voice barely above a whisper, she spoke to him. "I am ready, lover."

Raising her hand to his lips, he kissed her palm softly and laid it across his heart. "As am I, my Queen. I have been ready since I first laid eyes on you. I am with you, and I'll not leave your side. Never show them fear, you are Medici. Show them all what I see."

Turning, he led her as he did several nights ago. She was immortal now, their hearts and souls forever joined in love. As he led her to the Throne Room, no one was anywhere about, the house was still and quiet. Castello was feeling grand and glorious, a great night for all of those belonging to Medici.

Leading her along the great hall, there were many oil paintings of the past Medici reign, their ancestral history on display. He stopped at one grand portrait painted in oil, and Shade stood with Kate before the portrait of *Madre*, *Padre* and himself as a young boy and the memories came to him in waves.

Kate recognized this painting from her very first visit to Castello, the first night she fed from him. "Lover, your mother, she came to me again tonight."

She looked at the face of the boy in the portrait and Theresa was right, his loneliness showed in his face. Kate's heart broke for the child he was. She made a silent promise that his children would never know loneliness.

"Did she? I'm not surprised. Look at this painting, *mi amore*, I had been at camp several years when this painting was done. Look at her face, *bel*, she was so beautiful and happy, as was *Padre*. They were very much in love, in their way."

He reached out as his fingers glided softly over *Madre*'s face in the portrait. "I miss her very much. I am glad she came to you. It makes me feel comforted to know she is with both of us this night. She was a great queen, adored and loved." He squeezed her hand. "I have no doubt you will be the mightiest queen Medici has ever seen. Are you ready?"

"I'll do everything within my power to live up to her example, to be deserving of this title, to earn the respect and loyalty of your coven, and to be everything you need from me as your queen. I'm ready."

"Then let us begin our journey." Taking her hand, he led her to the side door of the Throne Room, speaking to her telepathically. **"From this**

moment on, *mi amore*, if you need to speak to me, do it thusly. I will guide you, I will be right here beside you, always right here."

Sliding his hand under her chin, he tilted her face up and kissed her lips gently, whispering in her ear, "*Ti amo*."

"Then know this, my king, my master, my maker, my lover, my eternal mate, you are everything I've ever dreamed of, and my love for you knows no boundaries. You lead, and I will follow."

Taking Kate's hand, Shade closed his eyes, letting their heartbeats synchronize. He squeezed her hand and felt her squeeze back and he knew they were ready. Willing the multitude of candles to light that surrounded the dais holding the two hand-carved, high back thrones, upholstered in red velvet, he was struck by the beauty and majesty the candlelight gave the room. How many times had his *madre* and *padre* sat there on these thrones, ruling with pride and glory? And now, their time had come.

The candles were low, to signal to the entire room the royal couple was about to enter. The small chattering noise of the gathered crowd hushed, and you could hear a pin drop inside the massive hall. Shade led her across the red carpet from the side portico to the center of the dais facing the throng of many. His highest ranked warriors lined the first five rows of the ancient hand-carved pews, worn smooth over the centuries. Seated behind the warriors were his household staff, members of the Medici coven, hand selected to serve the family. Following them were the highest masters of surrounding territories along with their mates. Many were here to show their respect and fealty to his queen.

"Keep your head down, *mi amore*, I will present you and then remove your robe. Keep your head down until I tell you to raise it."

Shade stepped forward, dropping his own robe and letting it fall ceremoniously to the edge of the dais and watched as Fiamma gathered it up quickly.

He addressed the crowd, "Welcome to Medici Castello."

All were seated, and the center aisle was wide, a luxurious red carpet lined its path to the carpeted dais. The many candelabras gave the entire room a beautiful, soft glow and all eyes were locked on him.

"I present to you my mate, Queen Katherine of Medici."

He turned and walked to Kate, her head still bowed. He faced her, blocking her from the audience's view. He slowly lowered the hood from her face, and her crimson locks fell to her shoulders, her beauty astounding. He winked at her. **"I will now stand behind you, *mi amore* and remove the robe. As I do, you must lift your head high, face your people, the masters, and the Council. I will not leave your side."**

Walking behind her, he reached around her shoulders, releasing the single button, and pulled the hooded cape from her shoulders. Her gown was as white as her skin and unfurled into glorious folds as he watched her head rise up. He willed the candles on the dais to burn brighter, encircling her in the light. *My beautiful lily white!* He watched as the entire congregation stood for her unveiling, in a giant wave to honor to his queen.

As he removed her robe, Kate felt a soft wind blow through her hair and around the layers of tulle that made up the skirt of her gown. Her adrenaline was flowing, and she could feel her fangs emerge as his entire legion of warriors dropped to one knee before her.

Shade's head was held high. They adored her and would give their very lives to protect her. He heard a small rumble of voices and looked to see Malachi approaching down the center aisle in his long green robe. He walked slowly and with dignity, authority, and power. His presence alone was daunting, and Shade hoped Kate could remain calm. **"Malachi approaches down the aisle, *mi amore*. He is from the Council. He will drink your blood and claim you immortal in front of all and give you his blessing on behalf of the Council. Do not show him fear, only respect."**

Shade stepped next to *bel* as Malachi approached the dais, his eyes locked upon hers. Kate's fangs had elongated, and her beauty was unrivaled. There was no doubt she was now immortal. Gi brought the gold and jewel encrusted bloodletting chalice to Shade on a golden platter. Shade took the chalice in one hand and lifted Kate's wrist to his lips. **"I will score your skin with my fangs and turn your wrist to bleed into the chalice. It is not painful. Malachi must drink your blood to claim you immortal."**

Carefully biting down into her wrist, the first hit of her blood still attacked his beast and Shade pushed him down. Tilting her wrist, he let the blood drain slowly into the chalice, then leaned to her wrist and licked the wounds, watching her heal immediately. He handed the chalice to Malachi and awaited his tasting and declaration.

For Kate, his bite was sweet, she felt a wave of desire wash over her, as his fangs pierced the tender skin on the inside of her wrist. She closed her eyes and took a deep breath, pushing back the sensations. When she opened her eyes, she watched as her blood dripped into the chalice. She felt the heat of his tongue as he licked the wound, and again, the desire for him arose. She used all her willpower not to respond to him. She saw the wounds heal before her eyes.

Kate turned her gaze to Malachi. His face was stern, emotionless, and she locked eyes with him. He was the Council who'd been here last night, the one who came to express his disapproval. Kate held his gaze and gave nothing away in her expression.

Malachi took the chalice offered by the Medici. Holding the cup with both hands, he lifted it to his lips and drank. As her blood touched his tongue, he was hit with its sweetness, its richness, and he felt the power of their joined blood as it rushed through him. He had never tasted mortal blood, and he'd anticipated a weakness of flavor and energy. But her mortal blood mixed with his royal blood had produced something unique and powerful. He closed his eyes as he swallowed, and saw Shade's gift flash before him... dream-walker, which Malachi knew already to be true.

And then he saw her gift of animalism. How very rare, and a powerful one at that! Malachi had served for centuries on the Council and had never once seen the gift of animalism. She would have command of all creatures to do her bidding and would be a great source of power for Shade. This would make The Medici a power to be reckoned with by all.

Then he saw something else, another gift? Not possible. Every vampire was imbued with only one. But there it was... day-walker. The Medici Queen would be a day-walker and protect her king. He handed the chalice back to the Medici. He would discover her gifts soon enough. Malachi acknowledged to himself that he and the Council owed Shade an apology; this mortal would not hold him back. Quite the contrary, this mortal would insure an even stronger legacy for The Medici. Malachi nodded his head to him and then to her, before turning to face the congregation.

"The Council declares her to be of immortal blood, as the blood of the Medici courses through her veins. The Council acknowledges her rightful seat on the throne as Queen Katherine, Queen of the Medici."

Shade had watched Malachi's face as he drank her blood, and the strangest emotions rolled over him. What had Malachi tasted that had made him have such a look of consideration on his face? Shade was curious. Malachi claimed her as his queen and there was no greater honor to bestow upon her. She was now Medici. He watched as Malachi left the dais and traveled down the aisle to stand at the back of the congregation, his presence still felt as he remained, observing from the middle of the aisle. He wouldn't leave until the crowning was complete. Only then would he take his leave and report back to the Council he had tasted her blood, she was immortal, and had witnessed her coronation.

Shade saw Marco stand up, holding a red velvet pillow. Atop it, lay the crown his *madre* wore for every occasion. This was the Medici crown that had been worn through generations. It held much pride, honor, and history. The crown spiked in gold stars, each star encrusted with a diamond in its center. Marco moved to the edge of the dais where Shade met him and removed the crown from its precious resting spot, holding it high in the air for all to see. He walked back to Kate and stood before her. **"Kneel before me, *mi amore*, and I will crown you my queen... for all eternity."**

Kate lifted the long skirt and walked to him, dropping down on both knees before him. He stood towering over her in the ceremonial leathers, the Medici crest on the center of his chest, and chain mail around his neck. She raised her eyes to his and drew strength from his steady gaze.

Shade felt her nerves, but she remained strong, his *bel rosso*. He took a deep breath, her beauty astounding him. He placed the crown upon her head, its beauty was something to behold. His eyes welled up, she was his queen now. Holding out his hands, she placed her hands in his and he lifted her slowly to her feet. He took her face into his hands and kissed each cheek, as was custom. He whispered softly to her, "*Ti amo*, my queen."

Taking her by the hand, he walked her to the center of the dais. He bowed deeply to her and then turned to the congregation.

"I am honored to present to you, Queen Katherine of Medici." He watched as every head in the palace bowed low. His warriors remained kneeling, heads bowed. Shade took her by the hand and walked her to the throne as she seated herself with grace and elegance. His heart was exploding with pride and love for the woman he had searched for his entire life. He took a seat beside her on his own throne and let his voice boom across the room. "Please take a seat. Marco, arise and approach."

Marco took the two small steps up to the dais. Raising his sword to his chest, he crossed the weapon over his heart, which signified he would give his life for hers. He was Second-In-Command of Medici, and in charge of all the warriors in this camp. He would be the first to pledge to her, and following him, each warrior of high rank would do the same. She was now their queen. Marco knelt on one knee before her, holding his sword out in front of him, point down to the dais, and bowed his head.

"My Queen, I am Marco, Second-In-Command to the Medici. I pledge to you my honor, and my eternal protection and fealty as a Medici Warrior. Our warriors honor you with our lives and give of ourselves to protect you from all outside evil. Hail to Queen Medici."

Laying a long-stem red rose on the dais at her feet, he remained with head bowed and on his knees until she acknowledged him, thereby releasing him to leave her presence.

Kate recalled the discussion with Theresa earlier this evening. She was wondering how much he'd want to protect her once he learned Theresa would be returning to the States.

"Arise, High Warrior. You honor me with your service, and you bring great honor to the Medici name with your command of the Medici Warriors, whose skill and bravery is unparalleled." She nodded to him in acknowledgment as his signal to rise.

As she spoke, her voice carried the confidence of her royal command, she was neither meek nor overpowering, but delivered her message with a voice that was light and lilting and carried through the large hall. Marco rose and was honored by her words. She had given him her blessing and nodded for his dismissal. Marco turned to Shade and bowed, then slowly walked backward off the dais, never turning his back to his master or his queen and took his place as first in line in the center aisle, standing and waiting for the next warrior to step forward and offer their pledge.

As the procession of warriors continued, Shade watched as the dais filled with red roses. His eyes kept going to her. He couldn't take them off her, for she was so regal and beautiful. Just the sight of her stunned him.

Marcello pledged and then a few more followed and then, here it came... Raven. *If that little shit doesn't tow the fucking line, I will rip his tongue out right here in front of everyone!* He watched closely as Raven toned down his usual dramatics and actually acted normal for a change. Next up was Fiamma, and he smiled at her as she pledged to honor Kate and awaited her acknowledgement and dismissal.

As Fiamma knelt before her, Kate realized Fee and the other female warriors faced the same discrimination from others as Kate did as a mortal mate. And Kate had to include herself in that group of self-doubters. Fee pledged her protection and fealty to her and Kate waited for her to finish. As Fiamma lay down her rose, Kate spoke loudly, wanting all to hear. "To Fiamma, and my sister warriors who bring honor to the Medici name, I respect your integrity in the face of adversity, and stand with you against those who doubt your strength and skills. Arise sister."

Kneeling before her queen was a high honor for Fiamma, for she wasn't yet alive to pledge to Shade's mother. Portia was long dead before Fee arrived in this camp. As Fee listened to her words, she felt the pride of being a female warrior fill her heart. Fiamma smiled at her. She'd be one damn almighty queen! Fee arose with her head held high and locked eyes with Kate. "You honor me, my Queen, as you do all our sisters this night. We are most honored that you stand with us, for we are all Medici."

Shade could hear the chatter in the congregation, and it almost made him laugh out loud. His queen was going to set some minds blasting tonight. Shade remained quietly seated as the remainder of the warriors stepped forward to pledge, each laying a red rose upon the dais and then taking their place standing in a long line down the center aisle of the room, lining both sides of the aisle, swords at their sides, standing tall, looking straight ahead. The procession of warriors was ending as Luca was next and the last to pledge. He was the Queen's protector, the highest honor of all warriors and suddenly, there was a lump in his throat. He knew Luca's *padre* and his own watched together this night.

As Luca stepped forward and knelt before her, her heart already wept for all he'd given, all he'd done. He placed his sword across his heart and then turned the sword tip down on the dais, as he began his pledge.

Luca bowed his head before lifting it to look at her. He felt the weight of the responsibility for her safety, and the pride of the moment. He was supposed to say the simple words, 'I pledge my protection and fealty,' the same as all the other warriors. But tonight, he must speak what was in his heart.

"It is my honor and privilege to serve as protector to the Queen. I pledge my life in service to my King, my Queen, and all the children of this union. Only death will part me from this sword, as I swear on my honor as a Medici Warrior, to always stand between my Queen, as well as the children of my King, against any foe."

Kate felt her tears flow as she remembered this gentle warrior who dragged her from the depths of darkness after losing the baby, who went against his master's orders in training her, who stood at Shade's side during the ambush. He had shown his loyalty time and time again. Kate slipped from her throne and knelt in front of him and heard the rumblings from the congregation.

"Luca, my loyal protector, my trusted friend, you have already demonstrated your strength of character to me who kneels, humbled before you. I ask that you drink my blood, and the blood of our children to come, so we may always be bound to you."

Kate heard a collective gasp from the crowd, and she watched as Luca looked to Shade. She knew she had broken protocol in leaving the throne, kneeling before this warrior, and asking him to drink her blood. From the corner of her eye, she saw Shade nod his approval to Luca. Kate extended her wrist to him, as he took it in his hands and bit into the soft flesh. She felt him draw the blood into his mouth, and watched him swallow, his eyes closed. As he pulled away, he licked the wound to heal it. She leaned forward, and kissed each cheek, then stood and retook her seat on the throne.

"Arise, my most trusted protector."

Shade stood and nodded to Theresa who came out upon the dais to collect all the roses and gather them for Kate. When she was done, she stood to give the roses to Kate and he held up his hand for her to stop. He turned to his *bel* and knelt on one knee before her, pulling from behind his back, three perfect red roses and held them out to her, their stems had been cut back, thorns removed. He looked up at her and smiled.

"My Queen, I present to you three red roses. They are sent with love from three separate hearts on this, your special day, from Lorenzo, Sophia and Natalia." He knew no one in this congregation had a damn clue who these three were, but *bel* knew.

She grasped his wrist tightly, as he held the roses out to her and tears flowed down her cheeks. They were tears for their lost baby, but also the promise of the three babies who waited impatiently to be born. She leaned forward, still gripping his wrist and kissed him. It was a kiss that should be reserved for private, not one issued in a room full of onlookers, but this was their private moment, a message from her lover of all the promise their future held. She broke away from the kiss, her eyes locked on his, and she was lost to him. She no longer knew where she began, and he ended. With a whispered cry, she spoke the only word that came to her, "Lover."

"*Si, mi amore*, I'm right here. But I have one more honor for you. You have given me so much, and there is still one person whose heart belongs to you this night."

Pulling a long stem white rose from behind his back, he held it to her face, and let the soft petals slide along her cheek.

"Our *dormire guerriero*, our sleeping warrior. The rose is not in full bloom, it is white and pure, as is he. But he is with us as well, *mi amore*."

He felt his own tears well up as he held them back. He beckoned Theresa forward and she handed Kate the large bouquet of roses from all the warriors, placing Shade's roses on top. He slipped her free arm through his and faced the crowd. "Are you ready, my Queen?"

"You lead, and I will follow, my King."

As Shade and Kate stepped off the dais to go down the aisle, Marco and Luca nodded to each other and all the warriors lining both sides of the aisle raised their swords in unison and crossed them over their hearts. Then they raised them high in the air and yelled "Hail the Medici and his Queen!" As the couple walked down the aisle, arm in arm, the warriors crossed their swords before the pair, a pact that each one would always surround them with protection and love.

As they got to the end of the isle, they exited the Throne Room and Shade led her down a long hallway, reaching a set of doors that led outside onto a balcony high above Castello. There was a small settee near the window. He stopped and pulled her into his arms as he sat down, holding her on his lap.

"*Ti amo*, my queen. You are so damn beautiful. I can't take my eyes from you, *bel.* There are many outside those doors who wait for us tonight. They all want to see their new queen, but before we do that, I just want to hold you, have a kiss, before I share you with the coven. Are you happy? Do you need to feed?"

"Lover, I'm beyond happy. I don't need to feed, but I do need a kiss. I didn't expect the flood of emotions tonight. So, hold me tight and kiss me, and I'll gladly meet your coven."

"That's my woman!" He kissed her long and passionately, letting his tongue slide into her mouth, moaning in agonizing need of her. He longed to be alone with her, but they had much yet to do before that happened and they both needed this sweet stolen moment. Letting his hands slide into the gorgeous crimson silk, he reached through her hair and held onto her crown, so it didn't fall as he kissed her.

Kate held the roses crushed between them, the scent of the flowers mixing with her own rose fragrance. She knew they were to go to the balcony next, and then there was the ballroom, but she wanted to leave with him now, go back to the private sanctuary of their bedroom and close the door, close out everyone else but them. She reluctantly broke the kiss because this evening didn't belong to them alone. She understood the celebration was as much for the Medici coven as for them.

"Let's go, let's go greet the coven."

"No, *bel*, not yet. I haven't given you my gift."

Lifting her off his lap, he stood her on her feet and spun her around with her back facing him. Reaching inside a breast pocket inside his leathers, he pulled out the diamond and ruby necklace and reached around and laid it across her beautiful neck, closing the clasp.

"There! The diamond and ruby necklace is from the vaults and was worn by my *madre*. Now we can go out on the balcony, *si*?"

He was saying rubies and diamonds. She couldn't see the necklace, but the sheer weight of it told her it was massive. She ran her fingers across the necklace, loaded with stones. Her emotions were already on edge and she fought back more tears. She caught a mental image of herself, at Bel Rosso, mucking horse stalls in jeans, a plaid shirt and a huge ruby and diamond necklace, and she had to stifle a laugh. Her title may be queen, but her palace would look much different from this one. Their life together would be much different from the people whose portraits lined the halls of this castle. She turned in his arms, her head against his chest.

"You spoil me too much."

"Oh, *mi amore*, I have just begun to spoil you." Reaching down, he tried to spank her ass through the many layered skirts of her gown. "Damn, I can't even find your ass in this dress!"

As they both laughed, he took her hand and they walked to the balcony. Whipping open the doors, they stepped out to greet the coven. Thousands of people shouted up in a cheer, the sound deafening. The cool night air felt refreshing and he watched her crimson catch the breeze and blow softly around her face. He saw the fireworks go off, lighting the night sky in glorious colors. The church bells began to ring and he could hear them all across Florence.

"I think they already love you, *mi amore*."

They waved to the throngs of people, who waved back and shouted up at them. A chant from the crowd was carried on the night breeze. "Kiss, kiss, kiss, kiss, kiss..." And what could they do but oblige them?

As they kissed, the cheers got louder and finally, he held up his hand to quiet them. It took him several minutes to calm the crowd until they were quiet enough that he could shout above them.

"To my coven and those we protect, meet your new Queen, Katherine of Medici. Hail Medici! Do you love her?"

They cheered and screamed, and he watched as Kate smiled and kept waving, her beaming smile was the brightest thing in this night. "Is she not beautiful?"

Pulling her close, he kissed her once more and then picked her up in his arms and carried her back into Castello, the sound of the crowd audible inside these thick walls. "Happy now?"

"Shade, I've been happy since the day I first laid eyes on you. You make me happy every day when I sleep next to you, and every night when I make love to you, or when you make me laugh, or cry tears of joy. You make me happy."

"*Si, mi amore*. I have loved you since the moment I set eyes on you as well. My beast roared up and slapped me upside my brain box. Come, I do believe there are people waiting for us to celebrate this beautiful night. I promise not to keep you too long, I do have plans for later this night."

Grabbing her hand, they ran down the hall together, their laughter ringing through the halls and he could almost see his *padre* shaking his head in disbelief.

3

The reception and gathering of warriors, friends and masters was well underway, when Kate and Shade entered the ballroom, after leaving the crowds they greeted from the balcony. Shade had the live band play a special song for his queen. Taking her hand, he led her to the center of the ballroom and watched as others dispersed and let them have the dance floor to themselves. Kate laid her head on his shoulder and they danced, moving together in a slow sway. This night couldn't be more perfect for him and he hoped she felt the same, as they listened to the song from Staind, *Tangled Up in You*.

As one song ended and a faster paced song began, he gave her a kiss and led her off the floor. He saw Marco, his old friend, approaching them with a grin like a fucking Cheshire cat on his face and hugged him, pounding him hard on his back.

Marco greeted him, "About fucking time, you old goat. You almost look like you're happy." Turning to his new queen, he nodded his head. "You did well, my queen and I'd be honored if the," clearing his throat, "king would oblige me a dance with you."

Shade held up his hand. "Whoa, not yet, old man. She belongs to me this night, you've not even danced with your own woman yet, you sure as hell aren't stealing mine. Where is Theresa?"

Marco shrugged. "She's fixing her face, and I'll never understand. If I love looking at her already, what the hell is there to fix?"

Theresa came back to the ballroom that was lit with candlelight and filled with the sounds of the band playing. Couples were making their way to the dance floor and the Midnight was flowing. She saw Marco from the back, he was talking to master and my lady. Theresa walked to them and slid her arm into Marco's, standing close at his side. Despite her decision, it still felt good for the two of them to be able to acknowledge their relationship in public and not hide it. "Here you are! I should have known I'd find you two together." She gave Marco's arm a squeeze. Theresa bowed her head slightly to Shade. "The coronation was beautiful, master. It was my first, and I can't tell you how honored I am to have been a part of it. A part of Medici history."

Shade smiled at Theresa as he took her hand and kissed it gently. "We are honored that you could join us. It's important to have my *familia* around me, and you are most certainly *familia*! Although, I'm not sure about this brut you hang around with. At some point, you should be having *bambinos* and creating a legacy of your own. You two need to get busy on that." He winked at Marco.

Marco grimaced. "My life doesn't accommodate *bambinos.* You should know that. But I don't mind that we will be practicing a bit more."

Kissing Terri softly, he saw her look away and could feel something was out of sorts with her.

Emma was nervous as she carried the tray filled with glasses of Midnight to the guests when she saw master and my lady talking with Marco and Theresa. If not for Theresa's decision, Emma would have been in the ceremony tonight. She would be packing and planning a new life in the States. She walked in their direction and offered drinks to all. "*Scusi.* Refreshments for anyone?"

Emma balanced the tray carefully as master lifted two glasses from it, one for him and one for their new queen. She turned and offered the tray to Marco. "You must be disappointed, *si*?"

Marco looked at Emma, wondering what the hell she was blabbering about. "Disappointed in what? You have more than enough drinks for me on that tray." He felt Theresa tighten up beside him. "Terri, what is it?"

Emma plunged ahead, unaware of the firestorm she was about to set off. "Well, that Theresa will be going back to the States. Of course, it's a great honor to be the Lady in Waiting, but still, I know you'd planned on her staying."

Marco felt his beast rise up and he rolled his eyes to Shade. "You did this, didn't you? You commanded her to return to the States. Is this retribution for the female warriors? " Grabbing a drink from the tray, he downed it quickly.

Theresa grabbed Marco's arm. "No! Marco, no! It wasn't master. Please. Don't make a scene on their special night. Master gave me the choice...to stay or go. The decision was mine. Please. We'll speak of it later, in private."

As she tried to reason with him, Marco stared at her and her words tore him to pieces. *She had a choice? She fucking had a choice and she chose to leave?* He nodded to her, trying to keep his anger at bay. Turning to Shade and his new queen, he bowed at the waist. "I wish you both health and happiness for all eternity."

He took Theresa by the arm and led her briskly out the open veranda doors and into the gardens. There was much they needed to discuss.

Shade could only observe the roller coaster of emotions play across his oldest friend's face and saw his turmoil. Shade had no idea Theresa had already made her decision. He turned to *bel.* She had been very quiet through this whole episode.

"*Mi amore*, did you know Theresa had made her decision to come back with us?"

"I did, but not until tonight, right before the ceremony when she was helping me get dressed. She said she'd not told him yet. I asked her to talk to him, to make sure. I told her if she changed her mind, I'd understand. I regret he's hearing it in this way. But something tells me you and Marco have very similar tempers. I think she was putting off this discussion because she knew it would be a difficult one. She does love him, but she said she'd always be second place to him. His first allegiance is to you, to being a warrior... So, go easy on him, even though he spoke harshly to you."

He pulled her into his arms. "It wouldn't be the first time Marco and I have fought with words. We do it often. We are warriors second, and brothers first. I have no intention of saying anything to him. Theresa will handle his temper, just as you do mine, *si*. But I find sometimes being a king brings me unhappiness, in knowing some of those I love the most in my life are suffering because they serve me. I cannot let Marco leave here, it is imperative he stay in Florence. I need to get the camp at home in full swing. I cannot be in two places at once. I gave Theresa the option because it was easier for her to move." He laid his head atop hers and continued, "I never thought she would want to come back without him. I couldn't be so strong as to leave you. I can only imagine the pain he feels now."

"Lover, I can't imagine it for myself. But I also can't imagine feeling I was second place in your heart. Theresa seemed very sincere in her wish to come back with us, and to take care of our children."

As they talked, she saw Luca, still in his ceremonial leathers, approach with Shannon on his arm. The path before them cleared as the vamps stepped back from her, all of them detecting her mortality.

"Master, my lady. Please let me extend my warmest wishes to you both. To you, my lady... For the honor you bestowed upon me. I'm afraid your actions have created a bit of controversy. And to you, master... Thank you for allowing me to bring Shannon. Nothing about your reign will be conventional or boring, that's for certain. I hear the chatter in the crowd as we pass."

Kate spoke up, "Luca, I really didn't mean to create a controversy. It just felt like... it just felt natural to me, to have you bound to me, and our children. I'm afraid I still have a lot to learn about what is proper protocol, but I think I'd have made the same choice, maybe not in a public forum if I knew it would be such a big deal. And Shannon being here, well, we knew that would be an issue."

Shannon didn't hesitate to weigh in with her thoughts, "Not an issue for me. This has been freakin' awesome! Getting to stay in this castle, going to Luca's home, being at this ceremony, and visiting Florence again.

You realize the last time I was here was with you? Right after college, we came here together. Too bad we didn't know these guys then. Oh... I think I have a picture of you on my phone, standing in front of Santa Croce Cathedral. She dug through her evening clutch, pulling out her cell phone and displaying the photo for Kate and Shade to see. “Here it is. Look how young you look.”

Kate looked at the photo. “Oh my god, I look twelve. Put that away!”

Shade grabbed the phone, smiling as he looked at *bel*. “You look beautiful, but not as beautiful as you do tonight. This night will forever remain a very special and memorable one.”

Turning to Luca, Shade gave him a brotherly hug. “So, you went home, did you? How did you find the homestead?”

“Master, I don't have the words to express what it meant to me.”

Shannon squeezed Luca’s arm and watched him blush. “Yeah,” she laughed, “I don't have the words either.”

Shade threw back his head laughing, picking up on Shannon’s private message to Luca.

Shannon took the phone back from Shade and started flipping through other images. "Wait. You have to see this one. We’ll call this Florence, Part 2, the food fight."

Kate looked at a picture of herself covered in whipped cream and eating a strawberry. “You didn’t take a picture of the food fight. Shannon! You always got me in trouble! Some things never change.”

Shade leaned over her shoulder and looked at the photo. “You look rather edible, *mi amore*.” He shared with her his wicked grin.

Kate laughed as she looked up to see Malachi approaching them, his face stern. Something told her he wasn’t coming over to congratulate them. “Lover... it's that Council guy...”

Malachi approached, still in his green robe. “Medici, a word please.” He gave Shannon a sideways glance before returning his eyes to Shade.

Shade could see Malachi wasn’t pleased, and he already knew what this was about, but the sooner this was over, the faster Malachi would retreat and leave them alone for the evening. Shade bent to kiss *bel* lightly. “I’ll return, my queen. I won’t be gone long, nothing to be concerned over, just business.”

Shade nodded to Luca, his signal for him to not leave her side and Luca nodded back. “Come, Malachi, I do believe a refreshing walk in the gardens will make your attitude much more pleasant.”

As they walked out to the veranda, Shade could feel his anger and he handed him a glass of Midnight. “Say whatever you need to say, Malachi.”

Malachi took the drink that was offered. “Medici, the Council was reeling over your choice of a mortal for a royal mate. I think I can quiet things down on that front. And then we hear of plans for a warrior camp in the States in the middle of Maximus's territory, and that has them in a stir. You say you have it handled, but that is yet to be determined. But tonight, you bring a mortal to one of our most sacred ceremonies? There is no possible excuse you can provide that will ever make that all right. And since she is being escorted by your queen's protector, I can only assume you gave your blessing. This is beyond unacceptable. This exposes our entire world, other masters and their mates, our rituals. I would ask, what you were thinking, but clearly, you were not! Your hospitality has always been unparalleled, and the masters looked forward to this occasion, but now, they all feel betrayed, exposed. They have been denied the very right to keep what they are private from the mortal world. How do you answer for this?"

Shade listened to him go on and on, and watched his frustration, and yet, Shade was happy inside. The Council would reproach him, and he'd need to answer for all they had witnessed.

"Malachi, I have chosen my queen. I am sitting in the middle of Maximus's territory, and I will deal with that issue when the time comes. My word and my honor should stand alone on that matter. For, if nothing else, I am honorable to my core. As for the warrior camp, that is my business, and where I go to build my empire harms no one here or on the Council, and you will benefit from it in more ways than one."

Taking a sip of Midnight, he let his gaze roam over all that belonged to him here and smiled. "I have worked hard to reach this point in my life. The mortal is of no harm to anyone here. She is under my rule and realm. I take full responsibility for her. She is Luca's future mate, and she will be turned in time and remain with my *familia*. I am the Medici, Malachi, and you are standing on my ground. We shed the blood of my elders to become even bigger. I dare you to ask even one of the masters here if they object, for we both know they will not express their discontent out loud.

"This is the new age, Malachi. I suggest you and the Council realize my power and money will make a huge difference to their life here, if they choose to start a war on my home grounds. Walk lightly, Malachi, I take neither this nor anything else I do lightly. If my queen wishes the closest person in her life to share in her day, then fucking suck it up and deal."

Malachi's anger boiled, but he dared not push him further. He'd share his sentiments with Council, and they wouldn't be happy, but the Medici provided much funding, so they'd only object so much. He was changed, much changed, since going to the States. The Medici was cast in their old world traditions and upheld them. But then he met her... this one mortal, and he was tossing their traditions aside.

"I will carry your message back to Council, Medici. We have tried to keep up with the changes of the modern world. Our kind has always struggled to find the balance between tradition and safety with the changes in mortal society in which we all must hide. We do our best, to protect the interest of all vampires. That is our role, our function. Your disregard for our rules and bylaws will be noted. I take my leave now, and I thank you for your hospitality."

Shade shook his head at him and chuckled. "Be on your way, Malachi, with our best regards and wishes. We are honored that you joined us and blessed this union. But I think you need to understand one thing about me before you leave. I believe deeply in the old-world traditions and beliefs, but I have learned we must change as the world and the times change, and I will raise the future of Medici, my legacy, to understand they must hold the old and new together in a much better state than the immortals of the past. If we are not prepared, nor prepare those around us, we will succumb to the mortal world and none of us will survive to tell the rich history of our kind. My *padre* would not move ahead, Malachi, and he lost his life fighting the hidden. I will not do such. I am king, I have come home, but I have brought with me experiences no one in the Council could ever imagine. I do not wish mortals harm, I wish to co-exist, and I hope for a future where we all can live together, without judgment."

Spinning on his heels, Shade headed back into the ballroom to find *bel* and never looked back. This was their night, and nothing would take away the joy he felt inside.

Walking back into the ballroom, the air was cooled by the doors that opened onto the veranda, and the room was packed with important masters, but this night, Shade only had eyes for one, his queen. As he slowly walked to her through the crowd of guests who were enjoying the Midnight that flowed most freely to their lips, he took his time and watched her, the sheer beauty of her and how she moved with grace and ease. She laughed with her best friend, and her face was beaming. He caught her eye as she turned and took his arm.

"My queen, I wish this night to be full of love for the two of us." Kissing her softly, he knew others are watching.

Luca had seen his return. Shade had been on the veranda with Malachi for some time, and although he appeared calm, Luca knew this discussion with Council was centered on him and his choice of an escort for tonight. "Master, is everything okay? With the Council?"

"*Si*, Luca, relax. It is just Malachi throwing his weight around."

Luca stood close to him, speaking in a lowered voice. "I haven't had much time with you here, so I haven't been able to thank you. For letting me bring her. I know it's gone against all of our traditions, but being able to take her to my home, and have her share that experience with me, I can't tell you what that means to me. And master... my home, it was so much more than I expected. Everything is as it was, and the lemon groves thrive. I'm forever in your service."

Shade hugged him tight to his chest and beat his fist on his back. "Luca, seriously, I owe you more than that, much more. Just don't go and walk off on me, I need you now more than ever. You will always be my *familia*, nothing will ever change that. I'm glad you went home. It belongs to you now, it is yours. So, let's not get so maudlin about all of this, this night is for celebrating!"

Luca raised his glass. "Then let us celebrate!" He turned to Kate and bowed to her. "My lady, may I have the honor of this dance?"

"It would be my pleasure, sir."

Luca led her to the center of the ballroom floor as people stepped aside to clear a path for them, and Kate could hear the whispers in the crowd. About her, about him, about Shannon... and she no longer cared. *We have made our choices, our choices, not theirs. Our lives, not theirs.*

Luca stepped in closer to her as they reached the center of the ballroom to begin the slow dance.

Shannon watched as Luca led her best friend to the dance floor and she turned to Shade. "Well, there's no way I'm standing here like a wallflower, besides, I've never danced with a king before. Come on, let's give them something to really talk about." She grabbed his hand and dragged him to the center of the dance floor.

Shade was startled by her abruptness. Taking her into his arms, he locked her in his gaze. "Is not the king supposed to ask the lady to dance first?"

Shannon laughed. "I wouldn't know. Like I said, you're my first king. Don't go all 'protocol' on me, your Highness. Just show me what you got."

Shade chuckled and slow danced with her, but as the song came to an end, he whispered, "Well, if this is how you truly want it to be, *mia dolcezza*, I think we need to change up the music."

Holding his hand up as the music faded, he spun his hand in a circle over his head at the musical director, and the whole tone of the night changed as masters and mates emerged onto the dance floor. He looked down at Shannon.

"Does this suit you better? Now, let's move some ass across this floor."

The band switched from the ballad to some head banging music by Disturbed, *Ten Thousand Fists*. Shannon broke from his hold. She reached up and pulled the pins from her hair and let it cascade down around her shoulders, so she could swing it freely as she moved to the music.

Smiling as he watched her bang her head to the beat, he saw Luca break his hold on Kate to change his dance to the new music as well. Shade slipped away from Shannon and walked up behind Kate, wrapping his arms around her and spinning her to face him, as Luca moved to be with Shannon.

"Would you care to dance with your king, my queen? I would be most obliged."

"Seriously? I'm wearing a gown that must weigh fifty pounds, and forty-nine of those pounds are in the skirt, and you want me to dance at the head-bangers ball?"

She laughed out loud as he twirled her around, the voluminous layers of tulle in the skirt swinging and swaying around her.

Nodding to the musical director, the music changed once again and he took her in his arms, and watched as the crowd circled them, watching them dance together, just the two of them on the dance floor.

She felt him sliding his arms around her waist as he pulled her close to his chest. *Into the Mystic* began to play... their song. She slid her arms around his broad shoulders and laid her head against his chest. She could feel him tuck his face into her hair, felt his breath. Their heartbeats synchronized as their bodies found the haunting rhythm of the music. This night was perfect.

"Rock my gypsy soul, lover."

Shade took a deep breath and inhaled all that was his *bel rosso*. She was finally his forever. "I love you, Kate. I will always love you."

Leading her around the ballroom, they made quite a show, but he saw nothing of the faces as they spun and twirled past them. He had eyes for only one, and she was his heart and soul. Suddenly, he felt a pull, a strong emotion very deep and his eyes roamed across the room. There in the corner, he saw them.

"*Mi amore*, look to your left, the corner of the ballroom, we have company."

She lifted her head slightly and looked in the direction he was nodding. And there they were, in their own embrace, moving slowly to the music, Portia and Christofano. They had joined them on this night.

"Lover, they have come to celebrate with us."

"*Si, mi amore*, as it should be, but I have a bit of a surprise for you."

Releasing her from his arms, he walked to the front of the crowd and nodded to the musical director. The music stopped, and an entire choir emerged and lined up. Holding up his hand, everyone turned to look at them.

"I honor this night, my queen, and my warriors, those of this household. But also, I honor the love and grace of my parents, Christofano and Portia Medici. Please join us in this ceremonial song that celebrates the joining of two souls, and was played at their own coronation. *Per sempre*, Medici!"

Taking *bel*'s hand, he led her to the center of the ballroom and bowed deeply to her and began to waltz with his beautiful mate, as he looked over to see *Madre* and *Padre* dancing beside them and his heart burst with love.

The band played a classical piece, *Una Stravaganza Dei Medici*, and the choir sang.

Kate saw his parents, as they moved from the corner and danced next to them, visible only to them. She saw they only had eyes for each other, remembering their own first night as king and queen, centuries ago, she imagined. The elder masters held their mates close as the classical music played and the chorus sang, remembering an era long past.

As the music ended, Shade watched *Padre* look to him with approval. "Look, *mi amore*, *Padre* is very happy. I think, for once in my life, I have pleased him. I only hope we will love like that and so much more, forever. Tell me you are happy, you do not regret your choice."

"Lover, there are no words for how I feel. I'll never regret this choice. I've left my mortal life behind, and I'm yours now, in a way I couldn't be before. There's so much ahead for us. I can't wait for it to begin, and at the same time, I want each moment to last. Eternity will never be enough."

Shade reached his hand to her hair. "I do believe we may leave our own ceremony now, *mi amore*. I think, perhaps, it is time we depart quietly and let the others celebrate. I want my alone time with you. Besides, I can feel you are getting hungry. Let us dance out the doors of the veranda and into the gardens and run like hell for our room. Ready to escape?"

"I'm so ready to get out of this dress, for more reasons than one. Let's go, you'll have to lead the way."

He took her hand and started to lead her through the crowd as the band switched back to more traditional music. They were almost to the door when they saw Alec and Rissa approach.

Alec held up his glass to Shade, in a silent toast. "Before you sneak away, please allow us to extend our sincere congratulations, brother. I think I can safely say I'm the only other master here who chose a mortal mate. I'm sure you've heard from the Council on that? They pestered me to no end on the matter."

Shade nodded to him. "Alec. We graciously thank you. Take no objection to Council's presence, you are both welcome here. Malachi is just testing his strength. The Council needs to move with the times and lighten up a bit, told him to suck it up and deal. Glad you could make it."

Alec turned to Shade's new mate. He must admit, she looked regal, and after the incident with Cuerpo, he was forced to reconsider his view of her. Not the weakling he'd thought. He offered his hand palm up, and she laid her hand in his. He lifted her hand as he bowed his head, kissing the back of it.

"And you, my darling, look ravishing this evening. Clearly, the two of you were trying to sneak away. I'll not keep you any longer, brother, from enjoying what is finally yours on this night."

"Thanks, brother, the night is young, and we are off. Enjoy the entertainment. Anything you need is at your disposal."

Kate nodded to Alec and looked to Rissa, who was obviously ignoring her, looking about the room at everything except her. Kate thought her old friend was jealous, but before she could even speak to her, Shade started to move away, and she felt his hand at the small of her back, guiding her in the direction of the veranda doors leading to the gardens.

"Well, that was a rather cool reception from Rissa, don't you think? She's staying here at Castello as our guest, comes to the coronation, and can't even acknowledge our presence? I can't figure her out, lover."

Once outside, he took her in his arms and teleported up into the highest parapet of Castello. Sitting her down lightly on her feet, he wrapped her in his arms as they stared out over the Florence skyline.

"All of this is yours, *mi amore*, as far as you can see. As for Rissa, perhaps she was simply overwhelmed."

"I know a cold shoulder when I see one, and that wasn't Rissa feeling overwhelmed, that was Rissa making a point of ignoring me. Clearly, you don't know Rissa."

"*Si*, I didn't bring you hear to discuss Rissa."

She felt him grab her unexpectedly, and before she could respond his mouth was on hers, his tongue exploring. She reached around his shoulders, pulling him to her, before breaking the kiss. "Call Theresa... or get me out of this dress please."

"Do you wish to keep the dress or have it in shreds? Vital info I need, *mi amore*, before my next move!"

"Lover," she started laughing, "I want to keep it. Please, don't rip it off. Just...get me out of this thing! One of our girls may want to wear this dress someday."

Picking her up in his arms, he teleported straight into their bedroom and found Theresa standing there waiting. He loved when his staff knew him better than he knew himself. "Do your thing, Theresa. I have a queen to accommodate. " He was flinging off his clothes as he headed to the bathroom. "Be ready, *mi amore*, when I get back!"

4

Marco quickly walked out of the ballroom, heading out the double doors onto the veranda and into the night breeze, and fuck if he didn't need it. This news had taken his beast and temper overboard. How the hell could she go back there with them? Teleporting quickly to a small grove of trees far beyond the coronation guests, he began stripping off the jacket of his ceremonial leathers. Flopping down on the grass, he sat there, trying to cool down and get his anger under control. He always thought he'd have Terri. "*Cazzo*!"

Theresa followed behind him, but watched as he teleported away from her. Damn him! She kept walking through the gardens as they neared the camp, and found him seated under a grove of trees, his jacket lying on the ground beside him. "So, do I even warrant the courtesy of a discussion, Marco?"

He stared at her. "You obviously didn't give me that courtesy when you made this decision, Terri. You couldn't tell me? I had to hear it from the staff? That tells me where the hell I rank in your life. Please, by all means," throwing his hands out, gallantly waving them about, "discuss."

"Marco, we're not mated. You've never even brought that up for discussion in all the time we've been together. You never asked if it was what I wanted. You never asked if I wanted children. You've been happy with the status quo, which was, you were free to pursue your life as a warrior. You were free to rise through the ranks as SIC, unencumbered by the responsibilities of a mate. And all the while, I was always available when it was convenient for you. I loved you, I still love you, but it was always clear to me I'd be second place in your heart. Tell me I'm wrong."

"*Cazzo*! Terri, you knew, you have always known, I'm a warrior, born and bred. But you never came to me, either, to tell me how you felt, never once. You left at master's command, as was your duty, just as staying is mine. It was the right thing to do for Medici, for the coven and for our master. We're not free to pick and choose. But you tell me now you were given a choice! And still you didn't come to me and tell me you wished to be mated. I'm older now, Terri, and more settled. Shade won't send me out to battle. He'll use my skills to train the younger warriors. But you left me out of the decision. I love you, and I'll always love you for everything you've ever given me. But my fate is warrior and I fight and love with that same heart. My allegiance, my heart belongs to that fate and my master, and if it could be different, it would be. But this is who I am."

She knelt beside him, "I understand you, Marco. I've always understood you. I've lived at Castello for several hundred years, surrounded by its warriors, so believe me when I say I understand the loyalty of the warriors. But I was nothing, Marco. I was a house maid, one among many. Why master picked me to go to Virginia, I'll never know. But he picked *me.* And now I run that household, and I'll be Lady in Waiting to the Queen. I'll raise the children of the King. It's an honor I could never have imagined for myself, and it's as important to me as being Second-in-Command is to you. I too have a loyalty and a duty. My lady confides in me, relies on me, just as he relies on you. Don't lay this on my shoulders. You knew I loved you. And since when, in our world, have women been allowed to make their desires known? We wait. We wait for the men we love to pursue us, choose us. Not the other way around. For all our enlightenment, our vampire culture is stuck in time. Women don't approach men about mating...about children. We wait. And I waited, Marco. I waited. I still love you. We'll visit here often. They'll have children, they'll return here, and when they do, I'll be with them. If you still want me... If you want this relationship to continue, then I want you to know, I still love you."

He listened as she opened her heart to him, and her words rang true. She too had come far within the ranks of the coven. He didn't want to deny her what she truly deserved. Watching as she turned on her heels and walked away, he quickly stood and grabbed her arm. Spinning her around, he took her in his arms, crushing her to his massive chest.

"Terri, please, I don't want us to separate like this. I'll never be able to rest knowing I've done this to you, made you feel less than what you are. You are an amazing woman and mate for any vampire."

Leaning down, he kissed her gently on the lips, sliding his fingers under her chin. "Go to the States. Find what you deserve, find your dream, and do your duty. You deserve so much more than me and what I have to offer. Be happy."

Smiling, his heart felt as though he'd been hit with a hammer. He released her and turned, walking back to grab his jacket. His innocent sweet Terri had come back a different woman. She had more spunk, was more vibrant. Her freedom and new responsibilities were giving her a greater sense of herself. He knew only too well that feeling, to seek and find yourself and discover your potential, without ties binding you. He turned to look at her and there were no tears in her eyes, just determination and pride in the woman she'd become. He turned and walked slowly to the barracks.

Theresa called out to him, "So this is it, Marco? All or nothing?

He answered her, his voice low, "*Si*, Theresa. Find your soul. Seek and find what it is you truly want. Go without obligation. It does neither of us any good to pine for what might have been, and I find it hard on my old heart. I've waited for you to return, and it damn near killed me. I won't wait more. You deserve to have this, Theresa. You truly deserve it."

He tried to say the words without breaking, but his heart was screaming. He put on his false bravado and never let her see his pain. He hardened his heart and the expression on his face.

Theresa sighed because it was as it had always been. Like it or not, women didn't hold equal status in their culture. Theresa looked back at him. If he couldn't have her on his terms, he wouldn't have her at all.

"Then remember I loved you, Marco of Medici, and we'll both break these bonds that have tied us together. I wish you only happiness."

She left him to return to Castello. She was sure my lady would be leaving the reception soon, and she'd be needed.

Marco watched the only person who understood him walk away. He felt something inside him die, but he couldn't let her see that. He must let her go to follow her fate, for she'd never find it here, or in him. He dropped to his knees once she was out of sight and placed his face into his hands. Tomorrow, he'd go on as always, the Second-In-Command of Medici and once again, he had given all he had to Shade.

5

Theresa helped Kate out of the dress, protecting the skirt with the layer upon layer of tulle, and carried it away to store it. Kate slipped out of her under garments, added a fresh spritz of her rose scented fragrance, ran a brush through her hair and climbed into that massive bed to wait for Shade.

Shade could feel her waiting, her anticipation high. It had been a long journey for them to get to this moment. But this night was important. She claimed him as her master, her king, and he was hoping he got to see more of the beast that lurked inside of her.

He walked into the bed chamber and saw her lying naked and face down on their bed, in wait for him. He didn't speak, just watched as she felt him close and lifted her head to look at him. He saw her eyes change to that beautiful hue of red, and her fangs instantly protruded. He let the towel wrapped low and loose around his hips slide slowly to the floor behind him, as he walked toward her.

She ran her hand over the empty space in the bed next to her. "We have waited too long, lover. Come. Join me in our bed."

He crawled in from the foot of the bed as his body slid along the backs of her legs, across her ass and up her back, kissing her spine as he went, flattening her body under his. Snuggling into her neck, he gripped a handful of hair and whispered, "Did you miss me, *mi amore*?"

Kate closed her eyes, skin on skin, was there ever a more delicious feeling? She loved the feel of him as he slid up her body, his kisses sending shivers up her spine, nuzzling into her neck. He grabbed a handful of her hair. It was his weakness, that hair. It was his kryptonite, and she knew it.

"Where should I start, lover?" She lifted her head from the bed so it was next to his, their lips only inches apart. She raised her hips in the air, pressing her ass against his cock.

In a whisper she inquired, "Soft kisses, or passionate ones? Or maybe you prefer bites now?"

She nipped at his neck with her fangs, and a small drop of blood appeared. She licked it slowly, and hissed at him. She would tease him tonight, past the point of no return. "Who do you want to come out to play tonight? Your gentle *bel rosso*, or do you want to see the beast inside your queen? Tell me what you desire."

Moaning as he saw her fangs, they excited him beyond anything he could have imagined. She teased and taunted him with those words. He was amazed at her control when she licked his neck and he gripped her hair harder. "Careful, my queen, I will show you who is master. I wish for something I have not yet seen. Does that beast want to come out and play with me?" He nuzzled her neck, licking and letting his tongue slide along her pulsing vein.

"Your queen wants what you want, lover."

He still lay on top of her. His weight had her pinned down to the bed. He slipped to her side as he struck her hard, the sound of his hand across her ass a resounding loud crack in the quiet room, and her beast began to emerge. She felt a throbbing in her fangs, an ache, a new sensation for her, as she hissed and growled at him. It had been hours since she'd fed, and she already craved him again. She rose up and rolled with him, pushing him down as she rolled on top of him, her mouth seeking his neck. She gripped his shoulders tightly as she sank her fangs into him, and drank deeply. The power of his blood hit her instantly, igniting the fire between her legs.

He moaned and felt those wickedly sharp fangs in his neck. It was the most erotic sensation in his life. He loved to feel her feed, feel her take his power, his strength, giving her life. In five hundred years, she was the only one to take from him. She drank deep and drew hard. He felt her body respond to the power of his blood when she pulled away from his neck and leaned in, biting his lip, sucking it into her mouth. He could barely breathe. Her beast was alive, wanting to come out and be tamed. Flipping her over and pushing her down hard on her back, he entered her fully, pushing her knees atop his shoulders as he started thrusting into her, then sinking his fangs deep into her neck. Her scent overwhelmed him, her body moved like a wave they rode together.

Kate's head was near the edge of the bed, and her hair cascaded over the side as her head fell back, her neck exposed. She felt him growl deep in his chest as he drank from her. She bit him again, drinking from him as he drank from her. Her hands clawed at him, gripping him, and pulling him closer, deeper.

He gripped his hands in her hair and rolled with her again, pulling her to his chest, kissing her with deep hard passion, his heart racing with hers. "Let her out, *bel*. I want you to let your beast go."

Letting go of her tresses, he slid his hands to her hips, gripping her hard as he guided her motions on his rigid cock, thrusting hard into her again and again, feeling her respond, her eyes glowing red in the darkened room.

She flipped him over, as she crawled on top of him, pinning him to the bed as she mounted him. Her beast roared back as her fangs elongated and the saliva dripped on his chest before she bit at him again. A savage bite into the strong muscle of his shoulder as one hand held his arm down, and the other gripped his hair, pulling his head back. Her hips rode the full length of his massive erection, slamming down hard against him, feeling his cock throb deep inside her.

He encouraged her beast. She must understand the full power of her beast before she could learn to control it. But he was still her master and he'd let her know it. His goal for this night was for her to learn he'd let her beast lead at times, but he'd always remain the stronger one. He was her maker and master. He slammed into her stroke after stroke, watching her growl and swing her hair from side to side as she thrashed her head in the air. Reaching up, he gripped her hair in both hands and rolled her onto her back and pulled her away from what her body craved. He was aching to drive back deep inside her and have his own reward, but his beast knew he must train her. Her arms reached for him, but he burrowed between her legs and slid his tongue inside her, sucking her juices, then suckling her clit, enticing her beast to either fight or submit. He knew she could feel his intent, knew he didn't do this to torment her or overpower her but simply to make her understand, her master would always rule. He slid his eyes to hers. "Do you want to cum, *mi amore*?"

He willed the music to play, its beat seductive. *Luscious Redhead Dark as Love* by Melissa Ritter

She arched her back and pushed her hips into him, as he denied her what she wanted most. She wrapped her legs around his shoulders, gripping tight as his tongue explored the depths of her. She did want to cum, but she wanted to feel him deep inside her when she did. He slowly crawled over her again, sliding his hand between her legs before pushing his member deep inside her. She wrapped her legs around his hips and he kept her pinned down, thrusting hard.

He kissed her deep and long, letting his hands explore through her hair, and along her face. His tongue licked at her neck and nuzzled her vein. He slowed the pace, letting her beast join with his, letting her feel how their power could be combined to take them to a higher plain. He thrust slowly, letting his cock glide in and out of her. Kissing her eyelids, he felt her hips come up off the bed to meet him and he let up from the pressure of holding her down, giving her free rein to move with him. "Take us there, my sweet lily white."

He kept pushing her to the edge, and pulling back, and pushing her to the edge again, and pulling back. Her body screamed for him, for the release only he could bring. She gripped her legs around him tightly and raked her nails across his back. As she heard his growl, she bit hard into his neck once again, and felt his fangs sink deep into her. Her growl was guttural. She clenched his cock hard with her sex, gripping him, pulling him deep, as her hips thrust against him. She unlatched as she threw her head back, screaming his name, as she felt him release into her.

The waves of pleasure rolled over them, spasm after spasm, and their bodies responding of their own accord. Their hips thrusting, as their orgasm took them to new heights before it started to subside. His body relaxed, their hearts pounding, chests heaving, and bodies glistening in a fine sheen of perspiration. He ran both hands through her hair, pushing it back from her face, before lowering his mouth to her.

"Mine, *mi amore*... All mine."

6

Shade felt restless, and he had no cause to be. What he'd waited for his entire life had happened this night. Kate was immortal, crowned his queen and was his for all eternity. He slowly slid from their bed, shifting her gently from his chest and covering her sleeping form with the soft blankets. Pulling on a pair of sweat pants that hung low on his hips, he walked to the window, opening the heavy drapes and feeling the cooling breeze of the Florence night blow across his skin. The moon shone down in its fullness, and hung low in the sky, letting him know daybreak wasn't far behind. The moonlight streamed into the room. He looked back at her, asleep on the bed.

He stood and let his mind wander. He replayed the events of the night over in his head, the coronation and how beautiful she'd looked. He let the memory sink in deep. It would be a tale to be told to his children and his grandchildren. The Coronation of Katherine the Medici Queen was legendary. The last Medici with that name and title had been from the mortal branch of their family tree. Queen Catherine de Medici was Queen of France, and married to Henry II. She had been a powerful queen, unloved by her mate, but she made sure her children all inherited the throne.

The memories played through his head, from the night he first saw her at Alec and Rissa's, to the coronation. He wondered if she'd made the right choice. All the things he'd deprived her of as a mortal, giving up family and friends, giving up daylight, it was more than he should have asked of her, and there was still much he hadn't shared. There were secrets he'd feared to tell her. He began to think perhaps the life he had to offer her would never be enough. He knew deep in his heart he didn't deserve the woman who lay in their bed across this room.

He turned his head to view her at rest and gasped at the sight before him. His *madre* sat quietly on the bed next to Kate, her blonde hair down, framing her face. Her cornflower blue eyes held his. She held herself regally, always the queen. But to him, she would always be *Madre*.

***

Portia watched him and felt his doubt. He'd grown to be the finest warrior the Medici had ever known. He'd finally outdone his own *padre*. She knew Christofano was pleased with their son and his choice of mate, knowing the future of the Medici coven was finally safe. She was more than grateful to her son for finally giving his father peace within his soul.

She and Christofano had watched him for years as he succeeded as a warrior but failed at love, failing to find his destined mate and failing to produce heirs that would secure their legacy. Although they were both long gone from his world, they resided in the spirit realm and never left Castello. Their life and love together held them here. And now, they welcomed into their hearts a new daughter. It pleased her greatly he'd come home, brought with him his bride who took her rightful place beside him.

But this night, he needed more than his mate to reassure him, to erase something he didn't allow himself to often feel, self-doubt. And like many times before, he was calling to her, to provide reassurance, comfort, and solace. Portia spoke to him from where she sat on the bed, next to a sleeping Kate.

"You, *mio figlio*, are more deserving than you could ever imagine."

"*Madre*, are you truly here?"

Portia held out her hand to him, her face lit with a soft smile, her eyes shining in the moonlight, her beaded gown the color of new corn, a golden silk that enhanced every beautiful thing about her. She was always the gentleness inside him. She knew his darkness, and understood the tangled web it wove around his heart, pulling him down. At one time, she was the only solace he'd known. *Padre*'s hand was heavy when it came to him, and hers had been the healing one, providing comfort as only she could.

"You have taken so long to come to me, *Madre*. I have missed you so."

Portia looked at his new queen and slid her hand gently over Kate's long crimson waves and turned to look at him, beckoning him to sit beside her on the bed.

"Come, *mio figlio*. Tis truly your *madre*. She sleeps, she will not awaken."

He walked to the bed and sat beside her, as her hand softly slid along his chiseled cheek. She looked deep into his eyes, even bluer than her own. She let her hand stray to his curls, black as coal, so like his *padre*'s. Pulling his head to her shoulder, she felt him come easily to her, and felt him sigh and relax. She caressed his head gently, kissing his cheek softly, just as she used to when he was such a small child. Now he was a grown man, a vampire beyond rival and her heart overflowed with love for him, for he was her only child.

"Your mind is tangling with your heart, and I think you need to separate the two, *mio figlio*. What is it you doubt? Surely, it cannot be the beautiful female that lies here, for her love for you is so deep and true. Has she not proven such to you? She came to you willingly, fought the demons to become yours. I have watched her for so long. Long before you ever saw her. She was chosen for you, led to you. She is your eternal soul mate. Of that, you could have no doubt, *mio figlio*."

Before his *bel rosso*, his *madre* was the comfort he had always sought in the darkness. It was her heart that lulled him to sleep with a knowledge that tomorrow would come, and he would hold his head high as a Medici and strive once again to be the vampire, the man, the king that was buried deep inside him. Closing his eyes, he breathed deep of her, felt her crawl deep into his soul and he let her inside. She was a part of who he was. Her hands brought a welcome healing touch he hadn't felt in so long. He relaxed, letting out a sigh. For a brief moment, he gave up the burden of being the strong warrior, the leader of so many, and the one everyone depended upon. He relinquished all this and became just Shade, her son. She took control. He no longer needed to be strong, as he could be weak with her. He felt her shift beside him, relaxing back against the many silken pillows and stretched out her legs, patting her lap for him to lay down his head. He knew this place so well. She had been his solace on many nights of grief and failure.

He lay down next to her, pulling the sheet over himself, and laying his head in her lap. Her warmth was as he remembered, her silken gown enfolded around him. Her hand slid over his shoulder and he reached up to hold it, kissing her hand. She wore her simple band of diamonds, the symbol she belonged to *Padre*. He felt her bend over and kiss his forehead. Her hand moved down his chest and lay across his heart, spreading her fingers to contain it, protect it, and feel it beat with her own. He'd never appreciated the treasure of their time alone when he was young, assuming she'd always be there. But now, her visits were a rare and priceless gift he didn't take for granted.

Portia felt him let her inside his soul, and felt the tears well in her eyes. She had longed to comfort him. She felt his *bel* inside him and he didn't push *bel* aside but allowed Portia to have a space reserved just for her. She kept one hand over his heart and her other slid through the curls in that beautiful head of hair. He was ready to talk to her, confess to her, and confide in her. Kate knew she was chosen by Portia to be her son's mate, and her soul accepted the bond that existed between Portia and her only son, a bond of love that only another woman could understand. Portia was comforted to know Kate protected him as he did her. Kate would give him that peace when he needed it. She had truly earned the title of queen and she would protect and serve this coven, as no other ever could. Her heart was pure in her love for him, for she was his light.

"Talk to your *madre*, *figlio*. Let your thoughts become my own. Rest and let me carry this burden that lies heavy on your heart."

Her words comforted, and he opened his eyes to look up and see her leaning down, smiling for him. He learned from his *madre* how the bond of two created one, strengthened both, and could last an eternity. And now, those lessons she'd shared with him he'd put into play with his *bel rosso*.

Shade knew well his *madre* had intervened, saw his wayward wandering, his lost and lonely soul, and put Kate in his path. He sighed deeply and voiced the thoughts in his troubled mind.

"I have taken so much from her, *Madre*. I have taken her soul. It belongs to me now and what have I given her in return? She is queen. She is loved deeply and will never want for anything, but I have left her so unattended at times. I left her out of much of what is our world, and then brought her into it, blind to what lies ahead. I have so much to teach her, guide her through to survive. I am grieved deeply by the thought of her becoming hardened, cold. I love my *bel rosso*. I love her softness, her vulnerability. What if she embraces her power as vampire and no longer needs the one thing I adore giving her, my protection. Perhaps, once she learns her skills, she will no longer need me to protect her. It will kill me. I don't want to let her down, disappoint her in this life. And what if she hates it? I cannot turn back the clock for her. She will always remain immortal. Am I strong enough to lead her, guide her? Can I give her all she needs? Can I love her enough? She knows another life, one I never did. Being immortal is all I have ever known. Can she let go of her past to always be mine? What if I cannot fill the void of what she left behind?"

Portia smiled and closed her eyes as his doubts came to life in words, letting her fingers wrap around a curl and twirl it without thought.

"Shade, *mio vampiro coraggioso*. Your *bel* will not miss what she left behind. She left heartache and the cheating hearts of mortal men. She will blossom with this life. She will discover places inside herself not even you have seen. She will embrace you, your coven, and your warriors. She has a soft and loving heart. She will never lose that, not with you. You adore and love her. Continue to love her as only you can, *mio figlio*. Teach her how to protect those she loves, and she will not abuse it. She will discover Medici is about *familia*. She has seen that, to some degree. Your warriors admire and love you, they also love her in the same manner and not because of you, *mio figlio*, but because she has already shown them her heart. She understands that giving and loving is returned to her in kind. Teach and guide her. Use what *Padre* and I have taught you, combine the best of both of us and give it to her. Deep inside her, she craves your protection. She likes that you take control of things, but she will have a feisty spirit when need be, I have seen that at work. She will not let you walk away from something she feels important to her heart, *figlio*. Respect that. Let her give you guidance and protection as well."

Portia slid her hand softly across his cheek. "She is the light in your darkest corners. But now, *mio figlio*, that light surrounds you always, embrace it. Let her light take away all the darkness and pain. Never shut her out of what is her means to love you and give to you. Always remember this."

"I love her so, *Madre*. I give her my all. There is nothing left of me, I give it all to her. She has seen our *bambinos*. There are three, *Madre*! Lorenzo, Sophia, and Natalia. I want them to be so loved. We lost a son, and I know it was not meant to be. It is a pain I can never take away for her, that painful mistake. And I made a choice, between her survival and the baby's, and I chose her. A decision she knows nothing about, and I wonder if she could ever forgive me for taking our child from her. I struggle to define my own feelings and loss. I fear I left her alone to deal with the loss. Without Luca, I may have lost her as well. He helped her through the grief she hid from me. I never want that to happen again. I want to share all of our feelings with each other, the good and the bad. Tell me I can do this, *Madre*. Tell me I can raise *bambinos*. Tell me I can give them what they need to survive, be happy and find their place in this life. I want them desperately, but I wonder if I can handle them, teach them, love them with a heart that is gentle and pure, but be strict enough to teach them the lessons they need to learn to survive in our culture."

Laughing softly, Portia swatted him gently. "*Mio figlio*, *bambinos* will lead their own lives. Show them what love and being immortal means and they will be fine. Love your mate, love her like you were taught and the *bambinos* will see and learn what love is. They only need to learn love, see it, and feel it, be raised in its atmosphere, and they will follow. The rest is mere books, tutors, and guidance. Have you not seen yet that your *bel* has a loving, mothering soul? Oh *mio figlio*, she was chosen to be the light for all. Your blood runs in her veins, she will have it all. She is the woman you have sought for your entire life. It is so simple, Shade. Just love her. Just *love* her. Stop worrying about a future you cannot control. Do what is right in your heart, and she will always remain your *bel rosso*."

He felt the death slumber crawl slowly over him and he whispered in a voice that was deep and yet soft. "I love her, *Madre*, I will always love her. She is all I have ever wanted. She is my light, she is my heart. No other will love me as she does. No other can comfort me as she does. No other can tame my beast as does my *bel*."

He felt his eyes become laden with the clawing hands of his death slumber and heard the sweet voice of *Madre* as she sang softly the old lullaby from his youth, one hand still combing gently through his hair, the other splayed across his heart. He reached across the bed and lay his hand over Kate's back and let the slumber take him. "*Ti amo, Madre. Ti amo, mi amore*."

***

Kate felt Shade's hand slide down her back, and she awoke to see him in his death slumber. It was so strange. Her sleep felt the same as mortal sleep. She didn't know what she'd been expecting, but unlike Shade, she woke easily from this slumber, and didn't feel pulled into it. She rolled closer to him, reaching out to him when she saw Portia sitting next to him on the bed and was startled. Kate gasped out loud before she realized who it was.

His mother sat quietly, her hand stroking his hair, a soft smile on her lips. She had appeared to Kate twice before, here at Castello, but only in the mirror, and now she sat here looking as alive as she was. Or was she only dreaming?

"*Madre*?"

"Si, figlia, tis me. Did I frighten you? I did not mean to." Looking down at her son as he was in his death slumber, she smiled, sliding her hand across his face. "He is so beautiful, *si*?"

Kate watched as Portia's hand stroked that face she loved. She reached out her own hand and touched his cheek. "He is more than beautiful. I think I call him distractingly handsome. He still takes my breath away, he always will."

Portia chuckled. "He is much like his *padre*, they can make you do things you never thought you would ever do, by just looking at you. But this is good, *si*? That you find him this handsome? What else, *mio figlia*, do you find distractingly wonderful about my son?"

Kate looked at Portia, as she had such adoring eyes for her only son. "I find him to be a gentleman, despite the leathers, and his warrior's heart, he is, to me, always a gentleman. He holds old values dear, honor and integrity, fidelity, and loyalty. You don't see those things very often anymore. I love the way he protects me, the way he makes me feel protected, and takes care of me. I don't mean taken care of financially, I mean he takes care of my heart. He cares how I feel. We've had our struggles, but I guess you've seen that. It wasn't an easy path for either of us to choose. I think he had a lot of fears about me becoming immortal, about whether I'd make it. I only had one fear, and that was losing him."

Reaching out, Portia pushed the soft red tendrils from her face and smiled. "You cannot lose someone who holds your soul, *mio figlia*. He loves you with his heart and soul. He is immortal, and his heart will only be given to one, but there is one thing that does disturb me, something I must ask of you."

"Anything! You can ask me anything."

"We have a bond, and it is something that has never been broken between us. But he has never found anyone who has taken his soul and flown with him, who fills his heart to the brim with love and tenderness. You give him light and chase away his darkness. It was something I always tried to help him through. But now he has his love, his light. I only wish to know if you feel there is still room within his heart for me. I know, perhaps, you may find this odd, but I believe the first time you hold Lorenzo in your arms and comfort him, you will understand why I will not be able to let him go."

Looking down at her son, Portia kissed his forehead softly. "He is my only son, his struggles have been hard, and I wanted him to find the right mate, I wanted him to find what he deserved, to be loved for himself and nothing more. It is why I chose you, led you to his path. You have all of him and I only want a small piece left for me." Raising her eyes to Kate, she almost begged. "He may never need me, he is so strong, and you give him everything he ever needs."

"*Madre*, you will always hold a place in his heart. You taught him those values he holds so dear, and I hope you'll always be there for him, for our children, and for me. I left everything for him. I had to leave my mortal family behind in order to protect him, and I have no regrets about that, so you must be my *madre* as well. Guide us both. Look over our children."

Portia reached over her son and took the hand of his eternal mate. "Have no fear, little one, I will always be here for you, for the *bambinos*. He tells me they have come to you. They are beautiful but will be taxing on your heart. But you must not fret, they will be born strong, and Medici, and you will be a great mother to his children."

Portia looked about the room. "So many memories in this room, it is where Shade was conceived. Tune into your gifts, your skills. They will give you all the answers you seek. Protect your children, love them. There are many in his coven who need love as well, some of them so lost. You must be their *madre* as well. You give him enough, *mio figlia*, you must believe that, for it is true. Do not look at me so surprised, I know what you feel, and so does he."

Kate looked at Portia with wide eyes and asked the question she always held in her heart. "Do you know what I feel? Do you know my fear? That, somehow, I won't be enough for him? That he'll grow tired of me? My life as a mortal is a short twenty-seven years compared to him and all he has lived and seen and done. And I have no illusions about his past. I know there were many before me, probably more than I care to hear about. I know he has loved before, but no woman has ever been able to hold his heart. And everything happened so fast for us, even by mortal standards, it was fast. For me, I feel an eternity won't be long enough to share all the love I feel for him. To watch our children grow, and their children. But then I fear this restless warrior who has seen so much, and done so much, will grow bored with me. I feel inadequate, and I feel jealous, even though he gives me no reason. He grows tired of my jealousy and gets angry because he gives me all and doesn't understand. Doesn't understand the weakness is not his but mine. My fear is he'll find another more appealing over time. That's my biggest fear, *Madre*. That he'll grow tired of me and I'll lose him to another."

Portia watched her face in worry and turmoil and reached out and pulled Kate to her chest, caressing her hair as she had for her son.

"Shhhh, now you must listen to me. He is a grown man. They all have their time where they discover, explore, their time to figure out who they are, *figlia*. They hone their skills, decide where they belong, all so when they find their mate, they know and can give them everything. *Si*, he has had many women, but not always by his choosing. Some played with his heart, and he knew deep down he had chosen the wrong path. He was seeking something above and beyond what had been laid before him. He was waiting for you. He had given up, *figlia*, given up finding his mate. I needed to push you in front of him, for I feared he would give up totally on love. He had accepted the darkness, and followed a very dark path, accepted the loneliness he felt, and it was breaking my heart. His warrior is not restless, he just seeks release. He is warrior to his bone. He will always fight, he is Medici. But he will never leave you. It is normal at first to feel this way, but you will soon learn, he will always be yours, in every way."

Kate let Portia's words wash over her, comfort her. Heartbreak and betrayal were her only experience with love before him. She too had given up on the dream of love.

"Do you see our future, *Madre*? Do you see our children as clearly as I do? They come to me, so eager to be born into this world."

"If I tell you I see your future, you will ask it of me, and I will not tell you such. It is for you to learn and explore. But I will be there. I see your *bambinos*. Ah, there is one who is most eager."

Portia laid her head upon Kate's. "She is the fiery redhead. She will bring you many smiles, and many heart breaks. He will fall deeply in love with her, *figlia*, give her more than she earns. But she will learn that pushing him too far will never win her his grace."

Kate looked at her. "You speak of Sophia. I feel her strongly, her spirit is willful and stubborn, and her temper a combination of the two of us. But she is also funny and curious and fearless. She will be a challenge, to channel what is best in her and try to keep her on the right path. To learn the Medici values of honor and integrity she must uphold for all, and to control the devilish imp without breaking her spirit, and everything that makes her so... Sophia. I dreamed she would break us, come between us..."

Portia laughed softly. "She will be fine, but she will challenge you at every step, be prepared and just love her. She will learn, with some helping hands, that to be Medici is not a right but an honor she must earn. It will take her time, *figlia*, because this one," kissing Shade softly on the top of his head, "will spoil her for far too long. But he will not put her before you, and he will see the ways of his willful daughter and take her in hand. He grew up so lonely, *figlia*. I feel that in him. And now, he will be surrounded by these children, who adore him, look up to him."

"I can feel his happiness, *Madre*. I feel the joy he will take in them, his pride for Lorenzo's strength, his indulgence of Sophia, his joy in his sweet Natalia. They are each so different and will enrich our lives immeasurably. It's such a blessing to me, to be able to give him these children, our children. I pinch myself, to remind me he's real. That what we have together is real."

"It is very real, *figlia*. And it is the fate of our world that you belong to him and vice versa. Never doubt that, and you will always have us both to guide and help you."

Portia felt his presence and looked up to see Christofano standing in their room. "My sweet vampire love."

Kate saw his father as he appeared, they looked so much alike, he and Shade, and yet, there was sternness about his father's face that she didn't see in Shade. She felt a wall, a barrier that he only dropped for Portia, and Kate understood why Shade felt such distance from him. And yet, he'd come to them in the chamber after the turning. "*Padre*." She bowed her head to him. "You honor me with your visit."

"*Figlia*." He nodded to her. "Portia, it is time you left them alone. They are no longer children, but adults, you will suck the life from them, *mi amore*. Now come, leave them to their life."

Reaching down, taking her hand, Christofano helped her up and kissed her softly. He looked down at his sleeping son and slid his hand through his hair and kissed his cheek as Shade remained in the grip of his death slumber.

"You are the Medici, *mio figlio*, and it lies within your hands. Love her as you should, and all will be yours."

He looked up at Kate and softly caressed her cheek. "Love him, give him a son. You are queen, and all honor you now." He kissed her softly and held Kate to his chest. "You are loved here, *mia figlia*."

Releasing her, he took Portia's hand and laughed as Portia said, "They will always be my children, Christofano, always."

"*Si, mi amore, si*."

Kate watched as he took her hand and they walked away, disappearing before her eyes. She knew why Shade loved to come here, because he saw them here, felt them here. She used to wonder why he chose to stay in the States, when he had this grand home here. But now she knew why he'd chosen to make his home at Bel Rosso. It was a fresh start. It freed him from his past. It allowed him to make his own path, outside the shadow of his father. She laid her head on his chest, felt his arm envelope her, pulling her close in his sleep.

"I love you, savage warrior."

7

Rissa was busy trying to figure out how to get her new purchases packed into her existing suitcases when Alec decided to amuse himself by exploring Castello. It had been a few years since he'd been here, and his previous visits were for far different reasons. It was definitely a different time in their lives, for him and Shade both. He went down the staircase and wandered down the grand hall. Somewhere down this hallway, there was a door that led to the area underneath the castle. He knew the chamber used for the turning was down there, but that wasn't what had him curious. He kept opening doors that led to one grand room after another until he found the door to the caverns.

He started down the stone stairs, the air musty, the lighting dim, until he reached the bottom. He let his memory guide him as he walked through the tunnels in search of that room. Surely, it was gone now. Surely, he had sealed it off. He took the final turn in the cavern and saw the door. He turned the door knob expecting it to be locked, but it opened. He reached inside the dark room and flipped on the light switch and stared in disbelief. It was all still here, the room for the Gorean Sex Cult. How many nights had they spent in this room? How many women? He walked past the rack, the shackles, the stockade, the whips, and paddles. Everything was here, exactly as he remembered it. *So, my brother, maybe things aren't quite as innocent with you as you pretend. Why else would you keep this room?* He ran his hand over the assortment of toys... Toys for very bad boys and picked up a collar. He ran the leather through his hand before slipping it in his pocket, leaving the room, and returning to their bedroom for Rissa.

***

Trying to cram as many things inside the suitcases as possible, Rissa had figured out a method and it seemed to be working. She had three empty cases brought in on the plane just for this purpose. There were a few items she'd shipped directly to G-town. Excusing Rosa, she took a long last look around the glorious room. They'd be leaving early tomorrow. The coronation ceremony last night was beautiful but, her wedding would be the talk of Washington, and she'd make damn sure the precious almighty queen was in attendance. *Where the hell is Alec?* Bending over to adjust the strap on her shoe, she heard him enter the room, and she purposely remained bent over longer than necessary.

Alec saw her with her ass in the air, the sheer fabric of her skirt riding up, showing a hint of the lace thong. He walked up behind her, sliding his hands beneath the skirt and cupping his hands over those smooth firm cheeks. “I brought you something, darling.”

She moaned softly and smiled, turning her head to look up at him, her hair hanging down around her face. “Something for me? Do tell, I love surprises!”

How convenient. She wanted to play games. He slapped her ass hard and heard the resounding crack of his hand as he saw the red imprint appear on her bare ass. “Stand up, take everything off.”

Her mouth watered and she felt the sting of his hand. She stood and flung back her hair, letting it cascade down her back. She did as he commanded and stripped slowly, letting his eyes take in every curve and well-toned muscle. She slipped her feet from the heels and kept her back to him.

He pulled the collar from his pocket and stepped behind her, feeling the curve of her ass as it pressed against his cock. He lifted her golden tresses, and slipped the collar around her neck, securing the buckle. He let her hair drop, then grasped her shoulders, turning her to face him, sliding one finger into a metal loop on the collar and giving it a sharp tug. “Now, what is this collar called? Refresh my memory, darling.”

“Slave collar, daddy.” Her voice was soft and sultry.

“Slave collar. Very good, baby girl. Now, just to be clear, you know what it means when I want you to wear a slave collar.” He tugged hard at the ring again as he spoke.

She felt her neck jerk. His lips were so close she could feel his breath on her face. “Yes, daddy, I’m your sex slave. I’m at your command, and I’ll obey or be punished.”

“Here are the rules, baby girl. Don't fuck up. Don’t speak. If I ask a question, you may answer, otherwise, do as you're told. Now put on a robe and follow me.”

She nodded and ran to the bathroom. She dropped her clothes to the floor and grabbed one of the long silk robes Kate had ordered to be made available for her and slipped it on. Sliding on a pair of heels, she looked in the mirror. She pulled up the collar of the robe to cover most of the slave collar and walked back out. She saw him head for the door and she followed. *Where the hell is he taking me?* Her curiosity was piqued along with her sexual appetite.

As they started to leave the room, he came to an abrupt halt, grabbed the collar, and pulled her face close to his. “A problem already, baby girl? Did I say shoes? I think I distinctly said, put on a robe. That means robe only. Remove the fucking shoes. Now!”

She kept her eyes lowered and quickly kicked off her heels. Her blood was pumping so hard, needing him, and wanting to feed. She took a deep breath and tried to relax and listen to his commands.

"Good girl. Now follow me."

He took her hand and led her down the hall to the staircase as they descended together to the grand foyer and then down the hallway with its opulent chandeliers. They reached the door to the underground and he pushed it open, turning to her. "Normally, I'd say ladies first. But I think it best you follow me, baby girl. And watch your step."

She followed behind him as he entered, and at first glance, it was dark, but her eyes immediately adjusted as they began a trek down stone stairwells. The smell was musty and old, and she wondered what in the living hell he was doing. They had to be underneath the palace by now and she kept following him when she felt something run over her bare foot. She jumped and started to squeal, but remembered his demand for silence. As they keep going further and further down, she stepped on something wet and felt it squish under her foot and she made a small sound of disgust and quickly bit her lip.

She followed him through the tunnels as they rounded the final corner and approached a large wooden door. He stood with his hand on the door knob until she had caught up with him, so she'd have a clear view of the room. He opened the door wide and reached his arm in and switched on the light. The room was revealed in a soft red glow.

"Welcome to paradise, baby girl."

As he swung the door open wide, Rissa saw a playroom full of toys, she stepped inside, looking about, trying to take in everything. Walking to the wall, she ran her hands over the old leather whips, hardened over time. The tables were old but conveniently fixed with chains and probes. A true paradise that looked like it was made for them. She looked at him, the smile on her face saying everything. **"Oh yes, daddy, baby girl loves this room!"**

He closed his eyes and puts his hands on his hips and issued a heavy sigh. "First of all, I didn't give you permission to enter. I expected more from you, so let's go back to basics, shall we. Master, I am master from now on, until you earn the right to call me daddy. Now remove your robe and get your ass on that table. Hands and knees."

She quickly disrobed and sat on the table, swinging her legs under her and getting on her hands and knees, letting her head hang down. She didn't speak, but she knew she'd pissed him off already, and was determined to please.

Alec grasped a handful of her hair and yanked hard, pulling her head back, so she could see his face. He kissed her hard, pressing his lips against hers, so her lips were pinned against his teeth, bruising her. He yanked her head back further to release the kiss, then tossed her head forward, releasing her hair. He ran his hand down her back, following the curve of her spine, over her ass, down the backs of her thighs and across her calves until he reached her feet. He ran the backs of his hands across the soles of her feet. He shackled her wrists and ankles to the table and then ran his hand across the soles of her feet once more before striking her feet with a thin hard plastic rod. He watched as she flinched in response to the pain.

Rissa curled her toes in response to the strike, but she wanted more, as the pain quickly subsided. She waited for the next exhilarating moment when he would strike her.

"My darling, I did say you couldn't speak unless spoken to. However, please feel free to scream at any point. Not that I will stop, mind you. But you may find it a release for the pain, the louder the better. Your screams excite me." And with that, he lashed out harder across the bottoms of her feet, striking that tender flesh again and again, as the memories of this room flooded over him.

She felt his beast emerge as he struck her harder with each lash. Each strike sent pain screaming up her ankles. They had spent many a night in this type of game play, but there was something different about tonight. This wasn't just the beast come out to play, but something darker and deeper than she'd ever seen before. He didn't stop and she cried out suddenly. His strikes were deep and she felt the blood running between her toes. She felt each lash drop like fire onto her feet and she screamed again and again, the sound echoing off the walls. She growled as her beast emerged, ready to tangle with him. Her screams were so loud it deafened her, no longer feeling pleasure, only agonizing pain.

Her screams excited him as he struck harder and watched her skin split open, the blood oozing between her toes and onto the table. He dropped the rod and leaned over her feet and ran his tongue over the wounds he'd created. As he licked away the blood, he watched her skin heal and heard her quiet sobs. He walked to the head of the table where he removed the shackles on her wrists and pulled her upright onto her knees as he pulled her arms behind her back, securing them with rope. He tossed the rope over a crossbeam in the ceiling, grabbing the lose end and pulling tight, watching as her torso was lifted and supported by her arms.

Rissa screamed out as she felt her shoulder joints pulled to their limits, but the burning was like a lover's kiss and she reveled in it.

Alec walked along the back wall. So many toys, he hardly knew where to begin. He left her suspended by her arms, as he sought what he was looking for. Picking things up, he remembered the last time he used them before replacing them back in their place. He picked up the nipple clamps and took them back to the table. Her head was bowed, and her hair hung around her face.

"Head up," he barked at her, and she lifted her head obediently. He placed a clamp on each nipple, adjusted it to its maximal tightness and watched as she gritted her teeth. "Now tell me that feels good."

Rissa was picking up on his thoughts, and realized he'd been here before. She could feel the memories flooding through him. She almost whimpered thinking he was remembering another lover he may have brought such pleasure to and it almost broke her. But she reminded herself he chose her.

He pulled the attached chain between the two nipple clamps up and toward him with one finger, stretching her nipples to a painful point. "Yes, master, this feels so good." She let out a moan, a mixture of pain and pleasure and watched the wicked smirk slide across his face.

"But not good enough, I think. Let's see if your master can make it better."

He attached the chain that held the two clamps to an electrode from the generator and flipped the switch as the electric current rolled through her body. His cock throbbed as he looked at her erect nipples, her skin twitching, and her jaw clenched. "Now, tell master it feels better."

The current sailed through her body and her eyes popped open wide. She found it hard to speak through her clenched jaw as the current controlled her. "Yes, master," her breath quickened, her voice sounding strange even to her, "better."

He walked down the length of the table, pulling off his shirt and letting it drop to the floor. He ran his hands over her ass again before sliding his hand between her legs to feel how wet she was. It made him smile to know her body responded this way to all the pain he inflicted. He slipped his fingers inside her, thrusting slowly before removing them. His fingers wet with her juices, he picked up the stainless steel dildo and slid his hand over it, getting it wet with her own sweetness, before inserting it deep inside her. He pulled another electrode cable from the generator and attached it to the dildo, adjusting the current, so it was low. She would feel the tingle, the arc of the electric current, but the pain would be mild... at least for now.

He felt the pain she felt. He felt the pleasure she took in the pain, and his manhood ached to be inside her. But the torture wasn't over, not yet, not for either of them. He picked up the hydraulic contraption from the floor and placed it on the table behind her. He lubricated his finger and slid it into that tight puckered ass. He probed her slowly, before removing his finger, and re-inserting two. He could feel her body spasm from the inside from the electric current pulsing through the dildo buried deep. As he felt her relax around his fingers, he positioned the pump with the rubber butt plug tight against her anus, poured the lubricant over the plug, and turned on the machine. It began its slow thrusting movement, pushing deep inside her in its evenly measured mechanical rhythm. He turned up the amps on the dildo and the nipple clamps.

Throwing back her head, the sensation was overwhelming. She felt him increase the current and it felt like a fire was going through her and she screamed, again and again.

She felt agonizing pain shoot through her body, connecting and arcing between her nipples, her cunt, and her ass. With each movement, her shoulder sockets screamed out from the ropes that kept her suspended. She couldn't control the jolting of her body, as it moved on its own accord from the power of the current and the ripping pain that coursed through her. Her screams echoed across the room, bouncing over the walls, rattling the chamber and she knew... He wouldn't stop.

He unzipped his jeans and stripped them over his hips, letting his cock spring free. He peeled the jeans off each leg and tossed them aside. Her body was no longer hers, but she had one more orifice to fill. He walked to the front of the table and climbed on, kneeling in front of her and grabbed a handful of hair. Yanking hard, he yelled at her to hush, and her screams stopped. As she looked up at him, her face and hair were wet with perspiration. He held his erection in his hand, and dragged it down her face, circling her lips. "Open wide, baby girl, daddy's going to fuck your mouth now. Don't you dare bite down."

Her eyes remained locked on his, as he slid his cock into her open mouth. She closed her lips around it, fighting the spasms created by the current. He slid deep before beginning his thrusting motions. She remained on her knees, suspended by her arms, so he held her head in his hands to guide her movements. With each thrust, he pushed deeper, watching her face as she struggled for air, his cock sliding down her throat and blocking her ability to breathe. Her face turned red, and her eyes watered and he listened to her make gagging sounds to get air. He kept thrusting deep until she started to go limp, and then he pulled back, allowing her to gasp for air, and then he started again... and again.

She felt the room going black. She wasn't getting enough air and felt the darkness settling over her. When he pulled out of her mouth, she gagged and gasped for air, spittle drooling down her chin, hair dripping sweat and her body jolted again as she came over and over from the current. He rammed his cock down her throat again. The darkness dropped over her, and she fell into the black vortex of unconsciousness.

As her body went slack, he withdrew his dick, still throbbing for release and his beast roared, vibrating these stone walls, and watching as the dust fell from the ceiling. He had pushed her body too far, but his beast wanted what it wanted. He angrily flipped off the switch on the generator ending the electrical current that flowed through her and watched, as her body stopped its uncontrolled quiver. He lowered the rope as her head rested on the tabletop. He flipped the switch on the hydraulic pump and removed both the butt plug and the dildo. He untied her arms, and lowered her shoulders, massaging the muscles in her shoulders and back as he heard a soft moan.

"Come back to me, baby girl. Daddy's not finished." He lifted her limp body and rolled her over on her back, brushing the damp hair from her face.

Gripping her hair in his hand, he lifted her face to his and licked the side of her face, starting at her jawline all the way to her temple, tasting the salt in her sweat. He let go of her head suddenly and let it drop back to the table, listening to the crack of her skull against the hard table. He spoke to her in a low growling whisper.

"That wasn't much fun for your master now was it, baby girl? I give you one orgasm after another, your body riding the current, and yet, my cock is still hard. You bring me no relief. And now I have to start over. Maybe I should've brought Jacks down here instead of you."

Rissa heard his admonishments, as she slowly resurfaced to consciousness. She wouldn't be compared to that warrior bitch! She sat upright and shouted at him, "Don't compare me to that whore!"

His beast roared back, sending cracks up the walls of the stone cavern and dust and small chunks of stone rained down on them as he mounted the table, crouching over her, his face inches from hers as he placed his hand in the middle of her chest and pushed her hard against the table. His eyes glowed red and the saliva dripped from his fangs.

He placed his other hand around her throat and squeezed. "Did I give you permission to speak? You dare defy me?"

He leapt from the table and pulled the whip from the wall and in a single motion, turned back toward her and snapped the whip over his head, hearing the sound as it zipped through the air and watched as it cut across the soft skin of her belly.

She screamed in anger, pain, and pleasure as she felt her skin open from the whaling lash. As he pulled the whip back, her hand reached out and she gripped the whip and yanked as hard as she could, drawing him to her as she bit his lip hard, drawing blood, and feeling his beast riding him hard to unleash. He let go of the whip and growled, sending vibrations rumbling through her body.

His face was only inches from hers. "You don't decide! I decide!" He grabbed her by the collar and dragged her from the table. This wasn't what he'd planned. He pulled her across the room and placed her in the stockades, locking her head and hands in place. He walked behind her, kicking her feet so they were spread wide. He grabbed the wooden paddle and swung hard at her ass and listened to the resounding crack. "Do you want to defy me again? Because I can do this all night, baby girl!"

She bit her lip, knowing she'd pushed him too far. She moaned as the pain warmed her ass and thighs. She felt the small trickle of her juices slide down her inner thighs and she wanted more. She wiggled her ass and braced for the next strike of his paddle.

He struck her again and again, watching as her ass turned redder with each strike, his cock throbbing for release. He released her from the stockade, and picking her up, he carried her to the table and dropped her down on her back. He shackled her arms over her head but left her legs free. He picked up the candles, lighting them, and held them over her face to see, before holding the candle inches from one nipple, letting the hot wax drip. Watching her flinch as the scalding wax hit her skin. He covered both breasts with the wax, before creating a trail down her belly. He pushed her legs apart as he knelt between them, letting the wax drip onto her clit, and watched as she responded.

Rissa felt the scorching hot pain as the wax dripped over her clit. She yanked on the shackles and screamed from the intensity of the sweet agonizing pain.

He grabbed the blade with its razor sharp edge and slid it slowly across her breast, peeling back the layer of wax. “Don't move, baby girl...don't flinch. Master doesn't want to make you bleed, unless you want to bleed. Do you want to bleed, baby girl?”

She felt the knife slide under the wax, and its cold steel surface felt amazing against her skin, from the painful burn, to a soothing cold. She loved the sensation of the wax being peeled from her body. “If you wish it, master, I only wish to please and pleasure you. I’m your slave.”

He drew the tip of the blade in a thin line from her naval to the top of her pubic bone, watching the skin open, the trail of blood beginning to flow, running down her sides. He ran his tongue over the wound, watching it heal, as her blood sang in his veins and he could take no more. He lifted her legs over his shoulders, as he slammed his cock hard into her, pushing deep, laying his full weight into her hips, and feeling her hips lift to meet him. He pounded her hard, the surface of the table beneath her unyielding, as he thrust hard and deep.

His hands were on either side of her face, his face only inches from hers, and her legs spread and held up by his shoulders, he watched the expression of pleasure on her face as he fucked her harder, bruising that tender skin. This is what she liked, what she begged and waited for. He lowered his mouth to her neck, and before he sank his teeth into her, he whispered, "Feed."

She had waited so long to feel him inside her. She gripped her muscles tight around his erection, sucking him deeper. She heard that sound of skin slapping against skin. She sank her fangs deep into his neck and felt that burst of blood into her mouth. She was starving for him.

He drew her blood into his mouth and it felt like liquid sex, as it rolled across his tongue and his cock throbbed and pulsed deep inside her with each swallow. Her body responded to him, her hips bucking off the table, riding him as hard as he was riding her. He unlatched and placed his lips on her ear and whispered, "Cum for daddy."

She felt his power roll through her, and she came like never before. She screamed and writhed beneath him. Her body convulsed hard against his and she loved him at this moment like never before.

As he felt her body release, he let go inside of her, pouring his cum into her after hours of holding back, feeling the ache deep in his balls, and his beast roared again with pleasure, as he slammed her hard against the rigid table. Riding her orgasm until they both faded, he dropped his weight on his elbows and looked at her face, her blue eyes glazed over and kissed her mouth, sliding his tongue deep into her throat. He ended the kiss and rested his forehead against hers, letting his heartbeat return to normal. "Now that is how you fuck, baby girl."

He rolled off of her onto his back, looking at the ceiling, listening to her heavy breathing beside him. He chuckled to himself. *Pretty sure the walls of Castello haven't echoed with these sounds in a few years, or have they? I'll have to ask Shade about why he kept this room long after the Gorean Cult was disbanded. Perhaps his mortal is not as innocent as he wants her to appear, and I for damn sure know he isn't.*

He dropped his feet to the floor, and picked Rissa up from the table. "Come on, baby girl, I'll carry you back to our room."

Leaving her robe and his clothes on the floor, he walked nude with her back through the cavern corridors and up the dark stairs and into the grand hallway. He headed up the stairs, calling to Rosa to get a bath ready. As they walked into their bedroom, Rosa was scampering out like a scared mouse, as he carried Rissa into the bathroom and lowered her into the tub of hot water, filled with the foaming bath salts. He climbed in the tub behind her, as she laid her head back on his chest. He dipped the natural sponge into the steaming water and started bathing her. Long slow strokes down her arms and legs, supporting her body while he washed her back. He dipped her back and wet her hair, poured shampoo into the palm of his hand, and washed her hair, rinsing it under the faucet. He let the hot water sooth her sore muscles before he lifted her from the tub, drying her with a towel, rubbing her skin until it was pink. He picked her up again and carried her to their bed, which Rosa had turned down for them and laid her down gently before crawling in beside her. She was exhausted and close to sleep when he nuzzled her neck and whispered, "Daddy loves you, baby girl."

8

Shade, Kate, Luca, and Shannon were all gathered in the less formal Family Room–if you could really call any room in Castello "less formal." They would all be going back to Virginia soon. Kate had seen very little of Luca and Shannon since they'd been here, and tonight, they were all together. Luca and Shade had decided the girls' skills at speaking Italian were decidedly lacking, and were trying, without much success, to coach them. Between the Midnight, or plain wine for Shannon, and their less than serious attitudes, the lessons weren't going well.

"*Bel*, it's *volare*! Not polare." Shade chuckled. "Let it roll off your tongue, put some pizazz into it, *si*?"

Kate was laughing as she tried to repeat the word, "*Vo-lare. Volare.* I can't roll my r's... wait... where do you put your tongue?"

Shannon howled with laughter. "Where do you put your tongue?"

Kate laughed. "To roll my r's, smartass!"

Luca put his face in his hands and shook his head then looked up at Shade and laughed.

"*Mi amore*, did you just say roll your arse?" Shade and Luca both howled with laughter. "You know I can do that quite well, but I don't suggest we do that in mixed company."

Kate shouted above the laughter, "R's, I said r's not arse! I already know how to roll my arse, thank you very much."

He grinned wickedly and pulled her over his lap and slapped her ass playfully.

"Oh *si*, *mi amore*, you roll that arse quite well."

They were all laughing when Shade picked up the sound in the distance. It was faint, and he hoped to fucking hell no one else heard that scream. *Son of a fucking bitch, who the hell is that?* There was only one master who'd been invited to stay at Castello for the coronation who remained here as a guest, and that was Alec. Shade knew Alec would remember the Gorean Sex Cult and the room in the caverns beneath the castle. He was a sick bastard, and it would be just like him to take Rissa down there. Shade would kill him for this fucking nonsense! He didn't know if Shannon could hear the faint sound, but he was damn sure Luca probably did and *bel* may have as well. Then it started again, and the screams continued, louder now and Shade caught Luca's eye and knew he heard them as well.

Luca locked eyes with Shade as he recognized the sounds. He knew they were coming from inside Castello. Luca recalled the years his master fell into that darkness, and Alec eagerly joined him in the escapades that took place out of sight, but not out of earshot. The staff and warriors were all relieved when Shade broke free, ending his relationship with Sabine and closing that room, ending the parade of depraved individuals who went there nightly. Luca glanced at Shannon, who was still talking, but Kate was starting to turn her head. She had heard the sounds as well. Screams, faint but getting louder.

Kate looked at him with a question. "Shade? Did you hear that?"

Shade exchanged knowing looks with Luca and they both knew who it was and what was going down.

He looked into her eyes as another resounding scream traveled through the house and he sighed. "*Si, mi amore*, I heard it, nothing to be alarmed about. Perhaps we should all take a stroll out into the gardens, get some air?"

As the screams got louder, it was now clear to Kate what she was hearing. She looked at him with questioning eyes, and then to Luca, who looked down at the floor. She turned back to Shade.

"That's a woman's scream. It's coming from inside Castello. I can't tell from where, it sounds muffled, but I don't understand. You're telling me not to be alarmed? A woman is screaming inside our home, and you say don't be alarmed?"

Shannon perked up. Her hearing was not as acute as theirs, but she too heard the screams. She walked to the doorway and listened. "Down there. Down the grand hallway somewhere. I heard it too."

Shade looked in her direction. "Shannon, step away from the door." He gave Luca a stern look. **"Don't let her go out that door."** As Shade closed his eyes, another scream ripped through the house, and he felt Kate ready to stand up from the sofa as he reached out to restrain her. "Stay where you are, *mi amore*. There are rules within the vampire community. Not all vampires are alike in how they treat their mates. But the most important rule we follow is you never tell another master how to control his mate. We still have guests within Castello. That's all I need to say."

The scream was piercing and filled with pain. Kate pulled from him, trying to break his grip. "I don't understand. What do you mean you don't interfere? It sounds like someone is being killed in our own home, and we're supposed to do nothing? Someone is in trouble. Do something!"

"*Bel*, relax please." He snuggled into her hair and held her tightly against his chest and whispered. "It is Alec and Rissa. I know you don't understand, but I cannot interfere. Please try to appease me on this. She is not being hurt."

"Rissa? Those are Rissa's screams? How can you say she's not being hurt?" Kate struggled to get free. Why was he holding her here, when clearly there was someone in danger? This was not like him, or Luca. "I don't understand. You're warriors. Why are you ignoring this?"

Shannon looked back at Luca. "I think someone should go check... at least check."

Luca stood and spoke sharply. "No! Stay where you are. This isn't our business."

Shade held Kate firmly by the shoulders. "Listen to me. It's Rissa and Alec. They are, *cazzo*, how the hell do I say this? They are in an underground chamber of Castello." He stared at *bel*, trying to make her understand. "We don't interfere with other master's mates, Kate."

He looked to Luca and shook his head. "Luca, please take Shannon back to your room, outside, take a drive, whatever you need to do that makes her more comfortable." Looking to Shannon, he said, "I apologize to you, I know you don't understand, but I won't interfere, not even in my own home. It is our code. Perhaps, Luca can explain it to you in a more understandable way."

Kate stared at him in confusion as he told Luca to leave with Shannon. Luca got up and took Shannon by the arm and led her back upstairs. After they left the room, she looked at Shade. "And perhaps you can explain to me in a more understandable way. What's going on? Why are they underground in Castello? The turning chamber? Are they in the turning chamber?"

He crouched in front of her, between her knees, as she sat on the sofa and he looked into those beautiful worried eyes. He laid one hand on her knee and slid the other hand along her arm.

"*Mi amore*, I will explain. But I need you to listen to what I am saying and hear me. They are not in the turning chamber. They are at the opposite end of Castello. They are having rough sex. Alec is a very different master than me." He looked down and shook his head. "He's a sexual sadist. He loves to hurt her, but you must understand she loves the pain, she does not fight it. It's how they get pleasure from each other and I cannot interfere."

Kate looked confused, but remembered Rissa's warnings from long ago, about vamps and rough sex. "Okay. I get that. I'm aware of the whole bondage thing. But it sounds...more than that. It sounds like more than just rough sex. And why are they down there? How would he know about the area underground? Why not in their own bedroom?"

"*Mi amore*, I promised I would hide nothing from you. I'm not proud of this, but it is in my past. Alec and I did some running around together. That's how we know each other. There are...tools, toys, and they are used for creating pleasure and pain. We belonged to a sex cult, the Gorean Cult.

It was custom at that time in Europe. We used these rooms for pleasure, for orgies and playing out sexual fantasies. For me, it was a phase, a dark phase. But for Alec, it is a lifestyle, one he maintains to this day.

"Alec was drawn to Rissa as I was drawn to you. But for him, he saw her darkness, her need to submit to his dominance, her desire for pain. This is what he likes, what they both like. He is very dark. He loves to abuse women with pain, it brings him pleasure. Please understand, I beg you."

Kate pulled away from him. "You built this room? You belonged to a cult? A sexual cult?"

She stood up and walked around the room, pacing the floor. It's what she had always feared. His experience so outweighed hers, he'd grow tired of her. Orgies? How did she compete with orgies? Had he made women scream out in pain? This wasn't the Shade she knew. Or did she know him at all? "But you kept this room? Did you think... Did you plan to use it?"

Watching her pace, he felt his heartbeat rise. He was going to kill that bastard for doing this in his home, making his own mate doubt him, doubt herself and everything she knew about him.

"No! Please don't think I ever planned to use it again. I had forgotten it, actually. I spend little time here at Castello. I was building my empire, gaining land, out being a warrior. I have not spent much time here in the past few years. And the room, it was simply forgotten."

He stood and ran his hand through his hair while she began to pace, and he watched as she put her face in her hands. "Please, *mi amore*! I'm not that man any longer. That is my past. I would never use it again. I had forgotten it was here! And yes, I did make women scream in pain. Yes, yes, yes to all the damn questions in your head!"

Kate squeezed her eyes shut as he said he made women scream out in pain and put her hands over her ears. *Who is this man?* She paced the floor again, her head spinning. "I need to see this room, lover. I need you to take me there."

Shade spun around and stared at her. "Why? Why would you want to see it, *mi amore*? You abhor it, look at you? It is already making you doubt me, wonder about me. Have I ever brought you such pain? No, never! I'm being honest with you. I am telling you my past, hiding nothing from you, nothing! And still, you want to see this den of sin?"

He realized if she insisted, he'd have to take her there and deal with the outcome. Alec and Rissa might still be there. He hadn't heard anything after Alec's roar, but he was making damn sure. **"Gi, can you make sure Master Canton and his mate are in their room?"**

Gi told him Alec had called for Rosa to draw a bath and had returned to their bedroom, carrying Rissa. Shade sighed, hoping to hell he hadn't killed her. Alec was one out of control bastard at this play, and even though

Shade knew Alec still engaged in rough sex with Rissa, Shade knew damn well Rissa experienced things tonight she'd never experienced before.

Kate spoke to him in a small voice, "I just... I need to see it. I need to understand." She wasn't sure herself why she felt the need to see it. But if she didn't, she knew her imagination would just try to fill in the blanks. "Please..."

Shade stood before her. "I don't like this, but I can tell you need to see it to understand it is not who I am anymore." Holding out his hand, she took it and he kissed her lips gently. "I can teleport us right outside the door, or we can walk, it is a ways to go, your choice."

"Teleport me."

He nodded and lifted her in his arms and teleported swiftly under Castello and stood outside the closed door. He sat her down on her feet and looked into her eyes. "We are deep underground, *mi amore*, far from the turning chamber. Remember who I am please, Kate. Remember this was years ago, and I am not this man any longer. I love you."

Watching her nod to him, he lifted the latch and swung open the door, willing on the lights. He held out his hand for her to enter and wondered how the hell this night with his mate turned into chaos.

She knew he didn't want her in this room. He reluctantly opened the door. He stepped in behind her, standing rigid, not moving. As her eyes scanned the walls, the ceilings, she walked through this den of torture and realized she was wrong. There was nothing in her imagination that could have prepared her for this. She was hit hard with the sense memory of him in this space, his emotions when he had come here, and it staggered her. Then she saw the images floating through her head of the women, the nameless, faceless legion of women who had been paraded through here. Some had come willingly, some not. She felt his darkness, and his loneliness. Sex had been used like a drug or alcohol, sex used to numb the pain, or make the body feel something other than a soulless emptiness. The women's pain had been his sick pleasure, followed by self-loathing, and a sicker desire to do it all again because feeling something was still better than feeling nothing, better than feeling lost in the darkness. Soulless sex. Mindless sex. There was no love here. There wasn't even passion here, only anger. This was the beast he always feared she would see. This beast only rejected and destroyed. This beast had no limits, wanted no limits. This beast felt like the demon that came to her in her turning, gripping both ankles and refusing to let her leave the hell that waited for her. This beast took and took and gave nothing in return, but pain and more pain. This beast pulled him deeper into the darkness and refused to let him go because the darkness and the pain fed his sickness. This beast rejected all that was light and good and held him in an unrelenting grip.

As she ran her hands across the table, she stepped over Rissa's silk robe, spattered with blood, and Alec's jeans. She walked past the sawhorse, the stockade, the chains, and straps, she saw the faces of the women, and heard their screams, as they all flashed through her head. And then she saw her...Sabine.

"She fed your sickness with her own dark desires. She held you in your pain and anger. She fed the beast and gave him more power, stripping away at your soul. She didn't love you, Shade. She couldn't love you because she didn't love herself. She needed a companion to walk through this soulless nightmare, and you were her willing partner. I don't know how you broke the grip of this place, how you came to resist its pull, only that you did. But it's still in you. And that was the darkness I saw in your eyes when I first met you."

This was what she intuitively felt made her fear him, resist him, and yet, at the same time, made her inexplicably drawn to him. She wanted to heal the pain, to shine a light on the darkness, replace the emptiness with love, and the soullessness with heart. **"Did you see that too? Did you know that when we met?"** she questioned telepathically.

She realized, yes, he did know, the beast knew, and *Madre* knew. Whatever fates conspired to bring them together, knew love healed all. Love filled the emptiness and filled the soul, soothed the pain, and ended the loneliness. The beast knew, just as Kate knew the beast. This was what Shade saw, when he had so much fear for her to meet the beast. He saw the beast that dominated this room, the beast that only knew destruction and pain. Kate saw the beast that was trapped in darkness and loneliness, and couldn't find his way out, but a beast that knew love conquered all. Love healed.

She walked back to him, slid her hand up his chest and around his neck. Standing on tip-toe, she pulled his face forward and gently kissed his lips, soft kisses. This room had never known soft kisses.

She whispered to him, "Come, lover, there is nothing for you here anymore. This is who you were, this is not who you are. It has no hold on you anymore."

She turned and led him out of the room, pulling the door closed behind them. "Leave it, destroy it. It matters not to me. I know you. I see you. I always have. You fear I'll be driven away by knowing the darkest parts of you, but you don't understand. I saw the darkness first. I fell in love with you in spite of the darkness, and there's nothing in your past that can push me away. Love conquers all, lover. Now come, we won't speak of this again."

***

Shade watched her closely as she walked through the room, standing back, there were no words between them, and none were needed. She felt it all, knew it all. Far beyond what he could ever imagine, she knew the depth of who he was. This is why she was his, why he wouldn't let her go, why he loved her with every fiber of his being. She understood him as no other female ever could. She was never afraid to love him, only afraid of herself.

He had never gotten over this part of his life, and it still lurked in the dark corners of his brain. She now understood what it meant when he told her she was the light in his darkness. He loved her. He too understood why his beast fell in love with her the moment he saw her. He knew she was the light he'd been seeking that would comfort him and the beast.

"*Si, mi amore*, love conquers all."

9

Soon they'd be leaving Castello and heading back to the States. Shade watched Kate sleeping, and knew she needed her rest. She wasn't used to all the changes in her body yet, but she was coping far better than he ever expected. Neither of them had discussed when they'd return, but he knew both of them were anxious to get back home to Bel Rosso.

He had a warrior camp in development that should be near completion and he was eager to get that started and get his ranks built there. As for *bel*, he smiled looking at her. He had some plans for her as well. A new *bambino* would keep both of them busy. As his thoughts went to her, he thought about Marco and Theresa. Their discussion at the reception was icy and he knew Marco didn't receive the news of her decision to return to the States well. Maybe it was time to have a talk with his oldest friend.

Shade liked walking to the warrior camp. It gave him time to clear his head, reflect on where he'd come from as well as where he was going. The Florence camp was very old school in its teachings and traditions, and he'd never change that. The Euro vamps were still different in their thinking and fighting skills than the American vamps. He liked straddling both worlds, it was a challenge he grasped with both hands. As he rounded the corner into the camp, he saw a feeder leaving Marco's quarters. She didn't see Shade, and he stopped to watch her leave. Feeders in the camp were forbidden, but Shade had always cut Marco some slack. Didn't take his brother long to decide on whether to work on his relationship with Theresa or let her go, and somehow, that made him sad. He knew if he didn't speak with Marco before he left, there would be unresolved anger between them, and he couldn't live with that. Both of them knew they either talked it out or fought it out, and they were both too damn old for that bullshit anymore. They needed to save their energy for the real enemies. Tapping on the door, Shade walked in and found Marco lounging, and watched as his eyes rolled up to greet him. "Brother, good night so far, I take it?"

"Good so far, old man. It should be better once I get a sword in my hand and my ass on the field. Something you want?"

Shade took a drag on the cigarette and exhaled slowly, "You know, brother, I'm too fucking old to be playing these games. So, I'm getting straight to the point. By the looks of the beauty that just strutted out of here, I take it you're letting Theresa go back to the States without a fight.

So, tell me," he sat down in a chair and threw one leg over the opposite knee. "What happened?"

Marco pulled his sweater over his head and flung it in a corner. Standing, he grabbed a glass of Midnight, downing it in one gulp.

"She made a choice, Shade. She chose you and your queen. She didn't ask me, she didn't tell me of her plans. I had the pleasure of finding out from a member of the staff. Let me see if I can get this straight now. If my memory serves me correctly, I'm a warrior, never bothered to talk to her about mating, children, and the like. In other words, I'm the bastard that was never going to give her fucking shit in her life. You come along, drag her ass to the States where she discovers she's a modern woman with choices, and likes being able to say whatever the fuck she wants, when she wants. I am assuming I have our gracious queen to thank for that. And you, well, brother, once again, you have bested me. Some things never change, Shade."

Shade sat and listened to his grief, silent and emotionless, until Marco finished his rant. "You done? Now you can listen to my side, old man. Look, I can't take you from here. I didn't know when I asked Theresa to come with us that you two were together. And by the sounds of this, she has been expecting something from you for a long time. I appreciate that you waited for her, but nobody is going to convince me your ass sat here celibate while she was with us. I know you, I know how you operate. You didn't just feed, brother, you fucked right along with it. So, I bring her back here to be with you, so the two of you can have some time together. I see it in your eyes when you look at her, she means something to you. I decided to give Theresa the choice, to go or stay. I did that for you, for both of you. I can't take you from here. I need you here to be my eyes and ears in the camp. *Cazzo*, brother, why the hell didn't you fight for her to stay?"

Marco slammed his fist on the table. "Fight? How the hell do you fight for someone who doesn't want to be here? Tell me! She needs to go, to grow and become who she wants to be. I hold her down here. She's never left this place before. She never will if she remains with me. Now she is the Queen's Lady in Waiting. She's going places I can't take her, *sì*? I let her go. I didn't want to, but I did that for her. I love her. I will always love her. She is tender and soft and loving, and took care of me when I needed it. She needs and deserves more. And she will have it with you. She has something special inside her, and your woman knows it. So, I concede my love to your mate, my queen. It's done. I want no ties to bind her to me. She deserves to find what she seeks, and it's not me. I am warrior. I am Medici Warrior."

Shade took a long sigh, stood and grabbed him in a brotherly hug. "I'm sorry. I never meant to take her from you. I hate to see either of you suffer, and I thought I was doing the right thing."

Marco let go of his anger. "Well, brother, we have a pact. No woman was ever going to come between us and that pact remains true. Just take care of her, protect her, and watch out for her. It doesn't matter that she doesn't belong to me, it matters that she is cared for and loved and is happy. I know it won't take her long to find what she seeks."

As he ended the hug, Shade stepped back and grimaced as he looked at him. "And you, brother? What is it that you seek? Because what just walked out that door is not it."

Marco gave him a sad smile. "Maybe not, but it works for now. I have no plans of becoming mated. I'm a warrior and a mate doesn't suit my lifestyle. You, you are the king, the Medici. It is different for you, but I know two things that will always be the same. I love you and, in your heart, you are a warrior like me. Now get the fuck out of here, I have a pack of pups to beat into shape!"

Shade slapped him on the back as he grinned. "You know where to find me. And yeah, I love you too, you old fucking coot!" As they fist bumped and laughed, Shade knew he'd be all right with time, and so would Theresa.

10

The whirring sound of the blinds opening in Castello woke Shade. The sun was setting, and he knew it was time to return to Bel Rosso and the Virginia mountains. Their time in Florence had passed much too quickly. The last two weeks had been a whirlwind of activity with the turning, the coronation and visiting old friends. Shade had taken his newly crowned queen to meet his coven and other masters in the surrounding territories. She had impressed and pleased him and all who met her, from the lowest in his coven to the highest. Her beauty had only been enhanced since the turning, and her feeding was now under control. He turned over in bed, reaching out for her, wanting to run his hand through that silken crimson halo that surrounded her head, and found the bed empty. He sat up slowly to see her wandering around the massive bedroom, already gathering things for their journey. She was ready to go home. "Did you not slumber, *mi amore*?"

"I slept, in your arms, as always. I feel your heartbeat beneath my hand, your breath across my cheek, and the protection of your arms. I sleep well, and dream well, thanks to you."

Shade let the smile in his heart break out on his face, as his gaze took in all of her. His queen was dressed in a red silk robe that clung to her curves.

"It is my duty, as your king, to make every aspect of your life happy. But we need to have a talk, come, *mi amore.*"

Holding out his hand, he watched her strut to him with a coy grin, she was, and always would be, his walking sin.

Kate climbed up on the bed and straight into his arms, those blue eyes calling to her. "And what do we need to talk about, lover?"

Snuggling her to his chest, rubbing her back, he nuzzled his stubbled chin into her hair. "We must return to Bel Rosso tonight, *mi amore*. Whatever you have bought, or want to return to the house, will go back on the private jet." He nipped her ear and continued. "I am not ready to have you teleport, the journey is long, and it takes much practice to be precise and I do not feel like traveling the world trying to find you. So, we will teleport together as we have always done. I want you to feel the difference this time, and keep your eyes open, look about you. It will feel and look much different now that you are immortal. Just enjoy the journey in my arms, *si*?"

Kate melted into him, laying her head on his chest. "Theresa has already packed most of my things, so I don't have a lot to do. And she said she'd stay behind to make sure everything was taken care of before she followed us home. Did you talk to Marco? About Theresa? I'm glad she's coming back with us, but I feel bad she had to make such a choice."

"*Mi amore*, I too feel guilt. But Marco is warrior, he will always be warrior. He had given no indication to Theresa of a future." Shade sighed, not sure he should divulge the information Marco had shared with him about his decision to break his union with Theresa. "He has..."

Kate waited for him to finish the sentence, sensing a reluctance to express what was on his mind. "What is it you hesitate to share?"

Shade smiled to himself. He had to remember she felt his emotions now as strongly as if they were her own. "Damn woman, perceptive as always, but now even more so. Marco loves her, *mi amore*, but he feels she deserves more than what he can give her. He has freed her to seek her own happiness. She would have stayed with him if he had given her the promise of mating. Marco knows she will move ahead, become so much more than if she stayed. I have one wish for you, now, king to his queen." Pulling her close, he tipped her chin up, staring deep into her eyes.

"You have one wish for me?"

"*Si*, I wish for you to promise me now, you will not disclose this to her. It will only make her feel the pain. Let her work this out on her own. Marco will do the same. They will both find their own paths. Sometimes, we must learn to let love have its own way in others' lives. Agreed?"

"I'd never say anything to hurt her feelings. I know this was a hard decision for her to make. I don't completely understand her choices, but I will, of course, honor them, and yours."

"*Grazie*."

Leaning over her, he covered her mouth with his, letting the kiss absorb her, take her from her thoughts straight into his heart and he felt her melt into him as his lips worked their magic on her. Slapping her ass lightly, he broke the kiss, smiling down into those eyes, now more amber than brown. Her beast sat just below the surface, waiting her chance to tangle with his beast, and he loved that she was finally his for all eternity.

"Come, let us dress and be gone. I am anxious to return. I will miss Castello, I always do, but Bel Rosso now calls to me so much stronger. The warrior camp should be done, and I am anxious to see it finished and begin what I was born to do."

Kate slid from the bed and pulled on jeans and a pair of sandals. The long gowns and elaborate crowns had been stored away as she returned to her more normal attire.

"Lover, I've missed it too. I can't wait to see what they've done with the camp. It will look quite different from your camp here since the architect designed it to blend in with the buildings on the property. And the high wall around the perimeter, I was a little concerned about how that might look. So, yes, I'm more than ready to return."

As Shade slipped from the bed, sliding on his low slung jeans, he pulled a sweater over his broad shoulders, listening to the happiness in her voice, and he knew Bel Rosso was her home as well. He knew, the moment he laid eyes on her, she would fit into that Virginia estate and restore its glory, make it a home for them both and now, all of his dreams had come to fruition. They were on their way to a new life together, where nothing and no one could come between them, and they'd conquer all, hand in hand.

Walking to her, he admired the beauty before him and the growl that erupted from him couldn't be held down. Sweeping her up in his arms, spinning her around, he lost his heart once more as she threw back her head, the crimson flying as her laughter filled the room. It was the most befitting exit he could ever wish for. All inhabitants of Castello would hear the laughter of happiness and love from their queen.

"Ready?"

"Take me home, lover. I'm ready!"

Shade pulled her close, letting his arm encircle her waist and felt her arms go around his neck. This time, as they teleported, he wanted her to experience the speed. No longer would he cradle her as before. This was her first lesson on how it felt to be immortal and ride the stars.

As they teleported out, Kate realized he'd always held back when he teleported with her as a mortal. She could feel the wind whip through her hair as they moved with greater speed, and he didn't hold her as tightly. As they moved across the night sky, he extended his arms and took her hand. For a moment, she panicked, thinking he'd let go, but then she heard his chuckle. "Not yet, *mi amore*, but soon."

***

As Portia and Christofano stood in the corner, they watched their *figlio* with his newly turned mate return to their home in the States. A blood tear slowly streamed down Portia's face, her hand reaching out to her only son.

"Journey safely, *figlio*. Cherish her, love her, and never forget we love you and await your return. Rule our lands with the heart of a king."

She felt Christofano reach out for her and pull her to his chest. Their son had finally found his place in the world. As Christofano tipped up her chin, his eyes shone with so much pride and his words were a comfort to her, for he'd finally realized their son had achieved all they could have ever dreamed for him.

"He is king, Portia, and he has found his queen as I found mine. Together, they will rule this world as no other, our legacy goes forward."

As he picked her up, he carried her to their bed. The night began for them as it had many centuries ago.

***

Shade and Kate landed in their bedroom as she staggered slightly when they came to a full stop and he reached out to steady her. She giggled as she caught her balance and grabbed for him. She felt a wave of dizziness wash over her as she regained her equilibrium. Looking around their room, taking in all that was familiar, it seemed ages since they were here. The last time she'd stood in this room, she'd been mortal.

She smiled at him. "Well, at least I didn't fall."

"*Si*, as if I would let you fall. It gets easier. *Cazzo*, it is much warmer here than I expected."

Grabbing the waistband of his sweater, pulling it over his head, he stood bare chested, jeans hanging low off his slim hips, his abs tight as a washboard. Walking to the armoire, he flung it open and stood with his hands on his hips.

"Damn it, woman, I can never find a thing in here! It is like a maze to me. I just need my jeans, leathers, tees and boots."

He rummaged through a few drawers, flinging clothes from one side to the other, growling in frustration as *bel's* laughter rang loudly in the room.

Kate shook her head. He'd been waited on hand and foot at Castello, his clothes laid out for him. No wonder he could never find anything.

"Shade, it's too hot for leathers. Just grab a t-shirt, if you can find it."

"Stop laughing at me. I am spoiled, but damn if you will not have some system laid out for me." Turning to her, his hands still on his hips, he gave her a pleading look. "Please? Be of some assistance to me, woman. Where shall we go first? Stables or the camp?"

Kate was amused that mortal or immortal, there were areas where all men were helpless. She walked to the armoire and pulled out a shirt for him and watched as he slipped it over his head, his dark hair falling around his shoulders.

"Come on, hold my hand. I'll take you to the stables."

"I heard that tone, *mi amore*. You will be punished duly when we get back to this room!"

He smacked her ass but she didn't flinch. Instead, she turned to him and purred and his beast growled back at her. "Lead on, my queen. Apparently, this king is completely inept."

They walked together down the stairs, the house quieter than usual as they waited for the return of the house staff.

"Lover, I was thinking about something since I'm immortal now. We have Reynaldo here and I'll no longer be eating. And the California house, we rarely have time to visit there. It seems a shame for it to sit there unused. I was thinking, what if we sent Reynaldo there, as a chef, and let him run that house as a bed and breakfast, or possibly an inn? We can lock our own bedroom suite there, and let him rent out the other rooms, prepare meals for the guest. It would draw people to your vineyard and promote your brand. What do you think?"

"Explain bed and breakfast, *mi amore*, because from what I have seen of you eating, breakfast is not such a big meal."

Kate led him through the house and out the back door, into the garden, taking the path that led to the stables.

"A bed and breakfast is like an inn or small hotel. People just come for one or two nights. They have a bedroom and then the B&B provides a lavish breakfast or brunch. The guests could tour the vineyards, go to the tasting room, and buy the wine while they're there. Many of the vineyards in Napa operate that way. People will take their vacations just to visit the wine country. It'll turn the house into a profit source, and also give Reynaldo a job."

Listening as they walked, Shade weighed the pros and cons of letting mortals further into their world, mulling over the advantages and disadvantages. He needed time to think this through.

"I will give it some thought, *mi amore*, I promise you. Let me do some research, have you spoken to Reynaldo on this yet?"

"No, of course not. I wouldn't speak to him without discussing it with you first. But talk to him as well if you are inclined to agree."

They walked hand in hand through the garden, now in full bloom, their path lit by the soft landscape lighting as they came into the clearing that led up to the stables.

"*Si*, let me think about this, and we will approach Reynaldo together." As they approached the stables, Angelo walked towards them, and Shade raised his hand in greeting. "Angelo, *buonasera*! How is my boy doing?"

"*Buonasera*, master. Welcome home." Nodding his head in a soft bow to his queen, "My lady, it is good to have you home, my congratulations."

Turning to master, he had no time for small talk but got right to the point. "Master, there is an issue I wish to discuss."

As Shade nodded his head for him to continue, Angelo stood before him, scuffing his boots in the dirt. "The horses have been bothered of late. There is a wolf, a large one. He comes to the stables almost every evening. He wanders here, stays close to the stables. It has the horses riled. They kick the stalls, doing some damage. It's a daily task to make repairs, so they don't bolt. I would ask your permission to shoot him the next time he appears. The shotgun is handy, and I keep it inside the stables with me at all times."

Shade found the information concerning. Wolves weren't loners, they traveled in packs, and if there was one, there were more, and that bothered him. He'd seen them high in the mountains when he teleported home. He knew they were about but being this close to the house and horses was not something he was comfortable with. He felt Kate tugging at his arm.

"Shade, no! Please don't shoot him. Let me try to send him away."

"*Mi amore*, we are not sure of the extent of your gift, neither of us. I do not like this. Wolves are dangerous animals."

Kate pleaded with him, "Please. I can already feel her. She's close by, and she's alone. Please, don't shoot her. I know she'll respond to me."

"She?" Running his hand through his hair, he looked to Angelo. "Don't shoot, Angelo, but keep the gun handy. If the wolf attacks my horses, she goes, *si*?"

Turning to *bel*, he took her in his arms. "I will concede that much, *mi amore*, do not push this issue. I will not lose expensive horseflesh to a wolf. Nor have her running this close to the house, it is not safe."

"We're fine, lover. I feel her intention."

Kate let go of his hand and walked across the field toward the line of trees that led into the dense forest. As she got closer, she saw the large female wolf standing in the woods, hiding in the shadow. As Kate approached, the wolf raced to greet her and Kate went down on both knees, extending her arms to her. The wolf ran playfully around her before bounding into her open arms, almost knocking her over, licking her face, and then lying down calmly before her. Kate rubbed her head briskly. The wolf looked at her as they locked eyes, and Kate nodded. "Aegis. Her name is Aegis, and she is here to protect us."

Shade and Angelo both stood watching with caution, as Angelo had the shotgun ready. Shade felt a moment of panic as the wolf raced toward her, and he teleported immediately to her side, ready to tackle the animal by the neck and watched as the wolf licked Kate's face and lay down in front of her. Angelo watched her pet the animal as if it were a house dog. Shaking his head, he couldn't believe what he'd witnessed. She'd tamed a wolf in an instant, with only the touch of a hand.

"*Cazzo, bel!* What the hell were you thinking? That wolf could have killed you." As Shade paced, he couldn't believe what he'd seen. "Aegis? How do you... I need a fucking smoke after this." Lighting up, he crouched a distance from the animal and Kate. "*Bel*, did this animal talk to you? Did she tell you her name and her purpose here?"

Kate sat on the ground and the wolf crawled into her lap, draping over her as the wolf laid her head on her paws. Kate stroked the thick coarse fur along her back. "She speaks to me, like you... In my head. Her name is Aegis. She says it means *shield*, and she's been waiting for me to come home. That's why she went to the stables every night, looking for me. I'll let her know to steer clear of the stables and the horses; her presence there only upsets them. See, lover, she's acknowledging me already, saying she meant no harm to the horses. She says she'll guard the house, just as your warriors guard the house."

As Shade watched her interaction with the wolf, he could tell she'd just begun to explore the power of this gift. His *bel* would be something to be reckoned with. "I am impressed, *bel*, you have taken to your gift well. Now, what the hell is she guarding us from? I feel no threat. Can you explain further, please?"

"She says there's no threat right now, but she'll remain close by, along with the others."

"Others? A pack then. I have seen them running in the mountains. Just make sure she stays clear of the horses. I don't want the others going there either. Ask her to warn them as well, for their own safety. I will advise Antonio, although, he may be a bit shocked, to say the least."

Kate nuzzled her face into Aegis's thick fur. "She says she understands. She'll stay away from the horses. She has a mate. She says wolves are like us, they mate for life."

"*Si*, they do." Holding out his hand, he let it lay on the ground. "Aegis, come. I mean you no harm. You seem to be protective of my mate. Come. Take my scent home to your mate. We wish to welcome you to Bel Rosso."

The wolf stood and walked slowly toward Shade, her ears back, her tail down, sniffing at his extended hand. Kate encouraged her, "Go, Aegis. He means you no harm. No one will harm you here." The wolf approached and lay at his feet.

Shade reached out gently, petting the thick coat of the wolf. "I do believe, *bel*, we need to let Aegis get back to her business. I will inform Antonio there is to be no shooting of anything." Standing, he walked to Kate and reached out his hand to her. "Come, let us check out the camp and let our friend go about her business, *si*?"

Kate stood and took his hand as they walked together toward the new camp, and Aegis followed along behind them. Kate laughed. "We have company. I'm afraid you'll have to get used to her."

Shade looked over his shoulder to see Aegis following after them. Shaking his head in wonder, he smiled at *bel*. "I have no problem with it, but I think we best inform the others of your gift. You amaze me, *mi amore.* Do you know how rare this gift is?"

Kate giggled as the large wolf followed along behind them, as docile as a family dog, and yet, she knew this creature was wild and capable of killing its prey. "I'm not exactly sure what I'm supposed to do with it, lover...this gift. Both you and Luca have said it's rare. I guess I'll just figure it out as I go."

As they walked down the new gravel road that curved away from the house to the new warrior camp, the high stone wall surrounding the camp came into view. The landscapers had already started planting ivy along the wall that would grow fast and soften the imposing structure. They approached the heavy wooden gates, not allowing an outsider a view of the camp that lay inside.

"*Bel*, look at it, just look at it!"

He pushed them open and led her inside the compound. Standing with his legs spread, taking in the entire grounds, his smile was huge, his heart racing with pride and excitement.

Kate followed behind him as the wolf danced and pranced around her feet. She reached down and pet the wolf as they followed Shade through the gates. "It looks beautiful. The architects did as we asked. The barracks look like a large home, not unlike the staff quarters, except there are several levels that are below ground. The building that looks like a detached garage is a weapons bunker, and there's a tunnel system that connects the barracks to both the bunker and the training center. The training center looks huge. It's a little hard to disguise, but at least the building materials are all the same, giving it the same feel. I'm glad they built the stone wall around the perimeter, though. This would definitely draw the curious."

"Oh, *si*, it will draw curiosity, but mortals are curious creatures to begin with. Let us go inside, I am anxious to see the layout of the place."

Walking inside, he led her and watched as Aegis sat beside the door, waiting for their return.

"Lover, there are rooms here for sleeping, with separate quarters for your female warriors, and separate shower rooms. They have an area where they can romp freely and other areas for those who need some quiet space. And you have a meeting room, where you can call them all together."

As they strolled on their inspection tour, Shade knew this place was ready to go, there was no more waiting and he was pleased with the outcome. "I wish *Padre* could see this, *mi amore*, I think he would be proud."

As they continued their journey, Shade admired the craftsmanship of each detail. Leaving the barracks, he headed for the indoor training center. "Damn, *bel*, this is amazing! Everything came out even better than I envisioned. What do you think? Happy with the outcome?"

"Very happy! It looks ready to me. I'll check with the contractors, I'm sure there are small details to be finished up, but nothing that should keep you from moving ahead. Marcello, Raven, Fiamma and the others could all move in here now. I noticed you didn't bring Olivia back with us to Virginia. Did she not make the cut? Or are you just leaving her to train in Florence?"

"Olivia was not ready for this assignment. She did well, but I asked her to remain back in Florence. She has much to learn yet, and being here was a great opportunity for her, but it showed me she was not yet ready for the streets. She too realized she needed more intense training in some areas. Marco will continue to work with her. She will be a force to reckon with in the future. But there will be others. You understand we will have females who will apply."

Kate looked at the floor of the new training center as he spoke. She knew in her head there'd be more female warriors coming when the design for the new barracks had dedicated space for women, but it was something she'd blocked from her mind. She liked Fiamma, and she trusted her. But did that mean she could extend her trust to every female warrior who walked through those gates? She understood what he was asking of her, what he needed from her. In her head, she understood this was her role now, as Medici Queen, but her heart still felt the cruel taunts from Sabine. She'd had such limited exposure to the female warriors, she wasn't sure she could extend open arms to all of them. But she owed him the benefit of the doubt. She had to push through and at least give the female warriors the chance to prove themselves to her, to earn her loyalty, as Fiamma had done, without pre-judging them. As he finished speaking to her, she lifted her eyes to him. "I can be what you need me to be."

He kissed the top of her head. "You are all I need, *mi amore*. Just love me and enjoy our life together."

Kate lay against his chest as his arms encircled her. "I'll always love you. Have patience. I'll figure this out. It's an adjustment. You spend much time with the warriors, and now, with the camp here, you'll spend even more time with them. It's hard for me to share you, but I'll deal with it."

"What you forget is, I will be home more now as well, do not forget that. Marcello is going to be my Second-In-Command. So, his responsibilities will be many. Speaking of which, I need to get to the Dead House tonight, check in on things there, and see what has been happening in D.C. while we have been absent. Come, let us walk back to the house, then I can get going, and get back to you for a long sleep in our own bed."

Taking her hand, they strolled casually back to the main house, each glancing at the other, soft smiles exchanged and huge hearts beating their never ending love for one another, as Aegis trailed behind them, tail wagging.

11

Shade prepared to teleport into D.C. He needed to get caught up on everything that had gone down while he was in Florence. He and *bel* had walked the property and checked out the stables and the new warrior camp, and he had seen, first-hand, his newly turned mate's gift. It was already exhibiting itself and he couldn't be prouder. And now, instead of a family dog, they had a wolf that had decided to protect them. Shade almost laughed, but he knew the only way for Kate to learn how to master her gift was to have the animals around her. Animalism was a rare gift for a born vampire, let alone a mortal who was turned. And he had no source of where to find information that might help her. He'd never known of a vampire who'd had this gift. Gifts were meant to be a defense mechanism, they helped with the vampire's survival, to either help them blend into mortal society, like day-walking, or used as a weapon if necessary, like dream-walking. He wasn't sure how *bel* would be able to utilize this gift as a weapon, but it was a gift he wished for no one to be aware of for the moment. This little secret needed to stay under the radar and the knowledge limited to those in the coven here in the States.

Shade made his rounds high above the Georgetown streets, and damn if it didn't feel good. Scoping out the night life and the activity of the people on the streets, he took a turn over Alec's residence. He found lights on in the house, but it was obvious neither Alec nor Rissa were home. Things appeared quiet and he rather liked that. He had a lot to accomplish in the coming months with the opening of the new camp and he had no time to be dealing with errant rogues on the rampage. Cuerpo was dead and so were his cronies, and good fucking riddance.

He teleported to the Dead House, landing outside in the courtyard. The place was quiet, and he lit up a smoke before going inside. It felt good to be home and getting back to doing what he loved. Leaning up against the ramshackle old Victorian house, he heard a stir and looked to see Tomas exit the house and light up as well.

Shade nodded at him. "Brother."

Things had been boring since Max had disappeared, and Tomas was ready to move on. His work here was done. He'd done well for himself, collecting his payoff from Maximus for being his spy on the inside, and also collecting his due from Canton, earning top dollar as Shade's Second-In-Command. It was time to do a little traveling. Europe was calling his name and after that damn fiasco Maximus had tried to pull off, he was more than ready to move on. Medici had this well in hand, and Tomas knew nothing else was coming from Maximus. He seemed to have completely disappeared off the face of the earth. Tomas had no idea where he was and could care less. He'd left without his little blonde honey hole, and Tomas was damn sure Maximus was hiding someplace with his tail between his legs, pining for the rich, highbrow whore who he'd failed to win. But what did he care? Tomas had played his part and had his money, and it was time to move on.

"Welcome back. Good to see you home. Congratulations on your mating. We need to talk, and now is as good a time as any."

Shade looked him over. Tomas looked well rested. It was obvious things had been quiet in Shade's absence. "*Grazie*, Tomas. Appreciate your work while I was abroad. What's on your mind, brother?"

Tomas took a long drag of his cigarette and turned his eyes to the Medici. "There's nothing going down here. No action anywhere. Since the disposal of Angel, we can't even find a damn vampire in this town that's not Medici or employed by Canton. I'm done here. I'm moving on. I gave it some time for your return. Owed you that much. But it's time for me to move on to the next job."

Shade had been expecting this, so he wasn't surprised. With no action, vampires like Tomas didn't stay long. "If anyone understands, it is me, Tomas. The call of the mercenary is one that sings in the blood. Being idle is not exactly something this warrior handles well, either." They both chuckled lightly. "I have no problems with you taking off. You've done well, you leave in good standing, and I'll be sure to tell Alec the same. Any business you need to finish up with either of us?"

Tomas knew Shade had no idea he'd been the inside man for Maximus, and he'd walk away with no one the wiser. Canton and Medici had no clue of the evil he'd helped pull off, and if Cuerpo had been successful, neither one of them would be alive. But even well laid plans get fucked up, and that fucking red-haired mate of his took out the evilest vamp around. It was time Tomas disappeared before anything came to light, like the fact Cuerpo wasn't Angel. Tomas doubted Max would ever divulge that bit of info. It was certainly to Max's advantage no one knew he was Angel, especially since his tactic failed.

"Canton's paid up. Your boys have things covered. Alec's original warriors are gone, except for Skelk. Your warriors are out there tonight, grids haven't changed. I leave with what I came with. I'll leave it up to you to tell Canton. I have no more business with him."

Shade took the last drag off his cigarette and stomped it out under his booted foot. "Then get your ass moving, Tomas, I know you are more than ready to head out of here. You know how to find me if you need anything. I'll tell Alec, not a problem. Appreciate everything you have done here."

As Tomas nodded, they fist bumped and pounded each other's backs. Tomas took off into the night as Shade returned to the Dead House. Damn, he had a few loose ends to finish up before he could jump into the new warrior camp full force, and he needed to get them in line before he called Alec to let him know he was back and Tomas was gone. For one thing, he was going to need a new SIC for the Dead House. It was time to call his warriors off the streets for the night. He let Marcello know he was here and to round them up and get their asses back to the Dead House.

It didn't take long before Shade could hear them teleporting in on the ground floor and heard the familiar, yet comforting, sound of pounding boots on the metal steps leading up to his command center. As they strolled in, each one took their turn fist bumping their master. There was a lot of back slapping and ribbing, and his warriors felt comfortable and relaxed.

"Take a seat, you bone-heads. Good to be back. Your queen is well and happy. I heard you bunch have been slack, with nothing more to do than piss away the nights in D.C. But for what it is worth, this is good news. Nothing is stirring up the territory. A few things I need to go over with you and then we can call it a night. The rules are not changing. We remain on watch. We keep the grids the same until further notice. Tomas has stepped down as SIC and is already gone, with my blessing."

Shade looked at Skelk and nodded to him. "Skelk, you're the only one left not officially one of my boys, but in my opinion, you have proven yourself invaluable to our efforts here. If you are agreeable, then I would welcome you into the Medici, put you permanently on the payroll and offer you accommodations at Bel Rosso. And with it, comes my protection as your master and your allegiance to my coven."

Skelk nodded his approval. Shade carefully eyed his warriors for their reaction to his announcement and was pleased when they nodded their acceptance.

"Excellent. Gather whatever you need and head out with the rest and Marcello will get you settled in. My mate has informed me our camp is ready for business. This is a dream come true for me, and a great beginning for Medici here in the States. I plan to hold an official meeting with everyone within the next week or so. Attendance is mandatory. Each one of you is here because I want you here, but I will give you options. If this isn't where you want to be, tell me before the meeting. No judgment is being made. I want warriors who will step up. This will be no walk in the park, so don't let the luxury your queen has provided you, fool your asses. I will demand one-hundred and ten percent, if not more. Now, get back to Bel Rosso and rest up."

Shade watched them scatter, their mouths running a mile a minute with plans. He was pleased knowing for each of them, this was a great opportunity to make something more of themselves. "Marcello, have a seat, I need to speak with you alone."

Marcello hoped this was good news. He'd worked hard while here and knew of all the Medici warriors in the States, his skills and leadership abilities were the most advanced. Marcello walked to the huge desk covered in papers, maps, and grids. He pulled out a chair, spinning it around backwards and sat down, propping his arms on the back of the chair. Shade plopped his large frame down in the worn leather office chair.

"Welcome home, master. Is everything good?"

"Couldn't be better. *Bel's* feeding is under control. My horses are in fine shape and the new camp is ready to roll. Few things need some finishing touches, but we are ready. Which brings me to why I asked you to stay behind, I need your opinion on a few things. You're my main warrior here, Marcello, you see it all, interact with the other warriors and they come to you with their needs. With Tomas stepping out, we have a vacancy. I need a SIC here in the Dead House. I want to spend as much time as I can at the camp, close to home and concentrate on building our ranks here in the States. I want this camp to be as big, if not bigger, than Florence. This is going to be permanent. I have Marco running Florence, but I will need help here at this new camp as well. I'm counting on you to step it up a lot more. Responsibilities are going to lay heavy on your head. I have no doubts you can handle this. You ready for that?"

Marcello took in every single word. This was the opportunity he'd been waiting for since he'd arrived. Being SIC at the Dead House would be an easy job to fill since he'd assisted Tomas frequently. "I'm more than ready!" Marcello could feel his blood pumping in his veins.

Shade nodded his head, swinging his legs up on the desk, crossed his ankles and whipped open the top desk drawer to find a pack of cigarettes. Pulling out a smoke, he lit up and flipped the pack across the desk to Marcello. "That's the answer I expected from a Medici Second-In-Command. But I want you to be my SIC out at the camp at Bel Rosso. You are far more valuable to me there than here. I need you to be in charge of operations, directly under me, recruiting and training new warriors. We have to walk hand in hand through this process, Marcello. You're the best I have."

Marcello heard an offer he wasn't expecting. *Second-In-Command of the new warrior camp? Fuck yeah!* He stood from the chair and began to pace, his heart hammering in his chest. It was worth it, all the years he'd spent developing his skills on and off the field, and this was finally happening. "Did you just appoint me SIC to the warrior camp, master? *Cazzo!*"

Shade smiled to himself. Marcello was still young, but he'd prove himself even further and Shade had no intentions of making it easy.

"You going deaf now? Settle the fuck down, Marcello. Relax, you heard right. You have done well here, earned it. But I won't make this a ride in the fucking park. This is no game, brother. I expect a hell of a lot from you. Prove to me, beyond a shadow of a doubt you can handle it and it will please me."

Marcello tried to control his excitement but remained standing, lighting up a cigarette. "I got this, master. I can do it without question. I'm the warrior for the job. I won't let you down. I was expecting, hell, I was expecting to be SIC here, not the camp!"

Shade chuckled. "Sit the hell down, you're making me itchy. Look, there is no one else I even considered for the camp. But that leaves me with a vacancy here, so I need your opinion. Who can I have step into SIC here at the Dead House? I have more warriors coming in from Florence to handle the streets and some to help at the camp. So, whoever the hell I choose has to know D.C. like the back of his hand, be ready to train and familiarize the Florence warriors in a hurry. Any thoughts?"

Marcello quickly got his head back in the game and sat back down, straddling the chair. His hands were playing across the back of the chair, he couldn't keep still. He was the fucking SIC of Medici Camp! "Two come to mind. My first choice would be Fee. She knows all the warriors back home, they respect her. It would be an honor as well, making her the first female SIC ever."

Shade dropped his feet to the floor and shook his head. "Not going to happen. Not that I don't want her here, but I have plans for her at the camp, brother. I'll have female recruits coming in, and I'll need a female to lead them. Only one I trust is Fiamma, and she'll report directly to you. Who is your second choice?"

Marcello hesitated to tell him his second choice. Shade had had some issues with this particular warrior, and he was far from ordinary. He took a deep breath, looked Shade straight in the eye and said, "Raven."

Shade threw back his head howling with laughter. "*Cazzo!* Your first duty as SIC is to give me someone who can command, and you give me Raven? Granted, that little punk is faster than a bullet, but he has a mouth to match. Hell, Marcello, are you serious? Explain to me why you would choose Raven? I cannot wait to hear this."

Marcello shook his head, he knew Shade would have this reaction and now he had to defend his choice. "He's changed, and for the better. Granted, he has a flare for the dramatic. Still does, but he wouldn't be Raven if he didn't. He's fast, faster than any of us. He can handle a weapon like a pro, and he can sometimes go places we can't because of his size. His dedication to Medici is solid. He belongs here. He fits in here much better than he did in Florence. He was a great help in getting Cory set up when he first came to Florence. If it weren't for him, the brothers wouldn't have given Cory a fighting chance with his leather skills. Now, they can't live without Cory. Cory is close with Raven too, and Raven has taken him under his wing. Look, if you have brothers coming in from Florence, this would be a good opportunity for Raven. He trains more now. Has his head in the game. Everyone loves the crazy bastard. He knows this city like the back of his hand. Hell, he can cover it faster than any of us. Give him a chance, make him work for it. If he doesn't cut it, send him back to Florence. Trust me when I tell you, he'll do anything not to go back. He won't disappoint. It's up to you, of course, but I don't see anyone else that can come close to accomplishing this job at the Dead House."

Shade liked the argument Marcello made. And Raven helping Cory? That sent a good feeling through him. Marcello made some good points. Shade knew he had to decide soon so they could step in and free his time for the camp. This meant he needed to sit down with Raven and talk things through. The kid needed to know what would be expected of him.

"So, Raven it is then. I'm putting my trust in you on this one, Marcello. I'll talk with Raven, get a feel for him, see how he responds to the proposition. In the meantime, until we have the camp meeting, I want no one to know what we've discussed. Keep the SIC position to yourself. I'll announce it at the meeting, along with whoever is chosen for SIC here at the Dead House. Otherwise, things go on as they have been."

Shade fist bumped Marcello and gave him a fatherly hug. "Get your ass home. Congratulations. You earned it, brother. I'll be back at Bel Rosso in a while. I have a few calls to make. Move!"

Marcello had one big ass grin on his face as he sauntered out of the room, his head held high.

12

Kate returned to their bedroom to find Theresa already unpacking their clothes and sorting things for the laundry. When Kate began to help, Theresa dismissed her, "I've got this, my lady, I'm almost finished here."

Kate headed downstairs to find Gi bustling around the house, opening windows to air it out, letting in the early summer breeze. Luca's door was open, and she could see him unpacking and sorting through his clothes as well. Everyone had something to do, except her. Kate laughed to herself, *what exactly do queen's do, anyway?*

She'd give Shannon a call, but she was sure, at this late hour, Shannon was asleep by now, her luggage left on the floor until tomorrow. Kate plopped on the sofa in the living room, watching as the drapes blew gently in the night breeze, the air fresh and clean. She picked up the scent of Aegis, and knew the wolf was close by. She smiled to herself, wondering what the heck she was supposed to do with a pet wolf. She scrolled through her cell phone, looking at contacts, deleting the names of the mortals, a symbolic motion as she deleted them from her life. She saw Rissa's name and paused. Kate was still confused by the cold-shoulder she received in Florence. Kate had gone out of her way to make sure she and Alec had been made to feel welcome there. She had hand-picked the room for them to stay in. Assigned a private butler and maid, made sure she had fresh flowers daily. Not because she felt particularly close to Rissa, they had never been close, but maintaining this relationship was important to Shade. She hesitated briefly, then hit dial.

When her cell phone buzzed, Rissa picked it up on the second ring without looking at the caller, her head buried in plans for the wedding. "Larissa."

"Rissa, hi, this is Kate. I was just checking on you. Making sure you both got home okay, and everything went well in Florence. I know I didn't have a lot of time to spend with anyone, but when I saw you at the reception, you seemed...distracted. Is everything okay?"

Rissa heard the bitch's voice and she growled under her breath. *Okay? Is she fucking serious? Like Kate cares what the hell I think!* "Kate, or should I say, your majesty? I'm fine, lovely event, we're both fine. Actually, I'm not fine, but why would you care? You can't possibly be pining for a thing. Or are you calling me to rub it in?"

Kate felt blindsided. "Excuse me? Rub what in? Of course, I care. And no, I don't pine for anything, but neither do you. I don't understand. What exactly do I have to 'rub in'?"

Rissa stood tall, her hand on her hip. "Don't you dare play the naive fool. You chased that warrior so you could own all of fucking Florence, and when that wasn't enough, you stole my Paris house. It was mine! But you had to be some badass hero and ask for my house on the Champs Elysees. It's worth a fortune! So, don't you dare act the innocent." Rissa was seething as she paced her office floor, wearing the rich carpet thin.

Kate stood up from the sofa. "What are you talking about? I don't own a house in Paris. And owning Florence? You know I don't really own anything in Florence, any more than you own D.C. The coven in Florence is under Shade, and you know, without him, I'm nothing. I felt the same disdain from the masters as you did, they'll never have the same respect for me as a turned mortal. I don't understand where this is coming from, Rissa. Are you angry that I fell in love with a vampire? If not for you, I doubt I would have met him."

"What am I talking about?" Rissa was livid and kicked the chair across the room. *Oh, you are not going to play the high and mighty bitch with me, sister!* "Oh please, Kate, you are Queen of Medici now. Alec is a master, not royalty. Use that pea brain in your head! Do you think, for one second, they care you were mortal once? Who in their right mind is going to say one cross word to that big-ass warrior? Seriously, grow up! Alec gave you my house is Paris. You killed some damn vampire assassin and as a prize, you get my house in Paris! I can't believe I'm having this conversation with you. And for the record, I told you to stay the hell away from him."

By this point, Rissa was screaming in the phone and she no longer cared. Alec wasn't around, and a good thing too because she was letting it all loose on this bitch, and it was about time she knew the score.

Kate was fuming. She couldn't believe Rissa was jealous about her relationship with Shade. She remembered all too well that Rissa told her to stay away. And all this time, she thought it was Rissa's concern about her. She should have known it was all about Rissa!

Kate took a deep breath. Shade still worked for Alec, and she needed to get a grip on her emotions. "Rissa, I honestly have no idea what you're talking about. If there's a house in Paris...something that was given to me..."

She had a flash of memory, a conversation with Shade, something about a reward for killing Cuerpo. Was that it? "Rissa... Oh my god, is this that thing over Cuerpo? Shade said there would be some reward, but I've been given nothing. If the reward is your house, I'll talk to him. I'll speak to Shade."

Rissa scoffed. "Speak to him? It's a master's deal."

Jacks heard the commotion and stepped out into the hall and heard a ruckus coming from Rissa's office. She didn't sense any danger, but something had blondie out of sorts. Knocking on the door, she waited for Rissa to answer. "Rissa, is everything okay?"

Rissa heard the knock on her door. It was the protector bitch from hell. Damn, she couldn't even talk on her phone without her nosey ass interrupting her. "Hang on a moment. We're not done, by any means!"

Walking to the door, Rissa opened it slightly to inform Jacks she was okay. If she didn't make nice with Jacks, she'd pay hell with Alec later. "Fine, I'm fine. Get out! I'm on the phone."

Slamming the door shut, she paced back across the floor, the cell phone clenched in her fist.

Kate could hear the side conversation. "You have company? I'm sorry, I thought you were alone. We can continue this conversation another time, but Rissa, I'm not dropping this. I'll talk to Shade when he gets home."

"Oh no you don't! That was the protector bitch from hell your warrior so graciously sent to fuck my vampire to hell and back as soon as she walked in the door. Thank you so much for that little present as well. Shade couldn't send a male? No, he sends one of the female whores from his harem to fuck my vampire right in the next room. In my own house! I owe you more than you could possibly know. Fuck! Everything is a damn mess in my life. I damn near lose my head from some rogue, then this bitch comes strolling in and decides she is taking over every second of my life and you come along taking my Paris house, become a damn queen and you wonder why the hell I'm emotional? No Kate, I'm not fine!"

Kate sat down hard on the sofa, letting Rissa's words sink in. Was she kidding? Was she goading her? All of Kate's fears and insecurities washed over her. She remembered meeting Jacks, the tall, dark-haired exotic beauty they interviewed for Rissa's protector. Kate welcomed her to their home. Shade assured her the women warriors were just like any warrior, and he saw them no differently. And now Rissa was saying Jack's had sex with Alec? Only a few hours ago, Shade was telling her there would be female warriors here, and more of them when the new recruits arrived, and it was something she'd need to get used to. What exactly was she supposed to get used to? "Rissa, is that true? About Jacks?"

Rissa took a deep breath. "I'm sorry, Kate, I lost my temper. Too many things have been happening lately. I've had such a busy season planned, and then there's the wedding. Alec is demanding it be perfect. But yes, it's true. Why would I make something like that up? She lives in my house, in the next room. It's like being in a cage. I can't leave the house without her, and she's on top of me every moment, even at home. And when Alec comes home, he doesn't come to me, he goes straight to her room."

Kate buried her face in her hand, her emotions a combination of pain, anger, and jealousy. "Rissa, I'm so sorry. I had no idea. I know we've had our differences, but right now, I'm speaking to you woman to woman. Get that bitch out of your house! I know it'll be a fight, and trust me, I've had a few, but don't back down on this. Get her out. If you need a protector, insist on a male protector."

Rissa held the phone from her ear and stared at it. Kate was giving her advice? How precious. "Listen, Kate, I'm working on it, I'm hoping this damn rogue ordeal is over and if nothing more comes of it, I can convince Alec to get her the hell out and get me a male. God, he must be spending a fortune on that bitch. Damn whore! I want her out of my house *and* my life, out of Alec's life. Where the hell does Shade find these women? Do they all look like this? My god, does he fuck them all as well?"

Kate felt her fangs punch through as she stood again and started pacing, a low growl building from deep inside her. She tried to control the beast, but she'd never emerged in anger before. Rissa's taunt went to the very core of Kate's insecurities. Kate wanted to scream at her, knowing it would only add fuel to the fire, but her anger was beyond being tamed.

"Rissa, Shade is not Alec... and I'm not you. I'm sorry the situation turned out as it did, and I can only give you the best advice I know. But I think it best we end this conversation before one of us says something we'll regret."

Kate ended the call without waiting for a response, as she felt her beast emerge. She threw the phone against the fireplace as it smashed into pieces and her roar could be heard throughout the house. Luca was there immediately as Kate bursts through the French doors and out onto the back lawn. Aegis responded, circling her feet, growling, when the lone wolf was joined by her mate, an even larger black wolf. And then the mountain lion showed up.

Luca followed her outside, but stood dead still as the animals circled around her, snarling, teeth bared, all of them protecting her. *Cazzo!*

"Kate, tell me what's going on? I feel no danger here." *Other than these three beasts that want to rip my throat out.*

Kate glared back at him, her eyes glowed red in the night, her fangs bared. *What the fuck set her off? There's no one here.* Luca felt his own beast emerge as his instincts to protect her took over. He growled back at the three animals that circled her feet, and watched as they all flattened their ears, snarling and growling, and lowered their bodies to the ground, ready to pounce. **"Master!"**

***

Shade sat in the Dead House, all the warriors gone for the night and it was quiet. He made a few notes, knowing he needed to call Alec and let him know he was back in town and Tomas had moved on to greener pastures.

He also needed to let him know he owed the deed for the Paris property to his mate and he would deliver it. Suddenly, he was slammed hard with her intense anger and his beast immediately surfaced. "*Bel!*"

As he teleported out, Shade heard Luca's call. He landed a few feet from *bel* and he couldn't believe what he saw, two wolves and a mountain lion. His beast went ballistic and he tried to figure out what the hell was going on. All three animals were ready to attack, and Luca was crouched ready to take them on. Shade stood opposite her, fangs bared and eyes glowing, with the animals in between. **"Luca, go! I need to talk her down. Get out of here. Now!"**

As Luca disappeared, the animals crouched lower to the ground, and *bel* glared at him like she wanted to rip his ass apart. His voice was soft and low, and he was ready if the creatures attacked, but he realized they were protecting her. They were only agitated more by his beast. He tapped him down and it wasn't easy facing his mate who was in full out beast mode. Shade felt his fangs retract and his eyes return to normal, he stood still, not moving a muscle.

"*Bel*, relax. Tell me what happened. I cannot get close to you. The creatures are protecting you, even from me. Look at me, *mi amore*. There is no danger."

Kate's anger was out of control and she didn't know how to reel it back. She was aware Aegis and her mate were circling at her feet and she saw the mountain lion join them. She knew they were there for her, to protect her. She took a few deep breaths, willing her heart to slow, pushing down her anger. As she did so, she felt her fangs retract and her eyes returned to normal.

She spoke to Aegis, "Calm down now, all of you. I'm fine. There's no danger here." The three creatures lost their aggressive posture and lay calmly at her feet, not ready to leave her unprotected yet, but following her command.

Shade watched as she calmed her beast and he was impressed. The animals relaxed as she talked to them, but they were not about to leave her. "That's my *bel rosso*. I dare not move, *mi amore*. You will have to come to me for them to understand there is no danger, and you accept my presence. We are learning this gift together, Kate. Move slowly until they understand I'm no threat to you. Come to me."

Kate walked to him and was swallowed in his embrace. The three animals stayed where she'd left them but remained watchful. "Lover, I didn't call them. I got angry, and when my beast appeared, I ran outside and they all came to me."

"Shh, *mi amore*, it's fine. Everything is fine. You did nothing wrong. We just need to figure out how to make them realize when you are in real danger and when you are just pissed off. Hell, this is going to take some doing. But I am pleased, you handled this well, handled them well too. A mountain lion? *Cazzo*, Kate! I would hate to see what comes crawling out of the woods if you were truly threatened."

Shade felt something brush against his leg and he looked down to see Aegis rubbing against him. Reaching down slowly, he held out his hand and Aegis nuzzled into his palm. "*Bel*, look down. You need to find out who these other two creatures are if you can. If they are permanent, I think it might be a good idea to know."

Kate looked down as Aegis was nuzzling against Shade, seeking his affection and approval. Kate looked at Aegis who locked eyes with her, and Kate nodded. "She says the black wolf is her mate, Night Stalker. And the mountain lion is named Riparo. It means shelter...or protection. She says they will all be here." Kate giggled. "She says there are others. I'll meet them in time."

Shade rolled his eyes and sighed. "Others? Great. Thank you, Aegis, Night Stalker, and Riparo. I am master here. I am her protector and mate."

As he emphasized the word mate, he looked to the black wolf that stood and approached. "*Cazzo*. If he attacks me, *bel*, please make him stop."

Shade chuckled softly as the wolf sniffed him, circling them both, then went to Aegis and nuzzled her neck. "Ah yes, one master to another, I got you, warrior."

Shade nuzzled into Bel's neck and then licked her face softly as she went into a fit of giggles.

"They know who you are. They are acknowledging your... What?" Kate looked down at Aegis, and laughed. "Okay, your dominance over me. Her words, not mine."

"Nice, Aegis. Not how I would describe it, for, you see, my queen has a mind of her own and apparently, a brigade of her own warriors. Now come, *mi amore*, let's go into the house. The sun is almost here, and if I cook in the sun, your warriors will have breakfast."

Lifting her into his arms, carrying her inside, he sat on the couch. "Start talking, now. I want to know what the hell this is all about, and don't leave out one detail."

As Kate recounted her conversation with Rissa, she felt her anger return and she didn't know where to start. "I called Rissa to see if everything was all right, if there'd been a problem in Florence and she practically attacks me over the phone... Something about me taking her house in Paris."

Cazzo, never fails, the bitch strikes again! "I should have known this was about Rissa. One of these days I am going to rip her damn tongue out." Shade slid his hands through his hair. "Anything else?"

Kate sat up straight, her back rigid. "Yes, as a matter of fact. That protector... That woman you brought here to our home. The one I welcomed here? She slept with him. She had sex with Alec. In their home! With Rissa in the next room. I try so hard to hear your words, to be re-assured about the female warriors, and I convince myself it's just me. But then I hear this. I told Rissa to get her out of her house. And I know I told Jacks she'd always be welcome here, but I'm telling you, I never want to see her again. I don't want you working with her again."

Shade felt his own anger rising. He understood her insecurities about the female warriors, but he bristled when she began to tell him what she expected him to do. Standing up, he growled loud and paced the floor. "You will not dictate to me who I work with and who I do not. Let me make that perfectly clear! Alec hired Jacks, I was only a source. I had nothing to do with what happened there. And if I need to conduct business, it will be done. You do not want her in this house, that I can comply with, but you will not tell me who I do business with. I am not Alec, *bel*. How he conducts his life is none of my business. I referred her. I cannot be responsible for what grown vampires do on their own time. Do you understand?"

Kate reeled at his response, his anger. They could never have this discussion without evoking his anger. She felt her beast flare again and she struggled, panting, getting up from the sofa and walking away from him, clenching and un-clenching her fist. She didn't want to fight him. That would resolve nothing. So, what was he saying? He wouldn't bring her here to their home, but if he wanted to work with her he would?

She took deep breath before answering, "I understand you aren't responsible for his actions, or hers. But I trusted her...because you asked me to trust her. And now you're saying you'll work with her in the future, and I'm supposed to... You want me to just turn a blind eye? Ignore what I feel?"

She knew that stubborn streak when she saw it. He had his heels dug in. Aegis was right...dominance. "Fine. Whatever you want, Shade."

He saw her beast rise up and it didn't take much, but this time, she was going to learn he was the fucking master when it came to business, and he was damn tired of her jealously every time there was another female involved. Stalking toward her, he walked her across the floor backward until her body hit the wall and he threw his hands on either side of her face, pinning her.

"You better settle down because I will not put up with this every time a female comes on this property. I'm your mate for eternity. I love you! Fuck, Kate, what the hell do I have to do to prove this to you? And why the hell are you so damn angry for Rissa? Since when did you become her confidant? Rissa is a bitch, a cold hard bitch, and the sooner you figure that out the better. Now, if you want to take that attitude with me, be prepared for the consequences because now you will feel it all, my queen. That beast crawling up and taking hold is not pretty now, is it? And if you think those creatures outside will protect you from me, watch your warrior show you how wrong you can be. Look at me!"

Clenching her chin, he kissed her hard, pushing his body into her and grinding her against the wall. Damn, she got his beast riled out of his mind!

"I love you, *bel*, I love only you!" Pushing himself off the wall, he turned and walked to the door and then stopped. His voice was calm. "I cannot keep going through this, Kate. It's killing me how you cannot feel how much I love you."

Kate pleaded with him. "Don't walk away. Please, don't walk away. It kills me as well. I hate this conversation. And I'm trying! I keep trying. Every time I think I have it worked out in my head that it's something I can deal with, something rips through my confidence. I hate this struggle. I hate my feelings of jealousy. Please, just don't walk away!"

Shade was slammed with the hurt and pain that rolled through her. He could barely breathe, as his own pain from her doubt of him almost crippled him. Taking a deep breath, he turned around and looked at her, held her with his eyes.

"Feel that, *mi amore*? It is my pain. I am not angry, just hurt. I can feel your pain too. I cannot live like this with you and I cannot live without you. Trust, love, protection needs to get us through. Do you love me?"

"Shade, I love you more than life. I would die without you in my life. You know that. And you're right. Love is not enough. I have to trust. There will always be women who will throw themselves at you. And I know you don't respond to them. I know that. But that doesn't make me hate them any less. I don't want to fight over this. I'm tired of fighting over this. Please..."

Kate held out her hand to him, waiting for him to walk back to her and for once, not walk away.

He stood there, dead still, even as she held out her hand to him. Closing his eyes, he took a deep breath. Slowly walking to her, he picked her up in his arms, cradling her to his chest. "*Ti amo, mi amore.*"

"I'm sorry. What happens between Rissa and Alec has nothing to do with us. I let her get under my skin. I love you, Shade."

He set her down and she stepped back, taking him in, his beast now gone. "Lover, we had an argument and didn't destroy the house! That has to be some kind of progress, right?"

He smiled at her words. "*Si*. Let us resume this tomorrow. I wish to speak to you more about the deed to the Paris house, and other things concerning Rissa and Alec. But right now, your ass is going to bed, and I have no energy left to argue. I just want to sleep in my own bed, wrapped around you, letting the death slumber take us away together, *si*?"

Kate slid her arms around his waist, glad to have an end to this discussion and more than happy to put off any further talk until after they'd slept. She couldn't imagine having him angry with her for their first death slumber here at home. "Come. Theresa has fresh linens on the bed. I can't wait to sleep next to you."

Picking her up, he took the stairs two at a time. He hit the door with his booted foot and flopped them both on the bed. "Get undressed, woman, and fast, I need to love some sense into your jealous brain!"

As they both tangled to undress each other, their laughter rang out through the house. The king and his queen had come home to stay.

13

Shade was in his study at Bel Rosso, opening the large window. The cool breeze moved the curtains as he sat at the large desk, staring out into the evening. The sun had not yet completely set behind the mountain range, and the sky was a brilliant burst of orange and pinks. He slumped back in his chair and looked down at the notes he was scribbling. There were so many thoughts in his head, duties that needed to be fulfilled, his new life with *bel*, the new warrior camp in the States, and the changes to be made at the Dead House. The thought of her ran through his mind. Closing his eyes, he could feel her in the house. She was with Theresa, working together upstairs, and he felt her happiness.

He heard a familiar laugh echo across the yard and in the open window. It was Raven, and he listened as the laughter and voices of his other warriors began to stream through the window. They were all up and about, waiting for the moon to rise before going into the Dead House and beginning their assignments. Shade needed to speak with Raven, one on one, and in private. The Dead House was not the place he wanted this conversation to take place, and he decided now was as good a time as any to get this done. Shade telepathically sent him a message and sat back and waited for the always dramatic arrival of his young warrior.

It wasn't long before he heard the patio door open. Shade went to the bar, pulled out two glass tumblers and filled them with a generous amount of Midnight. He knew he'd need one to get through this and make his final decision because nothing was easy with Raven. As Shade turned around, there he stood, his long black locks down to his ass, hanging loose, but clean and gleaming.

The first thing Shade noticed was his leathers. They were unique and stylish, more fit for the runway than a battlefield, and it looked like someone had sewn them onto his skinny ass. There were pockets and straps in places he'd never seen before, handy for the numerous weapons a warrior must carry. It was obvious this set of leathers was one of Cory's designs and Shade was impressed. Raven looked a bit nervous, and that amused him. Raven was never serious about much in life, except when he was facing the enemy, and then, he became deadly serious.

Raven watched as his master poured two large drinks and his heart began to race. *This sure as fuck can't be good!* He took a deep breath as Shade gave him the once over. "You wanted to see me, boss-man?"

Shade nodded to the chair opposite his desk, reminding himself to give Raven a chance to show him the changes Marcello told him had taken place. Shade set the glasses down on his desk and dropped comfortably into his chair. "Raven, take a seat. Just a few things I want to discuss with you, privately."

Shade pushed one of the crystal glasses across the desk in front of Raven and picked up the other for himself, his eyes never leaving Raven as he took a sip of Midnight. "Have a drink. Relax."

Raven took the chair opposite his master. *Relax? Was this some kind of joke?* His master's welcoming words and tone of voice didn't match his expression or the intense gaze he was giving him. He got a whiff of the Midnight and his mouth watered. That stuff the boss-man brewed was strong medicine and filled your veins with sweet harmony, but he'd sworn off drinking it before going on duty. Holding up his hand, he rejected the offer, wanting to get this the hell over with.

"*Grazie*, but no. I have duty tonight at the Dead House. Those are your rules, no drinking before or during duty." *Damn I could use a smoke bad, but no smoking in the big house.*

Shade set down his Midnight and kept his stoic look. "Did you give up all vampire vices or just the Midnight?" Shade needed to keep him on edge, he rarely had this warrior under the gun and he could feel his nerves.

Raven smiled that cocky ass grin. "Not all vices. I'm no saint, I'm Medici after all! Reputation to maintain and all that."

Shade chuckled and pushed the ashtray to him. "You can smoke in here, Raven. The queen has given me permission to smoke in the house, but I usually take it outside, since Luca and I are the only smokers in the house." Shade watched, with amused silence, to see if Raven would keep up this charade, or if he'd truly changed some of his antics.

"If my queen says no smoking in the big house, then no smoking. Pass. I respect her wishes." *Is he fucking trying to kill me here?*

Shade marveled at a Raven who followed the rules. "So, I see you have some unique leathers. I take it those are Cory's design." Picking up his Midnight again, Shade let the deep red liquid slide down his throat.

Raven swallowed hard. *Small talk, when master does this ring around the rosy bullshit, he's going to slam my ass with something bad. Cazzo! What the hell did I do?*

"Yeah, I like Cory. He has mad skills with leather. And he makes them fast. I give him design ideas and he tells me if it can be done, usually has some adjustments and ideas of his own. From there, we can come up with something unique. This is a new design. Accommodates my weapons, light-weight, and easy to move in. We get along really good, a lot in common."

Raven looked down and shuffled his booted feet under his chair then looked up to see master with his fingers steepled in front of his face, his elbows on the desk. *What the fuck did I do? Please don't send me back to Florence!*

Shade drained his Midnight and listened to Raven go on about the leathers. He used hand gestures once in a while, but the warrior he knew would have been flaunting his ass all over the room showing off his new leathers. This Raven was sitting still, and Shade did everything he could not to laugh out loud. This little meeting had him nervous.

"You *do* have a lot in common with him. Found both of you homeless and destitute in the worst parts of town, and basically, in the same situation as well. Except for my ceremonial leathers during the coronation, I have yet to have the honor of wearing anything Cory has made, but now he is back at Bel Rosso, all that will change. I appreciate your befriending Cory, I expected no less from you, Raven. You have pleased me."

Standing up, Shade grabbed his glass and filled it again with Midnight. "I asked you to come here because there are some major changes happening at Bel Rosso, at the Dead House and the new camp opening shortly. I have decided to change a few things with the warriors as well. I take it you have chosen to stay in the States and not return to Florence?"

Raven sat up straighter. He could only hope some of those changes included him. "*Si*, I'm staying."

Shade sat back down with his fresh glass of Midnight and smiled. "That is what I wanted to hear. What we're going to talk about remains between us, understood?"

As Raven nodded his agreement, Shade decided to let the warrior off the hook, give him the news of his decision and see what reaction he got.

"Once the camp opens here and we begin operations, Marcello will be my SIC in the camp. Along with Fiamma, they will help me organize and train the new recruits. I need you to be my SIC at the Dead House."

Shade paused and watched his face. "But there are some rules I expect to be followed. I'm giving you a chance here, Raven, to show me what you have in leadership skills. I'm bringing in some new warriors from Florence to fill in the gaps from all the mercenaries that left us. This will give you a complete battalion to run the Dead House. You'll need to get them familiar with D.C. and the grids, immediately. The Dead House will be under your immediate command. I'll be too busy here and I wish to spend as much of my time at the camp as possible. It will need much to be successful. If you can do this to my satisfaction, you are well on your way to bigger and better duties here at Medici. If you fail to comply and play games, waste my time and money, or let anything happen, you will be returning to Florence. This is vital, Raven, the Canton wedding is coming up, and that place needs to be locked down tight. His campaign is going to take off. We can't have a single episode. Think before you jump to answer, this is one hellish big step, but Marcello has recommended you, and I feel you can handle it. You have proven yourself in the time you have been in the States and earned this opportunity. But I want honesty, above all, so if you don't believe you can do this, perform to my standards, then decline this position. Understand?"

Raven's heart was slamming against his chest. *Holy fucking hell! He wants me to be the SIC of the Dead House!* Raven had to settle his mind to listen to the words coming out of the boss-man's mouth. He stood and walked to the window, his mind in a whirlwind. This was his chance to move up. If he could do this, and he knew he could, it would open the door to bigger and better things with his master. This was the break he needed, and it landed right in his lap. He tried to regulate his breathing and let his mind relax, staring out at the night sky. This was where he was meant to be, this time and this place, and he'd give it all he had. He never wanted to see the streets of Italy again.

"*Si*, I understand. I'm a Medici, all because of your leadership and guidance. No one ever gave me a chance. But you did. I know you think I never took it seriously, but that was just a front. I always feared my size would be a handicap and I'd never advance, that I might someday be dismissed, so I used my attitude as a shield. But in my heart, I knew I could use my size and speed to my advantage. I see what this country can do for me, where I can go. I belong here and not in Italy. I accept this position. I'll be the Medici you expect and show you nothing will stop me in my duties. This means more to me than I have words to express."

Shade watched him closely. He could feel his emotions. They were strong, and he knew Raven had taken a big step forward. "Good. Once we get you setup officially, if there are some changes you need to make, schedules, grids...any ideas, come to me. We'll talk them through and see how it goes. I'm letting you have some free rein in this. You have a good head on your shoulders, use that skill. As of right now, until we have the meeting for the new camp, things remain the same. I want no one to know of this. All of my changes will be announced at the meeting. If I find out anyone knows beforehand, this whole thing is off. I know I don't need to say it, but I will because this is new for you, code of honor, warrior. Anything you want to ask?"

Raven sat back down in his chair, still taking in all he'd heard. There was one thing he had struggled with since being in the States and he knew this was the opportunity to ask master and hope he wasn't overstepping his bounds.

"There is one thing. I struggle with the feeding. I know Marcello can hunt. The female feeders aren't to my taste. I prefer something...different. I need more, master. I want to hunt, find my own kind in feeding. I'll need my strength and need to feed more regularly to handle the job of SIC. I'm asking if that's possible for me."

Shade smiled, he'd heard a few rumors among the warriors about Raven, but he never paid much attention. "Males are more to your taste? Is that what you are saying?"

Raven raised his dark eyes slowly but with confidence. "*Si*."

Shade nodded. "Then we need to have that fixed. Hunt, do what you need to do, but the rules are the same. If you hunt mortals, seduce only, never kill. I expect you to be healthy, well fed, and ready to roll at any given time. If I call your ass while you are feeding, you respond immediately. I want you to be satisfied and happy. I need you to be at the top of your game. Anything we need to do to make that happen, you need to come to me. We can talk anything out. You don't go to Marcello any longer. You report directly to me on a daily basis once you become SIC. Anything else?"

Raven breathed a sigh of relief. He stood, ready to leave. "*Grazie*, master, *grazie!* I have nothing else at this time. Maybe some rogues to slice and dice tonight."

Shade stood and laughed as he walked around the desk and gave Raven a brotherly hug, pounding him on the back. "Congratulations. You have earned this, Raven, don't let me down. Show me what you have. Now get your runt ass to work."

Raven grinned from ear to ear and walked to the door, looking over his shoulder. "Not a problem, boss-man. I got this."

14

Kate and Theresa had finished unpacking the steamer trunks that arrived from Florence. Shade had been up for hours, working in his home office. Kate loved knowing he was here and close by, even if they weren't actually spending time together. After their argument last night, about Jacks and female warriors, she knew this was an inevitable part of her future and she'd given in to him, but it was still not an issue she'd come to terms with. There was still the issue of the Paris house to discuss. They never got around to that once she opened the powder keg of jealousy she always felt over other women, followed by his anger and her hurt. It was a vicious cycle that only pulled them apart and she needed to find her way through it, and she would.

She left Theresa and headed down the stairs, passing Raven in the hallway. He was wearing leathers that were clearly custom made for him, with wide stitches up the sides of each leg exposing a lot of skin. He bowed deeply when he saw her, sweeping one arm out to the side in a grand gesture, bowing his head, his hair draping to the floor. "My lady."

Kate stepped off the bottom step and giggled. "Oh, Raven, if I only had a fan."

With a flourish, Raven willed a fan into his hand and presented it to her, bowing again. Kate laughed and took the fan, opening it with a quick snap of her wrist, holding it in front of her face, peering over the top of the feathers before giving him a curtsy. "A bow as dramatic as that deserves a fan, doesn't it?"

Raven laughed. "Just one queen bowing to another, my lady."

She could hear his laughter ring through the house, as he walked back to the warrior camp. Kate giggled at him and headed to Shade's office. She stood in the doorway, looking at him bent over the desk, and scratching notes. She hesitated a minute before tapping on the open door. "Is this a good time?"

Looking up as she spoke, the smile on his face was soft and loving. "Any time is good when it comes to you, *mi amore*. And to what do I owe this honor?"

Kate held the fan in front of her face, peering over it at him as she entered the room. "I was wondering, sir, if we might finish our conversation? There appears to be a house in Paris that has my name on it and it has Rissa in a very angry state." She dropped the fan on the desk and crawled into his lap. "Seriously, Shade, what's she talking about?"

Laughing at her antics as she curled in his lap, he made no move to stop her. "Where did you get that fan? Did you get it in Florence? I want to know if you have some dandy you see on the side who gives you expensive gifts." Tickling her until she giggled and begged for mercy, he snuggled into her neck, kissing and licking her ear.

Kate squirmed to get away and picked up the delicate fan and whacked at him, laughing harder as the feathers floated free and tangled in his hair. "Your fashion warrior Raven gave me this fan. Don't make me have to call him back in here."

Shade threw back his head roaring with laughter. "My fashion warrior. Now that is an understatement. By the way, he is now the SIC at the Dead House and Marcello the SIC here at camp. So, if it would please my queen, I would ask you to communicate to your animal brigade that these two fine warriors will be entering the house more often and they need to let them pass."

"I'll will talk with Aegis, she'll understand the Medici warriors on this property are no threat to me. I think she leads all the other animals. Now talk to me about this Paris house." Kate pulled the feathers from his hair.

"Please make sure you get them all, *mi amore*. I would look quite the master addressing my warriors with pink and purple feathers in my hair."

Squeezing her tight and kissing her cheek, he smiled then got down to business. "There is something in our culture called a Masters Agreement. It is followed in all countries, but especially, in Europe. If the vital enemy or source of the conflict is killed, in this case, Cuerpo, the warrior who makes the kill is granted a reward, as well as the credit for the kill. Since you killed Cuerpo, it is your due from Alec to be rewarded. Do you understand so far, *bel*?"

"Yes, you'd mentioned something about a reward in Florence, but nothing about a house. And I know the warriors are very keen to have credit for the kill, it's important for their reputation. I understand that part."

"Si, very observant of you. Kills under their belt means a warrior can ask for higher wages, and become leaders within a coven, such as SIC's and Lieutenants. This is how warriors rise in the ranks. Now, normal rewards would be money. If another master makes the kill, the reward may be territory. I knew Alec had a place in Paris. We vowed to go to Paris every year to be together, and this will give us a place to reside, without using hotels. We can have more privacy. You love Paris, *mi amore*, and I thought you would appreciate the house as a reward much more than money, *si*."

"Shade, I love the idea of a house in Paris, a place where we can go and be alone together. Where I can take the children, and have a safe place for them. But if it's Rissa's house...how could he give away her house?"

He kissed her gently on the lips. "Listen to me. The property never belonged to Rissa. It is Alec's. Hell, he could buy her twelve houses in France, and she would still want more. The house was being rented, so Alec has arranged to have the tenants move and he will present you with the deed. That is his duty. And you will accept it."

She nodded, adjusting her thinking to his culture. "If this is what you want. We'll take this house in Paris, and I'll fix it up for us, for our children. And now we have another house to visit. Speaking of which, have you thought about Reynaldo? And the bed and breakfast?"

Stroking her crimson locks as her head lay on his shoulder, he never tired of her in his arms. "It is on my list, *mi amore*. Give me a little more time, I beg you. I have a lot of things that need to be done, and I still need to contact Alec with all the changes and get his ass over here to give you the deed. Alec has seen the head of Cuerpo, so he has no reservations about giving you this reward. You are quite the land owner, my queen."

Kate nodded in recognition of their growing property as she stood to leave. "Take your time with the decision on the California house. I won't mention anything to Reynaldo until you've decided. I just hate to see that property sitting vacant when I know it can be used productively. And I don't expect you to manage it. It's something I can oversee from here. But I'll let you get back to work. I know you're busy here."

She cast a coquettish glance at him over her shoulder as she left the room, flaunting the fan one more time, a promise of what the rest of the night held for them.

15

Shade adjusted himself in his jeans as he picked up his cell. His woman could drive him insane with passion. Her rose scent lingered in the air of his study and he closed his eyes for a moment and inhaled. *Work, old man, work!*

Not bothering to even look at the time, he dialed Alec and waited for him to answer. There was a lot of news to share and one item in particular Shade wanted taken care of immediately, the deed delivered to *bel's* hand.

***

Alec and Rissa had been back from Florence a little more than a day and were getting settled in their routine. After that little adventure in the chamber at Castello, Alec wondered how he could recreate some of that excitement right here. Clearly, he cannot create anything as elaborate. The houses here in G-town are close together, land is a premium, and he could not allow Rissa to scream out as she did in Florence. He knew Rissa would have no objections. She would in fact welcome it. He would think of something.

His cell vibrated against the table and he picked it up. Shade was on the caller ID. Alec was expecting his call, knowing he was back in the States.

"Brother, welcome to the life of a mated vamp. You'll have to figure out how to keep the sex exciting now, not that I don't think you have a handle on that already. I heard talk of your warrior camp, with a section just for females, a separate building away from your main house and your mate... And a valid reason to spend a lot of time there. Very clever."

Shade laid his head back against the huge leather chair and laughed. Some things never change, and Shade had enough of the arguments. If it is not one thing it is another, at least Alec is consistent. *Sick Son of a Bitch!*

"Mated life agrees with me very well, *grazie*. And exciting sex is never a problem with my mate. I do not need a Gorean sex chamber to make her happy, either. What the fuck, Alec? You had to go there? *Cazzo*, the whole damn palace heard you. I know Rissa is fine and back to her normal antics because she had my mate in one tormented outraged state last evening. You need to tame that blonde wildcat down!"

Alec chuckled. "Taming Rissa is a full-time job, my friend. What has she done now to get your new queen in such a state?"

"What hasn't she done? My queen called to thank her for attending, she was a bit upset at the cold shoulder she received from Rissa at the Coronation, but Rissa made up for that in spades, brother. She went off about Kate taking her Paris house. But that isn't all, not in the least. She fucking blew the roof off with her bitching about you and Jacks. Seems she is a bit ticked off you got your dick wet in that one. Then *bel* goes off on my ass because I sent Jacks over there. *Cazzo*, brother!"

Alec roared with laughter. "That is the beauty of Rissa. Life is never boring with that one. We both knew once her initial fear of that attack was over, she would fight tooth and nail over a protector. And brother, like it or not, you are the one who picked Jacks. Hell, you could have sent Skelk over here, but not my brother in deviant play. Oh no, you send me the hottest ticket in town, and one I just happen to have a little history with, and you act like you don't know what's going down? Come on, Shade. But the Paris house, I am sorry about that. She went off like a firecracker when she heard that one. Not really surprised at her reaction."

He has a history with Jacks? Damn, why didn't someone tell me about this? "Look, you wanted the best, someone who could handle her lifestyle, fit in and shut her ass down, Jacks was the one. Jacks is independent, makes her own deals. Look, I want the deed in Kate's hand and soon, brother, she earned that. And I never want to hear another word out of your mate's mouth about that fucking Paris house again. *Cazzo*, go buy her six more!"

Alec lit up a cigarette. "The deed is ready, and the house is empty. You can have it anytime. Hell, Rissa never leaves her damn business. I had to drag her to Florence, even though she did enough shopping to single-handedly boost the economy of Italy. I'll get her another house in Paris if she wants it, but I guarantee it will just sit there, just like this one did. That is why I had it rented out. Hadn't used it in years. So, what do you need, brother? You want me to teleport my ass out there again?"

Shade chuckled under his breath. "I do, brother. Check your schedule. Give me a call back when it's convenient, I will work it out to suit you. But moving on to another subject, nothing happened in D.C. while I was away. With Cuerpo gone, whatever remained of his coven seems to have moved on. Boys are not spotting any activity at all. Tomas has stepped down and already moved on to the next job. He said everything had been settled up with you. I am going to bring in some of my boys from Florence to fill out the platoon. Skelk is the only original mercenary of yours left, and he has pledged allegiance to Medici and is on my payroll now. So, now we have all Medici warriors on board. We'll need them with your campaign and the wedding coming up.

"Since Tomas was my SIC at the Dead House, I have appointed another warrior. I will be here at the camp most of the time, it will take much work, but you will benefit greatly in the outcome. And if anything goes down in D.C., my ass will be there, so don't worry."

Alec stretched his long frame out on the sofa as he talked. "Yeah, I heard from Tomas. He said it was dead here while we were in Florence. Told me he was moving on. That comes as no surprise. So, who is in command now?"

Shade has to hold back his laugh. Alec had met Raven once when he escorted him home from Bel Rosso, so this should be really good.

"Raven. You met him once."

Alec sits up on the sofa and shakes his head, did he say Raven? "That skinny runt in a kilt and a cape? Are you shittin' me? I know he's Medici, raised and trained in your camp. He told me his history. But I have to tell you, Shade, anybody sees that warrior will be asking for a dance not a fight. I hope you know what you're doing. My ass depends on it."

"I have raised and trained these warriors, Alec. Most of them were trained by my own hand. Raven is one of the best. Never judge a book by its cover. My runt has a head on his shoulders and he is one street smart warrior. He is faster than even your eyes can see, he can slice and dice before his victims even see or smell him. His size can be an asset. I have seen him at work. He will represent Medici, and he will take care of you and your territory."

"Shade, no harm meant. I never question your warriors. No one does. Look, since I have to teleport out, it won't take long, how about tomorrow evening? Does that work for you? I'll bring the deed. Just don't expect me to bow."

Shade chuckled. "No bowing necessary, brother. Tomorrow evening is fine. We are both free and it should not take long. Appreciate it, brother. Anything else?"

"Maybe you can show me the stables. Rissa said something about having a horse, and we sure the fuck can't have one here. Maybe I can get her a horse and you can board it?"

"Not a problem, I have plenty of empty stalls. We can talk about some horseflesh as well. I can bring them over here from Florence. Medici has a whole stable of horses born and bred there. Best you will find. I can have some photos sent to her by email and she can pick out the one she likes. There is one more thing for you to keep in mind. I am having an open call for warrior camp. If you could spread the word to surrounding masters, it will benefit us both."

Alec nodded as he spoke. "I'll talk to Rissa about the horse, and I'll spread the word about your camp, but I don't maintain much contact with the masters. I'll tell the few I stayed in contact with. See you tomorrow then."

"*Grazie*, brother, see you tomorrow." Shade ended the call and stood up, stretching his legs. This will keep Kate busy, another house to furnish. And Rissa wants a horse? Shade knew she could ride Alec like hell, but he wondered if she could handle a horse. Pushing the cell into his back pocket, he walked to the stairs and took them two at time.

"*Mi amore!* Where is my woman?" He heard her giggle and ran in the direction of the sound.

16

Alec tossed the phone back on the table. Maybe getting Rissa a horse would give her something to do besides work out in the gym. She could be outside, get some fresh air, and get away from the press. Hell, nothing was getting on that property in Virginia with that army of warriors there now. This could be a way to appease her anger over the fucking Paris house she never used in the first place. He poured them both a glass of Midnight. She'd been working to get caught up from their trip and could probably use a break. "Rissa! Join me in the family room, please."

Rissa hung up the phone with her dress designer. The wedding gown was complete. She just needed to get Alec's schedule, so the designer could be here at the house where she'd try it on, and make the huge reveal to Alec. She prayed he'd love the dress. Grabbing her schedule book, ready to find a time for such an appointment, she heard him call. *What in the hell is it now?* She ran the brush through her long blonde hair, and headed to the family room, taking the drink he offered.

"Ah, I could use a drink!"

"Sit darling, you've been working all day."

He took a seat on the large sofa, indicating with a pat of his hand that he wanted her to sit next to him. "I just talked to Shade. I'll be going out there tomorrow evening to wrap up some business, but you mentioned they had stables now. Shade said he'd be happy to find a horse for you. Are you interested? I think it'd be good for you, Rissa. Good exercise, fresh air, and you know you'll be safe there."

Rissa took a sip from the glass and settled next to him on the couch. She was happy to hear the news about the horses. "I'd love to have a horse, Alec. I used to ride when I was mortal. It was something I used to love to do. There's such a feeling of freedom when you ride. But if Shade picks out horses like he picks out protectors, I'd prefer to find my own, thank you. My schedule's so busy right now, and with the wedding, I'd have little time to ride."

Alec chuckled. She never missed a chance to get in a dig about the protector. "He said he'd email pictures of the horses he has bred in Florence. You can pick one out. He knows horses, my darling, and women, I'd trust his choice."

He knew this last comment would set her off and he downed the Midnight, getting ready to enjoy the ride.

Rissa was mid-sip when he uttered the smart remark. She peered at him over the rim of her glass. She felt the heat in her face as her fury rose to the surface, but she settled down. There were more ways than one to get her way. Sitting her glass down on the table in front of them, she crossed her legs.

"Oh, the warrior most certainly knows women, I have no doubt. He knows them almost as well as you. Trust is another matter, however. And although his choice in women has pleased you well, I'm sure that choice pleased him long before she pleased you."

Alec smirked at her, a twinkle in his eye. "My darling, I don't know for a fact that Shade was ever with Jacks, but if it's true, surely you don't think Jacks would be the first woman we've shared? That chamber of sexual delights was underneath his castle, after all. I can't tell you how many nights we spent there... but enough about that. Do you, or don't you, want a horse. I'm going there tomorrow. I can let him know if you're interested. He said there was plenty of room to board a horse for us, and the estate is large. You could ride without running into your good friend Kate."

He kept up the verbal jabs as she heard him refer to Kate and she growled. Uncrossing her legs, she stood and walked to the bar, pouring another Midnight. "Of course, I want a horse. Have him send the photos, and I'll choose one. I can teleport out there, which will save me time. No one will be the wiser." Turning to face him, she leaned against the bar. "Did he mention anything about rogue activity in the city?"

He was amused by her anger and her efforts to contain it. "He did give me a report. He said nothing went down in the district while we were in Florence. The mercenaries have all moved on to the next job, and it's just his warriors on the streets now."

Walking back to the couch, Rissa curled up and laid her head on his shoulder. "Alec, we need to talk about her. I know I need a protector, but nothing has happened in so long. Having Jacks following my every move is hampering my schedule. The press has backed off a bit, and to be honest, she intimidates the hell out of them. I think half the reason they're there is to get photos of her and not me, missing the entire point of my plan. I was speaking with Kate on the phone last night, in my own bedroom, and Jacks knocks on the door, simply because I was raising my voice. I had to interrupt my conversation to dismiss her. It's way too much, Alec. I'm doing everything I can to appease you, but seriously, will you consider something else for me? I have an idea that may work a bit better."

Alec thought to himself, *well this should be interesting*. "Of course, my darling. By all means, let me hear your idea."

Sitting up, her fingers wandered slowly up and down his thigh. "Since Shade has all of his warriors on our streets now, I think it may be a good idea if we have just one of them as my protector, instead of her living here. I feel safe in the house. It may help to get to know his warriors better, and I'd assume we'll need them for the wedding and the campaign. I think a male would stand out less, draw less attention from the press as well. It would look more normal, Alec. It would put the press coverage back on us. I don't think you have any idea how much interest she has stirred. Even some of my clients are a bit edgy with her around."

Alec laid his head back on the sofa. The truth was, he had tired of the constant riff between Jacks and Rissa and the tension it brought to this house. What made him think having two women under the same roof would be a good idea, especially with his diva and an alpha warrior with an axe to grind? He'd never intended to have a live-in protector in the first place, and now that things were quiet, there really seemed no reason to keep someone here twenty-four seven. Rissa would be tamer if he gave her what she wanted, a male warrior who only showed up when she left the house. The contract with Jacks flashed through his head. She got the same payout regardless of how long she was here. He almost had to laugh. Quickest million she'd ever made.

"My darling, if it pleases you, then I'll dismiss her. But not before talking with Shade tomorrow and having him assign someone the specific detail of escorting you when you're out. I know he has someone on this grid, just not sure who. He used to cover it personally when we had all the turmoil."

Rissa did a silent celebration in her head. *Battle won and Zena the warrior bitch is out of here!* The smile on her face spread quickly. He was giving her a gift in trusting her instincts, and she could handle a male warrior. Leaning into him, she hugged him tight and then retreated, knowing he hated affectionate outburst.

"Thank you so much, Alec. I'll be good, and I'll listen to the warrior. I have no problems with that. I know the rogue attack made me very unlike myself. But I understand, now, how dangerous it is, and I need to listen and learn from my master. I'll be pleased with whomever you and Shade appoint." Flopping back on the couch, she couldn't erase the smile from her face.

"I'm happy to see you've regained your confidence, my darling. I'll work out the details with Shade tomorrow. If I hear of any problems with you trying to outwit the warriors and slip away, then we go back to a twenty-four hour live-in protector, understood? I think we're out of danger, but I also don't want to be lulled into a false sense of security just because everything is quiet. We'll get you a horse, you can teleport out there, with an escort, of course, but once on his property, you'll be perfectly safe. The riding will be good for you. Good exercise, something different than the gym to change up your routine, fresh air. Consider it done."

Standing to leave, she turned to him, "I'll comply and thank you again, Alec. I won't disappoint." Walking to the door of the family room, she stopped and turned back to him. "The dress is done. I'll have Jenny send me your schedule for this month. I'll need you to be here when the designer comes to make alterations. Then you can see the dress and give your blessing. If you don't like something, we still have time to make changes. Anything else you wish to speak to me about?"

"Just have Jenny put it on my calendar, darling, and I'll make sure I'm here. I think we've covered enough ground for one night." He stood and poured himself another Midnight, and knew Jacks got one over on him good this time.

"Then I'll see you when you come to bed, Alec. I have work to do and I'm sure you do as well. I love you, Alec."

Rissa walked from the room, but once out of his sight, she ran up the stairs to the bedroom and acted like a small child dancing around with happiness. *The bitch is out of here for good!*

17

Alec wrapped up at work and had his driver take him home, so he could change out of his suit and into jeans. He had told Shade he'd teleport in tonight to bring him the deed. He picked up the document that had been transferred over to Kate's name and folded it, sliding it inside his jeans pocket, then teleported out.

He could see the vineyards as he came in over the estate, lush and green, and the warrior camp was visible from the air. To a casual observer, the buildings looked like another large house and possibly a large but elaborate barn, nothing that would raise too many questions with the mortals. The stables were placed on rolling hills, and the grazing pastures were all fenced in, and the fucker still had room to expand.

Alec landed in the front yard of the main house and was getting ready to walk to the front door when he was surrounded by two wolves, both snarling, lips curled back, and their teeth bared. "What the fuck?"

He heard a commotion behind him and looked over his shoulder to see a mountain lion, crouched and ready to pounce. His instincts told him to stand dead still, when he heard a loud screech and looked skyward to see a large falcon swoop down within inches of his head. Alec didn't carry weapons, and he wasn't sure what he'd use against this lot anyway. He was sizing up the wolves and his options when the front door opened, and Kate emerged.

He was about to warn her off when she clapped her hands and called out "Aegis." He watched with his mouth open, as both of the wolves turned away from him and trotted over in her direction, the mountain lion retreated into the woods, and the falcon settled in a nearby tree.

Kate called out to him. "Sorry about that. I seem to have inherited my own army of warriors. I didn't even think about how they'd respond to someone visiting our property. You're fine now, come on in. Shade is in the bunker, I think."

Alec creased his brow. "What do you mean you inherited an army?"

"Uh... well, apparently my gift is animalism. No one seems to know much about it, so we're just winging it here. This grey wolf is Aegis, her mate is Night Stalker, and the mountain lion is Riparo. They seem to be permanent additions to our household."

Alec looked skyward. "And the falcon?"

Kate looked at the huge bird perched high in the tree. "I never saw him before." The large grey wolf nuzzled against her leg and she reached down to pet her head. "Oh, Aegis says it's a she and her name is Danica."

Alec raised his eyebrows. "They talk to you?"

"Yes, telepathically, just like Shade. And I can talk to them. I thought it was just the three of them, but now the falcon shows up. Guess I need to keep an open mind about how many of them there will be. Come on in, I'll find Shade."

Alec looked around to see the wolves standing peacefully, panting, tails wagging, and he shook his head. He vaguely remembered hearing about the gift of animalism, but he'd never seen a vampire with that gift. He followed her into the house, as she called out to Shade.

Shade quickly pulled out an Italian dress shirt from the armoire, light blue and from one of his favorite designers. He had teleported from the bunker to change before Alec arrived. Buttoning up the front, he rolled the sleeves three-quarters up his arms and tucked the shirt into his jeans. He heard Kate call out that Alec was here. **"I could hear your army outside ready to attack, *mi amore*. On my way."**

Going down the stairs, he entered the living room and found *bel* and Alec. Shade went to Kate and kissed her on the cheek before shaking hands with Alec.

"Good to see you, brother. Good flight?" Shade smiled as Gi walked in with Midnight-filled glasses for all.

Alec gratefully accepted the Midnight, and took a big swallow. "That was quite the welcoming party you had waiting for me, brother."

Shade held up his hand in protest. "I have nothing to do with that. It seems my queen has her own army. Hell, they tried to keep me from her last evening. Interesting gift, *si*? So, let us all sit down, there is no pomp and circumstance needed for this."

Turning, he took Kate's hand and led her to the large couch, snuggling her to his side.

Kate took the glass of Midnight, the color a dark burgundy, like wine, only thicker. She sniffed at the mixture and it smelled like a heady wine, with a hint of copper. She tipped the glass to her lips and took a small sip, savoring the taste. The taste of the wine hit first, but the blood soothed, dulling the ever present hunger. *Jeez... no wonder they gulp down this stuff!* She sat down next to Shade, sipped again at the glass before setting it on the table.

Alec downed the wine and held the empty glass up for Gi who brought him another. Before sitting, he pulled the folded document from his jeans pocket. Sitting down, he unfolded the deed, laying it on the table in front of him and smoothing out the creases.

"As stipulated in our Master's Agreement, Cuerpo's killer gets to name their reward. So, for you, Kate, here's the deed to my property in Paris. It's a large building, on the Champs Elysees. It has three floors. Could be converted into three separate apartments if you wanted it as income property, but there's no elevator. That's not a drawback for this location, though. Or if you want the whole thing, it can be one very large house. I've owned it for years. I lived in Paris for a short period of time. But once I stopped using it, I rented it out. Rissa always thought she'd do something with it, but she never got around to it. If you want to live there, it would probably need a little work, some modernization, nothing major. But it's yours now." He slid the document across the table to Kate.

Shade picked up the deed and handed it to Kate. "Rewards are a nice thing to have, *bel*. Job well done, my queen." Kissing her softly, he watched as she eyed the deed and he didn't miss the smile working its way across her mouth.

"Thanks, brother, appreciate the time you have taken to come out and present it. It means a great deal to me."

Kate looked up, still a little dumb-founded by the fact she now owned property in Paris. "Thank you. I promise you, I didn't kill Cuerpo for any reward. I was just trying to save my own life. But thank you and we'll make sure the Paris property gets used. I'm truly sorry if this has caused a problem with Rissa. That was never my intention. I hope you know that."

Alec held up his hand. "Rissa can have all the houses she wants, don't worry about this one."

Shade chuckled and hugged Kate tight. "Now, Alec and I have some business to discuss, so go put the deed in my office. I will see to its safety, and before I leave for the night, I will come find you. And please, make sure your warriors are under wraps as Alec and I will be outside."

Shade turned to Alec. "Let's take a walk outside. And don't worry. Kate's army will be no threat. I want to show you the stables, so you can get a feel for them, then relay that to Rissa."

Alec downed the glass of Midnight then stood to follow Shade outside. "I did talk to Rissa last night, and she does want to move forward with getting a horse. Make sure you find her one that's already broke in. Rissa knows how to ride, but I want her to have a horse that's used to being ridden."

Making their way outside, Shade walked side by side with Alec. "Not a problem, brother, at least I know she can ride. But if she wishes for some refresher courses, Antonio is the stable master here, he will gladly teach her. He is in charge of all the horses. She is welcome to come at any time day or night. Antonio is day-walker as well. He will be instructed to accommodate her schedule. I already have one horse in mind for her, but I will send her the pictures of about ten to choose from."

As they approached the stables, Shade could see Aegis remained close at hand, but she was steering clear of the stables to avoid spooking the horses. As they got closer, Antonio appeared.

"Antonio, *buonasera*. This is Master Canton. He will be purchasing a horse for his mate. She will be boarding the horse here and riding at her leisure. Please accommodate her accordingly. We are going to have one brought in from Florence specifically for her."

Turning to Alec, he introduced Antonio. "Alec, this is Antonio, my stable master."

Alec shook his hand, giving him a strong grip, ever the politician. "Good to meet you, Antonio. My mate is a bit of a diva. Don't let her scare you off. Take control when you need to."

Alec took in the size of the stables, and the horses Shade had already brought over. He kept a wary eye on the wolf. “So, what's up with the animalism, brother? I mean, what the fuck do you even do with that?"

"Well, protection, for one. They had you immobilized, didn’t they? That would give me, or one of my warriors, time to assess the situation. It’s all new to me too. Not much research on it, either. And I prefer not letting this news get out. The fewer people that know about my mate’s gift, the better. At least until both of us can figure out how to control it."

Walking to one of the stalls, Impavido pawed the hay and snorted. "You remember this big guy, *si*?"

Alec nodded. "I can keep quiet about it. Not like I run in the immortal circles, anyway. I remember this horse, Impavido, right? He was one mean mofo as I recall."

"*Si!* But he went to Kate like a damn kitten. Could not believe it. Down there is Bravado, that is Kate's horse, and in the back is Meile, she is from my *madre*'s line of Arabians. As you can see, I have plenty of stalls, and I was bringing several more over anyway. It will be good to have more horses, they keep each other company. I’ll cut you a deal. Every one of the horses I’m offering is worth at least ninety to a hundred grand. But whichever one she chooses, I sell to you for fifty grand. You interested in riding as well, spend some time with her?"

Alec laughed. "Not me, brother. I'll stick to cars. Never had an interest in horses. No, Rissa can come here, get some exercise, something besides being stuck in the gym every day. And she'll be safe here, which brings me to our next topic. She wants Jacks gone, the sooner the better. I don't want a live-in, not even a permanent protector like Luca, but I think she needs some protection when she's out. You got someone you can assign? A male this time?"

Shade stared at him. "Do you blame her for wanting Jacks gone, brother? *Cazzo*, you could have at least taken it outside the home. Show Rissa some respect. Sorry, brother, not my place to judge, and Jacks will move on without a problem. So, you want a male, but not someone full-time. **"Marcello, who the hell is guarding Canton's house right now?"**

Shade and Alec walked back outside the stables as Marcello answered. **"Hyde has covered that grid. He's right here, you want him?"**

Shade guided Alec in the direction of the new warrior camp. "Let's walk over to the camp, brother, I want to show you around." **"Yes, I have a job for him, want him to meet Canton, send him out to the training field. We will both be out there."**

"Listen, brother, I think I have a solution for the protector. He covers the Georgetown grid that includes your house. He would always be close. He's a bit more mature. Good warrior, been with me a long time. He does not look like a typical warrior, more well-rounded, well educated, clean-cut and he likes nice clothes. He will blend in if Rissa has events in the evening or she needs him as an escort."

Alec followed Shade's lead as they walked toward the new warrior camp. The wall was high enough to obscure the view, but not so high as to draw questions. It could be scaled by a curious intruder, but based on the welcome party Alec received he doubted anyone would ever get that far.

Shade continued with his description of Hyde. "He likes finer things. He does not hang around the club scene. He's firm but not too heavy-handed. It may help with Rissa. She can be a royal bitch, brother!"

Alec chuckled. "You only see the tip of the iceberg. So, let's meet this warrior. What's his name?"

Shade took Alec inside the camp while he waited for Hyde to emerge. He showed Alec the basic training areas and talked about his plans until he felt Hyde approach. Turning, he saw Hyde standing against the wall, waiting for his master. Hyde walked toward Shade and Alec.

"Ah Hyde, I want you to meet someone. This is Master Alec Canton, you work his grid."

Hyde nodded respectfully, shaking Alec's hand. "Pleasure, Master Canton. Beautiful home you have. What can I do for you?"

Alec returned the hand shake, looking him over. He was very refined for a warrior. He'd pass well as a mortal. "Nice to meet you. So, you're currently protecting our grid? Have you seen Rissa? Do you understand our circumstances? I'm looking for a protector for Rissa. We both pose as mortals, live as mortals. She has her own business and her clientele is all mortal. I'll need someone who can escort her to whatever events she has, but not cramp her style. She doesn't like the idea of having a protector, feels it infringes on her freedom. You'll need to find that balance of being close enough to intervene if needed, without standing right in her shadow. She's a diva... Let's just put that on the table, and she won't make it easy for you. Are you interested in this assignment?"

Hyde stood as tall as Alec and met his gaze. "Master Canton, I've seen Miss Benneteau when she's been out in the evening. All the warriors are well informed of the activities and events taking place in the district, at master's insistence. It helps us in providing your protection. We always see you, but you may not see us. I can be wherever she wishes for me to be. I would be honored to serve as her protector in the name of Medici, if it so pleases you."

Alec took him in. Hyde didn't wear his hair long like many of the warriors, but had his hair cut stylishly close. He was clean-shaven. Put him in a suit and tie and he could be a businessman. He'd do well as a protector for Rissa, and hopefully, Alec could get his own house settled back into some normal routine without the pouting and the door-slamming.

"I think you'll work out fine. I do need to wrap up the details with her current protector, and as soon as that's done, you can begin your assignment. We're both day-walkers and keep a schedule similar to most mortals. We sleep at night, and once we're both home in the evening, you'd be free to go off duty."

Hyde nodded to him. "I see no problem with that, Master Canton. I'm also a day-walker. I presume that Miss Benneteau would like to meet with me before I assume my duties, and I'll let master take care of those details with you. Good evening to you and a pleasure to be working with you."

Shade observed Alec's reaction to Hyde and knew Alec was impressed. Hyde would be excellent for Rissa. "So, brother, I think you liked Hyde. I will get phone numbers exchanged, and schedules lined up. I have some additional Medici warriors coming in from Florence this week to replace your mercenaries. But I do suggest you get Jacks gone before you let him meet Rissa."

Alec shoved his hands into his jeans pocket. "Oh, don't worry there. I won't set up anything with Hyde until Jacks is gone. Now I have a proposition for you. When that rogue attacked Rissa, she got a couple of vials that fell to the ground. She wasn't sure what it was, but she grabbed them up. I sent them out for analysis and it looks like we may have Angel's potion that blocks the vampire's scent. Could be a very powerful weapon, don't you think?"

Shade raised his eyebrows. "What? You have the scent blocking potion? Genius! What is working in your mind, brother?"

Alec chuckled. "Believe it or not, I'm running out of property to pay your ass, since you seem to prefer real estate to cash. I was thinking of an exchange. I turn over the ingredients in the potion–my contacts with the lab can produce it for you–in exchange for your continued services. We're getting close to the one year agreement we started with, and I'll want to renew, especially with the wedding coming up, and the campaign. And now adding a protector dedicated to Rissa."

Shade thought this through, the potion in exchange for his security services. This could be a boost for his warriors, both here and in Europe.

"So, are you talking one more year of service for the potion?"

Alec laughed. "Brother... I was thinking a potion that allowed you to move about without detection for all time should be good for more than a year. I don't know what my future holds. I have the campaign, and I'll need some coverage, and if I win the election, then we really need to figure out next steps with the Secret Service everywhere. But one year? Come on, brother, get real."

Shade ran a hand through his hair. "Look, Alec, I need some time to think this through, discuss it with Kate. We are a team, we reign together. Give me a few days, *si*? But I like this deal. It works for both of us. We need to stay together as much as possible. And having Medici in your pocket is a weapon all its own. Give me a few days to give you an answer, *si*?"

Alec shrugged. "No hurry. We have some time before we renew the contract. Let me get out of here, get back home. I'll let Rissa know I have a new protector for her and take care of the situation with Jacks, and then I'll let you know when we can set up a time for Rissa to meet Hyde."

"Not a problem. I will send Rissa the pictures of the horses to choose from tonight, tell her to check her email. I will be waiting to hear from you then. Don't worry, Alec, Medici is on your streets, we own that town, you just be sure to rule it."

As they fist bumped, Alec teleported out. "Hope the bastard doesn't get lost. He would be one pissed off vamp if he ended up in Chinatown instead of G-town!"

18

Alec teleported back home from Bel Rosso, impressed, once again, with how much Shade had done with the property. The stables and the warrior camp were complete. He couldn't imagine what he'd do with the rest of the property, but he's sure it wouldn't sit stagnant for long. He didn't miss the point Shade made about discussing his business proposition with Kate, but on the other hand, he also noticed he still kept a tight rein on her as she rarely left that property without him.

Alec landed in the foyer of their G-town home and Santos greeted him, handing him a Midnight. Alec headed for his office but noticed the French doors that lead to the courtyard and pool were open, letting in the warm breeze. He headed for the outdoors and found Rissa seated in the courtyard, stretched out on a chaise lounge, a glass of Midnight in one hand and her eyes closed. He leaned down and kissed her forehead.

"Glad to see you're relaxing, my darling. Does this mean you're getting caught up at work?" He pulled a deck chair over closer to where she sat and sat down, propping his feet across the foot of her lounge chair.

As she felt the kiss on her forehead, she opened her eyes and smiled. He seemed in a very good mood. "I'm never caught up, but I came out to take in the beautiful night and decided to stay out here a while. I didn't realize it was so late. How was your day?"

Alec lit up a cigarette. "It was productive. I went out to see Shade. I saw the stables. He already had a few horses and was bringing in more. He's going to send you an email with photos of some of the horses he thinks you'd like. I told him they'd need to be already broken in. So, be on the lookout for that, and pick the one you want. I think it'll be good for you to get out of the city, enjoy the fresh air. Riding is good exercise and it'll be a nice break for you from all the hours in the gym. And you'll be safer there than anywhere else you could go. He has that warrior camp up and running. Right now, it's just his regular crew there, the ones he has on patrol here in D.C., but he's going to expand. Nothing will bother you there."

She nodded. "I'll check my email in the morning, but may I ask why you have a problem with me spending so much time at the gym? I know the attack was in the gym parking garage, but I thought this rogue thing was over." Swinging her legs over the side of the chaise, she waited for his response.

"Rissa, I'm aware of your stress level. You're tense all the time, looking over your shoulder. You were hesitant to go to Florence. You said it was because you were too busy, but I know it was your fear. You said you liked to ride, and now Shade has this place that is surrounded by vamps. It's the one place you can go where you can completely let your guard down. I do think the rogue attacks are over, but you'll continue to feel the fear of that attack for some time to come. This should help you get past all that, and do something you love in the process. You can still go to the gym. I just thought this might be something you'd enjoy. If I'm wrong, then you are under no pressure to go."

Rissa moved to his deck chair and snuggled into his lap. He hated that, but she wanted him to understand her happiness and appreciation of the gift he was bestowing on her.

"Alec, I don't mean to seem ungracious. I love riding. I'm always so jealous of my clients when they talk about spending their weekends riding. I'm a little hesitant yet, but that damn warrior bitch doesn't help. I've tried to relax and let her do her job, but it's like having a rod up my ass every moment. How much longer is she going to be here?" She kissed his neck softly.

Alec shifted her in his lap, uncomfortable with the affection. "Well that's the other news I have for you. I talked with Shade tonight about assigning someone else. I asked for a male warrior, so maybe your feathers won't get so ruffled, and he'll not be a live-in. He already protects this grid, so he's familiar with your routine. I met him, my darling. He looks very clean-cut. Not your typical warrior. He'll blend in well with your clientele. His name is Hyde. I'd like to set up a meeting, go over the ground rules. How does that sound to you?"

"Alec! Thank you! This means the world to me. Oh, I think I like him already. You approved of him already then?"

Alec nodded. "Yes, I met him. He's very refined. Highly educated, well spoken. In a suit, he'll blend right in. I told him I wanted him close enough to respond, but not to interfere with your work. He'll only be with you when you're out. He can teleport with you if you decide you want to go to Virginia and ride, but once there, he can leave you on your own. You can pretty much ride wherever you want on the property and be safe. It'll give you some time to be alone with your own thoughts, and yet, protected at the same time. So, when would you like to meet him?"

Smiling at him, she leaned into his chest. "The sooner, the better, any time will be fine. I can work around your schedule. He sounds perfect, Alec. Thank you for understanding how important this is for me. I have a lot to accomplish and with the wedding coming up, things are getting hectic. I've given Jenny the list of dates that are open for both the National Cathedral for the ceremony, and the Old Post Office building for the reception. There're very few openings, so I need you to choose the date that suits you, and quickly. Let me know, and I'll book the event and proceed with printing the invitations."

Alec nodded. "Good, I'll set something up for you to meet him. And whatever works on the calendar, you pick the date, my darling. That should be the bride's prerogative, I think. Just have Jenny mark it out in red. Now, if you'll excuse me, I do have some work to do...and a protector to fire, so I need to get to it."

Standing up to let him leave, Rissa knew he was going to her, that fucking bitch, and this would be her last moment with her master and in her house.

Leaving her by the pool, he directed Santos to bring her another Midnight as he left the courtyard. He headed to the office and opened the safe, taking out the final payment for Jacks. The deal was half up front, and the balance at the end of the assignment. He had originally booked her for a six-month stent, but she'd be leaving now, after one month, a million dollars richer.

19

As Alec teleported out of the camp, Shade teleported inside the house and felt *bel* in his study. He stood in the doorway, watching her on the computer as her fingers flew across the keyboard. "You seem pretty intense with your work there, *mi amore*. You didn't even feel me here. Care to share?"

"I was trying to see if I could find this property in Paris. To see what it looks like. If I have the right address, it's located right on the Champs Elysees. It looks huge! It has great architectural detail on the outside. I can't wait to see it. See what we can do with it."

She jumped up from the laptop and went to him, sliding her arms around his waist. "Thank you for negotiating that."

"It was my ultimate pleasure. I want you to be happy wherever we are, *mi amore*, and I think we will be spending a lot of time in Paris. It is a lover's paradise, *si*? Now come, sit down with me, I have some important things to discuss with you." Picking her up, she wrapped her legs around his waist and he snuggled into her neck.

Carrying her to the living room, he sat them both down on the couch, Kate facing him, as he slid a stray crimson lock behind her ear. "First of all, Alec has purchased a horse for Rissa, and he will be boarding it here. It will take a week or so for the horse to get here, along with some others I am having shipped over. Rissa can come and go as she pleases. Alec is paying for the privilege and wants her to have some fresh air, get some exercise beyond the gym and feel protected. Any problems with that?"

Kate shook her head. "No problems. She's a day-walker, and I may not even see her. But even if she comes in the evening, I'm fine with it. I'll have to deal with Aegis on her first visit. After that, she should be fine. I insist she be cordial to our staff, though. I've noticed she's quite dismissive with their staff, and I'll not have our people disrespected."

"Well, as it relates to the staff, Rissa should know better, but I will make sure she understands, and Antonio has already been given a heads up by Alec. Also, I have assigned Hyde as her personal protector. Alec is releasing Jacks from her duties. I should think that change will please both of you. Hyde was already assigned security on the Georgetown grid that includes their home, so he will be accompanying Rissa as needed, but he will resume his grid duties when not working with her."

Kate ran her hand over his chest, smoothing out his shirt. "I'm glad to hear it. You know Rissa and I aren't close, but I feel bad that this woman we sent to her home had sex with Alec right under her nose. I know it's none of our business, and they live very differently from us. I understand that. But for me personally, it raises issues of trust. You know how I feel about it, and we'll have to agree to disagree on the topic of Jacks. You still see her as a skilled warrior, I see her as a home-wrecker, so let's just leave it at that. I've seen Hyde. I don't know him, but Marcello and Luca speak highly of him. I think he'll be well suited as her protector."

"*Si*, as do I. He will suit her needs and he can handle himself among the mortals. Now, onto a more serious topic, Alec has made me a proposal, but this could affect our future, *mi amore*. Cuerpo had invented a potion of sorts, one that can eliminate a vampire's scent. Other vampires cannot detect your scent when you drink it. That is why we had so much trouble on the streets when the rogues were out. We could not smell them. When Rissa was attacked, that rogue dropped a few vials of this potion and she was able to grab them. Alec had them tested at the lab and he now knows the ingredients and how to reproduce it. Alec has made me an offer for this potion, which I could use very effectively with my warriors. I want your opinion. In exchange for the potion, he is asking I be obligated to him, to provide warriors for his protection for an extended period of time. We did not settle on a timeline. Give me your thoughts, Kate. This is important to our future."

Kate was caught off guard. This was the first real issue of major importance regarding his business that he'd consulted her on. She wanted to give him a thoughtful response. She mulled over in her head all she knew of the rogue attacks that he'd shared over the past year before answering him.

"Lover, I think having access to this potion would be a very powerful weapon, and absolutely necessary for your warriors. But I wouldn't assume you're the only one to own it. If Rissa found vials on the rogue that attacked her, that means other rogues from Cuerpo's coven may have had access to the potion as well. You can't know for sure if all of his rogues are dead, or if they've just moved on. I think the potion is invaluable, but I also think it would be a mistake to assume you'd be the only one to have it. Make the deal with Alec, but establish a term limit. If Alec is successful in his bid for President, protecting him will escalate to a whole new level, and will demand a lot of your resources. We don't know what the future holds, so to giving him a blank check is a bad decision. Give him a timeline. Five years, or maybe eight years if he is re-elected... whatever makes sense to you from the standpoint of committing your resources. But I could see him in a position where he would drain you, and all for a potion that could potentially be in the hands of every master over time."

Shade listened and stared at her thoughtful expression as she spoke. Damn, this woman was smart. He knew she'd reign beside him well.

"You are very intelligent, *bel*, and that is a good point. Alec is bothered by all of the property I have taken from him in these deals. He would take advantage, just as I probably would if I had the chance. Any idea how much I lo–"

Shade jumped bolt upright, stopping mid-sentence with Kate still clinging to him. "Vampire! *Cazzo*, its Jacks!"

Kate had picked up the scent as well, knew it was vampire, but she didn't yet recognize the scents of those vampires outside their own coven. She felt her heart pound, not in fear but anger. She heard the feral growl of the mountain lion and the two wolves, and she already knew, without looking out the window they had Jacks cornered. There was a part of her that wanted to issue a command to them now to rip her apart, but Jacks had done nothing to her, and Kate intended to keep it that way.

"Let me go outside. I need to call to Aegis They're holding her at bay now."

Shade nodded. "*Si*, I had no idea she was coming, *mi amore*, I swear to you. I knew Alec was releasing her, I do not know her purpose for coming here." Shade followed behind as they quickly made their way to the door.

Kate exited the front door to see the three animals surrounding Jacks. Aegis and Night Stalker were in front of her, teeth bared and growling, ready to attack. Riparo paced behind her, hissing and snarling, whipping her tail in an agitated state. Jacks stood spread-legged but still, her weapon drawn, ready to take aim at the first animal that attacked.

Kate walked out into the yard until she stood directly in front of Jacks and made eye contact before lifting her hand and asking Aegis to settle. All three animals dropped their aggressive posture and sat at ease but alert and ready to respond to Kate's command. "Put your gun down, Jacks, and explain your purpose here."

Shade stood in the open door and waited. He was curious to see how much control Kate actually had over the animals. He hoped like hell Jacks didn't fire off a shot. He would have no control over *bel's* beast if one of those animals was hurt. He remained quiet. This was his queen establishing her territory with another female not of their coven and he knew better than to overstep his bounds.

Jacks eased the Glock down, but didn't engage the safety. She thought she was landing in friendly territory, but she was no fool and this welcoming party meant business, including the new immortal in front of her with the flaming red hair.

"My lady, I've come to see your master before leaving the country. I've finished my assignment to Master Canton and only wished to let Master Shade know of my departure and to thank him."

Kate nodded. "Just so we're clear, Jacks. I've spoken to Rissa, and I know you had sex with her mate, in her own home, right under her nose. I can't, for the life of me, understand why she'd tolerate that behavior, so it's important you know...I'm not Rissa, and Shade is not Alec. Any inappropriate behavior on your part will be met with my beast. I understand you're an assassin of note, but then, so was Cuerpo. So, tread carefully. Do we understand each other?"

Jacks stared her down, her eyes never once leaving Kate's. Shade had chosen well, for his mate didn't back down, and she wasn't afraid.

"I understand completely. I came to wish you both good fortune on your mating and coronation, nothing more. I respect your master highly, as I do you my lady. I came to bear well wishes, and to thank Master Shade for the referral. I'll leave you in peace." Jacks nodded to Kate and then eyed Shade intently.

Shade walked outside, standing behind Kate, putting his arms around her waist. His eyes locked with Jacks.

"I appreciate your well wishes, Jacks. I am disappointed in how you conducted yourself with Alec. Revenge of that sort will never get you ahead, only a reputation and disrespect. I still consider you an ally and I am sure we will fight alongside each other in battle. I wish you no harm, but you are no longer welcome inside this home or on this property. Understood, *si*?"

"Understood, Master Shade. I'll take my leave now." Lowering her head, she showed respect to them both and teleported out to Greece. There was a master there she wished to contact for some relaxation and perhaps, some work.

Kate listened to his quiet reprimand of Jacks, and his decision to distance himself from her. It wasn't the conversation she'd expected, especially after their argument. She leaned back against him as his arms encircled her. Kate turned in his arms, sliding her hands up his chest as he leaned down to kiss her. Aegis and Night Stalker danced at their feet like playful puppies.

"My warriors approve, lover, and so do I. Now come inside, I'd hate to waste anymore of this night on business."

20

As Shade threw Kate over his shoulder, he slapped her ass and heard Aegis give a growl. Looking down, he laughed. "Master, remember girl? Take it easy, this is play."

Running back to the house with her as she giggled, he climbed the stairs and headed into the bedroom, sitting her down. "Now what were you saying about being done with business?"

Kate took one of his hands in hers and raised it to her lips, slipping his long finger into her mouth, and slowly swirled her tongue over the rough skin before sliding his finger out of her mouth. "Our business is never finished, lover."

Shade moaned from the warmth and wetness of her mouth as her lips closed over his finger. "You keep that up and I will never walk again. Damn woman, you make my whole body tremble with need for you." He watched as she smiled and backed slowly away from him, her body saying things words never could. "Teasing your savage lover, are you?"

Kate unbuttoned her shirt, showing quick flashes of the black lace bra against the contrast of her pale skin. "Am I teasing?"

"Past teasing, now you are torturing. A peep show, is it? Then perhaps I should get comfortable."

Standing where he was, in the middle of the bedroom, he lifted his tight fitting t-shirt over his head, exposing his broad chest and hard flat abs. Whipping the tee across the room, he slowly unbuttoned his jeans, one at a time, then reached in and grabbed his bulging cock and freed it from its constrained cage.

"I can give as good as I get, *mi amore*."

Kate giggled. "Oh, don't I know it."

She dropped the blouse on the floor and shimmied out of her own jeans, sliding them down her hips, revealing the black lace thong. She turned her back to him and bent over the bed, flipping her hair to the side as she looked back at him over her shoulder. "A little help removing these jeans, please."

"*Cazzo*! This game is a torture method, *si*?"

Walking to the bed, he lifted the thong with one finger and leaned over her, burying his nose into her hair and inhaled. He moaned from the scent of roses, now mixed with her immortal scent. He lifted her crimson locks from her neck as his tongue glided down her spine from the base of her neck to the beautiful black thong. Standing upright, he crouched behind her, still in his jeans and boots. He grabbed her jeans and slid them down, kissing each ass cheek, letting his hands glide down those silky white thighs, over her calves and down her ankles, allowing her to step free of her jeans. Kissing behind each knee, he stood and kicked off his boots and flung his jeans across the room.

Kate's eyes were closed as she honed all her senses to the sensations he created. Her temperature rose, even as the goose bumps appeared on her skin from his tantalizing tongue. She slowly pushed her hips back into him as she pushed herself upright, standing and flipping her hair back and turning to face him.

She grasped his hips as she squatted down in front of him. She ran her tongue from his naval to his pubic bone, before nuzzling her nose into that dark patch of fur between his legs, inhaling his male scent. She scraped her nails down the sides of his thighs before cupping his balls in her hands and running her tongue the full length of his shaft.

Shade was rooted where he stood. His eyes followed her tongue as it traveled across his olive skin and he felt his eyes turn red, his fangs aching to punch through, but he held back. His hunger for her was insatiable. As she buried her nose into him, his hands went to her hair, gripping tightly. Nothing turned him on more than that head of crimson. He rather liked her taking the lead. He wanted her to play and discover herself through him. He gave her a hint as to where he wanted her to go, and pushed her head down further to his feet.

Kate felt his hands in her hair and the gentle pressure as he pushed her head down. She was on her knees, bowing before him, her face at his feet. She licked the top of his feet, nipped at his ankles, her ass in the air, her hair draped over his feet.

He lifted her up and spun her around, walking her across the room and sitting her down in the chair. Walking back to the bed bare ass naked, he crawled onto the bed and lay down, propping himself on the pillows. With legs spread, he grabbed his cock and stroked slowly, his red eyes glowing and staring back at her. She was beautiful and he still couldn't believe she was his.

"Can you entertain me, *mi amore*? Do something that will surprise me. Don't hold back."

Kate looked at him spread-eagled on the bed, his cock in his hand. *Entertain him? Surprise him?* She knew his history. What could she possibly do that would surprise him? She sat back in the chair, head thrown back and arching her back, her legs spread, her ankles locked around the legs of the chair. She ran her hands over her breasts, stopping at her nipples, tweaking and twisting them, before slowly sliding her hands down her tight abdomen and between her legs. She let her fingers glide slowly in and out of her sex, already wet for him, and a moan escaped her lips. She raised her head, her mane of red hair falling forward as she locked eyes with his. She watched him, as he watched her.

He gripped his cock tighter, stroking slowly from the root to the bulging engorged head. His fangs punched as her slim fingers glided between the silken wet cleft of her sex, pink and protruding with aching need to clench tight around something thick and hard inside her. His eyes never left her as she threw back that crimson and he growled.

"Come. Let me taste you. Your fingers are wet and sticky with your sweet honey."

She got up from the chair, her legs already weak with desire, and walked to the bed, crawling up to him, sliding her breasts along the hard muscles of his chest, and slipped her fingers in his mouth. He drew them in, his heated tongue tasting her, as her heart raced. She dropped her head to his shoulder, nuzzled his neck, and licked the length of his vein pulsing beneath her tongue.

She came to him passive and playful and this wasn't what he or his beast wanted. He wanted her to let her beast out, feel what it was to have that strength and to learn to control it. She was still young to the idea since her turning, and she needed to learn, in a safe environment, what it felt like, and how to manage her beast to her benefit. As she snuggled into his neck, she needed to feed and this was just the advantage he was looking for. He wrapped her hair tightly around his fist and yanked her head back, looking at her startled eyes and saw the flaring beast beneath the surface. Grabbing her ass, he sank his fingers deep into her tender flesh and flipped her onto her back as he crouched over her and growled. "Earn your blood, my queen. Earn it!"

Kate was ready to feed when he yanked her away. She hissed and growled at him, baring her fangs as her eyes glowed a deep blood red. She wrapped her legs around his hips, and grabbing his shoulders, flipped him back onto his back, pinning his shoulders down, a growl deep in her throat. She grabbed his arms, pushing them over his head, and held his wrists in a tight grip. Her breasts brushed against his face and his tongue snaked out, licking at her nipples, sending a fire that settled between her legs. She concentrated her thoughts and willed his wrists to be bound, and was shocked as she saw the rope appear, binding each of his wrists to the headboard. She slid her body down his, licked his face and lips as she slithered further down his muscular frame. Her nails scraped down his chest as she settled between his legs, sliding her hand the length of his massive cock before slipping the bulging head into her mouth. She teased his cock with her tongue, sucking and licking at him. He lifted his hips and she pulled away, not giving him what he wanted. "Earn it? Before this night is over, you will beg me to feed from you."

His beast growled loudly in agonizing pleasure. *Careful what you wish for, Shade, your mate will give it to you in spades and then some*.

Throwing his head back against the pillows, he pulled on the ties, but to no use. His beast growled in frustration as she looked up at him through her tousled red hair. She slid his cock out of her mouth and climbed slowly up his body, impaling herself on his rigid, throbbing dick, as her own beast cried out in ecstasy and shook that head of crimson back and forth. Devil fucking help him, but she could take him alive and he'd let her.

She slid the full length of him, moving slowly, his hips matching her rhythm. She laid down on his chest, licking his nipple, nipping gently at his skin, drawing her nails gently down his sides. She sat upright again, locked eyes with him, and raised her hands to her head, lifting her hair, tossing it about before dragging her hands slowly over her breasts as she ground her hips into him.

Shade moved to her rhythm and embraced the torture, as she taunted his beast with her crimson. His hips lurched upwards, penetrating deep, but letting her set the pace. His body was aching for release, wanting desperately to touch her, let his fangs sink deep into the pulsing vein in the soft skin of her neck, giving him life and love and lightness. He withheld freeing his hands from the bonds and bending her beast to his will. He wanted this agonizingly slow torture of her teasing. "*Bel, cazzo!* Give me some release!" His body was covered in a fine sheen of sweat, his muscles straining and his fangs aching.

She responded to his plea by laying her body down on his chest once more, covering his mouth with hers, letting her tongue explore, tangle with his, as she licked first one fang and then the other, knowing this would push him to his limits. "Feed now, lover?"

His beast bursts free and there was no holding him back. She knew how to push him over the top as his beast growled "Yes! Now!" His beast broke the ropes that bound his arms, freeing his hands to grip fists full of her hair. He pulled her to his throat, inviting her to feed as he thrust his hips upward, hard and deep. Her fangs sank into the tender skin of his neck and he went insane with the love he felt for her. He sank his own fangs deep into her shoulder, drawing that sweet blood into his mouth, letting it wash over him in waves as his orgasm exploded, taking them both over the edge.

She felt his whole body tense as he broke free of the ropes and pulled her to his neck. She bit deep, feeling the rush of blood across her tongue and the immediate flash of heat between her legs just as he thrust hard and deep inside her. She felt him sink his own fangs into her as the orgasm washed over them, and they rode it together, wave after wave, as they swallowed the sweet nectar that sustained and bonded them to each other. As the sensations faded, she unlatched and kissed him, their blood mixing in their mouths, as his hand still firmly gripped her hair. She broke the kiss and laid her head on his shoulder, their hearts pounding in sync.

He never tired of how it felt to make love to her, feed from her, and he didn't think he ever would. He lay with her, letting their beasts retreat and their hearts and bodies recover. He realized he still fisted her hair and released the silk from his hands, letting his arms embrace her.

"I love you, *mi amore*. Devil knows how much I love you and cannot survive a moment without you. There is nothing on this earth that can hold me like you do."

Kate slid off him, lying beside him, her arm thrown across his chest. She licked the wound on his neck and watched as it healed. Outside, she heard the howl of the two wolves, and she smiled to herself.

Shade heard the howling. "Is that what I think it is?"

"Lover, it's Aegis and Night Stalker letting us know they approve of our mating."

He sat up chuckling. "Just make sure they know who the real master is around here."

Kate giggled. "We make enough noise on our own, now we'll have a chorus outside as well. There are no secrets in this house."

Shade rolled on his side, facing her. "*Bel*, I need to talk to you about something. It is really important to me. The meeting I'm having with the warriors, it is my first with them here in the new camp. I want to reign here differently than I did in Florence. I want us to reign together. Please, will you come with me and attend the meeting? I want you to know what's going on, be a part of everything. My grave mistake when you were mortal was hiding so much from you and it almost caused me to lose you and that was a wakeup call for me. I never want to make that mistake again. We are king and queen, and I want us to reign together."

Swinging his legs over the side of the bed, he sat there with his head down. "*Padre* kept business and the duties of his coven from *Madre*. She never had a say in anything. It was partly the times, but also his damn pride, he felt she had no place in his business. And he was so wrong. *Madre* could have made him so much stronger and powerful, but he was so damn blind to that. I am different, I want you to be here with me, know my business, be with my warriors, know them, help them, comfort them. I want my coven to love you for all that we do together to build and protect them."

Kate stroked his back as he sat on the side of the bed. "I have felt, from the beginning, I need to earn their respect. I know your warriors are pledged to me, are loyal to me. But I know that loyalty flows through you. You ask it of them, and they freely give it. But I want to earn it. I know there're skeptics outside your coven, and in the Council, that will always doubt my ability to fill the role of queen to this coven. But I'll prove them all wrong. I wish to be at your side, to be a part of building your legacy. To make sure our children carry those values forward into the next generation."

Turning toward her, he saw her face and it almost melted him. She loved him, his warriors, his people, and her heart was always given to them with everything she had. Pulling her into his arms, he crushed her to his chest.

"I care not about the Council, but I do care about you, and my *familia*. Please say yes, that you will come, be with me, stand strong with me always."

"I'll always be at your side. Even when you stand in battle, my heart goes with you."

His heart lit up and he kissed her passionately, pouring all his feelings through that kiss. "I love you, *mi amore*. Now get up and get dressed, we have some work to do outside." Winking, he slapped her ass then stood and grabbed his clothes. "Don't just sit there, move it, woman! You are not going outside bare-assed for the world to see. Come on, we have some teleporting lessons to work on."

Kate laughed. *Teleporting? What do I wear to learn to teleport? Something that will protect me if I crash land?* She went to her dresser and removed the leathers Luca had given her when she finished training and carried them into the bathroom to put them on. She slid into the butter-soft pants, which clung to every curve and slipped on the fitted jacket, zipping up the front, deciding not to pull up the hood, and left her hair free. She pulled on a pair of black knee-high boots and returned to the bedroom. "Ready, lover."

"And about time, wo-" As Shade turned to her, his heart did a flip inside his chest. His mouth hung open and he kept blinking as his cock responded to the vision before him. "*Cazzo*, kill me dead where I stand. You are looking hot. I mean scorching! How the hell am I supposed to teach you anything when you look like that? Damn, woman! Where the hell did those leathers come from?"

"They're mine. I earned them, just like I earned the crossbow. Luca had Cory make them for me when I finished my training. He mailed a pair of my jeans and a shirt over to him, so he'd know my size. I had no idea when I'd ever have the opportunity to wear them. It has a hood, and a mask that covers the lower part of my face so only my eyes are exposed. So, if you need an extra warrior...you know where to find me."

Shade shook his head. "Well, let's get some skills down pat first, and then we will discuss the warrior, *si?*"

They walked outside hand in hand, both of them in leathers, and Shade had never been happier.

21

As Shade led *bel* outside, the moon was high in the sky and the stars were out, a good clear night to teach her a few things about teleporting. He had no idea how this was going to go, but better to find out sooner than later. Walking her out into the open field far from the house, it took them a while to get there, but he wanted her away from anything she could crash land into.

"Now listen, *mi amore*. The first step is to think about your landing location. You have to visualize it in your mind. Keep your eyes open and keep your mind alert. As you go, you will learn speed and how to turn your body. So, picture the house in your mind, get a clear picture of it. Close your eyes and see it. Make yourself want to go there. Do you have it in your mind's eye?"

Kate closed her eyes and concentrated, seeing their home in every detail. "I can see it. Now tell me what to do."

Stepping close behind her, he put his hands on her waist. "Now, I want you to jump up at an angle. Not straight up in the air, lean into it, trust me. Take yourself there. Don't go too fast, just a comfortable speed. It's straight across the field. When you land, talk to me and let me know you have landed. Concentrate on where you need to be." Letting go of her waist, he stepped back. "Go!"

Go? That's my instruction? Go how? Kate focused her attention on the house and felt her energy build. As she started to lift, she gasped and clutched at him. Letting go of the image in her head in a moment of panic, she felt her feet back firmly on the ground as she clung to his arm. She was breathing rapidly. "Maybe you should go with me?"

"*Bel*, listen to me, you cannot be afraid of your skills, it will hamper you. If you fall, you heal by the morning. I'm right here. I will feel you if you fall, and I'll be there."

Taking her in his arms, he cuddled her to his chest. "Relax your breathing, come on. The house is over there, across that field."

He spun her around facing the direction of their home and let go of her. "Imagine this. Our *bambino* is afraid and screams out, get to him, *bel*. Go, he is terrified, go!"

Kate saw the house in her head again, a clear picture. She felt the energy build, like her cells were alive and moving at a high rate of speed. She let go. Let go of her fear and the pull of gravity and let her energy take her. She felt the lift again, and the forward motion. She could feel the wind in her hair and she watched as the house came into view. *Wait. Did he tell me how to stop?* She felt panic again and crashed to the ground. She rolled to a stop across the grass and discovered she was just outside their house on the front lawn, and Aegis ran to her, licking her face and whimpering.

Shade waited and felt her body hit the ground. "*Cazzo!*" **"*Bel*, get up, are you all right?"**

"I'm all right, lover. You didn't tell me how to land."

Luca had felt her panic and rushed to the front yard to see Kate in leathers sprawled across the grass, the wolf licking her face. "Kate? What the fuck?"

Kate laughed. "No problems, Luca. Flying lessons."

Luca held out his hand and Kate grabbed it and pulled herself up. Luca gave her some instructions, "Just picture yourself landing, the same way you picture your destination." He laughed. "Good thing you wore those leathers."

Shade sent her instructions on coming back to him. **"Okay, brush yourself off and this time, you come back to me, but land in my arms, they will be outstretched. Learn to control the speed and energy. It's energy and mind control, *mi amore*, that's all it is. You can do it. Now teleport to me, woman!"** Shade waited to feel her take off and held out his arms at an angle toward the sky.

Land in his arms? Is he kidding? She took a deep breath and looked at Luca. "Okay, well, wish me luck."

She envisioned the field where she started, and imagined Shade there, his arms open to her. She felt the flow of energy change as she lifted again, enjoying the freedom as she moved through the air, letting her momentum pick up. She saw him in the open field, waiting for her and envisioned herself there. She landed with too much speed, but right into his arms, knocking him off balance as he lifted them both skyward, before taking her safely to the ground.

"Well, much better. Now we need to work on your landings. You need to be able to land softly, quietly. Right now, every rogue in Virginia will hear your crash landings. Let's try something else. I am going to take off, just follow me. Don't worry about where we are going, concentrate on the energy of being with me and keeping up with me. You can do this, just practice, and once you understand how it works, you won't even have to think about it, it will just happen, *si*?"

He took off, rising slowly and heading for the mountain range. He could feel her trepidation, but then felt her lift and follow him. He turned his head and saw her catching up quickly. **"Slow down, *mi amore*. Breathe normally, and calm your heartbeat. Just glide and follow me. When you want to turn, just turn your body in that direction. It will go where your mind tells it to. Enjoy the beauty all around you."**

She followed behind him as he led her over the mountain range. She loved the freedom and the wind through her hair. She loved the view of their property from up here, and the realization dawned on her that any rogue vampire could teleport over them, see the lay of the land, the warrior camp, and she had a sense of their vulnerability against other immortals. She caught up to him quickly, not wanting him to get too far ahead of her, and reached over, taking his hand.

He took her to the top of the mountain before turning around and guiding her through the turn with ease, never letting go of her hand. He watched her face and felt her relax. They completed their turn around the mountain when he let go of her hand and went into a dive, speeding away from her. "**Come on *bel,* dive. I got you."**

She followed, picking up speed, and felt the smile spread across her face. She spread her arms and felt the wind on her face but realized by spreading out her arms it slowed down her speed. She pulled her arms in closer to her body and quickly caught up to him again.

"You've got it, *mi amore*. That's the way!"

He grabbed her hand and headed for the house, this time, going much faster, building up speed. Her smile was wide, and he knew she loved it. Shade let go of her hand as they teleported back and forth over the fields of Bel Rosso.

"Watch this." He went up high in the air and did somersaults, then teleported back to her and urged her to do the same.

Feeling brave, she decided to combine what she had learned with Luca, when he taught her to run the wall and do a back hand-spring into her new teleporting skills, and only hoped it didn't end disastrously. She dove for the roof of the stables and turned her body to land feet first. As her feet touched down, she pushed off and did a back flip before straightening in the air and lifting back up high into the sky. She could hear the horses respond as her feet hit the roof, and Angelo and a few stable boys ran outside, looking skyward.

Shade laughed as he watched her take his challenge and pull it off with ease. He teleported in and landed in front of Angelo. "It's okay, just teleporting lessons. Relax, I've got this one." Taking off again, he followed her and slapped her ass as he passed her, speeding ahead, higher and faster.

She raced to catch up, laughing out loud. He started to outdistance her, and she pushed hard, focusing on reaching him when she felt light-headed and lost focus. The dizziness overcame her, and she started to free-fall, unable to regain control, falling like a rock straight for the ground. "**Shade!"**

Shade could feel her as her body lost energy and she screamed for him. He back flipped midair and caught her in his arms, curling her into his chest. Landing inside the bedroom, he carried her and laid her down.

"I got you, *mi amore*, it's fine. Catch your breath and lay still for a bit. It takes a lot of energy to teleport. That's why you have to practice, and this is all very new for you. You did well."

He stripped himself of his leathers and boots, and helped remove hers as well. She was like a rag doll, her body limp from the expenditure of energy. Pulling back the duvet and sheets, he snuggled them in beneath the covers and pulled her atop his chest, his hands caressing and soothing her.

"Relax, your warrior has you, nothing will harm you. Sleep and dream. Tomorrow is another day. *Ti amo*."

She laid her head on his chest, feeling the exhaustion take over as her eyes felt heavy. She slid her arm around him and tossed her leg across his.

She told him she loved him, and then, just before drifting off to sleep, she whispered, "I'm going to be fucking awesome at this vampire shit."

Shade felt the rumble of his laughter roll up his chest and out of his mouth. "*Si, mi amore*. My queen is fucking awesome with her vampire shit and her wild menagerie of creatures. To top it off, she already talks like one of my warriors."

Shaking his head, he knew one thing; he loved this woman to her core.

22

The new warriors had arrived from Florence. Shade let Marco choose the five additional warriors he wanted here from the Florence warrior camp for the next six months or more. He'd give them six months, then decide if he wanted to keep them here, return them all or exchange a few. He now had seventeen Medici warriors residing at the Bel Rosso estate. Marco had joked with him, telling him he'd better come up with a plan for Florence. He was running out of fully trained warriors to come to the States.

Shade had made his calls and sent out word through the master's grapevine that he was having an "Open Call" for warriors. He was seeking interested warriors to come and be trained Medici style, becoming among the world's finest. His school in Florence took in young boys, as early as age ten, who grew up in the camp and learned their skills along with their basic education. Here in the States, he'd start the camp with vampires who were already adults, who'd been self-taught or trained by other warriors. Shade would break their old habits and retrain them his way. But first, all applicants would have to pass a basic requirements test to qualify for his camp. He'd put them through a rigorous test of their skill sets with various weapons, test their strength and stamina, and above all, their loyalty, respect, and honor.

In the end, he'd select only a few who could pass his strict admission codes and qualify to train as an elite warrior. This wasn't the first time Shade had begun from scratch. After the death of his parents, he'd had to start anew, and he'd made the camp bigger and better than his *padre*'s. He had every intention of refining that with even higher standards here in the States. He'd need scores of warriors here in the future, and this was where it would all begin.

But, for now, it was time to have his meeting with his current warriors here at Bel Rosso. They needed to understand his expectations and their new assignments and responsibilities. He'd rely on them a great deal and put them to the test. They'd have to give him 110%, but he'd give just as much, if not more. He had Marcello assemble them into the new training facility, as he wanted all to be present. As he and *bel* walked together down the road toward the camp, this was the beginning. History was about to be made, Medici style.

Walking through the gate of the camp, Aegis walked a few feet behind them, and Shade could hear the laughter and small talk of the warriors carried on the night air. He signaled to *bel* to be quiet as they walked to the training facility door, which was wide open to allow the soft breeze of the early evening to blow throughout the building. His warriors had no idea their queen would be attending this meeting, and he didn't want to miss their astonished faces when they realized she was with him.

Marcello had arranged for folding chairs to be set up in the middle of the facility floor. In front of the rows of folding chairs, someone had placed a plush, upholstered chair from one of their lounging rooms. Apparently, the bastards thought he was getting old and needed a cushy chair! He watched silently as some of his warriors stood in small groups talking, others lounged haphazardly on the folding chairs, ribbing each other. It pleased him to see them relaxed because tonight would be the last time they enjoyed such luxury.

Before he had a chance to announce himself, Marcello raised his voice loud and clear, "Master and his lady in the house!"

The warriors all turned their heads and jumped to their feet in respect. Their surprise at Kate's presence showed on their faces. Aegis had followed her through the open door and into the room, standing a few feet behind her. Raven quickly ran to another room and came back carrying an identical plush chair and placed it beside the other, their chairs looking like thrones before the royal court. Shade chuckled softly and led *bel* to her seat, leaning in and giving her a sound kiss on the lips.

Shade remained standing, holding up his hand. "At ease, warriors, take a seat. We have a great deal to discuss this night, but before we start, let me just say a few things. As you can see, your queen is present. Get used to her presence among us. I will not conduct my business without her. My *padre* believed our mates had no business in our world of master and king, but I do not follow that belief. We live in a different world, times have changed and right now, we begin a new future for Medici. I have learned well from my *padre*, but I am also a different master than he. My queen rules beside me in every aspect." Turning to Kate, he smiled. "Is there anything you wish to say, my queen?"

Kate had taken a seat in the chair and motioned for Aegis to sit. The wolf sat regally beside her, as if attending a meeting of vampire warriors was an everyday occurrence. Kate was caught off guard at Shade's request for her to speak to his warriors, but she was not unaware of how much he had ventured from protocol in this male dominated culture. As she stood to address them, Aegis stood as well, and all of the warriors stood in unison. She could hear the whispering and mumbling among them as they took in the wolf, some of them seeing the animal for the first time, confirming for them the rumor of the rare gift their new queen possessed.

Kate shook her head, waved her hand and indicated she wanted them to remain seated. "Please, sit. You have all honored me in pledging your fealty. I know you make that pledge out of love and respect for your master. You each humble me. I want you to know I don't take my role lightly. I understand my responsibility to uphold the legacy of Medici, to carry those traditions forward, and tonight, I pledge to you I'll do everything in my power to be deserving of your loyalty. As you protect me and mine, so I protect and honor you. I welcome you all here, to this new beginning." The warriors nodded their heads to her as she took her seat.

Shade smiled at Kate, as he took his seat beside her and began the meeting. "First of all, let me welcome our brothers from Florence. Please make this your home and feel free to ask questions. I know Marcello has seen to your accommodations and instructed you on the rules and the feeding schedule.

"There have been some changes in posts since our return from Florence and they will go into effect starting this night. Skelk, who was a previous warrior of Master Canton, has now pledged his allegiance to Medici, taken the blood oath and is on board with us full-time. I expect all of you to show Skelk our Medici honor, and respect and treat him according to our code of ethics. Welcome aboard brother!"

Shade made eye contact with Skelk and watched as he nodded his respect in return.

"Cory, our leather magician, is now in permanent residence here at the camp. I am damn sure most of you know where his shop is located already. He will be making the leathers for all of the new recruits as well as continuing to service your needs as well.

"Marcello has been promoted to my Second-In-Command here at the camp. He will be my right hand in overseeing all aspects of this camp, how it is run, and how all of you behave. You will take orders from him just as you did from Marco in Florence, there is no difference. I expect all of you to show him the respect of his station. Nothing less will be tolerated. And if I have my way, your asses will be too tired to give a damn to begin with. Understood?"

The group responded in unison, "*Si!*" Shade liked what he saw so far as the warriors appeared accepting of this announcement, but he wasn't too sure how the next one would go.

"The next promotion in rank is to Raven, he is now Second-In-Command at the Dead House." Shade watched them closely and saw a few doubtful faces, but not as many as he'd expected. "Same rules apply. He will be coordinating all grid assignments, monitoring warrior activity on the streets, and directing your efforts as required. You will obey his orders without question and follow his lead. I expect excellence out there. Medici rules those streets, and just because it is quiet now, does not mean it will remain so. If and when our enemies strike, they know they face Medici, so you must be prepared to defend and fight at all times. Understood?"

Another loud, "*Si,*" echoed off the walls.

"Marcello and Raven have the privilege of feeding and hunting off grounds. So, I want no shit about that. It was my decision and if either of them does Medici any dishonor, that privilege is taken from them.

"Our brother Hyde has taken a position with Master Canton, as his mate's protector."

Shade chuckled as he heard a loud groan from most of the warriors. They all knew Rissa and didn't wish that fate on any of their brothers.

"Calm down, Hyde has this under control and we wish him the best of luck." The warriors ribbed him some and gave up a cheer.

"Hyde will maintain his assignment on the grid of the Canton residence. He will work that grid alongside whomever Raven choses as backup. If Hyde is needed as protector, he will give advance notice and Raven will coordinate his replacement into that grid."

Shade stood to get their full attention. "My next order of business is the camp. Open call will start in one week. I will need everyone on board and all schedules in working order. This will be a test and it will mean some long hours for all of us. I will no longer be going to the Dead House unless needed. Raven will be in full charge of that area. My duties will lie here at the camp. You will have noticed we have separate quarters here for male and female. I have issued an open call to all warriors in the U.S. who may want to attend our camp. I will run this camp with a strict hand. The open call will bring in many, and we will keep only a few. We must keep strict control of their whereabouts and escorting them out of here if dismissed. I will make quick decisions of who stays and who goes within the first several days.

"Because I expect a huge influx of warriors, both male and female, at open call, I will allow them to stay within the walls of this facility. It will be cramped, get used to it. I do not want to hear any bitching from my own warriors. You set the example for proper behavior befitting a Medici warrior, or by all that is fucking holy, you will find yourselves on the streets."

Shade paced back and forth in front of them. "There will be no playing around with any females who enter the premises. The females will bunk separately inside the facility, away from the males. Any of you so much as makes a remark or touches any of them with disrespect and your fucking head belongs to me. We will keep whatever rotation has been set up for you for feeding. Right now, just deal with it. I have plans to change that up shortly, once we get settled in, but right now is not the time. Fiamma, come forward."

She lifted her shoulders, holding her head high as she walked to stand in front of him. Grasping her by the shoulders, he spun her around to face the warriors.

"I have one more promotion in rank. I would like to announce Fiamma is now Lieutenant of the warrior camp. She is the first female warrior in the ranks of Medici to hold a leadership position. If we are going to lead Medici into the future, our females need to be among us full force. Fee will be in charge of leading our females within the camp. She will over-see their training personally and help Marcello with any of their personal needs. So, beware, warriors, Fee will kick your asses you touch her females. Now move out!"

Shade could feel her stand taller as she turned to look at him. "You earned this, Fee. Don't disappoint me. The first female to hold a position of rank among my warriors is nothing to sneeze at. I need you here. I need your help. You are the only one I trust to help guide the females."

She nodded before turning and walking back to her seat, the sway back in her walk, her head held high and a smile that could charm the fucking snakes right off of the ground. Turning to *bel*, Shade reached his hand out to her. Medici was now well on their way to conquering the States.

"As you leave, you will receive a packet of information, grids, assignments, and rotations, also where you are to report starting tonight. This packet has been put together specifically for you, with your name on it. I suggest you get your asses busy reading it the minute you leave here and memorize it. Any questions or concerns can be directed to your respective SICs. I expect this place to rock and roll Medici style within a week, so get your shit organized, and be sure to feed. Be ready to lead, teach, and bring forth the new breed of Medici. You are in on the ground floor of a new beginning, history in the making. We stand united as one. We defend with honor, pride, and respect. All of you were hand chosen to be here. I wish for us to move into the future with hands clasped and swords raised in the name of Medici. Now get moving, pick up your packets and get to your duties."

23

Hyde had been assigned to protect the grid that included the Canton residence most of the evening. The arrangements had been made through master for him to meet Miss Benneteau and Master Canton at 10:30 p.m. Keeping his eye on the time, he teleported back to the Dead House to inform Raven he was now off duty, so he could get to his appointment, and another warrior could take his watch until the meeting was concluded.

He slipped out of his leathers and into something more casual for meeting Canton's mate. He knew he'd need to blend in with the mortals, so he wanted Rissa to see him as a mortal would see him. Teleporting out, he stood at the front door of the Canton's G-town residence and rang the bell.

Santos opened the door, nodding to the warrior. "You are expected, sir. Please follow me to the study. May I get you a Midnight?"

Hyde declined the offer and followed the butler into the study, where Alec was waiting. Alec greeted him and had him take a seat as Santos poured a glass of Midnight and handed it to Alec before leaving the room.

"Make yourself comfortable, Hyde. I'll bring Rissa down in a minute. I thought we should go over a few things first. Clearly, living in Georgetown, we're right in the middle of the mortals, unlike the way Shade lives. We try to keep our schedules very similar to that of a busy mortal couple. As I mentioned, Rissa has her own event-planning business, which she'd established when she was still mortal. She caters to only mortal clients, and I'm obviously surrounded by mortals in my role. We both drive instead of teleporting, except on rare circumstances. I keep minimal staff here. Santos has been with me for centuries, and I have a driver and bodyguard on call, Alto. I'll make sure you meet him. With my role, I do draw the attention of the press, and with our recent engagement announcement, Rissa also has more press scrutiny than usual. It's important we maintain a high profile in the press, but only in a positive way. Anything negative, anything that could possibly reveal what we are must remain off the radar. So, your role as a protector would be very different than if you were protecting someone like Kate.

"Your choice of weapons, how you move about in a crowd, must all blend in with mortal actions and not draw undue attention. Rissa will sometimes work from home, in which case, you'll not be needed. I only want you to shadow her when she's out. I think presenting yourself as her driver is a good cover. Our last protector was female, and although she was well qualified, I'm afraid my mate didn't take well to having another female in the house. You're probably somewhat familiar with our schedules already if you've been monitoring this grid, so you may be aware of my mate's temperament. We'll have a discussion, the three of us, but I honestly can't predict her behavior. She may or may not be compliant with your needs, so all I can say is try to be as flexible as possible, and if she becomes unmanageable, just let me know.

"I have a folder here with the floor plans of the house, just in case. Both our cell numbers, my admins number in case you need to reach me and I'm away from the office. Any questions before I bring Rissa down?"

Hyde carefully observed his surroundings as Alec spoke. He listened and smiled as Alec made comments about his mate. She was well known as the Darling of G-town and all of the warriors were aware of her temperament.

"Everything is clear, Master Canton. I'll work with Miss Benneteau and make sure she's well protected. As I've said before, I've seen her about the district and understand her schedule. There's one question I do have. I know you entertain a great deal here at your home. I've been on duty when we'd put extra protection on your home for such events. I'd like to know if you'd require me to be inside on these occasions."

"Good question, Hyde. That may depend on the event and the guest list. But certainly, for the upcoming wedding, we'll need warriors who are able to mingle among the crowd. Now, let me get Rissa."

Alec walked to the foyer and stood at the bottom of the stairs, calling up to her. "Rissa. Your new protector is here. Please join us in the study."

Hearing him call, Rissa stopped working, stood up from her desk, straightened her skirt and headed down the staircase. As she entered the study, her eyes went immediately to the handsome, well-groomed gentleman who stood as she entered. He wore a grey sports jacket over the black tee and jeans. He looked smart, clean, and stylish. She appreciated his short cropped hair and when they locked eyes, her knees went weak. His eyes were blue, a rare beautiful blue and they were stunning. So, this was a Medici warrior? He didn't look like any of the warriors she'd encountered before, and she liked what she was seeing. She turned to Alec and smiled. "Alec, would you be so kind as to make the introductions?"

Alec didn't fail to notice Rissa's eyes light up as soon as she took in Hyde. He made a mental note to remind her that his own code of conduct, as it related to infidelities, did not apply to her. "Hyde, please meet your latest challenge, Miss Larissa Benneteau, soon to be known in the mortal world as Mrs. Canton."

He turned to Rissa. "And for you, my darling, your new protector, Hyde. Let's see if we can keep him around a little longer than the last one, shall we?"

Rissa laid her hand on Alec's arm and smiled at him. "Of course, I'll do as you ask."

Smiling up at Hyde, she casually shook his hand and felt the sparks fly up her arm. He was strong, and he smelled like heaven. "It's a pleasure to officially meet you, Hyde. Please, call me Rissa. I appreciate you taking time from your duties to accommodate us, this evening. Please, take a seat."

Alec took a seat on the sofa, but Hyde remained standing until she was seated, and she found that quite gentlemanly. *Oh yes, he'll do quite nicely.*

"It's my pleasure, Miss Benneteau."

Alec keenly watched the interplay between them as he turned to Rissa. "So, my darling, Hyde won't be a live-in." He gave her hand a tight squeeze, letting her know he had already picked up on her piqued interest. "What would you like to share with him about your schedule and your needs when you leave the house?"

Rissa never took her eyes from Hyde and felt Alec's displeasure. *Jealous are we, Alec? How wonderful you know what it feels like.* "Well, Hyde, the day hours are busy with clients. In the evenings, I may attend fundraisers, and other events. If I have free time, I'll go to the gym. It'll be a great comfort knowing I have a Medici warrior near to ward off any attacks. Most of the evening events are black tie. I'd very much appreciate if you could blend in appropriately, but I don't think we'll have a problem with that. Alec has just recently agreed to give me a horse, which I'll be boarding at Bel Rosso. I'd ask that you escort me there and back. Do you ride?"

Hyde watched as she crossed her long slim legs and if she could spew pure sugar cane, she would. He could sense the tension between her and Canton and it amused him. They were definitely not like Master Shade and his lady.

"Yes, I do ride. But you'll find, at Bel Rosso, you're at the most protected place you could be. Antonio is the stable master. He's more efficient at handling the horses and dealing with your needs. Unless, of course, Master Canton wishes me to ride with you, then I'd oblige. I'll be at your disposal. It's vital we work together for your safety. I take my job seriously. You have nothing to worry about."

Alec nodded at him. "Oh, I think Antonio can handle the horses, he is the stable master after all. And Rissa is a skilled rider. I doubt she'll need anyone to accompany her on her rides, right darling? You always say your exercise is *me time*, time to be alone and clear your head. And as you said, there's no place safer than riding at Bel Rosso."

Alec lit up a cigarette and leaned back against the sofa as Rissa sat forward in her seat, her body language clearly displaying her interest. He laid his head back against the sofa as he inhaled deeply. He'd deal with this little infraction later.

Rissa could feel Alec's ruffled feathers and she was rather enjoying the moment. She knew she'd pay, but any attention from Alec was good, as far as she was concerned. "Well, of course, yes, Antonio would handle those things. Are you in this area every night, Hyde?" Rissa leaned over, placing her elbow on her knee and her hand under her chin, giving him an excellent view of her cleavage as she smiled softly.

Hyde felt the tension growing, although he didn't feel uncomfortable as it was obvious Canton was letting her lead the conversation. "Master Shade has modified my assignment, so I'll be on this grid every night. There will always be another warrior assigned as my backup in the event I must leave my post to assist you. I can wear an earpiece that is virtually invisible, and have an identical device for you. The speaker is small and can be designed to be incorporated into a bracelet or brooch. It'll pick up your voice, but also has a button you can push if you need to alert me in a crowd. I'd suggest we use them."

Alec looked at Rissa. "Oh, she'll definitely take advantage of that, both the earpiece and the bracelet. Right? And I don't expect any pushback this time around. We'll be toning down the drama, won't we, darling?"

Rissa never took her eyes from Hyde. "I'd love to try it. It sounds quite interesting. No pushback, none at all. There will be no drama. I've learned that communication is vital in my protection." Rissa turned to Alec and smiled. "I do believe Hyde will suit my needs quite well. Quite well, indeed."

Alec locked eyes with her. "Oh I have no doubt, my darling, none whatsoever. I'm more than aware of your needs. Do you have any further questions of your protector before you return to your work?"

"No, I don't believe I do. Hyde should have my schedule and numbers, which I'm sure you've taken care of." Rissa turned to Hyde and flashed him a smile. "Unless, of course, Hyde has anything to ask me?"

Hyde nodded as she flashed her innocent smile. "I don't believe there's anything else I require. I'll be reporting to Master Canton with any problems we may encounter, and we can work those out as they occur."

Standing, she approached Hyde and extended her hand to shake his. He stood immediately, taking her hand as she laid her other hand atop his. "Thank you, Hyde. I'm sure we'll get along quite well. I'm looking forward to having you around." She turned on her heels and swayed elegantly from the room.

Alec turned his attention back to Hyde. "Have a seat, Hyde. Just one more thing before you go."

Hyde didn't miss the extra touch and how close she stood to him. Her signals were very clear to him...and to Master Canton. But he wouldn't be obliging the future Mrs. Canton on any of her wicked ideas. Hyde took his seat, wondering what Canton was about to disclose to him and it piqued his curiosity.

Alec sipped from the glass of Midnight before setting in down in front of him. "I'm not familiar with your history, or how many jobs you may have taken as protector. I know different masters have different relationships with their mates. Different rules. But just so we're on the same page, despite my mate's obvious interest, you're being hired to provide protection services only. Is that clear? Or do I need to elaborate?"

Hyde almost laughed out loud. Master Canton was claiming his mate. Hyde held up his hand. "No disrespect, Master Canton, but I'm a Medici warrior. I've been with Medici since I was ten years old. I've had several protector assignments in my past, all of which, I carried through with honor. Medici warriors have a code of ethics, and if I were to do anything *but* provide protection, my master would deal with me accordingly and I think you can imagine how that would end up. I have no interest in Rissa outside of ensuring her safety. She's a job, and I'll not compromise my position and values as a Medici warrior, or violate your trust in me."

Alec nodded. "Glad we have an understanding. But make no mistake, she will test you, of that, I have no doubt. I'm sure you can handle it, but let me know if it becomes a problem. I do have my ways of keeping her in line. Now, if there's nothing further, I'd say we're done here. You have Rissa's contact information, and I'll make sure you're programmed in her phone. She'll be expecting you tomorrow."

Santos appeared in the doorway, Alec stood, shook hands with Hyde, and Santos escorted him out.

As Alec heard the front door close, he made his way up the stairs to find Rissa in her office, still working. He stepped inside and closed the door behind him, leaning his back against the door. "So, you seem quite pleased with your protector, my darling. You really need to work on your body language, it tells all. I can't recall the last time I saw you this engaged. Can you?"

Rissa never took her eyes from her work as she answered him. "I'm pleased he's male. He won't be bothersome or get up my ass like that bitch did. I feel a connection to him, but not what you're implying. As for my body language," she sat back and crossed her arms over her chest and stared at him, "I was quite engaged with my body language in the chamber at Castello. Remember?"

Alec smirked, "Oh, I remember quite well. But I don't recall you having much choice in that situation. Tread carefully. I'm forgiving in many things, and if you have an interest in a threesome to include another male, let me know. I'm sure I can arrange something for us. But one on one...without me...you know the rules."

Rissa smiled slyly and stood, sauntering slowly to him. She slid her leg up along his thigh and spoke in a low sexy voice close to his ear, "I know the rules. I've always followed them, but would you let me choose this third...the male? You've never given me such choices before and I'd gladly accept them."

Alec looked down at her upturned face. "Have someone in mind, do we? By all means, I'd let you choose. Watching you get fucked could be quite entertaining. However, I can't make any promises on what happens to them afterwards. Not that I could imagine you'd care."

Rissa purred, her excitement making her wet with anticipation. Alec had never offered her a threesome with a male, and she was beside herself. "I have no one in mind as we speak. But I'm sure I could find us something. So, you would just watch, not participate?"

Pouting, she pulled back and kicked off her heels as she glided across the room, her hips swaying an invitation she only wished he would accept.

"Rissa, surely you know me better than that. Of course, I'd participate. I would also direct and orchestrate. Don't plan on asking your new pet protector to join us. He'll not be your appetizer. Understood? But you should make sure you pick an immortal, I'm not sure a mortal male would be able to keep up the pace of what I'll demand from him."

With her back to Alec, she unzipped her skirt from behind and wiggled it down to her ankles, stepping out of it and bending down to pick it up, taking her sweet time so he could take in the view of her stockings, garters, and panties. Standing up, she flipped her long blonde hair back and laughed.

"Seriously, Alec, you cannot believe, for one moment, I'd choose Hyde over you. Have I ever given you cause to doubt me? You satisfy my every need. And I'd love to have you orchestrate my orgasms. He must be well endowed to pleasure us both."

Spinning to face him, she unbuttoned her blouse and flung it to the vanity chair. "For some reason, Hyde ruffled your feathers, and I rather liked that display of jealousy. It makes me proud to be yours, because I am, and always will be. No one has ever touched this body without your permission. No one ever will."

Alec watched her little game of strip-tease. "Jealous? I'm not sure I'd call it jealousy. But I know you well, my darling. I'm going to clone your phone, so I'll know when you make a call, and to whom. I've already spoken with Hyde, and I'm sure with that fucking Medici code, he won't be a problem. But I guess I do owe you something. After all, you did get me an engagement gift. I guess it's only fair I return the favor. Choose wisely, my darling... and make it soon before I change my mind."

He knew he had her worked into a state, undressing in front of him, teasing, and making her intentions clear. And he would leave her to find her own pleasures and think about his offer. He slipped out the door, closing it behind him.

Rissa threw her skirt at the closed door. "Clone my phone? Don't think that will stop me, master. Damn it!"

Heading to the bathroom, she drew a long hot bath and grabbed a bottle of Midnight. Tonight, she'd plan a fun evening for three, minus the hot luscious warrior that just left her house. She had no doubts she'd find someone even hotter and just as muscled for their threesome. In the meantime, she closed her eyes and thought about Hyde and all the nasty fucking he could provide her.

Alec chuckled to himself as he walked down the stairs, and heard her rant, tapping into the nasty little fantasies in her head.

24

Rissa came home from a long day of appointments. She had so many things to accomplish for the wedding and it was only adding to her already busy schedule. Her first day without the Amazon bitch was a great one and she couldn't help but be overjoyed. Alec was still busy at the office, and she was rather grateful. She drew a luxurious bath filled with scented oils and poured herself a glass of Midnight as the tub filled and the steam rose. She slid down into the hot water with a sigh, laying her head against the back of the tub, and sipped at the wine as it took the edge off her hunger. She needed to find a male for this threesome, and he'd need to be a strong, healthy, well-hung immortal. It would be the only way to stave off her hunger, and the only way Alec would let her feed, unless she begged, and she was in no mood to beg.

Alec had been very accommodating since their return from Florence and she wondered about the changes in him. He was still his self-absorbed, emotionally distant, workaholic self, but his demeanor toward her seemed a bit softer. He had gotten rid of Jacks, agreed to a male protector, and not insisted on a live-in, and now he was rewarding her with a threesome with another male. And on top of that, he was giving her the gift of her own horse.

Rissa sat straight up in the tub. "The horse!"

She yelled for Santos and instructed him to set up her laptop on a table beside the tub and bring her a fresh Midnight. She paid little mind to him, only barking out orders, after all, it was his job and he got paid well to cater to her every whim.

She opened her email and found what she was looking for. The warrior had sent photos of a selection of his finest horses from Italy. As she browsed, she noticed he'd written a description with each photo about the horse's lineage, size, age, as well as his assessment of each horse's disposition and temperament. Once she'd scanned them all, she went back and clicked on each photo to study them more closely and read his wisdom on each horse.

Rissa was excited. She hadn't had a horse of her own for a very long time. She scrolled through the ten selections Shade sent her. Her heart stopped as she opened the picture of the Golden Palomino. Shade had suggested this was a great choice for her in his commentary. The horse had a strong pedigree, was broken in, extremely friendly and easily ready to ride.

Her heart raced as she scrutinized the photo of the Palomino. Rissa could see herself riding this beautiful animal. She could be a good show jumper, but also, just a really good horse for pleasure riding. On the end of his note, Shade had attached a link to a video of this horse. Letting her fingers fly, Rissa clicked on the link and opened the video. Her heart melted as soon as she saw this magnificent creature. This was the horse she wanted! Her choice was made. She replayed the video again and heard a voice calling to the horse, and realized the volume was low on her laptop. She turned up the volume and heard a deep male voice calling to the horse... 'Biondo.'

"Biondo? What the hell does that mean?"

She quickly clicked on Google Translate and threw back her head laughing. "Oh yes, warrior, this is definitely the horse for me. Blonde, how perfect."

Rissa sent an email to Shade, telling him her choice was made and to move as quickly as possible in getting her shipped here. She didn't care how much it cost, Alec would foot the bill. She then forwarded the video and pictures of Biondo to Alec's email, so he could see her choice. She was about to have some much needed freedom riding. And the sooner the better!

25

Rissa was working from home after another busy day. Hyde was working out wonderfully, although he seemed resistant to her charms. She took a break from her work and stood up to stretch. It was almost nine and it was dark outside. She had a plan, and now she needed to put it into action. Pulling out her cell phone, she scrolled through and found Hyde's number. The briefest thought ran through her head, that Alec was cloning her phone now.

Hitting dial, the phone didn't even ring once and his sexy voice answered. Walking to the window, she knew he was out there somewhere, protecting this grid, and the thought pleased her.

"Hyde, this is Rissa. Could you meet me here, please, I need to be escorted to Annapolis? I have an appointment."

Hyde had just checked in to the Dead House when he got her call. As he listened to her request, he knew he had to go and told her he'd be there within minutes. He yelled out to Raven that he was on his way out to assist Canton's mate. The cat-calls and whistling began from the other warriors. None of them envied him, that was for sure.

He teleported directly to the Canton house and found her sitting in her sports car. Before he got close to the car, he watched her long legs swing out of the driver's seat as she stood to wait for him.

"Rissa. Good evening. I'm happy to assist you, but in the future, I must insist you wait for me inside. Now, where do you need me to escort you, this evening?"

Rissa stood with her soft leather trench coat wrapped around her slender frame. She fluttered her hand at his suggestion. "Yeah, whatever. I have an appointment in Annapolis. I thought, perhaps, you could drive us, and then escort me inside and wait for me? It won't take long."

Hyde didn't miss how she purred out her words. *What the hell is she going to Annapolis for at this time of night?* It wasn't his job to wonder, just do. "Of course, that's my job and I'm glad to help."

She held out her hand, placing her hand in his as he walked her to the passenger side of the car. He opened the door and helped her into her seat. He noticed how she intentionally hiked up her skirt as she swung her long legs inside, a bit of red garter belt peeking out. She could try, and Canton said she would, but her efforts would go unattended. Getting in the driver's side he fired up the Bugatti, glanced at her and smiled. "Where exactly are we going? The pilot needs some coordinates."

Rissa had him right where she wanted him. A good hour's drive alone in the car with him and she'd go home happy. She laid her hand on the taut muscles of his thigh and squeezed gently, feeling the hardness beneath her hand. "Oh, I'm quite sure you know the location. There's an underground club, for immortals and the gothic crowd. It's called Incendiary. I have some business there."

Hyde felt her hand on his thigh. "You do realize the nature of this club? It's an underground sex club for immortals. It can be dangerous. It's one of a very few of its kind on the East Coast. It's none of my business, but does Master Canton know you're going there?"

"Hyde, dear Hyde. Relax! Of course, he knows I'm going there, I have an appointment. And I've been there before, with Alec, naturally. I know the immortal I'm meeting. Now, let's be on our way, shall we?"

Walking her fingers up his thigh and toward his crotch, she was hoping to have a little fun on the drive. His scent captivated her, and she found everything about him attractive to her attention starved senses.

Hyde couldn't imagine she had any damn business in this club. He felt her fingers walking up his thigh, straight for the prize and his anger rose. *The bitch sure isn't subtle!* Grabbing her wrist with his leather-gloved hand, he placed it back in her lap. He heard her soft gasp, as this wasn't the response she was looking for. He'd teach her quickly, he was no toy, but a warrior and her protector. He got in her face and he could feel her tinge of fear mixed with excitement. "Let's get one thing straight. No touching. If you have a desire to play with something, I suggest you play with yourself, I have no need for it."

Sitting back in his seat, he could feel her trying to regulate her breathing. "Now, my suggestion is we don't drive but teleport there. The club is in a secluded area. If I need to get you out of there in a hurry, teleporting will be my option. It'll save time and will be our safest alternative."

Rissa had to bite back her anger. "So, are you counteracting my orders? Because it can't possibly be that confining to sit in this car and drive. I'm sure if I complained to Alec that you refused a direct request from me, you'd pay dearly for it."

Hyde laughed out loud. "Rissa, trust me when I tell you, your master will not care that I refused to drive you. Especially, if I tell him you wanted to fondle my cock while we made our way there. I think you'll find he'll side with me. But if you don't think so, call him, and plead your case. Now get your ass out of the car and head toward the side of the building, we're teleporting!"

Rissa's eyes widened. "How dare you talk to me like that! You're not my–" Suddenly, the passenger door flew open, and he yanked her from the car.

Hyde had had enough. He would show her who was boss, and she'd listen. She might be Canton's mate, but he needed to set down some ground rules, and manhandling her was going to be the only thing this one understood. She would try to talk her way out of everything, if he let her.

Pulling her from the car, he saw her hand go up to slap him and he gripped it hard. "Stop! Right now! You're acting like a spoiled child. Do things my way and life will be much easier, I promise you, Rissa. Just do as I instruct, and behave. Now, we're going to walk into the shadow of the building and teleport to Annapolis. Are you frightened?"

Rissa was shocked. No one but Alec had ever handled her like this. "No, I'm not frightened, but I don't teleport much. Will you at least hold my hand as we go?"

Hyde backed up from her and took her hand. "Of course, I don't want to spend half the night searching for you. Now come along, we've been arguing so long we could have damn near been there by now."

Walking to the side of the building, Hyde made sure there were no curious onlookers around and led her by the hand to the shadows. "You're safe with me. I'll protect you. Relax." They took off and teleported around Incendiary until he found a safe spot for them to land.

As they landed, Hyde decided it was time to make the rules clear. He didn't want any incidents while protecting Canton's mate. He could only imagine the chaos that would cause with Shade. He sure as hell knew, if anything happened here, there'd be hell to pay. Rissa probably shouldn't be here in the first place. He was already wondering what he'd gotten himself into.

Grabbing her arm lightly, he turned her to face him. "Let me make some things clear. You'll not be alone at any time. I'll be with you at all times. I'll hear and see everything you do, not that I care, but if there's danger, in any form, this is over. Do you understand?"

"Of course, I'm no fool. I've been here before with Alec. And I'm meeting someone inside that knows me. Don't worry, I'll introduce you as my body guard, no one will think anything of it, trust me."

Hyde growled. "You'll introduce me as what I am, your protector. You reek of Alec. They know you are mated to a master, so I wouldn't get any ideas. Now behave and let's get inside and get this over with."

Letting his hand slide to her back, he guided her to the double doors at the front of the nightclub. He could feel her smug attitude and knew how pissed off she was. Clearly, she didn't like being put in her place, but she'd soon learn, this was how he rolled, and it was what Canton expected.

Rissa wondered if he had any idea how damn sexy he was when he got riled up. As he commanded her, she laughed derisively. Before she could even respond, he was pushing her in the direction of the doors and she straightened her posture. A chill went through her from his touch. As they entered the club, they were immediately met by two brutes that were distinctly heavyweights. One of them bellowed out to them to state their business. Rissa stepped forward. "I'm Larissa Canton. Inform Colin I'm here. Now!"

Her voice was stern, and she watched as her name immediately got their attention. They sent a runner hustling to get Colin for her.

Hyde stayed on top of her. He hated the sex club scene, and this one seemed on the shadier side. He'd seen the inside of enough of them to know what went on, and he couldn't fathom what the hell she wanted here.

Rissa saw Elana gliding across the floor, her smile wide. They embraced and kissed each other on the cheek. "Elana! You look simply delightful. I'm so glad you obliged me tonight. It's been a while since I've seen you both."

Turning to Hyde, she casually gestured in his direction with a wave of her hand. "This is my protector, Hyde. He'll be joining us. Please, lead the way."

As Elana looped her arm through Rissa's, they strutted through the crowded club and Rissa paid no mind to the activities taking place around her. She could care less. She had one thing on her mind and one thing only. Hyde followed closely behind her, and Rissa rather liked having a puppet on a leash.

Hyde kept his eyes peeled in the darkened atmosphere. This was a protector's nightmare. His senses were on high alert. They were led to a small private room, decorated for sin and sexual pleasure, and he prayed she wasn't about to make him sit through some fucking and feeding session.

They entered the room to find Colin seated on a leather couch, practically naked. He stood and immediately came to her, kissing her hand. Colin had just finished his feeding session with a cute little blonde immortal. Colin eyed Rissa up and down. She was a delicious tidbit he'd love to fuck senseless for one night. Canton liked to play, but he'd kept this little gem to himself, so her request to see him this evening had Colin's interest piqued.

"Rissa, my beauty, I'm so glad to have your company this evening. I see Alec has put a tail on you. Care to introduce him?"

As Rissa introduced Hyde, Colin chuckled. Canton was never going to let this piece of ass off the hook. "I would assume you're one of Shade's warriors. Who else would Alec hire for his beauty?"

Hyde wanted to wipe the smug look off Colin's face, but he knew better. Hyde was aware of the sexual exploits that took place in the underground clubs, and the clubs were frequently used by many masters and their mates, but he had a bad feeling with this whole scene. And like everyone else, he'd heard some very disturbing rumors about the Canton's.

"Good to meet you, Colin." Hyde shook his hand. "I'm indeed a Medici. I'll be with Rissa the entire evening." Hyde stepped closer to Rissa and hovered over her. He would make it perfectly clear nothing was going to go down while he was here.

Rissa stood silently while the men did their chatting. She rather liked the idea that Hyde was protecting her. She liked the feeling of having a young strapping warrior at her beck and call. "Are we done with the formalities, Colin? Because seriously, I'm anxious to get on with business. I must get back to Alec, as well you know." She winked at Colin and he grinned wickedly.

"Please, Rissa, come sit yourself down and have a Midnight."

As Rissa moved to sit on the couch next to Colin, Hyde directed her to sit on the far end, putting some space between her and Colin, as he stood guard over her. Colin handed her the Midnight.

"Now, I've lined up several males for you to inspect. They're all immortal, and of course, they're discreet. They're all freelance and belong to no one. No master to call their own. I've selected them according to the descriptions you provided to Elana. Whichever one you choose, I'll personally make sure they arrive on the date and time you provide me. Just relax and I'll bring them all in. Take your time, and ask them to do whatever you wish, darling. They're here just for you."

Colin signaled to Elana to get the males and bring them inside the room. Rissa watched as four well-built young immortal males strolled in. She eyed each one carefully, envisioning her and Alec with them.

There was one that caught her eye. His hair was shoulder length and a beautiful chestnut brown, his eyes dark and his body was strong and muscular but not bulky. He appeared clean and well groomed. He wore nothing but a long V-neck knit sweater in a dark shade of blue that fell to mid-thigh, but was otherwise nude, all the way down to his bare feet. His posture was all alpha male and provocative and she wondered what was under that sweater.

Handing her glass to Hyde, she strolled over to all the males, walking around each one, inspecting them. They all stood still as she touched them, either on the shoulder or along their arm. When she came to the one she preferred, she walked around him several times, admiring his body. His head turned slightly as she walked around him, and he postured and flexed a bit to give her a nice view of his muscular legs.

Standing in front of him, she slid her hand down his cheek, and looked deep into his eyes. Oh yes, she could fuck this one good and would enjoy him abusing her body. "Name?"

As he smiled into her eyes, he answered simply, "Dalton."

"Mmm, Dalton. I like how that rolls off my tongue." Rissa leaned in to smell his neck, and his scent was intoxicating and all male. "Drop the sweater."

Dalton pulled the sweater over his head and tossed it to the floor, as Rissa stepped back to admire the body he revealed. His cock was thick and long, his balls shaved and smooth. His abdomen tight and hard, the perfect six-pack, and his chest chiseled and rock hard. He was perfect for what she was looking for. "Turn."

She watched him turn and his back was broad and well-muscled, his hips slender, and his ass was perfectly defined and tight. She licked her lips as her mind was made up. He was the one. Rissa turned with a smile on her face to Colin. "Do you think Alec will like him?"

Colin laughed. "Alec will find him quite perfect for both your needs. So, you've chosen Dalton then?"

Rissa turned back to Dalton and smiled. "Yes, it will be Dalton. Please inform him of my instructions. He'll be paid handsomely. Make all the arrangements with me, Colin. No need to bother Alec. Thank you, Dalton, that will be all for this evening."

Walking back to the couch, she took the glass of Midnight from Hyde, her hand remaining in contact with his a little longer than necessary. She turned to watch all the males walk out of the room. *Well worth the trip, Alec will be pleased with my choice.*

Colin nodded as he received her instructions. "Will you stay a while? Elana and I can be most accommodating. Hyde is more than welcome to join us as well."

Hyde growled and pulled Rissa to his side. Leaning down, he whispered in her ear. "We'll leave now, Rissa. Say your goodbyes. I don't participate in such activities. And Alec has given me strict instructions, so I suggest you listen well."

Rissa looked annoyed, but she knew the rules, and Alec would kill them both if she indulged in any of the delights here. "Colin, thank you, but I do need to get back. Thank you for helping me with my little surprise for Alec. I'll have a small gathering with the four us soon, I promise."

She kissed both Colin and Elana on the cheek, and hugged Elana close. "I'll be in touch."

She barely had the words out of her mouth when Hyde grabbed her hand and they teleported out and straight back to Georgetown.

Hyde wanted no trouble. He just wanted her ass back at their residence before something happened. He didn't trust her one bit.

As they landed, Rissa struggled to pull her hand from his. "Don't ever do that again! That's so rude. I barely said my goodbyes and you were dragging me out of there. They're friends. Go about your warrior business, I'm fine!"

Hyde stood with his arms crossed. "Are you done now? It's none of my business what you do, but I have a job to do and instructions to follow. And if you think, for one second, you're going out again, think again. Now get in the damn house!"

Rissa started to say something, and he held up his hand, pointing to the house. Rissa snapped back, "Fine!" *Damn warriors. Bossy bastard! How dare he?*

Hyde chuckled at her little tantrum, but at least she was listening. "Rissa, I'm going to walk you to the door and make sure you are safely inside. I suggest you cool off before you go in. I don't want Alec to think this isn't working. I'm not judging you, or your friends. I do care about you, and my job is making sure you come home to your master."

Rissa stood with her hands on her hips, staring at the front door of the house. As he spoke in a calm voice, she heard him say he cared about her, and instantly, her anger disappeared. She liked Hyde and she wanted him around. She liked how he made her feel and she knew he was right. Alec wanted no drama. He wanted her to improve, make this work, and she'd show him she could. "I'm not angry, thank you for escorting me tonight. I'm ready to go in."

He took her hand and led her to the front door.

26

Alec was working late in his study and kept an eye on the clock. He knew Rissa was safe and he felt no danger, but she was much later getting home than usual. This was her first week with Hyde. He was about to call out to her telepathically to see where the fuck she was, when he heard them at the door. He walked to the foyer and eyed them both. "A discussion please, with both of you, in my study."

Rissa could tell he wasn't happy. She turned and smiled at Hyde. "Don't worry, it's late, but he has no reason to be upset and if he is, it will be with me, not you." Rissa strutted to the study with Hyde following close behind.

Alec poured two glasses of Midnight and looked up at Hyde. "You still on duty? Or would you like a drink?"

Hyde shook his head. "No, thank you. I'll return to the Dead House to finish my shift when I leave here."

Hyde remained with his hands behind his back, waiting for anything Canton might throw at him. He was prepared to make his case if Rissa decided to argue about his method of managing her.

Alec returned to the sofa, offering a glass to Rissa as she sat beside him.

Rissa sipped at the Midnight. She really wanted to down it, but she tried to appear composed in front of Hyde, not wanting him to know how Alec controlled her by withholding feeding.

Alec noticed the look Rissa flashed in Hyde's direction. He took the glass of Midnight from her hands and set it on the table in front of them, just to make a point. "Now, perhaps, you'd like to explain why you're so late? You aren't in your gym clothes tonight. What kept you so occupied?"

Rissa stood and walked a few steps from Alec before turning to him. "Alec, please, do we need to have this conversation while Hyde's still present? I'm quite sure he has other duties to attend to. He made mention of it."

Alec chuckled. "Really, my darling? Clearly, whatever you were up to is no secret to Hyde since he escorted you there. Is there something you're hiding from me? Because I'm sure all that Medici code of honor crap will compel Hyde to tell me where he took you and what you were up to."

Rissa glared at him. "Hyde knows exactly what I did, what I said, and where I went. Oh yes, he's quite efficient. Here I am in one piece, safe and sound. And that code of honor crap you so blatantly refer to, I find rather refreshing, to be honest. So, let's see..."

Walking around the room, she purred her sweetness. "We teleported to Annapolis to visit the Incendiary. I wanted Hyde to drive us, he refused, insisting we teleport since, according to him, it's much safer. I had an appointment with Colin and Elana. We had a private room in the back of the club. Colin set up some males for me to choose from for our three-way. I chose one I thought we'd both enjoy. Colin asked if I'd stay, and, of course, Hyde took the reins and teleported us back home, escorting me inside. So, you see, Alec, I followed orders, all was perfectly fine."

Alec leaned back on the sofa, downed his glass of Midnight as he watched her little performance. "And did you find what you were looking for, my darling? Was there someone who got your attention?"

Cocking her head to the side, the smile slid ever so wickedly across her face, as she telepathically sent Alec the image of the young immortal male she had chosen. "Oh, very much so."

Alec smirked as the vision of the strong young male appeared in his head and he locked eyes with her. "Well, you definitely have a type, my darling. I just hope he knows what he's getting himself into. Check my schedule with Jenny, set up a night. And Hyde? Did that little fantasy of yours include Hyde?"

Rissa turned to face Alec and her eyes began to turn red. *How dare he say such things about her in front of the warrior.* She growled low and felt her body stiffen as she tapped down her rage. "Hyde? Oh no, my wicked vampire, Hyde has no place in my fantasies. But let me make one thing clear to you." She walked to the sofa, leaning down and looking Alec straight in the eyes. "Hyde is not the one you need to worry about. When other masters invite me in to play without you, I think it best you warn them whom I belong to, because I wasn't appreciative of their offer."

Alec's beast pushed for release as his fangs punched through. He hissed back at her as she got in his face. "You were at the Incendiary...it's a sex club. We're both well aware of Colin and Elana's exploits. The fact you were there without me might send him a message of your availability. I have no quarrel with his invitation, my darling, as long as you didn't accept. And I'm somehow highly doubtful you took offense."

Hyde could feel the tension building. The room was about to explode. He took a stance, ready for anything. He'd never seen a master belittle his mate in front of him before. Shade would never disgrace his queen in the presence of others. But then, his queen would never challenge him so openly either. These two fed off each other like a fucking game. Hyde couldn't defend Rissa if Canton went after her, it was their culture. A master ruled his mate and no vampire would dare interfere. Hyde would have to remain until dismissed, regardless of the outcome, and Canton appeared ready to take her down a notch or two, either with words or actions.

Rissa stood and grabbed her glass of Midnight from the table and began to walk to the bar and spun around to face him. "You know, Alec, Hyde was with me the whole time. His role was made clear to Colin when he was introduced. Colin knows better. And, of course, I didn't accept. Hyde teleported me out of there immediately."

Rissa waved her hand in the air, as she turned to fill her glass at the bar. "Colin could never satisfy me in a million years. He may be the master of Sin City, but he knows little of the sin I enjoy."

Alec smirked, amused by her anger. "What exactly would you have me do, darling? Call him out in a duel? Defend your honor? Are your delicate sensibilities that bruised? Colin extended an invitation, and you refused. Not unlike the invitation you extended to Hyde...and he refused. Oh yes, don't think I didn't pick up on your heightened level of sexual desire. I may be busy, but I still tune into you from time to time. Just make sure he doesn't creep into your fantasies when it's my cock you ride."

Hyde had to look down to hide his amusement. He'd wondered if Alec had picked up on her little explorations with him when they were in the car. All he needed was Canton wanting to take his ass out because of her fucked up sexual fantasies. When he looked back up again, he saw Rissa's expression and she was floored, and for once, speechless.

Rissa was embarrassed and stunned that Alec would go so far in front of Hyde. Her anger boiled to the surface, slow and hot. She walked to the table, slammed down her drink, and watched the red liquid splash over the rim and onto the surface of the table. Her body was shaking with fury as she looked Alec straight in the eye. "Are you done with your whore now, master? After all, I'm sure Hyde is quite entertained by your degradation of me and your impression of my behavior. I'm quite sure you wish to speak with him alone. May I leave now?"

Alec's beast was barely contained. He rose slowly from the sofa and put his hand around her neck, squeezing lightly. "I hear the words, my darling, but it would appear you have forgotten exactly who's master here. Hyde, please have Santos show you out. And I apologize for this display. It would appear my mate needs to be reminded of her role. I promise to have her more in line when you return tomorrow."

Bristling, Hyde didn't like the display he was witnessing. He contained his anger, and kept his emotions in check. As Canton dismissed him, he was glad to be gone. "As you wish, Master Canton, I'll return in the morning. Good evening."

Rissa saw the beast rise quickly, and he had his hand at her throat before she could blink. Her heart raced and her blood continued to boil. She was excited and frightened as his hand began to squeeze more tightly. She reached up to clutch at Alec's hand and tried to speak. He only squeezed harder, lifting her easily off her feet as she felt her airway close and blackness encroach. She struggled, to no avail, he wouldn't let her go. She made a grave mistake speaking to him in such a manner and she was about to pay hell for it.

Alec tossed her backwards into a chair, where she landed like a rag doll. "Why do you insist on provoking me, Rissa? You asked to be released from Jacks and I did that, and the first thing you do is go to a sex club. You flirt shamelessly with Hyde, and then have the nerve to call out Colin for propositioning you like you are some sweet innocent...when we both know better, don't we? What is it you want? Would you like me to kill Colin, like I did poor Senator Winston? Does that feed your ego? I give you permission to find us a male for a threesome, and I should have anticipated that only you could find a way to make even that into some kind of drama. I'm too angry to deal with you right now, so yes, it would appear I'm finished with my whore for the evening. Get upstairs before I hurt you beyond your body's ability to heal."

Rissa gasped for breath as she clutched her chest, her anger gone now with his disappointment in her. Her blood turned cold from his rejection of everything she'd done wrong. Standing on wobbly legs, she swallowed hard, biting her lip and ran head long for the stairs, going up them so fast she almost tripped at the top. She raced to her room, closing and locking the door behind her, falling to the floor, and wondering why she provoked him so. But she already knew the answer. She craved his attention, even when that attention was anger. She stood and faced the door, dropping her head against it as her blood tears fell.

She could fix this. She could make the changes he demanded and prove to him she was the perfect drama-free mate he wished for. But Rissa knew even as she swore to change, she'd never leave him. She was like a moth to a flame when it came to Alec. He was her addiction, her sick addiction.

Alec tossed the glass of Midnight against the stone fireplace, the glass shattering, and the wine dripping. How could she push him so far over the edge so fast? He'd had no intentions of arguing with her tonight. He'd only wanted to make clear to her that Hyde would be with her anytime she went out. He knew she was attracted to Hyde. He could tell that when she first laid eyes on him, but he knew it was harmless. How did she manage to turn every conversation into something confrontational?

Santos came in and started to sweep up the glass and clean away the wine stain. "Can I get you anything, master?"

Alec sighed as he dropped back down on the sofa, "Another Midnight. And a large order of patience, please, Santos."

27

Kate woke suddenly from her sleep. The room was still pitch dark, the light of day completely blocked by the electronic blinds. She sat up next to Shade who still slept soundly in his death slumber. Had she heard something?

She sat very still, honing her senses as he'd taught her to do. She could feel Theresa and Gi working about the house as normal. She felt Luca, calm and relaxed. She had a mental picture of him painting at his canvas. She sat still a minute more and heard nothing unusual and lay back down next to Shade, cuddling into the warmth of him.

Just as she closed her eyes, she heard Aegis howl. It was faint, but she didn't sound distressed. Kate sat up in the bed again. Was Aegis trying to tell her something? Kate looked at the clock and saw it was late afternoon, but still a few hours from sunset. She felt wide awake now and knew she wouldn't fall back to sleep. She turned on the light by the bed and slid her legs from beneath the covers, looking back to see Shade sleeping quietly.

She pulled on a sundress and stepped into a pair of sandals, and tiptoed from the room, closing the door quietly behind her. As Kate was walking down the stairs, she encountered Theresa on her way up, carrying a basket of clean laundry.

"My lady? Are you all right?"

"I am, Theresa. I woke early. I think I heard Aegis howl."

"Yes, my lady, she appears restless today. We've all seen her close to the house, occasionally with her mate as well."

Kate scrunched up her forehead. "Interesting, I wonder what she's up to."

Kate continued down the stairs and out of habit, wandered into the kitchen where she found Gi and Reynaldo talking. She climbed onto a stool at the kitchen counter and looked at Reynaldo. "I don't suppose you guys came up with a vampire version of coffee."

Reynaldo laughed. "No, my lady, only the Midnight."

Gi looked at her with concern. "Why are you awake, my lady? There are several hours until sunset."

Kate shrugged. "I heard Aegis. She woke me and then I couldn't fall back asleep. Shade says he thinks I wake up early sometimes because I'm new, and I need to feed more frequently. Whatever the reason, I may as well take advantage of it."

Kate left the kitchen and was about to walk to Luca's suite when she heard the scratching sound of paws against the back door, and Aegis' faint whimper. Was she hurt? Maybe Aegis was hurt and needed her. Kate changed direction and walked toward the back of the house. Without thinking, she reached out and grabbed the door knob, twisting the handle, pulling the door open as the sunlight filled the room. Aegis pranced on the other side of the door, excited to see her.

Kate stepped outside into the bright summer sun and the wolf jumped up against her, almost knocking her off her feet. Kate laughed and rubbed the wolf's head. "What is it, girl? What has you so worked up today?"

Shade felt her leaving the comfort of his arms, then heard her exit the room, but he didn't wake. He slid back into his deep death slumber, knowing Luca would be with her if she needed anything.

Luca felt her as she opened the door, his hand stopped mid-stroke against the canvas. He dropped the brush as he teleported to her. "Kate, no!"

Suddenly, Shade felt danger as Luca's stress slammed into him. He heard Luca scream a warning and Shade sat bolt upright, naked, and teleported to where she stood outside, instantly exposing his bare skin to the sun's intense heat. Falling to the ground, he could feel the pain building.

Luca had just gotten to Kate when Shade appeared.

"*Bel*, inside! Go inside!"

Shade couldn't see her clearly as the sunlight was blinding to his eyes. He stretched his hand out to her, crawling and feeling for her and felt a hand on his shoulder as he screamed in agony. The sun was beating down on his skin as it sizzled and burned, turning to a dark charcoal color. He couldn't survive in the direct sunlight for long, but his only thought was to get Kate inside. She was a newborn with no tolerance, and her lily-white skin would fry instantly.

Luca watched as Shade's skin reacted to the rays of the sun. Luca looked in confusion as Kate turned to them both, her skin untouched. Kate and Luca both made a grab for him, dragging him back inside the house. Luca kicked the door closed behind them, sealing out all light. Kate was in a panic, looking at the scorched burnt skin that covered most of Shade's body.

"Lover! Tell me what to do. Feed from me now."

Gi and Theresa came running with towels that had been soaked in cold water and started laying them on his body as he lay stretched out nude on the floor. Reynaldo was filling a large tub of cold water and carrying it to his side so they could wring out the towels and dunk them again into the cold water. Luca found a pair of sunglasses and placed them over his eyes, as Shade writhed in pain.

Kate could feel the pain he felt, and kept looking at her own pale white skin, unmarked in anyway. They could hear the warriors respond, as they all moved closer to the house, encircling it, standing guard, sensing their master's vulnerability.

Kate bent over him. "Lover, feed. I know you're in pain, but you must feed. It'll help you heal." She pulled her hair back from her neck as she bent over him, placing her throat at his now blistered lips.

Shade could smell the burning of his flesh. He felt her near as his fangs punched through, and the skin on his lips cracked as he blindly sought out her neck, sinking his fangs into her soft flesh. Her life blood flowed down his parched aching throat, her blood restoring him. His body convulsed and lurched as he took more, letting her blood seep deep into him, feeling its healing power in every vein, and he kept drinking.

"Feed, Shade. Heal for me. I'll not leave you."

Outside the door, Kate could hear Aegis, scratching, and pacing, agitated now and responding to Kate's own fear and panic. She felt them all gathering, Night Stalker and Riparo, and the falcon, Danica. And others. She felt the nameless others surrounding the house to protect her because he was weak. Shade continued to drink from her, drawing in her blood, healing him from the inside out.

Luca knelt beside him. "Master, Kate is fine. She's unharmed."

Theresa and Gi continued to switch out the towels, removing them as soon as they warmed up and replacing them with cold, wet towels. Kate remained leaning over him, her face close to his as she spoke to him. "Lover, I'm here, I'm fine!"

Shade broke away from feeding, as he tried to make sense of it. She was a day-walker? Not possible, she had the gift of animalism. He began to feel the healing, the cells replenishing and renewing as he shed the blackened ash of his burnt skin. He sat up slowly, blinking his eyes as he felt them adjust and focus. Reaching up, he removed the sunglasses and clutched her to his chest.

She clung to him. "What were you thinking? Why did you chase me into the sun?"

Shade looked at her with astonishment. "Why did you go out in the sun, Kate? Why the fuck would you do that?" His eyes scanned her body. "Are you hurt? Let me look at you."

Luca remained at his side. "Master, I don't understand it, but she's a day-walker, like us. She bears no sign of the sun on her skin."

Kate looked again at her own skin, and then looked at Luca. "I felt no pain. It felt good, in fact. It felt good to feel the sun on my face."

Luca nodded at her. "I could see that as soon as I got to the door, but master flew past me. He felt my panic for you. Kate, no vampire has two gifts. None. There'd be no reason for us to even look for this as your gift since the animalism already presented. Maybe when master is healed, he can shed some light on this, but right now, I'm going to get him up to bed."

Luca gently lifted Shade's body from the floor, still covered in the wet towels, and carried him up the stairs and into their bedroom, laying him on the bed as Kate followed at his side. Luca directed her. "Stay with him. There are still a few hours until sundown. He can fall back into his death slumber, and when he awakes, let him feed again, immediately. Lie next to him."

Theresa followed them into the room as Kate kicked off her sandals and climbed into bed beside him. Theresa carried a jar of salve. She opened it and together, Kate and Theresa spread the soothing balm on his skin.

As the balm worked its magic, Shade could feel himself being pulled back into sleep, his body knowing he needed to heal and rest. *Day-walker, day-walker, day-walker*, the words repeated over and over in his head, as he slipped into the deep comforting blackness.

She watched as the slumber took him, pulled him down into that deep sleep. Day-walker. It all made sense to her now. She'd never felt that pull into the death slumber. She'd watched him now for a year as she slept beside him, and watched how it grabbed him, pulled him under. After the turning, she'd waited for that feeling but it never came. She often woke before him, or lay awake beside him, and they both thought it was because she was new. She remembered her turning, that moment when she was falling back into the chamber, when she fell through the bright light, and the moment in the beginning of her turning when she felt the wolf crawl inside her. She had thought afterward, the wolf was her beast, but were they her gifts? Animalism and day-walker? Luca said no one had two gifts.

She lay down beside him but didn't drape her arm and leg over him, letting the salve, and his rest work their magic. She'd lie next to him until he woke, so he could feed. Her senses told her his warriors still encircled the house, and her brigade of animals stood guard, and she knew none of them would move until he was healed.

28

Shade could feel his body surfacing toward consciousness. He moved slowly and felt no pain. His body still felt stiff and he could smell the stench of the salve. Between the death slumber, the salve, and *bel's* blood, he was feeling better. He lay on his stomach and stayed there, not moving until he was totally awake. He listened to the electronic whir of the blinds rolling up and could hear *bel's* soft breathing beside him.

He knew she wasn't asleep as he lay still beside her. He moved his hand across the bed and felt her crimson silk and his beast rose quickly, wanting more, an ache that was the final step in his healing. More of her blood, and he would be 100%, but he pushed the desire down hard. He didn't want to frighten her. "I love you, *bel rosso*."

Kate reached out, pushing those dark curls back from his face, those ice blue eyes peering out at her. His skin was flawless and bore no scars from the burns.

"Shade, you scared me so. You must feed again. Luca said for you to feed as soon as you came out of your death slumber." She cuddled next to him, pulling her hair back, exposing her neck.

He snuggled into her neck and moaned. "I need you, I need you so much." Sinking his fangs into her neck, he drew her life blood into his system. Its affect was immediate, the taste uniquely hers, and he felt his strength return slowly, his body coming alive, recharged and renewed by her love and the life she graciously gave to him. Retracting his fangs, he lovingly licked the wounds and kissed her neck.

"I never meant to scare you. I feared you would die in the sun. Please tell me you are fine. Why did you go out there?"

Kate lay beside him, stroking his cheek as he spoke. "I heard Aegis. She woke me. I felt awake, so I went downstairs. She kept scratching at the door, so I went outside. I didn't even think about it. It was just habit. I never even thought about the sun. And then, when I went outside, the sun felt glorious on my skin, just as it did when I was mortal...only more. I had barely stepped outside when Luca was there and then you ran past him to get to me."

Shade moaned. "*Bel*, you need to think before you act. I could have lost you!" Pulling her close, he rolled onto his back and sighed as the pain was long gone and dragged her to his chest.

Gliding his hands through her hair, all he could think about was she was alive. "Day-walker. So, what do you think of this?"

"I don't know. Luca said no vampire has two gifts. I don't understand it myself. If I had opened the door and felt pain, I would've closed it right away. Do you feel stronger? Why don't you come with me to the shower, I'll wash away that salve."

"Si, and call Theresa as well, get these bed clothes changed." He slid from the bed as she followed him into the bathroom. "My skin is healed, but I will still need to rest, *mi amore*. The healing takes much energy." He looked at her quizzically. "I have never heard of any immortal having two gifts before. You seem to have some very rare attributes, *bel*. I will contact Council. They need to know of this, they will need to record it, for our history and for the bambinos to follow. It is vital in royal bloodlines."

He led her into the rain forest shower. "Let us wash away this episode, and relish in our love for each other, *si?*"

Kate stood with him under the water as she lathered him from head to toe, making him stand still as she applied a different kind of torture to his skin. Sliding her hands across him, washing away the salve and its strong odor, she could smell his own scent return. He pushed his hair back from his face, letting the water cleanse him, as her hands worked their magic.

He felt his hair had been singed. "My hair feels burnt. Can you wash it for me? Then trim it up, cut off the ends?"

"Lover, I'll gladly trim your hair after our shower. I'll make sure everything works as it should...everything." She slid her soapy hand between his legs and felt his cock as it throbbed and expanded in her grasp. "See? Still working."

Shade grinned. "Are you absolutely sure it works, without a doubt? I think you should test it further."

"You know, you're right. We shouldn't make snap judgments."

She slithered down his body and went to her knees in front of him, sliding his erection into her mouth, running her hands over the tight muscles of his ass, and gripping him tightly, pulling his hips forward, as she took him deep into her throat.

Hanging his head, his hair dripped over his face, the water streaming down his back. He stood spread legged like the warrior he was, with his woman on her knees in front of him, her mouth wrapped around his cock. Sinking his hands into her hair, he began to move her head back and forth, fucking her mouth slowly, controlling her movements and feeling her tongue work magic on his cock. He threw back his head, growling. Her hands massaged his balls and his breathing became ragged, as his eyes rolled back in his head.

Kate purred deep in her throat, knowing he felt the vibrations on his dick as she increased the pace of her thrusts, rolling her tongue over its bulging head. She felt his grip on her hair tighten as she brought him close and felt the weight of his balls in her hand as she massaged, feeling them tighten. With her free hand, she gripped his ass, sinking her nails in, pulling him closer, until she heard him growl and felt him thrust hard into her mouth, releasing into her.

He dropped to his knees and kissed her deeply and passionately. Speaking through his ragged breaths, he whispered, "I think it works."

Kate giggled at him. "Yes, I'd say everything is in perfect working order. Now, let's get you dried off, and I'll trim your hair."

"*Si!*"

As she toweled him off, she snapped his ass with the towel and took off out of the bathroom. Shade gave chase, quickly catching her in his arms, kissing her soundly and giving her own naked ass a sound slap that made her squirm.

As they both settled down, he sat by the window, and his beautiful *bel* trimmed the singed edges from his curly raven locks. He remembered a scene from long ago. His *madre* and *padre* in the same pose, his *madre* cutting his *padre's* hair. He only hoped his eyes reflected the same love, as his father's did that long ago night when he was so young.

29

Kate finished trimming his hair, still damp from the shower, then ran both hands through his long locks, tossing his curls, letting them fall naturally. They both got dressed and headed downstairs. "How are you feeling? Are you working in the warrior camp today?"

"I think I still feel out of sorts. I may go briefly to make sure things are lined up, but I will not stay. Is there something you want to do?"

"Nothing special. If you were busy, I was going to the stables."

As they reached the bottom of the stairs, Gi and Luca both appeared to check on Shade. Luca eyed him carefully. "Master, are you okay? Your skin looks healed. How are you feeling?"

Shade held out his hands. "I am fine, everyone needs to settle down. It was a scare, but I am fine. Healed, fed, and feeling good. Have all the warriors gone to their posts? If not, get them moving."

Luca told him not to worry. He'd take care of it and left to find Marcello.

Gi stepped forward. "My lady, the wolf has stayed at the door ever since master was burned."

Kate smiled at him. "Yes, I could feel them surround the house when he was hurt."

Gi nodded, "As master slept and healed, the others left, but the wolf remained. She still scratches at the door from time to time."

Kate looked puzzled. "Aegis is the reason I woke up the first time. The reason I opened the door. Is she still there?"

Gi nodded. "*Si*, my lady."

Kate grabbed Shade by the hand. "Want to come with me? I'm going to see what she wants."

"Oh *si*, I want to know what the hell made this wolf draw you outside. That sounds more like an enemy trick than a protector. That worries me, *mi amore*. You went straight to her without checking your surroundings. We don't fully understand this gift. You must be more aware before responding to the animals. But let us go find out what the hell she wants before she destroys our back door."

Kate thought about what he'd said. "Maybe Aegis already knew I'd be safe. Maybe she sensed I was a day-walker. I don't think she'd have tried to draw me outside otherwise. At any rate, I opened the door to the daylight out of habit. I might have done the same even without knowing she was on the other side."

As they approached the door, they could both hear the wolf scratching. Kate opened the door and the wolf jumped about, inviting her out to play. Kate followed her into the yard. "I seriously hope all this commotion was not about you looking for someone to romp with, Aegis."

Kate dropped down on her knees and sat on the ground, the wolf crawling into her lap. Kate got quiet, as the wolf was clearly communicating something to her. She stroked her fur and listened.

Shade stood over her. "Aegis and I are going to be at odds if she drew you out into the sunlight and my ass got charcoaled just because she wanted to play. So, spit it out Aegis, or you will deal with me."

"She's going to have pups! She's pregnant with a litter of pups. That's what she wanted to tell me."

Kate nuzzled her face into the wolf's thick grey coat. "Good girl, Aegis. Night Stalker must be so proud!"

Shade looked down at the wolf that was staring lovingly at Kate. "Pups? Meaning you will have even more creatures following you around?" He shook his head and ran his hand gently over Aegis's head and scratched behind her ears. "Well, Aegis beat us to the punch, *mi amore*."

Kate laughed but then turned silent, listening once again. "She says no...."

"No? Wait, what is she saying, Kate?"

Kate looked up at him with surprise. "Lover, she says we're having a pup too. A baby."

Shade's heart raced and he dropped to his knees, cupping Kate's face into his hands. "*Bel*, have you been aware? Did Lorenzo talk to you? Did you see him in a dream?"

Kate was beaming. "I always see him. I see all of them. But he hasn't spoken to me yet." Kate placed her hand on her belly. "It would be too soon for me to know anything. He'd have been conceived since the turning. But she knows... Somehow, Aegis knows. Just like she knew I could walk out the door in the daylight."

Shade crushed her to his chest. They sat in the yard outside the door, the wolf between them, as Shade rocked her gently. "*Mi amore*, my sweet *bel rosso*, a son. You carry our son, our legacy. I love you so!"

Kate spoke through her laughter as she was being held by Shade, and Aegis licked her face and danced around the both of them. "Lorenzo. Our Lorenzo. I can't believe this is happening. I didn't expect him so soon, but I'm so happy he's here!"

Aegis ran in circles around them, as Night Stalker joined her, sitting quietly with his chest out. Kate laughed at him. Two proud papas surrounded her.

"*Si!* Congratulations, Night Stalker! Come." He watched as the black wolf cocked his head slightly and stared at him. "Tell him, *bel*."

Kate held out her hand to the large black wolf that came to her side immediately. She stroked his head and told him, "Congratulations, proud papa. Maybe you can help Shade with his parenting skills."

The large wolf turned to Shade and placing both paws on his shoulders, licked his face.

Shade laughed as the huge wolf almost knocked him over. "*Cazzo*, he could take out one of my warriors if he had a damn mind to. Remind me to never piss him off!"

Aegis pushed Night Stalker away, growling slightly, placing herself in front of Kate, as Night Stalker calmed himself. Kate laughed. "Well, now we know who the boss in this family is. I'm fine, girl. You don't need to hover over me." She looked at Shade, "And that goes for you too. You don't need to hover over me, either. It will be very different this time. We've seen him. We know this baby survives. He more than survives. He rises to all the challenges his father puts before him."

"That may be so, Kate, but you still need to be careful, feed well, and not stress your body. Fuck! I have to get a hold of Council. I will need to talk to Malachi. I have a lot to do, come inside now."

She laughed as he grabbed her hand and pulled her to her feet, already ignoring her advice, and he was off and running. As if she'd expected anything different.

30

Shade made his way to the warrior camp. It was close to sunrise and he knew the warriors would be coming back in from their night duties at the Dead House. His heart was filled with love. *Bel* was pregnant with their *bambino*. His gait was faster, his stance taller, his heart filled with love and pride. His son, their son! He'd be arriving soon, and he must make sure Kate took care of herself. Even though she was immortal, he still worried about the health and well-being of both Kate and the *bambino*.

Walking into the barracks, he could hear the warriors talking and trading stories in the lounge area. As he entered the space, everyone turned and became quiet. It was obvious they had no idea he'd show himself so soon after the sunlight incident. As he looked around, it appeared they were all gathered.

"Close your mouths, I am fine. No harm done. Your queen is fine as well. This is nothing more than a small glitch in the schedule before we have open call for the new recruits. I will be returning with Kate to Castello for a few days, no emergency, just some business that needs to be tended to immediately. I will coordinate with Luca, Marcello and Raven if there are any changes regarding any of you."

A few of the warriors stepped forward, fist bumped him, welcoming him back to the camp. Raven and Marcello came over together and tied up some loose ends with him, but all in all, it had been quiet.

Shade noticed Hyde lounging on the couch, and he could only imagine what the hell was on his mind. He was pretty sure Rissa ran his ass ragged last night. He strolled over and plopped down in a large leather armchair, lighting up a smoke and nodding to Hyde. "So, how did you get along with the bitch from hell?" Both of them looked at each other and laughed.

Hyde shook his head. "She can be mouthy and wants her way. But she's finding out I don't tolerate her holy highness routine. She seems to like me." He rolled his eyes and Shade howled laughing.

Shade put out his cigarette in the ashtray. "So, the future Mrs. Canton has her eye on playing before being tied down. Alec really plays some games with her."

He watched Hyde carefully as he recounted his conversation with Alec, listening as he mentioned Alec had told him hands off and Shade shook his head.

"He believes in a whole different type of mastery. He takes what he wants from whomever he wants, male or female. But Rissa, no. She only gets Alec or whomever he chooses for her. She likes it rough. And he can deliver it. So where did she drag your ass to last night?"

Hyde sat back on the couch, his arm draped casually across the back. "She wanted me to drive her to Incendiary."

Shade's head snapped up and he stared at him.

Hyde nodded. "You heard right. I had the same reaction when she told me where she wanted to go. She said Alec knew she was going. She tried to get frisky with me in the car. I set her straight, and insisted we teleport. I had a strange feeling about it all along."

Shade looked confused. "What in the fucking hell would she want to go there for? That bitch is up to no good. Keep on your toes, she will have you fucked and drained before you know what the hell is going on if she has a mind to."

Hyde chuckled. "No worries, she wasn't long in finding out I don't play that game. Then I got the pouty face. She's an evil female, Shade."

They both laughed and stood to walk outside. Hyde said, "We got to the club and I still didn't understand her purpose there. But once inside, it became all too clear. She met up with Master Colin and his mate Elana in a private room."

Shade creased his brow. "Colin and Elana? They scrounge on the West Coast. She must really be up to no damn good to call them into Annapolis. This isn't sounding so good Hyde. Continue."

Hyde smirked. "She had Colin line up male immortals, young ones. Then he parades them around in front of her. She had a purpose all right. She's one piece of work, that one. She was looking for a third party for her and Canton...a ménage à trois. She found what she was looking for. She had him strip naked in front of us. She almost ate him alive."

Shade slapped Hyde on the back laughing. "Oh, she can do it too, believe me. Look, I am sorry she put you through that. I am sure it won't be the worst you see from her and if she has a thing for you, be on your guard. She will drag you into the most compromising positions. Did she act proper? Give you any shit about protection?"

Hyde laughed. "Oh hell no, she tried, but I shut that down quick. I know her kind. I got this, master."

"Be careful. Proud of you but keep that crazy bitch in line. Show her a Medici is always in control. Just keep your cock in your pants. If she gets to be more than you can handle, let Alec know, he will reel her ass back in. Get some rest, man, I am about to do the same myself."

Shade fist bumped him before he went back to the house. As he walked, he contemplated the idea of Rissa hiring an immortal male for a threesome. Poor bastard would be lucky if he survived.

31

Shade was ready to get moving. It was time to get to Florence and meet with the Council. He'd made his appointment, and was grateful Council was able to accommodate them on such short notice. He had a lot of concerns, mostly for *bel* and her gifts. He needed information and advice. The Council held all the historical records. They'd know much more than he would and perhaps, could help him in training and teaching *bel* the skills she'd need to master her gift of animalism, not to mention, they'd need to record she had the second gift of day-walking. He also wanted to note that his son was on the way. This was vital. There would now be an heir to the Medici line and this had been a long awaited event for his entire coven. It would insure stability into the future.

He watched as *bel* brushed out her hair and he was taken aback at how beautiful she truly was. He would walk with great pride into the Council meeting with his queen on his arm. "Have I told you today, how beautiful you are?"

Kate finished her make-up and spritzed on her rose fragrance, running a brush through her hair when he stepped up behind her. "Hmm, I think it's been a few minutes since you mentioned it. Have I told you how hot you are?"

He chuckled as he snuggled into her neck. "*Si*, I am hot for you, always. Are you ready for Florence? We have a big meeting. We need to get teleporting, not polite to keep Council waiting. And besides, we will need to get dressed once we arrive at Castello. Luca has gone to be with Shannon. I gave him strict instructions to feed, I do not think either one of them will complain. Any worries?"

She leaned back against him as he stood behind her, locking eyes with him in the mirror. "No worries, lover. Why are we meeting with Council? They didn't seem all that pleased to have me around the last time I was in Florence."

Shade smiled back at her. "Well, I expect that attitude will change with time. We have much to discuss with them, *bel*. Your gifts for one. They need to be recorded into the genealogy records. Ivor will handle that task. Then I need to inform them the heir to Medici is on his way. That alone will change their tune. I think you will do just fine. It is very business-like. Council rushes nothing, they can bore you to tears, but I think this visit will have a different outcome. Are you scared?"

Kate put down the hairbrush and turned to him. "Not as long as you're with me. Will you hold me while we teleport? I'm not sure my skills will get me to Florence."

He grabbed her up in his arms, kissing her soundly. "*Si,* I have no intentions of you getting lost. Are you ready?"

"Ready." She slipped her arms around his shoulders and laid her head against his chest. "Hold me tight."

"Always, *mi amore*."

Teleporting directly from the bedroom, Shade traveled quickly, feeling her cling to him. He didn't wish to take her on her first overseas teleport this way, but there was no time to teach her on this trip. He timed it, so they would make it before the sun rose at Castello. Their mission was important, and they were on a tight schedule. As they began to get closer to Florence, he spoke softly to her. "*Bel*, look around, take my hand. Let us enter our home teleporting in together for the first time."

He slowed down and felt her uncurl slowly from him and take his hand, the smile on her face beaming almost as bright as the stars as they took a few turns above the city.

Kate looked down on the city of Florence, lit like a jewel on the river Arno, and she could see Castello and its vast gardens just north of the city, the huge warrior camp visible from the air. She thought she'd never get used to the opulence of this castle. She held tight to his hand, teleporting on her own, yet tethered to him for safety. She looked at him and smiled. She knew she'd always be tethered to him, in love and safety.

Teleporting inside Castello to the grand foyer, he held her hand tightly, so she would land correctly and not in a tumble. Once on their feet, he steadied her. "Welcome home, my queen."

Suddenly, there was much activity and the house staff was bustling about, welcoming them home. Shade heard Emma's voice jabbering on above all the others and he shook his head as she rushed towards them.

"Master, my lady, you're earlier than we expected. I have everything ready for you. Theresa told me to prepare you for Council, my lady. Your dress is laid out, as well as your shoes, and your jewels have been removed from the vault. Your suite is ready. I have fresh linens on the bed, fresh towels out. And roses. I know you like roses, so I've picked them from the garden before you arrived. Do you have luggage coming? Is there anything you need for me to unpack?"

Kate had to purse her lips together to keep from laughing. She'd forgotten how nervous Emma was around her and Shade, and how much she chattered on. Kate looked to Shade. "I don't think we have luggage coming, do we?"

"No luggage. We will be meeting with Council and then returning here to take our slumber and leave in the early morning hours to avoid the sun.

Come along, we must prepare. Go on ahead, Emma, your queen will meet you there."

Shade took Kate's hand as they walked to the bedroom. He nodded and talked to a few of his household staff as they went. Once they were clear of the house staff, he turned to Kate. "Damn that one never stops talking. I wasn't sure I would ever meet anyone who fires questions at me as much as you or Shannon, but I think Emma has you both beat. Let her help you get dressed, *mi amore*. I have chosen something for you. If you do not like it, just say so, but I do know what is expected. I have asked it to be brought here for you. I need to get into my ceremonial leathers, and then I will come for you, *si*?"

Kate nodded. "I'm relieved the dress has already been chosen. You do recall how long it took me to pick out that red dress on the day we came here to interview all the warriors? I much prefer this process."

Kate followed Emma to the large bedroom that had once belonged to Shade's parents, recalling the events that had taken place here a little more than a month ago. She saw the long black formal dress laid across the bed. The last time she was here, she wore white for all the ceremonies.

Emma helped her remove her clothes then helped her into the sleek black gown. It had a scooped neckline and capped sleeves, and an empire waist that fell in a straight column to the floor. The hemline was cut slightly higher in the front with a very short train in the back. Emma pulled out a pair of classic black heels with no embellishment, and Kate stepped into them.

Returning from the dresser with a velvet box, Emma flipped open the top to expose a huge pear shaped diamond pendant, which she placed around Kate's neck before handing her two large pear shaped diamonds for her ears.

Emma whispered reverently, "They were *Madre's*. They're kept in the vault and brought out only for special occasions."

Kate could see her reflection in Portia's mirror as her transformation from jeans to royal court took place in a matter of minutes.

Shade finished dressing in his ceremonial leathers and tapped lightly on *bel's* door. He heard Emma respond and walked in to find his *bel* had been converted into the queen she was. Their eyes connected, and he walked slowly to her. He took in every inch and curve of her. She'd impress even the most doubtful.

Sliding his hand slowly around her waist, he pulled her hard into his chest and kissed her passionately. "*Madre's* jewels, a nice touch."

"They're stunning. Emma brought them out. I can't imagine wearing them at Bel Rosso, though."

She returned his kisses with soft nibbles on his lower lip. "Is there anything I need to know about this meeting? Any protocol I need to follow?"

Shade shook his head. "Just follow my lead. If they ask you a direct question, answer it honestly. Tell them how you feel. They are Council, but I want my queen to be my *bel* as well. Never change who you are for anyone involved in our world, *mi amore*. Do not be nervous. Come, we must go now. We will teleport outside the Council Headquarters and be lead in."

Taking her hand, they teleported outside the Council building and he could already feel her nerves were a little on edge. The Council resided in an old monastery that had been Council headquarters ever since Shade could remember. Some things never changed, including their archaic attitudes.

They were lead inside the great granite building and asked to wait. They were expected, and their presence would be announced appropriately.

"Relax, *bel*, this is your first time here, but it will not be your last."

The hall was massive, and even as he whispered, his voice carried in the large cavernous space of this old gothic building, their footsteps echoing down the long corridor. She knew Shade had had a very heated argument with one of the Council members before the coronation, and though he never shared the details, she knew it had been about her. But she wouldn't let him down. She swore then that she'd earn her place beside him and prove to them all she deserved to stand at his side.

"I'm ready."

A robed Council attendant approached and there were no words exchanged, it was simply custom to follow. Shade took *bel's* hand as they followed the attendant through the cavernous halls until they approached the main door of the Court. The entire place was guarded heavily, courtesy of Medici Warriors who were permanently assigned to this position, another long-standing tradition. Two guards stood at attention outside the massive doors that lead to the Council Court, and nodded to their former master. Shade hadn't seen them since they entered the Council walls. Once a warrior took on the assignment with Council, they never returned to the outside world again. The doors swung open wide, creaking on their massive hinges. The booming voice of the attendant echoed as he announced them to the Court. "King Medici and Queen Katherine!"

Shade squeezed her hand lightly and walked them to the front of the court chamber, where all vampires requesting an audience with Council were held. Neither Shade nor any other master had seen any of the rooms beyond the court chamber, as they were still held to secrecy and mystery.

As they approached the Council members, Shade saw them all sitting on their throne-like chairs behind a massive table. The room was paneled in old wood, elaborately carved, and gleaming from the oiling it regularly received. The carpets were red, and the chairs upholstered in the rich red brocade fabric with the European Vampire Council crest carved into the wood at the top of each high-backed chair. The room looked exactly as he remembered.

Shade held his head high. He saw all seven members of Council in attendance; Malachi, Jasperion, Agathian, Florian, Ivor, Citrichi and Onyx. In all matters before Council, all seven members must be present. As the attendant announced their presence, Council stood in acknowledgement of their royal status, but didn't bow to them. As Shade led Kate to the dais and stood before them, Council returned to their seats and Shade waited to be spoken to. He and *bel* were not allowed to sit until requested to do so.

Malachi remained standing on the dais in his emerald green robe, nodding to the king and queen. "The Council welcomes you and bids you be seated."

He stood while Shade helped his queen to the chair positioned before the dais, taking his seat beside her.

"What brings the Medici before this session of Council?"

Kate was looking at each of the seven Council members who sat expressionless before them, each wearing a brightly colored hooded robe of a different color.

Shade cleared his throat. "I have business with Ivor and Malachi. I have seen my queen's gifts. Yes, I said gifts. I wish for them to be recorded for historical and genealogical purposes. She has been gifted with two skills. One of which, I am here to ask for your guidance and help as to how I can assist her."

An attendant brought forth the huge leather bound books, and placed them on the table before Ivor.

Malachi looked at Shade. "I was aware, Medici, when I tasted her blood at the coronation that she had two gifts, and I can verify such to Ivor. Queen Katherine Medici displayed the gifts of both day-walker and animalism."

As he spoke the words, there was a mumbling among the Council members. Ivor picked up the quill pen and dipped it into the inkwell but hesitated before recording. Ivor wore a long hooded robe of ivory, identifying his role as archivist and historian, and the Council member who recorded and researched the genealogy of all of the vampires under the rule of the European Council.

Ivor looked to Malachi. "Are you sure, Malachi? The gift of day-walking is common now, especially among the newborns. But animalism?" Ivor turned his gaze toward Shade. "Have you seen evidence of this gift, Medici?"

Shade nodded in his direction. "*Si*. Several times. She can speak to the animals and they speak to her. As my queen has described this to me, it is much like our telepathy. They do as she commands. I have witnessed numerous animals respond to her. They respond unbidden when she is in an angry or agitated state. They proclaim to protect her."

Turning to *bel*, he leaned in and whispered, "Is there anything you may be able to call to you now?"

Kate looked at him with a confused expression. *Aegis? How could she possibly call Aegis from here?* "I'm not sure. Let me concentrate." She lowered her head, cleared her mind, and tried to pick up on the vibrations of any animal that might be near. From outside the building, in the spires of the Gothic towers, a raven sat, tilting his head. Kate called to him, pulled him to her, and saw in her mind as the bird took flight. She kept her head lowered with her eyes closed, and let the raven know where she was. As they sat in the closed chamber, they could hear a loud and persistent pecking at the large wooden doors.

Kate looked up. "If you'll open the chamber doors, the raven will enter."

Ivor nodded to the warriors who stood guard at the entrance, and they opened the massive wooden doors. The large black raven flew into the room, and landed on the back of Kate's chair, issuing a very loud and raucous, "Caw, caw."

Kate smiled. "He said his name is Poe."

Shade looked at *bel* and smiled, grasping her hand and squeezing it in appreciation. Looking back at Ivor he nodded. "Are you satisfied, Ivor?"

Ivor watched in amazement as the large crow settled on the back of her chair, already taking up a position to defend her. "Medici, may I address your queen directly?"

Shade nodded his head at Ivor. "Please, I encourage you to speak to her."

Ivor looked at her from under his ivory hood. "Queen Katherine, can you tell me please, about your experience with the animals? Are they random?"

Kate creased her brow. "I don't profess to understand this gift. But no, the experiences aren't random. They began immediately upon our return to our home in Virginia, after we left Florence following the coronation. There had been a wolf on our property, which had been upsetting to our horses. Our stable master said the wolf had showed up with the blood moon, which I understand to be the night of my turning. The wolf approached me on our first night home. I was able to communicate with her and she remains near our home. She has since brought her mate, who also responds to any intruders on our property. Later, a mountain lion joined the wolves, and the latest has been a falcon. The wolf, Aegis, appears to be in charge of the others, but through me. I can communicate directly with all of them, but Aegis appears to be their leader, of sorts."

Ivor nodded. "May I inquire of your turning, do you recall those events?"

Kate maintained eye contact with him. "I doubt I'll ever forget those events. I remember it well."

Ivor stood and paced. "I apologize to the Medici Queen for these questions. But this gift, it is extremely rare. In fact, we thought it extinct. We have not seen a gift of animalism present in over three thousand years, and there is no vampire alive today with this gift. And never have we recorded an event where a turned mortal was granted this gift. Do you recall anything unusual in your turning?"

Kate pondered this question. *Is he kidding? Was there anything about the turning that would be considered "usual"?* She ran the events of her turning through her head.

"There was this incident. I didn't understand it, but then, I didn't understand much of what occurred to me in the turning. But I felt the presence of a wolf, and I felt it being absorbed into me. I thought at the time it was my beast."

Ivor sat back down in his chair. "No, Queen Katherine. The wolf is your spirit guide. Any animal could have presented, but in your case, it was the wolf. That explains why the wolf waited for you, and yes, she will lead the others as you have observed. She is bonded to you, not unlike how your king is bonded to you. You will have the power to call upon all animals, just as you called the raven to you today. But the she-wolf will lead them."

Shade spoke up, "How do we harness her gift? Train her to use it? I have read nothing, seen nothing on how to use this gift."

Ivor shook his head. "I fear the Council will be of limited help in that area, Medici. It has been so long, as I mentioned. I will research the old texts to see if they offer us any guidance. It was a rare gift even in the old days, but a most powerful one, a gift to be envied for certain. I can tell you the animals that bond to her will go to their death to protect her, or anyone she calls them forth to protect. But other than that, I know little else." He picked the quill pen up again and dipped it back in the ink. "I have seen and heard enough, and have the testimony of Malachi, to convince me she, indeed, has this gift and it shall be so recorded, along with her gift of day-walker."

Shade felt perplexed, even the Council was of little help in understanding and helping him to help Kate learn and hone this rare gift.

"I would ask one thing of Council. This gift is rare, not yet understood by myself, my queen, nor anyone here. I would ask this remain secret as much as possible. This could be a potential risk for my coven, if any enemies were to hear of such. It is rare to have two gifts, and until she can master them, we are all at risk in Medici."

Malachi scanned the faces of the other Council members who all nodded their heads. "That is a reasonable request and we will honor it. What is recorded here shall remain sealed until such time you decide to make her gifts known. Do you have other business before this Council today, Medici?"

Shade stood, taking *bel's* hand and helping her to stand as well. "I do, Malachi. It is with great pride and honor that I announce the coming of my first born. My queen is with child. We will bring forth a son, the heir to Medici."

The Council members all stood in unison. Malachi beamed at him. "Step forward please, Queen Katherine of Medici."

Kate looked at Shade, who gave her a nod. She stood and moved to the dais where Malachi stood. He stepped around the table to stand in front of her, and as he reached toward her, the raven flew from his perch on the back of her chair and swooped across Malachi's head, a loud 'caw' echoing in the hall. Kate held out her hand and the raven landed there. She spoke softly to the bird.

The Council members responded with gasps and whispers. Kate looked at Malachi. "So sorry. I'm not used to them all yet and how protective they are. He means you no harm. Please proceed."

Malachi exchanged a knowing glance with Ivor before he placed his hand on her still flat belly. He closed his eyes as the room was so silent you could hear a pin drop. After a few seconds, he stepped back and smiled at her.

"The Medici Queen is indeed with child, and she bears him a son, a warrior. This is great news, Medici. An heir to your legacy is something we have all long anticipated and we are pleased. I hope you need no reminders that the *bambino* must be born here, in Florence, inside the chamber at Castello, and the birth must be witnessed by me to verify his birthright."

Shade stood tall, his chest out and his shoulders back. This was a moment he'd never forget. They never thought he'd settle down, that he'd mate, and they'd see a queen, let alone an heir to Medici. But today, all that changed. They would now treat him with deeper respect. Nothing could stop him now, not with *bel* at his side and his son to defend all that was their Kingdom. He felt such pride and love for her and saw an eternity of all his dreams coming true. He only wished his *padre* could witness this meeting.

"I am well aware of my duties to Medici and Council. They will be met with pride and honor, as things have always been done within Medici. We have no further business with Council unless my queen wishes to speak?" Shade looked to Kate and smiled.

Kate heard him present her with another opportunity to speak. She remembered well Shade's anger when the Council visited him at Castello. She turned and faced the hooded faces of the Council.

"I wish you to know I'm well aware of the disappointment of many in the community at Shade's decision to mate a mortal. I know you fear I won't live up to your expectations. You need to understand my commitment to him, to his warriors and his coven. You need to understand my commitment to raise his children in an atmosphere that will reinforce their responsibilities to carry forth the Medici legacy, and my own responsibilities to maintain that legacy. I feel that burden on my shoulders, and I carry it with pride. Above all things, I'll not fail him. I don't profess to understand the full power of my gifts, but I know in my heart that, together, we'll prevail through all things."

Malachi listened to her declaration and had no doubts she spoke the truth. The revelation of her gifts alone would turn the vampire community upside down. Malachi looked first to Kate and then to Shade.

"Whatever doubts I had about your choice of a mate have been removed this day, Medici. I apologize for the Council's warning on the eve of your coronation. Your beast was true in leading you to your destined mate."

Shade held up his hand. "Please do not speak your apologies to me. They are owed to my queen. She has already been an asset to this coven, my warriors, and me long before she was even turned. You doubted me, Malachi. You doubted my heart. If nothing else, my *madre* taught me one thing, your heart never lies. There is nothing that can come between us. Nothing."

Shade walked to *bel* and took her in his arms. "She is all to me. We would beg your leave now. I do not wish to tax my queen with travel and no rest. *Grazie* for your guidance this night. We wish the Council well."

Malachi turned to Kate and locked eyes with her. She held his gaze without blinking or looking away, her iron will and determination on display. "My apologies, Queen Katherine." He nodded his head to her and she gave him the slightest smile, as he read her thoughts, *You haven't seen anything yet.* Of that, he had no doubt. "If you have no further business with Council, then we dismiss you and your queen, Medici, and bid you a good evening."

Kate turned to face Shade, the raven still perched on her hand, as a warrior stepped forward to escort them from the Council Court. Once outside, he pulled her to him to teleport back to Castello when Kate laughed. "I think this bird is coming with us."

Shade laughed. "I think, perhaps he can find his own way to Castello. Come, it is late, we need to rest, we leave as soon as we can to return to Bel Rosso. I have already had you away long enough. I want you home, where you can rest and be with your menagerie of beasts."

As if he understood the conversation, Poe took flight, and flew in the direction of Castello. Although it was a short teleport to Castello, Kate's skills at teleporting were still new and untested, and Shade was feeling very protective of his newly pregnant mate. He pulled her to his chest and teleported them directly into their massive bedroom at Castello.

***

In the Council Court, the members sat solemnly around the huge table, absorbing the impact of all they'd learned tonight. Ivor was the first to speak, "Malachi, did you not know of her gift of animalism when you tasted her blood at the coronation?"

Malachi nodded. "I tasted both gifts, but I doubted what I tasted. I have never known another vampire to have this gift, so until she exhibited signs of the gift, I thought it best not to reveal it."

The black robed Onyx, responsible for the security of the Council spoke up, "We have all read of this gift, and while we do not know how to teach the Medici how to help her harness it, we are all aware of its potential. I know we were cautious in our words tonight, knowing she was once mortal, not knowing how strong this gift will present, but I don't think I need to give voice to what is in all our heads. If she can harness this gift, the power of Medici will change everything. He will be...together, they will be..."

Malachi finished his sentence, "Invincible. The Medici will be invincible."

The Council members nodded. Ivor scanned their faces. "This makes our alignment with the Medici more important than ever. He has never expected favors or asked to be given any advantage over other masters in our deliberations. It is his code of honor, and I do not expect that to change. But we cannot lose sight of what we have learned here, tonight. He has clearly expanded his reach into the States, and I think we have only seen the beginning. We must tread softly, my brethren. We cannot afford to make an enemy of the Medici. He may not fully realize the scope of his power yet, but the day will come."

32

On returning from Council, Shade and Kate spent the day at Castello, with Shade in his death slumber and Kate asleep at his side. Three hours from sunrise, he arose and teleported them back to Bel Rosso.

He recognized the landmark of the small town of Charlottesville. As they came closer to White Hall, he released her from his embrace, still holding her hand as they got nearer to Bel Rosso. He loved the look on her face when she teleported. He could see she loved the freedom.

"*Bel*, I want you to go on your own, go home to Bel Rosso. Let me see if you can manage it from here. I am going to go ahead and be there waiting."

Before she could argue, he was gone in a flash. Kate had wanted the freedom to teleport on her own, but with the safety of him beside her. Now, he had sped ahead of her and she felt a moment of panic. She started to lose altitude and knew she had to focus her attention. She scanned the landscape below her, trying to get her bearings, but found it more difficult in the dark. She was able to locate Route 240 and Crozet, and from there, she followed the roads, picturing Bel Rosso in her head until she landed in front of their home. Shade stood in the driveway, smoking a cigarette. Her landing wasn't graceful, but she remained upright as she laughed and walked to him, taking the cigarette from his hand and tossing it to the ground. She wrapped her arms around his shoulders and kissed him.

"How was that, lover?" She heard a round of applause and looked up to see Marcello, Raven, Luca, and Cory observing her from the garage.

"It was not exactly graceful, *mi amore*, but you are getting the hang of it. We will practice more. But you must learn now because once you advance in your pregnancy, you will not teleport." Kissing her soundly, he could hear the cheers and looked up to see some of his warriors lolling about.

Marcello elbowed Luca. "You know, you should teach my lady a few tips on teleporting, I heard she took a full roll in the grass the first time out."

They all laughed and slapped each other on the back as Luca grinned and closed the hood on the silver Jaguar. He climbed into the car and started the engine, backing it out of the garage.

Marcello called out to him, "Okay, what are you up to cousin, I know that grin."

Luca drove the silver Jaguar over to where Shade and Kate stood. As he got out of the car, he tossed the keys to Shade and said, "Since you're in the mood to teach, this is as good a time as any. Besides, you'll have a camp full of rookie warriors soon. You need to polish your skills on instruction. You were a good teacher, but not the most patient as I recall." Luca laughed goodheartedly at him.

Raven held back his laughter. Looking to Marcello, he grinned. "Want to make a bet? I bet boss-man will throw in the towel." Raven laughed as Cory said he wanted in on that bet.

Marcello responded, "You're on! He has patience with her, not like the warriors. She'll do well, I'll take that bet. If he can teach my lady to drive a stick shift, you buy me new leathers. If he can't handle it, I'll buy you leathers and I'll buy Cory anything he wants. Deal?"

Raven fist bumped Marcello as he grinned. "You're on!"

As Shade caught the keys of the silver S Coupe Jaguar, he shook his head at Luca. "You underestimate me, Luca. I think Kate has the skills to manage this easily. She just needs a little instruction, few ups and downs in the drive and she will have it. What do you say, *mi amore*? You can teleport now. Driving a stick is much easier."

Kate looked at him with doubt. She had tried to drive a stick shift before and had never gotten the hang of it. "I'm not sure there's much similarity to teleporting and driving, but I'll try it."

Kissing her forehead, he walked her to the driver's side of the car and handed her the keys. "I have faith in you. Now, do nothing until I get in, please."

Walking around to the passenger side, Shade watched as his warriors all stood in a line, laughing. Getting in the car, he began with simple instructions. "The pedal on the far left is the clutch. Middle is the brake. Right is the gas. Turn on the car by completely engaging the clutch and turning the ignition. Keep the clutch engaged while applying your brakes in order to safely release the emergency brake. It will keep the car from rolling forward. Let's begin with that step first. So, you can get a feel for it, *si*?"

Kate listened as he started giving her instructions. Clutch, gas, brakes, ignition, it all made perfect sense as he was saying it, but it was all a muddle by the time he finished talking. "Uh, okay. What was the first step again?"

"*Mi amore*, listen to what I say, push down the clutch, the left pedal, with your left foot, then the middle pedal down at the same time, that is the brake, and turn the key. Put the gear shift in neutral. Always make sure it is in neutral to start. As soon as the car starts up, release the emergency brake. You know what that is, correct?"

"Yes, emergency brake. This thing right here."

Kate depressed the clutch with her left foot, and it already felt awkward. She pushed in the brake and turned the key in the ignition and heard the rumble of the engine. Well, that wasn't so bad. She took her foot off the brake to move to the gas pedal, and put the car in first and the car bucked forward. She hit the brake pedal and the car stalled out.

Shade felt the car lurch forward and he grabbed the dashboard so as not to hit his head on the windshield.

"It's okay, *mi amore*. That's normal for first timers. Keep your foot on the brake and the clutch until I tell you otherwise. Now, engage the emergency brake again. And start over."

Kate nodded, bit her lip, and could feel her palms sweating. "Should I put the gear thing back in park first?"

"*Bel*, there is no park. You see the numbers on the gear shift, there is no park. The middle position is called neutral. You will feel it once you get the damn car started, so I can show you what the gear shift feels like. Now, start the car."

Shade looked over and could see the boys laughing and smirking. *Bastardos!* I will teach her if it kills me.

Kate wiped her palms on her jeans and then grasped the steering wheel again. "So, what gear should I be in?"

Shade sighed. "Neutral. The gear shift is already in neutral. Start the car. Left and middle pedal down, key turned. Keep both pedals down. Nothing else!"

Kate felt his frustration already, as she made sure the gear shift was in neutral, and then depressed the clutch and the break simultaneously. She released the emergency brake then sat still.

"Do I start the engine now?"

"Keep both feet down and turn the key. It is not that hard, *bel*, you can do it."

Kate signed, feeling tense. "So now? Start the engine now?"

"*Si*, now. Don't move your damn feet!"

Cory shook his head. "Sun will be up before she ever moves the gravel under those tires. It should be easy, but she doesn't seem to be understanding." They all chuckled and kept watching and waiting.

Before Kate turned the key in the ignition, she could hear Raven shouting out to Marcello, "I'm so getting new leathers, bro!" Their laughter made her more nervous as she turned the key in the ignition and listened to the roar of the engine again. She sighed before turning to him. "Okay, what next?"

Shade fought to maintain his calm. "Keep your feet down on both pedals." Taking her hand, he put it on the gear shift knob, his hand over top hers and wiggled it, so she could feel it was not engaged.

"Feel that, Kate? That is neutral. It is not engaged in any gear. Now, shift into first and keep both feet down."

She struggled to shift the gear into first, and watched him cringe as the gear made a scraping sound, but she kept both feet on the pedals.

"Okay... now what?"

"Now here comes the tricky part. Listen before you move! Take your right foot off the brake pedal and as you slowly give the car gas, ease off of the clutch. You want to match the pressure you apply to the gas to be the same amount of pressure you release on the clutch. If you feel like you are going to stall, push the clutch all the way back in and let off the gas and reapply the brake and you can avoid it. As the clutch is engaged, right foot on the gas, give the engine just a little gas and slowly let out some of the clutch. As you feel that catch point, the RPMs will start to drop, and the car will start to move forward a bit. Slowly give it more gas to keep the RPM's constant as you let the clutch out. The key is to give it enough gas to keep the RPM's constant until the clutch pedal is all the way out. If the RPMs are dropping, apply more gas."

Kate just stared at him. "Were you speaking in English? I have no idea what you just said."

Shade slid his hand through his hair and closed his eyes, taking a deep breath. "Okay. Take your foot off the brake and put it on the gas. As you let up on the clutch, you press down on the gas, same amount of each, to level it out. Once you get the clutch released, you should fucking be moving and we can shift into second... but at this rate, let's see if we can move."

Kate could feel his frustration level building and it wasn't helped by the chorus of laughter from the peanut gallery. The more frustrated he got, the more nervous she got. Kate moved her foot from the brake to the accelerator and tried to release the pressure on the clutch as she applied pressure to the accelerator. The car bucked forward with a sudden lurch, she released the pressure on the gas and the car stalled out again.

Shade threw up both hands. "Enough! We are switching, you watch while I drive. Maybe that will help."

Shade pulled the emergency brake and put the gear shift into neutral. Jumping out, he growled at the warriors loudly and it only antagonized them more. Switching seats with *bel*, he had to manually move the seat back before he could even slide in. Slamming the door shut, he looked at her as she slid into the passenger seat.

"Now, watch my feet. You ready?"

Kate glared at him, feeling close to tears. "I'm watching!"

"Listen and watch." Shade stepped on the clutch and the brake and turned the key. Releasing the emergency brake, he put the Jag into first gear. "Now, I am letting my foot up from the clutch and pressing on the gas, slowly, at the same time."

The car moved smoothly up the drive. "Once you are completely off of the clutch and up to around 3,000 RPMs shift into second gear by letting off of the gas, completely engaging the clutch, and then pull the gear shift down from first into second gear. After it is in gear, remove your foot from the clutch while putting your foot back on the gas, quickly before you lose any speed. This process will be slow in the start, but you will learn to do it quickly."

Shade gave it gas and then clutched and shifted into second and hit the gas and did a spin down the drive, slowing down and clutching, braking until he came to a stop, then turned the car around until it was facing the house. "Got it?"

Kate was exasperated. "Got it? Are you kidding me? What's an RPM and how do I know how many I have?"

He shouted at her, "Kate! How the hell did you learn to drive any car without knowing what RPM's are? Never mind, don't answer that. Please let's just try to get the car up the driveway. Switch seats!"

He put on the emergency brake and turned off the ignition. As he slammed the door to switch seats, he heard the laughter all the way down the drive. He shouted at his warriors, "Don't make me bust heads!"

Kate slammed her own door as she got out, changing seats again. "Does my Miata have RPM's? I just look at the speedometer. I don't need to know RPM's." She climbed behind the driver's wheel once again, her nervousness turning to anger. "Is this thing in park?"

He looked at her with exasperation. "Neutral, and *si*, it is in neutral."

Kate muttered, "Whatever," under her breath. She depressed the brake and the clutch, releasing the emergency brake and starting the engine again. As the engine roared, she shifted into first. She released the clutch as she floored the accelerator, and the tires spun, throwing gravel before the car lurched forward, fish-tailing. She slammed on the brakes, her seat belt holding her in place, as he was pitched forward in his seat.

Shade knew she was angry, but he was as well. "*Cazzo*, woman! Stay where you are. Don't move!"

Shade rolled out of the Jag and started walking toward the house, his temper overflowing when he saw his warriors, all four of them on the ground, damn near dying laughing, and that fueled his anger even more. As he got closer, they were back slapping each other and struggling to get themselves under control. Raven and Cory acted like they'd hit the jackpot. *Little bastards had a bet!* Shade shouldered past them and looked Luca straight in the eyes.

"Your queen needs assistance. Teach her how to drive that thing or at least get it back up the driveway and into the garage." Stomping into the house, he slammed the door and headed for his office.

Luca was biting down hard on the inside of his cheek to try to keep from laughing, as Shade told him to take over. He nodded to him, knowing if he opened his mouth to speak, the only thing coming out would be laughter. Marcello, Raven, and Cory were rolling on the floor of the garage, tears streaming down their faces.

Luca saw Kate getting out of the car and slamming the door hard. He shook his head, as he walked toward her. "Giving up, warrior?"

Kate glared at him. "Don't you dare make fun of me, Luca. I'm not in the mood."

He shook his head. "Not here to make fun of you. Want to try this again?"

Kate looked at him like he had two heads. "Seriously?"

He smiled patiently and nodded toward the car. "Get back in."

Kate sighed loudly and looked at him with complete exasperation. "If you start talking to me about RPGs and clutch this and shift that, I'm going to scream."

Luca chuckled. "Okay, no RPGs, just get in."

Luca climbed into the driver's seat and depressed the brake and clutch. Kate reluctantly slid into the passenger seat.

"Put your hand on the gear shift knob."

As she followed his instruction, he kept his feet on the brake and the clutch and had her shift through all the gears. Making her repeat after him which gear they were in. First, second, third, neutral, fourth, fifth, reverse. They sat quietly, his hand on top of hers as he made her go through the gears, over and over and over, repeating the numbers like a mantra. He removed his hand and called out the gear he wanted her to shift into and waited for her to maneuver the gear shift into the proper position. He made her repeat it over and over until she could do it in her sleep.

"Now, change seats with me." He had her take the driver's seat, as he climbed into the passenger seat. "Now, I want you to concentrate on the pedals. Don't worry about the gear shift. I will shift gears for you. Just focus on the pedals. Think of the pedals like a bicycle. One is up and the other is down. Release the pressure on the clutch and apply that same pressure on the gas. Don't worry if it's not smooth. It will take practice. If the car bucks, just keep going."

He let her practice over and over, as he managed the gear shift for her and she kept her eyes on her feet and the pedals. He chuckled, as he watched her concentrate on her feet. "Don't forget to look where you are going."

She started and stopped, over and over, until she could manage to move the car without having it buck and jump forward.

"That's enough for today. Tomorrow, I'll let you put the two steps together."

Kate just looked at him. "I don't know why I can't just drive my Miata."

He smiled. "You may not always have that option. A good warrior is prepared for anything."

Raven turned to Marcello. "You owe me leathers, brother, and I mean designer. Cory's best. I already have something in mind. That was the easiest pair of leathers I ever earned."

Marcello shook his head and turned to leave when Raven grabbed him by the arm. "Not so fast. You owe Cory something. You said anything he wanted. So, what is it, Cory?"

Cory looked at Raven wide eyed. "Are you serious? Anything?" He looked at Marcello as he nodded yes. "Well, I've never owned a car. Nothing new, a used one will do. Never mind, I could never ask for that. Just get me anything, Marcello, it's cool."

Marcello looked at him quizzically. "Hold up, Cory. You never owned a car? What kind of car do you like? Look, a bet's a bet. You won fair and square. I'm sure if I put up half the money, Shade would put up the other half. We can get you something you want. You've worked really hard and he appreciates all you've done. So, what are you thinking about?"

Cory stared at them. He couldn't believe his ears. Marcello would give him a car? Cory had never owned anything that expensive in his life. He had dreamed of owning a car, but he was always struggling to find food. The streets were no place to own much of anything.

"I couldn't ask master for a car. But I've been thinking, living out here, a truck would be good to have. I don't need a new one, just something used to get around in."

Raven flung his long locks over his shoulder. "Cory, you need a vehicle, bro. You need stuff in town, you can't always teleport everyplace. We live out here in the middle of nowhere. Let Marcello talk to Shade for you, he'll help, boss-man isn't the bully here, he takes good care of all of us, and that includes you."

Marcello nodded. "Let me talk to master about this, Cory, then I'll get back to you. Raven is right. You need a truck, a new one."

Marcello watched Cory's eyes light up. Kid never had a penny to his name. Just then, he saw Luca and my lady coming back with the car and she was driving it, somewhat.

"Come on, I think we better head back to camp before Luca walks back in that house and Shade finds out Luca managed to teach my lady." They all agreed and headed back down the road to the warrior camp.

Luca followed Kate back inside the house. They could hear Shade in his office, desk drawers being slammed shut as he muttered to himself. Kate marched to the door of his office.

"Really? You leave me in the car and you're the one having a tantrum?"

Shade stared at her and then at Luca. "So, from now on, I propose Luca teach you everything. For some reason, you respond to his teaching better than your own mate. I have taught hundreds of damn warriors, *bel*, hundreds, and look at the results. Luca being the best. How the hell can you not know what RPMs are? Who the hell taught you to drive? *Cazzo*, woman!"

Kate's temper flared, but she heard Luca snickering behind her and she had to laugh at the absurdity of the situation. "Well, I think it best we not let Luca teach me everything. There are a few areas I think we can agree you've mastered quite well. Besides, all I know about cars is steering wheel, gas, and brake. Everything else just gets in the way."

Shade shook his head in exasperation. "I just find it odd that you were ever able to make it around D.C. in that car without killing yourself or someone else after this episode. But I agree, there are some things no one can teach you but me. After all, I am master here, *mi amore*." Winking at her, he patted his lap.

She climbed in his lap and laid her head on his shoulder. "Traffic in D.C. moves at five miles an hour if it moves at all. I usually took the subway. And driving a stick shift in all that stop and go traffic would be maddening." She kissed his neck and whispered, "Don't be mad at me. At least, I can teleport."

As he held her in his lap, they heard a persistent pecking at their window and looked up to see Poe.

Kate looked up in surprise. "Oh my god! That bird flew here from Florence!"

Shade looked at the window and shook his head. "Imagine that!" Kissing her neck, he whispered into her ear, "I think we should tell Luca the news, *si*?"

Kate placed her hand on the side of his face, looking at those ice blue eyes, aware of the life they'd created that lived inside her. "I think you should be the one to break the news."

Shade looked deep into her eyes, and suddenly, driving a stick shift was long gone from his mind. Nothing mattered but the two of them, and the legacy she carried.

"Luca, some news. Your queen and king are expecting a prince. *Bel* is with child."

Luca was dumbstruck and stood open-mouthed. After watching the drama around the driving lesson, this was the last thing he expected to hear. "That's... that's... Congratulations, master! I think this calls for a celebration."

"*Grazie*, Luca. You are the first to know. It is why we went to Castello. We informed the Council of Kate's gifts and announced the pregnancy. I have been struggling with whether to let everyone know or to keep it under wraps for a while. Since we start camp shortly, I would feel better if everyone were aware of her condition. Kate carries our son and his name is Lorenzo. So, we know he is coming."

Shade picked Kate up from his lap and sat her on top of his desk so she was facing him. Looking into her eyes, he smiled. "*Mi amore*, I would like to announce to everyone our news. But I want them all gathered here inside this house, my staff, my warriors, and Shannon as well. I want to have some Midnight and a toast to our son."

Kate smiled back at him. "I'd like that. This baby is strong, healthy. I can feel his life inside of me. And I think he'll be a better driver, and like fast cars like his father. So, tell everyone."

Shade laid his hand on her stomach and laughed. "*Si*, that would be my *figlio*! Luca, I need you to get Shannon, can she come now, you can teleport and bring her here. Then I will contact the warriors, and the staff. Have Gi break out the Midnight. But no word to anyone. I want this to be a surprise for all. Can you get Shannon here tonight?"

Luca responded, "Of course! Let me give her a call to let her know I'm picking her up."

Shade looked at *bel* and grinned. "I think he might be a bit enamored with Shannon, *si*?"

Kate smiled at him. "I think they moved way past enamored. I haven't had time to talk to Shannon since we came back from the coronation, but I got the feeling things definitely moved along pretty fast while they were in Florence. Does this please you? I hope it pleases you, that Luca has someone."

Shade nodded to her. "I like Shannon, and she makes Luca happy. I am worried. He will have much responsibility now with the new camp and you being pregnant. It will take a lot of juggling to get him to her. So, I only hope she will adjust to his schedule when he needs to be with her. It will be the ultimate test of them together."

Shade could hear Luca on his phone right outside the office. "Luca, is your female available? I need to get the warriors ready. Does one hour work for you?"

Luca stepped back inside the door as he slipped the phone in his pocket. "She'll be ready when I get there. I can leave now, and I'll be back quickly."

Shade grinned at him. "Good job, get your ass to your female and get back here in an hour. That gives you some time."

Kate slid off the desk to the floor. "What do you need me to do? I can gather the house staff while you get the warriors."

"*Si, mi amore*. Do not tell them our news yet." Standing from his chair, he put his finger to her lips, then leaned down and kissed her softly. "Have Gi break out a good dozen bottles of Midnight, glasses as well. I want Theresa and Reynaldo here, Angelo too. I will let Marcello know to have the warriors who are off duty to come in. Some are on duty and need to remain so."

He pulled her to his chest. "*Ti amo, mi amore*. My heart can't take all this happiness. I am not used to being happy and fulfilled. It feels good to love and be loved. Our *figlio*, he is inside you."

Kate allowed herself to be gathered up in his arms, held tight against his chest. As she felt what he felt, it made her heart overflow. This time, it would be perfect. "Our son."

She slipped from his grasp and went in search of the staff, finding Reynaldo in the kitchen. "Reynaldo, could you join us for a family meeting in the living room, please? Do you know where Gi is?"

Reynaldo looked up. *A family meeting?* They'd never had a family meeting before. "My lady, I believe he went to the wine cellar."

"Perfect," she responded. Kate headed to the stairs and called down to him, asking him to bring up as many bottles of Midnight as he could carry. She found Theresa upstairs doing laundry and asked that she join them all in the living room. Once the staff was gathered, Kate paced. "You'll have to wait for Shade. He's gathering the warriors."

Shade quickly got Marcello to gather Raven, Cory, Skelk, Fiamma, and some of the other warriors who were not on duty. Angelo joined them from the stables. Hyde was out with Rissa, but he'd hear the news soon enough. As they all came into the house, there was a lot of noise and chatter, and he found Gi confused but opening bottles of Midnight.

"No drinks until we all gather, Gi. Need to find my woman."

Shade knew exactly where she was and found her in the bedroom, changing her clothes. "My queen, your subjects have gathered downstairs, we must make our appearance. Luca and Shannon should soon be here. Damn, I am a bit nervous."

"There's no reason to be nervous. This baby is eager to be here. I feel him more strongly every day. He says he's Medici warrior and he has much to do." Kate laughed. "Come with me downstairs. I think I can hear Shannon's laughter. I'd recognize that laugh anywhere."

Taking her hand, they went down the stairs together, confronting the throng of people. The nervous chatter was deafening, but as they entered the room everyone stopped and turned to them. Shade could tell everyone was anxious, calling them all to the house was unusual and he only hoped this was the first of many gatherings of this nature.

"Quiet down please. Gi, will you please pass out the glasses of Midnight? Everyone make sure you have a glass. Kate and I have an announcement to make."

Theresa made eye contact with Kate, and her eyes got as big as saucers, figuring out what this announcement was all about. Gi was pouring wine in everyone's glass, and Theresa jumped in and started helping him, knowing her master wouldn't speak until every glass was full.

Shannon looked to Luca, who just shrugged and said in a soft whisper, "You can be sure he's not about to toast her driving skills." Shannon gave him a quizzical look and Luca chuckled. As all the glasses were filled, every face in the room turned back to them.

Shade stood proudly among his family. "I know you are quite puzzled as to why I have called this meeting inside the main house. But this is where those I love are most welcomed. I want our home to be open to everyone. It is where love abounds and where we welcome new members to the fold. Tonight, I share with you the newest member to our *familia*... our son. Your queen will bring into the world the heir to Medici. Raise your glasses in a toast to our queen, my son, and Medici!"

As everyone cheered, they raised their glasses and drank, and then the chaos of noise truly began.

Shannon broke away from Luca and ran to Kate, wrapping her in a bear hug. "Are you kidding me? That didn't take long. I'm so happy for you!"

Kate laughed with her as she saw Theresa across the room beaming at her. They both knew this was a baby they would hold in their arms. The warriors surrounded Shade, slapping him on the back, fist bumping, chest bumping and Kate giggled. All that male energy and pride, like making babies was somehow as manly as fighting battles. She saw Cory standing quietly off to the side, drinking the Midnight, and watching the celebration, a melancholy look on his face. As the crowd broke up and the warriors sought out more Midnight, Cory slowly approached Shade. "Congratulations, master."

"Thank you, Cory. It is great pride I hold for my coming son. He will be my legacy. Medici has waited a long time for an heir. It only makes our coven stronger. Drink up!"

Cory took a small sip of the Midnight. "I can see your pride, master. It just makes me wonder about my own father. I never knew him, and he never even knew about me. Never knew I existed. I often wonder if he'd have been proud of me. I know my mother wasn't happy, and I didn't make things any easier. I'm sorry. This isn't the time to bring up such things. This is a celebration. I've just never been in a family before, where there was a new baby."

Shade put his arm around Cory's shoulder. "This is the perfect time to bring it up. Do you see all the male warriors in this room? All of them, I call my brothers. I have known most of them since they were about ten years of age. I don't know what your father would have thought of you, Cory. It may have made a huge difference in your life, had you known, depending on the vampire. But beyond all of that, there is something you truly need to know, you are part of my family now. You are like a son to me. I am proud of you, your accomplishments. You gave me a one-hundred and ten percent turn around in your behavior. It shows me you wanted to make your life better. Being in a family means you support, love, and cherish each other in good and bad times. That is what Medici is all about. A new *bambino* means we have more to love and cherish and care about. Just like when you came to my family. Never feel that you cannot come to me. I am here, always. Anything you need or want, or just to talk to me. I am available, not unapproachable. This is different than the life you knew, it is hard work, but we love just as hard. Have you contacted your mother to tell her you are back in the States?"

Kate listened to him as he spoke to Cory and she turned her head away to hide the tears. This man worried about being a father? She wiped the tears away as Cory told him no, he hadn't told his mom he was back yet. Cory looked at Shade with such devotion, just like his warriors.

"I'd planned to tell her I was back, but everything happened so fast, and I was busy getting my new shop set up. I was wondering if it would be okay with you, if I invited her to Virginia for a visit. She doesn't have to come if it's not convenient."

"Of course, you can invite her. I see no reason not to. Listen, here is what we will do. Talk to your mother and arrange when it is best for her to come for a visit. She can reside here in the main house as our guest. I will pay for her airfare."

Shade held up his hand as he saw Cory ready to protest. "No argument. You don't have to tell her where the funds came from, Cory, it's paid for. That's all she needs to know. I will make the arrangements for flight once we get a date settled. She will have to fly into Charlottesville via commuter from D.C. So that leaves us with one problem. I will need you to pick her up. Someone mentioned to me a bit earlier about a truck. Tomorrow night, you and Marcello go into Charlottesville, pick out whatever new truck you want, it's done. Drive it the hell back here, it's yours. That way you can pick up your mother from the airport and bring her to Bel Rosso. *Cazzo!* Do you know how to drive? Tell me you do!"

Cory laughed. "Oh yeah, I know how to drive. I never owned my own vehicle before, though." He gave Shade a surreptitious hug, feeling embarrassed at the display of affection.

Shade grinned at him. Cory had led a miserable life and now, he had some goals, a purpose, and someplace he belonged. "You earned it. Now go get some more Midnight. Hell, let's both get some more!"

33

Hyde arrived early at the Canton residence. The morning air was cool, for this time of year, in D.C. as they moved into early summer. Adjusting his sports jacket, he wore a simple pair of khakis and a dress shirt. His attire would take him through her schedule for the day and he could change easily enough, if needed, before an evening event. But so far, her schedule reflected no formal events for tonight. With Rissa, he was never sure what she might throw at him at the last minute. After the encounter with Canton last night, he expected her to be a bit tamer.

Hyde worried for her, with her unprovoked antagonism toward her own master. Canton had started out civil enough, simply stating the facts and reinforcing his expectations in a calm voice. Hyde had seen other master's react much worse when their mate got out of line. Their vampire culture was a male dominated world. Females, unless they were warrior born, were subservient to the male. Rissa had a great deal of leeway in her immortal life, living as a mortal, if she only understood that.

As Santos opened the door, Hyde walked into the foyer and stood waiting for his charge. "Please inform Rissa I'm here."

Santos nodded and headed up the stairs to inform Rissa of Hyde's arrival. Hyde noticed that Canton had already left the house, his schedule on the Hill an early one today, whereas Rissa's clientele didn't get their asses out of bed until late morning.

Rissa touched up her lipstick and was grabbing her sweater when Santos announced Hyde's arrival from outside her door. "He can wait. I'll be there soon enough, Santos."

She took one last glance at herself in the full-length mirror and was satisfied she looked one hundred percent professional. She grabbed her large purse and briefcase and headed down the stairs. She took note of Hyde's attire, dressed for success. He looked handsome and nodded his good morning to her. "Good morning, Hyde. Thank you for being on time and for waiting."

She handed him the keys, purse, and briefcase as she smiled at him. "You can drive. I think the schedule I provided was thorough enough that you know when and where we're expected to be."

Hyde took note of her demure behavior and that set off a few warning bells in his head. He knew Canton dressed her down and knocked the chip off her shoulder last night, but he didn't expect it to last too long. Opening the front door for her, he held out his hand. "Your carriage waits." He almost laughed as she rolled her big blue eyes at him and flung that blonde head of hair.

"Of course, it does." Rissa laughed and walked to the car as he opened the passenger side door. Rissa shook her head, "Back seat, please. I have some phone calls to make while you drive. It'll be easier for me, not so distracting."

As he opened the rear door, she noticed he kept her on the right hand side of the car, so he could keep an eye on her in the rearview mirror. How convenient, and Rissa liked the idea of having eye contact with him. It would give her a chance to tantalize him without looking as if she was doing so. She may have to heed Alec's warnings, but she was who she was, and she rather enjoyed flirting with him.

As they took off toward downtown, Rissa pulled out her phone and checked her email. Shade had informed her that the horses had arrived, and she could come meet her new friend any time she chose. She looked at her calendar and decided tomorrow evening's schedule would be easy to rearrange. This was a great way to start her morning! She looked up at Hyde and caught his eye. "Need to change my schedule for tomorrow evening. Seems as though my horse has arrived in White Hall. I'll need you to take me there if Alec can't escort me."

Hyde nodded as he maneuvered his way through traffic. "You'll be fine at Bel Rosso. Nothing will bother you there. As Alec said, safest place to be, but I'll escort you there and back, if Alec can't be there. Those are Alec's orders."

Rissa sighed and put her phone down, looking at him in the mirror. "He made that perfectly clear."

"Rissa, I know my job. I'll take care of you and make sure nothing happens. So, relax, listen to what he tells you. You seem to enjoy provoking him, and that's not a good thing. He wasn't commanding, just making his point clear. I've seen many masters relating to their mates, Alec was simply warning you his way. Don't be so negative. He gives you a wonderful life, you have your own business, and you basically do as you please. That's very rare."

Rissa huffed from the back seat. "Hyde, to be blunt, it's none of your business how we interact. Alec and I have an understanding."

Rissa stared out the window, not seeing anything, but she was remembering how she felt last night after Hyde left, facing Alec's rage.

"I sometimes take his words wrong. We're so busy, we never have time together. I know he loves me. As I love him. So, I'm listening now, doing what he expects, being the good little fiancé of Senator Canton. This wedding has to be perfect. It will be seen worldwide. My gown is coming in next week. If he doesn't approve, I have to start all over and I'm running out of time. I never seem to be able to please him." Her voice had dropped to a low and needy whisper.

Hyde looked back at her in the rearview mirror. "Then let's start over. I'm not the enemy. Let's work together and get you through all of your plans, without an episode. Take advantage of the horse and make it work for you. He gave it to you for relaxation and exercise, use it for that. I'll make you a deal. Once you get your horse settled, and you get used to each other, I'll ride with you sometimes."

Looking in the mirror, he saw her staring at him and he waited for some smart ass angry remark. But to his surprise, she smiled back at him. He nodded when she agreed. Maybe, with the right approach, Rissa could control some of the anger that ate away at her. Hyde knew that was all it was. She was lonely and insecure, and all the attention in the world would never make that go away. She was living proof of that. He knew one thing, no matter what happened, he'd never trust her. Pulling into the parking garage of her first appointment, he hoped their first full day was episode free.

34

"*Mi Amore*?" Shade called out to her as he walked in the door. The camp was ready to roll, but he and *bel* had company coming tonight, and he wanted to make sure she knew to expect their arrival. The horses had finally arrived from Florence and Rissa and Alec were expected within the hour to see Rissa's newest play toy. "*Bel!*"

Kate heard him call as she was pulling on a pair of jeans, stepped into her sandals and ran down the stairs. "Right here. What's going on?"

"Come, woman!" Shade held his arms open wide and watched as her smile lit up the room. She leapt up and straddled him, wrapping her legs around his waist, her arms tight around his neck. He kissed her deep and long, lingering after breaking the kiss, his mouth close to hers, his breath warm against her lips. "I needed that, my red-headed minx. Did you miss me? Lie if you have to, *mi amore.*"

Kate laughed. "I don't need to lie, I always miss you. Did you need me for something?"

"*Si*. The horses I had shipped over from Florence, including a palomino named Biondo, have arrived. He is to be Rissa's horse. They are on their way here now, to see the horse. I was hoping you would come with me to meet them."

"Well, if we're going to the stables, let me pull on a pair of boots." Kate released her hold on him and dropped to the floor, running upstairs for boots. "I can't wait to see the new horses. I guess I have to prepare myself for the fact Rissa will be coming here to ride."

Shade yelled after her as she ran up the stairs. "*Si*, but I do not expect you will see her, she will teleport in, most likely during the day. Nothing to worry about."

Shade was about to grab a quick Midnight when he heard Aegis howling. *Cazzo*! "They must be here. *Bel*, call off your warriors! Company is here."

Kate kicked off her sandals and pulled on a pair of western-style boots and headed back down the stairs. She could hear the less than pleasant greeting her welcoming committee was giving to their guests. She headed outside to see Alec standing by his car, and Rissa still inside. Aegis and Night Stalker were both poised at the passenger side door. Kate realized the animals had recognized Alec from his previous visit, but Rissa was a new intruder to them. As Kate walked outside, she clapped her hands and called to them. The wolves both turned their attention to her and immediately moved in her direction.

Alec looked at Kate with a frown. "I completely forgot about them. Is this going to be standard?"

Kate reassured him, "I don't think so. They weren't interested in you. They only seemed interested in Rissa. Once they meet her and understand she's not an enemy, it should be fine."

Rissa had been sitting immobilized in her seat as the two huge wolves circled their car with their teeth bared and growling at her through the car window. As the wolves retreated, she rolled down the window a crack. "Is it safe? Those animals look ferocious!"

Alec chuckled as he walked to the passenger side door and opened it. "Don't worry, darling. They cornered me on my first visit." He reached in. "Come on, take my hand, get out and let them get your scent."

Rissa looked at Alec with irritation. "My scent? I cannot possibly come riding here and go through this every time I want to ride." Taking Alec's hand, Rissa emerged from the car and stood perfectly still as the wolves paced at Kate's feet. She looked at Kate with astonishment. "Seriously, Kate, wild dogs? Are they your pets?" Rissa saw Shade as he strolled outside with a smirk lighting up his face.

Shade made his way to *bel*, his arms going around her waist. Cocking his head, he grinned at Rissa. "*Buonasera*. Problem, Rissa?"

Kate laughed as she snuggled into Shade. "I guess you could call them my pets. They've adopted me, I think. You'll be fine. They're very leery of newcomers, but once they understand you're no threat to us, they'll pretty much ignore you. You may not even see them the next time you come. You're safe here. Don't worry."

Rissa eyes never left the four legged beasts as they finally calmed and sat next to Kate. "Let's hope I never see them again." Directing her attention toward Shade, she inquired, "Can we please go see my horse? And thank you for Hyde. He does a wonderful job. We get along quite well."

Shade took Kate's hand and started to walk in the direction of the stables. "I am most glad to oblige you, Rissa. Hyde is one of my best. Now, shall we go to the stables? The horses arrived yesterday morning, the stable master, Angelo, got them settled in. Biondo made the trip fine, and I wanted the horses to have a good day and night to adjust before letting you come out. Angelo will attend to all your needs, he will take care of your tack and so forth, make sure Biondo is groomed and gets exercised on days you are not here. If you have any special requests, please take them up with Angelo. He will oblige you and he knows all of the horses quite well. The stables are open to you twenty-four seven. Angelo is a day-walker, so anytime you wish to ride, feel free to come out to Bel Rosso and enjoy our home." Shade wrapped his arm around *bel* as the four of them strolled casually to the stables.

Rissa still felt a bit on edge as she kept a tight grip on Alec's hand. Walking to the stables, she felt her excitement building. A horse of her own! The night was made even more exciting because Alec was with her, sharing time with her, and that made the evening perfect in her eyes.

Kate saw the raven circling in the sky above them, the raven that followed them home from Florence. He circled lower and lower and appeared agitated. Clearly, he could see she wasn't at risk. Before she could speak to him, he swooped down, diving at Rissa's head and grabbed a beak full of hair, ripping it free. Rissa screamed as she swung her hands wildly in the air, shooing the bird away.

"That fucking bird pulled out my hair!"

Kate yelled at him, "Poe! Stop it!"

The raven flew to Kate, the strand of long blonde hair held proudly in his beak. He dropped it at Kate's feet and settled on Shade's shoulder, before issuing a loud, "Caw, caw!"

"Rissa, I'm so sorry! This one is new. I had no idea." Kate looked at Poe who sat non-nonchalantly on Shade's shoulder, cocking his head as if to say, 'What's the big deal?' Kate telepathically sent him a scolding and told him to behave. He blinked his eyes a few times before flying off.

Rissa screeched, "Look at my hair! I have a wedding coming up. This will be a nightmare to fix. What in the hell is going on out here? It's like a damn episode of Wild Kingdom!" Rissa turned to Alec and glared.

Alec ran his hands through her hair, aware that Rissa had no knowledge of this rare gift. "Calm down, my darling. It's hardly noticeable. Kate has a rare gift, and she is still learning to master it. She'll be able to speak to animals. I'm sure the bird was just checking you out."

"Rissa, our apologies." Shade chuckled and shook his head. "You will have to forgive Poe. He is a new member to Kate's warriors. The wolves will be around, but they have been warned about getting too close to the stables. Perhaps, Kate can have a word with the raven as well. Come, let us go inside the stables before something else happens." Shade looked down at *bel* and grinned. **"I think I love that bad ass bird of yours!"**

Rissa took a deep breath and calmed herself. She talked to the animals? What was she now, some kind of Dr. Damn Do-little? "I'm trying to be calm. I just wasn't prepared, please, can we get inside? I just want to see my horse before something else crawls out, swoops down, or jumps me."

As they entered the stables, Angelo approached and Shade made the introductions. "Angelo, this is Larissa, Master Canton's mate. She will be riding Biondo as we have discussed."

Turning to Rissa, Shade introduced his stable master, "Rissa, this is Angelo, my stable master."

As Rissa and Angelo shook hands, Shade requested Angelo bring out the new horse.

Rissa was impressed with the stables. She'd visited the stables of many of the wealthy polo set, and this one would stand up to any she'd seen. Her eyes wandered to the many horses inside their stalls. "This is beautiful! I'm so impressed. I love it here."

Suddenly, there was a great ruckus inside one of the stables, as a large black stallion started snorting and kicking at the stable doors and Rissa hoped that wasn't her horse.

Shade raised his voice, "Impavido! Settle! That is my horse, the black stallion. He does not like females, unfortunately. Well, except for one." Leaning down, he kissed *bel*. "Could you please go over there and settle him, because he will not calm down until you go to him." Shade looked up at Alec. "Kate seems to have a way with him. Every time she comes in here, he is not satisfied until she visits him. Damn horse has betrayed me." Shade threw back his head and laughed.

Kate stepped up on the gate of Impavido's stall, reaching up to stroke his muzzle, leaning her forehead against his. "Easy, boy. We just have company. You settle down now." She stroked his long neck as he chuffed at her. Kate stepped back off the gate and joined Shade. "He's fine, lover."

Shade smiled at her. "See what I mean? *Grazie, mi amore*. Ah, here comes Angelo with Biondo." Shade watched as Biondo calmly walked in their direction, with Angelo guiding her by a lead rope. He waited for Rissa's reaction.

Rissa was entranced as she saw the most beautiful palomino she'd ever laid eyes on. She walked with elegance. Her mane was a beautiful blonde against the horses buff colored coat, which had been brushed to a high sheen. The horse swung her long blonde tail as if she knew she was commanding everyone's attention and Rissa gasped. This was hers! Her hand came to her mouth. "She's so...beautiful."

Shade was pleased with her reaction. He could see she was impressed with the animal and he knew there had to be a special bond between the rider and their horse. "Rissa, meet Biondo. She is straight from Florence, ready to ride. She is broken in, but she still has a great spirit. Come, say hello. She is yours now."

Rissa never took her eyes from the horse, her hand clutched to her chest as she smiled and slowly walked to Biondo. She extended her hand as Biondo nuzzled and sniffed her palm and then lifted her head up and down. Rissa slid her hand through the horse's gorgeous golden mane, the hair coarse but silky soft. Rissa continued running her hand along the horse's side as she walked all the way around her horse. Her beauty was astounding, and her spirit was gentle, yet Rissa could feel a fire inside her. Walking back around to face Biondo, Rissa nuzzled into her neck and heard a softy whinny. Rissa never took her hands from Biondo, always petting and reassuring her. "Biondo. You're such a beautiful girl." Scratching gently behind her ears, Rissa looked into the horse's golden brown eyes and there was an instant connection. Peeping around Biondo, she made eye contact with Alec. "I love her, Alec."

Alec stood with his arms crossed over his chest as he watched her circle the horse. "I can see that, my darling. I think Biondo is an excellent choice for you. You'll enjoy riding, I think."

Rissa smiled at Alec and had never felt so happy over a gift before. She quickly went to him and hugged him tightly, kissing him softly on the lips. "Alec, thank you so much. She's so beautiful. I can't wait to ride her!"

Before he could respond, Rissa returned to Biondo and fawned over her when, suddenly, there was a loud crashing and banging noise from another horse, which caused all of the horses to become riled. Biondo threw her head up and down, and Rissa moved out of the way just as Biondo reared up on her hind legs.

Kate felt the flow of fear as it ran through the new horses, skittish in their new surroundings. Angelo had stepped away to let Rissa bond with the horse, and now, there was no one attending her as Biondo was rearing up on her hind legs. Kate approached and held up her hand, speaking softly to her and the horse settled down, lowered her head for Kate to calm and comfort her. Kate called out to the other horses in their stalls and they all settled.

Kate turned to Shade. "That dark brown one got spooked, and the others just fed off of his fear. They're all fine now. She's fine, Rissa. They're all just getting used to their new environment."

Shade wrapped his arms around Kate's waist, nuzzling into her neck and kissing her softly. "*Grazie, mi amore.* I have a new stallion, he is not yet broken in. He was a bit much to get over here, and Angelo will need to break him in. I may need your gift to help him, *si*?"

Looking up at Rissa, Shade saw her jealousy and he was confused as to why. "Rissa, are you all right? Biondo is not normally like this, she is a calm spirit, but as Kate said, new environment and a riled horse can stir them easily."

Rissa stared at Kate. The bitch had this power over animals now? She had every damn thing in the world, all of Tuscany and queen too, and now she had to rule over the one thing Rissa loved, her horse! She watched as Shade moved with her, like a dance, they fit together like puzzle pieces, as he nuzzled and touched and kissed her constantly. They were so at ease with each other. *Bitch!* Alec never responded to her affections. He just commented that he thought she'd enjoy riding. She'd rather be riding him!

Rissa smiled softly at Shade, not wanting him to have a glimpse of her thoughts. "I'm fine, thank you. I've been around horses enough to know their signs. It's why I stepped away. I wasn't sure what Biondo would do." Nuzzling into Biondo's neck, Rissa whispered to her softly. "It's okay, girl, everything's fine, just you and me."

Kate stepped back from the horse, still holding Shade's hand. She knew Rissa and Biondo needed to bond, so the horse would respond well to her.

Angelo returned, apologizing profusely. "I'm so sorry, my lady, master. The horses were calm when I stepped away. I would not have left them had I thought they were still so restless. Larissa, do you want to ride her? I can get a saddle and bridle on her if you want."

Shade slapped Angelo on the back. "No problem, Angelo. Rissa, take Biondo for a ride around the main field here. Alec looks like he could use a Midnight, anyway. Join us inside, brother."

Rissa's eyes lit up, she wasn't expecting to ride tonight, but she was excited to get in the saddle and get a feel for Biondo.

"Oh, thank you, Angelo. I have my saddle, bridle, and tack gear on order. They're being handmade for me. Do you have a saddle I can use?" Rissa looked to Alec, biting her lip. "Please, Alec, can I ride her, just for a while?"

Alec looked at his watch. He hadn't planned on staying long. He still had some work to do at home, and they had driven here. "I still have some work to finish... "

Shade slid his hand through *bel's* crimson silk and looked at Rissa as her face dropped. Cocking his head to the side, he spoke to Alec in a nonchalant tone. "You know, brother, happy mate, damn happy master. Let her ride. If you had teleported your ass here, you would not have this dilemma. Let her ride."

Alec sighed. "Fine. You better have some Midnight waiting for me in that house, brother. Take a short ride, darling. Be careful. The horse is still skittish." Alec slid his arm around her shoulder and kissed her forehead. "Just come up to the house when you're done."

Hugging him around the neck, she was ecstatic. "Thank you, Alec, thank you. I promise I won't be long. Angelo, please can you saddle and bridle her? I would love to get the feel of her." Rissa walked off with Angelo, jabbering away about horses as he led Biondo off to be saddled.

"Smart move, I think she likes Biondo." Slapping Alec on the back, Shade laughed then swatted *bel* on the ass. "Come along, minx, let us get inside and have a glass of Midnight."

Alec allowed himself to be lead back to the house, as the scent of horses and hay hung heavy in the air. He really didn't understand what the attraction to horses was, but to each his own. "Lead the way, brother. I could use a drink. How's your camp coming along?"

Shade walked back toward the main house with Kate in tow. "Open call is in two days. I'm keeping things closed down tight while we pick and choose who will stay. The ones we cut will be personally escorted out of here. I am hoping to come up with twenty-five or more new recruits, just depends what shows up, brother. Could be less until word really gets around." As they walked inside, Gi arrived quickly and poured out Midnight for everyone.

Kate held out her hand as Gi poured. "Not too much for me, please. Just a sip. I'll have to stop soon, anyway."

Shade smiled down at her and kissed her softly. "*Mi amore*, it is okay to have a sip or two, no harm done, trust me. Alec, I am proud to announce that Kate is carrying the heir to the Medici legacy, our son, Lorenzo. We have just come back from Florence and meeting with Council to record her gifts and inform Council she carries my son."

Alec was a little surprised at how quickly this had taken place, but he knew Shade's need to have a son to secure his legacy was huge. Alec took the glass offered by Gi and raised it to the couple.

"Well, then, it sounds like congratulations are in order. I'm sure the Council was pleased to know they finally have an heir lined up for your coven."

Shade raised his glass in a toast. "*Grazie*, brother. We are more than happy. And Council was well pleased. They were quite taken with Kate's gift as well. The animalism can be used as a powerful weapon, but I asked the Council to keep it quiet for now. She will be a target to my enemies if they know of this gift. She is also a day-walker. Council has never, in history, recorded a vampire with two gifts. They were not much help in providing me information on her gift of animalism. They said they had not seen it in over three thousand years, and there was no vampire alive today with this gift. So, it will be a day by day learning experience for us both." Picking Kate up, Shade spun her around and kissed her soundly. "The *madre* to my coven, my *bambinos*, and the queen of my heart! What else could a master ask for?"

Alec's face turned red as he was embarrassed by the open display of affection. This wasn't the Shade he knew. This wasn't the Shade he'd spent night after night with in the chamber deep below Castello.

"Two gifts? I've never heard of two gifts before... for anyone. I doubt Rissa will ask questions about it. I can say Kate is a day-walker, but I doubt she's ever heard of animalism. If she asks further questions, I can deflect them and just say Kate can communicate with the animals. I'll keep your secret, brother."

"*Grazie.* Maybe you should think about *bambinos* yourself. You don't have anyone to continue your legacy either."

Alec laughed. "A horse I can deal with, but no babies, thank you. And I can't imagine Rissa with a baby unless it becomes the new designer accessory. I'd have to arrange a feeder for my... appetites. No, I don't think that would work. But I'm happy for you, if this is what you want."

Shade chuckled as he filled their glasses again. "No doubt I want this, Alec. I knew my future would include bambinos, I just never imagined it would play out like this. I never thought a mortal would entice me, but here we are."

As the conversation continued, they discussed business, the camp, and the Dead House. A good hour passed before the back door burst open and Rissa ran in, straight to Alec and hugged him like he was her lifeline. Shade chuckled as Alec was obviously uncomfortable with her display of affection.

Rissa was giddy with excitement. "Oh, Alec, I love her so much! She's beautiful and incredibly strong. She's perfect for me. Thank you! Thank you!"

Alec accepted Rissa's enthusiastic response. "I had no idea the horse would make you this happy, my darling. But it's getting late, and we still have a two-hour drive ahead of us. It'll be much easier when you teleport out. Are you ready?"

Rissa pouted. "Yes, but I hate leaving her." She turned to Shade and smiled, giving him a hug. "Thank you so much, she's perfect."

Shade was startled by the hug. "You are most welcome, Rissa. I hope she brings you a lot of pleasure. I will be in contact, brother. We still have a contract to work out as well."

Returning to Alec, she was all smiles and kissed him softly on the cheek. "We should be going, you still have work to do and I have to arrange my schedule for some riding time."

Alec nodded as he led Rissa to the door, "I hope you have time to consider my proposal. I look forward to hearing from you." As they exited the front door and walked to the car, Alec noticed the two wolves stayed hidden in the woods near the rail fence. It was clear to him they'd guard this property even against those visitors that were known to the family. Clearly, no one was getting past this security again. He opened the door for Rissa and she slid into the car.

As Rissa and Alec took leave, Shade stood and looked at *bel*. He said nothing for a long time and then crossed his arms over his chest and cocked his head to the side. "I think I witnessed two fucking miracles tonight. Alec actually showing a bit of affection to Rissa, and Rissa was happy. When the hell does that ever happen?" Throwing back his head laughing, he took *bel* by the hand and led her up the stairs. "I think it is time to have my queen lie down and rest a bit, *si*?"

Kate gladly complied, feeling tired after Rissa's visit. "*Si*."

35

Shade sent Raven and his brigade of warriors to the Dead House to patrol D.C. Hyde was on his own schedule with Rissa, and now it was time to get down to business with the new recruits coming into the camp. Shade strolled down to the camp to find it filled with warrior wannabes of all shapes and sizes. Marcello and Fiamma got the new recruits settled into the barracks, doubling up where necessary until the rounds of downsizing began. Shade had no need to identify himself as he walked through the camp wearing head to toe leathers. He was the Medici; he was known worldwide and recognized instantly. He strolled among the hopefuls, keeping his eyes and ears tuned to their conversations.

Once everyone was signed in and had their gear safely inside, Shade took the list from Marcello and read through it. He was a bit disappointed there were only a little over fifty warriors trying to get into the camp, but he knew this was their first attempt at reaching out in the States, and once they began, word would spread quickly. Shade planned to hold this open enrollment every year in the spring, and he knew the demand would grow with time. He was impressed with the number of females who had responded. He wasn't sure if this was a good thing or bad thing, considering *bel* would be happy if she never saw another female warrior, but she needed to get used to it. Female warriors were a part of this new age and their numbers were rising. He'd give the females no slack because of their sex or size, warriors were warriors to him. They must all pass the same test and meet the same requirements.

Marcello's list included details on each warrior's background, including their gifts, marking a star by every warrior with the gift of day-walking. It was vital in today's environment to have as many day-walkers as possible. They were needed within the ranks to provide the twenty-four hour protection to the masters, and a warrior who was a day-walker was lethal against a vampire who could only rise at night, as Shade well knew. He liked knowing the smallest of details about each recruit. These details could be valuable if he was on the fence about who made the cut. The recruit's gift could sway the decision to keep him or cut him loose. Shade memorized at a glance as much as he could about each recruit and then had them all gather outside on the training field.

Shade raised his hand in the air and everyone settled down. Marcello and Fiamma flanked his sides, and the rest of his Medici warriors lined up behind him as the new recruits stood before him. It felt good to be back at what he did best, training Medici warriors for the future.

"Listen up! I am Master Shade Medici. Welcome to the most elite, most strenuous warrior camp in the world. You have already met Marcello, my Second-In-Command and Fiamma, my Lieutenant. I expect your full cooperation. If you are given a direct order by anyone standing in front of you, I suggest your ass finds a way to make it happen. That is how I roll, no excuses. I tolerate no bullshit from anyone, not even those flanking my side. If you cannot deal with that, I suggest you leave right now and one of my warriors will promptly escort you out of here."

Shade paused to give them time to absorb his message, his eyes roamed across the crowd of would-be hopefuls and he noticed something odd. Most of the females had red hair. *What in the fucking hell?* Two male recruits stepped forward and Shade could already smell the attitude dripping off them. He nodded to Marcello who directed two Medici warriors to remove them from the property and make sure they were escorted far away.

Shade shouted out to the throng of recruits before him. "You have each been given a packet of instructions, schedules for the next two nights. We will easily be eliminating a third of you after tomorrow night's exercises. So, look to your left, look to your right, one of you is not going to make it. Sleep and rest when you can, we will provide feeders for you tomorrow, the schedule is inside the packet. The females will be separated from the males. Anything goes on that is disrespectful, you are gone. My brother and sisterhood are tight, we work as a team. This is about survival, protection, honor, and respect. We live by a strict code as warriors, you will learn it soon enough. If there are any serious injuries, Marcello and Fee will inform me, and we will deal with it as they come. And they will come. This is about showing me, and my warriors, you belong within our ranks. I suggest you give me one hundred percent, because I tolerate nothing less. Some of the tasks we will ask of you may seem simple, but I have done this a very long time, and I know exactly what I am looking for.

"For those of you who make it, the intense hard work is just beginning. Everyone here is vying for a position. All of you are freelance, so I expect loyalty and dedication to Medici if you are chosen. You must be willing to take the blood oath, bonding you to my coven. I will be watching and will be informed about each of you and your progress over the next few nights, so I suggest you give it all you have, because if you are not serious, this is no place for you.

"Marcello will be taking charge of the males, and all females will report to Fee, but you will work with both of them throughout your training. Remember one thing, all warriors ultimately report to me." Shade turned to Marcello. "Go for it. Show me you can be my SIC!"

Shade walked over to the stone wall that surrounded the camp and watched as Marcello and Fee went to work. Fiamma took a third of the group and began working with them on their sword skills. Shade was impressed when Skelk took another third and began working on their skills with a bow and arrow. Marcello stepped it up and led the rest in shuriken skills. Shade stood back and watched closely, making mental notes of each recruit, their skills, and their level of expertise with each weapon. He strolled among the groups and was impressed with his own warriors and their teaching skills. They'd not only learned how to be excellent warriors, but how to lead as well.

Shade made his way around to Skelk's group and watched for a while. A young female with flaming red hair was demonstrating some good skills with her bow, but her stance was not correct. He watched her closely and her body was well defined, muscular yet feminine, clad in form fitting leather. Her aim would be dead on if she could fix her stance. Skelk approached her and Shade intervened.

"I got this, Skelk. Continue on."

Shade eyed her. "Name?" He watched as her big brown eyes rolled up to his and she wasn't intimated by him as she answered, "Britt."

"Well, Britt, first of all, you need to fix your stance. It is throwing off your aim. I think you can hit that target dead on if you fix it. Let me show you what I mean."

As she smiled and nodded, Shade stepped behind her and put his hands on her waist and straightened her hips. He put his feet inside hers and used his heavy boots to move her feet further apart. "Now see the target, imagine the arrow hitting it. Tighten your core, and do not move your core. Feel the difference?" Shade stepped back away from her. "Lift your bow without moving your core, pull back, aim and let it go."

She did exactly as he told her and let the arrow fly dead center to the target. She quickly turned and flashed him a huge smile.

"See what I mean, keep your core straight, concentrate on that arrow going right where you want it to go. You have good bow skills." He put his hand on her shoulder. "Keep practicing and remember what I told you."

Shade moved on to a male whose shot was dead-on time after time. His speed at shooting the arrows was great. "Hold! Load your bow. Now close your eyes. See your target in your mind. You have shot enough arrows to be able to see it in your mind's eye. Let me see what you can do with the target without seeing it. Show me."

Shade stood tall and crossed his arms over his chest. He could feel someone watching him. His eyes slid to Britt and he caught her staring at him. He chuckled to himself. *You will hate me in the next two nights if I have anything to do with it.*

Shade heard the arrow whistle from the male's bow and watched it hit the target almost dead on. "Again!"

The male repeated it over and over at Shade's command until the arrows hit dead center. "Perfect! Liking what I see here."

The male nodded and then Marcello gave a whistle and the groups changed weapon stations.

Shade spent most of the night walking among the recruits, giving tips and making mental notes of what he witnessed. There were already a few he could see with potential as Medici warriors. He let Marcello know he was heading back to the house and shared with him his observations. As Shade strolled back home, they still had a few hours before the sun would rise and the camp would settle down, all of the recruits housed inside the new barracks. His chest was puffed out and his boots dusty from the nights work, but it felt good to him. He had begun his journey to the future, and the expansion of his legacy to be passed on to his *bambinos.*

He admired the moon and cool night air as he looked out over the fields. *You are home, old man. You traveled the world, but this is where your happiness lies, where your heart is content.* His eyes strayed to the vineyards, and his fortune would grow even bigger here.

He remembered he had to give *bel* his decision about the California house, in turning it into an inn and having Reynaldo move there to oversee the operation. Shade had done some research on his own and found it was a popular location in California for the mortals to take wine tours. He'd decided to let her do this, even though he'd never opened any of his properties to mortals before. Kate had a gift for making every house look like a home, creating a sense of warmth and coziness, even in a grand space. He had no doubt the California house would make a popular tourist stop. Smiling, he headed into the house, knowing she was waiting for him to come home.

Kate could hear the new recruits in the camp, as the metallic sound of sword against sword carried across the night air. She smiled to herself, thinking this wouldn't take long to get used to. The sound was music to her ears because it meant he was here, and safe, and not on the streets. She wasn't expecting him to return until sunrise but felt him when he entered the house with still a few hours till daybreak. She had been researching information online about the Paris house, but realized she'd have to go there and get measurements and a feel for the floor plan in person before she could get much done. Putting the laptop aside, she stood to greet Shade as he entered their bedroom, wearing leathers and a layer of dust.

"Lover, I wasn't expecting you this early. How's it going out there?"

"Marcello and Fee have things well in hand. I won't always be home this early, *mi amore*. There will be nights I am there until the sun peeps over the horizon. Once we really get moving, I will be heavily involved. What are you up to?"

"I was trying to see if I could get started on the Paris house, but it's difficult trying to plan anything from the pictures online. I'll need to go there. Will you have time? Or should I plan something with Luca?"

Shade sat down in the chair by the window and began unlacing his boots. Pushing back his hair with his hand, he raised his head and looked at her.

"We need to talk about this, don't we? *Bel*, I don't expect you to keep to my death slumber schedule. You are a day-walker, so is Luca, so you can do things in the daylight. You do not have to keep to my schedule. I won't like it so damn much, but I know there are things you have to do in daylight hours. As for travel, you can take the private jet or teleport, but you go nowhere without Luca or myself. If you want to go to Paris, you can have Luca teleport with you. Do you feel comfortable with that? Because I am telling you now, traveling alone is not an option. You get much bigger carrying our son, teleporting is out totally. So, talk to me, *si*?"

"I wouldn't go anywhere without you or Luca. I wouldn't even think of it. And I can take the jet if you prefer. I know I have a small window here because of the pregnancy. That's why I was thinking I should get the Paris house done now. As for day-walking, while I'm in Paris, I'll go out during the day. But as long as I'm home with you, I'll always try to keep my schedule aligned with yours. I love sleeping next to you, and I have no plans to give that up. So, which do you prefer, you or Luca? Jet or teleporting. I'll do whichever you prefer."

Shade stopped what he was doing and sat back and looked at her. "*Bel*, are you asking my permission?"

"Of course. Well, not permission as much as your thoughts, your preference. I'm not going to go if you think it isn't wise, or if you feel strongly about accompanying me yourself, and this isn't a good time for you."

"Come sit with me, please."

Kate grinned as she climbed into his lap. He curled her into his chest and snuggled into her hair, inhaling her intoxicating scent. "*Mi amore*, I want you to make these judgment calls yourself. Just let me know where and when. I'm sorry I have no time right now to help with these things. I trust your choices. You took this place and made it a palace and I love how I feel at home here. I have no doubts you will do the same with the Paris home. Spend my money, will you? Get whatever you want or need. Luca can go with you. I trust him completely. I do thank you for asking me, but I do not want you to be bottled up here so much. That will come soon enough as you advance in your pregnancy. The *bambino* will tire you, *mi amore*. Understood, *si*?"

Kate laid her head on his shoulder. "I'll always ask, because I want to know what you think. I want your opinion before I decide. But I do feel rushed to get some things done before I get too far along in this pregnancy. You said my pregnancy is only six months, and I must be a month in, so that doesn't give us a lot of time. That means this baby will be born in late November or early December. Is there a doctor I should be seeing?"

Shade slid his hand across her tummy. *"Si*, we have a doctor who has served our *familia* for centuries. I wanted to contact him while in Florence, but things did not work out, time wise, for me. So, I have asked Gi to contact Dr. Bonutti. I did not contact him with your previous pregnancy because you were mortal, he works only with immortals. Now, I have no reservations about having him be our family doctor. He too is immortal. He is very good, *mi amore*, I trust him. He resides in Florence, but I wish for him to come here for his first visit with you, so we can both be relaxed. Gi will let me know when he can be here. It won't be long, trust me, he has always been loyal to Medici and he will respond as quickly as possible. This is our son, Medici heir, and Dr. Bonutti will understand the importance of that. Will you be all right with that, Kate?"

"Yes, I feel better that this doctor is someone you know and trust. This pregnancy feels completely different from the last. I'm not sick, and I feel strong, but still, we didn't have the best experience with the doctors Rissa referred us to, so I prefer this, actually. And while I have your attention, did you have time to think about the California house? I haven't spoken to Reynaldo, but he's had nothing to do since we've returned. I know it bothers him not to be of service when everyone around him is so busy."

Shade chuckled. "*Si*, I have done a little research, and I like this idea. I think it will be beneficial to all of us. But I have said nothing to Reynaldo." He slid her hair back from her face. "I want you to talk to him, make sure he wants to do this. The staff loves you, *bel*, and you have a way with them. Take charge of that. I want you to have things to do. I do not want you to feel bored just sitting around this house. I want you to thrive in our life. This is something you can oversee and manage that is completely separate from what I do. Just keep track of everything you spend, make sure you leave the receipts on my desk in the study. I will handle the accountants."

Kate kissed his neck, as she ran her hands through his long hair. "I'll be happy to talk with Reynaldo, and work with him to get things started there, if he's interested. So, I'll be busy then, with the Paris house and the California house. And I'll need to get Lorenzo's room ready. Just let me know your schedule, so I can work around anything you have planned. I want to be here when you're here, and work on these things while you're busy in the camp."

"*Si,* maybe we need a secretary." Picking her up, he laid her on the bed, sitting down beside her. "I love you. I know I ask much of you. If it becomes too much, you need to tell me. But I know you enjoy the houses and it seems to be your talent. Things are going to get hectic with me and the camp. We will have to make time to be together. Please sleep with me if you can, I do not rest as well if you do not. Asking you to give up the daylight kills me, but I am selfish when it comes to you and I want that time to be ours alone."

"You don't even have to ask. Our time is as special to me as it is to you. I'll always lie beside you, lover. When you come home, I want to be here waiting for you."

"Then lay with me now, make me forget what is outside and remind me what is in my heart. I want to lay here, go to my death slumber with you on my chest."

Kate helped him undress, removing the leathers, kissing his skin, and tasting the salt of his sweat. He returned the favor by helping her slip from her clothes as they climbed beneath the covers.

36

Raven sat at the command center of the Dead House. He was SIC now and he took this seriously. Master was letting him make some changes and he was sitting at the computer, rearranging the grid. The warriors were covering a lot of ground and he'd re-designed the grid to what he felt would provide a more efficient use of their time. His fingers were flying as he rearranged the grid, playing with different options, combining territories. Although all of D.C. was densely populated, some areas needed more attention than others. He wanted to make the warriors' more effective.

Flopping back in the leather chair, he was staring at the screen when he heard Theo come in behind him. Theo was a great warrior and he'd started his camp days in Florence a while before Raven, but he was still young, and he loved being on the streets. He never bothered anyone, but he was social enough and he was doing a lot to help Raven in the Dead House. Theo had come over in the original group with Raven and Marcello and he had no intentions of going back. Like Raven, he loved the freedom of living in the States, and their home at Bel Rosso.

Raven looked up at him. "Any luck with getting everyone acquainted with the area?"

Theo stepped up behind him and stared at the screen. "Raven, if you just combine grids seven and eight, then split section nine and add it to section ten, you'd solve half the overlap. Last night, we crossed over grid seven two damn times. So far, it's been easy enough to get the brothers familiar with the city. Nothing is happening out there. But I'm seeing some shady vampires. They're not causing any shit, but damn, we should just scatter their asses out of town, in my opinion."

Raven took the cigarette tucked behind his ear and lit it up. Theo flopped down in the chair opposite him. Raven shook his head in the negative. "If they're not rogue and not causing any problems, not a good idea to stir them up. Keep your eyes peeled and watch them. If they become a problem, then we can move. I think they're just coming into the clubs. I watched a few the other night, they didn't even hunt or feed."

Raven focused his eyes to the screen again. He took Theo's suggestion and let his fingers work the keys, liking what he saw. "I think that idea worked. Let's try it out tonight. A few changes though. I want you to be in the Kennedy Center grid, something going on there tonight, bro. Hyde tells me Miss fancy pants has a big event going down in grid four, so send your guys over there. I'm taking up grid ten. But I'll make my usual rounds of all the grids."

Theo stood up and laughed. "What the hell are you doing in ten, bro? That's one seedy part of town, just some odd clubs and nothing much to be concerned with." He lit up a smoke and looked at Raven with a grin on his face. "Something I should know about?"

Raven flipped back his long black hair. "Don't worry about what I'm doing, worry about what I tell you to do! I need to check on some things down there, no big deal, brother. Where did you get those leathers? Cory?"

"Hell yeah, brother can kick some ass when it comes to leather. I'm heading out. I need to get some weapons. I have *no* idea why there's nothing out there to fight. And what the hell is with the wolves at Bel Rosso? That black one looks mean as the devil!"

Raven grinned. "They belong to our queen, so I'd not be going around busting their asses or your head is going to end up on a silver platter. Boss-man said they're her warriors. She has the gift of talking to the animals. I never heard of it before, but there's nothing ordinary about my lady."

Raven shut down the computer and walked out with Theo. It was time to start the night and he was ready to head into grid ten and find a few specific night spots for his feeding. Nothing was going on, and he was going to check out a few clubs before making his rounds and making sure this town still belonged to Medici.

37

As the sun set, Kate felt Shade stir in the bed beside her. She waited for him to open his eyes and lock her in that gaze of ice blue. She raked her hand through his tangled curls, pushing his hair back from his face before kissing him. "Sleep well, lover?"

Shade gave her a squeeze and a knowing smile, memories of their love-making flooding his mind. "*Si*, quite well, *mi amore*."

He slipped from the bed and pulled on a pair of jeans and laced up his boots. "I will be busy in the camp all night tonight, reviewing the new recruits. We must decide quickly who will make the cut. Why don't you join me, *bel*?"

Kate watched him dress from the bed. "Actually, I wanted to talk to Reynaldo, and then I was planning to find Luca and have him take me to the Cali house. Have Reynaldo join us. Reynaldo has never seen the house, and we can talk about what we need to do to get things ready. I can be back before sunrise. But I'd love to stop in on the camp. I'll check in with you before I leave. Is that okay?"

"*Si*, that is fine. Just be sure you go nowhere without Luca and let me know when you leave." He leaned over the bed, placing his hands on the mattress on either side of her face, bending down to kiss her. He peered into her eyes, more amber now than brown. "*Ti amo*."

Kate was lost in his gaze as she responded, "I love you more." She watched his broad back as he left the room. She reluctantly left the warm comfort of their bed, took a hot shower, dressed, and went in search of Luca. She found him leaning in the doorjamb of the door onto the rear patio, wrapping up a conversation with Marcello. He turned when he heard her enter.

"Kate? Do you need me?"

Kate nodded at him. "As a matter of fact, I do. I want to talk to Reynaldo a bit and then, if all goes well, you could teleport me to the Cali house. Can you be ready in about thirty minutes?"

Luca nodded and said, "No problem," as Kate headed for the kitchen to find a bored Reynaldo. Kate slid onto the bar stool at the kitchen counter.

"Miss me?"

Reynaldo laughed. "I miss cooking for you, my lady."

Kate gave him a huge smile. "Well, I think I have a solution for that, if you're interested. We have this huge house in California, much bigger than this one, and it's just sitting there. Shade has agreed to let me turn it into a bed and breakfast, or a small inn. It has seven bedrooms that could be rented out. We want to keep our own bedroom locked and unavailable to guests, but all the rest of the house would be open. I originally designed a suite for Luca on the main floor, but given the circumstances, that could easily be your living quarters. If you're interested, I'd love for you to become our chef there. In the beginning, while we're getting started, you'd need to manage the inn. As the business grows, we could hire a full-time manager, so you can focus on cooking for the guests. I'll talk with Gi and see if there's a housemaid from Florence he can recommend, and we can have her transferred there as well. What do you think?"

Reynaldo was momentarily silent. He'd been wondering if he'd be sent back to Florence once my lady was turned, or even if he might be released from Medici. He hadn't cooked in Florence in years and was happy to have my lady to prepare meals for. But now there were no duties for him here and he had worried he'd be let go.

"My lady, that's the best news I've heard in centuries. I'd be delighted to work again as a chef, prepare meals for the guests. If I could suggest, if you are open to the idea, I'd love to make it an inn, and serve three meals a day, not just breakfast."

Kate smiled back at him. "I like the way you think. Yes, absolutely. I'd like to teleport out there today. With the pregnancy, Shade will put a stop to my traveling soon, so I'd like to get it started as soon as possible. Luca will teleport me and you could follow?"

Reynaldo nodded enthusiastically. "Yes, perfect, anytime you're ready!"

Kate slipped from the stool. "Okay then, just give me a few minutes to walk to the camp, let Shade know I'm leaving and when I get back, we'll leave."

Kate headed out the back door of the house and walked to the camp. There were warriors stationed at the gates who nodded at her and let her in. She walked past the barracks, which looked like a large Tuscan villa and past the bunker, disguised as a large garage, to the open training fields. The new recruits had been broken out into smaller groups, each practicing different skill sets, being trained and supervised by the warriors from Florence. She scanned the field but didn't see Shade. She did see Fiamma with her flaming red hair and red leathers to match, surrounded by about fifteen female recruits, and all except one of them with red hair. Kate stopped in her tracks and stared as the group of female warrior wannabes suddenly took notice of her. Fiamma looked over her shoulder at Kate, flashed a big smile, and said something to the females before walking in Kate's direction.

Kate greeted Fiamma with a warm hug as she kept glancing at the women, all tall, toned, and beautiful.

Fiamma returned her hug but could feel Kate's resistance to the women in the camp when she told her, "Before you blow a gasket, I can answer the question in your head."

Kate's eyes never left the group of women gathered in a tight circle on the field, all of them staring back at her. Fiamma laughed. "Not one natural redhead in the bunch. They heard about your speech at the coronation. All of the female warriors have heard it now. And those that want to be Medici want to be a part of that sisterhood of which you spoke and have dyed their hair to honor you."

Kate scrunched up her face. "To honor me?"

Fee nodded her head. "They want to have the skills of a Medici, and the reputation that goes with it. But most of all, they want respect as women. To be seen as equals to their brothers."

Kate looked at Fee. "You do see the irony of this, right?"

Fee laughed loudly as her laughter carried across the practice field. "It's not lost on me, sister."

Kate joined in her laughter, shaking her head. "Seriously? I'm now the Pied Piper of Redheads, drawing a parade of women, all of whom want to impress upon my mate they are worthy of staying here? This was really not what I had in mind!"

Fee smiled and took her hands. "You have nothing to worry about. Master only has eyes for you. Now come, meet them. You're the reason they're here."

Kate allowed Fee to lead her across the field where she stood before the women, all except one of the female recruits nodded their head to her in a bow, even though they were not yet Medici and she was not yet their queen. There was one who locked eyes with Kate, taking her measure, looking Kate over from head to toe.

Kate smiled at them. "Welcome to Bel Rosso. I wish you all the best of luck in your trials here and look forward to seeing you wear that Medici crest on your leathers."

She shook their hands and gradually moved away, still looking for Shade. She spotted him as he exited the training facility in conversation with the massive warrior they called Skelk. Shade looked up and saw her, immediately stopping in his tracks and holding his arms open to her. Kate rushed to him, being lifted up for a kiss.

Shade set her back down, nodding at Skelk. "You have met Skelk, *si*?"

Kate smiled at the giant of a man, with his scraggly hair and his clear rejection of any custom leathers from Cory. She extended her hand to Skelk who seemed befuddled as he took her hand.

"We've not officially met. Welcome, Skelk. I've heard a lot about your skills. It seems we both have a love of the same weapon."

Skelk wasn't a social animal and he seemed completely taken aback, as his new queen greeted him. He'd not been part of a coven in a very long time, and never part of a royal coven, so he had no idea of proper protocol and shuffled his feet, as she spoke to him and shook his hand. He could feel his face turning red. He heard her make a reference to the crossbow and he looked up, catching her gaze and her open smile.

Skelk mumbled, "I heard you like the crossbow. Killed Cuerpo."

Kate was amused by his awkwardness. All the other warriors reveled in their alpha status and strutted around like proud peacocks. Kate thought there was a gentle giant inside that rough exterior. "Luca trained me, and he did a great job, but crossbow isn't his weapon of choice. Maybe you could teach me sometime?"

Skelk glanced quickly at Shade, waiting for a reprimand, wondering if his new master would be offended that Skelk would dare speak to his mate, but Shade seemed to be fighting back a smile of his own.

Skelk turned back to Kate. "Yeah, sure, uh my ladyship, I'd uh, be happy to." Skelk bowed his head and moved away before she could engage him in any further conversation.

Shade chuckled. "I think you make him nervous, *mi amore*."

Kate shrugged. "Seriously, he looks like a tank with hair. How could I possibly intimidate him?"

Shade slid his arm around her. "To what do I owe the pleasure of this visit?"

Kate leaned into him. "I just came to let you know I'm leaving now. Luca will teleport me to Napa Valley, and Reynaldo will follow. We'll be back before sunrise. This is just a preliminary visit, to get Reynaldo started."

Shade lifted her up as she slid her legs around his waist and kissed him. "Be careful, *mi amore*. I know Luca will take care of you, but I will worry until you return."

Kate laid her head on his shoulder. "Yes, I know all about worry. I'll be careful. And I'll be back by the time you wrap up camp for the night."

He slapped her ass and set her back down on the ground, kissing her palm before she walked away. He stood and watched her leave the camp.

"I can feel you watching me, lover."

He smiled. ***"Si*, always watching, *mi amore*."**

38

Fiamma led her team for the night out into the open training field. The other teams were organized, and the test rounds were beginning for skill level assessments. Tonight, they had instructions to *really* work their warriors and decide who should be included in the first round of cuts, and who had a chance of making it all the way through the training program. Fiamma had a pretty good idea which of her recruits should stay and who should go. She smiled as she saw Kate tackle Shade in a huge hug and he slapped her ass. It felt good to see him so happy and excited about life again, and it all had to do with one small redhead. Fee watched Shade stand with his arms crossed as Kate walked away from him and headed back to the main house.

Fee approached Shade. "So, our queen is not joining our fun tonight, master?"

Shade laughed and shook his head. "No, she is heading to California for the night with Luca, preparing our home out there for bigger and better things."

Breaking away from Fee to check on Marcello's group, Shade felt someone brush against him as they walked past. He turned to see Britt, the redhead he'd helped with the bow. He nodded to her. "*Buonasera*, Britt."

Britt flipped her red hair and smiled, as Shade continued in the direction of Marcello's group.

Fiamma took note as Britt walked past Shade, intentionally brushing against him. She knew Britt was messing in the wrong territory, playing a dangerous game with her master. Fiamma decided to keep an eye on her. She didn't miss that coy, seductive smile Britt flashed at Shade when he spoke to her.

As they began to work, Fiamma had the recruits throwing shuriken's at a moving target. She was helping a male warrior who she thought could make the first cut and spent a good deal of time with him. Her attention was drawn when she heard a group of male recruits laughing and looked over to see Britt had strayed from her group and was entertaining Marcello's group... and Shade.

Fiamma stood back and watched a few moments and saw Shade walk away from the group, heading over to observe Skelk's group of recruits. Britt's eyes followed Shade as he walked away and Fiamma knew she needed to have a word with her as soon as possible. This one had one thing on her mind, and it wasn't any shuriken, knife, or bow. Fiamma barked at her. "Britt, you belong in my group, not Marcello's!"

As Britt begrudgingly walked back to her group, Fiamma saw her look back over her shoulder to keep an eye on Shade's location. *Damn!*

As the night progressed, the recruits were pushing hard and long, without a lot of breaks. Shade wanted to make sure they knew that being a warrior was not just about weapon skills but stamina. Fiamma began to gather her group up and call it a night when she saw Britt, once more, walking with Shade and smiling. She hoped to hell Shade wasn't giving Britt any false impressions and he could see what this bitch was up to.

As Britt walked up to her, Fee took her by the arm and led her aside. Fee instructed her group, "Everyone go inside, the training is over for the night and tomorrow, we decide the cut. Rest, some of you will need it for your journey home."

Britt tried to wrangle her arm free from Fee's grip, but it only made Fee clamp down harder, holding her in place.

"Look, Britt. I have my eye on you, and this is a warning. I suggest you take heed. Master Shade is mated. You are here to learn to be a warrior and nothing more. I'm his Lieutenant and in charge of the females. So, I suggest you spend more time working on your skills than trying to put any moves on him. He's warrior at heart. And he expects all his warriors to be the same. Straighten up. Now, go inside!"

Britt gave her a look and flipped her long red hair back as she strutted back inside.

Fee smirked. "Mess with me, bitch, at least I'm a real redhead!" Fee shook her head as she walked back inside the barracks herself. Shade said he treated the warriors the same, but Fee knew he had a soft spot in his heart for the female warriors and had always tried to make a place for them in his ranks. He could bark at the male recruits, but he was a gentleman with the females and sometimes, kinder than necessary. Fee would intervene for Kate and always had her back.

She had known Shade a long time and had seen many a female wear the mark of Shade Medici on their throat like it was a badge of honor. Fee knew those days were long gone for him, but she also knew Kate was aware of his history and still had reservations about the feeders and the female warriors for that reason. Fee wasn't about to let Britt mess everything up for the female recruits that were here to learn and could be the new generation of Medici warriors.

39

Kate returned to the house to find Luca and Reynaldo waiting for her. She gathered up the California house plans, some information she'd researched on the internet about state license laws for inns, restaurants and B&B's, and her laptop and stuffed it all in a tote bag. She tossed the bag over her shoulder and held onto Luca, her own teleporting skills not well-honed enough yet for such a long trip. He lifted her up and they were quickly on their way. Kate kept her eyes open as they moved skyward into the night and rapidly moved westward across the country, landing in front of the huge Napa Valley estate.

Reynaldo landed only a few minutes behind and Luciano came out to greet them. "Shade told me you were on your way, my lady. He said you had big plans for this property. Follow me, I'll unlock the house and turn off the security system. I rarely go in myself. I stay in an apartment I developed for myself over the winery."

Kate looked at him with surprise. "Really? I assumed you just stayed in the main house."

Luciano shook his head. "It's more convenient for me to be near the vineyards. And I'm never in one place for too long, moving between all of master's vineyards. I always make a check of the property when I'm here, but other than that, the house is vacant."

Kate looked out over the rolling hills of the estate, the rows of grapes visible as they followed the curves of the landscape. Just like the Virginia property, there was still much land that had not been converted to vineyards.

As Kate looked at the rolling landscape, she addressed Luciano, "Has Shade considered expanding the vineyards? There's still so much property here."

Luciano shook his head. "Not that he's mentioned, my lady."

Kate surveyed the property, another idea brewing in her head, as Luciano threw open the massive front door and they all entered. Kate gave Reynaldo a tour of the house, with Luca staying close on her heels, before ending the tour in the large, well-equipped, modern kitchen. Luciano joined them there, as they each pulled up a chair around the kitchen table. Kate pulled all the papers from her tote bag and spread them across the table. "So, what do you think, Reynaldo?"

Reynaldo could barely contain his excitement. It had been so very long since he was able to fully use his skills. "My lady, the layout is perfect, and I can't wait to work in this kitchen. I can start the process of applying for all the state licenses we'll need to be able to open. I have no concerns about that. And running the kitchen, once we're busy, I may need a sous chef. But Gi would easily be able to procure one for me from Florence. There was a time when Castello was bustling with activity, but it has been many years now since we've been able to prepare meals. You mentioned Gi would select a housemaid?"

Kate nodded her head, not exactly sure what a sous chef did, other than assist the chef, but knew there was more than an adequate pool of people to draw from at Castello to help staff the inn. "Yes. I knew you'd be busy with meals, especially if we make it an inn instead of a B&B, and you'd need someone else to clean the rooms, do the laundry."

Reynaldo nodded. "Then have him send two, so they can rotate their schedule. Maybe not right away, but soon."

Kate agreed. "Of course, we can do that. I mean, we can always send someone back to Florence if this doesn't take off."

Reynaldo smiled. "Oh, I think it will take off. I'm an excellent chef, and I haven't had the opportunity to display my skills in a long time. Once we're open, word will spread quickly. I feel very positive about that, my lady. I do have one concern."

Kate looked at him, her brow creased. "And what is that?"

Reynaldo hoped he wasn't making this project more difficult than she'd planned. He didn't want to do or say anything that would discourage her.

"Well, I'm quite skilled at managing a kitchen, and it won't take me long to have that up and running. But I've never run an inn. I know how to deal with any guests and their meal request, but making room reservations, checking in guests, seeing to their needs outside the restaurant, these are skills I don't currently possess. Luciano can create our wine list, and he can even recommend a local sommelier, vampire, of course. I don't mean to make this complicated, but we may need a manager for the inn."

Kate bit at her lip. "How do we find a manager? He would have to be vampire."

Luca responded, "We have a network. Shade will know how to find someone from within the vampire community. They can come here, Reynaldo can interview them, weed them down to the best candidates, then you can come back here, meet them, interview them yourself and make the final selection."

Kate took a deep breath. She had thought this was as simple as bringing Reynaldo here, but it was quickly growing into something much bigger. "Where would the staff stay? There are only seven available bedrooms to rent out, and you're already talking about a staff of five."

Reynaldo shrugged it off. "There is room over the winery to add more apartments as well as space over master's large garage. Plus, whoever we hire as a manager may be local and have a place nearby. Don't be concerned with that. We can figure it out as we go."

Reynaldo decided to stay and start the process of securing their licenses and seeing what he needed to do to get the kitchen up to commercial code. He told Kate he'd have Gi pack up and send his personal items out to California, as he walked through the suite of rooms on the first floor that were originally designed for Luca. "This is perfect, my lady. Much grander than I'm used to." Reynaldo looked to Luca. "You're sure you don't mind?"

Luca laughed. "I'm seeing these rooms for the first time, brother. Make yourself at home."

Kate left him all the papers, made her rounds of the house one final time, making note to purchase a supply of high-end bed linens and bath towels to accommodate a daily room turnover.

As she wrapped up the meeting, she left Reynaldo to the task of getting everything started, then she and Luca teleported home to Bel Rosso. Arriving slightly past sunrise, Kate went directly to their bedroom where she found Shade, already undressed and in bed, fighting the pull of his death slumber. She stripped off her clothes and climbed in bed beside him, lying across his chest as his arms enveloped her.

"I missed you, *mi amore*. I was afraid you would not get home before the slumber took me." He kissed her as she snuggled into his neck, the room already dark from the blinds, blocking out the sun.

"I will always come home to you."

40

Shade opened his eyes, the blinds were still down, but he had a meeting with Fiamma and Marcello before the camp got started tonight, so they could compare notes. Tonight, the first round of cuts would be made and at least a third of the recruits would be sent home. They'd make their final observations tonight and decide on whom to keep in the camp by sunrise.

Bel still slept beside him, soft and beautiful, her crimson hair spread about her. He slid his hands through her hair and heard her moan softly. "Wake up, sleepy head."

She could feel the warmth of him as he lay next to her, his hand running through her hair, and his voice penetrated her sleep. She smiled even before she opened her eyes and rolled over to his embrace. Burying her head against his chest, she yawned, as he squeezed her tight and made her laugh.

Shade chuckled at her yawn. "The day-walker is sleeping like a vamp in a death slumber. Perhaps, I should give you more tasks to accomplish."

Rolling on top of her, he tickled her and they both began to laugh, he at her laughter and beauty, and her at his boyish games of tickling.

She giggled uncontrollably, pushing his hands away as he tickled her, making him stop. "I got a lot done yesterday, and I teleported to California and back...well, sort of. Luca teleported us both to California and back. Still, it was tiring."

"Oh, it was tiring? But training a bunch of would-be warriors is nothing? I see how this is going."

He rolled on his back, grasping her to his chest as her hair fell around them like a cocoon. Leaning up, he kissed her softly and smiled. "How is our son?"

"He's fine. He's strong and healthy, and eager to join you in the camp." She smiled at him. "He's so much like you. I can feel him. I never felt the other baby, his spirit. I think he must have been too weak, even from the beginning. But this one, this one will come out fighting, I think."

Shade quickly blocked the guilt that washed over him at the mention of their lost son, and the torture he still had buried deep inside. He'd never be able to tell her the truth, that he alone bore the fault for their loss. But while he felt the guilt, he knew his choice would be the same. If he had to choose between *bel* or the *bambino*, he'd choose her again. Quickly shaking the memory from his mind, he smiled up at her, letting his hands slide to the sides of her face, cupping it gently.

"He is Medici, he will come out a fighter, loving his *madre* with all he has, just like his *padre*. Dr. Bonutti will be here soon. So, tell me of your adventures last evening. Did you leave poor Reynaldo to fend for himself out there?"

She laughed. "I didn't leave Reynaldo. He asked to stay, so he could get started. He was very excited. He's looking into what licenses we need, but it looks like we're going to go with making it an inn instead of a B&B. I'm going to talk with Gi to see if there's a housemaid or two he can recommend we assign there, someone from Florence that might like living in the States. Also, since we're looking at making it an inn, we may need a manager. Luca said you'd have a network you could tap into? He said Reynaldo could screen the applicants, get them down to a few we could then approve. So, can you do that? Put the word out... Or however you do it?"

Shade shook his head. "Woman! Slow down. *Cazzo*! Some things never change." He gave her ass a slap as he sat up, resting his back against the headboard. Kate climbed into his lap and they sat in the large bed like two love struck teenagers. "Of course, I will do whatever you wish, *mi amore*. Let me just do my worldwide vampire call to the moon. It's like a howl, very striking, you know." She pushed his chest hard as she giggled. Fuck, he loved this woman!

Kate leaned over him, letting her hair cascade around his face, enclosing him in a curtain of crimson. "You haven't taught me all your vampire tricks, lover. Besides, I'm not sure they'd even answer my call. The only ones that listen to me have four legs...or wings. I think I'm still pretty much ignored by the vampire community. We'll change that, one day. Someday, they'll all see I'm worthy of being your queen." She leaned down and kissed him.

He grasped her hair tightly, pulling her hard into the kiss, his tongue grappled with hers and he moaned. "I don't care what the hell anyone thinks, you are worthy of being my queen and my opinion is the only one that matters. Damn! What time is it? I need to meet with Fee and Marcello about the cut."

Kate rolled off of him as he slid from their bed. "Do you mind if Luca takes me to Paris tonight? I think I should be home by sunrise, but if we have to stay over, I'll let you know. I know you'll ground me soon, and you'll have Gi and Theresa waiting on me hand and foot, so I need to try to get these things done as soon as possible."

"I told you, *mi amore*, that is fine. And *si*, you will be grounded soon."

He slid on his leathers and fastened his belt. Padding over to the armoire in his bare feet, he started banging around, flinging things to the floor. "I just need a damn black tee shirt, all I ask, a simple tee shirt!" Spinning around, he saw her laughing into her hand. "And what is so damn funny?"

Kate shook her head. "Second drawer. How did you ever dress yourself before me?"

Missing her sarcasm completely, he answered her, "Gi would lay out my things. I seem to have more clothing now than ever before."

"Maybe you should get Cory to make you some custom leathers. I'll have him design a pair for you like the ones Raven wears, with the cutouts on the pant leg." Kate pulled the pillow over her face to stifle her laughter at the very thought of her big bad warrior wearing pants with cutouts. "Or maybe red leather like Fiamma? What do you think?"

Shade stood with his hands on his hips and stared at her. "You think that is funny, now, do you?"

He took two leaps and jumped on the bed, making her bounce on the mattress and grinned at her laughter. "How is it you make me feel young and so alive? It's like I have been born again to see the world in a whole new light. Damn! I am late!"

As the electronic blinds rose, he knew his two warriors were already in his office, patiently waiting on him.

Kate pushed him from the bed. "Get going. I'll get dressed and come say goodbye to you before I leave."

He kissed her quickly, as he started to leave the room.

"Your boots! You forgot your boots!" She was still laughing at him as she headed for the shower.

"See what you do to me." Laughing, he quickly slid on his boots as his eyes followed her to the shower. He rushed down the stairs to his office.

Rolling into the office, he found Fee and Marcello both smirking. "Sorry, I had a few things to straighten up with *bel*."

Marcello laughed. "Yeah, we heard."

Shade flopped down in his chair. "I didn't ask for your input, just making a statement. So, let's get down to business. Show me your lists, give me your thoughts. I will let you know if I agree."

Fee shook her head. "Well, to begin with, the females are all pretty strong, but I'm on the fence with one. I think I'd like to keep at least three."

Shade looked over her list and then looked up at her. "Britt is on the fence? Fee, I like her bow skills, and although we don't have a lot of call for bow, I think it is important to keep warriors with some of the old world skills. If I recall, you were damn good with the bow when you started. Let us keep her this cut and see how she does."

Marcello nodded in agreement. "She isn't bad with the sword either. I agree."

Fee sat back and listened, she didn't get a feeling he was keeping her for any other reason than her skills as a warrior, but she had a bad feeling about this one. "Fine, but she better show us a lot more the next round."

Several hours went by with heavy discussion around each of the recruits on the list, as to who would make the cut and who wouldn't. Shade was adamant about keeping two males that were on the list to be cut who he felt had potential. Marcello and Fee had done their jobs well, and for the most part, they had all agreed.

"All right, it seems as though this task is done. We need to get our asses out there before chaos breaks out. We will post the list tonight in the meeting room of the barracks. Those that are cut will be escorted out immediately. Once we escort them out, we will give Raven a heads up to make sure they don't filter into D.C. and begin stirring things up."

***

Kate showered, dressed and coordinated her schedule with Luca. She went in search of Gi and they discussed having him select two housemaids to send to California. He said he'd get right on it, and he had several in mind who'd love to move to the States and who spoke English fluently.

She could hear Shade in his study, and it appeared his meeting was wrapping up. Marcello exited first and gave her a smile and a nod, as he headed out the back of the house. Shade emerged with Fee, and as he stepped forward to embrace her, Fiamma stepped back.

Kate slid her arms around his waist. "I'm heading out now, lover. We're getting a late start, but I've met with Gi and he'll work on housemaids for the Napa house. If I don't finish up tonight, Luca and I will stay over. I hate sleeping without you, but I want to get this project underway, at least to the point where I can work on it from here and coordinate things with the designers."

"I will miss you, *mi amore*. I never sleep as well without you." He snuggled into her hair and kissed her neck. "I will come to you in your dreams, *si*? Be careful, do not stress your body. It may be well to spend the night with Luca there. I want you to get your rest. But right now, I must be getting to the camp. We have much to accomplish. Medici is growing by leaps and bounds."

Kissing her soundly, he looked at Fee, she smiled and let him know telepathically she wished to speak with her queen. Shade nodded as he headed for the door. "I love you. Make our Paris home a place for our *bambinos* to thrive, *si*?"

Kate gave him a coy smile. "I was thinking more of a place for making *bambinos*, lover." She blew him a kiss and noticed Fee had remained behind. She turned her attention to the tall redheaded warrior.

"Love the red leathers, Fee. I told Shade he should wear a set."

Fee yelped with laughter. "I bet that went over well. I don't want to hold you up, my lady, but I wish to speak with you if you have a moment to spare?"

Kate took her hand. "I always have time for you." She led Fee into the living room. "Sit down. What's on your mind?"

Fee got down to business. "You know me, I'm just frank about things, never beat around the bush. I know you have concerns over the females, warriors or feeders. And I get it, from your standpoint. You haven't been exposed to the best sides of either. But I have a female warrior in the camp right now that is bothering me with her actions."

Kate sat up straight. She was pretty sure Fee wasn't here to talk about the warrior's lack of skills with weapons. "Actions? What are you trying to say, Fee?"

Fee carefully thought over how to choose her words, she didn't want to alarm Kate but wanted her to understand she'd not tolerate inappropriate behavior. "There's a female here, her name is Britt. She's a bit too familiar with master. I've dressed her down, warned her. I want you to know I have your back. I have my eye on her, I trust master with all my heart, he is the best master, but he does have a reputation. I know that's in his past, you need to know that as well. But some of the females don't care. They still want to be with the Medici. He had quite the reputation, and it was a competition among many females to be one of his conquests. I wanted you to know, so you could keep an eye on her as well. I hope I don't speak out of line, but sister to sister, we need to keep each other informed, protect what is ours. I love master and I love you as well. I feel I'm a good example of how most female warriors conduct themselves. But she's not like most female warriors."

Kate could feel her temper rear its head, her jealously rising to the surface. "Oh, I think I know which one you mean. And thank you for telling me. I'll keep an eye on her for sure and I appreciate you doing the same. I know if I try to speak to Shade about it, he'll get angry. He thinks I don't trust him, and I do. I tell him over and over it's not him, it's them! There are women who know no boundaries. I know he'll not act on it if they approach him, but that doesn't make me hate their actions any less. I'm going away again tonight and will possibly be gone until well into the second night. We have new property in Paris and I need to get things in order there before I get too far along with this baby."

Kate lowered her head and closed her eyes. "I'm very excited about the baby, and I know he is too. But you're a woman. You understand. The more pregnant I become, the less confidence I'll feel in myself around these women. I mean, look at you, look at all of you. You're so tall and have a distinctively unique beauty. I don't want to feel like I'm always competing with that."

Fee's heart almost broke. Reaching out, she hugged Kate and held the hug. "Kate, trust me, there's no competition whatsoever. He could have had any female in the world. He chose you. Have faith in him. Be proud to be his. No one can steal him from you, and every day, you become more beautiful in his eyes. I see that, we all do. He wants you, and always will. Please, don't worry, and I'm always here if you need someone to talk to."

Kate returned the hug, feeling the incredible strength in Fee's arms. "I know you're right. I can see it in his eyes every time he looks at me. Thank you for having my back. And I'll keep an eye on this one as well."

Kate broke away from Fee and stood, "Now, if I don't get going, I'll end up having to stay even longer in Paris." She smiled at Fee, realizing just how few female immortals she had befriended.

"Don't worry, she makes one false step, I'll get my way and she'll be gone. Now go, enjoy your new Paris house. I can't keep track of how many homes you have now." Laughing, Fee headed out the door and back to the camp. She prayed Britt would stay clear of Shade, but she had a really bad feeling that it was wishful thinking.

41

Luca landed them on a side street that crossed the Champs Elysees, surrounded in shadow and completely unnoticed by the crowd. He took Kate's arm and guided her back to the main thoroughfare. Kate looked around at the city she loved, on this warm night in early summer. The street was brightly lit as people still crowded the sidewalks, and the traffic was heavy as locals and tourists sought out their night spot of choice. Even at this late hour, there were still crowds.

She was surprised Alec would choose such a highly visible and populated area for a house. As they turned the corner onto the Champs Elysees, Kate was looking at the building fronts, and comparing them to the photo in her hand, looking for a house number. She saw the huge building in the middle of the block. It was a large, ornate Beaux Arts structure with many French doors on the facade that opened onto wrought iron balconies, all overlooking the broad boulevard.

She fished the key from her purse and unlocked the door. She and Luca stepped into the large open foyer with large black and white tiled floors and a curved white marble staircase with an elaborate scrolled black iron banister. The architecture was uniquely Parisian. They walked together through each of the three floors. The building was old, but was built in the 19th century, so it wasn't as ancient as Castello, and it had been well maintained.

Kate was making note of specific areas that would need some renovation, but she wanted to keep true to the buildings original architectural style. The bathrooms would need the most work, and the heating and cooling systems would need to be replaced. Almost every room had a fireplace, but she knew that wasn't a practical way to heat a home in modern Paris. She'd have a contractor check the electrical, but even without rewiring, there were light fixtures that would need to be replaced. She knew the merchants that helped her restore Bel Rosso to its traditional Tuscan glory, would be able to help her keep the same period feel for this house as well.

Alec had been right about one thing. The house was huge, and it could easily be renovated to make three separate apartments, and in this part of Paris, they could charge a fortune for rent. But if the point was to have a place for them to stay, a place to bring the children in the future, then she wanted to keep the entire property for themselves. She took photos in every room, and made copious notes, but found she was tired in spite of her enthusiasm. There was no furniture left here, so they'd spend at least a portion of the day in a hotel, so Kate could sleep, before coming back to take final measurements and meet with the designer.

Luca had arranged for a hotel nearby in the event they had to stay. He knew she was strong and healthy, but the pregnancy would drain her energy more quickly. "Come with me, Kate. I can tell you're tired. You got a lot done here and I promised Shade you'd rest. The sun is already out. We can walk to the hotel from here."

They walked down the wide stairs and back out into the streets of Paris. The sun felt glorious on her face. She wondered what it would have been like had she not been reborn a day-walker, to never experience the feel of the sun on her skin again. The tree-lined streets of the Champs Elysees were in full bloom, and every door had large urns filled with flowers. Kate lifted her face to the sun and took in a deep breath. Her heart broke that it couldn't be Shade walking beside her. That this was a pleasure he'd never know.

Luca led her to the Hotel Plaza Athenee on the Avenue Montaigne. They passed a small cafe with the strong smell of rich coffee in the air, and bakeries with glass front counters filled with baguettes and fresh pastries, their fragrant, sweet, doughy smell wafting from the open doors. She paused slightly as they passed, the memories of her mortal body responding to the scent. Luca smiled and pulled her away as they continued on their path. Kate smiled wistfully at him.

"I wonder if he ever misses this."

Luca shook his head, "You can't miss what you never had. These are mortal pleasures. Our bodies don't require it. We don't feel the same pull as you do. Your desire for mortal pleasures will fade with time."

Kate nodded as they walked arm in arm, the mortals on the street passing them by. "What about the sun, Luca. He can't walk in the sun. He only knows the darkness and a world of artificial light. I wonder if he longs for the sun."

Luca looked down at his feet as they walked. "Every vampire who must hide from the sun adjusts. Again, for those not born as day-walkers, they really know nothing else. I don't think Shade thought about it much until he met you. I know it bothered him greatly he couldn't be awake with you in the day. But just as you have adjusted your own schedule to sleep when he sleeps, we all do what we have to, right?"

She smiled back at him. "I'd change nothing."

They arrive at the Athenee and got checked in. They had a suite with two bedrooms, so he could be as close to her as possible.

"Get some rest, Kate. Sleep as much as you need. We don't have an appointment with the designer until this afternoon. Once you finish up with him, we can teleport back."

They both retired to their respective bedrooms. Kate barely noticed the lavishly appointed rooms. Her feet were tired from all the walking and this baby took what he needed from her first. She pulled the heavy drapes closed and climbed between the sheets, remembering the last time she was in Paris with him. She sent him her love and quickly fell asleep.

Kate slept soundly and dreamt of him, and Bel Rosso. She felt Shade as he dream-walked into her sleep, making love to her in Paris. She saw a young, dark haired boy running through the fields, squealing in delight, dragging a toy sword behind him and knew in her heart this was Lorenzo. She woke after a few hours of sleep and sat up on the side of the bed, shaking the sleep from her eyes. She walked to the bathroom and splashed her face with cold water. So much to do yet, and she wanted to get back home.

She called out to Luca who responded to her immediately. "Did you sleep well, Kate?"

She nodded. "I did. I was more tired than I thought, but I miss him beside me. Let's get back to the house, meet the designer so we can finish up and you can take me home."

They made their way back to the house and found the designer that had helped her so much on both the Virginia and California houses waiting at the door. Kate extended her hand to him. "I hope you haven't been waiting long."

He smiled graciously. He had served the Medici family for a very long time. They had made him a very rich man. What she didn't understand was he would stand here for hours waiting if necessary. "Of course not, madam. You are right on time."

Kate unlocked the door and the three of them entered together. Kate and the designer walked from room to room, planning out the space, taking measurements and discussing furniture. The designer had a large notebook of numerous furniture pieces he had at his disposal that he kept showing to her, making suggestions.

"And, of course, if there's something specific you want, just let me know. If I don't have it, I can certainly track it down."

They spent the remaining hours planning the rooms, the furniture, the drapes, and rugs. Kate ripped all the notes from her notebook and handed them over to him. "And here's the list of things that will need renovation. I'll need you to help oversee the contractors. I won't be able to get here as often, so I'll need your oversight."

He gleefully took the list, seeing dollar signs. "Of course, madam. We have done much renovation at Castello. We understand the Medici standards. Please, don't trouble yourself. I promise only exceptional work."

Kate had no doubt. As they finalized their plans, Kate gave the designer an extra key so he might come and go as needed and oversee the workers who'd be in and out. She bid him farewell and turned to Luca.

"Well, that's done. And I'm more than ready to get home to Bel Rosso. I'm surprised at how quickly this baby zaps my energy."

Luca pulled her close as they stood in the large foyer and teleported out. The sky was darkening, and he knew with the time change, it would be close to morning when they arrived back home.

42

Fee walked back into the camp and saw Shade, and she wasn't the least surprised to see Britt standing at his side. Shade saw her approaching and wondered why she'd stayed behind to talk to *bel*.

"Everything all right, Fee? Is *bel* okay?"

Fee smiled. "Of course, everything's fine, female chatter. I just wanted to wish her good luck on the Paris house. I know you'll be a grumpy ass tyrant tonight since she'll be gone, so I plan on staying far away from you."

Shade laughed and fist bumped her. "If she is gone too long, I will be going after her!"

Fee turned, and Britt was right under her feet. Fee grabbed her by the arm and steered her in the direction of the group. "You belong over here and you will stay over here!"

Shade worked through the groups, as they were put through their paces. He watched those they had decided to keep and thought they'd made the right choice. He gathered the warriors for a break and announced that the cut list would be posted at the end of the night in the meeting room of the barracks. Those not making the cut would be escorted out, but reminded them they could always try out again in the future. He let the warriors go for their last round of skill sets and decided to head back to the house. Things were fine here, and he was missing *bel*.

He needed to call Dr. Bonutti and see when he planned to arrive, and check in with Raven on how things were progressing in D.C. He worked his way around to the gate and headed quietly up the road to the main house.

Britt saw him leave the camp. He'd be hard to miss since she'd kept her eyes on him all night. She looked around and saw Fee was preoccupied with the women and decided to make her move. She heard Fee mention to him Kate was away, so he'd be all alone in that big house. Britt ran up behind him, catching up quickly as he took long strides on the path to the house. She reached out and grabbed at the waist band of his leathers. "Not so fast, warrior. I was hoping you'd maybe give me a clue as to whether I'm on the list to stay."

Shade's mind was so preoccupied, he'd had no idea anyone was behind him.

He was surprised, and a little annoyed to see Britt. He'd tried to be stern yet gentlemanly in making sure she understood he was master here, this was a warrior camp and she was a recruit, but she had stepped over the line and he was putting an end to this. "Britt, the list will be posted shortly. You will find out the results when the others do, and not before. So, I would suggest you go back and use your time wisely, *si*?"

Britt flashed him a coy smile. "I could go back, if that's what you want. But I heard your mate left you alone tonight." Britt stepped in closer, inhaling his scent. "Perhaps, you'd like some company in that big empty house. I have other skills you haven't seen yet, and I'd really love to show them to you."

She reached her hand out, brushing back those dark curls from his forehead, seeing the intensity in those blue eyes, even in the moonlight. She wanted him so bad he made her mouth water.

Shade sighed heavily. If she thought that was a line he'd never heard before, she was wrong. As her hand touched his hair, he gripped her wrist and growled. "I am master here, I am mated, and she is loved. You have no business with me other than to train as a warrior. You have overstepped your bounds. No more, Britt! If you wish to disrespect my commands, then you can leave now, and you will be escorted out of here. But I think you want to stay. I think you want to be a warrior. Tell me if I am wrong. Go now, before you stir my beast. Go!"

Shade turned and took a deep breath. He'd thought, once he was mated he'd be done with the nonsense of females chasing after him, wanting to bed him, to be his for one night. Fuck! His past would always haunt him in some fashion and now, he fully understood *bel's* anger when she saw any female around him.

Britt was surprised when he grabbed her wrist, but his strength turned her on even more. She felt the electricity of his touch and it ran straight from the strength of his strong grip on her wrist to the core of her sex, and she burned for him. She knew he was angry, but she also knew his reputation. This one wouldn't go for long without a woman to warm his bed, and if his mate stayed gone a while, Britt was sure she could wear him down. After all, he was the Medici, and there was a long list of conquest proud to be included on that list, and she intended to be one of them. She gave him a slow smile, tilting her head down in a submissive manner.

"Of course, master. Whatever you wish... However you wish it... You will have."

Britt turned and walked away from him, tossing her newly red locks and looking back over her shoulder at him, making sure he got her message as he watched her go.

43

Shade watched Britt walk back to camp, her message had been clear, he just hoped *his* message to her was just as clear! He thought he was done with all of this nonsense with females. What the hell did it take for them to forget his past, learn he was mated and in love and received that love in return tenfold? He took his time walking back to the main house, letting his temper cool down. He prayed *bel* hadn't felt the sexual advances from Britt. He was sure she wouldn't since his response had been nothing but anger and taking the vixen down.

Walking into the house, Gi nodded and handed him a glass of Midnight, which Shade downed immediately. He let Gi know he'd be in his office if he was needed. Gi filled his glass again and Shade walked to his office and picked up his cell. He looked at the pile of papers neatly stacked on his desk and sighed. He'd never been happier in his life, or busier, and there was only one thing he yearned for, his lily-white with the crimson locks.

He dialed up a few vampire masters he knew in California, asking them if they were aware of any honest and reliable day-walkers who might be good candidates to manage the inn in Napa. He had an idea what *bel* was looking for, as he gave the masters an overview of this venture. He silently hoped none of them sent him any female candidates. He'd had enough damn problems with females lately!

He glanced at the clock and could feel his death slumber coming slowly. Reluctantly making his way up the stairs, he knew she wouldn't be there and wouldn't be coming home today. How the hell did he ever live without her? He could feel her tiredness and knew she was pushing her limits, trying to get everything done before she was grounded. He chuckled out loud at her choice of words, but she knew him better than he knew himself.

Shade also knew, once the *bambinos* began to arrive, she would remain here. She'd want to raise them here at Bel Rosso. This was their home, their legacy, and he spent every second of his life making sure there would be enough to support them for an eternity.

Dropping his clothes behind him as he walked through their bedroom, he smiled to himself. He could imagine her disapproving stare as he left the trail of clothes behind him. He took a long hot shower then walked to the empty bed, naked and wet, his hair dripping small rivulets of water down his face and chest. He sat on the edge of the bed and noticed his cell blinking. Someone had called and left him a message. He grabbed his phone, hoping it was *bel*, but noticed it was Dr. Bonutti, returning his call.

Hitting redial, Shade didn't wait long before Dr. Bonutti answered in his jovial friendly voice. He had known Shade since his birth and had administered to the Medici family for centuries and there was no one better, in Shade's mind, to care for the next generation of Medici. "Doc, *grazie* for answering my call."

Dr. Bonutti laughed into the phone. "Medici, I apologize profusely for not returning your call earlier, but I have just come from London, a special case. I hear congratulations are in order in your mating and the crowning of your new queen. I am most honored to be of service to you and yours. Always a pleasure, I assure you."

Shade flopped back on the bed and grinned. "*Grazie*. I need you to come to the States as soon as possible. My mate is with child, we know it is a son. I need someone I can trust, someone who can make the journey here as often as necessary. She is not far along, but I need to have her examined, for my own piece of mind. She is newly turned and--" Shade swallowed hard as the loss of their first son slammed him hard every time he thought about it. "Well, she lost our first son when she became pregnant while still mortal. Both of us need some reassurance."

Dr. Bonutti listened and could feel the anguish of the Medici. "*Si*. Those pregnancies are rarely successful, Shade. This one, of course, will be fine and I will monitor the pregnancy and the birth for Council. I will come in two night's time. We will all meet, and I will answer any questions your queen may have. I am most excited to meet her."

"I appreciate it, doc. This means a great deal to me. I will send you the coordinates of our home, and we will see you then. *Buonasera*."

As Shade ended the call, he tossed the phone onto the nightstand and spread out on the bed, moaning. He wanted his *bel!* He wanted her to know the ache in his heart her absence caused him and sent her his love telepathically. Closing his eyes, he felt the slumber drag him under as the last words he heard were hers, whispering in her soft voice that she loved him and missed him too.

44

Through the fog of sleep, Shade heard the soft sound of the electronic whir of the blinds opening for the evening. He rolled over and moaned. His slumber had taken him deep and he slid easily into *bel's* dreams, making passionate love to her in the lover's paradise of Paris. He'd made her a promise in his dream, to come back here with her, and make love with her in reality, including the seedy alley where he'd taken her wantonly as others walked past. Reaching out for her, the bed was empty and cold. He missed the warmth of her curled against him, her head on his shoulder, her arm draped over his chest.

Before the ache for her could build inside him, he quickly showered, dressed in his leathers, and laced his boots. Tonight, would be a good exercise for the recruits. They'd cut a good number, so the group was smaller, and it was time to turn up the heat in the warrior camp.

As Shade made his way to the camp, he could hear the sounds of metal against metal and the swishing sound of swords waved high into the air, as mock battles were in full force. He walked inside the gates, across the training field, and watched as Marcello paired them up. The recruits were going at each other full force. Shade liked what he saw. He walked the perimeter of the training field, closely observing those he was hoping to keep. He tried to remain on the periphery of the field, out of their line of vision, so they weren't aware of being observed.

In Florence, vampires, as early as age ten, were brought to camp, grew up there, as they learned to be warriors. Here in the States, there were no such camps. These recruits were much older, and were self-taught, learning on the streets. Most were gypsy vampires, belonging to no single master, seeking to be hired as mercenary warriors, but their skills were not honed, and they lacked discipline. Shade was determined to find the best of them and make them Medici, trained and cared for properly.

Shade watched for hours, as Marcello and Fiamma worked them hard, making the warriors hold their swords high. He could see pain in their faces, and knew their muscles burned. He knew they felt as though their arms would drop out of their sockets from the weight of the sword. They must be trained for long battles, not just quick street scuffles. If his coven went up against another coven, it could be hours before the deed was done and won. Shade's warriors had to be prepared for anything. That was how the Medici warriors were trained.

Shade slowly made his way to the female recruits and watched them battle. He kept an eye on Britt but tried to stay out of sight. She moved well but managing the sword for an extended period of time was wearing her down. Fiamma was issuing her commands constantly and Shade could see Britt was getting tired and slow.

Two other female recruits were battling each other, and they were still going at it, full force. He stood and observed them for a long time, impressed with their skills. He walked to the cache of weaponry that was loaded onto a four-wheeler with a trailer. He picked up a sword of the same weight and caliber as the swords the females were using, as well as tucking about a half dozen shurikens into the pockets of his leathers.

He walked back out onto the training field, swinging his sword in a crisscross pattern above his head. All the recruits stopped their battling and stepped back, as the Medici swung his sword with ease. He walked straight to the two female recruits he'd been watching earlier and pointed his sword at the one with the dark hair worn in a single long braid down her back.

Shade barked out, "Name?"

The raven-haired recruit stepped forward, still breathing heavy. Fiamma moved to join them and Shade held his hand up to stop her.

"My name is Aislynn, master."

Shade heard her American accent and wondered where she came from with those skills, but there was plenty of time to find that out later. Right now, he wanted to test her skills further. "Aislynn, very beautiful name. Come to the center of the field. I wish to test you myself. Oblige me, *si*?" He saw her eyes go wide and he wondered if she'd decline.

Nervously, she replied, "Yes, master."

They walked to the center of the huge training field, the dust finally settling and all the other recruits made a large circle around them. Shade didn't miss the pissed off look in Britt's eyes. He had seen her make a move toward him when he approached Aislynn and saw Fee's firm grip on Britt's arm holding her back.

Shade stood casually before Aislynn; his sword held at his side. "Listen and heed my words, warrior. Do as I instruct you, try to kill me. Do not be afraid to hurt me or take me down. I am Medici. I have no fear because I know my skills. If you are to become Medici, you must be and think the same."

Turning his back to Aislynn, he told her to stand about two hundred feet back. "Now, attack me when you are ready. Understood, warrior?"

Aislynn took a deep breath, and Shade could feel her nervousness, as she answered, "Understood, master."

He could also hear the male recruits chuckling low, they'd not been paying much attention to the females or their skills, but they were about to get a valuable lesson on female warriors.

Shade stood still, closed his eyes, and honed his senses on her. She moved quickly and quietly, with stealth, and he heard her coming fast at his back. He could hear her lift her sword in the air and just when she was about to strike him, he back-flipped well over her head and landed behind her, sword held high in both hands. Aislynn spun quickly, moving her feet like a dancer and before Shade knew what was happening, she was flipping end over end above his head. They battled hard for some time, her strike swift and deadly, she meant business and didn't hold back. He was pleased. This was what he was looking for!

Her spins and turns were precise and her timing excellent. She had a great sense of timing and the ability to anticipate her opponent's move. That was a rare gift and not something that could easily be taught. It was something a good warrior had naturally, like Raven, speed like a bullet and timing to match.

He stalked her as they circled each other, each of them moving slowly, eyeing the other and waiting for the next move. Shade could see her muscles flexing, the sweat plastering tendrils of hair to her face. She had worked hard all night and he was pushing her farther than she'd ever been pushed before. Then she came at him fast, swiping for his mid-section and he quickly dropped and rolled before jumping back to his feet, pulling the shuriken's from his pocket and flinging them at her. She responded, not with shock but fight. She flipped through the air, missing one after the other as he threw them at her. She landed on her feet, sword raised, and her arms shaking with exhaustion. Shade was proud and impressed she'd never quit.

Lowering his sword tip to the ground, he felt exhilarated to be working his craft. "Stand down, warrior!"

He watched as Aislynn lowered her weapon tip to the ground and he approached her. "You have done well, Aislynn, your master is pleased. I hope to be seeing more of you in my camp. Keep up the hard work."

She looked up at him and smiled softly out of gratitude. "I am honored, master, thank you for the opportunity."

Shade held out his hand to fist bump and she looked startled but fist bumped him back. "That is what I am looking for, dedication, fight, respect, and honor. Skills that show me you have what it takes, and you will do whatever is necessary for Medici."

He turned to the crowd. "Aislynn has taken the challenge I laid at her feet, she takes this opportunity seriously and I hope all of you will as well. I reward those that give all they have for Medici. My coven works hard, whether warrior or not, we all strive to become a unit. Give me that and you will be staying. If not, you will be leaving here shortly. Nice work to all of you."

Shade walked back to the four-wheeler and laid his sword in the cart. He heard the chatter among the recruits as he headed out the gate and back up to the main house. He wanted to show the recruits what he expected of them, and he wanted to use one of the females to show the males he made no distinction. A good warrior was a good warrior. His point had been made.

Hearing the horses startle as he walked past the stables, he thought maybe the sword play had them a bit roused. He strolled inside to find Impavido. He stroked his mane and patted his sides, settling him down. "Good warrior. I know you miss that fight, don't you, boy? So do I."

45

Luca landed them softly in the foyer at Bel Rosso. Kate stretched her arms over her head and stifled a yawn. "It's still a few hours until sunrise. I think I'm going to take a quick shower, then surprise Shade in the camp." Kate rushed upstairs to shower and change, as Luca headed for his suite to call Shannon to let her know he was home and needed to feed.

***

Britt had looked on with envy as Shade challenged Aislynn. That should have been her! She couldn't take her eyes off of him as he battled, his arms held high, his dark locks falling in his eyes, the leather that sheathed his legs hiding nothing. As the battle ended, he made a speech to the gathering warriors then left the field. Britt saw Fee congratulating Aislynn and took this moment to slip away, following behind Shade.

She had heard from the other warriors his mate hadn't returned, so she knew he was still alone. Britt was convinced, with a little more effort, she could push past any reservations he might have. She was surprised to see him veer from the path and head for the stables but thought this may be to her advantage. She followed him, to see him soothing a massive black stallion, who responded to the stroke of his hand. Britt stepped inside the stables.

"I'd calm down too if I were stroked like that."

Shade's head snapped up as he heard Britt. "What part of leave me alone do you not understand? Apparently, you did not get your ass worked hard enough this night. Why are you here?"

Britt flashed him a smile and walked toward him seductively. She stepped up on the gate of the empty stall next to the stallion, who immediately responded to her presence.

"I just thought you needed company, master. I had no idea you liked to ride. But since we both seem to have a lot of pent up energy--I can think of a lot of things to tire us out. No one needs to know. I can be nothing if not discreet."

Shade couldn't believe the nerve of this one, brazen and no respect. Listening was key to being a good warrior, and this one just made a huge mistake, leaving the camp again, following him onto his own private grounds. Impavido began to snort and paw, shaking his mane violently back and forth.

"Relax, boy, just relax. I know it is not your *bel*, but calm down, I have this in hand." Stroking the horse, the huge stallion refused to settle. Shade climbed over the stall and grabbed his mane. "Come on, enough."

Turning to look at Britt, his anger was building. "A huge warning to you, this stallion does not like females. If he bolts out of here, you don't stand a chance to live. So, I suggest you back your ass off that stall, you do not belong here!"

Shade jumped over the stall and physically grabbed her arm, spinning her toward the entrance. "I am mated! So, I suggest if you have a brain in that bottled red head of yours, you march right back to camp because you truly do not want me to physically haul your ass over there."

***

Kate climbed fresh from the shower and spritzed on her rose scented perfume. She pulled on jeans and boots and headed for the camp, stopping at the door and going back to grab her crossbow. Maybe Skelk would be in the camp tonight and she could get him to come out of his shell a bit more. Luca said he was the most skilled vampire he'd ever seen with a crossbow.

Kate started down the path to the camp when she felt Shade's anger roll over her. Someone had pissed him off, and she was just glad not to be the target of that temper. She stopped in her tracks and tuned into him and could tell he was in the stables. She changed direction, walking toward the stables, wondering why in heavens name he'd be so angry. As she got closer, she picked up the scent of a female, and it didn't take a lot of thought to figure out which one. As Kate got closer, she could hear Britt laughing as she heard her response to him.

"Oh, the very idea of you hauling my ass anywhere has a lot of appeal. I'll go, but you know where to find me. Like I said, anything you want, anytime you want it."

Kate's temper flared as she saw the redhead strut from the stables, flipping her hair as she looked over her shoulder, casting one last lustful look in Shade's direction. Without thinking, Kate lifted the crossbow into position, and turned on the laser light. As Britt turned her head back around, the light was centered in her forehead and she stopped dead in her tracks, facing Kate with a crossbow aimed at her head.

Britt swallowed hard and held up her hand, speaking in a pleading voice, "I was only kidding around. I meant no harm. I'm sure he knows I was only kidding."

Kate took two steps forward, never lowering the crossbow, her eyes locked on Britt's. "Well, Britt, then you should know when it comes to Shade, I never kid around, and I do mean harm."

***

Shade's anger flared at Britt's smart-ass remark as she headed out of the stables. Before he could respond he was hit with the strong, intoxicating scent of roses and he felt *bel*. Her anger rolled deep and hard, her beast was waiting for a kill. He sensed Kate was close and then heard the conversation between the two women. Shade waited only a second before he quickly moved out the other end of the stables, so he could come up behind Kate.

He saw her dead aim on Britt's forehead, threatening her with her life. Shade slowly walked up behind *bel*, placing his arms around her waist, his eyes locking with Britt's.

"May I introduce my queen? She is deadly with this crossbow, killed the most heinous vampire in all of Europe, Cuerpo. I have no control over what she does, or whom she kills, but you have crossed the line with her mate. I, personally, would take you out for it, if the tables were turned."

Shade could feel *bel's* anger close to exploding. He squeezed her waist tighter and leaned into her neck, kissing it gently. "*Mi amore*, I think if you let her live, she may spread the word that Queen Medici does not let anyone mess with her mate. I also think if you decide to let that arrow fly, no one would miss her. So, this is your choice. I will let you make it and support whatever you decide."

Kate watched as the blood drained from Britt's face. Britt knew her fate rested in the hands of a jealous mate, and Shade seemed content to let her decide the outcome. Britt breathed a sigh of relief as she saw Kate lower the crossbow and told the wolf at her side to stand down. Kate realized her beast was close to the surface, and it was Shade who calmed her. She wondered if she'd have pulled the trigger had he not stepped up behind her. She shuddered because she knew the answer. With clenched teeth, Kate spit out her demand. "Get your things and leave this camp. You're not welcome here."

Britt mumbled her thanks and broke into a run back toward the camp. She quickly gathered her gear and teleported out without bothering to say anything to the other females in the barracks.

Kate dropped the bow on the ground as she turned to Shade and wrapped her arms around him. "I might have killed her."

He soothed her. "No, your heart would never have let you kill her. That was your beast, *mi amore*, wanting to take her blood. You thought before you took a life. Relax, my crimson haired minx, she is long gone, and nothing has happened except my queen claimed what is hers."

Kate sobbed quietly as he held her close. "Aegis was ready to attack her. She understands the threat of other females around her mate. I'm glad you were here. I'm not sure I share your confidence in my decision making. I think my emotions were ruling my choices and my anger was winning."

Aegis remained sitting as Night Stalker joined her. Aegis issued a low growl and cuffed Night Stalker on the head. Kate laughed. "Aegis just told him, 'See what happens when other females show up.' Come, let's go home. I have missed you."

"*Si*, it has been a long night for us both."

Picking her up, she curled into his chest and Aegis began to walk with them. Night Stalker picked the bow up in his mouth and trotted to the house ahead of them.

"I love you, *mi amore*. I will always love you and I think I finally understand how you see the females in my life now. Any time you want to shoot them or feed them to your warriors, go right ahead!"

Kate laughed out loud. "I'll try to be discreet, lover. I know they're not all deserving of my anger and jealousy." She laid her head against his chest, happy to be home, and in his arms.

46

Shade was dressed and pacing the floor in his office. Dr. Bonutti was scheduled to arrive shortly. He walked to the bottom of the stairs and called out to *bel*, "*Mi amore!* Are you ready? The doctor will be here shortly." For some reason, he felt nervous and yet, he knew *bel* and the *bambino* were fine. He still worried, nonetheless.

Kate heard him call. She'd lost track of the time. She knew their family physician from Florence was scheduled to come this evening, but she'd been going through photos of furniture selections the designer had sent to her by email and was letting him know which ones she preferred.

She set the laptop aside and scrambled off the bed. Stepping into a pair of sandals, she hurried down the stairs. "Coming!"

She found him in his office, pacing the floor. "Lover, you act like I'm in labor already." Kate summoned Gi and had him bring Shade a glass of Midnight. "You'd think you're the one having this baby. Is the doctor even here yet?"

Shade ran his hands through his hair, pacing the floor steadily. "I'm just worried, and I want to make sure things are well for both of you, and to know if there is anything I need to do. I want you to ask him any questions you have."

Kate took his hand and led him to the living room, pulling him down on the sofa beside her. He took a long drink of the wine before setting the empty glass on the table. Kate placed his hand on the small swell of her belly.

"Feel him, Shade. Feel his energy. This baby is strong." As she laid Shade's hand on the thin material of her sundress, he cupped his hand around the swell of his unborn child and felt him push back against the pressure of his hand.

"He kicked my hand, *bel!* He responded to me. Did you feel it?"

Kate placed her hands over his. "I feel him all the time. He recognizes your voice. He moves more when I'm around you, and you're talking to me. He knows his father already. I told you, this warrior's in a hurry."

Shade was still rubbing her belly when he heard Gi go to the front foyer to greet Dr. Bonutti. The doctor had been forewarned to teleport inside to avoid Kate's greeting committee of two wolves.

Shade smiled as he heard the doctor and Gi reminiscing about old times and how long it had been since they'd seen each other. Gi led the doctor into the room.

Shade stood as Dr. Bonutti gave him a hug, slapping him on the back. "Medici, you look well, very well indeed! And this home is beautiful. You are coming along well since leaving Florence. I am glad to be here and be of assistance to you once more."

Shade smiled as he remembered the years of his childhood when the doctor would visit. "Dr. Bonutti, welcome to Bel Rosso. Please, may I introduce you to your queen, Katherine."

Shade turned and reached for *bel's* hand, helping her up as he wrapped his arms around her waist. "Kate, this is Dr. Bonutti, finest there is. He has been with my family for many centuries."

Kate extended her hand to the doctor. "Welcome to Bel Rosso. I'm sorry you've had to come all this way, but I can't tell you how much better I feel having someone who's taken care of this family for years. Can Gi bring you some Midnight? Please, sit down. Let us know what you need."

Dr. Bonutti took her hand and kissed it softly. "I would go to the end of the world for the Medici family. And it is I who is honored to be requested to care for our new queen. There will be jubilation in all of Florence when this child is born. I brought forth the legacy of Shade and now, I shall bring forth the next generation of Medici."

After Gi had filled glasses for everyone, he excused himself and Shade sat with Kate beside him. "Do you need to examine her? Do we need to go up to the bedroom where she can lie down?"

Bonutti relaxed and smiled. "No, this is not like a mortal pregnancy. I can easily feel his energy by just touching her abdomen. I will feel if he is under any stress. Is that acceptable, my lady?"

Kate nodded. "Of course." She sat back down on the sofa and spread the dress across the swell of her belly. "Shade said this pregnancy would only last six months, and I have to say, I can feel him growing inside me, his energy. He's quite active. I feel great, unlike the first time when I was so sick. I get tired a little more easily, and I have the desire to feed more, but other than that, I feel no different. Is there anything I need to do?"

Dr. Bonutti knelt before Kate as she was seated on the sofa. He placed his hands over her tummy, shifting their position, putting a bit of pressure on certain areas. "My lady, just relax, this will not take long. You were sick previously because you were mortal. There is no fear of such, this time. I do not deal with crossbreed pregnancies, but I can tell you there was no damage from the first pregnancy. Ah, it is a boy. I can feel his male energy. Have you had visions of your *bambino*, my lady?"

Kate laughed. "Oh, I've had visions of this one as well as the next two. This is Lorenzo, and he'll be followed by two sisters."

Dr. Bonutti finished his exam and returned to his seat. "Having your *bambinos* appear to you in your dreams is quite normal. Now, a few things I wish to go over with you, but first, may I say congratulations, your son is progressing well. He is perfect, and I do believe within five months, your son will arrive without a problem." He held up his glass. "May I toast the new heir to Medici, Lorenzo!"

Kate lifted her glass as well and took a small sip. "I don't drink Midnight very often, but is it okay for me to consume?"

Dr. Bonutti nodded. "As long as it is in moderation, no more than one small glass a day. And, of course, whenever you have the desire to feed, your mate needs to accommodate you. You are aware, I am sure, Shade must stop feeding from you. I would suggest he not feed from you after another two weeks, at the very longest."

He looked to Shade again. "You will need to arrange for a feeder."

Shade nodded. "I have a feeder lined up already. Kate can only go two more weeks? I thought it would be longer." Taking *bel's* hand, he squeezed it gently, knowing this was a touchy subject.

Dr. Bonutti took notice of the slight tension in the room at the mention of a feeder. "Shade, you will need to feed on a regular basis, the blood will need to be clean and pure, no hunting. My lady will feed more and more as her term progresses, she will need your blood to settle not only her appetite but the *bambino* as well."

Shade nodded that he understood. "No problem, already arranged."

Dr. Bonutti looked at his queen. "My lady, you will feel progressively more tired. Rest when this happens, it is vital. The *bambino* will take much of your energy toward the end. When he is born, you will feed him exclusively for about a month. After that, you may wean him to his nanny and his wet-feeder and share the responsibility of feeding for about another two months. Shade can return to feeding from you during this time. We will see, once he arrives, how and when he needs to transfer. Some take longer than others. If you have any concerns, contact me. I will give you a private number to call, and I will come. Your activity during the pregnancy should be normal. I would suggest, as your pregnancy progresses, you stop teleporting any long distances. You will know when the time comes to cut back that activity. Exercise is suggested, it keeps you and the *bambino* healthy. Teleporting in, I could see the fine stables you have, and I know Medici is a horseman. Riding is fine, but as with teleporting, you will know when it is past time to do such."

Turning to Shade, the doctor continued on, "The *bambino* must be born in the chamber at Castello. I do not need to tell you, Medici, the Council must witness the birth. At least one member must be present during the birth as well as myself. Theresa is an excellent midwife, and I understand she will be the child's nanny. Having her in attendance will allow the infant to bond immediately to both his mother and his nanny. At any rate, you know I will be there. You must also be inside the chamber, so your son might bond to you immediately, as well as to bear witness to the birthing of your son and heir. The Council will want to record your presence there. Now, do you have any questions for me, please ask, I know this is a first for you both."

Kate shook her head. "No, of course. I understand the need for the ritual, and the witnesses. When should we come to Florence? How much in advance? I have projected the baby will be born toward the end of November or early December."

The doctor nodded. "I would think two weeks would be adequate. The baby will let you know when he wishes to be born, nothing will stop his progression. He is Medici, after all!"

Dr. Bonutti took another sip of Midnight, leaning forward in his chair. "Any other questions you have? I will come once a month to check on you, then twice a month in your last two months, depending on how you feel and if you wish to see me more often."

"I, uh, I know this is different from the first time I was pregnant, and we had so many problems. But, about sex, are there any restrictions?" She could feel her face turning red as she asked.

Dr. Bonutti smiled. "Please do not be embarrassed, sexual activity is a very important part of immortal life, my lady. There are no restrictions. If you feel uncomfortable once you are larger, then I do believe you should leave it to your mate to find a way to pleasure you. It is his job to take care of such things. And I have no doubt he will oblige you wholeheartedly. Just remember, Medici, you cannot feed from her."

Kate tried to stifle the giggle at the doctor's suggestion she leave it to Shade to find a way to pleasure her, as if that had ever been an issue. "We understand about the feeding. That won't be a problem." Kate looked to Shade.

Shade slid his hand over her tummy. "Anything else you want to ask, *bel*? I do not think I have any questions, at least, not right now."

Kate shook her head no. "I can't think of anything. If Shade has your number, we can always call if something comes up."

Dr. Bonutti pulled some papers from his pocket and handed them to Shade. "This is my private cell, use that number any time, day or night, I will arrive within the hour. The other is a list of wet feeders. You will need to interview and choose one soon. The wet feeders are pure breed vampires, bred specifically for this purpose. They will stay with the *bambino* through most of his young life, until you teach him his hunting skills. So, it is a good idea to interview and choose wisely. Arrange living spaces and such for them. This list is very exclusive, Shade, top notch, available only to masters and royalty. These are the best of the best."

Shade took the papers, folding them carefully. "Thank you for your advice and service, doctor. It seems we have much to accomplish before our son arrives. I know you have come a long way. We would be honored if you wish to stay with us until you can journey back."

Standing, Dr. Bonutti declined politely. "I do appreciate the offer, but I have other appointments. I am very used to traveling the world. My body has become used to it after all these centuries."

As Shade and Kate stood, Dr. Bonutti hugged his queen. "You have a very healthy son. Take care of yourself and if you have questions, just call. I look forward to serving you."

Turning to Shade, he hugged and back slapped him. "Congratulations. I know this is a moment all of Europe is waiting for. I am so honored to be chosen. I look forward to meeting Lorenzo."

Shade and Kate walked with him to the main foyer as Gi entered and they said their goodbyes. Dr. Bonutti teleported out as he came in. Shade turned and covered her in kisses.

Kate felt overcome with the reality of their situation, as if it was finally sinking in. "Oh my god, we're going to have a baby! And you... You, Shade Medici, will be the best father ever."

"And you, Kate Medici, will be the best *madre*. We are having a *bambino!* I need to do so much, *mi amore*, so damn much. Wet feeders, nursery, taking care of you, arranging things at Castello, making sure you feed. I am just so happy!"

Gi smiled to himself as he left the couple standing together in the foyer. **"We are all happy, master."**

47

At the end of the night, Fiamma walked with the female recruits back to their private quarters in the barracks. The decision about who she thought should be cut and who should stay was getting easier with each day's tests of their skills. The final decision was close at hand. She was going to push hard to have Britt cut. Fee hadn't seen much of her, but she'd been moving around a lot from group to group at Marcello's request, to watch some of the males. Shade expected their feedback on all of the recruits, and she wanted to have her opinions taken seriously. Although she was responsible for the females, she'd be called upon to train all recruits, both male and female, at some point.

So far, Shade had respected their opinions, and let them control the challenges established for the recruits. He'd made his rounds nightly, watching their progress. Fee knew she had been given a rare opportunity as a female to have a voice in this male dominated world. No other master would've ever given her this chance to learn, lead, teach and advise.

As they entered the female quarters, there was much chatter at the realization that Britt's personal items were missing, and her gear had been cleaned out. Fiamma hadn't seen her leave, but it was obvious, she was missing in action. Fee telepathically informed Shade of the missing recruit.

Shade smiled when he heard Fiamma inside his head. He could hear her concern, knowing she was responsible for all of the female recruits. If one had gone AWOL, she knew he wouldn't be a happy warrior and she'd have some explaining to do. Shade knew Britt was long gone and good riddance.

Fiamma grinned as she heard Shade telepathically respond to her and she laughed out loud. Fiamma knew Britt just had her first real taste of the legend that was Shade. He'd had females hang on his every move and Fiamma was glad Kate had taken the upper hand in controlling the situation. Fiamma was sure this wouldn't be the last time a female, mortal or immortal, would throw themselves at him. Kate better keep that crossbow handy!

Fiamma returned to the female quarters to find them all sitting on their bunks. "I've just been informed, by Master Shade, that Britt was asked to leave the camp, and not under good circumstances. Our queen has banned her from Bel Rosso, with the help of her crossbow. So, let's get something clear. Master Shade is mated. He's faithful and in love with his mate. You're all probably aware of his past reputation, but being mated is a serious matter to them both. You've all been invited here as warriors, not toys to entertain the master. You serve not only him, but his queen and this coven, with your lives. Britt was warned and took no heed of the warning. If either master or my lady warns you of something, I suggest you listen. My lady has a loving heart, but mess with her family, and she will take you out without a second thought. And she doesn't tolerate any behavior unbecoming a warrior. She's his chosen queen for a reason. She's very skilled in crossbow. She alone took out Cuerpo, one of the most legendary killers. She believes in our rights as females, that we be treated equally, given opportunities in our world, so let's show her what we can do. Let's not waste this chance to be female warriors in a male dominated world. Agreed?"

Fiamma watched as the new recruits stared back at her. She felt their shame that one of their own would be so bold as to try anything with Shade. The recruits all nodded their heads in agreement and Fiamma knew the few females remaining were here to become warriors, nothing more. Not one of them sitting here would ever let Medici down, and Fee felt that in her heart. She'd fight for them all to make that final cut, to become the sisters who'd fight alongside Medici.

48

Kate's head was swimming with the details of everything she'd need to take care of before this baby came. The nursery was no problem. She'd get that completed in no time. She knew Shade would go to Luca to feed. They'd discussed the wet feeders, and it was a concept Kate was still adjusting to. In theory, she understood the need that the babies fed until they were grown and old enough to hunt, which didn't occur until they were around eighteen to twenty years old. She knew her body couldn't sustain feeding Shade and a growing child, let alone multiple children, and her first obligation would always be to feed her mate. Still, the idea of placing her baby in the arms of a feeder went against the grain, and she didn't know how to get past it.

"Lover, the doctor gave you a list of wet feeders. Are you sure this is necessary? Maybe between Theresa and me, maybe we can handle it."

Shade could feel her mind reeling with all the things Dr. Bonutti had told her. "*Mi amore*, there is no way you can handle multiple *bambinos*, still feed me and keep your own strength intact. That is the purpose of the wet feeders, to relieve the stress on your body, give you time to replenish. Our son will still need his *madre*, never fear. Theresa will have many duties, the *bambino* will drain her energy as well. Perhaps, Theresa may be able to explain it to you better. Would that help you if we discussed it together?"

Kate nodded at the realization of just what a coven meant. They were all connected by blood, in some way. It helped her to understand this bond they all had. They all needed each other to survive. "Yes, I think we should include Theresa."

"She will be here shortly, *mi amore*, come sit next to me." Shade telepathically asked Theresa to join them. Before *bel* could get settled beside him, Theresa entered the room.

"Theresa, please sit. We have a few questions to ask of you." Shade leaned into *bel*, kissing her softly. "Do you wish to start?"

Kate twisted her hands, fumbling for words. This seemed like such a personal subject, but there had been wet nurses since the beginning of time in the mortal world. Was this really any different? "Theresa, we just met with the doctor, he left us a list of wet feeders. I was wondering if you've had any experience with them."

Theresa nodded. "Of course, my lady. I remember Shade's wet feeder well, and there were others throughout the years. What is it you wish to know?"

Kate looked at Shade. He'd had a wet feeder? But, of course, he would have. Why would she have thought any differently? It had just never occurred to her, he only spoke of his mother. "How do you pick someone? How do you know who to bring into your home, or trust to hand your child over to?"

Theresa smiled. "You meet them, and like in all situations, there will be someone who stands out to you. I know you haven't seen the wet feeders, my lady. Your only experience has been with the feeders we must all seek as adults. There's a vast difference between the two. The adult feeders are bred to feed, that is true, but also to provide sexual pleasure, to put out the flames of lust that accompany the feeding. In our culture, all feeders are female. So, the feeders are bred to service both male and female vampires. They are highly sexualized creatures and I know this is what you see in your head.

"The wet feeders are quite different. They're all female, this is true, but they're very young, asexual. They look angelic, androgynous...neither male nor female. The young vampires that feed from them don't have sexual feelings when they feed. That won't come until they reach their puberty and begin to hunt. The children don't bond to them. They will bond to their *madre*, who must feed them first, and to their *padre*.

"For the first month, they'll only feed from you. Then I will help you, we will share the responsibility of feeding, as they are weaned away from you to me and we begin introducing the wet feeder. I'll work with the wet feeder to wean them from me to the feeder. They'll still come back to you, not so much because they want to feed, but when they need comforting. When they are upset or frightened, they'll seek you out to feed. They'll continue to do that until they hit their puberty and begin to hunt and feel the sexual pull of feeding."

Shade listened to Theresa explain, and she went into great detail. He knew Kate must come to understand these things. This may be the first child, but not the last. "What Theresa speaks is true, there are no sexual feelings whatsoever for wet feeders. Lorenzo will have no emotional bond to his wet feeder, he will care for her, of course, but there is no blood bond. He will know his *madre*, you will be the first to feed him, and believe me when I tell you, he will never forget that. As he grows, and he needs you, he will still come to you for comfort. No one is taking him from you, *bel*, no one. This is just how we live and survive. Once I teach Lorenzo how to hunt, we will break him from the wet feeder, but not until I say so."

Kate nodded, it was her new reality and she needed to come to grips with it. She was comforted by Theresa's explanation, and knowing the bond to her child wasn't broken. "I think I'll feel better once the selection is made and I can see for myself. Thank you, Theresa, for your patience. I'm sure it won't be the last of my questions."

Theresa smiled. "Is that all, my lady?"

Kate nodded and Theresa exited the room. She curled up against Shade. "I don't mean to make this difficult. I'm trying very hard to understand, and I know you have made many concessions for me. Have you spoken to Luca?"

"No, not yet, but we need to talk to him as well, the two of us together." Shade laid his head back on the sofa and sighed loudly. "Do you regret being turned?"

Kate sat upright. "No! I have no regrets. There are things I still struggle to understand, some amuse me, like why these animals follow me around, and some confuse me...like why my children will feed from someone other than me. When I think it out, reason it out, it all makes sense. It's just different, and it takes some adjusting. I love you. I'm crazy in love with you. And I'll do whatever I have to do to make this work."

He let his fingers wander through her hair, the silky soft crimson always relaxing him. Standing up, he paced the floor in thought. "I just want what is best for all of us. I want you to be happy, enjoy our *bambinos*, enjoy raising them without worries."

"Lover, I can't feed you if I feed the babies, and my first obligation is always to you. Even as a new immortal, my body feels that. I know, as a mother, my job is to help our children learn and survive in this culture. It's what they must do. They'll spend their entire lives looking for a food source until they find a mate. They're not mortal children. I do get it. Our job is to protect them and teach them until they can survive on their own, and that includes providing them with a food source until they are old enough to hunt. You've already given me the one request I asked for, to not lie in the arms of another feeder. I'll learn to cope with everything else. Please, don't worry about me. I'll adjust."

Shade stopped his pacing and looked at her, their eyes locked and their hearts beat as one. "*Mi amore*, asking me to not worry about you is like asking me to stop breathing. I live to take care of you, cherish you and make your world perfect. Unfortunately, we live in an imperfect world, and you have a very imperfect mate. We will both have to figure this out as we go. It is a system that has been perfected through the centuries, that is why it still works, because we have had to make it work. We can tweak it to our own personal design, but the resources are here, *si*? I want you to go over the list with Theresa, narrow down the wet feeders, the both of you. Once you have done that, bring the top three here, then we can go from there. Agreed?"

She felt his love wash over her like a warm blanket. She knew he'd do anything for her. He'd attempt the impossible for her.

"Agreed, I'll take care of it. Theresa can help me narrow down the selection and then we can choose together, what is best for our son." Kate paused, touching her hand to the growing swell of her belly. "Our son. I love the very sound of it."

Shade walked to her, laying his hand over top of hers, snuggling into her neck. "So do I, *mi amore*, so do I. Luca is about, should we talk to him now? You know we need to reassure him we will be available to him, if necessary, when he tells Shannon. Have you thought about that?"

Kate's eyes opened wide. "Shannon! No, it never occurred to me. He hadn't even met her when I was pregnant before. What does this mean? That he can't have you feed from him? Shannon hasn't fed from him yet. No one else feeds from him."

Grabbing her into his arms, he rocked her softly. "Shh, settle down. He feels love for her, as I did for you. If she is to be mated to him, she needs to understand this world. Our bodies make no distinction when we feed, and the sexual desire is the same. Neither Luca nor I can ignore that for long. Let's talk to him together, *si*?"

Kate looked down, "I...yes...If you think I need to. I'm aware of what you feel. What you both feel. And it's only fair Shannon is aware as well."

Shade called out to him, "Luca! Come join us please."

Luca appeared at the door and Shade indicated he wanted him to take a seat.

"Luca, come in, we need to have a family meeting here. This concerns you, so get comfortable. You want a Midnight?"

Luca took him up on the offer and poured himself a glass. He knew the doctor had been here earlier, so he had an idea this conversation might be related. He was hoping there wouldn't be any problems with this pregnancy. He didn't think either of them could survive that again. As he took his seat, he knocked back a large gulp of the wine before setting his glass down. "What is it, master?"

Shade stood and paced. "I am going to ask you some personal questions, just be honest and give me your opinion. First of all, I know you feed from Shannon exclusively. How is your relationship going, and is this serious for both of you? Where do you see it going?"

Luca creased his brow. "Well, I'd say it's serious, especially after Florence. We talked about feeders, because I had planned to visit my old feeder and she asked me not to. I told her I'd been going to feeders here, even though I fed from her, I hadn't been seeing her frequently enough to make it exclusive. She asked what we needed to do to make that happen, since she wanted me to feed from her only. Since we've been back, I have honored that. I teleport there anytime I need to feed. She asked about feeding from me. I told her we weren't ready for that step yet. But I believe she's the one, master. I want to move slowly. I want to make sure she's ready, but at some point, I do see her as my mate."

Shade picked up Luca's glass and refilled it with Midnight and handed it to him. "Dr. Bonutti left a bit ago, and Kate and I have been talking a great deal. The doctor wants me to stop feeding from her within the next two weeks."

Shade looked up at *bel* before returning his gaze to Luca. Shade knew this was a subject that needed to be discussed among the three of them. "Shannon needs to know, Luca, she needs to understand what is going on with you, Kate and me. Because you feed from her exclusively, you are going to have to do so more often because I am going to be feeding from you. Although I am home more often now, I need you to still be strong for Kate. I will be doing a lot in the camp, tired and overworked. I will be relying on you, heavily. She is your chosen female, so tell me how she is going to handle this and how we need to go about it."

Luca ran his hands through his hair. He honestly had never thought about it. He'd talked to Shannon about feeders, and she understood. But he'd never told her, or anyone, that Shade fed from him during Kate's last pregnancy. He had no idea how Shannon would react.

"I honestly don't know. Kate had already lost the baby when I met Shannon. It was not a subject that ever came up, and she'd have had no knowledge of our culture to even inquire. But I agree. It's not something I wish to keep from her. It's a discussion I think I must have with her alone. But master, you understand my commitment to you. I'll make her understand."

Kate listened to him speak. She was trying to put herself in Shannon's shoes. Would she understand? Shannon knew now first-hand the power of the sexual desire that came with feeding. This choice for Shade to go to Luca was hers because she couldn't bear the thought of sharing him with another female. But would Shannon see it the same way? Or would she just feel betrayed? Kate knew she couldn't shift her own agony onto Shannon. If Shannon rejected this, she couldn't ask Luca to do something that would put their relationship in jeopardy. Kate knew it all hinged on Shannon now.

"You need to talk to her, Luca. I need to know if this is going to pull you apart, because if it is, then it's not the answer for any of us."

Shade slid his hand through his hair. "Kate, I will not feed from anyone but Luca. It is that simple." Shade turned to Luca. "I have no doubt about your commitment. We need to make her understand. And if it takes all three of us to do it, then we will. At least, if you need us for backup, we are all here together. Do this for me, *si*?"

Kate buried her face in her hands. She couldn't force her friend to do this if she didn't accept it willingly. She looked back up at both of them.

"Luca, please talk to her...alone. It's not our issue, Shade. I'll not ask Luca to put his relationship at risk. Explain it to her. If she says no, if it compromises what you two have together, then I'll deal with the consequences. Please, don't look at me that way. You made this decision for me, to put me at ease. But Luca was unattached then. It's not the path I want...if she rejects the idea, but I'll cope. Shannon has to come to this freely, willingly, or not at all."

Shade stood up, addressing her firmly, "This is our issue, Kate. Ours! We are *familia*, and she is not even mated to him yet. I am doing this for us. All of us. I could command him, but I will not do that. I could easily demand he no longer see her, don't push this issue with me. Luca is who I choose, Kate, who I trust. What the hell do you wish for me to do? Find a feeder from a coven? You would honestly give up your own damn sanity because of Shannon? No, I am feeding from Luca and that is final. Final!"

Kate was caught off guard by his outburst and her own temper flared. "It's my hope, Shade. It's my preference. But I won't force her, and neither will you! If she loves him as I love you, then I can't be the reason they're torn apart. If you care for Luca, and I know you do, you must think of his future as well. Please, I'm begging you. Let him talk to her. I don't want you with a feeder, but I'll find a way to deal with it. They don't need to live here in this house. Maybe the staff quarters or maybe you go to them. Shade...we may be arguing over nothing. Give Luca time to talk to her, and I'll talk to her as well if he asks me to. But it's between them, and only them."

Shade just stared at her and kept silent. He poured another Midnight, downing it quickly and pouring another. He turned his back to both Kate and Luca and downed the second glass. "Then take care of it, Luca. I am going to camp. I have a lot to think about and even more to do." Shade walked out of the room and headed for the camp.

Luca stood to follow him, and Kate reached out and grabbed his arm. "Let him go. I'm frustrated as well but give him time. He needs time. I've learned that, if nothing else."

Luca looked at her, feeling torn between her request and his master's turmoil. Kate stared him down. "I know you, Luca. I'm not blind to just how loyal you are to him. I know if he demanded it, you'd comply, and willingly, even if it cost you your relationship with Shannon. I can't ask that of you."

Luca pulled away, pacing the floor before turning to her to respond. "But that's my decision to make, Kate."

Kate shook her head. "No, Luca. If you love Shannon, if you think she's your mate, then it's her decision to make. You sacrifice enough of your life for us. If he has to go to a feeder, it's temporary, and I'll find a way to deal with it. But if you lose Shannon over this, that's permanent, and my conscience won't bear it. My happiness can't come at the expense of yours. Please. Just talk to Shannon, and let me deal with him, whatever the outcome."

Luca sighed and started back to his own suite. As he exited the door, he heard her say, "I thought it would get easier."

He turned and looked back at her. "What do you mean?"

She smiled a sad smile, and answered, "When I was turned, I thought the decisions would be easier."

He looked at her a moment before he responded, "Our hearts get broken the same, mortal or immortal. I'm afraid it doesn't get easier, Kate."

49

Shade stood outside the house, taking deep breaths, calming his inner turmoil. He needed Luca, he needed *bel* and he wanted to make both of them happy. They wanted Shannon to make all the decisions! Shade shook his head. Shannon was a loose cannon, and still mortal. One false move on Luca's part and she'd blow the lid off everything, including exposing them all to the mortal world.

He walked to the camp, his mind in chaos. He was leery of feeding from Luca for an extended period of time. He'd only fed from him twice when *bel* was pregnant before, and resisting the sexual pull had been a challenge. He knew it would become even more difficult with each feeding, but he knew he had no choice. Even if *bel* felt she could endure letting him be with a feeder, it wouldn't be the same for him now. Being with another female now, seemed as much of a betrayal to him as it did to her. He wanted Kate, no one else. He knew that wasn't possible, he had to protect his son and heir, and keep them both strong and well fed, which meant he must go elsewhere for his own nutrition.

He walked past the stables and stopped in his tracks. He could hear Impavido. "*Cazzo!*" Only one thing to do to free his mind and that was to ride. It didn't take him long to saddle up and head out. He could saddle that horse blindfolded in his sleep. He trotted out into the open field then leaned down over the stallion's head, grabbing the reins and snapping them down twice, his signal they were about to go full out. "Come on, boy, it's time we both let off some steam!"

Impavido reared back on his two hind legs and then took off like a bolt of lightning. Both of them free in the night air, the horse charging through the countryside of Bel Rosso.

***

Kate gave him time to blow off steam. She'd learned he had a short fuse, and he needed time and space after an argument, to think things through and calm down, and then they could talk. Not to mention, she had her own tendencies to fly off the handle. After about an hour, she decided to follow him to the camp. She walked the path through the garden, fragrant with roses and fresh lavender, and the scent calmed her. As she approached the camp, she could sense he wasn't there, so she stood still and focused in on him. *Riding, he's riding Impavido.*

Kate turned in the direction of the stables and had Angelo saddle up Bravado. She mounted the red mare. The horse's coat was brushed to a high sheen and led her out into the fields. Shade wasn't hard to spot in the moonlight. She set Bravado on a course that would allow her to intersect with him. As the two horses approached each other, Kate reined in Bravado, and waited for him to stop.

"May I ride alongside you? Can you slow that giant stallion down now and let him walk alongside me?"

Shade could feel her long before he saw her, and knew she was riding nearby. He slowed Impavido down to half pace, allowing Bravado to catch up. He saw her approach as he pulled the reins back and brought Impavido to a stop. Shade reached down, patting the stallion's side.

"*Si*, we can slow down." He didn't speak again, just kept his head straight forward as they rode slowly side by side in the moonlight.

Kate looked over at him, sitting tall in the saddle, silhouetted in the moonlight. "Shade, I don't want us to fight. Can we talk calmly about this? If you're not ready, I'll go back to the house, give you more time. Tell me what you're thinking."

Shade kept Impavido at a steady pace as he turned and looked at Kate. She looked amazing on a horse, her red hair flowing behind her in the night breeze. He almost choked from the worry he had for all things concerning her.

"I don't wish for us to fight either, sometimes that's why I leave, so I can calm down. My temper can sometimes make me say things that hurt you, and I cannot take back the words or the pain they cause."

Kate looked at him in the moonlight. "I know. I understand that now. I feel the beast rise up in me as well. I want us to give Luca time to talk to Shannon. We may be arguing over nothing. We don't know how she'll react to this. I don't want this to become an issue between us and cause hard feelings when it may be nothing at all. I feel your conflict, lover. Believe me, I have my own conflict to deal with. But we can't ask Luca to sacrifice his own happiness, if it comes to that. And he would. He loves you and is so loyal to you. He'll do whatever you ask. I understand you're his master, and I'm his queen. I understand we can demand it of him. But that doesn't mean we should. I know you love him too. And if you love him, then his happiness has to be important to you as well. I love you enough to endure anything. And I believe you love me enough to endure as well. We'll face whatever the future throws at us, and we'll face it together."

Shade pulled the reins on Impavido, making the horse turn his head and snort, the stallion balking at the slow pace, just like his master. He grabbed Bravado's reins and stopped him as well. Leaning over, he lifted Kate with ease from her saddle and plopped her in front of him. Her hair flew back into his face and he had an urge to just ride like the wind with her.

He released Bravado's reins and gave the horse a slap on his flanks, sending him back to the stables. With one arm around Bel, he took control of Impavido's reins in his free hand and dug his heels into the horses' side, as they took off at a fast gallop. They flew through the fields, *bel's* hair flung back by the wind around his face. This was what he'd dreamed of for a long time, riding together in the moonlight. He felt their hearts synchronize into one beat. He pushed Impavido hard and they rode close to the base of the mountain range and then began to climb a trail, Shade handling the stallion with ease.

Shade led the horse to an outcrop of rocks that formed a shallow cave into the side of the mountain and he pulled back on the reins, stopping the massive animal. He dismounted and held his arms up to her as she slid into him. He kissed her hard and deep. "I don't want to feed from anyone but you, ever, and right now, I just want to make love to you here."

She laid her head against his chest. "It's what we both want."

His arms encircled her as he towered over her. She loved the protection of his arms and how safe he made her feel. She allowed him to lead her to a bed of moss that grew thick on the forest floor, and he pulled her down beside him. The sky was clear, and the moon was bright, but the thick trees blocked much of the natural light. She could hear the crickets and the tree frogs, as they filled the night air with their song. She unbuttoned his shirt, sliding her hands across the smooth hard skin of his chest, exploring as if touching him for the first time. His warmth, his scent, the sound of his breathing as it became more ragged, called out to her as she slipped the shirt off his shoulders.

He tried to go slow, let her lead them, but his heart was pounding and his cock ached to break free. He unbuttoned his jeans, never taking his eyes off her.

He wiggled from his jeans as they fell to his ankles. He bent down, unlacing his boots with speed, kicking his jeans and boots to the side. He stood over her, naked as the day he was born into a world never designed to accommodate him. His eyes locked onto hers as a moonbeam broke through the trees like a spotlight from heaven straight down on her. Shade watched as she undressed, slowly and provocatively, just for him.

Impavido snorted and whinnied, shaking his head up and down as if in acknowledgement of what his master was thinking, and then wandered off along the trail, nibbling at the grass. Shade stared at her, his love for her making his heart feel as if it would explode, and he knew that whatever he had to do, he'd do it for her, always for her.

Kate slipped from her clothes, letting the sundress puddle at her feet, feeling the cool air of the dense forest on her skin. She unhooked her bra and let it drop, peeled the thong from her hips and let it fall, stepping out if it. She spread the dress on the ground and laid down, holding out her hand to him as he stood over her like a Greek god, carved from marble. "Come to me, lover."

Shade took her hand. He ached to touch her. Every second with her brought a lifetime of happiness.

"Take me wherever you want to go, *bel*, I belong to you. Make me feel everything will be okay. That whatever I have to do will be okay."

She took his hand and pulled him down to her. He knelt beside her and she stroked his thigh, his cock thick and throbbing, begging for attention. He leaned over her, kissing her mouth as their tongues explored. He lay down beside her, rolling onto his back and pulling her over on top of him.

Kate stroked his face. "Whether you feed from Luca, or you feed from..." Kate paused, closing her eyes before she finished her sentence, "or you feed from someone else, we'll be fine."

She had to believe they'd be fine. Any other outcome was unbearable. She leaned over him, letting her hair fall over his face as she lowered her mouth to his. She felt his hands on her hips, pulling, pushing, urging. She slid down his torso and mounted him, feeling his erection as it penetrated her, filling her, and she cried out with the pleasure he brought. She rode him slowly, lifting her hips so only the bulging tip of his cock remained inside her, before slowly sliding back down, relishing the feel of him.

He let her ride at her own pace and she teased him, as she brought slow pleasure to herself. He kept his hands tight around her hips until he could no longer take the painfully slow dance she led them through. He pushed his hands down hard on her hips as he impaled her fully and then sat up, penetrating her even deeper. His hands slid up her back, into that crimson and tangled there. He pulled her head back slightly, exposing her neck. His tongue traveled down that lily-white skin until he took an erect nipple into his mouth, letting his tongue roll over it, suckling like he was starved for her. He gave the other nipple its due, then pulled the nipple hard between his teeth as he heard her growl. Pushing her hair softly to the side, he slid his tongue up her neck and raked his fangs over her vein. His own growl was intense with passion and need.

"I cannot wait, *mi amore*, I need release now!"

Lifting his hips, he pushed his cock even deeper inside her, as he sank his fangs deep into her vein, his moan echoing off the mountain side. He heard a howl and then another answering the call and he knew it was Aegis and Night Stalker.

As his fangs sank deep into her neck, her own fangs punched through, aching for him. She felt the immediate explosion of heat between her legs as he drank from her, and her hips rode him hard. She clung to his shoulders, her head back, letting him drink his fill until her own bloodlust overcame her, and she tilted forward, sinking her fangs into his shoulder. His blood hit her tongue and it was like liquid sex. She felt her own orgasm wash over her, as she gripped hard with her hands, her nails digging deep into his flesh, her hips thrusting hard to take him fully. She felt his release, hot and wet inside her, the scent of their mingled sex hanging heavy in the night air. She drank deep and broke free, unlatching as she threw her head back, riding the waning waves of their orgasm before she collapsed in his arms.

He retracted his fangs and licked the wound, watching her riding out the orgasm. They lay back down on the soft moss as he cradled her on his chest. His hands caressed her back, keeping her warm as their heart rate and breathing returned to normal. "*Ti amo, mi amore*. I will do whatever I have to. I will accept if Shannon does not wish to let Luca do this. Just please promise me, you will help her understand this. Help her for us."

Kate laid with her head on his chest, listening to the beat of his heart. His voice rumbled deep in his chest. "Lover, I'll speak with her. You know how I feel. It's as important to me...maybe even more so. But I have to prepare myself for whatever the outcome will be. We'll do what we need to do, for us, and for Lorenzo, and those that follow." She kissed him lightly, feeling the soft fullness of his lips. "I love you, Shade."

"Come, you are cold, we need to get you back to the house, the night air is still chilly yet."

Lifting her from his chest, he gathered her dress and bra, and they both began to put their clothes back on. He gave a whistle and heard Impavido come crashing through some trees. "Damn, boy, if that was supposed to be a stealth move, you failed miserably!"

He watched as Impavido went straight to *be*l and nuzzled her neck and then looked back at Shade and snorted. Shade laughed and shook his head. "Damn traitor!"

Kate returned the affection to the large stallion, stroking his strong neck as she leaned her head against him. Shade mounted the horse and held his hand out for her. She stepped into the stirrup and grabbed hold of his hand as he lifted her effortlessly into place, seated in front of him.

They rode together back to the field where Bravado waited near the stables, grazing patiently, lifting her head as they approached. Shade reached out and grabbed her reins and she followed them back to the stables.

Angelo approached and took the reins for both horses and Shade dismounted and let Bel slide right into his arms.

"I want to stay at the house tonight. I do not want to go into camp. I want to be with you all night, *mi amore*."

"You'll get no arguments from me, lover. Come on. Let's go sit around the house like an old married couple."

Throwing back his head laughing, he grabbed her hand and they ran toward the house, laughing as they went. They would never grow old, and their hearts would always return to each other.

50

Raven took control of the command post in the Dead House and had his warriors out on the streets. So far, this night had not presented any serious threats, and that meant less for him to report to the boss-man, and some much needed time for him to make his rounds and check out grid ten. He needed to feed soon and had found a section in D.C. that catered to the gay scene. He could have a feeder, but all feeders were female. He preferred males, and now master had given him the freedom to hunt. At least there'd be some release for him in that area.

He liked getting dressed up, wearing great styles and lots of jewelry. He'd always been different from the other warriors. He knew he was fortunate his vampire culture didn't place the same stigma on his sexual preference as his counterparts in the mortal community faced. He teleported to "ZS", one of the gay clubs he'd found and decided, tonight, he was going inside. He'd been watching the clubs, seeing who was going in and out, and looking for males that reflected his style and taste.

Entering the club without fanfare, he didn't want to draw attention to himself. He found a feast of tasty treats waiting for him as he walked from table to table, checking out the clientele. Some were blatantly dressed in drag, while others were dressed more similar to him. He saw men of every shape, color, and size. Raven had done his research, and D.C. had a very active and open gay community. It wasn't New York, Miami, or San Francisco, but it would do until he could make his way to California. He knew, if he played his cards right, boss-man could eventually send him to protect their California estate and Raven could really rock it out there.

He made his way to the bar over all the flashing lights and loud music and ordered a whiskey. Of course, he couldn't drink it, but it looked good in his hand and helped him blend in with the mortals. He found a seat tucked close to the wall where he could observe all the action. He'd begun the night in the Dead House with his hair pulled back in a man-bun, but he'd taken it down now. His fingers were covered in rings and his leathers were unique, skin tight, and designed by Cory.

The DJ started playing Adam Lambert's, *For Your Entertainment*.

Raven sat forward in his chair and began to really pay attention. Male dancers strutted out onto the floor, dressed in tight jeans, leathers and no shirts. They danced on poles located around the dance floor and the entertainment began. As they performed, Raven couldn't believe what he was seeing. He'd hit the fucking mother lode! He watched as a crowd of young men joined the professional dancers on the floor, the men gyrating against each other as they strutted across the floor, coming closer and closer and Raven's mouth was watering.

This was the perfect hunting ground and although he knew he couldn't join in tonight because he was on duty, he'd finally found a place where he belonged, where he could dress as he pleased, be accepted and feed without judgment. He could cut loose in this place, and Raven loved to dance.

He stood from his seat and watched as one of the hard-bodied dancers slithered up to him. He moved sensuously around Raven and let his hand slide through his long black straight hair. Raven wanted what was in front of him, but he held back. He was on duty and if he screwed up, Shade would send him back to Florence with his dick rammed down his throat. Boss-man took no shit and Raven had no intention of throwing away this opportunity.

The dancer was clad in tight leathers. His cock was huge and straining against the soft material. He wore sunglasses inside the dark club, and his hair was short and spiked. Raven could barely stand still, it had been a long time since he'd fed from a man and he knew if he made a move, he could have this one easily. The dancer moved around Raven and slid his body along Raven's ass, tempting him, and Raven's beast wanted out to play. The dancer leaned into his neck, and Raven knew he was mortal and he wasn't sure how much longer he could contain his urges.

The man whispered in his ear, "Don't be nervous, gorgeous, just dance and let go."

Every cell in his body screamed to just go with him, dance and find a quiet dark corner to feed and let his beast have some fun. But Raven shook his long mane in the negative. "Not tonight. I need to leave, but I'll be back another time. Will you be here?"

The dancer grabbed his hand and licked Raven's palm. "Pretty much every night. Until we meet again, gorgeous."

The hard-bodied dancer slipped back into the crowd, as the beat of the music seemed to be slamming harder and harder. Raven made a mad dash for the door and headed around the building into the alley. He leaned against the brick building, sucking in deep gulps of cool night air. "*Cazzo*!"

Once under control, he teleported back to the Dead House and as far from the temptation as he could get, but soon, very soon, he'd have a night off and he knew exactly where he was going, straight into the bowels of that temptation.

51

Luca paced on the patio outside his suite, smoking a cigarette while holding the cell phone in his free hand. He was caught in the middle, once again, between Shade and Kate. He knew his allegiance to Shade was unbreakable that he'd sacrifice everything for him. But he understood the conflict and what he was putting at risk. This wasn't something he'd ever discussed with Shannon, and he knew Kate's own loyalty to her friend, and to him, would leave her riddled with guilt if Luca's choice resulted in the end of his relationship with Shannon.

Luca already knew his choice. He loved Shannon and wanted her as his mate. But she'd have to adapt to this. She'd have to understand that, in his world, his allegiance would always be to Shade. Luca sighed then dropped the cigarette on the ground and put it out with his boot before hitting dial. He heard her sweet voice on the other end of the phone. "*Mia belleza*, tell me you have no plans for the evening."

Shannon purred, "Well, it sounds like I do now."

He chuckled then told her he was coming over. "We need to talk, Shan. There are some things going on I need to keep you informed of."

Shannon's tone changed as her concern bled through the phone. "Is something wrong, Luca?"

"Nothing wrong, *mia belleza*, but things we need to discuss."

Shannon felt confused but welcomed any reason to be with him. "Of course, babe, come now. We'll talk, and you can sleep here with me. I've missed you."

Luca told her he'd be there shortly. He sent a message to Shade telepathically that he was leaving. He felt Shade's acknowledgement, and knew he was wrapped in his own turmoil.

Within minutes, Luca teleported out and landed inside Shannon's condo in Alexandria. Shannon greeted him with a kiss that left him stunned and staggering for his breath. His fangs ached with need, and he'd feed from her while he was here, unless this conversation went badly.

"*Mia belleza*, as much as I'd like to take you to your bed right now, I feel we must talk first."

Shannon sighed and plopped down on her sofa. "Luca, you're such a buzz-kill. Sit down next to me and spill the beans."

Luca smiled at her as he sat down, taking her hand. "So, we haven't talked to each other since you heard the news of Kate's pregnancy. You're pleased to hear this, yes?"

Shannon beamed at him. "Of course! I think it's awesome. Will this make you an uncle of sorts? Maybe I'll be an unofficial auntie. Kate has always felt like a sister to me."

Luca smiled at her enthusiasm as she curled into him. "Don't get any ideas, *mia belleza*. There will be no babies in our future for a while."

Shannon laughed. "Oh, don't worry! I'm not ready for that in my life yet. Although, I'm very happy for Kate. She told me briefly about the loss of their first baby. I know this is what she wants, what they both want, so really, I couldn't be happier for them. You don't think there will be a problem, do you? Is that your concern? Is that why you're here?"

Luca shook his head. "No, her first pregnancy came when she was mortal. It's not impossible for a mortal to give birth after mating with a vampire, but it's very rare. The infant rarely survives, and often, the mother will die as well. We all feared for Kate during that pregnancy. But now, as an immortal, she'll be strong, and the baby as well. So, no, to answer your question, there should be no issues with this pregnancy. In a few months, Shade will be holding his new son, the heir to the Medici dynasty."

Shannon was beaming at him. "I'm so excited for her. How long have they known?"

Luca shook his head. "It was only just confirmed by the doctor, and the only people who've been told are Council and the people at Bel Rosso. But it's also why I'm here, Shan. Why we must talk."

Shannon could see his mood shift as he became more serious. "Okay, so what do you need to tell me? That you'll be protector to her children as well? You'd already mentioned something about that. Are you saying your time with me is going to be even more challenging?"

Luca looked away from her as he gathered his thoughts. "Yes, I'll be protector to her children, along with other warriors who'll be assigned, but that's not what I need to discuss. It's about the feeding."

Shannon creased her brow. "I don't understand. What does Kate's pregnancy have to do with your feeding?"

Luca bit at his lip. "This is complicated, Shan. I want you to listen to everything I have to tell you before you react, please."

Shannon sat up straight, bristling a little in anticipation of what he was about to say. "Okay, Luca, I don't know where this is going, but I've managed so far."

Luca was wishing he had a glass of Midnight, but took a deep breath, instead, before starting his explanation. "During her pregnancy, just like for a mortal, the baby grows fast and takes his nourishment from the mother. Kate will need to feed more often from Shade to sustain herself as well as the baby growing inside her."

Shannon nodded her head. "Yeah, okay, that makes perfect sense."

Luca took her hand, rubbing his thumb gently over her hand as he continued his explanation. "However, because the baby needs everything from her to grow and be healthy, Shade won't be able to feed from her. No male can feed from his female while she is pregnant. They must all seek another source to feed."

Shannon tilted her head. "Okay, I can see why that would be the case. So, he has to go to a feeder then? Like you were using before me?"

Luca looked down. "Normally, that's what's done. The male goes back to a feeder during the mate's pregnancy and for a short time afterwards while the female feeds the newborn, until the baby is weaned to a wet feeder."

Shannon shook her head. "A what?"

Luca looked up at her, glad for a chance to slow down the inevitable. "A wet feeder is a special breed of feeder, young, virginal, androgynous. They are selected to feed an infant and remain with them until the infant reaches puberty, which doesn't occur until they are between eighteen and twenty. Neither the child nor the feeder feels any sexual attraction during the feeding. It is nourishment only."

Shannon screwed up her face. "Seriously? Why wouldn't they just feed from the mother?"

Luca explained to her, "Because the female's first obligation is to her mate, not her child. I know this is strange in your culture. If the female continues to feed the child, she can't feed her mate, and her mate is at his strongest when he feeds only from her. Also, if the female has more than one child, she can't possibly feed both. The wet feeders are bred specifically for this function, just as feeders are bred for the non-mated adults. This has protected and preserved our culture and limits the frequency that vampires feed from mortals. It protects us from exposure and has preserved our race. Do you understand?"

Shannon nodded. "Yeah, it sounds very strange to me, but yeah, I get it. So, what does this have to do with you?"

Luca paused. "Not unlike you, Kate has always objected to feeders. During the first pregnancy, she asked Shade to promise he wouldn't seek out a feeder, and he promised her he wouldn't."

Shannon shook her head. "I don't understand. You just said males go to a feeder. He has to feed, right?"

"Yes, he has to feed, or die. Kate didn't want him with another female, because as you are aware, with adult vampires, it's not just feeding but sex. She couldn't get past the image of that in her head, Shade with another female. He could, of course, hunt, look for unsuspecting male mortals. But with hunting, the blood you find is not always pure. There are mortal diseases, drugs, other contaminants. So, it's not always a good option. It will keep the vampire alive, but not at their strongest. And Shade is a warrior, he must always be strong."

Shannon creased her brow again. "So what are you trying to tell me? How did Shade feed?"

Luca looked up at her, locking her in his gaze. "From me, *mia belleza*, he fed from me. And during this pregnancy, and all future pregnancies, he will continue to feed from me. You need to know he never asked this of me, I volunteered, and he gratefully accepted. They both gratefully accepted. I didn't know you then. But I can't tell you my decision would be any different. You know my loyalty to him."

Shannon pulled her hands away and asked, "So when he feeds from you. Do you feel...does he feel...?" Shannon stammered over her words, trying to process the information.

Luca didn't make her formulate the question in her head. "Yes, *mia belleza*, he feels the same desire you feel when I feed from you, only more intensely, since he is feeding from me."

Shannon stood up from the sofa and paced in the room, quiet for a few minutes as she absorbed what he'd said.

"Okay, but do you act on those desires? I mean, can you ignore them?" She already knew the answer, she knew the power of the desire she felt when he fed from her, and the ability to ignore it would be impossible.

Luca shook his head. "No. We don't. You understand, in our culture, we make no distinction between sexual encounters with male or female, even though every vampire has a preference. There is no stigma in our world around sex. We don't even have words for homosexual or heterosexual. That's a mortal construct. We understand the mortal meaning. We just don't understand your dilemma."

Shannon didn't look at him and continued pacing the floor. "So, you're with Shade in a...sexual way? And Kate knows this?"

Luca watched her closely, trying to read her mood. "I was with him, and yes, Kate understands there is a sexual component to our feeding. After her pregnancy ended, I was no longer with him. He'd never seek me out when Kate is available to him, do you understand? It's only while she's pregnant. Shade loves her, wants her. And I want you. I love you, Shannon. But this is our culture."

Shannon felt like her head would explode. She put both hands to her head. "This is too much. Too confusing. Because, if I understand everything you're saying, it's a choice! He could go to a feeder. He doesn't need to go to you."

Luca nodded, answering her softly, "It's a choice, *mia belleza*. But it's my choice as well as theirs."

Shannon stopped pacing and looked at him. "So, are you saying if I asked you not to offer yourself to him, you would...you'd tell me no?"

Luca held her gaze, seeing the pain and confusion in her eyes, wishing he could take it away. But this was who he was, and his loyalty to his master would always take precedent.

"I'd say no, Shannon. But it's in no way a reflection of how deeply I love you. I know you'll struggle to understand, but he's my master, he's done more for me than I can possibly repay. I'm bound by blood to him, and to her. But I want you to know Kate didn't want me to make a decision that would put you and I at risk. She was adamant that if you objected, I was to ignore any commitment to her or Shade. I've searched my heart, and my honor as a Medici requires I remain true to my master. I could keep this from you, hide it, keep it secret. There'd be many opportunities for me to be with Shade and you'd never have reason to know, but I won't keep anything from you, Shannon. I promised you from the beginning. And if this is the life you choose, to stay with me, then you need to know everything."

Shannon cried soft, silent tears. He saw them wet her cheeks and his heart was breaking. Luca stood and went to her, pulling her close to his chest.

"Shannon, I'd do anything to take away this pain."

Shannon pulled away. "That's not true. You won't change your mind about allowing Shade to feed from you. Why can't I be first, Luca? In anything, why can't I ever be first? You just said Kate would free you from any obligation. So, this is your choice to make!"

Luca let her pull away, giving her space. "Shan, I don't know how to explain to you my commitment to him. He raised me when my father died, I was trained at his hand, I was chosen to be protector to his mate. I'll stand at his side for the rest of his life, and her life. I'll guard his children. He saved my father's homestead, preserved it for me. He maintained the lemon groves, which have produced a lot of wealth that has been accumulated for me. He owed me nothing and gives me everything. In return, he asks for loyalty.

"Please try to see this through my eyes. I understand, in your culture, you have aligned love and sex, and a mate who strays to another for sex is a betrayal of love and loyalty. I have watched Kate struggle with that as well. But in our culture, while there is an expectation of fidelity once mated, there are circumstances where one or the other partner may have to go to a feeder. It's a matter of survival. Don't misunderstand, a vampire can betray a mate, a vampire can be unfaithful and indiscriminate in seeking out partners for sex, and that is generally frowned upon, unless it's an arrangement both have agreed to. But when the selection of another partner is related to feeding, it's not viewed as betrayal. It's complicated by the fact that our feeding is so closely tied to heightened sexual arousal. It comes unbidden."

Shannon looked back at him. "But does it have to be you? If Kate feels threatened by the idea of Shade being with another woman, then I understand that. If she feels more comfortable with the idea of Shade being with a man, why does that man have to be you? Why not one of his other warriors?"

Luca shook his head. "We are linked, the three of us. It's the solution that brings the most comfort to all three. Kate knows me, understands my intent, she understands my love for Shade is in no way a threat to her and what they have together. Shade and I have a bond that I've already explained. It's the choice that feels most natural and comfortable for all of us."

Shannon dropped her head. "Except me. Do you even care how this makes me feel?"

"If I didn't care, I wouldn't be here. It's my hope I can help you understand. If we were to someday mate, you and I, and you were to become pregnant, then I too would have to seek out another to feed. Do you understand? This is not a reality we can avoid."

Shannon dropped down in an armchair, placing her head in her hands. "I'm trying so hard."

Luca sat on the arm of the chair, gently caressing her back. "I know this, *mia belleza*. I feed from you and I can feel your pain. If you choose this life with me, there will be much you'll have to adjust to. It's why so many reject a union with a mortal. I can only follow my heart, Shan, and my heart has led me to you. I hate that my love brings you such pain. But there's more."

Shannon lifted her head from her hands. "More? I'm not sure I can handle more, but go ahead. Let's get it all on the table."

Luca stroked her hair, tucking her thick brown locks behind an ear. "Once Shade starts to feed, it's one way. I don't feed from him, he only feeds from me. That means I'll need to feed more often. I'd need to come to you more often."

Shannon blinked away her tears as she looked up at him. "Luca, that's the only really good news you've given me tonight."

Luca bent over her, kissing the top of her head, stroking her cheek. He whispered her name, his lips brushing her ear. "Shan, I feared you'd reject me. Turn away from me. I can't change what I am. And I won't turn my back on Shade. But I want you in my life. I need you in my life. I need you to come to me willingly, freely."

Shannon lifted her face to him as he cupped it in his hands. "Luca, I know your heart. You need to feed tonight, don't you?"

He nodded his head. "But I won't impose on you, *mia belleza*, if this is not something you can live with."

Shannon stood and took his hand, leading him to her bedroom. “I love you, Luca, heaven help me, I love you. I can't imagine a life without you now. I'm still not sure how I feel. There are things I need to work out in my head. But I can't let you go."

Luca sighed, closed his eyes, and stopped in his tracks, pulling her to his chest.

She clung to him. “I can't let go."

He rubbed her back as her head lay on his chest. "Nor can I leave you, my beauty."

52

Shannon woke to find herself in his arms. She lay quietly before moving, running the events of last night through her head. Her life had been turned upside down since she'd fallen in love with Luca. She could understand why Kate created the lie for all her old friends and family when she made the choice to move in with Shade. It had been somewhat easier for Shannon to maintain the illusion with her friends since Luca was a day-walker, and Shannon had continued to work and live on the same schedule as before. But she knew she'd move heaven and earth to be with Luca now. This latest revelation, that he'd make himself available to Shade to feed, didn't feel threatening to her. She knew she wouldn't lose him to Shade. Luca's devotion to her wasn't questioned. It came back to that same feeling she'd had when he explained to her that, in a situation where Kate was in danger, he must respond to Kate first. She understood his explanation, his duty and honor would always come before his love, and it made her feel like she was in second place. And yet, she knew he'd die protecting her as well. As she lay in his embrace, she felt his hand gently stroke her bare back.

Luca had felt when she awoke, and knew she was processing everything they'd discussed before he followed her to her bed last night, feeding from her, making love to her, feeling her soft warmth in his arms as he slept. He didn't want to lose this woman, but her decision to follow him would have to come to her freely. He'd watched Kate and Shade closely over the last year and knew there'd be as many conflicts in their path as well if Shannon decided to stay with him. It would break his heart were she to walk away, but his path was clear. "*Mia belleza*, you are awake."

Shannon stretched and moaned as he smiled at her, brushing her thick brown locks from her face, kissing her nose. When she opened those huge doe eyes and locked them on him, his heart skipped a beat.

"I'm awake, babe. Did you sleep well?"

He gave her a knowing smile. "As a day-walker, sleep has never been important to me. I can go days without sleep. But lying next to you makes me want to spend eternity in this bed."

Shannon flashed him a look and a sly smile. "Not all of it sleeping, I hope."

He pinched the firm flesh of her ass, as he laughed. "Very little of it sleeping, *mia belleza*. You have me entranced. You have cast a spell, I think."

Shannon shared a wistful smile. "Have I, Luca? Cast a spell?"

"Shan, I hate that my actions give you any doubt." Luca pulled her close to his chest, enfolding her in his arms.

From her cozy spot nuzzled against his chest, she asked him, "Would you take me back to Bel Rosso with you today? I need to talk to Kate. Can you do that for me?"

Luca looked at her, his face serious. "I can, Shannon. And I'm sure Kate would love to see you. But please tell me you're not going there to try to influence her about my decision to allow Shade to feed. I'll not change my mind, and I don't want Kate or Shade to feel anymore conflict about this than they already do."

Shannon shook her head. "No, I understand. But if I can talk to her, maybe it will help me to accept what is. I love you, but that doesn't mean everything comes easy...for either of us."

Luca nodded in agreement. "Then let's get dressed, get going. Theresa will wake Kate for you." They climbed from bed, showered, and dressed. Shannon downed coffee and a cup of yogurt before Luca teleported them both to Bel Rosso.

Luca landed inside his suite with Shannon in his arms. He set her down gently and Shannon started to explore canvases that he'd stacked against the wall, displaying his latest work. Luca sought out Theresa, and asked her if she'd wake Kate, and let her know Shannon was here to visit. Luca returned to Shannon while they waited.

"Reynaldo has left for California. Kate is turning the California house into an inn and Reynaldo is going to be the chef there, but there's still food in the kitchen. Is there anything you want?"

Shannon looked up briefly from the canvases, smiling at a few portraits he'd been working on of her. "Is there any coffee in there?"

Luca smiled and nodded at her. "Plenty of coffee, *mia belleza*. I think coffee is as important to mortals as blood is to vampires."

Shannon laughed as she stood up to follow him to the kitchen. "Only more so."

Luca led her to the kitchen where Shannon started brewing a pot of coffee from fresh ground beans, and the rich aroma filled the air. Upstairs, Theresa entered the pitch black bedroom where Kate slept next to Shade and gently shook her shoulder, whispering to her that Miss Shannon was here. Kate aroused from her sleep, groggy and warm, as she lay curled against his warm body. She stretched and moaned as she slipped from the bed.

Theresa turned on a small table lamp as Kate pulled on a sundress, her jeans already too tight for the growing swell of her belly. She searched for her sandals. Theresa was following behind her, brushing her hair as Kate headed for the door.

"What time is it, Theresa?"

Theresa responded it was almost 10:00 a.m. Kate headed down the stairs, picking up the smell of coffee and followed her nose to the kitchen, where she found Luca admiring Shannon as she sipped at the large mug of liquid energy.

Kate groaned. "There's a part of my DNA that still cries out for coffee."

Shannon looked up as she heard her dearest friend enter the room, and slid from the stool at the kitchen counter, wrapping her in a big hug.

Shannon stepped back to admire her. "You can tell you're pregnant already!"

"This pregnancy only lasts six months, so everything moves faster, but I have to say, it doesn't give me much time to adjust to the idea." They both slid onto the bar stools at the kitchen counter. Kate looked at her friend. "I didn't know you were coming. I would have stayed awake."

Shannon swallowed down more coffee as she answered, "I didn't know I was coming either. It was sort of spur of the moment. I guess your pregnancy doesn't give either of us time to adjust."

Kate flashed a look at Luca, his eyes telling her everything she needed to know before she locked eyes with Shannon. "Luca talked to you...about the feeding."

Shannon nodded. Kate reached out, placing her hand on Shannon's arm. "Shannon, you're okay? You understand?"

Shannon stared into the depths of the empty mug. "Understand? I don't...I guess...I think the decision is made, regardless of what I understand."

Kate shook her head. "No. That's not true. I told Luca this couldn't come between you."

Luca answered her in a soft voice, "Kate, the decision is made. I've made my choice. Shade will feed from me. I went to Shannon to tell her. This isn't up for discussion."

Kate looked at the two of them. She knew better than anyone the depths of the loyalty that lie between Shade and Luca, and knew from his tone, he wouldn't bend on this. He'd sacrifice everything. She turned to Shannon, laid her head on her shoulder. "Do we need to talk, Shan?"

"I'd like that. And Luca...I love you, but..."

Luca nodded. "You want privacy. I understand, *mia belleza*. I'll be in my suite." Luca left them and returned to his room.

Kate slipped from the stool and took Shannon's hand. "Come on. Let's go for a walk outside. Everything's in bloom in the gardens. Maybe we'll walk down to the stables." Shannon followed her as Kate led her out the rear patio doors and down the garden path.

Shannon hesitated as the large grey wolf approached slowly, and Kate held out her hand, scratching the wolf behind the ears. Kate looked over at her. "You know about them, right?"

"Yeah, Luca told me, but seeing it is a little surreal."

Kate snapped her fingers at the wolf and pointed, and Aegis wandered back to her spot on the patio and curled up in a ball.

Shannon breathed in the fresh air and the strong scent of the lavender mixed with the roses. "It smells heavenly out here."

Kate nodded, still holding her hand. "I know, right? I love the lavender. I was thinking of planting more, a lot more. Like big fields of it. We have the land. I'll have to look into it, see what's involved. But you didn't come here to discuss gardening. Talk to me."

Shannon looked at her feet as she walked along the gravel path. "Luca says Shade fed from him before...when you were pregnant the first time."

"Yes, he did." Kate led her to a garden bench under a large maple tree and pulled her down beside her.

Shannon sat on the bench, pulling her knees to her chest. "And the sex thing..."

Kate nodded. "I know, Shannon. Trust me, I understand your conflict. It's taken me a while to come to terms with it. But you know for yourself, the feeding and sex go hand in hand. Part of my conflict comes from my mortal views of sex, and there's no amount of explanation that can make that go away. Maybe with time, I'll view it differently now that I'm immortal, but who knows, right? All I know for sure is Shade loves me, and is faithful to me, in the only way he can be. He can't change what he is, or what his body needs to survive. His heart belongs to me. His soul is bound to mine. The first time I was pregnant, I asked that he not go to a feeder. The very idea of him lying with another woman, regardless of the reason, was more than I could bear. But now that I'm turned, even he seems more adamant that he not go to another female to feed. We know Luca. We love him. Luca isn't a threat to our relationship. Do you understand? Even knowing what I know, about what they both will feel, what they'll experience, I know it will enhance their bond to each other, but not in a way that takes him away from me. I'm speaking to you woman to woman, friend to friend. Does that make any sense to you?"

Shannon sighed and laid her chin on her knees. "Oddly, yes. I still can't tell you this doesn't hurt. But I understand what you're saying, on an intellectual level."

Kate leaned forward, laying her head against Shannon's. "Shan, if you choose this path, to stay with Luca, and my heart tells me it's the path you want to follow, then you may find yourself in this situation someday. If you become pregnant with his child, he'll need to seek out someone to feed from. Which option would you choose? Male or female?"

Shannon lifted her head and looked at Kate. "Would he go to Shade?"

"I don't know how it works exactly, but I can tell you if that's their course, then I'll stand by you. I understand your conflict, and his need."

Shannon nodded and took Kate's hand. "I know he loves me. I don't feel threatened by it. Not in the sense that I feel like I'll lose him or anything. I think it's more a feeling of coming in second."

Kate gripped her hand. "But you aren't! You aren't second. I've struggled with the same emotions of where I fit. Mortals, even turned ones, are seen as second-class citizens in their culture. And Shade's obligations to his coven, to his warriors...trust me, we've had more than a few battles over that. It's taken me some time to see through it, to see his complete devotion to me. He struggles too. Everyone in his coven is reliant on him, their survival depends on him, and even the Council has expectations of him in maintaining the legacy and ensuring the coven's survival for the future of their race. It took me a while to come to grips with that and understand that, despite all the demands made on him, he still places me above it all. And Luca does the same for you, within the constraints of their culture. If we'd both been born immortal, we'd not be having this discussion, or feeling this conflict. It would be understood. The very fact that Luca seeks ways to make you at ease with this decision, shows his love for you. Can you see that?"

Shannon nodded her head, "I know he loves me, Kate. I've never met anyone like Luca. He keeps nothing from me, and he's totally transparent. I always know what he's feeling. You know me. I'm not the insecure, jealous type. But I've never had anyone that meant this much to me before."

Kate smiled at her. "He has already carved out a spot for you in his life. And he'll always bend when he can. But you'll need to let go of some of your mortal concepts and meet him halfway."

Kate laughed out loud as she heard her own words. "Oh my god, I'm listening to my own advice, and wishing I'd had someone to talk to when Shade and I were starting out. We had some fights that literally shook the house. But I'd never walk away from him. And he'd never walk away from me, no matter how conflicted we were. Listen to me, Shannon. You know me, maybe better than anyone, and I'm the last person who'd have ever told you to trust a man. How many times was I left disappointed and betrayed? But I'm telling you now, trust him. Luca loves you, and he'll never do anything that will intentionally hurt you."

Shannon slipped her arms around Kate's shoulders as the two hugged each other. "I know you're right, Kate. Let's go back inside. He needs to hear from me. I'm not saying this won't still take some time for me to come to grips with it. But he needs to know I accept this."

Kate smiled as they stood from the bench and the two friends walked back to the house, Shannon heading for Luca's suite and Kate returning to the bedroom to sleep next to Shade.

53

Rissa had worked hard all day, Hyde escorting her everywhere, their relationship working better with each passing day. She was pleased with how he protected and cared for her, always a gentleman. He'd come to feel like a friend in how he advised her, and she was getting used to him being here, and sometimes, he even made her laugh.

Hyde had escorted her home early today. She had an appointment with her dress designer, and she was excited to finally see her wedding gown. This would be her final fitting before the wedding, and her first view of the completed gown she'd wear when she officially became Mrs. Alec Canton. It was well worth the enormous price for a one-of-a-kind gown from a famous designer. It was also worth the price to have him personally come to her home to make the final fitting and provide Alec the opportunity to give his approval.

Rissa was aware the press was hounding her more and more as they got closer to the wedding date, looking for anything to give them a headline. This gown had been the best kept secret of the year. Rissa wouldn't even reveal the designer until the wedding day.

Alec wouldn't be home until later, so she'd have some time for the final fitting and any last minute alterations before he saw it, making sure the elegant gown fit her body like a glove.

Rissa rushed into the foyer to find the designer and his seamstress waiting. They hurried upstairs so she could try the gown on and see the finished garment. She quickly pulled her hair up into a softly swirled bun, letting tendrils hang loose around her face. She slipped on the heels that were custom designed to go with the dress. She closed her eyes. Santos had brought in three full-length mirrors, so she could see herself in full front and rear view. The designer and seamstress helped her slip into the dress, then fluffed and straightened before she opened her eyes to see the finished garment. As they stepped back, she gasped at the sight of herself. She looked like a princess. She stood taller, with her back straight and moved her arms to the sides, looking at how the gown clung to her torso before it flowed across her hips and puddled at her feet.

The front on the gown was cut in a deep yet narrow "V" almost to her waist, her breasts discreetly covered. The back was cut low as well, the bodice a lace confection enhanced with seed pearls. The train wasn't long but would look beautiful as she walked down the aisle. She only hoped Alec would approve.

She smiled at the designer and he returned her smile, his finger over his lips, tapping softly as he walked around her. The designer and seamstress placed some pins in a few seams, making sure the garment hugged her perfectly. The alterations would be minimal.

They decided it was time for Alec to see the gown and give the final verdict. She'd felt him come home about thirty minutes prior. Rissa called to Santos and asked him to inform Alec she was ready for him, and to ask if he wished to see her in their bedroom or downstairs. She waited nervously for his answer, as Santos left to go downstairs. She'd had a huge hand in the design of this gown and she loved the end result. If Alec didn't approve, she'd be disappointed.

Santos had already informed Alec when he got home the dress designer was here for the final fitting. He could hear Rissa's voice from time to time as it rose in excitement. He smiled to himself as he worked alone in the study. Santos returned to let him know Rissa was ready, and he followed Santos to the foot of the stairs. Alec started up the steps to the bedroom, where he could hear Rissa giggle like a school girl. The door to their bedroom remained closed and he could hear the soft conversation of the designer and seamstress as they prepared Rissa to be seen.

He tapped lightly on the door. "I know I'm not supposed to see the bride in her gown before the wedding, but I don't hold with those superstitions, are you ready, my darling?"

Rissa's breath caught in her throat, and the designer nodded his head and stepped to the side. Rissa took one last look in the mirror. "Yes, Alec, please come in."

Alec entered the room to see her standing with her back to him. The dress had long sleeves of lace, but the bodice had a cut-out that exposed much of her well-toned back. The gown clung to her frame as it followed every curve before falling gracefully into a puddle of silk, lace and elaborate beading at her feet, the train fanned out on the floor. Her pale blonde locks were piled on her head, exposing her long graceful neck, and she slowly turned her head, looking at him over her shoulder, her eyes lit from the inside, her smile reflecting her pure joy at wearing a gown that had been made to emphasize everything he found so beautiful about her. Alec put his hand over his heart. "My darling, I've never seen you look so beautiful. If you weren't already mine, I'd ask you to marry me."

Rissa felt something warm and beautiful roll through her. He liked her in this gown. "Please let me introduce you to my designer."

Rissa turned to the designer, her face reflecting her joy. "May I introduce my fiancé, Senator Alec Canton."

Rissa laughed as the designer appeared flustered, shaking Alec's hand and asking him if he could interpret his reaction as an approval.

"The dress meets with my approval. You may have to make a second one if Rissa wishes to hang onto it as a keepsake. I can't promise this dress will survive the aftermath."

The designer laughed and blushed at his remarks. Alec returned his attention to Rissa. "Turn around, my darling, let me see the front."

Rissa smiled at the exchange and knew Alec could charm anyone right off their feet, male or female, the ultimate politician. As the designer and his assistant rushed quickly to help her, she turned slowly as they rearranged the train at her feet. Rissa raised her eyes to his and held her breath. Her heart felt as though it would beat out of her chest. She stood tall, looking elegant in the gown. Her hands lay softly at her sides and suddenly, she felt extremely vulnerable under his gaze.

Alec took her in as she turned. The dress was cut in a deep but narrow "V" that discreetly exposed her breasts. Rissa's tall frame and long torso were emphasized in the long column the dress created. She was a vision of elegance and sophistication, and Alec knew this dress would be on the front page of every newspaper. "It's perfection, my darling. Change nothing. You are perfection."

Rissa smiled and almost screamed from the rooftops in her happiness. She walked to him slowly and laid her hands on his shoulders. "I wanted to make you proud of me, let the world know, we'll always be together. I want to be the most beautiful bride for you, Alec. I want them all to be jealous that I belong to you. But what matters most is how you see me. I love you, Alec."

She knew he didn't care for public displays of affection, but there were mortals in the room, and she knew as well as he did, every word and action would eventually make it to the press, so she casually kissed his cheek, letting her hand follow along his strong jaw as her huge diamond caught the light.

Alec slid his hand along the bare skin of her back as he bent his head to her, kissing her lovingly, gently, aware of his audience at all times.

"And I love you, Rissa. I think the women will all be jealous, but not of me, my darling. They'll be jealous of you in this beautiful confection of a dress. Careful now, don't tempt me. I'm not sure your designer has time to create another one before the wedding."

Rissa laughed softly as did the designer who remarked that it was quite the compliment and one he'd never heard before. Rissa shooed Alec from the room.

"Then let us finish up and I'll be down shortly once we're done."

Rissa's head was still spinning with his approval, his kiss, and his compliments. They'd be the couple of the day, both of them stunning, showing the world they'd conquer and rule

54

Shade, Fiamma, and Marcello had been working for hours, going over the results for every new recruit, reviewing their scores on the various skill sets and deciding who'd make the final cut. They had the final list of both males and females they'd chosen for the first class of the Bel Rosso warrior camp. There'd been a few heated discussions over several males Shade was on the fence about, but they'd finally reached an agreement, and all felt they'd chosen well.

Marcello set up a long table in the barracks meeting room. They'd meet with each recruit individually and let them know the outcome. Shade insisted on the one-on-one meeting, so he could review with each warrior their performance and the reasons for his decision.

Shade took the seat in the middle, with Fiamma and Marcello flanking his sides. He'd likely do most of the talking, but he wanted both Marcello and Fiamma to participate as well, to give their input and start to learn from him the delicate art of cutting those warriors who didn't make the final cut. It was a balancing act, because he didn't want to make enemies of those being cut, and many would be able to return again for another tryout if they worked on specific skills. Shade felt as though those not making the cut were probably already aware they'd be leaving. They'd tried to be fair in their assessments as they'd gone along, giving feedback, so every recruit had a good idea of where they stood. He didn't want them to feel blindsided.

Many of the recruits that had come here to be a Medici warrior had found this was no game, and much tougher than they'd expected. And for those who made the cut, this was just the beginning. There was a more grueling path ahead before they'd ever take the blood oath to Medici.

The first few male recruits to be seen had been selected to move forward. Shade let Marcello give them the good news and he handled the situation well. Shade said a few words to each new recruit, welcoming them as the next generation of Medici warriors, before he dismissed them. Shade looked down at the list and saw Riley was next. He wasn't making the cut and Shade sat up straighter in his chair as Riley walked in. He motioned for him to take a seat and Shade laid his hand on Marcello's arm as a signal he'd take the first warrior being cut. Shade wanted both Marcello and Fiamma to understand how this was done, how important it was to appreciate the recruit's efforts and send them off with some hope for the future. He always tried to keep their dignity and pride intact and honored their efforts.

"Riley, I would like to thank you for coming to my camp. I appreciate your efforts and the dedication you have shown, even in this short amount of time. Unfortunately, I will not be able to use you at this time. But please do not think this is permanent."

Shade saw the disappointment on Riley's face. "Every spring, I will be holding these tryouts for warrior camp, right here in the same place. There are a few things you can work on to improve your chances. I would like to see you focus on your stamina and speed. I know you are young, one of the youngest to apply. Do not see this as an end to your journey, but a beginning. Work on these areas and if you are still interested, come back again to try next year. Build your stamina. Do not hesitate. It will become your death. Your sword skills are good, but that lack of speed hampers you. In the long battles, you become winded and slow. My suggestion is you work daily on those things and your skills will come with time. Work with that sword until it becomes an extension of your arm and never hesitate in battle. This was a group decision, nothing personal. I wish you the best of luck out there. If there comes a point where you need assistance, contact me personally. We will see what we can do here at Medici to assist you."

Standing up, Shade shook Riley's hand, as he handed him his personal card. He liked this young man, but he needed more street time and experience. Shade knew he'd see this one again. His gut told him the kid was hungry and motivated.

As the night progressed, each recruit came in one by one to receive the decision. Fiamma was firm but soft-spoken in delivering her message to the female recruits. Marcello was more abrupt with the males. He felt both of his top warriors had done an excellent job. He was proud to have them on his team, to always have his back.

Shade looked up as Aislynn walked in. He held out his hand for her to take a seat, as he indicated to Fee he'd take this one.

"Aislynn, I want to thank you for coming to my warrior camp. I appreciate your dedication to this effort, and I am pleased to tell you that you have been accepted as a student of Medici." Shade watched as her eyes became huge and the smallest of smiles spread across her face.

"It is my wish to build the number of female warriors in the camp, and in addition, warriors with crossbow skills. With Skelk now on board, he will help my warriors become better skilled in the use of this weapon. Your hard work is just beginning. Being a warrior is a combination of skills, heart, soul, and bravery, mixed with intense dedication. I have watched you closely. You have all of those attributes and we hope to enhance them here at Medici. Once we are done with all of the interviews, Fee will come and get you settled into your permanent quarters in the barracks. She will instruct you on our daily regimen and anything else you will need to know. Congratulations and welcome aboard."

Shade stood to shake her hand. He didn't know her full story yet, but he'd know soon enough. It's vital he knew his warriors' history, and what motivated them to take this path. He heard her utter a small 'thank you' as she nodded to Fiamma and Marcello and exited the room.

Fiamma remembered that feeling well. It had been many years since she'd been accepted into the camp in Florence, and she never thought she'd had a shot. "She's going to make a great warrior. She has what it takes."

"Oh, I know she does, Fee, and you are going to make damn sure she turns out just as I expect. I need my female numbers increased, not many showed up this year, and we accepted all but one into the ranks. You have your work cut out for you. I will not be any easier on them because they are female."

She punched him in the shoulder. "Like that's something I didn't already know. I think being mated has made you a bit slow."

Shade reached out like he was going to throttle her, but she leaned away from him and laughed. Their relationship had changed over the years. She had once felt intimidated by him, but now she only felt admiration.

Shade laughed at her antics. "We have several more to get through and then you two need to get your asses in gear and get everyone settled in the barracks. I need to get back to my woman!"

As Fiamma sorted through the dwindling stack of papers in front of her, he felt his energy lagging. He was tiring more easily. He hadn't been feeding from Kate or Luca and he was feeling the effects. He knew he could push himself at least another week, but the signs of his weakness would start to be visible, and he couldn't afford to have his warriors see him in a weakened state. He cleared his mind quickly, as the next warrior came in and sat down. Just a few more to go and he'd get back to the main house, where he'd feed from *bel*, a pleasure he'd have to soon relinquish, while Fee and Marcello got the new warriors settled, and made sure the ones being cut were escorted off the property.

55

Shade heard the electronic blinds go up. The sun had begun to set, but there was still light in the sky. The days were getting longer, and he loved the coming season. Although he couldn't tolerate direct sunlight, the filtered light of early dawn and dusk was manageable. That gave him time to inspect the grounds in natural light and see what needed to be done. He loved sitting on the fence-line in the late evenings, watching the night emerge.

Opening his eyes, he knew *bel* was still asleep. She didn't even budge and that was a bit unusual, but he'd felt her leave their bed during his death slumber. She'd been gone for some time before she returned to snuggle on his chest. He slid his hand through her crimson waves and down her back. He slipped his hand over her hip and rubbed the rising bump that was their *bambino*, growing healthy inside her. He closed his eyes and smiled as he let his hand rest there. Every day, their *figlio* grew inside her and she became more beautiful. The pregnancy was making her slender body more voluptuous, her skin glowed and he couldn't imagine anything more beautiful in his world.

He felt her move as she turned her head on his chest, looking up at him. He kissed her gently on the forehead. "*Mi amore*, let me move you. I need to get up."

Kate yawned and stretched, as she felt him slide from beneath where her head rested on his broad shoulders. She realized as her belly swelled with their growing baby, this wasn't a position she'd be able to sleep in much longer. She rolled from their bed and grabbed a light silk robe, wrapping it around her. "Shannon came for a visit today."

Shade stopped in his tracks on his way to the dresser as he asked, "A visit with whom?"

"Luca brought her here to visit with me. Did you feel me when I left our bed?"

Shade found a pair of jeans and slid them on, leaving them unzipped. He turned to face her. "*Bel*, whenever you are away from me, I feel it."

Kate followed him to his dresser and slid her arms around his waist. "I'm never really away from you, you know. You carry my heart."

Sliding his hands through her hair, rubbing her back, he laid his head atop hers. "*Si*, as you carry mine. So, has Luca's mortal accepted the feeding process? I need to know, *mi amore*. I need to know all four of us accept this and can remain intact. Talk to me."

"She has. She struggled with it, not unlike me. But she knows what's in Luca's heart."

Shade released Kate from his arms and sat on the edge of the bed, his face in his hands and sighed. "He chose me over her, did he not? She is upset about his choice. I am glad she came to talk to you. I hope you told her this does not change their relationship."

Kate sat beside him on the bed, stroking his thigh. "Luca will always choose you. And I think she struggles with his choice. It made her feel like she was in second place. But we talked about it and the conflicts she and I have both faced as mortals. I think she understands now. Or, at least, is coming to understand."

Shade looked at her through his raven locks, still tossed from sleep. "I never meant to hurt her nor Luca, you know this, *si*? I want Luca to find love, especially now that I have found you. I want the same for him. I want him to be loved like this. He deserves it, *mi amore*. I need to speak with him, *si*? I want to know he is fine with all of this."

"Of course. Go to him. I'll take a quick shower, and then we can do whatever you have planned for the night."

As Kate stood, he grabbed her hand and looked into her eyes. He took the silk sash of her robe in his hand and tugged it softly until her gown opened and he kissed the rise of her tummy.

"I love you, Kate. You know I love you. I will return once I am done speaking with Luca. We have made the final cuts in the camp. Those that remain will now be trained as Medici warriors. And this warrior inside you, the one we have created together, he will grow to become the most powerful Medici in history."

Kate ran her hand through his hair as his lips brushed the swell of her belly. "Well then, he better be strong, he'll have big shoes to fill. Go, talk to Luca. Find the peace you seek. I'll be waiting for you."

Shade watched her walk to the shower, then finished dressing. He could feel Luca outside as he went down the stairs. He stepped outdoors to see the sun had almost set, but the sky was a brilliant kaleidoscope of colors and he raised his face to the skies and smiled. He never missed an opportunity to take advantage of that transition of day to night nor night into day, for it was a time of magnificent beauty to him and one he didn't take for granted. He let his senses lead him and found Luca sitting against one of the trees along the main drive leading into Bel Rosso. It seemed both of them were contemplating much lately.

Luca heard him approach and started to stand up. "Master?"

"Relax. I just woke up and spoke with Kate. Sit down." Shade sat down next to him, stretching his long legs out in the fresh grass. He pulled out a cigarette and offered one to Luca. "Go on, you know you need it, probably more than I do at this point."

Luca took a cigarette and they both lit up.

"Luca, I need to say something to you. Just hear me out. You know I love you. I have loved you like *familia* and that is never going to change. I rely on you and put a lot on your shoulders because I trust you like no other. It is a heavy burden to carry. But I understand love now. I understand what it feels like to have that love returned to me one hundred times over. I want you to have that love, find it for yourself. I know Shannon was here today and talked to Kate. So, I am going to assume the two of you have talked as well. I'm not asking you to share what you have with her, just tell me where we stand right now."

Luca took a deep drag on the cigarette and exhaled, as he watched the smoke being carried away in the light evening breeze.

"Master, I knew when I accepted this role as protector that I'd be bound to you in a completely different way. I've pledged my loyalty to you, and to Kate, and for me that must always come first. But I do love Shannon. In time, I hope to have her feed from me, to have her mated to me, but I feel the need for that to move slowly, for both of us. It's not a question of how deeply I love her or her me. It's more a matter of giving her time to adjust to our world, to accept those things that seem so foreign to the mortals. I understand Shannon's conflict, but my decision was made before I ever approached her about this. She was torn, I won't lie. But we've talked, and I brought her here today to talk to Kate. I can't tell you she is completely on-board. But she understands and has accepted my decision. She'll come to grips with this in time. I can tell you, it's not something that will drive a wedge between us. Shannon and I are in a good place. And I remain committed to you, as always."

Shade pulled Luca to his chest and kissed the top of his head. "Good. I do not ever wish for you to lose her because of me. Mortal women are hard to deal with. But I think we both fell in love with two extraordinary mortal women. *Cazzo*, Luca, I never thought I would have been in this position five years ago. Now I am mated, have a *bambino* coming, have a new camp, and my responsibilities just keep growing. Sometimes, I worry I cannot be all I need to be to everyone. How the hell did my *padre* deal with all of this?"

Luca laughed as he put the cigarette out. "He didn't. His mate was immortal and didn't have these struggles with our customs, and he had one small camp, not two large ones. The coven was much smaller. In many ways, it was a simpler time, although they had their challenges, for sure. But you'll manage. Your *padre* kept Portia on a pedestal. He didn't seek her council. You rule your coven with Kate at your side, and I think she'll bring you great strength and power. We have yet to see what she's capable of achieving with her gifts. And we've both seen first-hand how stubborn she is. She won't be one to let you carry these burdens alone."

Shade howled laughing. "Oh, she is stubborn, damn is she ever! I think it is fate that I chose a mate that keeps me in line because she is so stubborn. But *Madre* had a lot of power as well, although it was never shown to the outside world, she kept *Padre* in line. He probably was never aware of just how much at the time. I miss her. Sometimes, I wish she could be here to see the things I have now, to see how beautiful it is here. I think she would have loved it here, to have grandchildren to hold."

Shade sighed and stood up. "Come, let us walk back to the house. Kate should be done with her shower and I believe she has something in mind for me tonight. I just hope to hell it is not another damn driving lesson!"

56

Cory was nervous and excited. He'd driven to the Charlottesville Airport to pick up his mom in his new truck. She was arriving this afternoon. Marcello had gone with him to buy the truck. He picked out a red Ford F-150. While they were in town, Marcello directed him around Charlottesville, helping him get familiar with the area. Charlottesville was nothing like Florence, or San Francisco. He'd have no trouble finding his way around here, navigating the narrow streets of this small town nestled in the foothills of the Blue Ridge Mountains.

Heading to the airport, he used the trucks' GPS system to guide him. He pulled into the parking lot and went directly to the terminal to wait for her. He was pleased to see the flight was on time. He spotted her as she entered looking around, confused, and nervous. He waved at her and her face lit up when she saw him.

Cory was anxious for his mom to see where he lived now, what he'd done with his skills and how he'd made something of his life. He'd been given a chance and he wanted her to meet the man that made this all possible for him. He'd always felt drawn to Shade, back when he used to come in the clubs in San Francisco. He was one of the few who'd ever shown him any kindness. Cory looked up to him, respected him and now that he'd given him this opportunity to change his life, Cory felt deep gratitude for him.

***

Rachael stepped into the terminal to see her son, looking healthier than she'd ever seen him. He'd gained weight, and his color was good. There was a gleam in his eyes she couldn't remember ever seeing before. For so many years, Cory had been lost to her. She knew his life on the streets had been slowly killing him, and yet, her pleading with him was to no avail. She'd been cautiously happy when he'd called her, almost a year ago now, to tell her about the vampire who was giving him a home and a job.

When she'd discovered she was pregnant those long nineteen years ago, she'd gone back to the club in search of the man she'd spent several weeks with, but she never saw him there again. She had a difficult pregnancy, but feared seeking medical care, knowing she'd sought out the adventures and sexual exploits offered by the vamps in that club. When Cory was born, she wondered if he'd even survive. As he grew, it became clear to her he wasn't entirely human, and not entirely vampire. When she went back to the club seeking advice, she was shunned by the vamps there and Cory even more so. He didn't fit in her world, and he didn't fit in theirs.

Once Cory moved to Europe, she'd heard from him several times while he lived in Florence, but now he was living back in the States, she'd get to see him again. Their bond had always been a strained one, him blaming her for his life, and rightly so. She walked toward him, dragging her luggage behind her, and stopped, holding out her arms to him, hoping with a mother's hope that he'd welcome her.

Cory saw his mom dragging the heavy piece of luggage through the crowd, she seemed older than her years and very frail. She had lived a hard life too and he hadn't been of much help. He'd always had so much anger inside. Maybe now they could start over. He'd finally found a family of sorts, someplace he was accepted, and he was making money. As she held out her arms to him, he hesitated, but then scooped her up in a hug. Shade had shown him family was important, and she was really all he had. Hugging her quickly, he took her luggage in hand.

"Have a good flight?"

Rachael took his face in her hands, this beautiful boy with the delicate features. "I did. You've never looked better! Are you happy?"

"Yes, I'm happy. I'm doing well, make good money. I make custom leather clothing and I really like what I do. I want you to see where I live and meet the man who's responsible for this. He's given me a chance to make a better life. I'm accepted there, Mom. My truck is parked outside, home isn't far. I hope you'll be proud of me."

Rachael walked along beside her son as he carried her luggage. She could feel his sense of pride, something she believed he never felt before.

"Cory, I'm so happy for you. I tried so hard to find a place where you fit in. I can't even count the number of nights I laid awake, worrying about you. But look at you! This man, this master, he is respectful of you? He doesn't take...advantage?"

Cory stopped and glared at her. "No, he doesn't take advantage! He took me away from the hell I was living in, and gave me a chance to work, improve my life, learn, and grow. He's amazing and honorable. He's a great master. He pays me well for the work I do for him and his warriors. I was living in Florence, and now he has brought me here, to live at his home. I knew you wouldn't understand."

"Cory! Please, I don't mean to upset you. I know how you lived on the streets. I couldn't be happier that you've found a benefactor. I'm grateful someone in a position to make a difference in your life, was able to step in. I went to many in the vampire community after you were born, but I was turned away. I want to see where you live, where you work. I want to meet these people. I only hope they'll be as accepting of me, as they clearly are of you. Nothing has made me happier than knowing you've found a home and found acceptance. Please, don't let our old wounds spoil this reunion."

Cory calmed down, trying hard not to let the patterns of their past intrude. "Let's just go, maybe if you meet him and his wife, see where I live and what I do, it will help you understand everything is very respectable, and I have friends there."

Leading her out to his truck, he opened the door and helped her to step inside. Throwing her luggage in the back, he headed back to Bel Rosso.

Cory pointed out a few places of interest to her as they drove and talked. "The estate where I live is called Bel Rosso. That's Italian for beautiful red. The master's wife has long red hair and he named it after her. She's very nice to us. There's a building for staff quarters to house those that work for him and a barracks for the warriors in the camp. He lives in the main house. There are horses and a lot of fields and mountains, way off the main road."

"It sounds beautiful. I can't wait to see it. Did he loan you the truck to come pick me up?"

Cory drove away from Charlottesville and headed west to White Hall. "No, Mom, this truck is mine. It was a reward for all of my hard work. I earned it, fair and square. He's very giving. He recognizes how far I've come, and how much I do for his coven and his warriors."

Rachael looked at him with surprise. "Yours? Cory, that's wonderful! This truck is brand new. I've never owned a new car in my life. It sounds like you've made quite an impression."

Rachael reached across the console that separated their seats and brushed back his long, dark brown hair. Hair not quite as dark as the man who fathered him. He really bore little resemblance to that man. That vampire was tall and dark-skinned, with intense blue eyes that left her paralyzed. Cory was of average height for a mortal, his eyes brown like her own, and his frame was slight, his features delicate, almost feminine.

"I'm proud of you, Cory. You've come such a long way. It's one thing to be given an opportunity but quite another to take advantage of it. Clearly, you've made the most of this opportunity, and made this master proud as well."

Cory tilted his head to the side, uncomfortable with her touching him, but he understood she cared about him. His anger had never allowed her to get too close to him. He'd always held her at bay. He knew he was the result of some affair she'd had with a vampire she met at one of the clubs. He knew she was abandoned by him, and he'd always been torn between wanting to meet the man who was his father and wishing him dead.

As they pulled into the long drive leading to Bel Rosso, he couldn't wait for her to meet Shade and see what a master vampire was supposed to be like. "I respect and admire him. I want to be like him. He notices me, is always encouraging me to do more and be more. Look, there's the main house where he lives, further down this lane is where I live in the warrior camp. He's a great vampire and warrior, but I'm too weak and small to be one. So, instead, I make the leathers they wear. We'll go to the camp first and you can see my quarters and my shop."

Rachael's mouth was hanging open with shock, as he pulled into the long private drive that led to a beautiful Italian-style villa, visible from the private road. It was the kind of house you'd see in a high-end magazine like *Architectural Digest*. The grounds were breathtaking. The property covered acres of rolling green hills, with the mountain range on the horizon. As Cory took the fork in the driveway that led away from the house, she could see sections of the property included large vineyards, and another section was dedicated to stables, with fenced in fields for several magnificent horses that grazed in the pastures. This land looked like something out of a fairy-tale. He drove down the private drive toward a stone wall and two massive wooden doors. Two men, that Rachael clearly recognized to be vampire, smiled at him and opened the gates. Inside the compound was another house that looked even larger than the main house but styled in a very similar Italian villa design.

"Is this the camp, Cory? This looks like a giant house?"

"Yes, Mom. This is the warrior camp. The house is really a barracks where we all live and bunk down."

Cory pulled around to the side and parked. Walking around the vehicle, he opened the door for his mom and helped her down from the truck. The sun had gone down and the outside lights had begun to come on. There was noise coming from the barracks as the warriors were preparing to get out on the training field, so Cory decided to take his mom into the shop first and show her where he worked.

"Let's go into my shop, I'll show you some of my work and what I do here."

Rachael followed her son into the large building. She'd never encountered vampires in their world. As a teenager, she'd been into the Goth sub-culture, and used to seek them out in the underground clubs of San Francisco. But she knew of no mortal who ever mingled with them outside of the clubs. Mortals went to the clubs for the thrill of the sex and to be fed upon, and they were clearly seen as disposable. But she noticed the warm smiles Cory received from the warriors who called this camp home. They gave them both a warm welcome, even though they looked imposing enough to rip them both to shreds without breaking a sweat.

"Lead the way, Cory."

Cory took his mom into his large shop where bolts of leather lined the tables and the tools of his trade were spread throughout the large workshop. Cory explained the basics of what he did, as he walked throughout and pulled out some custom bright red leathers he was making for Fiamma.

"This is for Fee, she's a female warrior. I custom fit everything. They need the flexibility, plus some custom features to accommodate whatever weapons they use."

Pulling out a leather chest-piece, he showed her the detail work he created in replicating the Medici crest for the coven. "This is the master's crest and it goes on their dress leathers. They have special events and wear only dress leathers for those times. Every warrior wants something different, so I work with them to come up with a design."

Just as Cory was about to show her some of the patterns, Raven stuck his head inside. "Cory, bro. Oh, sorry, didn't mean to interrupt, just wondering if you have my shirt done? I might need it next week, if I get a night off."

Cory grinned at Raven. "This is my mom. Mom, this is Raven, one of the top warriors."

Raven extended a dramatic deep bow to Cory's mom. "Nice to meet you, Cory's Mom."

Cory turned back to Raven. "I have it done. I'll bring it to you later when you get back from the Dead House."

Raven fist bumped him. "Oh man, that's spectacular. *Addio*, bro!" Cory laughed as Raven disappeared out the door.

Rachael was overwhelmed with the scope of the workshop. It wasn't some little hole in the wall but a business, fully stocked with high quality leather, and every piece of equipment for cutting and hand-tooling imaginable. There were industrial sewing machines for stitching together the leather garments, and large tables for laying out the leather and cutting out the patterns. Cory had finished garments hanging and ready, and several that were in various stages of completion. Her son had finally found a home. A place he fit in, more than fit in. A place he was welcomed.

"Cory, this is amazing! And your work is impeccable. These clothes could be sold in high-end stores."

Cory smiled at her. "It's funny you say that because master's lady said the same thing. It was her idea to have me make the warrior's clothes. I work very hard, and I love being here, having a purpose. This is my family now. I'm not exactly family, but we're all treated like one big family and work together, and I like that. I feel like, for the first time in my life, I'm accepted. I think it might be safe now, to take you into the barracks where I live. Master said I could show you around, it's really busy here right now. We have a lot of new recruits as the camp is just beginning. The one in Florence is well established and has been there a long time and is much bigger. This is a new camp master is just starting."

Cory led her into the barracks and showed her the main rooms filled with couches and comfortable armchairs. He explained they all lived in a barracks-type environment, but everyone got along like family. Several of the warriors threw up their hand in acknowledgement and then Marcello appeared.

"Cory! This must be your mother. It's really nice to meet you. My name is Marcello and I'm Second-In-Command. Cory's doing a great job here. We couldn't manage without him, not even sure what we did before he got here." Marcello turned to Cory. "You're going to be busy. We made the final cuts, now the recruits will need new leathers." Marcello bowed his head to Cory's mom. "Enjoy your visit."

Cory grinned and fist bumped Marcello and led his mom into his living quarters. The building had emptied out now, as night was falling, and everyone was preparing to get to their duties.

"This is my bunk room. It's simple, but I like it, I get to be part of everything that's happening."

Rachael was struck by the size and scope of the building, and the camaraderie that he shared with all the vampires. Clearly, this master had the power to dictate terms to his coven. She'd learned throughout the years that half-breeds, like Cory, were rejected by the vampire community at large. She had no idea how this master would accept her presence here, but if nothing else, she hoped she could meet him to, at least, thank him for the life he'd given her son.

***

Shade made his way quickly to the camp, the time seemed to fly by very quickly of late, never enough hours to accomplish all his tasks. He walked through the high gates then stood back watching the new recruits on their first full night of becoming Medici warriors. He'd given Marcello and Fee the strict regimen he expected the new recruits to follow.

It felt good to be back in his element, in the camp, training warriors. Shade saw Raven blow him a kiss on his way out to the Dead House with his team of warriors, and Shade flipped him the finger. Damn runt was going to be the death of him yet, but Raven was taking his responsibilities and new post well. Raven was a good scout. He had street smarts and hadn't disappointed him in his new role.

He walked the perimeter and spotted Skelk with Aislynn. Shade stood in the shadow, watching her perfect her stance under Skelk's direction. She was going to be a damn good asset to him. She was young, with a natural talent, and he could mold this one, like he had with Fiamma.

He walked further into the camp when he picked up a scent of a mortal female and his head snapped up. He saw Cory walking out of the barracks with an older woman and then he remembered Cory's mother was arriving today.

Cory escorted his mom outside onto the huge training field, the lights now on, illuminating the space. "These are the master's new warriors. The ones wearing the leather, those are the older warriors who came here from Florence. They will teach the new recruits."

"*Cazzo!* I had forgotten. Damn, maybe I am going daft," Shade commented.

Shade made eye contact with Cory, watched him say something to his mother as Shade moved across the training field to the other side of the camp to welcome her. *Cazzo*, he needed to get them the hell out of here. These were new warriors on the field, and it was a dangerous place for a mortal to be. These young skins were learning new weapons, and ammo tended to travel in all directions.

Cory could feel his mom shaking, and he wasn't sure if it was from fear or excitement. Not many mortals would ever see this sight and it made him feel special that master would allow him to do this. He felt eyes on him and looked across the field to see Shade making his way over to them. Shade was easily spotted anywhere with his height and confident walk. He even walked like a warrior and vampire of high importance. Cory knew he'd never be like him but ached to have his approval. Shade had been the only male role model who'd ever given him the time of day.

Rachael saw him as he walked across the campgrounds in their direction. His height caught her eye as he stood taller than the vampires around him, and those raven locks hung in loose curls around his face, those long muscular legs, and his cocky, confident stride. It couldn't be!

She glanced at Cory who was watching him with adoring eyes, then back at the tall, handsome vampire walking right to them. He was close enough to them for her to see his eyes now, those piercing blue eyes that had melted her nineteen-year-old soul. She could feel her body shaking as she reached out to Cory, taking his arm to steady herself.

"Cory...that man...is he your master?"

"Yes, that's Shade Medici. Don't be scared, Mom, he's very nice. He knows you're coming."

Rachael's knees buckled. Shade! She never knew his last name, but she'd never forget his first name. She closed her eyes. Would he even recognize her? She looked nothing like the pretty nineteen-year-old girl who'd eagerly climbed into bed with this man. The years had not been kind to her, and they showed on her face, making her appear much older than her thirty-nine years. Her face already bearing deep wrinkles around her eyes, her hair carrying a little grey, making her look closer to fifty than forty. What if he rejected her, threw her out of the camp when he realized who she was? What if he rejected Cory? Taking away the only good thing to happen to him in his life.

Rachael felt her stomach churn. She felt ill. She knew enough about the vampire culture, in her search for a solution for Cory all these years, to know that half-breeds were never recognized in the vampire community. If her presence here cost Cory his only shot at a decent life, she thought this would be the final straw, for both of them.

Shade smiled as he approached but noticed Cory's mother looked a bit sick and he knew this was more than most mortals could comprehend. Walking up, he slapped Cory on the back. "I see you made it back from the airport without incident."

Cory beamed up at Shade as he felt his mom leaning more of her weight onto his arm. "Master, this is my mom. Rachael Robbins."

Shade gently took her hand and squeezed it lightly. "Welcome to Bel Rosso. I am Shade Medici, Master of the Medici Coven. I am Cory's master and I am honored to have the pleasure of your acquaintance. You have a fine son. Please, you are shaking, let us go into the main house and sit down. I think you would feel much more comfortable and Cory can get you something to drink."

As Rachael made eye contact with him, her heart pounded with fear he'd recognize her. His impossibly blue eyes locked with hers, and she was flooded with the memories of the two weeks he'd spent with her. He stayed in her apartment in the Haight, seeking his death slumber in the day. She used heavy quilts to cover the one dingy window to block out the sun for him. She recalled the nights and felt a rush of blood to her face. He fed from her as they'd had the kind of sex she'd only read about, his appetite insatiable for both the blood and the sex. She remembered how empty she'd felt at his sudden departure, and then she never saw or heard from him again. She took the hand he offered, and she felt the same jolt she felt in the club the first time she saw him.

In a shaking voice, she answered, "I'm so happy to meet you. And I can't thank you enough for what you have done for my son." In her head, she was screaming, *Our son! He is our son!*

"Miss Robbins, please, I have done little for your son. I only gave him a chance to make a life worthy of his incredible talent. He made those changes himself. And I may add, very well. He is part of my *familia* now. I take care of my coven and those that serve me. Cory has proven to me, and to those you see around you, he deserves to be here, he is a talented vampire within my ranks."

Shade looked at her closely, there was something familiar about her, but he shook it off. He'd met so damn many people in his life. "Please, let's go inside. Cory, go on ahead, get your *madre* some water or wine, no Midnight. If you will allow me to escort you inside, we can sit and relax, it tends to get quite noisy out here."

Shade took her arm, entwining it with his so she didn't fall, and led her inside, helping her sit down in a comfortable chair in the living room. She seemed so frail and he had pictured Cory's mother to be much younger than the woman sitting across from him now.

"Rachael is a lovely name. Have you always hailed from California?" Shade smiled politely at her. He could feel her nervousness, and her voice, there was something about her voice. *Cazzo*, he was losing it! Throwing one leg over his opposite knee, he ran his hand through his hair trying to relax, and in doing so, hoping to help her relax.

Rachael heard his questions and tried to focus her attention. "California, yes, I grew up in Southern California, but then ran off to San Francisco as soon as I got out of high school. I couldn't wait to get out on my own. I got a little apartment in Haight-Ashbury. I used to frequent the underground clubs. That's where I met...where I ran into Cory's father."

Rachael looked around the beautifully decorated room, crossed and uncrossed her legs, trying to get comfortable. She'd worn her best dress to meet Cory, and she tugged at the scarf she always wore around her neck, feeling a little warm here in the South.

Shade watched her closely. She was quite nervous. She pulled at her scarf, a tick he found charming. He caught a glimpse of a tattoo on her neck, hidden by the scarf, and he smiled. He knew, from Cory, she'd paired with a vampire in one of the underground clubs, so she wasn't new to the vampire club life and its incessant sex and feeding.

He nodded at her. "San Francisco had a few clubs back in the day. I visited there a few times. I now own some vineyards north of there. That is my business, producing wine. I do not mean to be rude, Miss Robbins, but did you know Cory's father well? Would you know his name? I may be able to help Cory find him and let him know he has a son in this world. I am not unaware of how half-breeds are treated in our culture, but it goes against the code of honor I was taught growing up in Florence. I hope I do not speak out of line here. It is none of my business, but it does annoy me that he abandoned you. Please understand he may perhaps have had no clue you were pregnant. Did you try to seek him out?"

Cory walked in with a glass of wine and handed it to his mother. Rachael took the glass offered and fought the impulse to chug it down. She took a large sip from the glass as he was asking her if she'd looked for Cory's father. Clearly, he had no memory of her, and she was somehow relieved and disappointed at the same time.

Rachael smiled at Cory as he took a seat on the sofa near Shade. It almost broke her heart. All those years...lost. She hadn't eaten on the plane and the wine went straight to her head. She felt the flush of heat again and tugged once more at the scarf she wore to cover the tattoo. That foolish tattoo she'd gotten in her youth, written in Gothic script across the side of her neck, 'We Are Not Angels'. The tattoo, those underground clubs, the indiscriminate sex, so many mistakes, and both she and Cory had paid the price for them.

"Yes, I did try to find him. I went back to the club. People remembered him, but he wasn't from the States." Should she tell him? She looked at him directly, holding his gaze. "He was from Europe, from Italy...like you."

Shade listened carefully, this vampire was from Italy? He had to know who the hell he was. *Cazzo*! Who could it be? He watched as she downed the wine quickly and pulled again on her scarf . As she did, her scarf slipped from her neck and drifted to the floor. He quickly reached down to pick it up and leaned forward to hand it to her and saw the tattoo on her neck.

He made a noise deep in his throat, sounding strange even to him. Images flashed through his head as he remembered that tattoo, San Francisco, and Haight-Ashbury...Rachael!

Shade almost fell to his knees with the memories that flooded his brain. The several weeks he'd spent with her, in her dingy one-room apartment, feeding from her often, lying with her. He slid his hand over his heart and shook his head. His head snapped around and looked at Cory. How the fuck did he not see this before? The dark hair, the high cheekbones, and full lips, but he carried her dark eyes, and his features were softer. His world began to crash around him. Cory was his son. His son! Quickly getting up, he turned his back and walked away from the couch.

"Cory, I need you to... Please, could you leave us alone for a while? I wish to speak with your *madre* alone. Go!"

Cory looked at Shade who appeared rattled as he asked him to leave the room. He looked to his mom, the color draining from her face. She nodded at him, encouraging him to leave.

"What's going on, Mom?"

Rachael looked at him with sadness. She could only hope the outcome of this visit didn't mean the end of Cory's chances for a better life. "Please, Cory. Just give us a minute."

Cory stood and reluctantly left the room, walking toward the back door that led to the patio. He stepped outside and plopped down in a deck chair, confused and hurt by the events playing out inside.

Shade tried to breathe. This changed everything. Everything! And he had no idea where to begin. She looked so old. Nothing like the beautiful young woman he'd made passionate love to and fed from for weeks. He'd been in the States on business, only there for a short period of time to make some contacts. So many things began to churn in his mind. He couldn't comprehend them all at once. What had he done?

"Rachael."

She looked at him, her eyes filled with sorrow. "I'm so sorry, Shade. Cory never said your name. In all the times he spoke to me about you, he called you master. I had no idea. I did look for you when I found out I was pregnant. The vamps at the club remembered you, but they said you weren't a regular. The pregnancy was hard. I was sick the entire time. He was born prematurely, and I wasn't even sure he'd live. He'd take formula, but it wasn't enough. I went back to the club, tried to find someone to help me. But they said he was a half-breed and not worth their time. One of the female vamps there did tell me he'd need to feed. That he'd eat both human food and blood. He's had a hard life. I tried to homeschool him, but he was so angry, so confused. He didn't fit into my world, and he didn't fit into yours. He kept running away, living on the streets. As he got older, I knew he was hanging out in the underground clubs, trading sex for blood. I cried myself to sleep almost every night. I couldn't reach him, and I couldn't help him. Then he called to say a master had hired him and he was moving to Florence, and he never seemed happier. Please, I beg you, don't punish him because of me. If you don't want to tell him you're his father, I'll understand, just don't send him away. It would kill him!"

Shade felt his heart breaking. He'd done this. His foolish life of sex and pleasure had produced a child that suffered and a woman who suffered even more. He remembered the pills, the guilt of his selfish love for *bel*, and their child he killed with his own hand. Did this mean *bel* would have survived that pregnancy as well as Cory? Shade stood with his back to her, her words like knives ripping at him with every stroke of her tongue. He turned slowly and looked at her. He saw the ravages of her suffering. Her face and body bore every moment of grief and agony he'd laid on her. He walked to her, crouching down at her feet, taking her hands in his.

"I didn't know. I did not know. Please, I beg you, forgive me. I cannot bear the hell I have put you both through. Please, believe me when I tell you this is not the man I am inside."

Kissing her hands softly, he reached up and slid a stray lock of graying hair from her face. "Rachael, I am mated, expecting my first son. But Cory is a part of my *familia*, more now than ever before. He is accepted here, and he will be accepted in my life as my son. He cannot be given the legacy of my throne because he is a half-breed. I am royalty, a king. But he will have all I can provide for him. I will never abandon him, never. I accept him. I accept my mistakes and if I could take back your pain and agony, I would. But I would never change the time I spent with you, or his birth. Please, please Rachael, forgive me!"

Shade begged of her, and he must make retribution for all he'd done. Never did he once think he might already have a child on this earth. Laying his head on her hands, he made one last plea, "If you have a heart, I beg you to forgive me. Let me make amends for all the suffering I have laid at your feet."

Silent tears ran down Rachael's face, as he knelt before her and begged her forgiveness. As he laid his head down, she reached one hand into his hair, the memories of him, of them together, hit her like a lightning bolt as she stroked his hair. There were other men after him, but none like him. She remembered every detail of their time together.

"You couldn't have known. It was my mistake too, not just yours. I'm just so thankful for what you've given him, the opportunity for a life here. He's a different person now. He's never known happiness, Shade, until you took him in."

Upstairs, Kate was sitting on the bed, "resting" as Shade had insisted, her laptop opened as she researched some information on lavender. The climate was right here in Virginia, and she was thinking about planting several acres. The retail applications for lavender were seemingly unending. The plants would not only look beautiful, they could be profitable. She was scratching some notes about the average return on investment for the sale of the lavender in its various forms when his feelings slammed into her. Her fingers stopped on the keyboard as Shade's emotional pain washed over her, overwhelmed her. "Lover?"

Kate pushed the laptop aside and slid off the bed, not bothering to put on her sandals, but running barefoot down the stairs. She entered the living room to see him kneeling on the floor, his head bowed into the lap of a woman she didn't recognize, her hand slowly stroking his hair as her tears dropped. Kate was confused by what she saw.

"Lover? What's wrong?"

Shade knew Rachael would forgive him, but he was fearful now of *bel's* response. He stood and walked to her, taking her in his arms, kissing her neck and holding her tight. Speaking softly in her ear, he prayed to all the fires in hell she understood this because their life could be made or broken in this moment.

"Listen to me, *mi amore*. Please hear all I have to say before you respond, *si*?" Kissing her softly, he led her into the living room. "Kate, this is Cory's *madre*, Rachael. She has come for her visit with Cory, but we have discovered something you need to know."

Shade looked to Rachael. "This is my mate, my queen, Kate."

Rachael smiled back at her, looking nervous, as Kate greeted her, welcoming her to their home.

Taking Kate's hand, he led her to the sofa. "I knew Rachael a long time ago. I did not recognize her, but she recognized me. I don't know how to say this..." He took her face in his hands and stared into her eyes, reaching his heart and soul out to her, letting her feel his love and undying devotion to her. "Cory is my son."

Kate felt his anguish mixed with the love he was sending to her. She heard the words he spoke, and it took a moment for them to register. "Your... Cory? Cory is your son?"

Kate remained silent, blinking her eyes, as she recalled the first time she saw Cory in the club in California. He'd looked so thin, so pale and fragile. She recalled how gentle Shade was with him, and how she'd encouraged him to reach out, to help him. "You knew? When you saw him in California? Is that why you helped him?"

Shade shook his head. "No, *bel*. I had no idea. I didn't recognize Rachael. And she had no idea Cory was living with me. He never told her my name, just called me master. Please, *mi amore*, I need to know you can accept this, accept him. He's my son, and I can't send him away. Tell me you understand."

Kate nodded her head, still feeling dazed. "Of course, I accept him. I could never ask you to turn your back on your son."

Shade stood and paced the floor, running his hands through his hair. "*Cazzo!* Cory is outside. Should I bring him back in? Talk to him alone. I do not like feeling out of control and I feel like everything is spinning out of control."

Kate put her hand on the swell that held their child. This woman carried his child once too. Kate looked at Rachael, and saw a woman worn down by the years, who was closely watching their reactions. A woman who'd been young and pretty once, full of life's promise, only to have it all stolen away. She stood and went to Rachael, kneeling before her. She was a mother in pain, and Kate knew that pain.

"Rachael, we love Cory. He's blossomed here. He's happy here. I think he has an opportunity to really make something of himself. And I know this man. I know his heart. Shade would never have left this child to try to make it on his own in this world had he been aware. Cory is his blood. Half-breed or not, I promise you, it makes no difference to him. I was a mortal girl too, and we had a child...or...lost a child. He still wears that scar on his heart. I don't want to replace you or push you aside. I'm begging you to let us share him. Let us love him. The three of us together, maybe we can make up for all those lost years."

Rachael gripped Kate's hands tightly, trying to stop her own hands from shaking, as her tears flowed freely. "I'd never take him away from his father. I don't think he'd leave, regardless. I recognized Shade as soon as I saw him. I feared he'd send me away. Send Cory away. I've spent years researching. I know half-breeds are rare, and completely rejected. That you'd still want him..." Rachael broke down into sobs and Kate held her close, feeling her tears on her shoulders.

Kate looked up at Shade. "He needs to know, Shade. We need to tell him. Let him know he's loved."

Shade's voice was shaky. The level of emotion filled this room and his love for Kate had never been greater. Shade walked outside, composing himself as he saw Cory slumped in a chair. Cory swung his head in his direction. Shade walked to him, laying his hand on his shoulder.

"Cory, I need you to come back inside now. We have some things to discuss. Nothing is wrong, just a lot of information to absorb. Come."

As Cory stood, it took everything Shade had not to grab him into his arms and hold him. *His son! His son!* The words kept repeating in his mind.

"Am I in some kind of trouble, master? I thought it was fine to bring my mom here. Did I do something wrong?"

Shade shook his head. "No, Cory, you did nothing wrong. Just come inside, your *madre* and I have some things to tell you."

As they walked back inside, Cory went to his mother and hugged her, sitting down beside her, his eyes huge in his head and Shade knew he was scared out of his mind that he was going to be told bad news. Shade wasn't sure of the reaction he was going to receive from Cory when he heard what they had to say. Shade sat down across from Cory and his mother and pulled Kate next to him.

"I don't know where to begin. I am still trying to comprehend it all myself." Shade looked at Cory and locked eyes with him. "The first thing you need to know, Cory, is everyone here loves you, everyone in this room loves you. And that is never going to change, *si*?"

Cory nodded his head in acknowledgement, and Shade never took his eyes from him. "I lost my parents when I was young, and I had to learn to rebuild my life without their guidance. So, I understand why your life was hard and I completely understand why you were doing what you were doing when I found you in the clubs. I think that is one of the reasons I was drawn to you from the very beginning, but I have come to find out, today, it is not the only reason. I used to haunt these clubs for feeding and sex. One night, I met a beautiful young female, she was friendly, and she could dance. She enchanted me with her wit, her personality, and her offer to let me feed and all that comes with it.

"She knew me only by the name of Shade, and she knew I was vampire. She willingly accepted my advances. We danced the night away, we drank as well, and we went to her place. I fed, and we made love until the sunrise. She was kind to me, gave me a place to stay while I was there. I didn't know much about her, and I didn't care. I didn't have much care for anything back then other than managing my coven and my warriors, and I was only there for a few weeks. Every night, I would haunt the same club and she was there, so I just stayed with her. When my venture was over, I left town, said goodbye, and left her some money. Her name was Rachael."

Cory listened, his mom reaching over to hold his hand. Shade held him in his gaze. Cory wasn't sure he heard him correctly. *Shade knew his mom? Shade got his mom...* "Are you saying what I think you're saying?" Cory looked at his mom and then back at Shade.

Shade nodded at him, "She had a tattoo on her neck, it read, 'We Are Not Angels' and I will never forget that, ever. When I saw your *madre* today, I did not recognize her, but time has not changed for me, so she did recognize me. Cory, I am your *padre*...your father."

Cory was stunned, he couldn't move, but he glared at Shade as he felt the rage growing inside him. He was conflicted, his emotions all over the place. First rage and then relief, but then the memories of the hell he'd been through his whole life ripped across his heart. Standing, his face was contorted with emotions he couldn't seem to control.

"You made me a bastard! You left her alone, pregnant, and then went out whoring and fucking your way back to your rich life. You left us alone. I was born a bastard, and a half-breed. I hate you! Look at what you did to us. Why? Why?"

Rachael grabbed him, held tight to him. "Cory, no! He never knew. He never knew about you."

Kate leapt from Shade's side and went to him. "Not a bastard. Never a bastard! You're his son. Our son. All of us, you belong to all of us. We can't change the past, the mistakes that were made, none of us can do that. But we can change the future...your future. You know this man, Cory. You know him! You know what's in his heart. He was drawn to you from the beginning and you to him. I could see it myself, and I was still mortal then. I understand your pain and your anger. But don't throw this away. You're loved here."

Shade stood. He knew the rage Cory had inside him. He recognized that with clarity. "Enough!" He walked towards his son and opened his arms. "Cory, come to me!"

Cory stared him down. Shade watched as Kate and Rachael clung to each other for support, Rachael in tears. Shade lowered his voice. "Cory, please come to me." Shade watched Cory come to him slowly, his anger still bottled inside.

Shade embraced him. "Come to me, son. Come to me."

Cory nearly fell into his arms and Shade held him tightly. "Let go of your anger. I have taken your blood, *si*? You knew then it was different. I love you, Cory. I want you in my life. You are my son. Cory Medici. Your life starts now, filled with love. Don't leave me, *figlio*. I need you. We need each other." Shade felt Cory sob and shake in his arms, and Shade's own blood tears flowed.

Kate watched them embrace as they both shed tears. She felt Shade's love for this child, and his guilt. She knew he'd move Heaven and Earth in his attempt to make up for the lost years with him. She saw Cory let go of his anger, an anger he'd carried like a chip on his shoulder all his life. It would take time, for both of them, to heal all the wounds, but they'd taken the first step. Kate went to them and wrapped her arms around them both.

Kate stroked her hand through Cory's hair, "You're his son, his blood. You're Medici, Cory. He'll never let you stray very far from him. Open your heart to him. Forgive him. He has only love for you. Even I can feel it. He'd never have let you grow up alone if he'd known about you. And forgive your mother. She faced hard choices and had few options. So many mistakes, and you had to bear the burden of all of them. But that's behind you now. You belong here."

Shade let go of Cory and watched him go to his mother. Shade took *bel* into his arms, holding her close and kissing her, he whispered against her lips, "I love you, *mi amore*. I know this is more than you expected, but I am going to make this right. I don't know how, but I will do this for him and Rachael."

Shade summoned Gi, who brought refreshments for everyone. Shade downed two glasses of Midnight quickly and got his mind back to the present situation.

"I have a few things I need to do. First and foremost, I will let Council know Cory is my legitimate son. I will deal with them in my way, but Cory may have to come with me back to Florence. They will need to see proof. This is the highest honor I can bestow on you, Cory, to have it recorded in the ancestral books that you are my son, I claim you as my blood. Secondly, everyone else within my coven, all of my warriors need to know as well. I cannot leave you my legacy as king, I regret that immensely, but it is what it is. You will have every other opportunity as if you are my legitimate first born, but as a half-breed, that is something I cannot change."

Shade looked at Rachael. "I can never make up to you the loss of your youth, the hardships you bore. But I never regretted being with you. It was something that brought forth a gift to us both. But I will tell you this, I will make sure you never struggle another day in your life. I want you to be comfortable for the remainder of your years. You will be welcome here in our home whenever you wish to visit. But I am asking you to let Cory stay with me. He needs to be here among us, where he is accepted and protected. I give you my dying oath, I will protect him. Please, Rachael, I ask only this from you, and I know it is a lot, I have already taken so much from you, but I ask you to let him stay here with us."

Rachael wiped away her tears. "Of course, he can stay. I feared you'd send him away, reject him like all the others have rejected him. I don't fit in his world, as much as I've tried. You can help him. Only you can make a difference in his life. As long as I can still see him that's all I ask."

Kate turned to Shade. "He needs to live here, in this house, not the barracks. He'll have his own room here."

Kate turned to Cory. "You're still free to come and go on your own schedule, but the son of Medici won't be living in the barracks. You have your shop inside the camp where you can work and be close to Shade and the other warriors, but you'll live here."

Shade smiled at *bel*, already planning. "Of course, can't have a Medici living in the barracks. Are you all right with all of this, Cory?"

Cory shrugged. "I guess so. I just want my mom to be okay, I don't want her to worry anymore. I'm going to live in the big house? Wow!"

Kate turned to Rachael. "Do you have luggage? We need to get you settled in the guest room. And you must be starving. I was never much of a cook, but the kitchen is fully stocked. I'll fix you something to eat. You must be exhausted after your travel, and all this emotional drama."

Shade laughed. "We get rid of Reynaldo, and within the damn week, I have two mortal women in this house who need food! *Mi amore*, make sure you arrange a bedroom for Cory in Castello, and make room for him in the Paris house as well."

"I'll talk with Gi and we'll find the perfect room for Cory at Castello. There's no shortage of space there. And I'll make sure he has a room in the Paris house." Kate stood and headed to the kitchen. "Just give me a few minutes, Rachael, I'll fix something for you, and then we'll get you settled in. You'd probably like a long hot bath."

Shade watched as Kate took control and rushed off to the kitchen, then he looked at Rachael. He took her hands and lifted her from her chair, hugging her to his chest.

"Rachael, *grazie* for all the things you did for me long ago. But thank you most for giving me the gift of his life. I only wish I had been there to experience it all with you both. I can never repay you for that, but I am going to make life much easier for you. You may visit Cory as often as you wish." Shade kissed her cheek softly, and then leaned in and kissed the tattoo that he'd kissed many times years ago. Looking in her eyes, he smiled. "Yes, you are an angel."

Rachael laid her head against his chest, his scent so familiar to her. This man she'd searched for after she was pregnant, and for years after Cory was born. She'd loved him and hated him at the same time. Wishing he was back in her life, taking care of her and their son, but hating him when she struggled for so long with Cory, feeling she'd lost him to the streets for good. It was clear Shade loved another, was bound to her. But at least she had this. At last, she had acceptance for their child, and security for his future. And it was enough.

"I'm hardly an angel, either one of us. But I thank you for accepting him, and yes, I do want to visit my son, our son. I'm sorry. I'm not intruding in your life. It's clear to me how much you love her, and our time is long past. But you should know I never stopped loving you."

Shade heard her declaration of love for him. "She is my soul mate, Rachael. I spent my whole life looking for her. And it's okay to have feelings for me. Because Cory is the son we created together, and it came from a mutual consent to give each other what we needed at the time. I cannot say I ever loved you, that would be a lie, and you'd know that. I was a warrior and a true son of a bitch, many times. But I worked hard to become who I am now. I would die for Kate. I can't turn back the clock, and I do not wish to, but I am trying to make amends for those things I did in the past that hurt others. I will take care of him. He is our son."

Gi came in to announce he'd lead Miss Rachael to the kitchen, as my lady had tried to prepare something edible. Shade threw back his head and roared laughing. "She was mortal once, Gi! *Cazzo*, old man, she had to be able to fend for herself at some point."

As Gi led Rachael to the kitchen, Shade saw Cory staring out the window, deep in thought.

"Let's take a walk, son. I think we both could use some air."

57

Shade and Cory walked outside and down the road to the warrior camp. He wanted to give them some privacy and give Cory the chance to express whatever he was feeling, letting go of any unexpressed anger about the past, or fears of the future. Shade knew he'd held a lot inside over the years and it would be released at some point, and not always in a good way. He didn't want Cory to begin their new relationship in this manner. Shade was already struggling with his own concerns about being a father, and now the task was upon him even sooner than expected.

"Let's take to the fields and talk it out, *si*?"

Cory nodded but wasn't sure he was ready to talk much yet. He was still processing all the information that had been dumped in his lap. He'd often thought of meeting his biological father. Everything he ever thought he'd say or do if he met him, didn't play out as he'd imagined. But then, he never imagined Shade Medici was his father, either. A whole fuck load of emotions poured out. For years, he'd carried so much anger and shame, and now he felt relief and something like love for this man. His head was churning with confusing and conflicting emotions. He loved his mom, but they'd never been close. Cory knew that was more his fault than hers. He'd pushed her away, even when, deep inside, he'd wanted to be cared for.

He walked beside Shade as they moved along the fence line, down to the vineyards. The night sky was clear and the light from the moon and stars glittered and sparkled around them. Shade stopped and climbed onto the fence rail and Cory could almost hear it groan as it took his weight. Cory climbed up beside him, and they were a picture of opposites. Shade was tall and muscular, and Cory thin and wiry. Despite the turmoil in his head, Cory admired him, and knew if he could have wished for a father, Shade was it.

Shade didn't really know what to say, but he began with what was in his heart. "You know, Cory, there was something my *padre* taught me that has stayed with me. It is something I live by and I hope maybe, this will help you. He always said to follow my heart. Never mind the rules, what others expected or thought, follow your heart. If you listen hard enough, it will always guide you to the right path. I'm following my heart here, because I know there is so much bottled up inside you and has been for a very long time. This news has brought out a lot inside of me as well. I don't expect you to change who you are because of me but know that your future is open. I will help you achieve whatever it is you wish to pursue.

Your life will be longer than a mortal's, but eternity is not an option for you. That will be something I will have to suffer through when it happens.

"I have already lost a son, he was like you, a half-breed, and he never made it to see a day of his life. If I had known you existed and survived, that would have changed my life drastically. I have to accept what is in the past, but we can change the future, together. Mine is looking great, the best it has ever looked in all of my life, and right now, I would hope yours is as well."

Cory looked sideways at his newfound father, his black hair blowing in the cool air. He seemed relaxed, as if nothing ever shook him up much. But Cory had learned to read his eyes, he'd watched him a lot since moving here, and listened to him even when Shade didn't know he was there. He knew Shade was good for his word, he did what he said, and he meant the words he spoke. Cory decided to speak from his heart as well. "The first time I saw you in the club, I couldn't stop looking at you. My heart was telling me then, you were different, and I seemed to be drawn to you. When you fed from me, it felt different. With the others, I always got a heightened sexual thing, but I didn't with you. It was more like...love or something. It felt so weird. I'd never felt that before, you know? The night you brought my lady into the club, I watched you with her, and I was jealous. I was so excited to see you back, but I could see she had you pretty hard. I was happy for you, but I followed my heart that night and approached you. I don't regret any of that time we had together. But right now, I feel like everything I've ever known has been turned upside down. Like, somehow, my whole life has been this bad dream and now I finally wake up and everything I ever wanted is here." He sighed and shook his head.

Shade listened and understood. This was just what he wanted Cory to do, speak his heart. This kid was his blood. He had to take him now by the hand, give him dreams for his future, and be a father. Shade reached his arm around Cory's shoulder and pulled him close as Cory laid his head against him. Shade ran his fingers through his son's hair. It was soft and hung in waves, like his.

"Cory, I know how you feel. You can talk to me, you know. You can ask me anything you want to know. I am always going to be here now. You can come to me for anything and everything. If you need me, just come to me. I will stop whatever I'm doing for you. And that is how this is going to roll with us. We have to work at this together, because you never had a father and I never had a son, so now we are rowing the same damn boat, but we can get wherever we are going if we work together, *si*?"

Cory didn't fight the comfort of his closeness. It felt good, for once, to have someone who understood everything about him. With his head on Shade's shoulder, feeling his arm around him like a warm blanket, his struggle was over. He was home. "This is going to sound really stupid, but what do I call you? What do I call my lady?"

Shade chuckled softly and squeezed Cory tight. "I hope you will call me dad, but if that feels awkward to you, then call me Shade. It may seem strange calling me dad in front of the warriors. It doesn't bother me, but you might get some heavy ribbing about it, no matter what. I'm still your master. I am master to everyone in my coven. And I am damn sure you will feel my wrath at times, just like they will. You will call your queen, Kate. She is your queen as well, just like I am master. But she is not your mother. She is going to love you to death if I know anything about her, and she will spoil you so damn bad. But that is who she is, loving and caring."

Cory smiled. "I can do that, Shade. Dad. That sounds so strange, but I'll get used to it. What's going to happen to my mom? I've been sending her money from my pay, it's not a lot. I just want her to be okay."

Shade had heard from Marco that Cory had been sending some of his pay back to his mom, and it made him proud.

"That is no longer your worry, son. I'm going to get her a house, wherever she wants to live, something very comfortable in a safe neighborhood. Then, whatever debt she has, I'm going to pay off. Give her a clean slate. She can stop working and struggling, and maybe we can extend her life a few years. It's important you have her in your life as long as possible. And I expect you to build a relationship with her, fix what is wrong. Get closer to her son, she is your *madre*, and you only get one of those. Trust me, when she is gone, you will be grateful for all the time you made to be with her."

Cory sat up and looked at him, eyes wide. "You'd do that for us? I mean, you'd take care of her in that way? I don't...I can't believe..." Cory jumped off the fence and hugged him tight. He was overjoyed that Shade would take responsibility for his mom and help her as well.

"I will do whatever it takes to correct my mistakes. She was someone who showed me kindness, and in doing so, it destroyed her life. I can't undo the damage, but I can make sure her future is pleasant. And like I said, we will make this officially right in our world as well. We will go to Florence and get your name in the ancestral records. I am acknowledging you as my son. I'm not even sure anyone has ever done this before, but we are Medici and we break new ground. You will have to come with me, and so will Kate. We will take the jet to Florence as soon as possible and take care of that. Then get our asses back here because we both have some serious business to take care of concerning this camp. You are still going to work. I think if I told you not to do the leather work, I would have a damn riot on my hands and the warriors would beat the living hell out of me!"

Cory laughed. "I don't think anyone could beat your ass, well, maybe Kate."

Shade threw his head back with laughter. "Oh, my woman can do it too. But I think I would enjoy it too much. On a more serious note, just because I am the Medici, does not mean we are all safe. There are those who will take whatever they can from me, and that includes you. So, we will work on some basic weapon skills, so you can defend yourself. You need to pay attention, Cory, always be aware of your surroundings, especially when you leave these grounds. I do not want to frighten you, just make you aware. You are Medici now and there are some that will want you dead just because my blood runs in your veins. You call to me whenever you need to. I will speak with everyone in my coven, they will know you are my son and their allegiance will be to you, just as it will be to all my *bambinos*."

Cory looked up to Shade and stared at him. "Does your blood run in my veins? I never fed from you. I know I was not allowed. But I never took the blood oath as a warrior, like the others did. You sent me to Florence and then, when I came back, we were so busy." Cory's eyes dropped to the ground.

Shade pulled him close and Cory buried his face into Shade's chest. Shade tipped his chin up and looked deep into those dark pools. "Of course, my blood runs through your veins, but say what is in your heart."

Cory had watched as each new recruit had joined the coven, and drank their master's blood from the chalice, bonding them to the Medici. He'd never been invited to share in that ritual, and never expected to. He felt he lived among them but wasn't one of them. Even here, he felt accepted, but was still an outsider. He'd kept his hope of having a blood bond to the coven bottled inside, telling himself to be content with what he'd gained, but now his heart was screaming to have what he wanted more than anything. "I want to feel the blood bond to the coven and drink your blood from the cup."

Shade felt the boy's pain wash through him, and it almost broke him in half. Shade reached out and put his hand around Cory's head, pulling him to his neck.

"Feed, *mio figlio*. Take me inside you. Feel your *padre's* blood inside you. You will drink from me, not from some chalice."

Shade felt no hesitation as Cory sank his fangs deep into his neck and something inside him opened up, warm and bright. He could feel his power swirling through him and into Cory, feeling everything Cory felt. Shade could feel his son's heartbeat synchronize with his and the cells pulsating throughout his small frame. Shade knew then, this was where his whole life had led him...to become a father, to have his sons exist and thrive, and Cory was just the first to arrive. In that bright crystal-clear moment, as his half-breed son fed, he saw a vision of Lorenzo, his face a reflection of Shade’s, his body strong and vibrant. He knew he’d love them both equally.

Shade whispered to his son, *“Familia."* Nothing would separate them again.

Shade and Cory walked back to the house. Shade’s arm was draped casually around Cory's shoulders. As they entered the main house, Cory seemed a bit confused about where he should go, and Shade advised him to go back to the barracks for the night. His mom was already asleep, and no one in the barracks was aware of this news yet. Tomorrow he could get his things packed, and Kate would get a temporary room ready until she created a permanent space for him. Cory agreed and hugged his father, letting his guard down as he allowed himself to feel the new bond. Something had changed inside them both tonight and it was all for the good.

As Cory left, Shade headed to the bar, poured himself a large Midnight and gulped it down. He’d not fed from Kate in several days and he was weakening. Cory's feeding from him didn’t help. He knew he should be going to Luca, but he was trying to delay that change as long as possible.

58

Kate had taken Rachael to the kitchen where she'd prepared a light meal for her as Gi and Theresa took her luggage up to the guest bedroom. Theresa turned down the bed, ran a hot bath and had everything ready when Kate escorted Rachael to her room. Giving her a hug, Kate told her good night.

"I'm sure you're exhausted. Take a long bath. Theresa has laid your night clothes out for you. Get a good night's sleep. Shade and I are up at night and sleep during the day. But Cory will be going to bed soon himself and the two of you will have all day to visit tomorrow. There are books here if you want to read a while. And feel free to call Theresa if there's anything you need."

Kate left her and returned to her own bedroom, waiting for Shade. She knew he'd left with Cory, just the two of them, and she could feel when Cory fed from him. She sat on the bed with the laptop on her legs, not able to really concentrate with everything that had transpired in the last few hours. She felt Shade enter the house and come up the stairs.

Shade had to face her now, he knew she was waiting. Once again, he felt like he'd put her in a bad situation, and wondered if that would ever end. "You all right, *mi amore*?"

She looked up as he entered their bedroom, reaching her hand out to him. "I'm fine. I'm more concerned for you." She pushed the laptop aside and patted the bed beside her. "Come, lay down beside me. Talk to me."

Shade sat on the edge of the bed, unlacing his boots, and kicking them off. Sliding his tee over his head, he flung it to the corner and rolled to her, burying his face in her hair.

"I'm sorry, *mi amore*. I am so sorry for all of this, I seem to put you into situations that are awkward and hard to handle, and they all stem from my past. I am so tired. I think I'm being emotionally drained, slowly but surely. So much is going around in my head. Cory fed from me."

Kate pulled him to her, letting him lay his head against her shoulder as she ran her fingers through his hair. "Shh, rest now. I can feel how tired you are. I could feel him feed from you, and you'll need to feed tonight from me."

She put her finger to his lips as he started to protest. "I feel strong, Shade. I'm fine. And you don't owe me an apology. This is certainly nothing I saw coming. It's not the way I saw this visit with Cory's mother playing out, but I've never loved you more. He's your son, and it would have broken my heart had you rejected him. I welcome him to our family. I'll make a place for him here in our home, and I promise you, I'll love him as I love our own children."

"It blindsided me too." Closing his eyes, he breathed deep, taking in her rose scent. "I love you so damn much! We will have to go to Florence, take the jet. You will have to come with me. I want this done as soon as possible. I am going to set Rachael up with a house, something comfortable. I plan to pay off any debt and then I'll have my accountant put her on the payroll. Give her a decent income, so she can live out her life in comfort with no worries, it's the least I can do."

Sitting up, Shade rubbed his eyes, letting his hands run through his hair, the agitation never leaving him. "What have I done, *bel*? How many could there be out there? There could be more half-breed children I know nothing of, growing up without guidance, and rogue in the streets. I could have killed one of my own sons. Damn it all to hell! I can't stand this. The thoughts that go through my head at what I might have done. The damage I may have caused other innocent people in my past."

Kate reached out to him. "Stop. Stop tormenting yourself. None of us can change what's in the past. The important thing is you found this child. And I believe you were destined to find him. You were drawn to him, and he to you. If there were more children out there, then they'd have been drawn to you as well. The power of your blood in them would draw them to you. You'd feel them. You know this is true. You have a rare chance with Cory, to make up for the mistakes of the past. You've already altered the course of Cory's life by bringing him here. And now, by claiming him, it will open more doors for him. And Rachael, you can change her life as well. I'll gladly go with you to Florence and stand before Council with Cory at our side. I want them to know I accept this child, your child. And he'll spend the rest of his days as a Medici, with my full blessing and support."

Shade clutched her tightly, wanting to climb inside her with his whole being. She brought him so much comfort and light and love. "I would die without you. I don't deserve all of this; all you keep giving me."

His tongue snaked out as he licked the vein that pulsed in her soft white neck, moaning in sweet agony for her. He kept nuzzling, nipping, and kissing like a starved beast, needing her to fix all that was wrong in him.

He spoke with his lips against her throat, "Lorenzo, he came to me."

Kate slid her hand into his hair, pulling him closer as she lay back against the pillows, propped against the huge carved headboard. "Lorenzo? You saw him?" She smiled. "He'll be just like you, a warrior tall and strong. He's so eager to get here. I feel his spirit get stronger every day. Feed from me, lover. Feel him. Feel his young warrior spirit."

There was no hesitation as Shade sank his fangs into her neck and drew deep. Her blood spilled across his tongue, sliding sweetly down his throat and hitting him with a swell of comfort. Her light and love traveled through him, filling every cell with desire. His body jerked awake and his beast stepped forward, taking over. Shade had waited too long to feed from her, and the beast wouldn't be tamped down. He drew deep, knowing he needed to slow down but couldn't stop. His body writhed against hers, his fists in her hair, not able to get close enough to her. He heard a small moan from her, and he unlatched, throwing back his head, her blood trickling down his chin and onto his chest. His eyes were ablaze, making the room glow with the tones of his red-hot love.

Tugging at his jeans, he quickly removed them. He slid her gown up to her hips and buried his face into her heaven. Sucking and lapping at her sex, the beast wanted her to cum and cum hard, and he wanted every drop of her. His tongue pushed deep inside her while his fingers caressed her clit, as she responded to his greedy hunger.

Kate felt the heat build between her legs as he moved swiftly to feed. She knew he'd waited too long to feed out of his concern for the baby inside her, and he'd resisted going to Luca. He drank deep from her, ravenous in his need, and she gave herself freely. She felt his beast emerge, as his mouth settled between her legs, lapping at her in the same hungry fashion his lips had sought out her blood. She gripped her hands in his hair, and lifted his face, drawing him up to her as he climbed on all fours over her body. She wrapped her legs around his hips, pulling him down, feeling his cock slide into her as his weight settled on top on her. She clung to him, her arms around his back, and her mouth locked to his. Joined to him in every way she could. She rode the rhythm of his hips, as his cock slid deep, pulsing inside of her.

The beast was still greedy and unrelenting. He rode hard and deep, as the passion built to a breaking point and he came hard inside her, holding her against his chest as she thrashed hard in her release.

His breathing was ragged as he rolled onto his back, taking her with him as he held her tightly against his chest, still buried deep inside her, his dick pulsing as her orgasm receded. Her locks of crimson clung to the sweat on her beautiful face, her eyes glowing in their reddish amber beauty, a color uniquely hers. Her beast wasn't done, and he grinned. She was only beginning to understand the beast wouldn't leave until fully satisfied.

"Coming out to play, *si*?" Slapping her ass hard, he prepared for whatever pleasures her beast intended to deal to him.

Kate growled deep in her throat, as she pushed him back on the bed. As he lay on his back, she straddled him, running her tongue over his rock-hard abs, up his chest, his neck, and bit at his chin. She nipped at his bottom lip, drawing it into her mouth, tasting a hint of his blood. She ran her hands the length of his arms, pushing them over his head, feeling the strength of him. She sat up, sliding her hips down slowly, mounting him once more, and moaning as she felt him fill her. Her hair fell forward on her face as she rode him, and his hands moved down, grasping her hips, guiding her movements as his hips lifted and thrust to meet her.

Shade watched every move she made, her delicate white hands touching his dark, olive skin, her tongue trailing over every inch of him, she consumed him, body and soul, and then she impaled herself on him again as she flung that crimson mane over his chest. Wildly and unabashedly, her beast took him whole. "Fuck, take me, make me cum again. Fuck!"

Grabbing fistfuls of her hair, he pulled her head to him and sank his fangs into her neck again; drawing the life he needed from her and felt himself once more ready to explode inside her. His moans were loud, and he felt her muscles tighten, ready to cum hard for him and he unlatched and pulled her lips to his neck. "Feed, *mi amore*!"

Kate sank her fangs into his neck at the base of his shoulder. She loved the feel of the hard muscle against her lips. She drank from him, for both her and the baby, and felt the power of his blood as it ripped through her veins, igniting every cell, and lighting the fire between her legs. Her mouth broke free as the orgasm hit her full force, her head thrown back, his blood still on her lips as she cried out with pleasure, her hips grinding hard against him as his hands gripped hard, pulling her down hard against his cock. She dropped onto his chest as the orgasm faded, out of breath and heart pounding.

Shade slid his hands across her back, rubbing her softly, letting his fingertips glide slowly along her spine, their chests rising and falling quickly as they gasped for air, waiting for their breath to return to normal. Leaning down, he kissed the top of her head. "No one can love me like you."

Kate laughed softly. "And don't you forget it, buster."

Shade felt the chuckle rolling up through his body. "Like you would ever let me forget."

Kate giggled as she rolled off him, lying in their bed beside him, her head on his shoulder, her hand stroking his chest. "I love having you home more, even when you're working in the camp. I love knowing you're here, close to me."

Rolling to face her, his eyes ate her alive, he didn't have to touch her, just look at her and his love overwhelmed him. "I am rather enjoying it myself. This will be the last time I feed from you, *mi amore*. I won't put you or Lorenzo at risk. I hate stopping the feeding. It almost drives me mad, because I love that more than anything, feeding from you, it's the strongest bond I have with you."

Kate stroked his face. "The bond never goes away, Shade. We'll always have the bond. Nothing can change that now. I'll still feed from you, and I carry your child inside of me. We'll still make love. I've never felt closer. It was different before, when you went to Luca. I was still mortal then. But I want you to feed. I need you to be strong, so don't deny yourself, thinking you are protecting me. Feed from him."

Wrapping his arm around her, he kissed her passionately and closed his eyes. "I will always love you, *mi amore*." He felt the pull of his death slumber coming quickly. The emotional drain of events and lack of feeding were taking him down faster than he'd realized.

"*Ti amo per sempre*..."

She felt him slipping into his death slumber. Kate pulled the blankets over them, tucked him in as she curled up next to him. She kissed his chest, "I love you more."

She heard the soft whir of the blinds as they lowered, blocking out all light and sealing them in darkness.

59

Rachael stayed at *Bel Rosso* for a long weekend, spending most of her time with Cory as he escorted her around Charlottesville and the surrounding areas. In the meantime, Shade called his accountant and set up a monthly income for her. He also wished for her to have a house and would explain that detail to her before she left. He made sure all her debts were taken care of and she'd have a fresh start. Shade waited for Cory and Rachael to meet with him before they left for the airport, he heard Kate coming down the stairs, talking to Rachael. Kate led her into his office. Shade stood and asked everyone to take a seat. He had some details to go over before Rachael returned to California.

Gi entered the room with a tray of Midnight and a refreshing cool drink for Rachael. Cory followed behind him, joining his mother. As they got comfortable, Shade sat down behind his massive desk.

"I have a few details to go over with you, Rachael. I promise it won't take long. I hope your stay with us was a joyful one and you were comfortable and well cared for while in our home."

"It was a wonderful trip. Cory was never a happy child. He has always struggled to find his place in the world. I can't tell you how much it eases my burden to see him somewhere that makes him happy."

Shade smiled at her and then glanced at Cory and winked. "Well, I think the things I am about to tell you will ease more of your burden. I have arranged to purchase a house for you, something comfortable, and in a safe neighborhood. I have made the arrangements through a realtor in California. He will be contacting you shortly. I have given him instructions to help you find whatever you want, so you need to pick the house and location. I don't want you to ever worry, taxes, insurance and maintenance on the house will be handled and paid by me. My realtor and accountants will work hand-in-hand arranging the packing and moving trucks for you . It will all be taken care of. You just need to relax, let the realtor show you some homes, pick the one you like best and it is yours."

Rachael looked to Kate and back at Shade, her mouth open. "Oh, I can't ask that of you. That's too much!"

Shade held up his hand. "Rachael, I do this of my own accord. You do not have to ask. I feel this is my obligation to you for all the years you have struggled, so I ask that you forgive me, let me care for our son, and let me, at least, make the rest of your years comfortable. I never want him to worry for you, this is important to me." Shade looked at the shock and happiness in her face and he'd just begun to fill her in.

Rachael's eyes filled with tears and Kate handed her a tissue and Cory rubbed her back.

Kate spoke to her softly, "Please, in accepting this, you help Cory, and you help us. I know this man. The guilt he feels for all the years you struggled, for all the years Cory struggled. It's the only way for all of us to heal."

Shade looked at the three of them, his mate, his son, and this woman whose life he'd destroyed. "I have to heal, Rachael, as do you and Cory. I never want you to think I am taking him from you, you may visit whenever you wish, for as long as you wish, and he will be allowed to visit you as well. Never worry about that. I have contacted my accountant and all your outstanding debts have been paid. You start with a clean slate. I have also arranged for a steady income. My accountant advised me to have this paid out to you in monthly increments, so expect a check to be automatically deposited into your bank account every month."

Shade picked up an embossed envelope with the Medici crest and walked to her, crouching in front of her, placing the envelope in her shaking hands. "Rachael, live your life, travel, do all the things you could never do. I'm always here if you need anything, as is our son. I just want you to live your life, be happy and know it's all fine now. Cory will be fine and loved as well."

Rachael accepted the envelope then covered her face with her hands, sobbing freely. Cory leaned his head against hers. "You deserve it, Mom."

Rachael looked up at Shade as he still crouched in front of her and stared into those piecing blue eyes she remembered all too well, unchanged these past twenty years.

"I can't thank you enough. You have no idea what this means to me. I never blamed you. I want you to know that. I was a young, reckless girl who made some foolish choices. I know Cory carried a lot of anger for a very long time, at me, and toward the father he never knew. I never in my life expected to find you again, and certainly never expected this."

Shade smiled softly as he stared into her face, aged and worn down from the angst and hell he'd unintentionally put them both through. Deep in her eyes, he could see the young heart that was carefree so long ago, the young girl who'd offered him a few weeks of feeding in his lonely stay in the States.

"Foolish is the wrong word, Rachael. We were all such when we were young. It is one of the reasons I helped Cory when I saw him. I know what kind of life lies in those streets, how dangerous it can be, but that is all behind us now. I hold my own remorse for the suffering I caused and the careless way I left you. But we will move forward, so you must promise me," Shade lifted her chin, smiled into her eyes, deep and long, "...that you will move forward, find happiness in your own life."

Leaning forward, he kissed Rachael's cheek softly and stood. "Cory, be careful taking your *madre* home. See that she gets on the airplane safely, act like my son and show her how a Medici treats all the women in his life, *si?*"

Cory's heart almost exploded with joy for all the gifts his father was now giving his mom. She deserved them all. When he watched how tender and caring Shade was with her, he knew deep inside, his mother would begin to heal. They could both begin to heal from this, and they'd finally find the peace they'd been looking for. As Cory stood up, he took his mom's hand and helped her stand.

"You got it, Dad! Mom are you ready? We need to get moving or you'll miss your flight. I have your luggage loaded in the truck. It's parked out the side door here."

Rachael stood and hugged Kate, whispering, "Thank you," before turning to Shade to hug him good-bye. She couldn't help but wonder what her life would have been like had she been *the one*. Had he fallen in love with her the way she'd fallen in love with him. She knew that would never be but was so grateful for his kindness and generosity. She smiled at them both as she left with Cory, heading back to start her life over in California.

Shade watched them leave and stood there for a while before he spoke. "I hope she will be okay. I hope I have done enough, and she can live how she deserves for the rest of her life. The ravages of time have not been kind to her."

"She has had a hard time, both of them have. Look how Cory has flourished in the past year. Rachael will do the same. She'll have a roof over her head and be relieved of the burden of debt and wondering how she'll pay her bills. The stress of that takes its toll. It was the right thing to do. I'm so proud of you."

Shade placed his arms around his *bel rosso*. "No one is prouder than me. You amaze me, *mi amore*. You took Cory in, like all the others in my life, gave him love and hope. Then, discovering he is my son, you accepted him with open arms, while you carry our own inside you. I could read Rachael's thoughts before she left, they were of loving me, wondering what it would have been like to be the one I fell in love with. It makes me rather sad, for she could not have tempted me even then. I was waiting...waiting on you...my whole life."

Kate smiled up at him. "Somehow, Shade Medici, I think she's not the only woman who has fallen in love with you. My guess is that would be a pretty long list. I'm not sure what you saw when you looked at me across a crowded room, but I'm just glad you saw it."

Turning, he took her into his arms and lifted her up, her legs wrapping around his waist, her arms around his neck. He stared into those big beautiful eyes, her crimson hair falling softly around her face.

"I saw love, pure and simple. I saw passion, waiting to come alive. But I think, most of all, I saw a female who would love me like never before, be the light in my darkness, be my comfort when in pain, and make wild beastly love to me when I wanted a bad girl."

Kate dropped her head back and laughed. "I don't think I was a bad girl until you came along."

Shade snuggled into her neck and moaned. "I have made arrangements with Council. We are going to fly to Florence two nights from now. But I need a favor before we go, something I think your delicate touch can handle. You will oblige me, *si?*"

Kate tilted her head as he snuggled into her neck, his breath hot against her throat. "I will oblige you anything, lover. Name it."

"I don't want to make this sound like I am a snob. But is there a way you can make sure Cory is properly dressed for our meeting with Council. Cory dresses fine for here, but he is being presented to Council as my son. I need him to be dressed appropriately, *mi amore*. His hair needs to be trimmed up. I don't even know if he has a proper suit. I have no idea how to approach this without offending him. Can you help me here?"

Kate laughed softly. "Of course. I'll take him into town with me, and Luca will be with us, so he won't feel like it is a girly shopping trip. I doubt he'll agree to cut his hair short, but we can get it trimmed. Do you want him in a suit?"

"Definitely a suit for Council and make it something of quality. I have no problem with how he dresses here. Hell, he never goes anywhere. But he needs a wardrobe that befits his station as my son. I need them to see him as my son. That is important. The Council puts much emphasis on image. That is why I am always directing you how to dress when we go there. I am royalty and I go before them appearing as such. Cory needs to do the same, as will all our *bambinos*. I hope that doesn't sound too demanding."

Kate shook her head. "Not at all, but I can tell you now, Lorenzo will live in leathers and jeans! Don't let that concern you though, because Sophia and Natalia will break the bank with their wardrobes. They'll have no problems looking royal. In fact, Sophia has already informed me she plans to sleep in her crown."

Shade chuckled. "Just set Cory up is all I ask, *mi amore*. Help him pack. He knows about Castello, but not like he is about to know it. I am not ashamed of him in any way. I never want to change him, just help him look the part. I cannot make Cory a prince since his bloodline is not pure, that title will belong to Lorenzo. And our daughters will be princesses and have all they desire, spoiled with crowns and gowns, jewels, and shoes."

Kate flashed him a look. "They won't have all they desire. They'll have all they deserve. There's a difference. I don't want spoiled children who think they're entitled to whatever they request. They'll learn that rewards come from hard work, not just the privilege of being born to someone with money."

Shade laughed. "*Cazzo*, you sound like my *padre, bel!* I want to spoil them, love them, and give them all the things they need."

"Your children will be spoiled. I have no doubts. I just want them to understand not everything comes to you on a silver platter."

Shade nodded. "*Si*, you are their *madre*, and you will make sure they grow up proper. Damn *bambinos* already turning my hair gray!"

Shade smacked her ass as he set her down on her feet. "Now, I need to get to work and make some money, what are your plans for this evening?"

"I have a call scheduled with Reynaldo to discuss plans for the inn and how that's going. And I've been looking into planting lavender. We still have 1,000 acres of undeveloped property. I have more research to do, but I was going to talk to you about that, unless you were planning to use the land to expand the vineyards."

Shade walked back to his desk, shuffling through the stacks of papers. "*Si*, I want to expand the vineyards, but not for a long while. Lavender? *Bel*, what in the hell do you do with lavender? Explain to me why you need that much land for lavender, *si*?"

Kate leaned against the side of his desk. "Lavender oil is extremely profitable, and the plants are very low maintenance. One acre will generate about thirty thousand dollars a year in gross profits. I was thinking about two hundred acres of lavender fields. I'm still researching, but that would gross roughly six million dollars a year. I have to figure out the cost to plant and maintain the fields, how much it will cost to harvest the plants, what it costs to transport the harvested product to the buyer. So, I still have some research to do to have an idea of what the net returns will be. But it's a lovely crop, fragrant, and it will help distinguish our vineyards from the others."

Shade sat down hard in his desk chair. "Did you say six-mil? Where in the hell did you get this information?"

Kate straightened the pile of papers on his desk, not making eye contact. "Well, I have lavender in the garden, planted among the roses, and it's so easy to grow, and it smells so good. Every time I go into a shop, I see lavender soap, and lavender lotions, lavender sachets. We'd harvest the crops and sell the lavender to the industries that use it in their products. The thirty thousand per acre is a high number and depends on good weather and a good crop yield. I just started researching on the internet. The climate is right, and we have the land. I thought we could try it here, start small with a few acres and expand as we learn, see how it works, and maybe duplicate it in California."

"*Bel,* you are going to be raising our *bambinos*, when do you propose to have time for all of this?"

Kate laughed. "I have no plans to work the fields. Luciano already has a network of migrant farmers he uses to maintain the vineyards. I thought we could tap into that. For six million a year, I'm pretty sure we can afford to find someone to oversee the operation. Just as you have Luciano to oversee all your vineyards. I'm not going anywhere."

Shade slapped his hand on the desk. "So, kiss your savage lover, and let me get to work. Do what makes you happy, *mi amore*. I just want you to be happy. Just don't forget me."

Kate ran her hand through his hair. "Forgettable? That would be the last word I'd use to describe you. Now go to work, before I decide to give you the night off."

"Temptation, woman, you drive me wild!" He watched her strut out of the office and grinned. She was his for all eternity and he'd always cherish the ground she walked on. She had him heart and soul.

60

Sitting in his office, Shade waited impatiently for Marcello, Raven, and Fiamma to wrap up their meeting. He wanted to make sure they were aware he was returning to Florence and would be gone for several days. He'd have to take the jet, which would only make the trip longer, but this was too far for Kate to teleport on her own, and it would be a challenge for Cory as well. *Cazzo*, he hated flying.

Gi entered and informed him, "The plane is waiting in the hanger and the car is loaded with the luggage. My lady and Cory are ready to leave whenever you're ready." Shade thanked Gi and as he left the office, his three warriors entered, looking a bit confused.

"Don't get comfortable, this won't take long. I will be returning to Florence for several days. I will be taking the jet. *Bel* and Cory will be coming with me. No need, at this time, to explain why that will come in time. I need all three of you to run the camp and the Dead House. If you have any problems, contact me immediately and I can teleport back home. I am leaving Luca here if you need him. He will be in charge of the estate and available for anything else that may come up, *si?*"

Marcello didn't like the sound of this. Shade's departure seemed much too sudden. "Any problems, master? Anything we need to be aware of?"

Shade grunted. "If there was, I would tell you. Just do your jobs as expected. This is not a protection issue. I will explain everything when I return. Now, move out."

The three warriors walked back to camp, talking amongst themselves. They were all confused as to why Shade would be taking Cory. They'd noticed a change in their master over the past few days since Cory's mother's visit, but none of them had a clue as to why Shade was leaving and taking Cory with him.

Fiamma listened to the chatter. "He does have a lot of business to take care of and not all of it is in the States."

Marcello shrugged. "Sure, yeah, business, but what does that have to do with Cory?" They continued on their way, each of them wondering what in the hell was brewing.

Shade walked to the bottom of the stairs. "*Bel*, let's move! Cory, roll!"

Luca and Cory came out of Luca's suite when they heard Shade calling. "We're heading out now, Luca. Warriors have been advised, let me know if you need me, I can be here quickly."

Luca responded, "I've got this. Don't worry about anything. Dante has filed the flight plan and has everything ready for takeoff. I'll handle anything that comes up here. Just have a good trip and I'll see you when you get home."

"*Grazie*, Luca." Shade gave him a hug and fist bumped him.

Kate hurried down the stairs, carrying a purse and a small tote bag. "I'm ready."

"There's my *bel*. You have more luggage? What in the hell do you need this for, *mi amore?* You probably have ten suitcases on the plane, you need take nothing. Everything is there for you." Shade looked at Luca and rolled his eyes.

Kate kissed him and laughed. "I saw that. Come on, the car is waiting." Kate turned to Cory and held out her hand. "Are you ready?"

Cory nodded his head and took Kate's hand. His heart was hammering in his chest. He was nervous and excited. He'd never been inside Castello, and he knew Council was a big deal. "I think so."

Shade slapped him on the back. "Come on, son, the plane takes much longer than teleporting, but we have no choice now, teleporting is no longer an option for Kate."

Heading out to the car, Shade got Kate buckled in the passenger seat and Cory climbed into the back, as he climbed behind the wheel. Shade drove to the hangar quickly, anxious to get this over with and back home. Once they pulled into the hangar, Dante was outside waiting for them to board.

"My main man, Dante!"

Dante smiled and slapped Shade on the back. "We're ready to go, just let me know, master. Carolyn is our new flight attendant and is inside waiting to meet everyone and is prepared for anything you need."

Shade thanked him and led Cory and *bel* up the small steps to enter the plane. He almost laughed as Cory looked like he was about to hurl with nerves. "It is okay, you will enjoy it."

Kate immediately noticed Issa was no longer the flight attendant for the private plane and sighed with relief, flashing Shade a look of appreciation. Carolyn smiled and extended her hand to introduce herself.

"My lady, I've just been assigned to master's plane. I'm an experienced attendant, but I've never worked directly with our master before, so please let me know if there's anything you require."

Kate thanked her and let her know they'd work out their routine over time. She directed her attention to Cory who appeared nervous.

"Cory, Shade will sleep on the flight as the sun will be up soon. There's a bedroom in the back of the plane. I'll be with him if you think you're okay. I brought you my iPad and some books to read, and there's a TV with a lot of movie options you can watch. I'm sure Carolyn can help you get settled."

Carolyn nodded and stepped forward. "Of course! I was informed you may need some refreshments, so we have food and beverages on board."

Shade laid his hand on the small of Kate's back. "Let's get you settled, *mi amore*. I want you to rest as well. It is important we are all fresh when we land. We meet with Council a few hours after landing."

Shade got *bel* settled inside the small bedroom cabin and then turned to Cory. "Let's go to the cockpit. Dante and Ciro fly this bird with precision. I think we should join them and see how she goes for a while. You up for that?"

Cory couldn't believe it. The plane was like a house with wings. Everything Shade touched was gold. "Wow, you mean fly it?"

Shade laughed. "Well, I think flying the bird might be a bit much your first time, but if you want to spend some time up there with Dante and Ciro, I am sure they won't have a problem with it."

The takeoff was a breeze, and the pilots explained things to Cory as they maneuvered the jet through the takeoff procedure. Cory was inquisitive and firing questions at them, his excitement overcoming his nerves. Shade knew Cory had skimped on his education. The thought created a knot in his chest, thinking about the opportunities Cory missed because of him. But he loved how his son went with the flow, and he hoped Council would be cordial in their acceptance of him.

Once they were airborne, Shade made his exit and Cory decided to stay in the cockpit. Shade made his way back to *bel*. His slumber was coming on quickly. "Damn, I hate flying! Come cuddle up with me."

Kate climbed into the bed in the darkened cabin as he closed the door behind him. "I welcome any opportunity to cuddle up to you. I'm so proud of you, lover. For the way you've embraced Cory. I know it goes against everything in your culture, but it's the right thing to do. He'll flourish as a Medici. Now lie down beside me and sleep, you look tired."

"It is nothing, *mi amore*, just a lot of emotions, and a lot to finish up in camp. I want this over and done with before Lorenzo's birth. I want Council to accept Cory."

Moaning, he felt the slumber hitting him hard, too hard. Putting his arms around her, his eyes closed, and he let the slumber pull him under.

Kate curled up next to him, her head on his shoulder, and fell into a light sleep. The night passed quickly, and she felt the plane touch down as Dante landed on a private runway at the Firenze Airport. A car was already waiting, and she could hear the luggage compartment being opened and their luggage being removed. Kate shook his shoulder gently, kissed his ear as she whispered to him, "Shade, wake up. We're here."

Shade could hear her voice, like the song of the angels, or at least if he ever heard an angel, he thought they would sound just like *bel*. Moaning softly, he pulled her onto his chest.

"Already? I feel like I drank too much Midnight." Shaking his shaggy mane, he opened his eyes. "Look in that small closet, see if I have a clean dress shirt in there, *si*? I need to look the master to introduce my son to the staff."

Kate scrambled across the bed to the small closet. "You have everything in here, a complete change of clothes."

"*Si*, help me dress and then we can get to Castello. Did Cory do well on the flight?"

"I haven't checked on him yet, and no one interrupted us during our sleep."

Kate slid the fresh shirt across his broad shoulders, and he slid his arms into the sleeves. She buttoned up his shirt and he pulled on a pair of dress pants. Kate slipped from her nightgown and pulled a summer dress over her head and stepped into a pair of ballet slippers. As they stepped from the bedroom cabin, it was clear Carolyn had served Cory an in-flight meal of steak and potatoes. He was laughing with her as they battled it out over a video game.

Shade laughed. "Well, someone seems to like flying. Cory, you need to put that game away. We need to get to Castello. In a few hours, we meet at Council, we all need to prepare. Come."

Taking *bel's* hand, Shade exited the plane with Cory on their heels. Dante had left the cockpit and climbed behind the wheel of the Bentley, as the three climbed into the back seat and Dante drove them to Castello.

As they entered the grounds of Castello, Cory was feeling uncomfortable. He'd lived in the camp for almost a year and saw the castle from a distance but had never been inside. When they pulled up in front of the ancient castle, he saw the staff lined up in two rows at the entrance and he wondered what in the hell was about to happen.

"Why's everyone outside?"

Shade smiled. "Well, Cory, you are about to have your first introduction as my son. Meet the staff. It will settle your nerves before meeting Council."

Cory sat up straight and stared at the huge number of people, all dressed in their formal black and white uniforms. Damn, living this life would take some getting used to and suddenly, he felt like that juicy steak was about to come back up.

Kate sensed Cory's nervousness and remembered the first time she'd met all the staff. She rubbed his back and whispered to him, "Don't worry. They're all part of Shade's coven, and completely loyal to him. Because he loves you, they'll love you. And we're both right here beside you."

Shade took *bel's* arm and entwined it with his. "I love this dress, *bel*, shows off my son growing inside of you. By the way, they all know. So be prepared for a lot of attention."

Taking Cory's hand, Shade squeezed it lightly. "Come, it's time you are introduced to my staff. Just smile, say thank you, and shake hands if you are comfortable with that."

Shade felt Cory squeeze back, as he walked toward the staff and they were lined up awaiting his arrival. Antonio, the new majordomo, stepped forward, welcoming Shade and Kate back to Castello. Shade thanked him and stood tall and proud, addressing everyone.

"It is good to be home at Castello, home of my birth and the future birthplace of my *bambinos*, one of which is well on his way. Your queen is healthy as you can see. The young vampire beside me is the newest addition to my family and the Medici Coven."

Letting go of Kate's arm, Shade pulled Cory in front of him, putting his hands on Cory's slender shoulders. "May I introduce you to Cory Medici, my son. You will treat him with the utmost respect and honor, as you will all of my *bambinos*. His birth was a surprise to me, but there is no doubt he is of my blood and I am proud and honored to have him as my son. His mother was an acquaintance in the States. She is still living and has been accepted into our *familia*. She is mortal, making my son a half-breed. Some of you will recognize him as the master leather artist for the Medici warriors, an honorable accomplishment on its own. Please welcome him into our *familia* with love."

Shade leaned down and whispered to Cory, "Just breathe, son. This is just introductions."

Taking Cory by the hand, Shade reached for *bel*, and they began the long line of introductions. Shade stopped, as always, to speak to each of the staff about their families. There was much exchange between the staff and their master as he congratulated them on the many milestones in their life, and they each clamored for his attention.

Cory was taken aback at Shade's words. Shade was claiming him as his son in front of all his staff. Cory felt his insides do a flip, but Shade's strong hands on his shoulders made him feel protected and proud. As the staff gazed at him, he felt like crawling into a hole. He was nothing like his father in size and importance, but then he began to see the welcoming smiles and nods in his direction.

As the introductions were completed, the staff scattered quickly to their posts. Shade led *bel* and Cory through the halls, explaining several things to Cory on the way.

"I am sorry this is a short tour, son, but we do have an appointment and Medici's are never late when it comes to seeing the Council."

Leading them to the upper floors, he walked to the master bedroom and looked at Kate. "*Cazzo*, what room is supposed to be Cory's? Do you know, or should I summon Antonio? I am sure Cory's luggage is being taken there."

Kate smiled and pointed down the hall. "Two doors down, next to Luca's. I asked them to give him that room. It has a nice view of the rear gardens, and he can see the camp."

Shade nodded. "*Si*, I will show him." Shade led Cory to his room, a male servant already inside, putting away the things from Cory's luggage. As Shade opened the door, Cory gasped.

Shade chuckled. "Make yourself at home. This is yours now."

Cory stared wide-eyed around the elegant room filled with antique furniture and classic paintings. The pile of the carpet was thick and deep. The bed was big enough for eight people and Cory wondered how the hell you ever grew up with all this elegance and came out like Shade.

Shade nodded to the butler. "Ah, Cezare, you are a good choice for my son. Cory this is Cezare, he will be your manservant whenever we are here. He will be on duty just outside your door. He will attend to your dressing, your hair, your bathing and if you need anything, he will be the one to help get it for you."

Looking up at Cezare, Shade instructed him, "We leave in an hour, have him ready. I think Kate provided appropriate dress and shoes."

Cezare nodded. "*Si*, master, one hour, your son will be prepared to leave."

Cory scowled. *Manservant? Was he joking?* "Dad, I have my own butler?"

Shade laughed. "*Si*, you do son. Get used to it. Cezare will help you get ready. I need to get ready myself. Cezare will bring you to our room when it is time. Just relax, we will be together through all of this."

Shade hugged him tight, holding him a moment longer. "You are Medici now, and this is how we live, Cory." Shade quickly exited, his emotions on overload.

Kate scurried into their room with Emma running behind her, as she rushed to get dressed for Council.

"My lady, do you wish a bath?"

Kate pulled her hair up on her head and Emma helped her pin it in place. "A quick bath Emma, and let's keep my hair dry. I don't have time to wash and dry it."

Emma ran the tub of hot water, pouring Kate's favorite bath oils into the steaming water. Kate stepped into the tub, rinsing off the dust of her travels as Emma washed her back. When she stepped from the tub, Emma wrapped her in a thick towel and Kate washed her face and applied fresh make-up.

Emma unpinned her hair and brushed it to a high sheen. Stepping back into the bedroom, Shade was already dressed in his ceremonial leathers. Emma lifted the pale blush colored gown over Kate's head and let it drop into place. It was a simple chiffon empire waist gown that floated effortlessly to the floor and covered the swell of the baby. The color complimented her skin and her hair, giving her a glow. Emma brought her a pale blush lipstick, and pinched Kate's cheeks.

"There, my lady. Now, step into these shoes, and you are ready." As Kate stepped into the satin slippers with the slight heel, Emma spritzed her with the rose fragrance.

Shade smiled. "You look beautiful, *mi amore*. Every day you carry our *figlio*, you become more beautiful. Your skin glows, my lily-white."

He kissed her softly at first, and then deepened the kiss. Emma giggled and backed slowly out of the room. Shade chuckled. "I think we embarrass Emma with our display of affection."

There was a knock on the door, as Cezare announced that Cory was ready and Shade answered, "Enter!"

As Cory walked in, there was a dramatic change in his appearance. He'd dressed in a suit hand-tailored to his frame and appropriate for his station. Cory seemed uncomfortable in his own skin. Shade knew Kate had taken him shopping and guided his hand in selecting what he should wear. Shade watched as Kate went to him, looking over the new suit, brushing off his shoulders, straightening his tie and making a fuss over him. Shade shook his head, she had such strong mothering instincts, and he adored that in her.

Kate brushed Cory's hair back from his face, "Don't hide that beautiful face." She stepped back and looked at him, as he stood in the new suit. She smiled. "You are much too handsome for your own good, just like your father."

Cory was embarrassed with the fuss and the clothes. He wasn't used to this much attention. He smiled as he looked at his father, wearing the ceremonial leathers that he'd made for him, bearing the Medici crest. Cory had spent hours making them perfect, not knowing at the time Shade was his father. Cory walked up to Shade and hugged him.

Shade returned that hug. "It is overwhelming, I know. But you will get used to it, I promise. Everyone ready? I am sure Dante has the car ready to go."

"Ready, lover." Kate linked arms with the two of them, as they headed downstairs.

Entering the grand foyer, the staff was in attendance once again, and this time, Marco appeared. Shade broke away from *bel* to give his oldest friend a hug. "Damn good to see you, old man!"

Marco had already heard the buzz about Shade arriving with a new son and he was anxious to hear this story. "Damn, can't get rid of your old ass, did you not just leave here several weeks ago?"

As they both laughed, Marco bowed to his queen. "Welcome back home, my queen. We are honored, as always, to be of service to you."

Kate nodded to him and smiled as she laid her hand over the swell of her belly. Cory seemed nervous again in Marco's presence, and was watching his face for any signs of disapproval.

Marco looked at Cory and nodded. "Welcome home, Cory. You are truly missed here, but the leathers you make for the warriors arrive weekly. They are appreciated. Welcome to Medici. It is my greatest honor to serve and protect you."

Dropping to one knee in front of Cory, he paid him homage as a Medici son. Cory looked down at him and then rolled his eyes to Shade, his mouth hanging open in complete astonishment. Marco was bowing to him.

Shade watched Cory's face and bit his lip trying not to laugh. "Marco is pledging his protection to you, as is his duty as my SIC and warrior of my coven. Rise, warrior."

As Marco stood, he nodded to Cory and stepped back. Cory looked to Shade. "Am I supposed to do something?"

Shade smiled. "Well, you can crack him over his hard head if you like or kick him in the shins. You can even attack him if you want, he won't fight back. His job is to protect you. But I would suggest you just thank him. That is most appropriate."

Marco looked at Shade and scowled. "*Grazie*, master!" Their laughter rang out, echoing off the walls. Cory couldn't believe how comfortable Shade was around all these people. He did everything with ease and grace.

Cory nodded to Marco. "Thank you, Marco. It feels weird, but I'm told I'll get used to it."

Marco smiled at him. "You will, trust me. Not looking too bad in that suit either, you should make yourself some ceremonial leathers."

Marco nodded and left, as Shade led his family out to the car and the serious business of Council.

61

As they rode in the car to Council, Shade began to explain to Cory some rules of etiquette. It could be a frightening experience facing the Council for the first time. Shade was pretty sure no half-breed had ever stood before Council before, and he had no idea what kind of reception they'd receive.

"Son, while we are on our way to Council, a few things I wish to explain. We will be announced to Council before we enter the chambers. There are seven Council members, and, like warriors, they are born to Council. It is their birthright and they serve as Council their entire lives. Each was born to a High Master, and they are identified at birth. They oversee the activities of all the covens, and monitor adherence to our laws and practices, as well as hear grievances between masters. Each one has a specific duty to our community.

"I will address them all today, but it will primarily be Malachi and Ivor who will make the final decision. I will be requesting they record your birth in the official records as I claim you as my son.

"We do not sit until bid to do so. I will do most of the talking. The Council will address me personally. If you are asked a question, speak and answer honestly, but under no circumstances are you to speak until spoken to. Council means us no harm, but to be honest with you, I have no idea what I will be up against going into this meeting.

"Our community does not recognize half breeds, as you are painfully aware. This won't be easy, but their anger will be aimed at me, not you. They will most likely ignore you. The place is daunting, but Kate and I are with you, you are well protected and safe."

Shade turned his head and looked at Cory who was staring down at his hands. "You are Medici now, Cory, hold your head up, be proud and never let them see your fear. Council needs me and the money I bring to their coffers, so they won't give me too much grief, but if they do, things could get heated. Let me handle them. You just hold yourself with honor and respect. If I think things are getting too intense, I may ask you to escort Kate outside of the meeting chamber. Do whatever I ask of you, without argument. There is one other thing, they may want to taste your blood, it's no big deal, but they need to know Medici runs in your blood, it is only for verification, *si*? Any questions?"

Cory listened intently. He was frightened but didn't give a voice to his fear. That would be showing weakness, and he never wanted to show that to his dad. He looked up at Shade, their eyes locked. Shade held his gaze for a long minute and Cory felt him inside, giving him strength and calming his fears. "I want to make you proud of me. But explain the feeding. Not sure I like that idea."

Shade smiled. "They will score your skin at the wrist, bleed you into a chalice and then drink from that. They will not feed from you."

Cory felt a flood of relief wash over him. He'll do whatever he had to for his dad and his newfound family, but he was relieved no other vampire was going to feed from him again. "Good because I made a promise to you, and I've kept it. No one feeds from me any longer. I'm a Medici now."

Shade reached over and hugged him around the shoulders. "You will be fine, son. I have no doubts."

When they pulled up in front of Council, Dante exited the car and opened the door for Kate, taking her hand and helping her out. Cory and Shade exited the car and Shade took *bel* into his arms.

"Just relax, things may get a bit heated, but you are safe, and no harm will come to those I love. As always, just be my queen. I know you love Cory, let them see that."

Kissing her, the three of them walked inside the grand hall. An attendant greeted them and took them to the chamber hall where they waited their announcement to Council. Shade watched as Cory sat up straighter, his hands restless. Shade could feel Cory's nervousness of whatever was to come.

"Relax, son, this is about me, and they will focus on me."

The large wooden doors opened, and the Medici warriors flanked each side, as the announcement for their entrance boomed loud and clear through the Council Chambers. The attendant called out, "King Shade Medici, Queen Katherine and Cory Robbins."

Shade led *bel* on his arm with Cory flanking his other side. They walked to the long table positioned in front of the Council, seated in their colored robes on the raised dais. The expressions of the Council members looked foreboding as they prepared to hear the case before them.

The Council members had been speculating all evening on what matter could be so important to require this special session. Once they were all gathered in the Council Court, the attendant announced them, and the Medici entered with his queen, and a half-breed.

Onyx stood in his black robe, his face obscured by the hood and banged the gavel down hard, calling for the guards. There was a loud murmur that ran through the remaining Council, as they reacted to the presence of the half-breed. No mortal or half-breed had ever breached the walls of Council.

"Stop right there! Medici, what is the meaning of this? You know our protocol. No mortals. No half-breeds. The only vampires who may present before Council are masters and their mates once the mating has been sanctioned by Council. Children of masters must have their birth witnessed by Council and may only be present accompanied by their parents. Coven members can only be recognized here by their master, they cannot present in person. We mean no disrespect, Medici, but you have brought a half-breed in our midst. I must respectfully ask that he be removed."

Shade felt the guards walking toward him and the growl ripped from him. "Back off now! I know the rules, Onyx. You mean no disrespect, but you attack me before I enter your chambers. I was not born yesterday. I bring forth this half-breed in your presence for a damn good reason. Let us sit and explain. I am asking you to trust me!"

Shade gripped *bel's* hand and pulled Cory closer to him. Shade's eyes moved instantly to Malachi. "I asked for a meeting with Council and I expect to have it. I have good reason to be here with him, I would not otherwise have asked. Give me a chance."

Malachi stood, his green robe draped around him, holding out his hands to the guards. "Medici, we have convened as you requested, but your actions were not anticipated. Onyx is only doing his job. We will grant you some leeway to hear your case but understand this is unprecedented. Take a seat and state your case, but I cannot imagine any argument that would justify the presence of a half-breed in our chambers."

Shade nodded. "*Grazie*! I plan to claim my justification to the Council."

Leading *bel* to her chair, he pulled it out and seated her as he nodded to Cory to take a seat. Cory looked like he was about to jump out of his own skin. "Cory, sit on my right side. Relax, no harm will come."

With everyone seated, Shade could feel the tension building with Council and he knew he'd have to proceed with caution. "May I have leave to speak?"

Malachi looked around the dais at the other Council members who all nodded reluctantly and silently. He looked at Shade and nodded. "Make your case, Medici."

Shade took a deep breath, clearing his mind and preparing to announce something he knew had never been heard inside these walls.

"The young half-breed you see with me is known as Cory Robbins. I met him recently while visiting California. I hired him and brought him into my coven as my leather artist, sewing the leathers for my warriors. Through a course of events, I discovered his mother was a mortal woman I had met and had a relationship with many years ago while traveling in the States on business. Cory is my son. I claim him as my own, as does my coven and my queen, and I wish for his birth to be recorded within the ancestry books."

The volume of noise increased drastically as the Council members all spoke at once and Shade stood, ready for anything they threw at him. Shade held up his hand. "I am claiming him! I want this Council to verify his bloodline and record it. I know I am breaking all rules, setting a new precedent. But no child of mine, with my blood in their veins, will be thrown to the streets like trash. That is not in my code of honor. Cory is accepted into my *familia* as my own, and I wish for that to be officially recorded here."

The room erupted in chaos as the members of Council all raised their voices, each trying to out-shout the other in their objections. Onyx banged the gavel hard against the table several times, restoring order. Onyx, Malachi, and Ivor were seated with their heads together, speaking in a low whisper. Malachi rubbed his face. Never in the thousands of years sitting on this Council had any vampire ever tested their bylaws. They faced a dilemma in their need to honor their traditions, and yet not fall out of favor with the Medici. He trained the warriors that secured them, and his money went a long way toward maintaining them. Malachi must reason with him.

"Medici, are you sure you wish for your queen and the half-breed to stay in the room for this conversation?"

Shade glared at Malachi as he leaned across the table, his hands spread across the tabletop. His anger was close to the surface, his beast ready to take action and fight for what was his son's right.

"*Si!* Do I have reason not to have them with me? This is my son. He is Medici! Do not push me, Malachi, I warn you. Do not push me further! The fires of hell will be on this Council and if it is a fight you want, Medici can bring it. Think carefully, Malachi, give me honor and respect. I know this is not within our laws, I am breaking ground here, but my son and my queen have a right to know what faces them. We are *familia*, and we rise and fall together."

Onyx started to stand but Malachi held out his hand. He knew the Medici, and his father before him. Both of their tempers were legendary. It was best not to add fuel to the fire and antagonize him further. Malachi knew he must proceed with caution.

"There is no need for such, Medici. Please, be seated. I am sure we can discuss this rationally. This Council has ruled for thousands of years. It is our sacred trust to protect our species and ensure we will thrive for future generations. It is why we must validate all matings between master's and their mates. It is why we must be present at the birth of all children born as a result of that mating. Ivor keeps very accurate records that go back as long as our race has existed on this planet. We encourage purity of blood to secure our species and our longevity. It is why we discourage matings with mortals."

Malachi looked to Kate. "I mean no disrespect in my comment, Queen Katherine, I am merely stating our protocol. This Council has fully recognized your mating to the Medici."

Returning his attention back to Shade, he continued, "A half-breed is not immortal. He will live longer than the average human, assuming he does not meet with an accident, but he does not have that gift of immortality. He cannot breed vampires. Were he to mate, his children would be only quarter vampire, and with each generation that followed, the offspring would have less and less of our power until there was none left. He cannot turn a mortal. His blood does not have the strength. I am sure he is a day-walker as most half-breeds are. They keep that trait from their mortal roots. The half-breeds do not have our physical build or strength. They do not have our immunity to mortal disease, and despite our efforts in the past, they are not able to be turned. It is for this reason the Council does not recognize these offspring between mortal and immortal. They cannot sustain our race. I have no doubt this half-breed is your offspring if you bring him here and speak with such conviction. My question to you, Medici, is why you can't just continue to care for him, as you obviously are doing now. See to his well-being and that he is taken care of. It more than meets any obligation you have to him. He cannot inherit your legacy and rule over your coven. You have a full-blooded son in your mate's belly now, and that child will eventually rule. Why must you insist this half-breed be recorded? For centuries, the half-breeds have been ignored by our kind. You have already done more than your share by taking him in. Why must you insist on having him recorded as your seed?"

Shade moved behind Cory, placing his hands on his shoulders. "Because it is time someone takes responsibility for their lives. I care not that he cannot inherit nor manage my legacy. He already knows these vital facts, but you forget one thing, Malachi. I accept my past, where my travels have led me. It makes me who I am. My *padre*'s generation would have killed him or let him die at the hand of rogues. Today, they are ignored, left to their own devices, and rejected by both mortal and immortal worlds. I cannot live with such. I am a wealthy, successful vampire, a master. And this vampire, half-breed or not, deserves dignity, deserves to know who and where he comes from. He deserves honor and respect. I am not the only master who rules that has half-breed children, there are many I am sure, and more are to come. But I will not stand down and let others berate my child and make him less than what he deserves. He is my son, a product of my loins. His mother willingly gave her own blood to me.

"Had I known of his existence, I would have taken him in then. You speak of survival of our kind, yet you would see them suffer, live among us on the streets, kicked aside like garbage. This is not the age I live in now, not what our world needs. If we are to survive and thrive, we need to recognize their presence among us. I do not mean for them to rule of any sort, they are not able, but you demoralize them, treat them as less. I bring a full immortal son into my life, while welcoming one I knew nothing of. I love him. I love this half-breed as my son."

Shade returned to his seat and grasped *bel's* hand. "Malachi, I understand if you need to have a closed door discussion on this before making a decision, but let it be known, I will not walk from here until Cory Medici is on record in my own family history as my son."

Malachi and Ivor exchanged glances and Malachi sighed heavily. "I must address your queen, Medici. Permission to do so please?"

Shade looked to *bel*, she nodded to him as he responded to Malachi, "With my pleasure, please do so."

Malachi turned his attention to Kate. "Queen Katherine, your king and master has brought forth to us, today, a child not of your womb. In your mortal world, I believe you refer to these as bastard children. Even in the mortal realm, bastard children are not always officially recognized. What your king and master is requesting of us means you too must accept the half-breed as your child. We cannot record the half-breeds mortal mother in our records. The record will reflect he is a half-breed, and future generations may or may not know his true story. In our genealogy records, many may assume the half-breed was your child, born to you while still a mortal. Do you freely accept this child into your home? Are you prepared to teach him and prepare him for his role as a Medici, in as much as he is capable?"

Kate stood to face the Council. "The blood of my king and master flows through the veins of this child, as his blood flows through my veins, so he is already part of my blood. I accept him fully into my home, as I accept his mortal mother into my home. I love him as my own, as my king and master loves him. We are aware of his physical limitations, but he'll know this child in my belly as his brother, not his half-brother. There will be no distinction in our home between full-blooded children or half-blooded children. They're our children, and they'll all be loved and raised to understand their role and rights as Medici. I stand with my king and master in that we'll not leave until this child is recorded as his rightful son...our rightful son."

Shade's heart pounded with pride for his mate. He knew in his community she was going above and beyond, she was giving up her own status in his family history by recognizing this half- breed as family. **"I love you, *mi amore*, *grazie* for giving him your heart as you have given me your own."**

Shade looked to Malachi. "You doubted her too when I chose her, you did not wish for me to make her my mate and queen. And yet, you see the power and prestige she brings to my coven. She has a gift considered extinct among our kind and is the only vampire of record with two gifts. She carries inside her my strong *figlio* who will rule Medici. Now you hear her speak of my half-breed as my own son as well. Yet still, I can feel your trepidation to have this done, even after all I have shown and proven to you. Step up, Malachi, move with the coming times, move the Council into the future. "

As Cory sat quietly, he listened to their arguments and could feel the Council practically snarling at him. Their body language was closed off and negative, he'd seen it many times before. They'd never accept him for who and what he was. Cory listened to his father defend his rights, his legacy, and his existence, and Cory knew even if no one else here accepted him, Shade and Kate always would, and that was all that mattered. Cory sat up straight and stared straight ahead, refusing to concede to their negative ideas of what he could be. He was Medici and he felt that power sitting in this room. Shade squeezed Cory's shoulders when his anger flared and he came to Cory's defense at every harsh word.

When Kate spoke, Cory almost broke, fighting to keep his emotions in check. He had found where he belonged, and he would fight and speak his own defense if given the chance. This was his place and time to become something no half-breed ever got the chance to be, to become something more. Prove they could give back to the vampire world, and suddenly, he knew his actions would affect the coming generations of all half-breeds, and he was ready to take that on.

As the Medici made his final argument, the Council sat in silence. Malachi looked to Florian, in his robe of blue. Florian was responsible for the enforcement of their bylaws, and any changes to protocol would require his final approval. Malachi raised his hands in a shrug as he looked at Florian, as if to say he was at a loss for how to proceed from here.

Florian had been scrolling through the books of ancient texts as he listened to the Medici's plea, searching for any history of a break in this protocol in the past, but he found nothing. The Council met independently on a regular basis to discuss these matters and review these ancient rules imposed in a modern time, as they knew there would be circumstances where they must adjust. The key was in knowing when to give in to the demands of the modern world, and when to hold fast to the old traditions. Florian locked his gaze on the half-breed, addressing him for the first time.

"Stand and face the Council, half-breed."

Cory gulped hard, looked at Shade and when Shade nodded, he stood. He tried to concentrate, appear strong, when something inside him went into overdrive, a rush of his father's blood in his veins. He couldn't explain it, he just knew that whatever was about to happen, it wouldn't change how much his dad or Kate loved him. Standing tall and locking eyes with Florian, he refused to be intimidated.

Florian looked at the frail youth standing before him. He guessed him to be at the age of puberty for a vampire, around eighteen or nineteen. "You have heard the testimony of both your father and the female who, should we decide it so, will be recorded in our records as your mother. Tell me, half-breed, how you see yourself contributing to the Medici coven. You have heard the limitations on your life. How do you commit to be a productive member of this most powerful coven, and not just a drain on its resources? If this Council records you as the son of Medici, there will be much expected of you, half-breed or not."

Cory never dropped his gaze from Florian. "My name is Cory, Cory Medici, not half-breed. I already provide to the Medici coven. I'm the master leather artisan. I design and make every piece of leather the Medici warriors wear. I've been doing this for a while. Master Shade took me off the streets, not knowing who I was. I already love the brothers and sisters in the coven, we're a family. What I give to them is because I want them to be the best at what they do, which is to protect everything that is Medici. That's my contribution. Shade is my father. Kate isn't my biological mother, but she's given me more love than I could ever expect in my life. Both of them have. I'm not born to be a warrior, I'm not born to lead. But I'm born with a right to contribute, love and be loved, respected, and honored. I know you don't understand. I never expect you to. But someone has stood up for me, and taken me into a family where I've been taught there's much I can accomplish. The vampire community just kicked me aside. They never gave me a chance to show anything of what I could become. Shade saw something in me, he gave me a life with an opportunity to flourish, and it changed my entire world. He opened a door for me, giving me a chance, long before he knew I was his son. I come from the streets, where we are less than dirt, abused, beaten, and treated like sex slaves by the immortals, having to do whatever is necessary to survive.

"I stand here as one of those, but a rare one, because I was given a chance to get out. I know many who have killed themselves because of how you think of them. I'm Medici. I will always be Medici. And my actions will show that. I didn't ask to be born, but your community disowned me. Call me whatever you wish, but I call myself Cory Medici, son of the Medici."

Cory remained standing, his gaze never leaving Florian. If Shade and Kate had to fight for him, he would fight right along with them. These vampires were important, but suddenly, he didn't care, he was just a son who was loved.

As Cory sat back down, the Council remained silent. Florian took the lead and asked for a recess. "The Council must discuss this matter before us. We ask that you leave the chamber and wait outside in the vestibule. The guards will escort you and we will call you back in when we have reached our decision."

Shade nodded and stood, leading *bel* and Cory to the huge wooden doors, the guards escorting them to a comfortable sitting area secluded down the long hallway from the Council Chamber. Shade paced back and forth, running his hand through his hair.

"I apologize to you both, I did not know how this would go or what they would say or do, but I knew it would not be pleasant." He flopped in a cushioned chair, his hands covering his face.

Kate felt his frustration and ran her hand up his back. "Regardless of their decision, Shade, he's your son, he's our son. We don't need the permission of a bunch of decrepit vampires in rainbow robes to dictate our lives. They called him half-breed like he's not a real person. Their decision, one way or another, changes nothing in my mind. He's Cory Medici!"

Shade took her in his arms. "They need to fucking understand I will not tolerate this behavior any longer. Cory knows he is my son, he knows how I feel, he knows how you feel, but what I want is change."

Standing, he embraced Cory to his chest. "I am sorry for all you have had to bear, and that I put you in this position. It is a lot to ask, but you have to be the role model for all of the half-breeds who have suffered and will continue to do so. Even if they consent to this, it will still be a hellish stigma to them. And it will take years for the change to bring about any results. I am the strongest vampire in Europe. I need to lead the changes for our kind, even the half-breeds. I lost one son to this fucked up stigma, but I won't lose another."

In Shade's embrace, his words made Cory proud to be a half-breed. It was the first time in his life he'd ever felt that. "I'm proud to be the role model. They sit there and have no idea what life is like for us. I just hope I said the right words. I'm so angry at them! They judge me because of my birth. They don't even know me. I'm so tired of that mindset. I should have shown them my scars, shown them how I was beaten, abused to just live and feed."

Shade's gripped Cory even tighter in his embrace, his small frame felt delicate and fragile under Shade's strong arms. Burying his face in Cory's neck, they both felt the emotions rolling over them, bonding them together. "I love you, son, I will always love you, protect you and nothing is taking you from me."

The guards approached and one of them cleared his throat, interrupting the emotional display between the Medici and his son. "The Council is ready for you to return." The guards led the three of them back into the chambers and had them take a seat.

Malachi stood. "The Council has discussed your unique situation and we have decided, pending verification of his bloodline that we will record the half-breed, heretofore known as Cory Medici, into the records. The attendant will bring the chalice, please."

A robed attendant appeared with the gold chalice and handed it to Malachi who stepped from the dais to the table where Shade, Kate and Cory were seated. "We ask the Medici to score his wrist and drain his blood into the chalice."

Shade nodded to Malachi, reaching over, he took Cory's wrist in his hand and sank his fangs into the vein. Shade held his son's wrist over the chalice, watching the thick red blood drip into the cup. Once the chalice was a quarter full, Shade lifted Cory's wrist to his mouth and licked his wounds, watching them heal. He handed the chalice to Malachi, his eyes issuing a challenge.

"Drink it, Malachi."

Malachi nodded. "It is my intent, Medici."

He took the chalice from Shade's hands and tipped it to his lips, tasting the blood of the half-breed. It was diluted, but he clearly tasted the distinct flavor of the royal Medici blood. He closed his eyes as he waited to see if any gifts would be displayed. Other than day-walker, which he fully expected, there was nothing new. He set the chalice down on the table and looked the Medici in the eye.

"I declare before this Council the royal blood of the Medici runs through his veins. Let it be recorded that this half-breed is the son of the Medici and Queen Katherine, and he shall be known as Cory Medici."

Ivor stood and opened the large leather-bound journal, dipping the quill pen into the ink and recording the entry into the Medici ancestry. He stamped the entry with his official seal and then proclaimed, "So be it."

Malachi turned back to Shade, "Is there any further business before Council?"

Shade felt like a great weight had been lifted from his shoulders. "I am grateful for this meeting and for the outcome. I am pleased with the progress of the Council and thank you for your wise decision and compliance with my request. I have no further business with Council at this time."

Malachi nodded. "That is reassuring to hear, Medici. You have brought us more drama in the last year than we have seen in the last thousand. May our next encounter be less stressful? We bid you good evening. The guards will see you out."

Shade stood and nodded to each member of Council. He took *bel's* hand and placed the other around Cory's shoulder as they followed the guards outside and into the waiting car.

"Home, Dante. Take us the hell home!" Shade laid his head back on the seat, his eyes closed. "Some nights, *mi amore*, being a master is very tiring on my soul."

Kate laid her head on his shoulder, as her hand stroked his chest. "Lover, you make me proud. I see why your warriors will follow you into battle, why they pledge their loyalty to you. You give them loyalty in return. I couldn't love you more."

She looked at Cory who was seated on the other side of Shade. "I know I'll never replace your biological mother. I'd never presume to do that. But I meant what I said in there. You're my son now too."

Cory watched as she comforted Shade, and once again, he wondered how it would have been different if his real mom would have been in her place. "I know you had to say that to them in there to plead my case. I appreciate it, I'm grateful." Cory looked out the window of the large Bentley and watched the skyline of Florence pass him by, his heart content that he was now legally the son of the Medici.

Kate spoke to him, "No, Cory, I didn't have to say it. I said it because I meant it. You're Shade's blood. I was mortal, turned by him. He made me as much as he made you. We're both joined by his blood. We're blood family. When we get back to Bel Rosso, you'll move out of the barracks and into the main house. I have contractors working on your room. I'm converting the attic space into your space. There are bedrooms on the same floor as mine and Shade's bedroom, but they are reserved for the babies to come, who will need close attention. I thought long and hard about where to place your room. I thought if I convert the attic space then you'll have more privacy."

Shade looked over at Cory, felt his confusion, hesitation. When Cory didn't acknowledge *bel*, he decided he needed to speak. "Cory, answer Kate. Speak your mind. Do not hide your feelings from her, nor me. We are *familia*, we need to share to grow, *si*?"

Cory looked straight ahead, not directly at Shade or Kate. "Thank you. I'm not used to the love and attention. I'm fine. I mean no disrespect. It will just take me a while to get used to all this. I was just getting adjusted to being accepted in the camps and now all of this has happened. It's a lot for me to absorb."

Kate smiled at him. "That I can understand. I've had my own share of feeling over-whelmed. So, it will be important for you to let us know what's going on in your head. I want you in our life, but I understand you're not a child and you need your own personal space. Just let us in, Cory. Shade and I have had our issues adapting to each other, merging our two worlds. So let us know when we crowd you or move too fast."

Shade pulled Cory to his chest, ruffling his hair with his hands. "It's okay to feel like you have been through hell and back because you have.

We love you, and you can come to us for anything, good or bad. That's all we can ask. We love you without judgment. I am here for you, so is Kate."

Dante pulled into Castello and before Shade could even move, Cory had opened the door and headed inside, walking fast and alone. Sighing, he knew his son needed some time to process this change. Shade let Dante help *bel* from the car and they walked hand in hand back inside.

"My life seems to be complicated as hell lately, but I would change nothing. Not one moment of it. Tell me it will get easier, *mi amore*."

Kate smiled up at him, as she took his hand and placed it on the swell of their growing baby. "Easier? I don't think so, lover. But always worth it."

62

Alec arrived home later than usual. Santos met him at the door, taking his suit jacket and handing him a glass of Midnight. He made his way to his office to drop off his briefcase when he saw the wedding invitation placed front and center on his desk. He picked up the invitation, enclosed in its own box, and examined the diamond broach. Alec dropped down into the office chair. *Did this woman attach a diamond brooch to every invitation?*

He shook his head, and finished off the remainder of the Midnight, calling Santos for a refill. He took out his cell phone and gave his business manager a call, asking for a quick summary on what she'd spent for the wedding so far. When he heard him say $30 Million and counting, Alec took another big gulp of Midnight. It wasn't that they didn't have it; it just seemed an unnecessary extravagance. He should have been prepared for this, he knew how jealous Rissa had been of Kate's Coronation and she was determined to top it. He heard Rissa as she entered the front door with Hyde. Alec walked out to the foyer to greet them.

Hyde was helping her off with her coat as Rissa smiled and reminded him tomorrow they needed to start out earlier than usual, she had much to do. Hyde told her he'd be here early and nodded to Alec before taking his leave.

"Did you have a good day, darling?"

Rissa moved slowly in Alec's direction. "I had a very long but productive day, and you, Alec?"

"Not bad. Could always be worse. I was looking at the invitations."

Rissa tried to assess his mood. "Oh good, I'm so glad you found time to give them a glance. I think they turned out well, don't you? Have to impress, right? I have appointments tomorrow with the florist, and I need to pick up my hair clip from the jewelers. I should just have that delivered. It would save me a trip."

Walking to the living room, Rissa went to the bar, picked up the Midnight and poured herself a large glass full. "Do you want one, my wicked vampire?"

Alec followed behind her. "Yes, please. A large one, and tell me, was that invitation reserved for special guests? Or is everyone on the guest list getting the diamond brooch?"

Quickly downing her drink before pouring herself another, she poured one for Alec. She handed him the drink, as she took a seat across from him on the sofa, pulling off her heels.

"New shoes, killing me, I broke a heel today, I stumbled and it broke, so I had to stop and buy another pair. I abhor breaking in new heels when I'm on my feet all day."

Looking at Alec, she raised her eyebrows. "Did you ask me something? Oh yes, the invitations. Of course, everyone gets the same invitation. I'm having the special guests hand delivered, the others will be posted. Is there a problem?" Sitting back, she closed her eyes, downing the tumbler of Midnight.

Alec shook his head, it's not as if any of it could be undone at this point, and he'd known, going in, it would be a lavish affair.

"No problem, my darling. Just try not to bankrupt us before I can make it to the Presidency. Could you bring me the cigarette box, please?"

"You never gave me a budget, Alec, you said to do it my way. I assumed you'd have no problem. You do want to impress everyone, the goal being to draw attention. Most of the guests are mortal, so we have the cost of food, and you said not to skimp."

Standing to get the cigarette box, her head swirled and she almost fell over before regaining her balance. She stood still for a moment, massaging her temples, her heart rate dropping.

Come on Midnight, do your magic. She needed to feed but she knew he'd been busy lately and she could manage a few more days without. Carrying the cigarette box back, she handed it to him and settled back down on the couch. "Any news on the political front I should be aware of?"

Alec saw her stagger slightly as she made her way to the cigarette box and the comment about stumbling and breaking her heel took on new meaning.

"It's not a reprimand, my darling. I asked you to make it memorable, and I'm sure it will be. There will be those who'll be impressed, and those who'll scoff at the amount of money spent, but you know what they say, there's no such thing as bad press, and I'm sure your wedding will be front page news."

He moved closer to her, looking closely at the paleness of her skin, its transparency making the blue veins visible beneath the surface. That was never a good sign.

"My wedding? Oh, so this is *my* wedding now? Tell me you'll at least be present."

Alec brushed the hair back from her face, pale despite the make-up. "I'll be the one standing at the end of the long aisle waiting for you. When was the last time you fed, Rissa?"

Rissa looked away, trying to escape the intensity of his stare. She hated when he had to ask. He couldn't remember, and it was a stab to her heart that he didn't seem to care enough to recall, and made her almost beg for his attentions.

"I don't remember, Alec, why? I'm feeling fine, a bit tired, but nothing more. I should go take a long hot bath and then get some sleep. I have a lot to do tomorrow, and I hope I can find some time to ride later in the evening as well. I'll leave you to your work, no need to worry."

He gripped her wrist as she stood to leave and pulled her down into his lap.

"I believe we've discussed this once before, my darling. You need to tell me if you've gone too long. I'm older. I can survive much longer between feedings."

He loosened his tie and pulled it free from his neck, unbuttoned the top buttons of his dress shirt and exposed his neck. "Feed. It's not a request."

She couldn't resist his scent or the closeness of him. Rissa snuggled into his neck, moaning softly. Sinking her fangs deep into his neck, that first hit of his blood made her head spin as his strength pumped through her, giving her an intensive high. Every part of her being screamed for him, ached for him, and wanted him. As she slid her hand around his neck, her body came alive, as she took more of his precious life's blood to sustain her.

Alec brushed her hair back from her face as she fed. He laid his head back on the sofa, exposing his neck freely to her, allowing the erotic sensations to wash over him, feeling his cock grow hard.

"It's not just your wedding, my darling. You seem to forget, I was born immortal. My world has no such ceremony for weddings. You were wed to me the night I turned you. That's the night that lives in my mind. This wedding is for the mortals, you're already bound to me in ways no mortal can ever understand, bound beyond simple vows surrounded by pomp and ceremony. My blood gives you life, sustains you. No wedding can replace that. Now drink your fill."

Rissa finished her long feeding, retracting her fangs, licking clean her lips, her body on fire for him but knowing he'd never give himself to her tonight. As she laid her head on his chest, the hunger for his blood was fulfilled but the desire for his body wasn't satisfied. She pushed down her desire for him.

"The mortals need to see with their eyes I belong to you, Alec. I don't care about this wedding but making it perfect is something I do for us both. To show the mortals you're a rich and powerful man, and to show them what I can do. This is my business. Weddings are where I get the most exposure and make the most money. I just want you to at least pretend you take it seriously and have a good time when it happens."

He kissed her forehead, "I'll not need to pretend, my darling. I do take it seriously, and I promise to have a good time. Now, go. Finish your work."

Kissing his neck, she climbed from his lap, grabbed his glass, and refilled it with Midnight. Picking a cigarette from the box, she lit it, took a drag, and then handed it to him.

"Don't be up too long, Alec, you need rest too. And thank you for... well, for being understanding about the money. I'm actually enjoying putting it all together."

Gathering her things from the hall, she rushed up the stairs and headed for a long hot soak in the tub, where she pleasured herself to relieve the burning heat between her legs. Tomorrow was another day and she'd start out with master's blood inside her.

63

Shade lay with *bel* inside their suite at Castello, insisting she rest for a few hours before taking the flight back to Bel Rosso. Not letting her get overly tired was important to him. He knew this pregnancy was completely different from their first experience, but he wouldn't take any chances with her. He gently rubbed her back until she fell asleep. Lying beside her, his mind was still occupied with the events of Council and Cory.

Once he knew she was asleep, he quietly slipped from their bed and left the room, walking to the room that had served as his office at Castello for centuries. This was the room where he'd overseen his business interests, as well as managing the issues of the camp and the coven. It had been a while since he'd sat here among the volumes of ledgers that had been maintained over the ages. As he entered, he stopped in his tracks when he saw his *padre* sitting at the desk, and the memories of his childhood flooded over him.

Christofano would hold court in this office as Shade was summoned before him to be emotionally dismantled for all the things his *padre* thought he lacked. Shade was never able to live up to his expectations of being a warrior and the son of the Medici, ready to take on all the responsibilities of managing the coven. Shade knew his *padre* had finally come to see him for the man he'd become, but the pain and disappointment of never having his *padre*'s approval when he was young remained in Shade's heart even today.

Christofano looked up as his son entered the office, his face showing his clear dissatisfaction of Shade's actions this night.

"You bring a half-breed to this *familia*? You fathered him, claim him as your own and ask your queen to do the same? Do you have no shame? They have no place in this *familia*! No place in your life. Have you learned nothing? You walk into our home with a half-breed who is weak, who brings shame and degradation to us and act as though you rule the world with no care of what you have done. What have you to say for yourself? I can barely stand to look you in the eye."

Shade walked to the chair opposite his father's desk and sat in the familiar seat. Not much had changed. Once again, he'd failed in his father's eyes. Shade stared at him a long time, wondering how his father ever ruled the coven with such harsh thoughts and impossible standards. But he knew it was a long time ago, and times had changed. Shade was born to make the changes necessary to make their immortal world stronger.

"I have a lot to say for myself. Your grandson is now growing strong inside my mate. The empire you once built is flourishing and larger than anything you could ever have imagined in your time. Medici has expanded from one continent to another. There are now two warrior camps. I have more money than I could ever spend. The wine business brings in much wealth. My mate is gifted with not one but two gifts, one of which is rare and will bring to our name great power. None of that was your doing. It was my doing, my reign that reaped it all. I am the Medici now. The son I had with a mortal female is in my past, and yes, my actions were a mistake, but I can't let his life be a mistake. He is of my blood, and he deserves my name. I was born to become a warrior, a master, a king. I had no choice. My path was set for me at my birth. I did my duty with diligence, with my own blood spilt and my spirit broken at times. But I have come to believe my real purpose is to make the changes necessary to see our immortal world flourish, grow in numbers and learn to survive and integrate invisibly with the mortal world. I am making those changes in the name of Medici."

Christofano pushed the chair back from the desk. "You have been to Council and they accepted these terms? Your queen has allowed another female's *bambino* into her heart as if he were her own? She allows such? You have done well, *figlio*, but this boy you claim, what value does he bring to the Medici? The true son of Medici grows inside her, strong and full blooded, heir to king and coven. This half-breed is a waste of your time and energy."

Christofano leaned back in his chair, shaking his head at his only son. "Help me understand this new way of thinking, I see things very differently."

Shade chuckled and crossed one leg over his opposite knee. "*Padre*, I am not sure you will ever understand how a half-breed can become a vital part of Medici. You are trapped in your time, not able to comprehend the massive changes of life on the earthly plane. Immortals from the States are different, their lifestyle and standards are nothing like how I was brought up. You taught me well, but I teach differently. The legacy you left gave me a head start, but the coven I lead now needs to be guided with love, understanding, and a firm hand. Kate is open-minded, she loves me like *Madre* loves you, and she supports me, loves what is mine. We work together, not separate. Cory is part of my blood. He suffered greatly because of mistakes I made, as many like him suffer. The half-breeds have suffered for ages and I want that to stop.

"Cory does not deserve to suffer for my carelessness. His mother gave me comfort in a time when I felt none. I claim him as my son because I love him. I want no child of mine to be abused and left to suffer and starve. Look deep inside your heart, *Padre*. If I had come home with a half-breed son when you were still alive, could you have so easily discarded him? Think before you answer. Could you have thrown him to the wolves with no care when you could have made a difference for him, given him a life that had meaning and purpose within our *familia*? Could you have watched as *Madre* suffered, knowing you left a *bambino* with Medici blood out on the streets to agonize alone and defenseless? You and I both know, *Madre* would suffer for that action. She may not have spoken against you as it was her nature and place to accommodate your rule, but she would have felt the pain of your decision, nonetheless. Think about those things before you judge my decision. Cory possesses great talent, with education and direction, he can become much more. He is my son. Nothing will change that simple fact."

Christofano listened intently to his son explain this half-breed and he felt Shade's deep love for this child. He was proud of his son, where he'd gone, how he'd survived after their demise, bringing the Medici back to its regal status, above and beyond anything he'd ever dreamed.

Christofano nodded. "Portia would have been brokenhearted to know a child of my loins or yours may die without assistance, but it was not something done in my day. I knew of one who paid to keep his *bambino* safe and well but moved him far from his rule. Malachi must have been beside himself to agree to such. The Council changes no laws easily. But I understand the love for a child. It is a love that is entwined in your soul. It is a love unlike any other and something I had never felt until the day of your birth. You will feel that soon when your own son is born. This half-breed, your other son, he too will feel your love. But he will need much from you to flourish in our community."

Shade looked across the desk at his father. "He has already given back to me, *Padre*. He is accepted among my warriors. My queen loves him as do I. It will take him time to adjust to being a Medici, but we will work together as *familia*, and that, *Padre*, is one lesson you taught me well."

Standing, Shade walked to his father and they embraced. Christofano accepted the affection even though he was never one to show great emotion.

Shade told him, "You have a grandson, *Padre*, his name is Cory. Do not scare the fuck out of him while he is here. Just love him, accept him, and accept his presence in my life. My life is different, and you have to accept the changes that come with that. Take pride in me. Take pride in what we have accomplished. But know that, through it all, the lessons you taught me are still with me, and I use them every day of my life. *Ti amo, Padre*."

Shade watched as his father walked to the door of the office, giving up his position for the night to his son. He turned to Shade and nodded. "*Ti amo, figlio*."

64

The flight home from Florence was long but uneventful, everyone sleeping as much as possible, the stress of the events at Council taxing Shade. As they landed, the sun was not set. Dante had the limo waiting in the private hanger, where their luggage was transferred and they climbed inside. The dark tinted windows on the limo and his sunglasses made it safe enough for Dante to drive them back to Bel Rosso.

Once inside and settled, Shade was in his office going over a few details around the plans he had for a new feeder compound. It looked like a promising concept but explaining it to *bel* was another matter. He had to explain this to her, help her understand this was the most financially feasible option, as well as the option that provided for the greatest safety for his warriors. Telling her he planned to build this compound on the grounds and bring the feeders into the camp, he knew she'd blow a fuse. He felt if he could make her see the sense in it, she'd agree. Taking the stairs two at a time, he found her inside the room she was planning for Lorenzo's nursery and he thought this was a good start. She'd be in a good mood and perhaps not argue as much. Who the hell was he kidding, this was his *bel*!

"Nursery?"

Kate looked up as he entered. "Yes. I want to get this done. I have the contractors renovating the attic to make a private space for Cory. And then we have the nursery, the Paris house, and the inn in California. I need to get this project started since the doctor said I may not have as much energy as the pregnancy progresses. I think I'm just going to go with a traditional blue color...or maybe a soft grey." Kate flipped through the paint swatches, holding them up to the wall.

"*Bel*, if this is too much for you to handle, it is easy enough to get professional decorators in. Just give them direction and they will do all of the work for you." Shade scrunched up his face, crossing his arms over his chest as he leaned against the door jamb. "But I have a feeling you are much like my *madre*, she was not satisfied unless she attended to every detail in person."

Kate laughed. "There's no way I am not doing this myself. Look at this paint sample. Maybe not grey, too stark...maybe a bluish grey. Yes, I think I like that better."

Shade shook his head. "He is a *bambino*, he will not notice. You could make the room pink with orange polka dots and he will not know."

Kate sighed. "But he won't stay a *bambino*. He'll grow up in this room. And he'll notice. He'll love his room. Don't you love this house?"

Shade treaded lightly, not wanting to upset her before this conversation even began. "Of course, I love this house. It is our home, as will be every house that has your touch. I just have one stipulation, something I want. I do not care what else you do in the *bambino*'s rooms, you have excellent taste."

Kate looked up at him. "And what's your one stipulation?"

He walked to her, wrapping his arms around her, snuggling into her crimson. "I wish to have a cradle inside our bed chamber. I want the *bambino* close to us when he is first born, *si*? I would like the cradle that belonged to me brought here for Lorenzo. It was hand carved by Medici artisans."

She smiled at him. "You had a cradle? I'd love for Lorenzo to sleep in your cradle. And I think, for the first month, when he feeds from only me, he should be in our room. The doctor said after the first month Theresa and I would share feeding, so I'll need to move him to the nursery then. Theresa will have a nanny's bed in here as well, in addition to her own room."

Shade nodded. "*Si*. I will have the cradle shipped over immediately. But first, I have something I want to discuss with you before I go to camp. They will be getting ready to begin classes shortly. Come to the bed chamber with me, *si*?" Holding out his hand, he kissed her cheek.

Kate took his hand and followed him back to their bedroom. "What do you need to discuss?"

He led her to the large overstuffed chairs in their bedroom, as she took a seat opposite him. "Before I even begin, I want you to give me a chance to explain completely, hear me out before you judge, *si*? At least give me a fighting chance to say what I have to say, because this is something you feel strongly about and not in a good way."

A million thoughts flew through her head, and she mentally prepared herself for whatever he had to say. "Okay, I'm listening."

"I have made a business deal, one that will be more practical for my warriors and the new recruits. I have arranged with the feeder coven located outside of D.C. to have some European feeders from Italy brought in."

Holding up his hand, he could feel her temper flare. "Hear me out, *mi amore*. I am going to need more feeders to keep this large group fed and nourished. I will employ feeders from Europe and the States. We have a wide variety of warriors now, with a variety of taste. But it is not always safe to have my warriors' teleporting to the feeder coven, nor can I conspicuously have them brought back and forth, it draws too much outside attention in this countryside. I want to build a compound for them inside the camp. I want it to look in line with the Tuscan feel of the camp and our home. It will look like a house sitting among the rest of the buildings. The compound will need to be designed with private rooms where the feeders live and receive their clients. I want a tunnel leading from the feeder compound into the warrior camp. The warriors can easily access them without being exposed. I have asked Gi to have a female brought in from Florence, one who personally knows how I operate to provide supervision of the feeders. She is older, and this is her profession. In her youth, she too was a feeder, and now she serves to oversee the young ones. She is called a Matron. She is in charge and responsible for their actions as well as reporting to me any problems with the warriors. It is the easiest and most efficient way to handle this large group of warriors. But I am going to need your help. You are my queen and I know you hate the idea of having the feeders around, but with the tunnel, you will never see them. It saves me time and money, and keeps my warriors fed, protected and everyone involved is in a stable, controlled environment. Give me your thoughts."

Kate absorbed what he was saying. She did as he'd asked and listened to all he'd said. She stood up and walked to the window, looking out over the rolling hills of Bel Rosso in the dim light of the dusk.

"They'll live here?"

The memory of the voluptuous feeder that climbed him like a tree flashed through her head, as well as his response to her. He fought her off, but his sexual arousal and desire was like a force field that moved across the room in a powerful wave.

"Lover, you're asking a lot of me."

"*Si*, I ask much from you. And *si*, they will reside here. You are my queen, there are some things you will have to comply with even though you do not like them, *mi amore*. I need you to be behind me, support me in all things. I could easily do this without telling you. But that is not how I want us to be. *Padre* would have just done it, never told *Madre* and be damned. But I want you involved."

Standing, he paced, sliding his hands through his hair. "If you have any other suggestions for a better system, please share it with me. But this is how I think it will work the most efficiently for our warriors and the feeders."

Kate could feel him pacing behind her. She leaned her forehead against the cool glass of the window pane. She was still coming to grips with the idea of wet-feeders for her children. Shade described them as asexual, but she'd never seen a wet-feeder. This was her world now. There was no escaping it. But he was asking her to accept a house full of feeders on their property?

"Help me understand. When the feeder came to our house...the one Rissa brought here, she had a power over you and Luca. Her appeal was almost hypnotic, unavoidable. Your response to her was not even voluntary but primal. How will you...avoid them?"

Shade stopped his pacing and stared at her. He could feel all the worry that rolled through her, her thoughts like a living entity in the room. He'd known this wouldn't be easy for her and he was asking a lot. Walking to her, he wrapped his arms around her waist, pulling her back into his chest, rubbing the mound of his unborn son as if to comfort them both.

"That is the reason for the tunnel. I won't see or hear them. Yes, the feeders exert a very strong sexual draw on any vampire, power that is difficult to fight. Their blood is pure, never tainted. They release a scent that stimulates desire. *Mi amore*, I love you, I know you can feel that inside you. And your experience with feeders has been an extremely bad one but a reality check of their power. Marcello will be in charge of the feeder compound, he will inform me of any problems, but he will handle everything with the Matron. I want you to know, I will never go there, never step foot inside the house. This is why I need you to assist me. If it makes you feel better, I can have Fiamma oversee the design of the compound. She can come to you instead of me if there are needs or concerns. I have no intentions of ever seeing the inside, but it is my duty to care for my warriors, *bel*. This provides a controlled environment. Feeders have been a staple in our community for as long as I can remember, it is how we have survived all these years. It limits our interaction with mortals. *Si*, they are highly sexual creatures, but as you know, sex and feeding in our world goes hand in hand. Please try to understand. This is not about me. It is about those I care for in my coven."

She was immortal now and understood even more the power of the sexual attraction that came with feeding, and she also knew the hunger that gnawed at her when she needed to feed, and the weakness that quickly followed if she didn't. She understood it was survival. He'd never given her a reason not to trust him, not ever. He'd made every effort from the very beginning to assure her of his fidelity, and she had no doubt about his commitment. But what if they sought him out? Like Britt?

"I believe what you're saying, Shade. I do. But what if they come to you?"

Spinning her in his arms, he pushed the beautiful stray crimson locks behind her ears, letting his hand slide gently across her cheek, his thumb rolling slowly over her lips. His blue eyes looked, with love, into her amber ones.

"*Mi amore*, feeders are bred to serve. They know nothing else. It is their role in our society. They do not seek a specific partner. Their life is devoted to serve and feed. Vampires seek them out, not the other way around. They are carefully bred and trained for this specific task, and they would be lost if let loose in our world. They are carefully housed and taken care of, groomed to be alluring, sexual and irresistible, it is their only job in life. So, a vampire must seek them out. They do not wander in our immortal world. I have no need for them. I have all that I will ever need in my arms. But it is a master's duty to provide such for his warriors, either in leading the warriors to a feeder coven or bringing the feeders to the warriors. It is my duty, do you understand?"

Kate laid her head against his chest. "I do understand, Shade. And I'll do as you ask. I'll help design the house, so it blends in, and connect it to the underground tunnels. All I ask of you is to let me coordinate it. I'll work with the Matron and set the rules. I'd like to have Fiamma assist me, help me with the parts I don't understand. I'll feel more comfortable if I can control it. Is that okay?"

Shade smiled as he kissed the top of her head. "*Si, mi amore.* Thank you for understanding. I hate putting you under more stress and piling on more things for you to do."

This wasn't a project Kate was looking forward to, unlike the nursery and the Paris house, or her plans for the inn, but she'd add it to her list. At least she'd have some control, and that made her feel better. Not much, but a little.

Shade led her to the bed, sat her down and crouched between her legs, kissing his unborn son. "One more thing. I have asked Cory to stay here in the house tonight. I do not want him at the camp until I can have a general meeting with everyone, letting them know Cory's status as my son. I plan on having that meeting tomorrow night, will you join me?"

"Of course. Now that his mother has left, he can use the guest room until I have his suite completed upstairs. And I'd love to be with you when you share the news."

"That's my *bel*! While I am in the camp tonight please talk to Cory. He never had a room for himself. Can you let him help with choosing the things in his room? I would like him to feel as if this room was not just given to him, but something he had a hand in choosing. I want him to be comfortable here, not just a place to rest, *si*?"

"Lover, I'll be happy to have his input. I'm adding a bedroom, living room and bath for him upstairs. He'll have his own private suite."

Shade chuckled. "As always, you spoil them all. No wonder they never want to go back to Florence. Thank you, *mi amore*, this means much to me." He kissed her tummy, sliding his hands over her baby bump. "*Ti amo, mio figlio*. I must get to the camp and make sure everything is running smoothly. It is never ending."

Kate ran her hand through his hair. "Then go. I'll send a message for Cory to come to the house. Gi can get his room ready for him tonight. Cory can see the floor plans the contractor has drawn up and we can talk about what he likes. Get going, the sooner you go, the sooner you come back to me."

65

Shade was pacing in his office, he'd told Marcello to make sure the warriors were assembled, new recruits included. No one was to go out tonight until he held this important meeting, mandatory for all. He wasn't nervous for himself or *bel*, but for Cory. He knew they'd look at Cory differently once they knew the truth, and Cory would probably be subjected to some good ribbing. But it was vital Cory be known as his son and that he was accepted by Shade and Kate. Shade expected the same from his coven and warriors. Luca left earlier to make sure all was prepared. Even he didn't know this news. As *bel* walked into the office, Cory was close behind. Shade stopped his pacing and smiled at them. "We ready to walk over?"

Kate went over to Shade, sliding her arms around his waist. "I'm ready when you are."

Cory looked around the office, feeling nervous. "Yeah, I think I'm ready."

"Then let's go." Taking Kate's hand, they all strolled to the warrior camp. The weather was beautiful, and the gardens were in full bloom, Shade enjoyed the outdoors. He got to spend little time with *bel* in the waning hours of daylight. Entering the camp, the noise level was out of control, as the warriors were letting off a little steam before taking to the training fields.

Entering the large lounge room, they were completely ignored, as the warriors were rough-housing with each other.

Shade issued a loud whistle that brought every head turning in his direction. "Get your asses in the other room and settle the hell down! We have business."

The room suddenly went quiet when they all realized his presence here. The warriors and new recruits filed out of the room into the meeting hall, where Shade, Kate and Cory followed.

Shade led *bel* to the three chairs that had been placed for them at one end of the meeting room. He waited until the entire crowd filed in and got seated and he nodded for Cory to sit with *bel*. Once everyone was settled, he could see their curiosity as to why Cory had been singled out to sit in one of the three seats designated for their king and queen.

Shade held up his hand, "Let's settle down, I have two important announcements to make. First, I wish to address our feeding issue. We now house a great number of warriors with our newest recruits, so shuffling warriors and feeders about is more time-consuming, and unsafe all around. I have come up with a workable plan. We are building a feeder compound. It will sit near the barracks and look like the rest of the buildings here on Bel Rosso. There will be a connecting tunnel underground, no warriors or feeders will ever be exposed to the outside world. This tunnel will have a security code like all the other tunnels. Marcello will be in charge of overseeing the feeder compound, and Fee is also going to be working closely with your queen in the management. Once we have completed the building, I have arranged for American and European feeders to be available. You will still attend to your feeding on a scheduled basis, but for all concerned, you will not be leaving Bel Rosso to feed. That is important for everyone's safety and protection. I will be bringing in a matron who will run the compound and you will follow her rules or you answer to me, or worse, to my queen. So, I suggest if you do not want to end up like Cuerpo, you behave yourselves." As he turned, he took *bel's* hand and brought her to stand beside him. "My queen, do have anything you wish to say to your legion of warriors?"

Kate was caught off-guard as he invited her to speak. She never felt prepared to address the crowd. "Uh...just to be clear, as Shade stated, there will be a connecting tunnel to the feeder compound. Like all the tunnels, it will require fingerprint ID to enter. The tunnel is designed for one-way traffic. You may enter the feeder compound, but the feeders may not leave the compound and come into the camp. The feeder compound will be well appointed, designed for your comfort as well as for the feeders that live there. I'm fully aware that you could use your fingerprint ID when exiting the feeder compound to bring one of the feeders out with you. This is against regulation, and I will demand your removal from this camp immediately should this ever occur. There will be no first warning...this is your first and only warning. Your rank, your skill level, your tenure here, none of it will account for anything in granting you leniency if you break this rule. Am I clear?"

Shade was impressed, but he knew when he put her in charge, she'd rule this bunch of wild beasts with a firm hand. He looked out to see if anyone had any questions and saw Marcello stand to be addressed.

Leaning into *bel* he whispered to her, "When one of them stands, they are showing you respect and asking to speak, you have to acknowledge and let them ask their question, and more than likely Marcello is asking on behalf of the entire group."

Kate nodded at him. "Is there something you wish to add Marcello?"

Marcello bowed his head to her. "*Grazie* my queen, I do have a question. Does this rule apply to our master as well? I am sure we'd all like to be clear on that point, especially if I am in charge of the proper security within this camp."

Marcello tried to hide his smirk as the warrior's lean forward, waiting to hear their queen's response. Shade crossed his arms over his chest and went to speak when Kate quickly laid her hand on his arm and he shut his trap immediately.

Kate was aware she was being teased by Marcello and put on the spot in front of his warriors. "Good point Marcello. Your master will *not* have security clearance to the feeder compound, and if any warrior is discovered trying to sneak him in, you will find both yourself and your master banned from this camp." Kate glanced at Shade. "Any more questions?"

As the smirks and cat calls rose from the warriors, Shade turned to his queen and bowed. "I assure you, my queen, there are no questions. You have made your point quite clear." As he leaned in, he kissed her soundly and the wolf whistles began. Leading her back to her chair, kissing her hand, and winking he turned back to his warriors.

Marcello returned to his seat and he could see that Kate was more than able to handle the warriors, her king and anything else they could throw at her. He liked that she was cordial, could joke with them and took them all in stride.

Shade held up his hand to settle them down. "Now that we have that cleared up, it is time for us all to get serious. As most of you know, Cory's *madre* came to visit us. While she was visiting, some information was revealed. Many years ago, I was visiting the States on business, California as a matter of fact. When I went back to California years later, I visited the clubs and came across a young half-breed with whom I felt a distinct connection, never knowing the reason why. This past year, I saw his potential, his skills, and took him off the streets and invited him into my coven. That young half-breed is Cory. I have recently found out that Cory is my son."

Shade saw the mixture of disbelief, bewilderment, and shock on their faces. "Cory has already been established through Council as my legitimate son. He is my firstborn, but because he is a half-breed, he cannot inherit my legacy. That obligation still lies with my immortal son your queen now carries. I make no other distinction as to how or where Cory was born. He is my flesh and blood, welcomed into my heart as my own. Your queen has the same feelings and you will as well." Shade let what he said sink in and turned to Cory nodding for him to step forward.

Cory tried to hold his head up, but the more Shade talked the more he tucked his head. By the time his speech was done, Cory's head was hanging low. He felt Shade reach his hand under his chin as Cory lifted his eyes slowly and took his hand. Walking to face the warriors, who only yesterday he considered his brothers and sisters, he wasn't sure how they'd respond to him. He looked out at their faces, and they were looking back at him in awe. He felt his stomach doing flips and he hoped he didn't hurl where he stood.

Shade embraced his shoulder, pulling him close. "It's okay, hold your head up, you're my son and everyone here needs to know."

Shade reached back and took *bel's* hand, pulling her forward to stand with them. "This is the Medici family, your queen, your king, and their son Cory Medici. You will honor, respect, and protect each of us with your lives. This only adds to the legacy that is Medici. Rise and bow before the son of Medici. Honor him as you have honored all of the Medici's that proceeded."

Cory gulped and squeezed Shade's hand tight as he watched every warrior in the room stand and drop down on one knee. In unison, they pledged, "*Per sempre* Medici."

As the warriors arose, they remained on their feet. "I will not tolerate Cory being treated any differently. He is still your leather artisan and your brother. I expect him to be treated with dignity and respect. He will now reside in the main house of Bel Rosso and not the barracks. You are dismissed."

As the room thinned out, Raven approached Cory with a huge grin. "Coming up in the world, bro!" Taking a deep bow, he did a quick hand flourish in the air and laughed. "You're still a runt brat to me, no matter what the hell your last name is."

Cory laughed, and they fist bumped and hugged. A few warriors surrounded Cory and the noise level rose through the roof once again.

Fee approached Shade and Kate as they stood talking to each other. "Congratulations on your newly discovered son. Might I beg a word with the queen?"

Shade looked at Fiamma. "Reluctantly, Fee, because I never get enough time with her as it is." He kissed Kate before leaving. "I will go talk to my warriors, when you are ready to go back to the house, let me know. I will take you back and then I need to get back to work, *si?*"

Walking out into the crowd, there was much ribbing and fist bumping as Shade walked among his warriors.

Kate grabbed hold of Fee's hands, smiling at her. "So, it looks like I'm mother to a son approaching adulthood. Never saw that coming. What's on your mind, Fee?"

"Well we all adore Cory. He has some wicked skills with leather. I just wanted to say, way to handle this bunch of crazy males. They take you at your word, they'll listen to you, and they admire and respect you. I want you to know that." Fee looked at Kate's baby bump. "You're beginning to really show. You make him happy Kate, like never before."

Kate smiled at her, "He makes me happy...like never before. I can't wait to put this baby in his arms."

Fee grinned. "On another note, I know you aren't fond of feeders. I know this can't be a comfortable position for you, handling the feeder compound. But in our culture, the feeders are looked upon with great respect, and the warriors learn to care for them in their own way. They understand the value of the feeders to their very existence. I don't think we'll have any problems. Do you know who the matron is yet? Is it someone from here or Florence?"

Kate shrugged. "No, I haven't met anyone yet. Shade said the compound would house some feeders from Florence and some from the States. He said Gi was selecting the matron, so I'd assume she'll be from Florence. I'd really appreciate your help in overseeing the compound. I want them to be comfortable and safe of course. But there's also a reason why all the feeder covens are isolated. I understand Shade's logic, in placing a compound here, but it's not without its challenges."

Fee smiled. "I'm honored to help in any way, you know that. Shade gave me a chance to move up in a world where females are still looked down upon. He understands our value and knows in order to have enough warriors to carry us into the future he must train and integrate the females and males. I think you had a great deal to do with that."

Kate shook her head. "I doubt that. He's so protective of me. I think his view of female warriors was already well established in his head. He knows he has to mold the vampire culture into the 21st Century and modifying the roles of women is a part of that."

Fee spoke in her animated fashion, "He doesn't make the female/male distinction when it comes to his warriors, but he's no ordinary master either. Most European masters still have no use for females as warriors. Shade has changed a few of their minds. But no female has ever been assigned to protect the Council yet. I'll never live to see that day." As they both laughed, Fee noticed Aislynn gazing in their direction and she motioned her forward. "Kate, I'd like you to meet Aislynn, have you met her before?"

Kate welcomed her into the circle. "We've not officially met, but I've seen her on the training field. You're an impressive warrior Aislynn."

Bowing her head, Aislynn smiled softly. "Thank you, my lady. I'm honored to be a Medici. It means a great deal to me and I intend to do my best to take advantage of this opportunity to learn from Master Shade and those that serve him. May I ask you something? I don't want to overstep my boundaries, but I've heard you're amazing with the crossbow. May I ask who taught you your skills?"

Kate looked down before answering. "I'm afraid I was taking some unauthorized lessons, but Luca trained me, and he said Shade trained him. I understand Skelk is the real master at cross-bow however, and I'm hoping he'll work with me. He seems like the reclusive type though, so it may take me a while to break down those barriers."

Kate saw Aislynn blush when she sought out Luca in the crowd. Kate turned to look at Luca. He was totally preoccupied with the other warriors and was taking no notice of Aislynn.

Kate felt a sense of protectiveness for her guardian. "Luca is spoken for. You might want to try to catch the eye of one of the other warriors."

Aislynn gasped. "Oh, my lady, no. Luca is very handsome, but I have no interest in him."

Fee laughed. "Relax, Aislynn, if I thought for one moment you had your eye on Luca, or any of the males, you wouldn't be here. We already had one episode of that. Kate was just reminding you Luca was off limits. And I think, at this stage of your training, you're best to leave the males the hell alone. Who would want one of these brutes anyway?"

Kate turned to Fee. "Does that mean your heart is so hardened you can't find love, sister? I hope not."

Fee caught a glimpse of Marcello and quickly looked back at Kate. "I learned long ago to shut my feelings down. It's been a hard road being taken seriously as a female. I had to fight every day to win this respect, and it wasn't easy. I don't know if my heart is hard, some say I'm stone cold, but I can still fall in love. I'm a warrior first, but perhaps someday, a male will see me for more than warrior."

Looking down she quickly ended the conversation and grabbed Aislynn's hand. "Come on, we have work to get to and I'm sure our queen has a million things to tend to."

Kate watched as the two females walked away. She knew strong women made a choice, mortal or immortal, and it would take a strong man to accept them. She hoped Fiamma could find him. She turned and looked around the room, finding Shade surrounded by his warriors, all vying for his attention and approval. She smiled and sent him a message. **"I am ready to go back to the house."**

Shade heard her voice in his head and his eyes locked with hers. How the fuck he ever won her heart he'd never know. Excusing himself from his warriors, he commanded them to get to their posts and get busy. Walking to *bel*, he bowed elegantly.

"May I have the honor of escorting my lady home?"

Kate flashed him a coy smile. "Oh, I hope so."

"I am a mere warrior my lady, but I assure you I am most respectable, and I will protect you with my life."

He let his hand slowly slide around her neck and through her crimson silk and he sighed. He wrapped her in his arms, cradling her into his chest.

Kate giggled. "Not too respectable I hope. I'd be disappointed if you didn't make advances."

Leading her out the door, a cheer went up from his warriors as they all scattered to their duties. Tonight, he'd let her feed and then return to his warriors. As always, his *bel* came first.

66

Once Shade returned to the camp, Kate made her way to his office and picked up the floor plans for the attic space that would now be converted into a suite for Cory. He'd have his own living room, bathroom, and bedroom. Kate talked to Gi to make sure the kitchen stayed stocked as well, since Cory still ate some human food.

Cory wandered back in from the camp, still a little shell-shocked from the reception he'd received from the warriors. He sat down with Kate to review the floor plans and was blown away by the amount of space he'd have. He worked with Kate to pick out the kind of furniture he liked, but he'd seen Luca's suite, and Shade's office, and he knew she wouldn't make his room all frilly.

The contractor dropped in and Cory suggested a few changes. Everyone was happy with the plan and the contractor said his crew would have everything done in a few days. In the meantime, Cory would continue to stay in the guest bedroom.

Kate followed up with the designer working on the Paris house, and gave Reynaldo a call about the progress in California. Both projects were moving along well. At the end of the night, she headed upstairs to wait for Shade. He returned to her after a grueling night of putting the new recruits through their paces. The night sky was starting to lighten as she heard the electronic blinds come down. She switched on the lamp on the bedside table and watched him as he stripped from his leathers, moving slowly. Kate calculated in her head how many days it had been since he'd fed from her, and knew he was waiting too long.

"Lover, when did you last feed? You look tired. Haven't you gone to Luca yet?"

His body was weary and tired. He wasn't even fighting real battles, only teaching his new recruits in mock battles. Looking over at Kate, he knew she could sense his body slowing. He'd been putting off feeding from Luca, knowing that once he started, he wouldn't feed from his mate again for a long while and that made him feel like hell.

"I do not remember the last time I fed. I believe it was the night we went riding in the moonlight. I have not gone to Luca. I am tired, that is all, *mi amore*, nothing more. A lot has happened lately, I am more concerned about your condition than my own at this point, *si?*"

Kate looked at him with concern. He'd pushed himself with the trip to Council to address the issue about Cory, making the final cuts in the camp and getting the new warriors on a schedule. His color looked pale and it worried her. He'd continued to feed her, and had taken nothing in return. "I'm well taken care of. You've seen to that. Now, please, before you climb into bed, go to Luca."

He could feel her deep concern and love for him. He'd hoped to figure out some means of being with Luca away from the house or go to Luca when she slept, so as not to make it difficult for her. The memories of her tears from before had made it hard to go to Luca.

"*Bel*, I will find the time, trust me. I just..." He flopped down hard on the bed, throwing his hands over his eyes, sighing. "I can manage this. I can go a few more nights without, I do not feel well, and I know you can feel that, not lying to myself. But I can go longer."

Feeling his beast growl inside him, it was getting harder to be near her and resist. His beast was hungry, and he'd have a hard time controlling him if he began to starve. In his head, he knew he could be putting everyone here in danger.

She could feel the depth of his hunger, the gnawing pain and the need. Why the reluctance? They'd already discussed this with Luca, and Shannon was reluctantly onboard. She knew Luca was in his suite. She'd seen him there just before coming upstairs. She feared his reluctance was based on his concern for her. How difficult it had been for her during the last pregnancy, knowing what went on behind the closed door of Luca's suite.

Kate would make him feed, in the only way she knew how. She rolled over close to him, slid her hand over his bare chest as she laid her head on his shoulder. She licked and nipped at his chest before moving to his neck, letting her tongue slide over the length of his vein.

His growl vibrated through the room, his fangs punching through instantly as his beast rolled through him, ready to feed. Gripping the sheets, his knuckles white as his body began to shake, and he was losing control. "*Mi amore*, please, you torture me, I cannot bear this. I can barely stand to be near you without feeding. Why are you doing this to me?"

Rolling her off his chest, he stood from the bed, his hunger like a live entity, demanding to be fed. His fists were balled up tight at his sides, his eyes lighting the room in a brilliant red as he growled, trying to regain control.

Kate slid from their bed and took his hand. "Come with me, Shade."

She led him down the stairs and into Luca's suite. Luca looked up from the easel as Kate entered, holding Shade's hand. Shade's fangs were bared, and Luca could feel his hunger from here. Luca looked at her quizzically, as she led Shade to his bed. Kate lay down and pulled him into bed bedside her. Shade was almost more beast than man as he climbed into the bed, the saliva dripping from his fangs, his need to feed overpowering him. A light bulb went off for Luca, as he realized what she was doing. Shade hadn't feed from her, or from him, and she brought Shade to him tonight. Kate slid her hands into Shade's dark curls, and kissed him deeply, as Luca undressed and climbed in the bed from the opposite side, with Kate sandwiched between them.

The beast became more aroused the closer he was to *bel*. His fangs ached, his body rigid with need and wanting. His beast was alive, angry and hungry. Denying the beast was dangerous, but Shade continued to fight, trying not to let him have full rein, but the beast was winning this battle. Shade finally relinquished control as the beast now followed *bel's* lead. He responded, pushing his tongue into her throat, his moans guttural and aching in his deepest darkest need for blood. He could feel Luca close at hand, but no longer cared, with the realization it was her beast that was leading him where his beast needed to go.

Kate felt him respond to her, returning the kiss, his tongue exploring deep inside her mouth. She slid her hand over his abdomen and down to his rock hard cock, feeling it throb in her hand. She stroked him slowly, knowing he'd need little encouragement this night. His hunger had him pushed to the edge of endurance. His hips responded to her touch, thrusting against her.

Kate could feel Luca's breath on the back of her neck as his own beast emerged. She let go of Shade's cock and reached behind her, taking Luca's hand and pulling it over her, leading Luca's hand to take hold of Shade's erection. She could feel the sexual tension build between the two male beasts, seeking release. Kate broke her kiss and lay back on the bed, as Luca leaned over her, his mouth connecting with Shade's. Kate watched as their tongues battled, before Shade grabbed Luca's hair, pulling him hard against his lips as his primal growl filled the room.

Kate slid under Luca as he rolled over her, their hard, muscular bodies now joined. Luca stroked his cock hard, as she saw Shade pulling him closer. Kate walked from the room and closed the door behind her. She'd wait for him now in their bedroom.

Shade picked up Luca's scent and their mouths locked, tight and sweet. His beast knew he could take Luca, feed and achieve release by the strong hand that stroked him, the grasp tight around his cock, knowing how to bring him what he needed. Letting go of all reservations, he pulled Luca tight against his body as he felt *bel* leave. He was beyond the point of no return, as his beast wanted what he wanted.

Breaking the kiss, he rolled Luca to his back, letting his hand slide to his neck, growling with deep sexual intent. As they locked eyes, Luca's fangs punched and his tongue snaked out as he leaned up and licked Shade's neck. Shade sank his fangs deep in Luca's neck, as that first burst of young warrior blood slammed into his system, driving him into erotic overdrive. His body responded to the blood lust and his hips grinded against the hard male body beneath him, feeling Luca's erection against his stomach. Drawing even deeper, Luca's growl only fed his own desire and his cock was like steel. He wanted more than blood to satisfy his beast.

As master fed, Luca slid his hand between them, gripping both of their dicks in his hand. He could feel the throbbing heat in his hands as he stroked them both simultaneously, and they relished in the feel of his hand and the friction of cock to cock, sliding against each other. Shade drank deeper, letting his hips ride the rhythm of Luca's strokes.

For Shade, the feeling was erotic, the hunger was abating but other desires rose to the surface. The beast hungered for more than blood and Luca's beast responded in kind. Unlatching his fangs, Shade slowly licked the wounds in Luca's neck. His beast liked the feel of masculine muscle under his tongue and his mouth quickly sought out and encircled a hard nipple, as Luca's body writhed beneath him. Shade's hand slid into Luca's hair, as he gripped a handful of hair and hoarsely whispered his name, "Luca."

Feeling Luca's release was close, Shade slid down his body slowly, letting his tongue leave a wet trail across the hard muscle. Shade's hard cock slid over Luca's muscular thighs, as his lips kissed his narrow hips, and Luca's moans vibrated the bed beneath them.

Gripping Luca's erection, it felt rigid and thick in his hand. Beginning to stroke him from root to tip, letting the head bulge, his beast fed on the sounds, the smells, and the release he knew he'd bring to Luca. Stroking slowly, his hand gripped and released as he stroked. Shade slid his other hand down Luca's hip and thigh. He stroked his balls, squeezing them lightly, bringing Luca even more pleasure. His own cock aching as well, his strokes were deep and strong as Luca's beast writhed beneath him.

"Take release, Luca."

Shade's hand moved faster and his grip was hard, as his hand slid up and down the thickened hard cock. Luca called out as his cum shot skyward before sliding down Shade's hand. Shade's beast growled in response to Luca's scent of raw sex, as it filled his nostrils and stimulated his own aching need.

Luca's chest heaved as he gasped for air. He rolled onto his side, reaching for master's cock. He felt Shade crawl slowly back over him as Luca gripped him hard, stroking with one hand as his free hand circled Shade's hips, and Luca gripped the rock hard muscle of master's ass. Luca threw his head back, exposing his neck once again as he felt Shade sink his fangs into the muscles of his shoulders. Luca's body responded as the current of sexual energy flowed through him, and he stroked hard, twisting his hand, as he slid it the full length of Shade's rigid sword.

He could feel his master drinking deep again, as his cock throbbed harder in his hand. Luca squeezed and released his cock, sliding his hand faster up and down the thick shaft. Luca gripped the muscle of Shade's ass tighter, mixing pain with pleasure as he created a twisting, rolling motion with his hand over the bulbous head of master's dick, feeling him explode in his hand, his hot cum dripping through his fingers as his growl vibrated through the room.

As Shade unlatched from Luca's vein, blood seeping down his chin, he threw back his head, taking in air, his body satisfied sexually, and his blood-hunger gone. Pulling Luca to him, they locked eyes and his beast still moved inside him, both of their bodies still alive, not yet releasing the other.

Luca's tongue whipped out and licked his own blood from Shade's chin and Shade returned in kind, kissing him, his hands sliding to Luca's cheeks, holding his face steady as his kiss deepened. Feeling their beasts retreat slowly, he broke the kiss, pulling Luca's head to his shoulder, Shade whispered, "*Grazie*."

Luca lay with him quietly, held in a gentle embrace as their breathing returned to normal. He knew the death slumber would pull Shade down quickly now that his needs had been met, and he felt him slip from his bed.

Luca watched him as he left the suite and spoke softly to him, "Don't wait so long next time, master."

Shade stopped but didn't turn around, feeling revived, yet the death slumber slowly creeping into his body. "I'll need you again, but then I always need you for protection of my most valued, *bel*. You serve us both with heart and soul, and I am grateful Luca, always."

Walking out the door, he closed it behind him, heading up the stairs. He cared not that he was naked, only that his needs had been satisfied, but still aching to have *bel* in his arms for his slumber. Opening the door to their bed chamber, he walked in and saw her lying on their bed and he took a deep breath, suddenly not sure what he should say, if anything.

Kate had waited for him in their bed. She could feel his hunger as it was abated, and the intensity of sexual desire as it rolled through him. She could hear the sounds of their mutual pleasure and the power of the release. She heard his footsteps on the stairs and then he opened the door to their room. She looked up at him from their bed and flung the covers back, making room for him beside her. He slipped silently into the space she'd made for him and she immediately curled around him. Her hand stroked his face, the stubble harsh against her tender skin, as she lowered her mouth to his, kissing him as before. She laid her head on his chest and wrapped her arm across him. "Sleep now, lover."

He could feel her acceptance, her acknowledgement that this was how it must be. He felt no remorse, no pain, no agony from her as before, but only love, love so deep it almost made him weep. His arms encircled her, hugging her as one hand slid to her bare ass, the other wrapped into her crimson. The scent of roses encircled them both. She was his home and his light.

"*Ti amo, mi amore*." His eyes closed as the slumber took him, and he walked with her in her dreams.

67

Kate had made the final walk-through with the contractors who'd remodeled the attic space and staircase that led to Cory's suite. He'd have his own living room, bathroom, and bedroom. The contractor was able to add another fireplace into the existing chimney along the outer wall, so Cory had a fireplace in his bedroom. The interior designers had been working night and day to get the new furniture in, including the large flat screen TV and the video gaming system.

Kate shook her head. It was the only TV in the house. Cory remained with one foot in the mortal world as he lived among immortals and maintained his love of mortal pastimes like skateboards and video games. His suite looked masculine but very well-appointed. Not overly opulent and fancy as Cory requested, but he'd have everything he requested and more. Both Cory and Shade had been in the camp all night. Cory was busy making leathers for all the new recruits who made the final cut, and Shade was busy with their training. Kate turned to leave the suite, pleased with the results. As soon as the men returned from the camp, she was ready to show Cory his new space and have him move from the guest bedroom into his own rooms.

Shade was pleased with the new warriors. His team from Florence was working hand in hand with the new recruits, making great progress towards his goals. Leaving camp, he walked up the path to the house when he saw Cory up ahead. Shade picked up his stride, catching up easily.

"You are in a big ass hurry son, what's on your agenda?"

Cory felt Shade's arm go around his neck and he laughed. "My stomach!"

Shade punched his arm playfully as they came stomping into the house, rough-housing with each other. Shade watched as Cory headed to the kitchen. Shade took the steps two at a time as he headed for their bedroom. He found his beauty, mid-term in her pregnancy, her long red locks hanging loosely around her shoulders and wearing a sundress that left her shoulders exposed. Her feet were bare, and her toenails painted red. She gave him a soft smile that beamed just for him.

"A sight for these tired sore eyes. Come give your savage lover a kiss. Your warrior is home, woman!"

Kate allowed herself to be swallowed up in his embrace, happy to have him home. "Did I hear Cory come in with you?"

"*Si*, but his stomach was making demands on him. That boy is going to eat us out of house and home. I never saw a mortal eat that damn much! He is not even a warrior and he consumes a lot. He is so fucking skinny. Where in the hell does it all go?"

Kate laughed. "He's like every teenage boy, still growing and always hungry. His rooms are ready. I was waiting for the two of you. This is a big day. Your son will officially be moving into his own rooms. We sort of skipped over the whole nursery and going to school stuff with him. How do you feel about this? Are you adjusting? Is he adjusting?"

Shade looked down and shuffled his feet. His guilt at missing most of Cory's life up until now was still a sore spot in his heart. "We are both adjusting *mi amore*, he still refers to me as Shade sometimes, and that is fine. I try to call him son when we are alone and Cory when we are among the warriors, so as not to make him feel out of place. The warriors are adjusting better than we are it seems. They rib him a bit, but not as much as I thought, and always good-naturedly. They like him, have bonded with him long before this came about. As for me, I am proud to have him living here."

Shade kissed her soundly on the mouth, as he heard Cory coming up the steps and stand in their doorway, taking another bite of his apple.

Cory cleared his throat. "Excuse me, don't stop on my account, but get a room!"

Kate laughed. "We have a room, a lot of them in fact. But more importantly, you now have your own rooms. Are you ready to see them?"

Cory grinned. "Hell yeah, they're ready?"

Kate led the way, letting Cory follow her. Shade walked behind them both, eager to see Cory's reaction for himself once inside what he was sure to be rooms fit for the son of a king.

Kate led them up the new staircase to the third floor, which had been entirely given over to Cory. The stairs opened into his living room, with the large sectional sofa, shelving for books and video gaming equipment, and the huge 70" flat screen TV. The walls behind the sofa featured a gallery wall of art, all provided by Luca. Paintings of warriors from the camp, the horses in the field, a painting of the main house at Bel Rosso, portraits of Shade and Kate, as well as a portrait of Cory, and Cory's mom. The ceilings had been left to show the exposed beams and pitched roof, which added to the masculine feel of the rooms.

Cory stopped in his tracks. He couldn't believe what he was seeing. The room was large, and decorated in neutral tones of beige and brown, the exposed wood making everything feel homey. The lighting was amazing with windows and a skylight. His eyes went to the huge flat-screen television.

"Sweet!"

Shade chuckled. "Damn, this room is bigger than Kate's old condo in D.C."

Cory walked around the large room, his eyes getting bigger and bigger. His mom's old house wasn't this large, and he'd never had anything this special of his own. He looked at the wall over the sofa and spotted all of the paintings and his eyes lit up. Walking over to them, he stood there staring. He saw himself and even his mom. There was one of Kate and Shade, as well as some group images of the warriors. He could clearly recognize Marcello and Raven in the action scenes.

Turning, he looked at Kate. "These are Luca's paintings! I mean, this is one of my mom."

His hand slid slowly over the painting of his mom. He hoped her new living conditions would be this luxurious. He knew Shade would take care of her as he'd promised. Cory rolled his eyes to Shade and they locked eyes with each other. Shade could feel his emotions, how overwhelming this space was for him, his surprise that this was actually his.

"It's all yours, son. This is where you live now. This is where you deserve to live. And the things you need will be provided for you."

Shade walked over to where Cory stood, putting his arm around Cory's shoulders. "Luca has a great talent. Look at your *madre* in this picture. He has captured her love for you in her eyes. Just like you can make leather into something artistic, Luca can do the same with a canvas."

Kate stood back and watched Shade with this man-child. Too old to be held, and yet needing so much to make up for all the lost time. She'd asked Luca to paint the portraits and made sure to include Cory's mother, letting Cory know he belonged to all of them now. This was his family. Her heart melted as she watched them together and knew their bond grew stronger with every day. She cleared her throat to get their attention. "Okay, well do you want to see the bedroom now?"

Kate led them from his large living room into the bedroom. The stone fireplace was the focal point in the room. His new bed was King-sized and layered with a feather bed and luxury down-filled linens, in shades of light brown and a brown tartan plaid. The windows gave him a bird's eye view of Bel Rosso from the third floor. The new hardwood floors gleamed and a large antique Persian rug covered the floor for warmth. There were side tables and overstuffed leather chairs. He had a huge closet that Kate had filled with the new jeans, high-top Converse sneakers, t-shirts, and the plaid long sleeve shirts he wore routinely. He had a small desk area, with a laptop, and a new iPhone.

Cory followed Kate into the huge bedroom and he couldn't take in everything fast enough. He walked around in a large circle looking at everything.

"That's my bed? Just for me? I never had..." He felt the tears well up in his eyes and he went to Kate and embraced her. "I never had my own room, my own bed. It was a mattress on a floor. Living in the barracks was a luxury for me. I really don't know what to say. I feel like I don't deserve this, I love it so much."

He let go of her, feeling a bit awkward and then his eyes landed on the far wall and he yelled, "No way! My boards! You hung my skateboards on the wall. Fucking sweet!"

Walking over to the wall, he pulled his favorite board down and looked at Shade. "You know we're building a board ramp and some other stuff at the camp. I'm teaching Raven how to skateboard. He's good, but he can't touch my skills."

Shade shook his head. "Great, Raven on a fucking skateboard. That is all I need!"

"Do you want to see the bathroom? This way." Kate led him to the bathroom which had a long counter made of reclaimed lumber, against a stone wall. There was a large sink mounted into the counter and a big shower stall.

Shade stood in the doorway of the bathroom, arms crossed over his chest and winked at *bel*.

"Cory went to the middle of a huge bathroom that was his alone, and ran his hands through his long dark brown hair. "I feel weird because I don't know what to say, but I have a few questions."

Shade nodded. "Questions are good, let's sit in the living room and talk a bit."

Taking *bel's* hand, he led her back out to the large sofa, pulled her to sit next to him and watched as Cory sat cross-legged on the other end.

"Speak your mind, son."

Cory stared at his newly found parents. "I know I can come and go whenever I like. You said I could have company. Kate doesn't want feeders in the house, and I know that's for real. So, I guess I'm asking if I use the feeders at the compound?"

Kate looked at Shade, then back at Cory. How did they get *here* so fast? She had no experience at being a mother and the first thing she had to do was have the *sex talk*!

"Cory, this is your home, and I want you to feel at comfortable here in every way. You're free to bring your immortal friends here. If you bring mortals, we need to know about it before hand, so we're careful and don't expose ourselves. That's for our safety. Understand? The only mortals who come here now are Shannon and your mom. When you need a feeder, then I must insist you go to the compound. Someday, when you meet someone, when you have a girlfriend, someone you feel attached to, then you may bring her here. But no feeders inside the house."

Cory stared at Shade. Shade nodded. "This is her decision because I have to live here with her Cory, she is my queen. Feeders are something we have decided on together, and I will not go against her wishes. But I want you to be able to voice your opinion. If ever there are other things you don't agree with, do not just disobey them. Voice your objection to them from the beginning, when the decisions are made, then voice why you disagree. It is the only way to be heard."

Cory listened intently. "I agree. But can I bring the warriors up here if we want to play X-Box and watch movies?" Cory leaned back against the sofa as he blushed. "I don't have any girlfriends or anything like that."

Kate laughed. "Of course! Bring all the warriors...well maybe not all the warriors, bring your friends. I know you're friends with Raven and Marcello. They're all welcome here. And use the kitchen whenever you want. Gi knows to keep it fully stocked. I forget to cook anything since I no longer eat human food, but if there's something you want, I'll be happy to cook for you. Just tell me. I'll fix it for you. And don't worry about the girlfriends, they'll come with time, trust me. You have your father's looks and his charm, so it won't take much, believe me."

Shade nodded. "Son, just do not bring mortals here without talking to one of us first. We have to keep a low profile. And don't be skateboarding in this house."

Cory laughed along with them, feeling appreciated here. "I feel love here. I never had anything like this. My mom did the best she could, but I never got to be myself, I was lost, and I didn't make it easy for her. I feel like I've found myself here, and now I can allow myself to feel emotions. Before, I had to shut everything down, so I didn't feel. It was too much when I was on the streets and at the clubs, and what I had to do to survive. I like this me. I want to be a Medici and I want..." His eyes locked onto Shade's, he could feel the tears roll down his cheeks, and he didn't feel embarrassed. "I just want to be your son."

Shade felt his heart scream with emotions as he watched Cory's tears fall, and his words made Shade's heart burst. He held out his arms and beckoned Cory to him. Cory flew off his end of the couch and into his arms, burying his head into Shade's neck, sobbing. Shade slid his hand up and down Cory's back, his own blood tears spilling forth.

"You are my son. You are Medici and I do love you."

Kate laid her head against Cory's and wrapped her arm around his back. He was enclosed now in their embrace. Her own tears fell, for this child that had suffered so long, had now found his place, and for this man, who had a heart with so much capacity for love.

"And I love you, Cory. I'll love you as much as the children I'll bear for Shade. You're home now."

Shade had no words, his emotions overflowed for a child he never knew existed, born into a world where he wasn't wanted and now loved beyond all means. Wrapping his arm around Kate, he held them both. "*Si*, home. We are all home now. *Familia*."

68

It was a soft, summer evening and Rissa teleported with Hyde out to Bel Rosso. The sky was brilliant in glorious hues of peach and pink over the mountain range, as the sun slowly sank below the horizon. They teleported into the stables and Angelo had Biondo saddled and ready for Rissa to ride. She'd made it a routine to come out and ride at least two evenings a week, interchanging it with her rigorous gym workouts. She felt amazing, her stamina was better, and her body was still feminine and curvy, yet stronger to take on the demands of Alec's sexual appetite.

Hyde mounted one of the other horses to ride with her and they took off riding a few trails, moving at a slow gallop to warm up the horses. Rissa loved this part of the ride. She felt such freedom and it relaxed her. It was the only time she could be alone without the press who were beginning to follow her wherever she went. Alec was right. This was her down time, her stress free zone where she was fully protected.

After riding several miles at the base of the mountains, they headed back to the open fields near the stables to practice some basic trick riding that Angelo had taught her.

Once back inside the fenced in field, Angelo had set up a series of jumps. Rissa encouraged Biondo, using her thighs and heels to get the horse to jump and make sharp, quick turns. Every time they successfully completed an obstacle, it built more trust between rider and horse. Hyde sat atop his horse and called out commands and advice to her, getting her to repeat the jumps and obstacles until she and Biondo worked together as a team.

Riding over to where Hyde sat along the fence line, Rissa's smile was wide as she patted Biondo, praising her. "I think we have that last jump down. It's high, but she understands what I need her to do."

Hyde nodded and smiled at Rissa. He'd seen less aggressive behavior from her lately and she listened to his directives. Riding the horse, here in the beauty of Bel Rosso, was where she was the happiest.

"Put your heels down even harder Rissa, let her know you mean business."

Rissa looked at Hyde and shook her head, "I'm going to dig my heels into your sides if you don't let her have a chance to take a break."

They both laughed, and it felt good to relax, when movement caught Rissa's peripheral vision. She turned to see Kate and Shade walking along the path from their house and she noticed how much Kate was showing in her pregnancy. Rissa observed as Shade walked with her, holding her hand, not able to take his gaze from her and Rissa only wished Alec would give her half that much attention.

As Kate walked with Shade on his way to the camp, she needed to catch up with Fee and finalize some of the plans for the feeder compound. She saw Rissa and Hyde. She waved at Rissa and tugged at Shade's hand. "Come on, we need to stop and say hello. Angelo says Rissa comes out about twice a week to ride, but I rarely see her."

Kate led Shade over to the fence where Hyde and Rissa were both mounted on their horses. Kate stepped up on the first rung of the rail fencing, Shade grabbing her waist, steadying her.

"Careful, *mi amore.*"

Kate giggled at him. "I'm not going to break, Shade." She turned to Rissa. "You look good out there on Biondo."

Rissa observed their closeness and was green with envy. Shade was so protective of Kate. Biondo let out a loud snort and whipped her head back and forth. Rissa realized she'd been tightening the reins in her hands. She was envious of their love, the attention he paid to every breath Kate took. She wondered if Alec ever really loved her and shook it off. Of course, he loved her, he chose her as his mate.

"Thank you, Kate. She's a beauty! Easy to train and she takes commands with such grace. I'm actually thinking about joining up to ride and play in a few charity polo matches. My skills are getting better now that I'm riding again. You look, uh, quite radiant in your pregnancy. When are you having that... When is the baby due?"

Kate ran her hand over the growing swell of her belly and felt Shade's hand cover hers. "He's due in late November, but I often wonder if he'll wait that long. He seems very eager to get here. I still ride Bravado, but no jumping for me. I have to be content with a gallop or Shade will ground me altogether. But you look skilled at jumping, and Biondo would probably make a great horse for polo. She has great speed, and she's not intimidated easily around the other horses."

Rissa smiled at her comment, knowing Biondo was no polo horse. "Well, I wouldn't ride Biondo in polo, I'd never want her damaged in any way. I'd choose another horse for that type of event." Rissa looked at Hyde. "What do you think, am I ready for polo yet?"

Hyde reached over and pushed her calf down hard. "Heels down, Rissa, if you don't remember, your precious ass is hitting dirt. But I think a few more lessons and you can try a run at polo."

Rissa smacked his hand away. "Never good enough. Push, push, push!" Laughing, she looked at Kate. "He's a grueling protector. I'm sure yours is as well. He just never lets up!"

Kate laughed. "Trust me, between Shade and Luca, I'm surprised they let me walk up the stairs unassisted. I'll be glad when the baby is born, and we can return to being normally obsessive instead of overly obsessive about my safety."

Shade kissed the top of her head. "I will be as obsessive as is necessary when it comes to your protection, as well as our son's."

Looking up at Rissa, he noticed her boots. "Rissa, if you decide to compete at polo, you seriously need to change your boots. You would do much better in the stirrup. Does Alec know you are playing polo? He hates riding and I know he hates those damn polo matches."

Rissa grinned. "Well, you just answered that yourself. He has no clue, nor would he care what I did, as long as it is good press. He'd only be worried about whether our team won."

Rissa laughed softly but it was a laugh she didn't feel. Alec had no desire to know what she did. He rarely ever accompanied her to events any longer. Hyde was now her only companion and that made her feel sad. She watched as Shade nuzzled softly into Kate's neck, his hands always caressing and touching her. Alec rarely touched her except when they had sex. Seeing Shade and Kate together made the differences between her relationship with Alec starkly apparent, and that pained her.

Eager to be away from them, Rissa maneuvered Biondo away from the fence. "Well, I don't want to hold you up any longer, I want some time to ride in the fields before I head back home. I hope you can ride with me sometime, Kate, even if it's just for a short ride. It's so beautiful and peaceful here. You're lucky to live out here."

Kate smiled and nodded at her. "Very lucky, Rissa. I'm grateful for this place every day. Enjoy your ride. We won't hold you up any longer. We both have things to do. Say hello to Alec for us."

Shade lifted her down from the rail and they continued in the direction of the camp. Rissa watched them as they walked hand in hand. She looked over at Hyde, kicked Biondo in the sides gently and slapped the reins hard. "Let's ride, girl!"

Taking off like the wind, she took the last high jump in stride, Biondo clearing it easily as Rissa leaned down over the horse's long neck. They rode like hell, full out into the fields. The night moon was rising, and Rissa let go of all the things bottled up inside her. Alec loved her, but he just loved her differently than Shade loved Kate. That's all this was. She could come and go as she pleased, do as she pleased, and answered only to Alec when it concerned what he needed and nothing more. Spinning her head around, she saw Hyde riding up behind her and passing her in a cloud of dust.

"Damn you, Hyde!" She pushed Biondo harder, trying to catch up, and it felt good to feel the wind in her hair. At least she had Hyde, and she enjoyed his company and his protection.

69

Shade stood in the large meeting room of the barracks, surrounded by his warriors and new recruits, as they waited for the beginning of one of the most vital ceremonies in any warrior's life, The Blood Oath. This was where the new recruits would drink the blood of their master and pledge their loyalty and protection to the Medici Coven, becoming one with the master who led them. It had been a tradition since the birth of Medici warriors, his own *padre* continuing the tradition that each warrior must be able to bond with their master, to feel his emotions to better protect and serve.

Shade saw Kate sitting on the high-backed chair that served as their makeshift thrones when addressing the warriors inside the camp. She was talking and laughing with Fiamma. He looked around for Luca and Cory but didn't see either of them.

Marcello gave out a whistle as the crowd settled down and Shade headed to the front of the room, taking a seat next to *bel*, hoping Cory wouldn't forget to attend. The small side table sat next to Shade's chair, holding the jewel encrusted chalice that bore the Medici crest. He'd lost count of how many warriors had drunk from this chalice, bonding them for life.

Rows of chairs had been lined up in front of them, with a center aisle between them. The new recruits took their seats, while his tenured warriors stood at the back of the room to observe and witness. He turned to look at *bel* and the smile she gave him, reassured his heart. He had waited weeks before having the ceremony, making sure the recruits would work out and were willing and able to stay with Medici. He wanted no warrior bonded to him who wasn't able to commit mentally and physically to his coven.

The room suddenly became silent as Shade looked up to see Luca and Cory entering the room from the rear. Shade swallowed the lump in his throat as Cory walked down the center aisle, carrying Shade's ceremonial sword. To see his son carrying his sword was an emotional moment. Cory stood tall and proud as he lifted the sword in the air, crossed it over his chest, and then grasped it tight as he passed it to Shade. Their eyes locked as Shade put his large hand over the hilt of the sword, taking it from his son.

"*Grazie, figlio*"

Cory had spent the morning with Luca learning how to carry and transfer the sword properly. The damn thing was so heavy, Cory felt like his arm was falling out of the socket. But he was determined to make his dad proud of him and show the rest of them he was truly his son. Luca had explained the pageantry of the ceremony to him, and its importance to the warriors taking the oath. Cory developed tunnel vision, seeing only Shade and nothing else as he carried the sword to the front of the room.

When Shade took the sword from him, he nodded to his son, then pulled him to his chest, hugging him tight. Cory beamed with pride and went to his seat beside Kate to watch something he was sure he'd see repeated many times in his future.

Shade waited for Cory to be seated and gave himself a moment for his heart and mind to settle. Everyone he needed was in the room, and the expansion of his reign in the States was official. Raising the sword high in the air in his right hand, the new recruits became deadly quiet and all eyes were on him.

"Today we bring into our ranks new warriors who will serve and protect in the name of Medici. This is the first Blood Oath that has ever taken place outside of Florence for the Medici coven. Today, you take my blood and we become as one, brothers and sisters. You take this Blood Oath as your official acceptance into my coven. An honor dealt to few. I am your master, your leader, your brother, and you will now follow."

Each warrior stood and in unison recited the words that had lived long in the history of this coven. "*Per sempre* Medici!"

Shade took his seat in the high back chair and the warriors seated themselves once again. Placing the sharp-hooked scoring ring on his right index finger, he picked up the chalice. Scoring his left wrist, he let his blood pour into the chalice, filling it. Licking his wrist, it healed immediately.

He lifted the chalice in the air. "*Per sempre* Medici! Let us begin."

Aislynn was the first warrior to approach and went down on one knee before him, head bowed. He noticed all the female warriors were in the front row, and he appreciated that Fiamma had seen that the females were given first opportunity ahead of the males.

"Drink and become Medici."

Aislynn reached out and took the chalice, taking a small sip and feeling the immense power of her master's blood course through her, almost knocking her over. It was the most powerful thing she'd ever felt in her life and she believed she could conquer the world single-handedly. Her veins surged, as his blood rushed into her. Handing back the chalice, her eyes locked with his and she repeated the words drilled into them, the pledge.

"I am Medici Warrior. I protect, honor, and serve this coven with my life. Medici is my *familia*, my master, my king, his mate my queen."

As she bowed her head once more, Shade raised the sword in the air and lowered it to her right shoulder, touching it slightly and then repeating the process to her left shoulder. Taking the tip of the sword he gently slid it under her chin and raised her head up, never once breaking her skin. Their eyes locked and there was deadly silence, a defining moment for any warrior.

Lowering the sword, Shade's voice carried through the room. "Rise warrior and be presented."

Aislynn felt her heart beat like a drum, her strength felt as though it had tripled with his blood. Turning, she faced the throng of new warriors.

Shade's voice boomed out as he presented her. "Aislynn of Medici, warrior of Medici coven."

All the warriors recited again, "*Per sempre* Medici."

Aislynn walked back to her seat, filled with pride as she tried not to shake. She was now an official warrior of Medici and she knew this was a rare moment in any warrior's life, but to be a female and part of this prestigious coven was more than she'd ever imagined.

The procession was repeated with each recruit, until each had been sworn into the coven. As Shade stood before them, they all rose, standing at attention, every warrior in this room now belonging to him, his responsibility, and his coven here in the States. He couldn't help but look back at the changes that had taken place in the past year.

His *bel* had changed him from the hardened cold warrior filled with darkness to this, the leader and master of a coven rivaled by none and becoming more powerful every day. When his parents died, something inside him died as well. But he'd been renewed with her love and light, helping him to be the master he'd always wanted to be.

He walked to her and went down on one knee before her. "My beloved queen, I give to you our warriors, to protect and serve our coven. They give their life for you, as do I, your king. They are my gift to you as my mate, my queen, the mother of my children. *Ti amo*."

Shade handed her a perfect long stem red rose as he kissed the swell of her abdomen where his son grew strong inside her. Standing, he kissed her on the lips, his hand sliding gently across her cheek. Taking her hand, he helped her from her chair and watched as Cory joined them, and they walked down the center aisle as the warriors stood at attention. As they passed hand in hand, each warrior dropped to one knee to show their allegiance and servitude.

As they reached the back of the room, his warriors from Florence dropped to one knee before them, their swords held high in the air, their heads bowed. Today, Medici was on course to rule the world and nothing would stop him, with his queen and his son at his side.

70

Gi informed Kate the new matron for the feeder compound was arriving today from Florence. The compound was located inside the walls of the warrior camp, and the construction of the compound was finally completed, including the underground tunnel that connected the compound to the camp, the stables, and the staff quarters, so all of the coven could freely access the feeders. There was no tunnel connecting the main house to the feeder compound.

Each warrior had specific security clearances for the various underground tunnels allowing them to move about the property from building to building without exposure to the sun, but also to protect them in an ambush. Shade had been allowing the warriors to continue to use the compound located just outside D.C., which wasn't too bad for Raven's crew, but inconvenient for all the warriors based in the camp.

Kate had asked Fee to join her for this meeting with the matron. They'd take a tour of the facilities, so Matron could see the layout. Fee had already gone over the floor plans with Kate and made suggestions, and now all they needed to do was complete the furnishings and bring in the feeders. Fee arrived at the main house wearing red leathers and Kate just shook her head.

"If your intention is to distract your opponent, then just let me say, that outfit screams 'mission accomplished'!

Fee flashed her megawatt smile, a weapon in itself when needed. "What, these old rags?"

As they both laughed, Fee got serious. "You know Cory made these for me. That kid's a magician. I hate calling him a kid, he's really not a kid, but he knows how to measure, so your leathers fit like a glove. Sorry if my leathers offend you, but they become a weapon themselves. We sisters have to use every weapon we have at times."

Kate shook her head. "It doesn't offend me at all, and you look great in them. I don't think I could pull off a leather bodysuit in my current condition, so I'm just jealous of your figure. Are you ready to head to the compound? Gi says he took Matron there."

Fee chuckled. "Your figure is perfectly fine. Have you not realized yet Shade cannot take his eyes off of you? I just wish...oh never mind. I'm more than ready, are you sure you're okay with all of this Kate? I know he asked you to do it, but are you comfortable with the process?"

Kate sighed. "Yes, sort of. Well, not really. I mean, I understand his logic, and from that perspective, I totally get why he wants the compound on the grounds. It makes perfect sense. And I understand more than ever the need to feed, the hunger. Maybe if I'd been born immortal, or if we hadn't had that incident with the feeder Rissa brought here, then I'd have no reservations. You know I trust him. But I've seen the effect the feeders have on the men. Their reaction to the feeder comes unbidden, like it's out of their control. And I understand feeders were bred to create that response. Does it affect you that way? Do female vamps have the same uncontrollable desire to be with the feeders?"

Fee nodded. "Yes and no, but it's not as intense for the female. The feeders secrete a female pheromone. The female vamps respond to it, although it's much more intense for the male. I asked Cory about this, he's like a lab rat for us, unfortunately, because none of us has ever associated with half breeds. He says he feels an attraction to the feeders, and it comes unbidden, but his sense of smell isn't as great as a full-blooded vampire, nothing like what the other warriors tell him it feels like to them. I wish I had the words to describe it. It's just a natural part of our system as immortals. It's part of our survival instinct. If we're not mated, we may sometimes wait too long before we respond to the hunger. If we wait too long we can become violent, our beasts respond, and we lose control. That's the reason for the feeders, to protect our kind, to encourage us to feed and provide a source to feed that limits our exposure to mortals and controls the beast. Come on. Let's get over there. I'm anxious to meet this matron."

Kate walked with Fee over to the camp. "We'll have to use the tunnels, the door and windows you see in the feeder compound are for visual effect only. There's no way to enter except through the tunnels. We can test the security access with your fingerprint."

As they entered the warrior camp, Fee took Kate to the barracks and the stairwell that led to the long tunnel. As they approached the doors made of steel, thick and intimidating, Fee pointed out the security access panel.

"Okay, here we are, according to Marcello we just place our hand inside this small opening, it lights up when it reads our hand print, and if you're authorized to enter, it records your identity and a time stamp, and automatically opens the door."

Fiamma slid her hand into the space, laying it flat against the glass plate. A green light scanned her hand, and the door opened quietly without a sound. "Well, that was ingenious. After you, my lady."

Kate entered the corridor and Fee followed, as the door automatically closed behind them. Fee noticed the camera mounted in the entry and knew they were on the security feed monitored inside the camp, as well as inside the main house. Fee pointed out the hand scanner panel mounted on the inside. The vampires must use the scanner to exit the building as well, which would record the time they left. The feeders wouldn't have security clearance to exit.

Kate and Fee walked up a flight of stairs into the main hallway of the feeder compound to find Gi and an attractive older woman, dressed very professionally.

Gi nodded to Kate and Fee. "My lady, this is Matron. All matron's go by their title of matron, and not their names. It is considered impolite to inquire about the name they used when they were feeders."

Kate shook the older woman's hand. "I'm very pleased to meet you. Thank you so much for coming. You come highly recommended. But I apologize, I had no idea you were once a feeder as well."

Matron bowed to her as she took her hand. "It is true my lady. Feeders are bred as you know to attract our kind, entice them to feed, but as we age there are chemical changes that come as a result of allowing so many to feed. Eventually, the feeders no longer exert the same power to attract. Once that happens, they are released from the feeder compounds and can live among the immortals. Some choose to find mates among those who have fed from them. Feeders are not allowed to feed from their clients. But once they are freed from their service they're allowed to mate. Others, like me, choose to stay in this life. It's a much-protected environment, and it's where I feel safe. I have served the Medici family for centuries, servicing the warriors in the camp in Florence, back when Shade's father was still alive. When my time came to be released, I chose to stay on, to oversee the new feeders, and I have been a matron ever since."

Kate listened carefully. The matron was discreet, and she gave no indication Shade had fed from her. Kate had a feeling she'd not get an answer if she asked, but the matron clearly recognized Fee as they exchanged a greeting.

Fiamma wasn't surprised when she saw who'd be matron at Bel Rosso. She was highly sought after by masters of Shade's class, but she never strayed from Medici. Fee had heard the young feeders speak of her and shared stories of her beauty, her elegance, and her power as a feeder. Fee liked Kate's response to her, she got a good feeling that Kate was comfortable with her and that was vital. Fee knew Kate needed to feel comfortable with everything that happened here.

Fee reached out and took her hand. "Matron, I'm so happy to see you again, it's been a long time. Welcome to the Medici at Bel Rosso. I'm Lt. of the warrior camp here, and in charge of the female warriors. I'll be working alongside our queen to help her in any capacity, so I hope you'll feel free to let me know if there's anything you need."

Gi excused himself and said he'd return to the main house, and to let him know if Matron needed him. Matron gave him a warm hug and Kate raised an eyebrow. *Gi? Really?* She smiled to herself.

Kate turned to Matron. "If you'd like, we can tour the compound. We had contractors from Florence help on the design, and then Fee also had some input. Shade said it wasn't necessary to make it opulent, but I had a different plan in mind. We can talk about it as we walk through."

Kate looked around the main hallway. "This is the main foyer from the front door, but as you know, we built a tunnel system to connect to the other buildings. All of the coven will use the tunnels. The front door is not fully operational and can only be accessed by a special code in the event we need service personnel that we hire from time to time, or it needs to be used as an emergency exit. If you'll follow me..."

Kate took Matron by the elbow and led her into the main parlor. It was a massive room with Venetian plaster walls and a huge fireplace.

"This room is where the feeders can gather when they're not with a client, or when they're off-duty and don't wish to stay in their room. There's another room off of this one, where the warriors will enter and choose which feeder they wish to be with. Both of these rooms will be lavishly furnished. I want the feeders to be comfortable here, and I want the warriors to have a place where they can escape."

Matron was in awe of the massive parlor with the plaster and stonework, and the huge fireplace. They had a nice compound in Florence, but nothing like this.

"My lady, this is much more than what we are used to."

Kate shrugged. "Not all of the furniture has arrived, they're still bringing that in, but the parlor will be very comfortable. You'll have your private bedroom here on the first floor, and away from the rooms for the feeders, so you can have some privacy." Kate opened the door to a bedroom, sitting room and bath that looked like a very high-end luxury hotel.

Matron stepped into the rooms and ran her hand along the large bed before walking into her private bath. The compound in Florence had large bathrooms that everyone shared. Kate had never seen the Florence compound, or any other feeder compound, for that matter, so she watched Matron's face expectantly, trying to gauge her reaction. She was pleased to see the smile that spread across her face.

Fee spoke up, "Matron, I worked with our queen to design the compound. She wanted this to feel like a home for the feeders. I was often told by our feeders in Florence they wished the facility was designed to allow for more camaraderie with each other. So, our queen designed a place for them to be together and still have their own private space for themselves. Our Florence compound was built in a time when, well let's face it, luxury wasn't an option considered necessary for the feeders. Master has built the new warrior camp here to incorporate the newest technology and designed the accommodations for the warriors to be comfortable, to help them thrive and be healthy. Our queen understands that completely. The rooms here will be much larger and more private, the baths as well, this also helps the warriors as they can bathe here before going back to the barracks. Master will never enter these premises. I cannot speak for his son, or the queen's protector, as to whether you'll see them here. I know the warriors understand the code of conduct, and they'll treat the feeders with honor and respect as is custom."

Matron smiled at Fee. "I lead with an iron will, our feeders will understand the code, I will make sure of it. I will want to personally approve every feeder that comes here. I know the feeders that have been selected from Florence, but I understand we will have feeders from the States as well, to accommodate all taste. We will meet regularly, to review what makes our clients happy, and to make sure the feeders always conduct themselves with the utmost decorum as is befitting a Medici. I promise you, I will not tolerate any foolishness. If there are warriors who have been told this compound is off limits, I promise they will not be here for long my lady."

Kate laughed, she had no doubt this woman could lay down the law. "There's only one who's forbidden to enter, and he belongs to me. If you find him here he'll have to deal with the both of us."

Matron gave a hearty laugh. "Ah yes, our master. He was a frequent guest in the past, and a favorite among the feeders, but I promise you we've not seen him since he found you. Our business dropped off dramatically when he moved to the States. The feeders heard about you very quickly, long before you were queen."

Fee raised her eyebrows and then covered her mouth trying not to bust out in hysterical laughter. "Shade, putting the feeders out of business!" Fee held her sides laughing. "I'm sorry Kate, but you have to see the funny side of this."

Kate shook her head and laughed in spite of herself. "Yes well, if I ever find him here I will put *him* out of business. We have security access through the tunnels Matron, so only those authorized to enter may come in. That will protect you and the feeders as well. Shade has a son, a half-breed named Cory, and he'll come here. Luca is my protector, and I think Shade wanted him to have access in the event he needed someone in an emergency situation. He has a mortal girl he feeds from, but he'd have to teleport to her. If Luca were injured, he may not have the energy to teleport. If you'll follow me, I can show you the feeder's suite. There are 35 suites right now, on three floors. We have the ability to expand if we need to later. I'll show you one room. They're all pretty much identical." Kate led Matron down a long hallway of Tuscan stone, with doors leading off both sides of the corridor.

Matron followed her down the hall with Fee close behind. Kate opened one of the doors and led her into the room.

“Every bedroom has a large king sized canopy bed and a chandelier light on a dimmer. The private baths have large tubs that will accommodate two, as well as large shower stalls for those warriors who want to play in the water. The rooms have a large closet and comfortable chairs for the feeders and their clients. What do you think?"

Fee looked around at the luxury of the rooms, the attention to detail. "Play in the water, oh yes, someone is mated to a warrior.” Fee bit her lip and grinned at Kate. "I think personally, every feeder on the planet will want to be working here if you ask me. And from the point of view of a warrior, this will be a welcome respite from the barracks and camp life. *Cazzo* Kate, most of our warriors haven’t seen anything like this!"

Kate looked at the two of them. “Is it too much? I mean, they have to live here all the time. And the warriors have such a sparse life in the barracks. I thought this would be a peaceful get-away."

Fee shook her head. "I know you never saw the barracks at Castello, Kate. I’m glad you didn’t, if you think the warriors’ life here at Bel Rosso is sparse. This is over the top opulence for us. As for the feeders, I can’t imagine how they’ll react. But I know you. I know how you want to take care of the coven in the best way possible."

Kate looked around the room. "Well, I like it. I wanted it to look like a place I’d want to spend time in. So, what's next, Matron?"

"Well, my lady, I have already chosen the feeders from Florence and they will be arriving soon. They have no idea what they are in for. I can tell you, they will be quite happy here. I still need to interview the feeders from the U.S. Gi informed me that several compounds, including the one near D.C., had candidates that wanted to transfer, so I think I have about thirty to interview, and I will choose ten. I will work with Gi to set up those appointments, if that is all right with you."

Kate nodded. "Of course, call on Gi anytime."

Matron walked back to the main parlor, taking in her surroundings. "Do you wish to be here my lady, when I interview the feeders?"

Kate shook her head. "No, I’ll leave that to you. I have no idea what you’re looking for in a feeder, and besides, I’ve not had the best experience with feeders. I'm afraid I’d only pick ugly ones."

Matron and Fee both laughed, as Matron spoke, "There are no ugly ones, my dear. That would defeat the purpose."

71

The day couldn't go by fast enough, but Rissa had finally gotten the wedding invitations mailed, and those that were to be hand-delivered into the hands of the messenger service. She finalized the details with the caterer and the florist, and things were finally coming together for the event of the year, but she had an even bigger surprise scheduled for tonight.

Rissa has arranged with Alec's secretary, Jenny, to have his schedule cleared for the evening. She'd given Hyde the night off, as she planned on staying at home. Glancing at the clock, she knew the 'surprise' would be ringing the doorbell at midnight and he came in a luscious package and went by the name of Dalton.

She was preparing for the threesome Alec told her they could have. Brushing out her hair, applying the makeup and red lipstick perfectly, she was slipping on her gloves when the doorbell rang. She heard Santos answer and waited, knowing Dalton would ask for her.

Dalton had been given strict instructions and made sure he was at the correct address. At exactly midnight, he rang the doorbell, dressed in leather from head to toe. A tall elderly man, dressed in a black suit and white shirt, answered the door, and looked a bit grumpy. "I'm here to see Miss Benneteau."

Dalton was asked inside and told to wait in the foyer. He scoped the place out as he waited for the blonde who'd picked him out at the club. This was some ritzy ass neighborhood, but then, every master who solicited his services could afford to throw around the green stuff.

Alec heard the doorbell and the mumble of conversation between Santos and some unexpected guest. He inhaled deeply, picking up the male vampire's scent but didn't feel any danger. He looked at the clock on his desk. It was almost midnight. Rissa hadn't mentioned anything about company. He got up from the desk and walked to the foyer to find Santos and some leather clad stud.

Alec chuckled to himself as he smirked at the young male. "And you are?"

The male saw the master vampire and was shocked to recognize him. He's that senator he saw on TV all the time. Holy Fuck! No wonder the blonde had paid him so much money.

"My name is Dalton. Rissa hired me one night at the Incendiary, told me to be here at midnight."

Alec shook his head and called out to Rissa, "Rissa, your toy is here!"

Rissa grinned wickedly. Oh, he's definitely a toy, but not just for her. She slowly and seductively walked down the staircase, wearing only a red lace bra and thong, black fishnets and a pair of red patent stilettoes. Her hair was down and flowing around her face and her hands clad in black fishnet gloves. She looked at Dalton and licked her lips for effect. She stepped directly in front of Alec and answered him in a seductive voice, "You called, my wicked vampire?"

Alec watched her come down the stairs, prepared for a night of play. He loosened his tie and looked over at Dalton. "I hope you're well rested."

Dalton laughed, but felt a little nervous now that he was here. These two looked like a serious tag team and he thought he'd earn every penny of her hefty fee.

Alec slid the tie from his neck, spun Rissa on her heels so she stood with her back to him and he bound her wrists with his tie, and then slapped her ass hard. "Get back upstairs."

He turned to Dalton and barked out, "That goes for you too."

Dalton nodded and watched her thong clad ass wiggle up the stairs, a fine red handprint forming on her beautiful round cheek.

Rissa threw back her head and shook her long blonde mane, taking her time climbing the stairs. What she wouldn't give for that damn Castello sex chamber tonight.

She led the two men into the large bedroom and stood spread eagled in the middle of the room, her back to Dalton and Alec, waiting like the perfect submissive for her next instruction. Her body was alive, and she could feel the shivers of excitement and anticipation rolling through her. Alec was in control and he'd never let her have a three-way with another male before.

Alec entered the room last and closed the door. "So, what will it be tonight, my darling? One cock in your cunt and one down your throat?" He grabbed her long blonde locks and forced her to her knees.

Jerking her head up, she saw Alec look down at her with a wicked grin, but his beast was only riled, and she wanted the beast to emerge full force. Growling, she licked her lips. "I want every orifice filled with cock, thick and throbbing, master."

Alec chuckled. "Maybe you should have hired two men, my darling. Well, I'll see if Dalton and I can live up to your expectations."

He started to unbutton his white dress shirt and nodded at Dalton. "I suggest you strip out of those leathers."

Dalton started to peel off the soft leather until he was standing nude in their bedroom. He watched carefully as the senator removed his clothes and tossed them in a chair. Dalton was usually in charge when he was hired for a threesome, but his instincts told him to step back and wait for direction with these two. Alec walked over to Rissa and released the necktie, freeing her hands, and pushed her forward so she was on her hands and knees. Using his bare hands, he struck her ass several times, watching her skin turn pinker with each strike. He grabbed a handful of the firm muscle in her ass cheek and squeezed hard until he heard her yelp out in pain.

Alec looked over at Dalton. "This is foreplay for my darling Rissa. Don't be gentle, Dalton, or she'll eat you alive."

Dalton watched him carefully and didn’t blink. Elana and Colin had told him this female was into pain, and he could see her master liked inflicting it.

Rissa felt the sharp sting of Alec's hand on her ass in repetition. Closing her eyes, she moaned from the glorious pain and how wet she got when he spanked her. Lost in the sensation, she was taken off guard when he squeezed so hard she yelled out.

Alec walked around in front of her and dropped on his knees, his cock hard and throbbing. He lifted her chin and held his cock in one hand, slowly stoking. "Open wide, baby girl.”

Rissa couldn’t take her eyes off his hand as he stroked his dick. She opened her mouth for him as she wiggled her ass for Dalton who still remained standing behind her.

Alec slid his erection into her mouth, and across her tongue, pushing until he felt his cock hit the back of her throat. He grabbed handfuls of her hair as he guided her head and thrust his cock in and out of her mouth. Her eyes were closed as she concentrated on taking all of him.

Alec looked up at Dalton. "Well, don't just stand there. Fuck her...hard."

Dalton quickly got on his knees behind her. He ran his hand between her legs to find her wet and ready. He stroked his cock with her juices, and ran the head over her wet sex, already swollen with desire. Taking his lead from Alec, he entered her in a single thrust, pushing hard and deep as he gripped her hips.

Rissa was enjoying the hard driving abuse from both ends. She could feel Dalton’s hips slamming against hers as he gripped her hips, digging his fingers into her and fucking her hard, his balls slapping against her. She sucked Alec deep into her throat as they all moved in unison.

Suddenly, Alec pulled his cock from her mouth and she moaned. "No...please no."

Alec stood and walked away but remained in her view. He watched as Dalton fucked her from behind, her hair and breasts swaying with each thrust as he pounded her hard. He saw her face as she responded to him and waited until he could tell she was ready to cum when he demanded that Dalton stop and withdraw. The young male looked startled, but did as he was told.

Rissa bucked hard, pushing her ass back in Dalton's direction, her moan one of anger and frustration. She wanted to cum. She looked up at Alec and growled, her fangs punched through and dripping. She wanted more and now!

Alec growled back at her, his fangs punching through as he grabbed her by the hair and dragged her across the floor. He lifted her hands above her head and used his necktie to tie her wrists to the bedpost, leaving her seated on the floor.

Stepping back, he grabbed the young male and pushed him down on his knees in front of him. Dalton slid his hands up Alec's thighs and licked at his cock. It was clear, now, this master wanted to tease her, and Dalton knew the drill. Alec slid his cock into the young male's mouth, in clear view of Rissa, letting her watch each stroke.

Rissa watched as his beast emerged but still not in full force, and it excited her. She'd bring that bastard out if it killed her. As Alec grabbed her hair and dragged her across the floor like a rag doll, Rissa grappled with his hands, clawing at him, knowing it only served to anger him. As he tied her to the bedpost, she kicked and growled. She watched as he tortured her with Dalton, as the young stud took her master's dick and sucked him to perfection. She thrashed her head back and forth in protest, as Alec's beast emerged fully and she yanked on the bedpost, wanting that cock. This was no longer any fun, but torture at its worst, and she was pissed off, feeling her body ache with need.

Alec stood with his legs straddled as the young male swallowed him whole, sucking hard and deep. He grabbed a handful of his hair as he thrust hard, releasing his cum deep into the back of Dalton's throat.

Dalton swallowed and licked at the head of Alec's prick, smiled up at him and said, "What's next?"

Alec walked over to the dresser and took a cigarette and lit it, offering one to the young male who shook his head no. "What's next indeed? What do you think, darling?"

He looked at Rissa who was straining against the necktie. Alec picked up his cell phone and scrolled through the contacts, hitting dial, waiting for an answer on the other end. A female voice said, "Hello."

Alec stared at Rissa who was watching him expectantly before he answered. "Jenny, I know it's late, but I'd like you to drop by. My butler will see you in."

Rissa's beast was out of control as she heard Alec speaking to that fucking snotty ass little bitch of a secretary. Her growl rattled the walls and she screamed at him, pulling at her restraints.

Alec finished the cigarette and put it out in the ash tray. Walking to the closet, he dragged out a large rectangular iron frame with a heavy leather strap in each corner. He leaned it against the wall before untying her and dragging her to the frame. "Help me out here, Dalton."

Alec strapped one wrist above her head in one corner of the frame while Dalton grabbed her other hand and wrestled with her to strap it onto the other corner. Her feet were kicking wildly, and Alec laughed and gave Dalton a warning, "Watch she doesn't take out your jewels."

He grabbed her leg and strapped it to the bottom corner of the frame and Dalton managed to grab her other leg strapping her down. She was now spread-eagled against the iron frame. She was shaking her head from side to side, her blonde mane flying as she screamed at him.

Santos called up from the foyer, "Master Alec, you have another guest."

Alec smirked. "Send her up."

Jenny scurried up the stairs. She couldn't believe her good luck. She'd been chasing this man since the day he hired her.

Jenny stepped into their bedroom to find Alec and some other young buck completely nude and erect, and his fiancé from hell strapped down and screaming her head off.

Jenny flashed Alec a look and he smiled back at her. "I told you to be careful what you wished for."

Jenny started to remove her clothes, never taking her eyes off of him. "And what makes you think this isn't exactly what I wished for?"

Alec threw his head back laughing, as her fangs punched through.

Rissa screamed at her! How dare he even look at her, he would *not* fuck that cow in front of her. Struggling, she could feel the leather straps slice into her wrists, drawing blood. She could feel the contraption rattle and move, she was desperate to break free. She looked up to see Dalton directly in front of her, just staring, like she was some circus act he is admiring. "Fuck off, Alec! Get me the fuck out of this thing now. Do it now!"

Alec approached Jenny slowly, sliding his hand into her light brown hair. He lifted her face and kissed her, letting the kiss slide from her lips and down her neck. Dalton approached her from the rear, kissing and nipping at the opposite shoulder, his hands sliding around her waist. Jenny moaned, and leaned her bare breasts against Alec's muscular chest, letting both men explore with their hands and mouths. She laid her head back against the young male's shoulder, as she felt Alec's hands slide down across her breasts and onto her hips. He lifted her up and she wrapped her legs around his hips, as his cock sought out her sex. She felt him penetrate her and she cried out with pleasure. She had watched him every day, wanted him every day. She held onto his shoulders as he easily held her weight in his hands and slid her along the thick shaft of his erection. She felt the young male probing from behind as he slid his dick into her ass and pressed hard against her back, sandwiched now between two strong males, and she gave herself up to them.

Rissa watched Alec's face, how his eyes glazed over in passion. She knew that look, his beast was being pleasured and her heart beat faster. Rissa's body went rigid. Yanking hard on the restraints, the contraption rattled, getting his attention and his eyes bored into hers. She licked her lips, letting her tongue glide over her fangs. His wicked grin rolled over his face and she instantly felt that connection to him, as he telepathically made her cum so hard her eyes rolled back in her head. Screaming as she came, she heard him roar as he came hard inside his own prey. The power of them together was overwhelming and even though she couldn't move, he still gave her intense pleasure without touching her physically. Her head hung down, her hair swinging forward, as she slowly lifted her eyes to see what he'd give her next in this blissful torture.

Alec came hard inside Jenny, as he felt her thrusting her hips forward to take in all of him, and back to take in Dalton. Alec's release triggered Dalton, followed by Jenny as the three of them convulsed with the power of the orgasm that raged between them. Alec felt Rissa's orgasm as well as the four of them rode out the waves of pleasure. He stepped back as Dalton held Jenny upright, her body limp now with pleasure. He nodded at the bed and Dalton lifted her and put her on the bed.

Alec picked up a riding crop that lay on a duffle bag of Rissa's gear, something from her recent trips to Bel Rosso, no doubt. He slapped it across his hands as he walked toward Rissa, the sharp slapping sound getting her attention. As she looked up, his eyes bored into her. He used the riding crop to lift her hair back from her face, before gently caressing her cheek with it.

"Poor baby girl. Not what you expected?" He flicked the tip of the riding crop against her erect nipple.

Alec turned to Dalton. "Release her."

Dalton obeyed and unstrapped her wrists, and Rissa massaged the deep red marks left by the straps. He released her ankles and she brought her feet together, relieving the pressure on her legs. Alec ran the riding crop down the middle of her breasts to her abdomen, to the cleft between her legs. "Get on your hands and knees, baby girl."

Rissa quickly scrambled to the floor, dropping to her knees.

"Fuck her, Dalton. Fuck her until she begs you to stop."

The young male dropped on his knees behind Rissa and grabbed her hips, entering her roughly and pounding at her. Alec watched as he mounted her, watching his thick cock slamming into her over and over.

Rissa let him ride her, and she loved every moment. His member was throbbing and felt like hot steel inside her. She matched him stroke for stroke. She never let up and began to control the pace, pushing him faster and deeper until he came hard inside her. She felt his sweat dripping on her back and she thrust so hard back into him, it almost knocked him over. Young pup. She'd show him! She brought him to orgasm again as he draped over her back, breathing hard.

Reaching behind her, she grabbed a handful of his hair and whipped him over her head to land hard on his back in front of her, his face starring up at her in amazement. Purring, she bared her fangs and nipped at his shoulders and neck, and then slid her tongue along his vein, feeling him come alive once again. She kissed him deep and hard, pushing her tongue down his throat.

Alec lit up another cigarette and watched the performance, as the young male struggled to keep up with her. Jenny was beckoning him from their bed, but he was currently entertained by the floor show and ignored her. Alec smirked when Rissa tossed Dalton head over heels, landing him on the floor in front of her.

Alec snapped the riding crop along his leg just to remind her he was still holding it, before he walked behind her, striking her hard across the ass with the leather crop. He slid the crop between her legs, letting it slip into the crevice of her swollen sex, as he slid it up and down. "More, baby girl?"

The crop snapped and Rissa sizzled. She loved how he handled it, spinning it in his hands Feeling it slide between her legs only fired her more, she shivered on all fours wanting to cum but wouldn't.

"Baby girl wants more!"

Alec dropped on his knees behind her and grabbed her hips, lifting her off the floor as he slammed into her. "Suck him, baby girl. Let daddy watch you suck dick."

Dalton rolled off his back and knelt in front of her, grabbing her hair and lifting her head. Alec paused in his relentless pounding to give Dalton time to get his cock in her mouth, and then he resumed his pace, hitting her so hard that Dalton need not move. Every thrust from Alec pushed Rissa's mouth deeper onto Dalton's erection.

Rissa moaned. Alec's movements were fast and hard, as he pounded her over and over again. She heard Dalton moan, and felt him explode in her mouth and she swallowed his cum. She could tell Alec was also close. His breathing was fast, his hands bruising her tender skin and digging into her hips. Dalton fell back off his knees, drained once again and Rissa begged, her body on fire and she couldn't hold back any longer, the need to cum causing physical pain.

"Daddy, please, please!"

"Cum, baby girl, and take me with you."

Throwing back her head, she slammed her body hard into him, feeling him explode inside her, the rush of pleasure like a volcano erupting. Thrashing and shaking her head, her body quivered as they became one.

He collapsed on top of her, putting his hands on the floor on either side of her so she wouldn't be crushed under his weight. He rolled off her to the side, both of them breathing heavily.

Jenny hung her head over the edge of the bed, looking down at him. "What about me?"

He opened his eyes and looked up at her. "What about you?"

She looked at him coyly. "Well, what does this mean? What happened here tonight?"

He chuckled. "It means nothing, Jenny. You were a toy, a prop in the night's entertainment, nothing more. In fact, you can go now. Santos will show you out."

She climbed from the bed in a huff, gathering her clothes and dressing as she left the room.

Alec looked at Rissa. "How about you, baby girl? You good now, or do I need to have Dalton fuck you again?"

Sliding her eyes to him, she slid her hand over his cock and felt it instantly harden, stroking him a few times, she grinned. "I think daddy saved the best for last. Get rid of him."

Alec nodded at Dalton as he gathered up his leathers and started to leave.

Dalton paused at the door and told them, "Call me anytime."

Alec looked at Rissa after he exited. "He was a gift. And he's gone now. You ever fuck anyone without me and I'll kill you. You know that, right?"

Rissa sat up as she watched Dalton stroll out the door, clothes in hand. "Well, I hope your gift giving spirit never dies. But there's one thing I'm interested to know." Standing up, she walked to the dresser, pulled out a cigarette, lit it and strolled back to Alec. She laid her head in his lap, putting the cigarette to his lips. "You can't seriously let him walk out of here, he recognized you instantly. He cannot be trusted no matter what Colin and Elana say."

Alec took a drag on the cigarette, then slowly exhaled. "That was taken care of before he ever showed up here. Glad you're not emotionally attached, as that's the last anyone will ever see of Dalton. Santos has it arranged."

Rissa sighed. "How disappointing! I was hoping you'd be my knight in shining armor and kill him for me. I wanted his dead cock handed to me on a silver platter." Pulling her hair to the side, she exposed her long neck. "Please, Alec, you haven't fed, you need it."

Alec took another deep drag on the cigarette and exhaled. *Oh, my darling, you have no idea when I feed, or who I feed from*. He stroked her hair, not in the mood for her drama if he were ever to reveal that piece of information. Just because he made her wait to be fed didn't mean he should ever do without. He put the cigarette out in the palm of his hand, listening to the sizzle, and watching as the burn healed. "Of course, my darling. How kind of you to offer."

He leaned over her, licked her long neck, and sank his fangs deep into her tender flesh.

72

Gi entered Shade's office to inform him the cradle from Castello had arrived and that Kate and Fiamma were currently at the feeder compound and would be there some time.

"*Si, si!* What is she doing at the feeder compound?"

Gi smiled. "She is meeting with Matron. She arrived today while you were in your death slumber. My lady is meeting with her to tour the compound and discuss the arrangements for the feeders."

Shade didn't miss the large grin on Gi's face when he spoke of Matron, and he wondered who in hell they had come in from Florence to take the position. Shade's interest was piqued by the look on the old man's face, as Gi clearly approved.

"Gi, let me carry this thing upstairs, I wish for it to be in our bed chamber. Perhaps you could assist me with where to place it?"

As Gi complied, they walked to the kitchen where Gi had the cradle uncrated. The cradle was solid wood, and very heavy, yet Shade lifted it easily to his shoulder as the two of them made their way up the stairs to the master bedroom. Gi advised him to place it in the corner near the window and once done, they both stood back to admire it. Both Gi and Shade decided Kate would want it closer to the bed, so it was moved until they were both satisfied with its placement.

The cradle had been used by Shade when he was a baby, and by his father and grandfather before him. Hand carved from a solid piece of wood by Medici artisans, the cradle weighed close to a hundred pounds. Its dark wood was worn smooth in spots where loving hands had rocked it. The intricate Medici Crest was hand-carved into the headboard.

As they stood back and admired their work, Shade slapped Gi on the back. "I think we both deserve a glass of Midnight, my man." They headed back downstairs to Shade's office.

As they entered the office Gi went to pour some Midnight and Shade interrupted him. "Old man, sit down, let me get this one."

As Gi settled himself in a leather chair, Shade poured the Midnight, handed it to him and settled his large frame at his desk.

"Things are a bit busy around here Gi, and I apologize if we're keeping you at your paces. I promise to make it up to you. You need to let me know if you need time for any personal business."

Shade watched his face closely, and as he figured, the smile of his faithful longtime servant was a warm one.

"Master, I have served Medici my entire life, and although I am older now, it is with much happiness and honor to keep serving. Our queen has much heart. The sounds that abound here and at Castello are of happiness and joy. I might add we are all looking forward to the sound of small feet rushing through the halls again. As for my feeding, it will be much easier on my old bones now."

Shade chuckled. "I can see in your face, you have a bit of color. Something sure as hell has sparked your interest, and it is not that damn cradle. Give it up!"

Gi sipped the Midnight slowly, savoring its bouquet and the burst of intense energy as it hit his tongue. "I have been going to the feeders in Florence for centuries. It was your *padre*'s command. We fed just as the warriors did, from the feeders selected to service the camp. Once his death came, there was not much for us to do. You were a strapping young vampire, intending to take over the world, you were never home much. There was more freedom for the warriors and the staff to hunt and search out whatever we wished for. But I had already found a feeder to my unique taste. She served your *padre* and his warriors, and yourself as well, Master Shade. I never had to hunt, nor leave the walls of Castello to find my own satisfaction and life source."

Shade sat forward and leaned on the desk. "Are you saying what I think you are saying Gi? You had the same feeder the entire time you served at Castello? Impossible!"

"Not impossible, master. Some of us find a feeder that enlightens not only our blood but our hearts and minds as well. Such was one of the feeders that serviced the barracks. I fed from her for many years. We have a bond, and I am fortunate enough to still have the extreme pleasure of her company."

Shade slapped his hand down on the desk, roaring with a laugh. "*Cazzo*, old man! You mean to tell me you teleported back to Castello every time you needed to feed? This female must be extraordinary, and obviously, I have to know her. Who is it?"

Gi didn't miss the anticipation in his master's voice. He was more like his *padre* than Shade would ever care to admit.

"I could not go to her every time I needed to feed, time would not allow, but I did go back to Castello as often as possible. I think she is most extraordinary. I am quite sure she is familiar to you. But I do not think our queen would wish for me to reveal her name."

Shade scowled. "What does Kate have to do with any of this?" Shade was confused trying to think why Kate would care if Gi had been going to Castello to feed and then it hit him like a brick upside his Italian head. She was the new matron here at Bel Rosso!

Gi watched Shade's face and could see the moment Matron's identity hit him. "*Si*, she is now the matron here at the feeder compound. I personally chose her to come here. She is the best at what she does, and it relieves me from teleporting, leaving me to attend to the *familia* here at Bel Rosso, and of course, she is quite obliging to accommodate me."

Shade hadn't paid much attention to the details of arranging for feeders in Florence. Gi had worked hand in hand with Marco to make sure the needs of the staff and warriors were met. Shade had used the feeders, although he preferred hunting and clubbing and meeting women outside of the feeding community. He was the Medici, and before mating to his Bel, females clung to him like bees on honey. Finding a feeding partner was never an issue with him.

"There have only been three matrons at Medici that I can recall, but if she went back as far as *Padre*..."

Shade left the sentence hanging as he recalled a beauty and a name that, at one point in time, he overheard his *madre* and *padre* discuss at length in a non-friendly manner. Velia, it had to be her, no one could rival her beauty and the distinct allure of her blood. It was rumored she had fed many a warrior, and Shade had lain with her himself. She was extraordinary in her power, and she chose with whom she fed, a rare privilege in the feeder community. Warriors choose their feeders, not the other way around. She was known to satisfy any immortal male in all areas and Shade rolled his eyes to Gi.

"You old goat! You mean to tell me you have been tapping into Velia all this time. It is Velia. Has to be!"

Gi felt a blush creep across his cheeks and he sat up straighter. Velia was the only female for him. "She was quite the beauty in her time, still is to me. She was bred as a feeder, so her course in life was set. But once she retired, we sought each other out, and we have remained true. She has been a loyal subject to the Medici coven, she deserves to be here and rise with you and the *familia*. She is a stern and caring matron. She runs a tight ship with the feeders. You have no need to worry. And from what I can see, the queen and Velia get along most agreeably. The compound has been constructed luxuriously, it has our queen's touch, and it will be quite accommodating for the feeders and the warriors."

Gi paused a minute as he sipped at the Midnight. "I would suggest we keep this conversation to ourselves, master, your mate may not care for the fact you are, shall we say, well known to the matron, or that I currently have a relationship with her. I prefer that to remain between us."

Shade ran his hands through his hair and flopped back in his leather desk chair. "I agree, I rather enjoy my family jewels and if Kate were to become aware of Velia's history, I would miss them."

Gi laughed heartily at his words. The queen kept a tight lock on those jewels, but he knew his master would never ever stray, his love and devotion to her was unrivaled.

Gi lifted his glass to him. "It shall be our secret. I know you will never see Velia, nor venture inside the compound. Velia will choose the feeders herself. She will bring some from Florence and choose the American feeders as well. The warriors will be well fed and pleasured, I assure you. Velia will keep them in line. I know you remember her to be soft and kind, but she has learned to manage the feeders, as well as the warriors."

Shade laughed. "And I have no doubt you keep her at the top of her game as well, old man!"

Gi stood to leave. "A gentleman never reveals his secrets or conquests, master."

As Gi left to continue with his duties, Shade's mind drifted back to the days of his youth when he was sowing his wild oats. Velia was a beauty, soft and voluptuous, but a handful even then. He pictured her in his mind and smiled. She had taught many a warrior the ways of sexual gratification and had even shown him a few tricks. He realized if she was matron, she'd be teaching the young feeders a few of those tricks as well. *Cazzo*, he'd have his hands full with these warriors.

He tried to picture Velia with Gi, and he shook his head. Gi! First, it was Marco and Theresa and now Gi and Velia. How in hell had he never seen either of these relationships, as they happened right under his nose?

He heard Kate as she came in the house and he made himself busy with his paperwork. He remained grateful beyond belief he'd found his own love and mate, and she was more than he could have imagined. She gave him something no female ever had, her unconditional love and light, and a happiness and peacefulness inside him that had been missing for so damn long.

73

Kate left Fee in the camp and walked back along the garden path to the main house after the inspection of the feeder compound. As she entered the house, she stood still a second to feel him. He was in the office, so she set her course for him when she bumped into Gi.

"Gi, I met Matron, and I couldn't be happier with your choice. I think she'll work out perfectly."

Gi smiled and nodded his head in a respectful manner, extremely glad his queen was pleased with Velia as Matron, and she would be staying on. "I am most happy to hear this news, my lady. I do feel she is the best matron for the position here. She comes highly recommended." His smile widened as he stepped aside. "You will find master in his office attending to business."

Kate noticed the wide smile across his face and was amused. Gi was always so serious. "Thank you, Gi." Kate headed to the study to find Shade at his desk, head bent over a stack of papers.

"Our majordomo seems in an extremely good mood."

He looked up as she entered. "*Si.* So, do you want to tell me how you have learned to block images and conversations from me already?" Grinning, he stood and moved to the leather sofa, patting the empty space next to him, inviting her to sit.

Kate slid in next to him, laying her head on his shoulder, laughing at his comment. "Now how would you know what images I've blocked? And what good is a secure tunnel and compound if you can travel there in your head?"

Shade laughed. "You never cease to amaze me. You have mastered the art of keeping every single female at a distance from me, even in my head! So, tell me, I am interested to know if you approve of how things are going. Do you like Matron?"

"The compound construction is complete, and some of the furniture is in. Everything should be in place in a few days at the most. Fee says it is much more than what they're used to, as did Matron. I liked her a lot. She'll run a tight ship."

Kate lifted her head and looked at him. "She had no problem remembering you, lover. Seems you almost put them out of business when you left Florence and came to the States. And Gi seems more than a little pleased with Matron. Is there something I need to know about?"

Cazzo! She picks up on everything. "Well, I don't think I put them out of business. I didn't use the feeders as much as you may think, but I won't lie, I did use them." Snuggling into her hair, he closed his eyes, taking in her rose scent. "As for Gi, the sly old fox is very happy at the moment, he chose Matron for a reason. He asked me not to speak to you on it."

"I knew Gi picked her and had a say in the other feeders that are coming over from Florence as well. Matron said she was retired as a feeder. She said she was free to live with other immortals now but chose to stay on in the capacity of matron. So, what are you saying? That she and Gi...have a thing?" She shuffled her position on the sofa, so she could turn to face him as he answered.

"It seems as though Gi has been feeding from Matron since the beginning of time. During *Padre*'s day, servants fed with warriors at the barracks. And he has never stopped feeding from her. Did you know he was teleporting back to Castello since being here just to feed from her? I don't want to hide anything from you, *mi amore*. Her name is Velia. She was an extraordinary feeder in her day. But I have been advised by Gi she is a strict matron."

Kate was shocked to learn Gi had been teleporting back to Florence just to feed from her. "Why didn't he say something? We could have brought her here earlier. I think my hatred of the feeders had everyone walking on eggshells. And maybe when I was still mortal I wouldn't have been as open to the idea of bringing a feeder here. I feel bad he had to go to such extremes, but I'm glad she's here now. For him, and because I think she'll do a good job of keeping order in the compound."

Raising his eyebrows at her, he was more than a little shocked. "Are you feeling well, *mi amore*? You have never had one good thing to say about feeders. But, in their defense, they are a vital part of our culture. And perhaps in the future, other things will become clearer now that you see through the eyes of an immortal. *Grazie,* for doing this."

Kissing her, Shade slid his lips along her cheek, and nipped at her ear. He whispered, "I have a surprise for you."

Kate leaned her forehead against his and purred, "Do you now? And what might this surprise be?"

He slide his arms under her, lifting her as he stood and carried her from the room and up the stairs towards their bedroom. "Well, since you are curious, perhaps I had best just take you to the surprise."

As he approached the closed door of their bedroom, he told her, "Now close your eyes."

She closed her eyes as he opened the door and carried her into the room, setting her down on her feet.

"Keep them closed. No peeking!"

He positioned her directly in front of him, blocking her view of the cradle. "Now, open your eyes and find your surprise."

Kate slowly opened her eyes and looked about. Sitting by their bed was an ancient wooden cradle, elaborately hand-carved. She gasped as she knelt beside it and reached out to run her hand over the surface. The wood was worn and smooth to the touch. She pushed against the cradle as it gently rocked, despite the weight of it. "Lover, this was yours?" She felt Lorenzo stir as she placed her hand over the swell of her belly, quieting the life inside her.

He watched her face, the smile and appreciation. He knew she'd love the old traditional cradle, passed down through the generations.

"*Si*, was mine, and several generations before me. *Madre* has worn it down a bit. Apparently, I was a cranky *bambino*. *Padre* rocked me as well, so the stories are told."

Watching her hand go to the swell of his *figlio*, his heart felt as though it would explode inside his chest. He wondered how he could possibly hold this much love. Walking around the cradle, he slid his hands over the wood, the smell of Castello filling his nostrils. Kneeling beside her, placing his hand over her tummy, he only hoped he had enough inside him to take care of them all, keep them safe, and give them the love they all deserved.

"Lorenzo knows, *si*? He knows we are here with him, that we love him. The sons of kings slept inside this cradle. He will one day be King of Medici. I only hope I can be a good *padre.*"

Kate placed her hand over his, so he could feel the baby move beneath his touch. "Feel him, lover. He'll tell you everything. He's a proud Medici already, and he can't wait to follow in your footsteps. He knows he's loved, and he wants so much to please you. He'll be a fierce warrior, and a good man. His children, and his children's children, will rule Medici for centuries to come. That's his message."

As she pressed her hand slightly into his, he felt their *figlio* kick, and he laughed softly. "I want him to know his past but forge his own future. I also want him to have your soft heart, so he can rule fair and true. I want each generation to improve Medici rule. I want our *familia* to be the leaders of the future and what is to come. Wait! Did you say his children? *Mi amore*, can you see his children?"

"I can't see them yet, but he can. I see him, growing up, chasing after you in the camp, eager to start his training. He looks just like you with his long dark hair and his blue eyes. He has tears in his eyes because he's only two, and he can't lift your sword. He wants to fight beside you. You hold him to your chest and tell him, 'In time my *figlio*.'"

As she spoke, he felt their son do a somersault in her tummy. Quickly pulling his hand back as if he was burned, his eyes grew huge and he stared at Kate. "Did that hurt? Are you all right?"

Kate laughed. "I told you he was eager to get here. He already practices his warrior skills. And no, it doesn't hurt. I love feeling him move."

"He is strong, *si*? I like feeling him as well, and he will be here soon. I am excited, but also somewhat nervous."

Kate smiled at him from the floor. "He already loves you and wants to be just like you, Shade. He will be quite the ladies' man, so it seems he'll follow in your footsteps in more ways than one. He'll work hard, and play harder, and make no mistake. He'll be a handful."

"*Si*, like his *padre*." Leaning down, Shade kissed his son through Kate's swollen belly before taking her face in his hands. "*Grazie* for this gift you give me, *mi amore*. *Ti amo!*"

74

Raven scooted in the wheeled office chair across the control room in the Dead House, checking the security monitors that tracked the locations of every warrior on the streets. The new grid arrangement seemed to be working well, as the warriors were becoming familiar with their new territories. He'd taken Theo with him several nights, making rounds. Watching the monitors was one thing, but nothing took the place of checking up on the warriors in person. Shade had taught him that. It gave Raven the opportunity to make sure nothing was left unattended or unprotected and made sure they'd worked out all of the bugs in providing adequate coverage for all of D.C.

He sat in front of the large console, logging in the activity of each of the warriors when he heard the sound of familiar boots walking across the creaky wooden floor above his head. Warrior or not, nothing was sneaking up on him in this damn place without someone hearing it. He recognized the heavy footfalls of the boss-man. Clicking the key to save the document, he finished up just as Shade walked in.

Raven looked up. "Well, well, well, to what do we owe this special appearance?"

Shade chuckled and popped Raven on the back of the head. "It's royal, not special, get your damn titles correct if you are going to bust my ass, SIC."

Raven spun around in the chair, his long hair flying, as he turned to face Shade. Raven pulled a smoke from behind his ear and lit up. "I finalized the grid layout, made a lot of changes. Interested in taking a look?"

Shade plopped down opposite him and lit up as well, as his booted feet flew up on the table, crossed at the ankles. "Not on that thing, no. I need to see it up close and personal. Showing me on a screen does nothing for my old head." Taking a long drag, Shade blew smoke rings above his head.

Raven responded, "No problem. I can print it out for you. Or better yet, we can take to the streets and I can show you."

Shade grinned. "*Si*, so stop yapping your mouth and let's do this."

They both teleported out as Raven pointed out to him the new grids, and which warrior he'd assigned to each. Things were quiet. The warriors were all at their posts and making their rounds. Raven and Shade stayed out of sight, allowing Shade to observe the warriors at work.

He was impressed with the changes Raven had made. He'd made the warriors time more efficient and effective. They were close enough to each other at all times to respond quickly to handle any situation. As they stood on top of one of the older buildings in the metro, the nightlife was beginning to really kick into high gear. Shade felt good to be away from camp for a night and back on the streets.

"You do well, runt, impressive. Shows me you have a head on your shoulders and it's about time you started using it. Let's find us a good bar and have a celebration drink. I think you deserve it!"

Raven was bursting with pride. He'd been given the responsibility for the Dead House and he was making it better. He had a lot more ideas he wanted to implement, but right now, he was satisfied to have a night out with the boss. It was rare they got to spend much time together beyond working, and Raven might have a chance to share a few other ideas he had once they were in the club.

"*Grazie,* boss-man. Two blocks northeast, good club, they have Midnight and it's usually pretty packed in there. We won't stand out."

Raven took off over the rooftops, swooping down to street level in front of the club before Shade even had time to process what he'd said.

"Goddamn, runt!" Shade took off in pursuit, swooping down behind him.

Raven mocked him. "Christ, you're getting slow!" Raven bent over laughing as Shade shook his head.

"Get your ass inside, now!"

Walking inside the crowded club, they scoped out the guests. Shade didn't feel any other vamps present, but the night was still young. "Many vamps come in here?"

Raven pulled his loose hair back as they made their way through the crowd. "Sometimes, but it's a little early for the vamp crowd boss-man. This place attracts everything. What do they call them? Yuppies? Young white rich kids, trying to make it big in the city."

Shade nodded "Yeah, I can see that."

As they made their way to the bar, Shade took in everything around him. There was definitely money in this place. This was the white collar work crowd, the ones who partied early and got home to bed before the stroke of midnight. Most were well dressed, their noses in the air, looking for booze and ass. He ordered two Midnights and threw a twenty on the bar. It didn't take the bartender long, as he nodded to Raven and served their drinks. It was obvious to Shade the bartender recognized Raven.

The two of them settled in, leaning against the bar with their Midnight and watched the crowd. Shade's eyes roamed over the mortals closest to him when he suddenly felt eyes on him. He let his gaze drift in the direction of a tall, lean blonde mortal male. The mortal was surrounded by women, all of them fawning over him. He was dressed well and holding court with the females when their eyes met. The mortal looked away.

"So, tell me Raven, how is Theo working out?"

Raven took note of how boss-man operated, always aware of his surroundings, never letting his guard down. "He's working his ass off, just like me. He knows what he's doing. If I want to go street level and check out the warriors, I can leave Theo in charge in the Dead House. He can handle it."

Shade nodded, but still felt the eyes of the mortal on him. Shade took notice of the mortal's body language, and how he was posturing with the women, his manicured hands making frequent contact. None of the women objected to his advances and it was clear the mortal didn't expect to leave alone tonight. The mortal was tanned like he was airbrushed, he was in his element, the consummate player.

Shade turned his attention back to Raven as he answered, "I'm glad to hear it. We always need to have warriors being trained to step up to the next level, make advances in the organization."

Ethan saw the tall dark haired man at the bar. He was pretty sure this was the guy his buddies had pointed out as the man Kate was with now. He continued to flirt with the bevy of females around him but kept looking at the man with the stylishly long black hair and blue eyes. He shifted his position at the bar. Ethan edged a little closer until he could hear snippets of their conversation. The man stood with another guy, with even longer black hair. Both of them spoke with an Italian accent, and Ethan was sure now this was the guy.

He and Kate had been engaged, but then she broke it off when she'd discovered him with one of his "groupies," as he liked to call them. Ethan remembered the heated argument with Kate, and how she threw the engagement ring back in his face. He chuckled to himself, still amazed Kate would think he should be monogamous. I mean, it wasn't his fault he was a chick magnet. And what's a guy to do anyway? Deny himself all the pleasures of life? He sipped at his drink and kept glancing at the tall dark Italian. He looked older than the men Kate usually went out with. Not her type at all. The alcohol was making him brave, as he approached the two men at the bar and extended his hand to Shade.

"Hi. I'm Ethan. Ethan Young."

Shade felt him creeping closer. This one could be trouble. As the mortal stepped up and introduced himself, Raven immediately stepped away, so he stood at the mortal's back. Shade never had to worry, his warriors knew the routine. Shade took a long sip of his Midnight and leaned against the bar. The mortal's hand was extended, but Shade had no intention of shaking it.

"Shade. Shade Medici. Am I supposed to know who you are, Ethan Young?" Shade could smell the cockiness rolling off him, and the alcohol rushing through his veins. He had no idea what this punk was up to but was sure he was about to find out.

Ethan gave him a big smile. "Well, I'm a little surprised if you don't. I was sure she'd have mentioned me."

Shade casually pushed himself upright off the bar and stood tall, towering over the mortal. "There have been a lot of *she's* in my lifetime, Ethan Young. Perhaps you would care to elaborate?"

Ethan laughed. "So, she jumped out of the frying pan and into the fire? How typical. Kate, of course, I'm speaking of Kate Reese. We were engaged. She dumped me, said I was a player. But it looks like she must be drawn to players. Maybe she should have stayed with me."

In an instant, Shade saw the visual in Ethan's head, and it turned him dead cold inside. Her soft white skin, that plump sweet ass, and crimson hair. The mortal's words hit him, and he growled. His Kate! So, this was the scum sucking bastard that had played her. Well, aren't we going to have a little fun tonight!

Shade looked at Raven and knew he was ready at a moment's notice to take this piece of shit down. Raven was just waiting on his word.

Raven knew immediately what was going to happen when he heard the mortal utter Kate's name, and felt the boss-man's blood boil. Raven telepathically called for Theo to come and wait outside the club, just in case Shade lost it inside this place. Raven knew Shade was not usually one to make a scene, but this mortal was talking about Kate, and that changed everything.

Shade kept his voice low as he locked eyes with the mortal. "She dumped the right one, you useless limp dick bastard. Now, she has me. You see, where I come from, men honor their commitments to women. We kill bastards like you."

Shade took a step closer to him, looking down into Ethan's face. Raven had him boxed in from the back. Shade heard Raven in his head, warning him this wasn't a good idea and they should take it outside.

Shade got in Ethan's face. "But before we kill them, we slice off their cocks and ram it up their ass. Then rip their heart out and push it down their throat. It is called retribution for abusing and cheating on a female who gave you her trust."

Ethan held up his hand. "Hey, man. Take it easy. Jeez, you are *way* too serious. I mean, don't get me wrong. I miss Kate. Wish she'd stuck it out with me. Breaking up was not my idea. I mean, she was a great piece of ass, but you know that already, right? If she hadn't broken up with me, you wouldn't be able to sample my leftovers."

Raven took a deep breath when he heard Shade growl and he knew Shade wanted this bastard dead, now!

Shade looked deep in Ethan's eyes, locking him tight in place so the mortal couldn't move. His voice was a deadly low deep growl that sounded like something had crawled straight up from hell. His beast was out and wanted his due for his mate. Shade growled out the words, "Turn around and walk out the door."

He watched as the bastard mindlessly followed the instructions, walking in a trance out the door of the club. Raven saw the mortal head for the door, and stepped in front of him, leading the way. As they made their way to the door, Shade was shaking with anger, the longest fucking walk of his life. He would see to it his *bel* had her revenge, and this scum would never walk the face of the earth again.

Once outside, Raven continued to walk as the mortal mindlessly followed down a long street, finally turning into a darkened alley. Theo saw them exit the club and dropped in behind Shade. Theo wasn't sure what had gone down, but clearly, the mortal was about to see his final minutes on earth.

As they entered the alley, Shade slammed the mortal's back up against the brick building and unlocked his mind. He wanted the mortal to see and feel everything. Shade showed him an evil grin, exposing his fangs as the mortal bastard pissed his pants. Shade grabbed the mortal's cock and squeezed hard, as Ethan's scream echoed off the walls.

Shade's eyes flashed a brilliant red. He released Ethan's dick and grabbed his throat, lifting the bastard's feet from the ground as he writhed in pain. Shade roared like thunder in the night. "Scared, little man? How does it feel to be alone and vulnerable? Hurt and in pain?"

Shade felt Raven and Theo crouching behind him, keeping a look out, both their eyes glowing and fangs protruding.

Shade wanted to feel the mortal's fear before he took him out. He willed forth the music of a heavy metal band, so it sounded like it was coming from a nearby club, to drown out the sounds that would emanate from the alley.

Ethan looked around, confused. He was walking down a dark alley. *What the fuck? How did I get out here?* He felt himself getting slammed against the brick wall and the face of the dark haired Italian was inches from his. Ethan's heart started to pound as he watched the face transform, the eyes glowing red, and the appearance of fangs. Ethan shook his head. *No way this is happening! What the fuck was I drinking in there, anyway?*

He was about to plead for mercy when the vampire grabbed his junk and squeezed. Ethan screamed as it felt like his balls would rupture. He noticed two other vampires standing behind this one. *Kate is with a vampire? Someone needs to warn her!* He heard his own scream cut off as the monster slid his hand around his throat and applied just enough pressure to block his air. Ethan flailed lamely, pounding his fist on the man's impossibly hard chest, then grasping at his own throat, trying to pull the monster's hands away as he gasped for air.

Squeezing Ethan's airway, Shade watched him flail, the mortal's perfectly manicured fingers clawing helplessly at his hand. Shade released his grip on Ethan's neck, just enough to let him draw a breath.

The saliva dripped from Shade's fangs, he was so eager to take the mortal down, but he wanted him to feel every minute of the agony. Shade punched Ethan hard in the chest, pushing his fist quickly inside his chest, and squeezed his heart. "Feel that, player? Hurts, just like you hurt her!"

Yanking the mortal's heart outside of his chest, Shade knew he had little time left before the man died. Shade held the beating heart in his hand in front of the mortal's face and squeezed it as it oozed between his fingers, and watched the life fade from Ethan's fear-filled eyes, knowing the last thing he saw was his own still beating heart being crushed in Shade's hand.

"You crushed her and now I crush you. For my queen! Death to you, bastard," he snarled.

Shade held the mortal in place, as his blood started pooling on the street. He could hear his warriors' growl as the smell of blood lured them. Shade could feel the sword coming at him, as Raven threw it to him. Shade caught the sword in midair with one hand and with a forceful strike, beheaded the bastard who'd never hurt his *bel* again.

Shade held the blonde head high in the air, as the mortal's limp body dropped to the street. Shade's roar echoed above the booming music. "*Per sempre*, Medici!"

He pitched the head in the alley, throwing the bloodied sword down. Walking out of the alley, he left the dead mortal for his warriors to dispose of. He felt his body tremble and shake. He didn't typically slay innocent mortals, but this was no *innocent* and he'd taken revenge for the only person that ever meant something to him, his light in the darkness. She'd always walk in the light with him for now and all eternity. This was for her and her alone. He couldn't erase her past or her memories, but he could remove the source of her pain.

75

Kate checked her calendar, trying to fit in everything she needed to finish at the Paris house, help Reynaldo get the house in California converted to an inn, and finish the nursery before Shade grounded her completely. Even though she felt great with this pregnancy, she knew he would always worry. She picked up the cell phone to call Reynaldo when she got an incoming call. Kate looked at the caller ID and saw Shannon's name. A smile spread across her face as she answered.

"Hey, Shan. What's up?"

Shannon immediately started talking, "Hey. Have you been watching the news?"

Kate scrunched up her face. "The news? I rarely turn the TV on anymore. Why, is something wrong?"

Shannon tugged at her hair as she paced the floor. "Well, weird, for sure. I thought you'd want to know. It's Ethan."

Kate rolled her eyes. "Ethan? Really? You called to tell me about Ethan? What's he doing now?"

Shannon shrugged. "Kate, he's missing. The news said his family filed a missing person's report about a week ago. He hasn't been at work. His apartment is untouched, no sign of forced entry or foul play. They found his car parked downtown near that bar where we all used to hang out. He's just...missing. He's just disappeared."

Kate was silent on the other end of the phone. She had a flash memory of Shade returning from D.C. last week, his shirt and jeans covered in blood, something she'd not seen in months. He was silent when he arrived, hurried in to take a shower and offered no explanation. And as usual, she didn't ask for one. He came to her after his shower, holding her, caressing her. They'd made love and he whispered no one would ever hurt her again. She'd thought it an odd thing to say, and when she asked him what he meant, he just smiled and kissed her. She shook her head, coincidence, it was just a coincidence. Why would Shade ever hurt Ethan? She's pretty sure she'd never mentioned Ethan by name when discussing him with Shade.

Shannon waited for her response, listening to the silence. "Kate? Are you still there?"

Kate's attention was pulled back to the present. "Yes, I'm here. I was just...thinking."

Shannon paused a minute. "You don't think...you know...I mean..."

Kate stopped her friend from finishing the sentence, "I'm sure he'll turn up. You know Ethan. He probably found some girl and they took off for the Bahamas or something. It's nothing."

Shannon paced, biting at her lip. She could feel Kate's tension, as they both danced around the possibilities of what they both knew.

"Yeah, I'm sure you're right. He'll turn up. Well, I just thought you'd want to know. No big loss, right? Just one less asshole in the world."

Kate nodded her head. "Yes...one less."

Shannon told her goodbye and told Kate she'd call if she heard anything, both of them knowing the world had heard the last of Ethan Young.

Kate responded, "Yeah, okay. See ya, Shan." Kate ended the call and walked to the window, looking out into the dark, seeing her own reflection in the glass. *What have you done, Shade?*

76

Shade left the warrior camp. It was time to go home. He loved the sound of that word as it rolled through his mind...*home*. Coming in through the patio doors, he stopped at his study, unloaded his weapon onto the desk and headed up the stairs to find his *bel*. As he walked inside the bedroom, he found her on the bed, the laptop balanced on her legs. He watched her for a few moments, her feet bare, and her belly round with their son.

"You look engaged in something, care to share, *mi amore*?"

Kate heard him as he came up the stairs. Her mind had been in turmoil since the call with Shannon. Her instincts told her there was a correlation between Shade and the disappearance of Ethan. But what if she was wrong? She'd been scanning the news reports online, looking for some clue. She didn't learn anything other than what Shannon had already told her. She remembered the bar mentioned in the news article. It *was* one they used to frequent, one of Ethan's favorites. She never liked it much, as it was just a *meat market*. Ethan would have her on his arm, but he'd always make eye contact with every other single female in the place. They fought about it often. She looked up at Shade when he spoke. "Shade, do you know Ethan?"

Blocking his thoughts from her immediately, he looked at her with a questioning expression. *I know he is dead, as the fucking bastard should be*. "Ethan? Doesn't ring a bell." Sitting down, he started unlacing his boots. *Who the fuck let the cat out of the bag? She knows!*

Kate watched him as he avoided eye contact. She felt the shield go up as he blocked his thoughts from her and busied himself, pulling off his boots. She studied him for a minute. He never looked at her, never flashed that smile. "You know, you're good at many things. Lying isn't one of them. Shannon called me today. She saw on the news where Ethan was missing, has been missing for about a week. I'm not angry, just confused. What are you keeping from me?"

Shade dropped his boots to the floor and looked up at her, pushing his hair from his eyes. "First of all, who the hell is Ethan? And why was he on the news? You are confused? Well, include me in that count, *si*?"

Kate pushed the laptop aside and slid off the bed, his agitation revealing more than he knew. Did she even want to know the answer to these questions? She walked to where he sat in the armchair and slipped into his lap.

"Ethan was the man I was engaged to before I met you. I'd just broken up with him. I don't think you ever met. In fact, I don't think I ever mentioned him by name. You never inquired about my past, and I was happy to leave him behind, and all the memories associated with him. So maybe it's nothing? But you don't go into D.C. very often, now that you have Raven in charge. So, perhaps it's a coincidence. Ethan's disappearance and you coming home in blood stained jeans and a shirt beyond cleaning."

Wrapping his arms around her, he kissed her neck gently. He knew he should tell her, she would eventually figure it out, if she hadn't already. He hated exposing her to the ugliness of the kill, and how fucking much pleasure it brought him to take that bastard out of this world.

"So, his name is Ethan. Is there something you want me to do? Do you want me to find him for you? As for my bloody clothes, it is not the first time you have seen them, Kate. Nor will it be the last."

Kate laid her head against his chest. Her instincts were telling her he knew exactly what happened to Ethan, but he wasn't going to open up to her about this. "I don't want you to find him, Shade. Ethan means nothing to me. You do whatever you need to do."

She knew. He could feel it. Shade ran his hand through her hair as she rested her head against his chest. "Let me ask a hypothetical question. What if I did make this Ethan disappear, how would that make you feel? I'm curious now that we seem to be on the subject because you more or less assumed I already did it."

Kate sat upright and locked eyes with him. "A hypothetical?" She knew this was no hypothetical. She looked down, processing the information. Shade wouldn't just randomly attack and kill him. Ethan would have done something, threatened him, or her.

"Honestly, lover, I feel nothing. Ethan used people. He felt privileged, like the rules didn't apply to him somehow. He was very charming, in the beginning. He was good at manipulating people to get what he wanted. But he had a cruel streak. I loved him, and he used that against me. He mocked me when his infidelities caused me such heartbreak. He laughed at my concept of romantic love, that one man could love one woman. He told me I'd better get with the times if I expected to keep a man. We broke up, and I'd been through so many disappointments with men, I thought he was right. That it was me, and my expectations were unrealistic. I'd sworn off men, and relationships, and then I went to Alec and Rissa's party, and there you were. I felt connected to you immediately, and it scared me to death. That's why I took off the way I did. Why I couldn't find my words. Later, Rissa warned me you were a player, and I couldn't bear the thought of having my heart broken again."

Kissing her lips, he let her feel the love he had for her, let it wrap around her like a cocoon.

"I was a player, mi amore, but in a different sense. My darkness and my beast made me do things I have come to regret. But a true love means devotion and loyalty, respect, and honor. Mortal men are capable of it, so they tell me. But I am very happy to hear you feel nothing for him. That if I had disposed of him, it would not bring you heartbreak. That pleases me. Some men deserve their ends, Kate. I hate what he did to you, how he made you feel, but in a way, I am very glad for it. I wanted you to know what love is, a soul that dances with your own. I just hope you never regret anything I ever did to be with you."

He had answered without answering. Kate knew he'd never speak of the details of what happened to Ethan. She knew that Ethan was no longer alive and the mortal world would find nothing. No clues would lead them to Shade, or anyone else. Ethan Young had just ceased to exist, and they'd never speak of it again.

"I've never regretted anything in our lives together. And I can't imagine I ever will. I no longer exist without you."

"Good. Then come to bed with me, I want you next to me in my death slumber."

Picking her up, he carried her to the bed, lying her down gently. He stripped from his leathers and climbed in and she curled onto his chest. They both knew, without saying the words that the world held one less bastard.

"I will always love you, mi amore, I will always protect you, and nothing in this world will ever hurt you again."

77

Luca sat with his feet on the desk in Shade's study, scanning the security cameras, the images flashing across the screens every few seconds. They had added cameras now to cover the drive and main gate to the warrior camp, as well as the perimeter of the wall around the camp. With the exception of the one incident about a week ago when Shade came back from D.C. in blood-soaked clothes, the activity at Bel Rosso and the Dead House had been slow, which was fine with Luca. Luca had made an inquiry of Shade at the time, asking if there was something happening in D.C., but Shade shrugged it off as nothing. Like Kate, Luca had also heard from Shannon about Kate's missing ex.

Shade was in the camp almost every evening now, and the rogue situation in D.C. seemed to have totally dissipated. Luca stood and stretched, thinking he'd take a smoke break when he saw two Virginia State Police patrol cars enter their property. The lead car paused as its headlights illuminated the sign that read 'Bel Rosso Vineyards', and then both cars continued up the drive.

"Fuck!" Luca sent a telepathic message to Shade right away. ***"Cop cars on the property, master. Taking the driveway to the main house."***

Luca stepped into the corridor outside the office where he saw Gi. They both exchanged a knowing glance and Gi told him he'd greet them at the door and stall for time. Luca teleported upstairs to the bedroom Kate was working on. It would soon be Theresa's, where he found both Theresa and Kate.

"Kate, cops are here. Stay upstairs until Gi calls you down. And for fuck sake, don't let Aegis respond to the cops!"

Kate looked at Luca, their eyes locked, and they both knew this was about Ethan. Kate felt a moment of panic and fought to gain control. She must protect him at all cost. She closed her eyes and called to Aegis, telling her to stay out of sight.

As soon as Shade heard Luca's warning in his head he knew exactly what this was about. This could be serious trouble. Teleporting from the camp inside the bedroom, he was a blur, changing out of his leathers and into jeans. Damn fucking bastard was still causing his woman chaos. Kate stepped inside their bedroom. Shade nodded to her, telepathically giving her instructions, ***"Play it cool, I am teleporting down to the study, show them in if you need me. Go!"***

She left the room, and he could feel her nervous anxiety as he immediately teleported into his study to wait their arrival. Tuning into her, he could feel and hear everything that was said. Making himself look busy, he looked like any other mortal businessman working in his study in the evening hours.

Gi responded to the doorbell, opening the door and greeting the police. "Good evening officers. How may I help you?"

The two policemen glanced over his shoulder, taking in the interior of the house as one of them spoke, "Does a Kate Reese live here?"

Gi nodded. "Well, she is Kate Medici now, but yes."

The officer made a note. "Could we speak with her please?"

Gi nodded. "Of course, please follow me."

He led the two officers to the living room where he asked them to be seated. "May I get you some wine?"

Both officers shook their head and gave him a weak smile. "No, thanks. On duty, you know. Maybe another time."

Gi nodded. "Make yourself comfortable and I will get Mrs. Medici." Gi walked to the foot of the stairs, and saw Kate standing at the top, waiting for him to summon her.

She had quickly run a brush through her hair but left her light sundress and sandals on. The loose fit of the dress skimmed over her belly, exposing her pregnancy. As Kate entered the living room, both officers stood.

Kate greeted them. "Officers? How can I help you? Please, have a seat."

The two men glanced at each other as they sat down. A petite pregnant woman didn't make a very good suspect in a missing person's case where the missing person was a six-foot man and foul play was suspected. The one officer cleared his throat.

"Sorry to intrude, ma'am, but we have a few questions we thought maybe you could help us with."

Kate sat down across from them. "Of course, whatever you need?"

The second officer threw a question at her. "You know Ethan Young?"

Kate nodded. "I do, yes. Ethan and I were engaged. I got a call from a friend a few days ago telling me he was missing."

The first officer asked her, "When was the last time you saw him?"

Kate scrunched up her face. "Last summer? We broke it off in August, so a little over a year ago."

The officer referred to his notes. They had been interviewing Ethan's friends. All of them said Kate was the one who broke off the engagement, and all of his buddies stated they'd never seen or heard anything from Kate after the break-up. Both officers took in her pregnant state.

The first officer nodded at her. "And you're married now?"

Kate smiled at them. "Yes, and expecting."

The second officer said, "That was quick."

Kate laughed. "Yes, it was. I met him in September, and well, everything happened really fast."

The second officer inquired, "Is your husband at home, Mrs. Medici?"

Kate nodded. "He should be working in his office. We have the vineyards here, plus more vineyards in California, as well as in Italy and Greece. Would you like to meet him?"

Both officers nodded. "If it wouldn't be any trouble."

Shade could hear them coming and had been listening `to their conversation. He knew they had nothing on him, so it was just a matter of providing an alibi for them both and sending them on their way. As the door opened and Kate introduced the officers, he quickly stood. Shaking their hands, he offered them a seat. "Shade Medici. Welcome to Bel Rosso Vineyards. How may I assist you this evening?"

Shade played it cool. This wasn't his first encounter with mortal law enforcement, and manipulating mortals was second hand to him.

The lead officer shook his hand before sitting. "Sorry for the intrusion on your evening, Mr. Medici."

The officer looked at his partner as they exchanged glances. This guy was huge, over six feet, and looked like he trained for the Navy Seals. Could he have experienced a little jealous rage over the old boyfriend?

"So, you must be aware of the missing person's report on your wife's ex, Ethan Young. You two know each other?"

Shade could feel their trepidation over his size, and he didn't miss their eye contact and the silent exchange between them.

"I am sorry, but I had never heard of Ethan Young before a few days ago when my wife told me about his disappearance." Looking to Kate, he smiled. "When I met my wife, it was through mutual friends. As you can well see, we fell in love at first site and are expecting our first child. She mentioned a breakup when I met her, but never mentioned his name. But I am sorry to hear he is missing."

The lead officer was flipping through his notes. All of Ethan's buddies said to the best of their knowledge, Ethan had never met Shade Medici. They'd heard through mutual friends Kate had hooked up with some Italian guy, but none of them knew him personally.

"Hmm. So, you never met him then? He never made any attempts to contact your wife?"

Chuckling, Shade made direct eye contact with the cop asking the questions. "I had no desire to meet him. He was not someone I ever cared to know. I am not aware of him ever trying to contact Kate after we were together. I feel she would have mentioned it. But I understand you must investigate all avenues of his disappearance, so I am more than willing to help in any capacity, as, I'm sure, will my wife."

The lead officer scribbled away in his notepad. This looked like a dead end. Kate Medici was too small and too pregnant to have dragged Ethan Young off. Plus, he couldn't think of why she'd want to. She'd clearly moved on. This Medici guy had a lot of money and looked like the guy who always got what he wanted, including the girl. He couldn't imagine he'd be intimidated by the likes of Ethan Young. He and his partner would continue to look for anyone that might have seen Kate and Ethan together, although that looked unlikely. But Mr. Medici didn't look like a husband who'd share his toys, so to speak. Any hint of old Ethan sniffing around his wife might be enough to push his buttons.

"One last question, if I may? Could you both verify your whereabouts for the night of Ethan's disappearance?"

Shade smiled. "Well, I don't think I even know the night of Ethan's disappearance, but I don't have to check the calendar. I'm afraid we live a very boring life. We are always here in the evenings, both of us. Feel free to interview the staff, our butler, or our housekeeper. I manage the vineyards from here, and both of them can verify that we're always home."

The two officers stood up. "Thank you for your time. Again, sorry to bother you."

Turning to Kate the lead officer asked her, "If you should by any chance hear from Ethan, you'll let us know?"

Kate nodded quickly. "Of course!"

Gi appeared at the study door, ready to escort the two police officers out. Kate and Shade followed along with them, saying goodbye to them at the door. They listened as the cars pulled around the driveway and headed away from the house.

Kate turned to Shade. "Please tell me they'll find nothing."

Shade took her in his arms, rubbing her back. "Relax, I do not need you upset. There is nothing to find. It is done now. And I am pretty sure he will not contact you. But trust me, if he did, I will deal with it."

Kate looked up at him. "Lover, we both know Ethan won't be contacting me. You have no secrets from your mate."

Leaning down, kissing her forehead, he smiled. "*Si*, none. So, let it go please? This is over and done with. No more."

Kate should ask why, but it didn't matter. Whatever the trigger, she'd forgive him anything. She'd seen his beast and knew that whatever happened to Ethan no mortal would ever discover. She stared back into those blue eyes and he revealed nothing.

She nodded her head. "Done. We won't speak of it again."

78

Gi sorted through the daily mail, tossing the nonessential mailers and sorting the mail for master and my lady. Among the day's deliveries was a very elaborately wrapped small flat box from the Canton's. Gi climbed the stairs to the nursery where my lady had been working with the designers on setting up the new baby's room.

"Excuse me, my lady, but this package arrived in the mail. It is addressed to both of you, but master is in the camp and I thought you might want to see this right away."

Kate looked up from the fabric swatches she'd been matching to the blue-grey paint on the wall. "Thank you Gi."

She stood up straight, placing both hands on the small of her back as she stretched, the swell of her belly prominent now. "I could use a break anyway."

Kate took a seat in the rocking chair as Gi brought her the small package.

"You look well today, my lady."

Kate laughed, placing her hand on her belly. "We feel well Gi, thank you."

She took the package and slid the satin ribbon from the box and lifted the lid, exposing the hand written invitation with a diamond broach affixed. Kate raised an eyebrow. "Well, it certainly has Rissa's style."

She read the invitation to the wedding, four months out. She leaned her head back against the rocker, closing her eyes as she gently rocked in the chair.

"Looks like I'll be going to a wedding, Lorenzo."

As she rocked in the chair she heard the clamor of boots on the tiles on the floor below and knew he was home.

Shade came in from camp. The nights had been long, but the new warriors were learning what they needed. The instruction had been intense and was becoming more so every night. He knew there was still much to be done, but he was pleased with their progress. The smell of roses wafted in every corner of their home and he headed up the staircase, letting his nose lead him. Peering around the corner, he found her sitting in the nursery, rocking in the huge chair. His smile was wide as he watched her belly grow every single day. In her lap was a small box, and she held a card in her hand.

"You look beautiful, *mi amore*."

His eyes scanned the room, taking in the details of the décor she was creating for their son. Walking to her, he leaned down and kissed her softly before crouching down beside her.

"I love coming home to you."

"And I love when you come home." She ran her hand through his dark locks. "Your son has been active today. I think he knows I'm getting this room ready for him."

Shade placed his hand over her belly, looking up and smiling at her. "Active is a good sign. But you will tell me if it takes its toll, *si*? Do not overdo. Others can be told how and what you need done. I have a feeling our son will become more active as his time to be with us nears."

Kate held up the elaborate invitation. "We have an invitation to Alec and Rissa's wedding. Lorenzo will be a few weeks old, still too young to be among mortals. Typical Rissa, she's pulled out all the stops. The wedding is at the National Cathedral, and the reception is in the Old Post Office building. I can't imagine what this wedding is going to cost, but I assume our attendance is pretty much mandatory, especially since they came to Florence for the coronation."

Shade looked at the extravagance of the invitation and laughed. "I am sorry, *mi amore*, but I find it amusing she is spending Alec's money as if it is endless. And yes, to answer your question, attending will be mandatory and there will be a lot of work on my part. Medici warriors will be providing security for the biggest event in Washington since the last inauguration. This city is hard enough to control, but this wedding will bring in many outside dignitaries. Most will be mortal, but there will be a few immortals as well. It will be very different than your coronation. Council is not keen on his antics of portraying himself as mortal. And they are not exactly happy with my participation in such."

Shade took the invitation and read the detail. "December, it is not far off. I have been preparing the new warriors to oversee the security of Bel Rosso while the experienced warriors will be assigned to D.C. I need to talk to Alec about this. It will be here before we know it."

Kate ran her hand over the swell of her belly. "I can't believe how fast the time is flying by. Luca will stay here, right? He'll be here with Lorenzo, along with Theresa?"

Shade let his hand slide along her cheek. He knew she'd be protective over their babies. "*Si*, Luca will stay here. There will be times, even when he is small that you will need to leave him to do other things. Leaving him in the hands of others to protect, *si*?"

Kate locked eyes with him. He knew her heart and how tightly she'd cling to this baby. "I understand, lover...and I know Luca will protect him, but it's still hard for me to let go."

Never taking his eyes from hers, he took her hand in his, placing it over his heart. "We will always protect our prince. No matter what comes, we are both immortal and he will be much stronger than any mortal *bambino*."

His words poured over her like honey, and she knew she could trust him, with her life and the life of their children to come. There was nothing he'd guard more closely. "Of course, I'll follow your lead, but you know I'll never really let go. Not completely."

Shade kissed her gently, sliding his tongue over her lips, nipping them softly. "*Si*, I expected nothing less. I need to speak with Alec, so I will be down in my office, is there something you need?"

"No, I'm fine, and I still have some things to finish here before your slumber. Go finish up your work and come find me when you're ready for bed."

"*Si*." Kissing her once more, then leaning down he kissed her tummy, talking to Lorenzo in a soft but stern voice. "As for you, *figlio*, lay off the warrior activities, your *madre* is tired, she has much to accomplish! You know I love you, and your time will come soon enough, but for now, give your *madre* a break!"

Standing, he kissed the top of Kate's head, her crimson locks soft against his face and he inhaled deeply. "I will try not to be too long, *si*?"

Walking downstairs, he went into his office, closing the door.

***

It was early morning, before sunrise, and Alec slept lightly, feeling Rissa curled tightly against him. He rarely required deep sleep, and the older he got the less sleep he required. He was lying still, waiting for the alarm when he heard the soft vibration of his cell phone. He reached across her to the nightstand and picked up the phone to see Shade on the ID. Slipping from beneath the covers, he threw his feet to the floor, seated on the side of the bed, running one hand through his hair. He answered the call as he reached for a cigarette, lighting up, the red glow of the cigarette bright in the dark room. He exhaled before speaking.

"Hello, Shade. What's up?"

"A lot. I know it is damn early for you to be up, apologies, but we need to have a serious conversation on a few key things coming up in the future. One of them being this mortal wedding you plan on pulling off. Tell me when you can meet to talk with me, Alec. Both of us are going to get busier and the planning needs to start now. I have a son arriving and I want this down pat before that happens."

Alec took a deep drag on the cigarette and exhaled again. "Ah yes, the wedding. The President will be there, as will most of Congress, so the place will be crawling with Secret Service as well as the D.C. police. But there will be immortals there as well. It was scheduled for evening, so we could accommodate the immortals, and because Rissa wanted formal. So yes, we'll need your warriors out in full force. God forbid we have an incident in full view of all the press. We can wipe memories, but not photos and video coverage."

Shade threw his booted feet up on the desk, leaning back in his chair, thinking about the nightmare this could end up being.

"We can handle this. I need you to relax. My warriors know their shit. I am having everyone out in full force. I will work with Raven and we can coordinate everything we will need once we get closer. Secret Service can handle almost any mortal threat. We will focus on the immortals, and remove any problem long before the mortals know they are there. How is Hyde working out with Rissa? I will need to have him on the inside, brother. He will be at her side before the ceremony, close at hand during and then it's up to you how you want to handle things with her once this show is over. Tell me they are getting along, because I have no damn time to come up with another protector beforehand."

Alec chuckled. "Oh, Hyde is working out fine. Rissa is quite enamored with him, in fact. He's played it cool, and remains very professional, much to her dismay, I think. But they're getting along fine. So, have him in a tux if he's working inside, and you may want a few others on the inside, just in case. You'll have to clean them up to look civilized and stick them in a tux. I'll inform the Secret Service that I'll have private security as well, so maybe if your goon squad could tone down the leathers for one evening and look a little more mortal."

Shade smirked, always the fucking prancy-ass. "Those goons keep your ass alive, remember that. I have a few I will put on the inside. Fiamma will be one of them. They never look for female warriors. We will have rooftop to ground coverage brother. Just curious, did you give Rissa full reign of your damn bank accounts? We got the invitation tonight, she went all out. You would fucking think you were the damn president already!"

Alec flicked the ash of his cigarette in the ashtray. "As for my bank account, I've found it's easier to let Rissa have her way. She was quite jealous of the coronation, so I was prepared to see her go all out on this wedding. You know Rissa. She'll have the last word."

Shade smirked, he knew Rissa all too well. "At least she has accepted Hyde. He seems fine with the arrangement as well. Once the event gets closer we will coordinate and make sure there is nothing we have missed. I've been busy as hell out here. Have the feeder compound up and running now as well, camp is doing fine. The new recruits are working their asses off. We need to get this potion business settled as well brother. I have talked to Kate about it."

Alec took a drag on the cigarette. "Does this mean you're accepting my offer on the potion?"

Shade's feet hit the floor, he walked to the side door, lighting up a smoke once outside, the sun almost ready to break out for the day.

"Look, Alec, I want this potion, I want everything that comes with it. This is a weapon that is vital and can make my services the most elite in the world. I'm building. I have big plans, and the potion could be part of those plans. But we need to talk seriously about what you expect out of me in exchange. Protecting you and yours for all of eternity is out of the question. Who the hell knows what is ahead for us. We both have enough enemies to ignite a war like no immortals have ever seen."

Shade stubbed out his smoke and waited for Alec's response.

Alec lay back on the bed, turning his head slightly to see Rissa still sleeping soundly. He knew when he asked that the potion was a powerful tool, and requesting Shade to accept it for payment for all services in the future was a stretch, but he had to at least ask.

"So how long then? How many years does the potion buy me? It's another year before I start actively campaigning, and if I win, then we're looking at a minimum of four years in the Presidency, and hopefully, I'll win a second term and go for eight. So, ten years? Certainly, you can give me ten years. After that, who knows where I'll go anyway."

Walking back inside, Shade listened and knew *bel* had gone to their bedroom and was waiting for him. He was careful how he committed his time these days, things were very different in his life now. Walking back into the study, he paced the floor, running his fingers through his tangled locks.

"Ten years is fair, Alec. It will take me a while to get where I need to go, my son will have to be trained, prepared. Neither of us knows the future. But you get that Presidency, you have my backing. I'm here in Virginia for the long haul, brother. This is home for me now. I have invested my future here. You want ten years, let's do it, once ten is up, we will talk. But I want the rights to that potion exclusively, free and clear. Deal?"

Alec sighed, wondering at his path and where it would lead. "Deal, brother. Don't you ever grow weary of it old friend? Don't you grow tired of all the scheming, the hiding, all the game-playing?"

Shade heard the tiredness in his old friend's voice and wondered at the strangeness of his inquiry. "I lost it all once, Alec. I had to start over and it brought me here. I'm never done. It keeps me moving, keeps me alive. Once I let it all go, something will trip my ass up and it will be the death of me. Now, I have even more to lose, my mate, my son. It's a new life for me now. I see things differently. All that fucked up hell in my life was bringing me here to her. What the hell has you talking like this, not like you to be getting all philosophical on me? Perhaps you have become too involved with the mortals, their petty bullshit, you need to step back into the immortal world and get your bearings."

Alec chuckled. "Nothing. It's nothing. I didn't mean to turn this into a therapy session. You have a different life, a different motivation. Makes me wonder about my choices. But that's my path to follow, and your job is to protect my ass, so let's just keep it at that, shall we? So, ten years and then we renegotiate. I can live with that. Anything else on your mind?"

Shade knew Alec. He was never philosophical, never doubted. Something had him in knots. "Nothing brother, nothing on my mind. Look, I got everything covered. I'm here if you need me. You know the number."

Hanging up Shade heard the electronic blinds going down for the breaking dawn. He could honestly say that was the oddest phone call he'd ever had with Alec. Tossing his phone on the desk, he headed to the bedroom, his death slumber knocking hard and he wanted his woman in his arms before it took him.

79

The nursery was almost complete, as Kate supervised the placement of the furniture, including a sleeper sofa that Theresa could use when she needed to sleep in the baby's room, even though she'd have her own room in the house soon. The designer and the workers took their leave and Kate looked around the room. It looked completely different than the first nursery. She wanted nothing that seemed the same. Instead of the gender-neutral red checks, she'd gone with a bluish-gray color on the walls and a crib that was black enamel. The bookcases were white, as was Theresa's sofa. Kate added color to the room with bright storybook animal print throw pillows on the sofa and the curtains. There was one last piece to add, and it was a large, colorful abstract oil painting Luca painted in primary colors that Kate wanted to hang over the crib. Walking to the top of the stairs she called down to Theresa, "Theresa, could you help me in the nursery please?"

Theresa was making a sweep of the downstairs living quarters with the duster, keeping busy. The house was growing with the new addition for Cory, and the baby on the way. Hearing Kate call to her, she quickly slid the duster into her apron pocket and rushed up the stairs to the nursery.

"You called, my lady? Oh, the nursery looks beautiful, a good choice of colors!"

Kate dragged the large canvas out from behind the crib. "Thanks. I want to hang this over the crib, and then I'll be done. But I think I'll need some help with it."

"My lady, you shouldn't drag such things. Please let me help you. I see they've hung two nails and leveled those, so it will be easy to hang, just awkward."

As they lifted each end, they attached the painting to the wall and stood back to admire the work.

"Oh, my heaven, my side is a bit tilted!" Theresa shifted the painting slightly, aligning it to hang properly, she stepped back with her hands on her hips. "I think that should do it."

Kate admired the art. There was nothing about the piece that indicated it was created for a nursery. But Kate knew the baby's eyes would be drawn to the bright splashes of color.

"Thank you, Theresa. Would you like to help me make up the sofa bed? Your bedroom will be close by, and I know Shade wants Lorenzo to stay in the cradle in our bedroom for the first few weeks, at least, while he feeds exclusively from me. I thought having a place for you to lie down might give you more rest on days...or nights, the baby is restless. I guess we'll have to wait and see if he's a day-walker like us or will be pulled to his death slumber like his father. Either way, both of our lives are about to dramatically change."

Theresa smiled at her, she loved Kate. She knew deep in her heart she'd be a good mother to her babies.

"I love this room, my lady, and so will Lorenzo. It will transition well from baby to small boy. His gifts will be known to you soon enough. Although they're small, they're different from mortal *bambinos*. They'll walk and talk earlier and be very intelligent and curious about the world around them. It will be a task to keep them in hand, but one I'll enjoy. I'm so happy to be here and honored to be serving you and master."

As she helped fluff pillows for the sofa bed, she knew Kate had yet to think about the wet feeders and she needed to attend to this.

"My lady, have you given any thought to the wet feeders? I don't wish to speak out of turn, but you should be taking care of that as soon as possible. I know you're busy, but it will be important to have that ready to go ahead of time."

Kate sat down on the sofa bed, smoothing the blanket with her hand. "I think about it. I have the list Dr. Bonutti gave us. I keep putting it off because I'm not sure I know what to look for."

Theresa sat down beside her. "Did you know what you were looking for when you chose Luca as your protector?"

Kate looked up at her. "No, I didn't. Shade told me to follow my heart. He had already selected warriors who were qualified, and said I should find the one I felt a connection to."

Theresa nodded. "*Si*. And you found him, because something inside told you he was the one, am I correct?"

Kate smiled as she remembered her nerves on that day. "Yes, there was a definite connection to him, and he's been perfect for me, and for Shade. But a feeder, I'm not sure I'll feel any connection with a feeder."

Theresa laid her hand on top of Kate's and could feel the tension even this conversation gave her. "You may not feel a connection, but the *bambino* will. He'll give you a sign when you find the right one. It's a feeling you get. They're quite harmless, the wet feeders, but the *bambino* must connect with them to feed. I've known very few who did not match well.

"Dr. Bonutti gave you a list, it's easy to have the feeders come here at appointed times. I can arrange that for you. I can be with you while you speak with them."

Kate nodded her head. "Thank you. I'd appreciate your help, and whatever guidance you can provide. I know I've put this off, so if you don't mind setting something up. Everyone's told me they're different, not like the feeders for the adults, but it's a hard concept for me to grasp. The list is in Shade's office. Would you...take care of it?"

Theresa patted her hand. "You let me worry about that. I'll gladly do it and help you in any way I can. My lady, they feel nothing sexual, just as the baby feels nothing sexual when he feeds from us. They are a food source only, allowing the female to return to feeding her mate. The feeder won't live here in the house, but in the staff quarters. Please don't upset yourself. I know this is new and must seem quite strange to you. But after you meet them, you'll understand, they will bond with Lorenzo, become someone who is a source of comfort to him. They take nothing from you, or Master Shade."

Theresa smiled at her, "You look so beautiful, my lady. You glow from this pregnancy. There are so many that are waiting for the little Prince. I know I'm so excited to welcome him into the world!"

Kate beamed at the thought of him. "I can't wait to hold him. I feel his energy every day and he grows stronger. He'll be so much like Shade."

Theresa stood and shook her head. "Heaven help us!"

80

Theresa set up the patio in the back of the house to meet with the wet feeders. It was a beautiful late summers' evening and the garden was in its last glory. She set out a few bottles of Midnight along with some wine glasses and put some flowers from the garden in a vase, at the center of the patio table. She lit many candles, and created a soft and relaxing atmosphere.

She'd arranged for the feeders to meet with Kate one at a time. Dr. Bonutti had given them a list of ten names, and Theresa had narrowed it down to three based on what she knew Kate would be drawn to. She'd arranged for the wet feeders to teleport in and held them now in her room in the staff quarters. Theresa felt holding the interviews on the patio might be less threatening to Kate than having the wet-feeders in her home until she was comfortable with this idea.

Theresa let Kate know everything was ready, and Kate joined her outside. Aegis appeared immediately, and Kate calmed the wolf, rubbing her head as the wolf curled up at her feet.

As the evening progressed, Kate had interviewed two of the prospective wet-feeders and Theresa thought she'd managed it well, even though she sensed Kate's nervousness. Kate returned to the patio after taking a small break, Theresa smiled at her.

"There's only one more, my lady, her name is Nita. Don't feel pressure if she's not someone you wish to have, there are more feeders on the list from Dr. Bonutti. Would you like a glass of Midnight?"

Kate sat down at the table, accepting the glass of wine Theresa poured for her. "Thank you, yes. Maybe that will help." Kate took a small sip. "They were very nice Theresa, and not at all what I expected. They're so young, just girls really. They look almost nymph-like. I'm relieved, but still, putting my child in their hands. I have to feel something! Let's see this last one please, so we know if we must continue this search."

"Relax, my lady, as I've said, Lorenzo will let you know."

Theresa walked over to the staff quarters to find Nita waiting patiently. Leading her out along the garden path back to the house, the young wet-feeder seemed entranced by her surroundings. Theresa made the introductions and took her seat quietly next to Kate. Nita bowed slightly, as she was introduced to their queen and took a seat at the table across from her.

"I'm honored to have this opportunity. It's my first time in the States, it's beautiful here. It looks a bit like Tuscany, my homeland."

Kate smiled at the sound of her voice. It was soft, angelic, and almost musical in its lilt and soft Italian accent. It soothed her instantly, and Lorenzo who'd been busy kicking all night suddenly settled down as well.

"Welcome, Nita. We've tried hard to make the property look as much like the Tuscan home Shade is used to. The house, of course, is designed very much like a Tuscan villa, but yes, these rolling hills and the mountains, the vineyards, they all look very much like Tuscany. So, the other wet-feeders spoke of their experience with other families where they've served. Would you like to tell us about where you worked before?"

Looking down quickly, Nita fumbled with her fingers as a nervous habit. Raising her large eyes, she smiled, hoping the next statement wouldn't keep her from being selected as the small prince's wet feeder. "My Queen, I've not worked for any family. This will be my first baby to wet feed. If you wish for me to leave, I'll understand."

Kate felt Lorenzo roll over inside her at the same time she reached out to Nita, taking her hand. "No. Don't leave. It pleases me that you haven't fed others. You'll be pure for my son. He's a prince, and he'll be a warrior like his father. He'll need pure blood to make him strong, powerful. Your voice soothes me, as it soothes him. You understand you must live here, leave Italy permanently...or at least until Lorenzo is old enough to move to the camp in Italy. Then you'd be required to follow him back to Florence."

As the queen grabbed her hand, Nita felt something warm and giving flow through her, something caring and understanding. She'd heard the queen was kind and loving to her people and Nita was finding that to be true.

"Oh, *si*, my queen, I'm most willing to be here for however long you wish me to be here for the prince. I have very pure blood. I have experience with babies. We are all trained in their care. We are trained how to feed, cuddle, and hold them properly. We know how to soothe them when they are agitated. I also sing. It comforts them, helps them relax and feed. I know many Italian lullabies. I'll learn American ones as well, if you wish. If you choose me, I'll serve you and the prince well. It's what I was born to do, and I'd spend my entire lifetime with him, if necessary, to see him grow and be strong like our king."

Kate knew in her heart Nita was the right choice, but Shade should meet her as well. He'd want to have a say in who nurtured his son. **"Shade, please join me on the patio. I want you to make the final choice on Lorenzo's feeder."**

"I'm sure you can be happy here, Nita. Theresa will be his nanny and live inside the house. But the staff quarters are well appointed. Our chef has recently relocated to California, and his suite can be modified to your taste. But before we decide, I've asked Shade to join us."

Shade was helping Skelk set up some moving targets when he heard *bel* ask him to come meet a wet feeder. He quickly excused himself from Skelk. Teleporting into the main house, he peeped out the window where he could see Theresa and Kate at the patio table chatting with a young feeder. He quickly went upstairs, washed up a bit, getting the dirt and grime from his face and hands. He threw on a clean tee shirt, tucking it into his jeans, as he headed outside.

Nita suddenly became very nervous hearing her master and king would be arriving. She didn't know she'd be presented to him. She saw him walking out and she stood and lowered her head in respect. Shade acknowledged her and asked her to sit, as he stepped up behind *bel* and kissed her neck softly.

"Lover, this is Nita. Theresa and I have met with other wet feeders this evening, but I'm most drawn to Nita." Kate took his hand and placed it on her belly. "As is your son. Talk with her and let her know her fate. Is she the one?"

Shade looked at the small girl that sat meekly with her head still bowed. "Nita, please look at me."

Nita heard his low voice and was almost frightened. He was powerful, and she'd only seen him from a great distance. Wet feeders were quite sheltered, raised to be pure and clean, feeders for the children of masters. Raising her eyes, she responded, "Master."

Shade smiled at her and cocked his head. "Well, it seems my queen likes you and if my *figlio* approves, you have crossed two very huge hurdles. I only have a few questions. Where in Italy are you from?"

Nita swallowed hard, hoping her voice didn't squeak from her nerves. "I'm from Tuscany, master. I grew up in Poggio a Caiano, not far from the Medici's summer villa."

Shade chuckled. "Ah yes, the villa. I remember it well. It slipped from the hands of the Medici's over the years. It is now open to the tourist, *si*? It was a grand home, purchased originally by another Medici, a mortal named Lorenzo. This is a good sign, is it not? Might I offer you a drink of Midnight?"

Nita held up her hand. "No. I don't drink, master. I've never had alcohol. I thank you for the offer though."

Shade turned to *bel*. "Is there anything special I should know about Nita?"

"Only that she is pure. She's never fed another. Her voice soothes Lorenzo even now."

Shade sat down in the chair next to Kate, sliding his arm around her. "Pure is important for his growth as a warrior, Nita. You must stay with him until he is grown or has no more use for a wet feeder. You will be well paid for your dedication and service to my son. Is there anything else you wish to tell me? Convince me you wish to be here."

Nita cleared her throat to speak. "Master, I know your son will be a warrior, a strong and courageous Medici. While he's small, he will need to feed and sleep to help his growth. I can sing. I love to sing, and it helps comfort the baby."

Shade nodded to her. "Then, by all means, Nita, let us hear your voice and let us see how my *figlio* reacts to such."

Nita stood and began to sing, her voice soft and sweet and echoed in the summer night as she sang an Italian lullaby. *"Dormi dormi bel bambino..."*

Nita sang with the voice of an angel, and Lorenzo did a slow stretch and turned over in Kate's womb, before curling up again in a tight ball, quiet and still. Kate ran her hand across her belly and smiled. "Your son has chosen, lover."

Shade leaned over and kissed *bel* softly. He laid his hand on the swell of her belly and could feel his son comforted by the song.

"*Si*, he has chosen, and so has his *padre*. We welcome you, Nita. You hold a great responsibility to the Prince. It is an honor to serve me and the Medici coven in your duties. I hope I will hear that voice on many a night, as it will give great relief to your queen and me to know he is held with love and comforted by your blood. Kate will see to getting you settled in when the time comes."

He turned to *bel*. "You have made a good choice and I am most pleased."

81

Shade had tucked *bel* into bed and made sure she was resting, her insistence she was fine was lessening, and she was more open to his request for her to rest. The baby was taking his toll on her energy and endurance.

As he walked to the camp, he realized the sun was up much less now as they moved into the beginning of fall. Before long, the mountains would be flush with color, as if they were on fire. He heard very little noise coming from the camp and knew the night was just beginning for his warriors. He made a quick detour to the stables, talking with Angelo, making sure things were going well and the horses were healthy. Checking on Biondo, he was glad to hear Rissa rode often in the evenings. Hell, he was glad someone was making use of the horses and stables. He never seemed to have enough time to do anything pleasurable lately.

His mind was preoccupied with the coming of the Prince of Medici. He'd made arrangements so Castello was prepared for their arrival at a moment's notice, he was taking no chances. He had Dante on standby with the jet and Theresa was prepared to go as well. Now, if he could just settle his mind and calm his nerves. Becoming a father was more than he'd bargained for and the closer the time came for Lorenzo's arrival, the more anxious and worried he became that all would go well. Leaving the stables, he headed into the camp where the recruits began their nightly warm up and soon, they'd start their regimented lessons for the night.

His eyes scanned over the warriors and he felt their movements seemed sluggish. He walked around the training field and every one of them appeared as though they were coming off some wild night. Then it struck him. He knew that feeling, and it came from one thing, overindulging in blood. Damn feeders! He didn't need this shit going down in his camp.

New, young warriors were susceptible to the lure to overfeed if they weren't regulated with a heavy hand. He saw Fiamma working her group and his temper flared. He looked for Marcello, but he was nowhere to be found. Marching across the field, his temper building quickly, he spotted Raven leaving the main barracks. Shade whistled and yelled loud enough for them to hear him in Charlottesville.

"Raven, send your warriors to the Dead House. You stay the fuck here with these warriors until I return."

Raven raised his hand in acknowledgment and strolled out onto the field. Shade made his way straight to Fiamma as she stood dumbfounded, staring at him.

"Inside, now!"

Fiamma nodded and followed him inside, wondering what in the hell had him so stirred up. He'd been acting a bit off lately, but he was about to blow a fang and she knew this couldn't be good.

Marching inside the barracks, Shade turned on Fiamma. "Where is Marcello?"

Fiamma looked at him and had to think for a second. "He's down at the feeder compound tunnel, checking on the door."

Shade stood with his hands on his hips. "Checking on the door? Damn it, Fee! Are you blind? What in the hell is going on with the feeders and the warriors? This is not a fucking vacation!"

He paced, his hand immediately going through his hair, his temper flaring as he tried to keep his anger under control.

"Master, please, Marcello goes down in the evenings and makes sure the warriors return from the compound. He's doing his duty."

Shade spun around on her. "Well, someone is not doing something right! The recruits are slow. *Cazzo*, can't you see they have overfed? What the hell is going on?"

Fiamma took a deep breath, her temper flaring. "I beg to differ with you, master. We have a great matron who runs it with a strict hand, so before you go off the handle with me, perhaps you should figure out what the true dilemma is."

Shade went toe to toe with her, their noses almost touching, eyes locked. "Don't push me, Fee, I am in no mood to take your backtalk. Who in the hell sets up their feeding schedules? You? Are you doing it?"

Fiamma locked eyes with him and didn't back down. What in the hell is wrong with him? "*Si*, I make the feeding schedules, regulate them, rotate the warriors. I have no complaints, nor have I noticed any major issues."

Shade backed away and growled. "Apparently, you give them way too long to feed. They are sluggish, overindulged in blood. *Cazzo*! The American warriors are young and not used to the purity of the Euro feeders."

Marcello entered the room, his master's bellowing heard loud and clear in the tunnels. The two warriors behind him stopped dead in their tracks, as Marcello quickly sent them out another door and out to the field with their brothers and sisters.

Marcello looked at Fiamma and knew she was taking the brunt of his anger. "Fiamma is doing her job well, master. We all are. I could hear you in the tunnels, what's the problem?"

Shade spun on his heels and stared at Marcello. "Well, I am so glad you heard me in the fucking tunnels! What in the hell is going on, you are my SIC for fuck's sake? I have got warriors who are overstimulated with blood. Guarding the fucking tunnel door, are you?"

Marcello stood with his head high, he knew his duties and Shade had been under a lot of stress lately. He knew Shade clearly wasn't feeding regularly either and they'd all bear the brunt of his anger and stress.

"I escort the warriors back up to the barracks from the tunnel, making sure they get their asses back when they're supposed to. No feeders come with them. That's what our queen and Fiamma agreed upon. Did you wish to change that?"

Shade slammed his hands flat against the barracks wall. "No! They need to have a shorter period to be down there. Fix it. There is a lot these warriors need to learn. Damn it, Marcello, you know the wedding is coming quickly, I need to have some of these warriors on the streets with us in D.C. when it goes down."

Spinning around, he growled loudly. "Do you think they are ready to take on D.C.? Because what I just witnessed out there is not up to Medici standards. Not one fucking mistake can happen at this event. My fucking ass and reputation are going to be on the line! Every single warrior will be put to use that night, either here at Bel Rosso or in D.C. And we have one hell of a lot to accomplish and only two months to get them ready. This lies on my head. Mine! I spend hours with Raven going over grids and arrangements for one damn night. So, fix it!"

Marcello listened as he saw Shade's anger go off the charts. His emotional state was barely under control and Marcello could only hope that once the queen had their son, he'd begin to calm down.

Marcello nodded. "Consider it done. Fiamma and I will work together and cut back their feeder time. It won't happen again. The recruits are coming along fast, much faster than either of us expected. We'll begin, within the week, to send them out to the Dead House with Raven to work the area, become familiar with it. Give us a chance to make it right, master."

Shade hung his head, taking a deep breath, his eyes closed. He knew he was asking a great deal from them both, and it was taking its toll on everyone. He needed to get his act together and be the Medici and master they expected.

"I apologize to both of you. I have a short temper, right now. There is so much to plan and be prepared for. This camp is different, run different than Florence. I want it to start off right, continue on schedule. I knew changes would be necessary. Just shorten their feeder time slots, and we will see how that goes. I am not used to having a damn feeder coven housed on the grounds. I suppose I have forgotten what it feels like to live in the barracks, feed on a schedule, and work my ass to the bone. I know my mind is on many things lately."

Without looking at either of them, he marched out the door, already beating himself up for taking out his frustrations on the two warriors he knew were doing more than expected to make Medici stronger and powerful.

As Marcello watched him leave, he turned to Fee. "You okay?"

Fiamma shrugged. "Of course. But I'm worried about him. Not like him to go off like that so quickly. I didn't see the recruits as being sluggish at all. I was out there with them."

Walking to her, he gave her a hug. "Well, I think he's never been a father before either, even though Cory is his son, he wasn't there to witness a birth, nor have to deal with all that comes with it. I think once the baby is here and he gets to feed from the queen again, and this damn wedding is over with, he should get back to normal. But until then, we need to do all we can and humor him."

Fiamma closed her eyes and gave herself up to the small gesture of the hug. Marcello was her brother-in-arms, but she knew the rules, no fraternization among the troops. Secretly, he was someone she wished would see her more as a female, and not just his sister-in-arms.

Fiamma chuckled. "Humor him. Easier said than done!"

As they both laughed Marcello fist bumped her, and they headed back out on the field, but they didn't see their master anywhere in sight. Marcello released Raven from the field and they settled in for the long night of working the warrior's asses off.

Shade had teleported straight from the door of the barracks to the wall outside the warrior camp. He wanted no more contact with the warriors, he'd lost his temper and he knew he needed to cool off. His booted feet began walking heavily and fast to the stables. Out of nowhere, he saw Night-Stalker pacing and prancing ahead of him. It appeared someone else was just as worked up as he was. Night-Stalker paced beside him.

"This *padre* thing makes me agitated as hell, *si*?" Night-Stalker howled and Shade shook his head as they both kept making their way to the stables.

Cory heard Shade yelling from his workplace in the barracks and stepped outside his door, listening intently. His father was royally pissed off. He could feel him when he teleported out and Cory decided to follow him, keeping some distance behind his dad. He saw the black wolf, and heard Shade as he spoke to the wolf who howled in response.

Cory knew his dad was stressing out, but he never thought he'd see him lose it like that. He was always in control, always thinking things through, but for once, Cory sensed he needed help, and Cory hoped he could make a difference.

"Dad! Hold up."

Shade heard Cory and turned to see him jogging up behind him. Would he ever get used to someone calling him dad? "Cory, what's wrong?"

Cory caught up with him and shook his head. "Nothing's wrong with me, what's wrong with you? Where are you going?"

Shade took a deep breath. "A lot of things need to be done, that is all, and I seem to not have control of them, at the moment. I was headed for the stables. I need to ride, let off some steam. You want to come along?"

Cory laughed. "Uh, no. I'll walk with you, but I have a lot to get done myself. And the only thing I ride is a skateboard."

Shade laughed and threw his arm around his son. "To each his own."

Cory walked with him and decided to defend his brothers and sisters. "You know everyone is working really hard at the camp, including me. No one's slacking. Everyone is really aware of what's coming. They take their responsibility of being a warrior seriously. You gave everyone their duties and they're doing them. We're all working together for Medici. It's cool to be a part of this. See how it works, how everyone has a place and a job. It's okay to get stressed out. You have a lot on your plate."

Shade stopped walking and looked at Cory. Shade locked eyes with him and stared. "I know I ask a lot from everyone. Sometimes, it gets more than even I can handle. I have stretched myself thin with properties, the coven, and the camp. Trying to keep it all in line, even with a great coven to help me, is not always easy. I am glad you understand what I do, what it takes. But do not ever worry, I am fine. I just need to step back and let those I give responsibly to have a chance to carry them out. My own *padre* flew into rages often, and I never understood it. He had so many people helping him, just like me. Made no sense how in the hell you could have so many others doing the work and yet, you could get so angry. Now I understand. Hell, my *padre* didn't have half of what I have now."

Cory placed his hands on his dad's broad shoulders. "You're not your dad. You are your own person. And we are going to help you to get it right and keep Medici the best."

Shade let go of the anger and stress. Hugging Cory to his chest, he sighed heavily. "I don't know when or how, but you became Medici right before my eyes, son."

Cory pulled back and grinned. "It's the hair, man!" Cory turned and headed back to camp, as he heard his dad roar with laughter.

82

Dr. Bonutti had spent the evening with a colleague at Johns Hopkins. The immortals always kept an intense eye on the discoveries of blood pathology. Keeping tabs on their work in the mortal world was important to make sure mortals never uncovered any discoveries related to the immortals. He decided while he was so close to Virginia, he'd take a chance and visit his king and queen while in the States. Besides, after spending the few days in Baltimore, a visit to their beautiful estate with its clean air and beautiful mountain views would be a nice break.

The Medici had become a powerful vampire in his years and now his lovely queen was bringing forth a son, an assurance of many more years of Medici rule and that pleased the doctor. Having been forewarned by Gi about Kate's gift of Animalism, and given an open invitation, he teleported directly into the foyer of the Virginia estate. Teleporting directly into any vampire's home without their express consent was an automatic death sentence from Council, as it gave the vampire no forewarning. It was viewed as an act of aggression against which the vampire had no time to defend themselves or take action against such an invader. It was a high privilege to be granted such consent, especially by a vampire of Shade's standing, and Dr Bonutti didn't take it lightly. Gi greeted him immediately and showed him to the living room.

"Doctor, what a pleasant surprise. Was my lady expecting you? She didn't inform me of your visit."

Dr. Bonutti shook his head. "I apologize if this is an inconvenience Gi, but I was at Johns Hopkins with a colleague, and I thought perhaps I'd stop in and attend to our queen, check on her progress. She's getting close to term. Would you ask if she's willing to see me?"

Gi smiled, he was glad to see the doctor and knew Kate would love this visit. "My lady is doing well. Please come into the living room, and I will announce your arrival. Would you like a Midnight?"

Dr. Bonutti followed Gi into the living room and made himself comfortable. "Yes, that would be quite enjoyable. Medici does know how to make a drink that soothes the vampire soul and palate!"

Gi handed him a drink and made his exit, heading upstairs to find Kate in the nursery, hanging small clothes in the closet. "Excuse the interruption, my lady, but Dr. Bonutti has made an unexpected visit while here in the States. Would you be willing to see him? He's waiting in the living room."

"Of course! I'll be right down. Could you summon Shade and have him join us?"

Kate left the nursery and rushed to the bedroom. The summer was coming to an end and the vineyards were filled with migrant workers during the day, harvesting the grapes. The camp was in full swing now, and Shade was busy with training the new warriors every night. The Paris house was done, and Reynaldo had completed the changes he needed to bring the kitchen up to code in the California house, and had several candidates he was interviewing for the position of manager. It had been a busy summer and the days had passed quickly. She was barefoot and wore a knit sundress that conformed to the swell of her belly and brushed the top of her bare feet. She slid her bare feet into a pair of ballet flats and ran a brush through her hair before turning to go downstairs to greet the doctor. She found him seated in the living room, sipping on Midnight.

"Dr. Bonutti! I'm so glad to see you. Shade should be here any minute."

The doctor stood as the queen entered. Her cheeks had a healthy pink glow. Sitting down his glass of Midnight, he stood and gave her a delicate hug.

"My lady, you look beautiful! I apologize for the unplanned visit. I was with a colleague in Baltimore and this beautiful place couldn't keep me away. I hope I'm not imposing." Stepping back, he admired her. "You look beautiful in your pregnancy! But, we shall wait for master and then talk, *si*?"

Shade had been in the camp, observing the recruits as they ran obstacles when Gi telepathically told him the doctor was at the house. Teleporting into the living room he found Dr. Bonutti and *bel* chatting.

Kate looked to Gi and asked that he bring Shade a glass of Midnight, as he took a seat next to her.

Shade accepted the glass of the wine. "So, what brings you to the States?"

"I was in the area. I thought while here, I'd pay you a visit, check on the queen's progress, see if there were any questions you or the queen might have."

Kate shook her head. "I don't think I have any questions. Everything's gone beautifully. Lorenzo is very active, and I feed regularly from Shade. My energy level is good. I sleep well. There've been no problems."

Dr. Bonutti nodded. "That's all good to hear. I'd like to examine you while I'm here. It involves placing my hand on the queen, as before, to make sure the baby is well positioned, and growing as he should. Would you allow me, my lady?"

Kate sat up straight on the sofa and stretched the fabric of her dress across the growing swell of her rounded belly. "Of course."

The doctor placed his hands on Kate's abdomen, as they glided easily around its shape. He deftly moved his hands across her mid-section, carefully feeling the shape of the small prince that lay within her. Pushing and prodding, he felt the sleeping form kick and roll inside her and he grinned. Removing his hands, he returned to his chair and took a seat.

"Well, the baby's energy is strong and healthy. By the size and feel of him, I do believe your son will be born in late November, early December at the latest. You must begin to make arrangements now, the time will pass quickly. Don't be surprised to find your energy waning from this point onward, especially the last four weeks. You must feed more frequently as well, for the baby will take what he needs from you and will leave you quite tired. This is the last stage of pregnancy. Watch your activity, no teleporting of any distance. Feed often. Sexual activity is fine for the mother and of course safe for the baby. But I'd suggest nothing too strenuous. Have you found a wet feeder yet?"

Kate smiled at him. "Yes, from the list you provided. We selected Nita as our wet feeder. She'll come back to the States after Lorenzo is born. I think she'll work out beautifully, and Lorenzo responded strongly to her presence."

The doctor nodded. "Ah yes, Nita. She's a good choice, she's very pure. This will be her first assignment as a wet feeder. She'll serve the prince well. I do believe she also sings, if I remember correctly, a pleasing gift. The baby will grow to have a strong bond with his wet feeder, but you must never feel she competes with you for your son's affection. Lorenzo will always need your blood, and in a few weeks, his *padre*'s blood as well."

Shade sat up and leaned forward. "I do not recall feeding from my *padre*. Is this something new?"

"Nothing new, master. Your son will need a strong bond with you as well. You would have been too young to remember, but your father fed you several times. The baby will seek you out to feed when he's ready. In the meantime, you'll need to feed your queen more often. How are you faring in keeping yourself fed?"

"Oh, feeding. I'm fine. Everything is good. No problems." He slid his hands on his thighs and smiled at Kate. "Do you have any questions?"

Kate looked at Shade quizzically, he seemed ill at ease with the question. "I think I'm fine, lover, at least until the delivery." She directed her attention back to the doctor. "Is there anything different I need to do? I know we'll go to Florence, and back to the same chamber where I was turned. But is there anything I need to know?"

Doctor Bonutti answered, "My queen, as with the coronation, there is much ceremony. But the labor will be fine. We need do nothing specific. The Council will be present for the birth. As will I. Theresa is your mid-wife, and she's quite skilled, and of course Shade will be there also. I think this baby is anxious to be a part of this world and meet his family. Council will witness the birth of the child, enter him into the official records, and establish his birthright and legacy. Once I examine him, we'll leave you in the chamber. It's a time you will feed your baby and spend alone time with your king. There's no law as to how long you must be there. Whenever you wish to leave the chamber is your choice. But once you leave the chamber, he must be presented to the coven as the Prince of Medici. All must see him, to assure the lineage and protection of the coven. "

Kate sighed. "Well, that sounds simple enough, especially after all the pomp and circumstance around the coronation. This will be a piece of cake."

She rubbed her belly, as she felt a sharp kick from Lorenzo. "I better rest now because I have a feeling he'll have me running in every direction once he's here."

Shade chuckled. " Come, rest, *mi amore*. I will take you up to bed."

Standing, he shook the doctor's hand and Gi arrived to see him out, as they said their farewells. The doctor again reaffirmed that all was fine and to please contact him at any time.

Shade took her hand and led her up the stairs. Inside their bedroom, he settled her on the bed, and lifted her dress over her head. He crouched in front of her, removing her slippers. Rubbing her feet and massaging her ankles, he smiled at her soft moan of relief.

"You need to slow down, *mi amore*. I have put too much on you to accomplish and now you suffer for it."

Kate smiled at him as he massaged her ankles and feet. "Lover, I'm fine. And we're in a good place. Cory's moved in, and the nursery is done. The Paris house, the California Inn...everything's moving along."

Kate stretched out on the bed, lifting her hands above her head in a deep stretch. "I'll be glad when he gets here, and I can get my shape back. I never realized how heavy he'd feel."

She rolled onto her side as Shade's hands moved to the small of her back, massaging the muscles deep. She moaned quietly at the pleasure of his touch.

He applied a little more pressure along her spine, as he massaged up and down her back. "You are so damn beautiful." He climbed into bed beside her as his hands began a journey all their own, sliding down the curve of her ass and onto her thighs, sensually massaging. He slid his hand between her legs, playing carefully, feeling the wetness of her sex as her body responded to him. "Mmm, wet and needing. Just how I love you."

She leaned her back against his chest, turning her head to meet his lips as they searched for hers. His touch was electric as always, igniting a fire in her. She missed her slender body and the way she was able to climb over him so freely, her movement restricted now by the baby she carried. His fingers explored, and she pushed her hips against him, feeling the hard shaft of steel.

"I need to be inside you, *mi amore*. I can no longer bear this. I need to feel you. I am so lost without us."

He glided his cock into her soft wet sex, feeling her heat and his beast reared instantly. His chest heaved as Shade pushed him down, not allowing the beast to touch her.

Her moans enticed and encouraged him. Gliding the bulging head of his erection inside her, he moved slowly, stretching her gently to take him. "You are so tight and hot, *mi amore*, you set me on fire."

His hand slid over her hip, gripping her tightly and pulling her hips back against him, as she took him inside her. He leaned over her, kissing her, her hand tangled in his hair.

"I love you," she whispered against his lips.

"Let go for me, cum for me, let me love you always."

Snuggling his face into her hair, closing his eyes, his body craved her blood. He was like a starved animal and he ignored the pain it created, inhaling her scent of roses, the smell of her sex surrounding him in a cocoon of desire. His body moved of its own accord, wanting to explode inside her. He felt her tremble from hunger and sexual need. He pushed deep inside her and felt the release.

She felt him cum inside her, as he timed his own release to wait for her. Her body shuddered in the aftermath of the climax, as he held her tightly to his chest. She rolled onto her back, seeking his throat, as she ran her tongue over the throbbing vein in his neck before sinking her aching fangs deep, drawing his life's blood into her mouth. She felt his power with each swallow, and the fire between her legs ignited again. Her body demanded his blood now, to satisfy her hunger and the growing baby, and she took without reservation.

He felt the ecstasy of having her feed, but the agony of not being able to feed from her. It was the price he paid to have a *bambino.* He felt her love and intense need, his own son demanding his blood. He fed them both, giving them all that he was. She continued to drink deep, draining him, and it was more than he could handle.

He needed her to stop or he'd lose control. He rolled away from her, as he stood quickly from the bed, swaying from the dizziness caused by his own loss of blood, and not feeding.

He slid to the floor, his back against the bed, pulling his knees to his chest, his head hanging down, his body weak and in agony. "No more, *bel*. No more."

Kate crawled across the bed to him, leaning her head over the side of the bed, her hair cascading down around his shoulders as she slid her hands down his chest. "Shade! You're not feeding!"

His beast screamed inside him, starving. Balling his hands into fists, he slammed them into the floor, fighting back the pain. "I hate hurting you. I hate I cannot have you as I need. I fight it for as long as I can."

Kate ran her fingers through his hair, calming him. "You don't hurt me by going to Luca. You hurt me by abstaining. You need what he can give. And I need you to be strong. Lorenzo needs you to be strong. Go to him, lover."

Looking up as she leaned over him and kissed him, it was a kiss of consent. "*Si*. I love you. I will always love you with my life."

Standing he slid on his jeans, not buttoning them, and made his way to the door, turning to look at her. He placed his hand over his heart, smiling at her as he headed out the door, closing it behind him.

Standing outside the door, he took a deep breath, relaxing his body before he went to Luca's quarters. The walk seemed to take forever, not realizing how desperately he needed to feed. Before he could tap on the door, it opened and Luca beckoned him in.

Luca had felt his presence before he reached the door and opened it to greet him. The two locked eyes. Luca knew why he was here. It had been more than a week since Shade had fed from him, and Luca knew Kate fed from Shade almost every day now.

"Master."

Luca extended his hand, taking Shade's hand in his. "I was about to take a shower. Why don't you join me?"

Shade locked on Luca's hazel eyes and his mouth watered. He nodded and felt the warm skin of Luca's hand within his. He always dreaded this, until he was here, knowing this was the safest option he had, and somehow, Luca knew how to make this easier on his soul.

Following Luca to the shower, he watched him strip naked, his body tight and hard, the muscles ripped and his skin a golden caramel. Shade's eyes never left Luca as he watched him turn on the water, the steam beginning to rise, just like his hunger and need. Luca turned to face him, their eyes once again locked tight to one another. Luca's hands glided across Shade's hips as he slid the jeans down, running his hands over Shade's thighs and down his calves, as the jeans dropped around his ankles and Luca looked up at him.

Luca let him step out of the jeans as he tossed them from the shower stall into the bedroom. He ran his hands back up the strong calves and powerful thighs of his master, before letting his tongue lash out at his groin, feeling the strong pulse and pull of his master's blood. He knew he wouldn't feed from Shade. He'd only take his master's blood to save his own life, and only then if offered, but the scent of him was a powerful aphrodisiac. As Luca stood to his full height, he ran his hands over his master's chest and across his shoulders, letting his tongue taste the salty skin at his throat. Luca stepped back under the flow of the hot water streaming from the shower and pulled Shade with him.

The water was hot and beat down on his skin like a drum, leading the beast to his prey. Luca's tongue flicked and played, but he knew his limitations. Shade let him have his way for only a few moments, and then slammed his back hard against the shower wall, the water running rivulets between their bodies, hard and aching. Shade placed his hands flat against the shower wall on either side of Luca's head and went straight to his mouth, but never letting his lips touch. "You tempt me."

His voice was deep and low, almost a growl. Reaching for the toiletries that lined the shelf in the shower, Shade grabbed a shampoo and squeezed some into his hands; the scent was musky and all male. Nipping quickly at Luca's shoulder, he commanded him to turn around and as Luca complied, Shade's hands went into his long dark hair, working up a lather and massaging his head, the fragrance filling the air. The softness of his hair and firm hardness of his body took Shade to another level and his beast appreciated all of his senses coming alive.

Shade pulled Luca against his chest as they stood under the streaming water, letting it rinse the shampoo from his hair, as the sudsy water ran over his shoulders and down his back and ass. Shade put his hands on Luca's slender hips, his lips leaving kisses along the pulsing vein in Luca's neck, slick, wet and warm from the water.

"Oh yes, you tempt me."

Luca's eyes were closed as he gave himself up to the ministrations of his master, feeling his hands in his hair before sliding down his body. Luca laid his head back, exposing his neck as he let his arms drop to his sides, slowly stroking his master's thighs. He could feel the engorged shaft of his master's hard cock as his own cock throbbed, hard and exposed.

"Let me tempt you, master. Take what is yours."

There was no stopping the beast now, he reared full force and his fangs punched, his eyes radiated, lighting the shower in a glow of crimson. Snaking out his tongue, he let it slide from across Luca's shoulder, as he growled deep in his chest. Shade sank his fangs deep, the first burst of Luca's blood like a flow of hot lava into his system. Shade felt Luca slump against him, his knees almost buckling under him from the deep draw he took.

Shade's hand slid under Luca's chin, letting his head rest there as Shade drew even deeper, unable to stop. He was parched and starved beyond his own limits and he should have known better than to wait so long.

Shade's other hand sought out Luca's steeled cock, filling his large hand and his own cock lurched. His moan was loud and gravely as his body ached in need.

Luca let his master support his weight as he relaxed into him, feeling the hard slow strokes on his cock and the erotic sounds of his master taking his fill. His mind reeled with the thought that it is his blood that sustained his master. Luca's mouth was open, as his moans of pleasure echoed in the shower, building as his master pushed him closer to orgasm, stroking harder, faster, even as he drank deeper. He felt the release wash over him as he exploded, his shaft throbbing as his cum spilled from him, and over his master's hand, closed in a tight grip around his dick. Still pulling, stroking, milking that last drop from him as Luca screamed out with his release, his knees buckling as his master held him upright.

Unlatching his fangs, licking the wound, Shade shook his head, the water drops flinging from his hair. The water ran over his body and he felt like he could conquer the world in that moment, young warrior blood pumping in every vein. Pulling Luca up, he kissed him deep, his tongue snaking around his warm mouth, diving deeper into his throat.

Luca responded, his own tongue darting and playing and Shade moaned with the incredible feeling he had ripping through him. Luca's hands went into his hair, as he gripped fistfuls, pulling his master tighter into the urgent kiss.

Shade broke the kiss, knowing Luca's beast was on the edge, wanting to feed. "Easy."

Their eyes locked. Reaching out, Shade slid his hand over Luca's cheek and he nuzzled into his neck, licking, nipping, and working his way up Luca's ear. "Take me in your mouth."

Luca dropped his head back against the wall of the shower stall, gulping air as he fought the urge to feed from his master. At Shade's urging, he let his body slide down the wall until he was on his knees in front of him. His master's cock was still hard and throbbing. Luca ran his hands up Shade's thighs and encircled his massive erection. His tongue lashed out, teasing the bulging head of his master's dick and he heard the sharp intake of breath from Shade. Luca slowly slid his mouth over that hard knob, letting his lips play before sliding the shaft deep into his throat and beginning to stroke Shade's cock with his mouth. He felt Shade's hands in his hair, gripping tight, guiding his head faster. Luca could feel the throbbing shaft in his mouth and knew his master was close.

Closing his eyes, Shade let the sensations roll over him, the blood, his cock deep down Luca's throat, and Luca's tongue as it lashed and licked, taking him deep, sucking him. His hands gripped Luca's hair, as he guided him deeper with each stroke. His beast wanted his due and Shade let him free. His hips lurched forward as his balls tightened and Luca devoured him. He felt Luca's hands grip his balls and stroke as Shade exploded hard and deep, his body shaking and his scream loud. Dropping his head back, his eyes rolling back in his head as Luca sucked him dry, draining every drop of him. Shade slid his body down the slick wet wall until his ass hit the floor. Luca knelt between his legs, as Shade pulled him to his chest, his voice cracked. "Luca."

Luca lay with his head against Shade's chest, both of them spent. "Master, I am yours."

Shade kissed the top of his head. Without him, he'd be lost, and so would *bel*. "I need to go back to her. You need to rest and go to Shannon. Bring her here, if you think it best. I need you to stay strong for me. *Ti amo*."

Luca stood and reached his hand down for Shade to grab. Stepping out of the shower, Shade toweled off and slid on his jeans. His hair still wet, he went to leave and turned to look at Luca. They both knew this time they shared would soon be ending, but it would come again. It was a bond that only brought them closer, a necessary bond that neither spoke of, but locked them tighter for all eternity.

Shade walked out and closed the door behind him, hastily making his way to the bedroom. He found his *bel* sleeping. She slept on her side, her hair spread like a flame of crimson love across the white pillow. He dropped his jeans and walked to the bed, watching her sleep peacefully. This was his world, all wrapped into one small lily-white female. He crawled into the bed beside her. Her shape no longer allowing her to sleep draped across his chest, his son, even now, encroaching on their rituals and he almost laughed.

Spooning his large body around her, his arm went protectively across her belly, his body tight against hers. His head snuggled into the sweet smell of roses that arose from her crimson locks and he was home. He felt the pull of his death slumber yank him hard. Closing his eyes, he felt her move slightly, his confirmation she knew he was there now. His son kicked beneath his hand. "*Ti amo, mi amore*. Your lover is here."

83

Kate paced in their bedroom as she talked on the phone with Reynaldo. He was filling her in on the details of opening the inn. Reynaldo had suggested they name the inn *A Touch of Tuscany*, and Kate had quickly agreed. They had already had several guests without even advertising, and Reynaldo had narrowed down his options for a manager. He felt very strongly about one of the candidates, but Kate knew she was too far along in the pregnancy now to teleport out there.

"Reynaldo, I trust your instincts. If you feel this is the right person, then just move ahead."

Reynaldo informed her this immortal had experience in managing inn's and had worked at several well-known boutique style hotels in Europe. All of his references checked out and he had excellent endorsements from his previous employers. He was French but had lived in the States for many years and was very knowledgeable of the Napa Valley region. He had also been schooled as a sommelier.

Kate heard Shade enter the room as she continued her conversation. She looked up at the window to see the sky was beginning to lighten. She hadn't realized how late it was.

"Let's move forward with it, Reynaldo. You said his name is Mica? Go ahead with the final interview, if you think he's the one, we can have him teleport here, and make him an offer. If he accepts we'll put him on the payroll. Okay? And give me a call if anything changes. Thanks, Reynaldo. Bye."

Kate set the phone down and went to Shade as he sat on the side of the bed, pulling off his boots, pulling his shirt over his head, shaking out his hair. "Lover, you look tired."

Shade had a long night. He'd overheard Kate issuing instructions to Reynaldo in California when he entered. She was firm and decisive and he almost laughed at how much she had changed since the first time he met her. She had been so timid. She could barely speak to him. Now she moved through business deals like a true pro, all of her projects in line. "There's a lot going on, but I can manage. It seems you are just as busy if not more so. Sounds like you have found a manager for the California house, *si*?"

Kate kissed his bare shoulder and ran her hand across his chest. "Well, Reynaldo has found someone. Normally I'd go out there and interview them myself, but I think it's too late for that now. I could fly out on the jet, but I know that would make you nervous as well, so if he thinks this guy is the one, I'll have him come here. Reynaldo has handled everything else I've asked of him. I trust his judgment. Don't you?"

"*Si*, I trust his judgment, but you seem very casual about throwing someone on my payroll, woman."

Laughing, he flopped back onto the bed, massaging her back as she remained sitting on the edge. "I know I have asked a lot of you, *bel*. I am proud you have taken it all in hand. This manager, he is immortal and a day-walker I hope. You have planned well, and it will be a good business."

Kate closed her eyes as he massaged her back, his strong fingers probing and relaxing the tight muscles. "Yes, he's immortal and a day-walker, and also French. And speaking of business..." Kate turned and lay back on the bed next to him, her arm across his chest. "I need an answer from you on the lavender fields. I won't be able to plant until spring, but if I'm going to convert that land, some of it will need to be cleared, and then it will need to be plowed and fertilized. I know you have other things on your mind, but what do you think?"

Shade closed his eyes. "*Bel*, if this is what you want, then do it. I know the vineyards in the States will take some time to mature before we show huge profits here. Vineyards are not an overnight endeavor. You have done your research on the lavender. There is no reason why this won't be successful. "

"I've thought about it. Even if the lavender doesn't work out, and I have no reason to believe it won't, the land would already be cleared for expansion of the vineyards. It's not an irreversible decision. So, I'll move ahead with that then. Oh, and one other thing."

Kate rose up, supported on her elbow so she could see his face. "When I had Luca go with me into town a few days ago, I noticed the property that adjoins ours is up for sale. I went online to check out the details. There's no house on the property, but there is a barn, and the stream that runs across our land cuts through there as well. There's a paved access road and a few unpaved roads around the barn. I think we should buy it. It's 1500 acres, so half the size of our property here. It's priced at $7000 an acre... so that's about $10 million. You said you wanted to expand the vineyards. It would be a shame not to take advantage of it, don't you think?"

Shade listened to her logic about purchasing the property. He opened his eyes and stared at her. "*Mi amore*, we are both dead tired from managing properties. Expanding the vineyards is in the plan, *si*? What do you have in mind?" Shade sat back up, pulling off his leathers.

"Lover, we've been here a year, and look at what's changed! The staff quarters were renovated and it's already full. I completed the house renovation and then we had to add an expansion to the house to make room for Cory. We added the warrior camp and the feeder compound. We added the stables and established fields for grazing. You want to expand the vineyards. I want to add lavender, and maybe sunflowers. I hear you speak of the camp and how you want to grow your presence here in the States. If you expand the camp it will cut into the land we use to produce revenue. I think it's also a smart move to keep our perimeter as large as possible. If we don't buy the land, it'll be bought up by a mortal. We don't know what they'd plan to do with the property, but it would limit us in some ways. We've been lucky the land wasn't occupied before now. It gave us even more isolation. I know you usually fight or negotiate for land, but this is a circumstance where I think buying it makes sense."

He lay back down on his stomach and propped himself up on his elbows facing her, kissing her soft lips. "The warrior camp will need expansion in the coming years. We already know you see at least three *bambinos* coming. Damn, it is like we have built an empire in only a year. So, here is my proposal. I want you to call Luciano, have him call my lawyer. Both of them handle my properties. You let him do the work. Get them over there, let him negotiate the price. I don't know how long it has been sitting there, but a cash offer will usually be accepted at much lower than the asking price. Once they purchase the land it is going to sit there until after Lorenzo is born. *Bel*, *bambinos* take a great deal of time and energy. I don't want you running yourself into the ground with all these projects. Our *figlio* will need his *madre*. I like that you want to do things, have interests. That pleases me immensely. You have a good business head about you. Luciano has already told me he's seen this in you. Deal, *sí*?"

Kate wrapped her arms around his shoulders as he leaned over her, his dark curls tumbling forward around his face. "There's nothing I'm looking forward to more than holding and taking care of this baby. Lorenzo will be my top priority. But we're building our future here. For Lorenzo, and the other children that follow him. I must say, when you moved me from my condo to this isolated house in the foothills of the mountains, I could never have envisioned all it would become. And if it's changed this much in one year, what lies ahead for us? I'll do as you ask. I'll let your lawyers handle the transaction and I'll rest and wait for this baby."

Moaning his consent, he snuggled into her neck. "*Grazie*. I know you will love him, take care of him, just as you do me. I have no doubt of that, but it is a task, and as he gets older and the others come, this will be a mad house. They will need discipline, but I don't wish for them to be brought up as I was, it was too strict. I want them to be able to play and learn, be loved and happy. I want this to always feel like home to them. If I had never met you, this house would still be as it was, empty with no life or spirit inside it. You have given me so much, *mi amore*. You have filled my life with love every day. I can never repay you for all you have given me. Do you know how much I love you?"

Kate brushed his hair back from those intensely blue eyes and locked into his gaze. "I feel your love every second of every day, Shade. When you're with me, and when you're away. You make sure of it. I only hope you feel my love the same."

Looking into her beautiful face, it glowed with love and happiness. "*Si*, I feel it so deep. My soul has never been so happy. I keep waiting to wake up from dream-walking to find all of it is gone that you were just a vision. Every night when I wake from my death slumber and you lie beside me, I breathe a sigh of relief. Speaking of which, I feel like a damn sledgehammer is hitting my head, sun is rising."

Kate gave him a wicked grin, before pulling him down on top of her. "Then you better get busy."

The electronic whir of the blinds blocked out the early rays of the sun. Kate reached over and turned off the lamp by the bed before turning her full attention to him, and the taste of his lips on hers.

84

Shade and Raven sat in the study, laying out a grid for the venues to be used in Alec and Rissa's wedding. They'd need more intense coverage around the National Cathedral and all along Embassy Row, as well as the route Alec and Rissa would follow over to the reception site at The Old Post Office Building. They'd keep minimal coverage in the rest of the District during the event. They'd been in the study for what seemed like hours when Shade stretched, and turned to Raven. "Anything else we need to get squared away, besides who still needs some training on the streets?"

Raven looked over the grids one more time. "Boss-man, I'm going to need a guest list I can circulate among all the warriors."

Shade nodded. "The guest list is coming. But keep an eye on all the immortals. Quietly remove anyone that makes a scene. Every vampire there will be aware of the security. I don't think we have anything to worry about."

Raven folded up the grids to take with him. "I'm going to make sure Aislynn gets a challenging assignment. Skelk and Fee are both impressed with how quickly she's advancing. We're going to speed up her training, and I'll give her an inside assignment for the wedding."

Shade nodded. "That's fine. I have been watching her, her skills with a shuriken are deadly."

***

Kate was waiting for the arrival of the new manager for the inn. Reynaldo had conducted his final interview, and Mica should be arriving any minute. Kate wanted to be ready to respond to him immediately, since Aegis and Night Stalker stayed so close to the house. Aegis had already had her pups, and she kept them close by in the woods near the house. Her pups made Aegis even more protective and volatile, and Kate didn't want Mica startled on his very first visit.

Kate felt the energy of the air around her change as he teleported down into their front yard. She exited immediately to greet him, calming Aegis and Night Stalker as they both approached him, sniffing. "Never mind them. They'll not harm you. They're my own little welcoming committee."

Kate extended her hand to him. "I'm Kate. Please come in. Reynaldo has spoken quite highly of you."

Kate looked him over. He was tall and handsome, but then she had yet to see any of the vampires that didn't possess their own unique beauty. His hair was a light brown, not quite to his shoulders and styled. His eyes were dark. He wasn't as muscular as the warriors, but clearly fit and strong. He wasn't as young as some of Shade's warriors in the camp. Kate was guessing he was closer to Shade's age.

Mica nodded at her, taking her hand. Reynaldo had warned him about the animals, but even with the knowledge beforehand, it was startling to see the wolves. Mica kissed her hand. "I'm most pleased to meet you. I am of course familiar with Shade Medici, although we've never met."

Kate smiled at him. "Well, his bark is worse than his bite, but don't tell him I told you so. Come in, we're expecting you."

She led him into the house and down the corridor to Shade's office. "He was meeting with his warriors earlier, but he knows you're coming."

As they reached the door to the study, Kate saw Shade bent over the desk, still with Raven. "Shade, Mica is here. Should I have him wait in the living room until you wrap up?"

Shade looked up to see Kate and Mica, as he stood to greet him. "No, we are done here." He nodded in Mica's direction, waving his hand to enter. "Shade Medici, please come in, welcome to Bel Rosso. Let me clear these things away here. May I introduce you to Raven, one of my top warriors?"

Raven looked at the vampire standing next to the queen and was dumbstruck. He was older than Raven, and no warrior. His eyes were dark and mysterious. His clothes were very stylish, and looked designer, or at least hand-tailored. Raven could only manage a nod. Their eyes locked and he felt an immediate connection. Suddenly, he was interested in finding out who this was and why he was here. His heart raced inside his chest and his beast went haywire. *Mica? What the hell kind of name is that and where is this handsome vampire from?*

Shade was speaking, and Raven looked away. "Raven, you are dismissed. I will contact you once I speak with Alec. Take Aislynn into D.C. as soon as possible."

Raven nodded. "No problem boss-man." Raven turned to leave the room, but not before bowing to his queen. "Until we meet again my lady."

Kate laughed at Raven as be performed his deep dramatic bow, and she slapped at his shoulder. "Raven, meet Mica. He's here to interview for the manager position at the California property. He'll be working with Reynaldo."

Kate couldn't help but notice while the deep bow was for her, Raven hadn't taken his eyes off Mica, and Mica seemed as interested in Raven.

Mica extended his hand. "Raven, is it? That's an Interesting name, very dark and mysterious. And are you as dark and mysterious as your name suggest?"

Raven took Mica's hand and the sparks flew up his arm. The two men held their grip, their eyes locked. "As dark as you like, and if you need mystery, I can provide it. Mica? That's an unusual name also." Raven smiled and liked the smile he received in return.

Mica laughed softly. "It's French. Mica Moreau. "

Shade stared at the two of them then cleared his throat. "Raven, you have duties and I have some business to attend to. Out!"

Raven never took his eyes off Mica and released his hand. Swinging his hair over his shoulder he headed for the door. "Boss-man, some day you are going to figure out, you have shitty timing." Closing the door behind him, Raven headed back to camp and found his steps were much lighter.

Shade shook his head. "I apologize, Raven has a mouth with no filter. Please take a seat and fill me in on what you think of the inn. May we offer you a drink?"

Mica watched the young warrior leave and took note of his flippant remark to his master. Clearly, he had the trust and respect of his master to respond in such a casual manner. Mica shook his head, knowing this one would be a handful, but one he hoped to experience.

Mica nodded to Shade. "A drink would be most welcome after the long teleport. I sampled the Midnight from the Napa vineyards. Do you produce Midnight from the vineyards here as well?"

Shade nodded. "Of course, and we will produce much more as the vineyards mature. We are still shipping Midnight into the States from my Italian, French and Greek vineyards. So, tell me a bit about yourself. You have already said you are French. We have just purchased a home in Paris. My queen has been working hard to get it furnished. She decorated the California home as well."

Standing, he poured three Midnights and handed one to *bel* first, kissing her softly before handing a glass to Mica. Returning to his desk chair, he sipped his own, waiting to see how Mica would handle himself.

Mica remarked, "Reynaldo had informed me that the queen had decorated the California house as well as renovating this one. May I say you have excellent taste? I've most recently worked at a boutique hotel in San Francisco. I'd been there for several years, but I'm tired of the city and prefer the calm of Napa Valley. Prior to that, I worked at several inns in France. I believe Reynaldo forwarded my resume and my references. Your Napa house is in a beautiful location. The vineyards and the winery alone would be a draw to tourists. But the house, it's magnificent. And Reynaldo is quite the chef. Most of the inns in Napa Valley are family owned and operated, and they prepare the meals themselves, and many only offer breakfast. Very few have professional chefs. It will be a huge draw. I see a lot of potential for this property, and I'd love to be a part of it, getting in on the ground floor. I have no doubt the rooms will stay full."

Shade nodded in his direction. "You have an impressive resume. I am glad you are interested but I must admit this is Kate's project. She had the vision for the inn." Looking to Kate, he flashed her a huge smile. "Drill away, *mi amore*. This is your project."

Kate spent the next hour talking with Mica, both of them planning and throwing out ideas for the inn and how to market it. Kate felt immediately connected to him and loved his passion and enthusiasm.

"Tell me, Mica. I've had two house maids sent over from Italy. Reynaldo and I thought two would be plenty to start. You'll have to let me know if you need more. There are more people in Florence we can draw from."

Shade listened to their conversation and liked Mica, he was intelligent and his experience and knowledge of the industry were obvious. He could tell Kate had already made a connection with him. He realized this was no little project Kate had taken on just to fill her time. She'd used her business sense and marketing skills and this place was going to generate some huge money.

Shade started thinking long term about this property, and its real value. "I just realized that even though the California property is in Alec's territory, we may need to have some warriors out there for protection. This sounds like a serious business endeavor that could take off quickly under Mica's guidance. I don't feel comfortable leaving my assets with no protection."

Mica nodded. "I must say I was surprised when I went there to see how large an operation it was, and to find no warriors. I've met Luciano briefly. He's in and out, and of course Reynaldo. I doubt you'll draw any immortals as visitors, but even with mortals, there can be problems. The California territory has been stable for years. I haven't been aware of any challenges for territory in the time I've lived there. But this is a serious enterprise. I'd expect there to be warriors."

Shade poured himself another glass of Midnight. "Master Canton owns the California territory, so there is no immediate threat to my property. We are business partners and I provide his protection needs here in D.C. One of the main reasons I am based here. I think I should send one of my warriors out for a few days to observe and determine what we will need to provide adequate protection. I will see to that as soon as possible. If you're hired for this position, I will have Kate contact you with the details of when they will arrive and you can take it from there."

Shade turned to Kate. "So, my beautiful queen, do you wish to hire Mica for your castle in the Napa Valley?"

Kate beamed at him. “If we haven’t scared him away with our wolves and our flamboyant warriors, then yes, I’m ready to hire him."

Mica smiled. "And I’ll gladly accept."

Shade grinned at her happiness, he could feel her excitement and pride in this project. "Well, I think you have definitely found your man. Welcome aboard, Mica. It is a pleasure to have you on staff. I appreciate it more than you know."

Standing, shaking Mica’s hand, Shade wondered if he sent Raven out there to conduct the inspection if anything would be accomplished. Something about these two had been an instant hit.

85

Raven had finally scored a night off, and his ass was heading straight to club ZS in the metro area. He'd found it while making rounds in D.C., but this was his first free night to spend some time there.

His needs could be met by the female feeders, and he did what was necessary to survive, but when it came to sexual gratification, he found the females sorely lacking. His new assignment as SIC of the Dead House gave him little time lately to do as he pleased, and that was getting under his skin. It didn't help he'd met that hot, delicious French pastry Mica, and his appetite was raging for release.

Dressed to kill in black leathers, his hair down, he knew he'd attract just what he was looking for. Raven added black kohl eyeliner around his already dark eyes. He slapped on a hat, added some bling, and checked himself in the mirror. He had a ring on every finger of both hands, and chains around his neck. He glanced one more time in the full-length mirror and he was ready to roll. He had no intentions of coming home until he got exactly what he wanted, which involved alcohol, dancing, feeding, and a hot body to soothe his inner beast.

Walking into ZS's, the club was dark, the only lights creating a strobe effect in sync with the pounding music. The club was crowded and offered a buffet of trouble, just how he liked it. Taking in his surroundings, Raven stood on the edge of the crowd, noting the number of immortals that were mingling with the humans. He walked to the bar and ordered a Midnight. He was still new here, and he was taking stock of his surroundings before he made a move. Growing up on the streets of Florence, poor and abused, taught him many lessons and he was well indoctrinated on the protocol in the clubs. He still couldn't forget his station, his position as SIC to the master. He was young and boss-man had entrusted him with a lot of responsibility. He'd come far in his short life with Medici and he wasn't about to throw it all away over a piece of ass with a huge cock.

He grinned, as he recalled the teasing his brothers were always throwing at him. They knew he was different, but they also knew in a battle he'd always have their backs.

Deep inside, he craved someone of his own, someone who'd feed from him. The loneliness and hardships of his life on the streets never left him, even though he was now part of a brotherhood that loved him. He wondered if he'd ever find the intimacy or the connection he saw the mated immortals enjoy.

He took a drink of the thick wine and shook his head. That was enough of those thoughts. That wasn't what he'd come here for tonight. His eyes were glued to the one male pole dancer who was giving a show. Raven was pretty damn sure this guy made his living by dancing, and whatever followed after hours. His style was unique, but Raven knew he could make this dude look like an amateur on that pole.

He felt a warm body slide up behind him, close and tight, a hard cock rubbing against his tight leather pants. "Good to see you again gorgeous. That pole has your name written all over it. Want to give it a try?"

Raven felt his heart race. Closing his eyes, he took in the scent of the male behind him. It was the dancer who'd approached him the first night he walked into ZS. Raven moved his ass against the male and felt him breathing heavy on his neck. All he wanted was to dance and feel that hard oiled body sliding over him.

Without saying a word, Raven took his hand and led him to a pole in the center of the dance floor. Raven grabbed a chair and shoved the male dancer into it. Leaning down, he kissed him on the lips, before letting his tongue slide down the sweet pulsing vein in the dancer's neck, as a moan escaped him. He was going to have this fine piece of ass before he went back to camp tonight. He needed a release!

Raven shrugged off his jacket, tossing it to the male and then lifted the hat from his head, placing it on the dancer's head, winking at him. Already they were getting some attention from the crowd.

Raven strutted to the pole, ripping his shirt off and flinging it at the gathering crowd of males who were curious now about what this immortal could do on a pole. Raven crouched on his haunches, the pole to his back. It seemed as though the world had stopped, and the spotlight was on him, he wasn't about to disappoint. He slithered his back up the pole into a standing position, undulating his hips, his eyes locked on the man sitting in the chair in front of him.

The music started and what came next was a floor show like none they'd ever seen, or ever would again. He worked that pole, made love to it, his strength allowing him to make moves that looked almost impossible to the mortals in the room. Raven let himself disappear into the music, let his body translate his aching need, and every eye in the club was on him. He used the pole from top to bottom, climbing, sliding, undulating, and moving his body to the beat of the electronic house mix. When he was done and the music stopped, he glided to the floor, crawling like a snake, slinking to the male in the chair.

The male dancer's eyes were glazed over, focused on Raven and that's right where Raven wanted him. Raven took his hand and led him away from the now cheering and over-stimulated crowd. They walked to the back of the club and slid into a secluded booth where Raven's beast was rewarded and he took until his sexual appetite was sated and his hunger gone. Raven fed like a starved animal, but he was careful to make sure he didn't drain him.

The man's eyes were already drooping with soppy intentions, hoping to stake a claim on Raven. "What is your name?"

As the male asked, Raven took his face in his hands. "Welcome to Raven's world."

The male had yet to realize he'd remember nothing of this night, except the hot, long haired beauty that made love to a pole like it was human. "When will I see you again?"

Raven laid his hand on his forehead, erasing the memories of the intense sexual gratification they'd both shared. "When you see me."

Teleporting out, Raven had finally satisfied the need he'd waited five months for, since being in the States, the need to escape the warrior world and be who he was.

86

Marcello walked down Rugby Road in Charlottesville. It was early fall and the fraternities were going at it full speed. The University of Virginia was starting a new school year, and as Marcello walked along the cracked sidewalks, there were females in every size, shape, and color he could ever imagine. He stood outside one of the stately old houses, watching the activity as the young students came and went, enjoying their first taste of freedom from parental controls. Most of them had been drinking, and that would only make his job easier. Fuck, he loved the states. The females here were friendly, open, and generally trusting. They were drawn to him like flies on honey.

Marcello had rock star good looks. His brown hair streaked with blonde hung to his shoulders, his skin tan, his eyes a brilliant blue surrounded by lashes any girl would die for. He stood tall, and buff, but not overly muscular like some of his brothers. He dressed in jeans, torn at the knees, and a t-shirt featuring a local band. His attire would allow him to blend in with the throng of other male students, but his intensely good looks would always make him stand out in a crowd.

He enjoyed having the feeder compound close to the barracks, it was convenient and pleasurable, but nothing replaced the thrill of the hunt. He loved being SIC of the Warrior Camp but there came a time, when a warrior needed to bust loose, walk away from all his responsibilities and see what was on the outside. He'd spent a lot of time in D.C. checking out the area when he was assigned to the Dead House. There was a big club scene in the District, and the Georgetown campus was close, but he found he preferred this small town setting with its dense concentration of students. He chuckled to himself at the unfair advantage he had, like shooting fish in a barrel.

Marcello pushed his way through the throng of people crowded around the doorway of the frat house, into a room of young people dancing to the loud pounding music. He immediately picked up the scent of other vampires in the place and he was on full alert. His eyes scanned the crowd and it didn't take long to single them out. He pushed through the crowd, using his elbows as he made his way to a spot where he could easily see all the action. He stood quietly and observed, as the two vamp warriors were talking up some females across the room. He kept his eyes on them and knew they were definitely aware of his presence as well.

Marcello never lost sight of the fact they sat in the middle of another master's territory, but he'd never encountered warriors from Max's coven before. He sure as hell didn't want an altercation right in the middle of campus, and so close to Bel Rosso. Shade would kill him if he did anything that exposed their coven or put them at risk. Marcello knew there'd been no problem between the two masters. But he also knew warriors were extremely territorial and protected their own at any cost. He leaned against a makeshift bar, where the young people were making a sport of emptying a keg of beer, and wished he had a Midnight about now. He slid his hand into his pocket and withdrew a pack of cigarettes. He noticed no one else was smoking, as he lit up and made eye contact with one of the vamps from the rival coven. The two rivals exchanged words and casually made their way in Marcello's direction. His weapons were well hidden but easily accessed, but this was the last place he wanted to fight. *Cazzo*, all he'd wanted was a night to relax and feed!

***

Tyler and Haden were chatting up the new freshmen who'd been doing shots and drinking beer, taking advantage of their new found freedom. Early fall on the UVA campus was easy pickings for them, but their instructions from Max were clear. They could hunt, feed, and fuck, but be sure to wipe their memories, and this was a strict no-kill zone. Avoid conflict at all cost. The two of them had been hunting here for years, and never left hungry, but tonight they detected the presence of a new vamp and they were on high alert. They were aware of the Medici's estate in the middle of Max's territory, but Shade Medici had kept a tight rein on his warriors and neither Tyler nor Haden had ever encountered any of them in town before.

Tyler smiled at the drunken girls. "Excuse us a minute, ladies, I think we see an old friend. Don't go anywhere." The girls giggled and assured him they'd be waiting.

Tyler turned to Haden. "Over near the bar, where those guys are playing beer pong, must be one of Medici's. Stay cool brother, but watch my back. We don't want any trouble."

The two walked through the crowd, making their way to where Marcello stood. Tyler never took his eyes off Marcello, and Marcello had him locked in a stare as they sized each other up. Tyler approached with caution, raising his hand to fist bump the new vampire.

"Brother? I'm Tyler. This is Haden. Are you new around here?"

Marcello returned the fist-bump. "Medici. Is this your usual hunting ground?" He could feel their curiosity. They already knew where he hailed from. His accent was a dead giveaway. He also knew they were on full alert, just as he was.

Tyler looked him up and down, they were about equal in size, but he wanted no fight, and certainly not in the middle of the campus. Max would have their heads. "I'd say this is one of our more lucrative hunting grounds. Easy pickings. And enough to go around if you're planning on hunting here. No reason to battle. It's a large campus and a lot of fraternities. In addition to the female students, you have the townies, trying to crash the frat parties. The townies tend to be on the young side and you'll learn to spot them. Max wants us to keep it clean. Not draw any negative attention. Don't go after any girls who aren't showing interest. Wipe their memories. Don't let them feed from us, and absolutely no-kill. You got a problem with those rules?"

Marcello shook his head. "It sounds like we have the same rules, so I don't see a problem. Name is Marcello, by the way."

Haden spoke up, "We know about the Medici's. You're just the first one we've seen. We have no quarrel with you being here. Like Tyler said, there's more than enough to go around, but Max doesn't want us to do anything that will draw negative attention from the mortals. Hence the rules. You follow the rules and we got no problem."

Marcello took a drag from his cigarette, acknowledging their comments. "And what the hell are townies?"

Tyler boldly claimed his territory by removing the pack of cigarettes from Marcello's pocket and lighting up, handing the pack back to Marcello. "Townies? They're the local girls who are still in high school, sneaking into the party. They're usually underage and easy pickings, but Max says hands off."

Marcello leaned against the bar facing the throng, unphased by Tyler's brashness. "Our master also insists we not prey on mortals who are under age, or who don't show an interest. Sounds like Medici has the same rules of etiquette as you."

His eyes caught a beautiful dark haired beauty who'd been dancing alone, clearly trying to draw his attention. She winked at him, and he knew she could easily be his entertainment for the evening. "Someone is calling my name. If you'll excuse me, I think I'll mingle. Nice meeting you."

Fist bumping them, he turned his back on the rivals and walked away. He knew for sure their eyes would be following his every move all night long.

87

Sitting at the command center in the Dead House, Raven reworked the roster for the upcoming week, as he pulled in a few of the new recruits to work with his experienced warriors. The recruits needed some street time before the wedding. He'd worked with boss-man to determine which of the new recruits were ready for the challenge to begin rotating through D.C., and who'd be staying at Bel Rosso to provide protection. They needed every warrior, old or new, and it was Raven's responsibility to get them ready. Tonight, he'd brought Aislynn with him. She was his first pick of the new recruits and she seemed eager to learn, but Raven had no intentions of making this easy for her.

As Aislynn sat beside him, he went over the grids, explaining how they were being covered and who he'd assigned in each sector. He pointed out key hot spots for immortal activity, highlighting the clubs. "Any questions?"

She looked closely at all the screens, memorizing them instantly and smiled at Raven. "No problem, I'm familiar with the D.C. area, remember I'm from the States. So, I'm hoping I can learn faster than some of the others."

Raven lit up a smoke and sat on the edge of the huge table that held all the monitors and security equipment. "Big hopes and dreams. That's a positive, but don't become too relaxed out there because you think you know the area. It can become disorienting when you're working the rooftops, teleporting from one building to another. This is no game, sister. And you need to use every skill you have. Keep your wits about you, use your gifts, and hone them. This wedding will be huge, and if anything goes wrong, I'm losing my job and my ass along with it. I'm *not* going back to Florence. I intend to make sure every warrior out here, under my command, knows their shit!"

Theo walked in as Raven was lecturing the new female warrior. He stood casually in the doorway with his arms crossed over his chest, listening. He eyed her up, she was small and young, but he'd heard enough good things about her. Her hair was pulled back in a long braid down her back, a red leather strap braided intricately throughout her black hair. Theo was more than glad she wasn't one of the females that had dyed their hair red to look like their queen. Every female he'd seen lately was wearing her hair red, in honor of the queen, but there wasn't a damn one of them could match the unique color of the queen's crimson locks.

Aislynn's body was fit. Her slender, yet muscular frame, looked poured into those black leathers she was wearing, clearly more of Cory's work. She was pretty to look at, but he knew the rules when it came to a sister in arms. She was off limits, but if he could, he'd surely go there.

She was making a good name for herself. She could handle a crossbow like a true warrior, and he'd heard she was equally good with other weapons. Master had his eye on her too. He knew if master chose to personally move your ass up the line, and give you pointers, you'd better take it and run with it. Few ever caught his eye in the hundreds of Medici warriors that served him.

Raven finally shut his trap and looked over at Theo, flipping him the bird. Theo returned the favor with a laugh. "So, what's the plan for the night, bro?"

Raven could read Theo's thoughts plain enough. "The plan is for you to keep your beast in your pants, off limits, brother. This is Aislynn, new recruit right out of camp. I'm working with her tonight and leaving you at the command center. I want her to get a feel for what goes down on the club scene, Grid 7. Let her see the number of immortals that hang out there, who hunts there."

Fist bumping Theo, he looked over at Aislynn. "This is Theo, he's from Florence. Harmless basically, I'm still trying to break him of thinking with his dick instead of his brain, but we're still in the early stages!"

Aislynn stood up and watched, as the two men laughed at their own jokes. She was used to their antics now. It was constant at the camp. "I'm looking forward to getting out there."

Theo shook his shaggy shoulder-length mane. "Oh, I'm sure you are, sister, but you haven't seen the creatures that roll out of this place at night. But you will soon enough."

Raven issued her instructions. "Grab some weapons. Load up on shurikens, sword, no crossbow tonight. I'm going to take that away from you. You need to learn to defend without the safety of your favorite weapon. Best way to learn how to use the other weapons. Let's roll, sister!"

They headed out, Theo staying behind in the command center, recording any kills, and remaining in communication with every warrior on the street.

It was close to midnight and Raven and Aislynn had been keeping a close eye on Grid 7. The clubs and bars were thick in this grid, and the party people were out in droves this Friday night, seeking sex, alcohol, and drugs.

Raven took Aislynn to the rooftops and let his other warriors stay ground level. They'd checked a lot of the surrounding grids, all by teleporting on the rooftops. Raven pointed out to her how to keep track of her surroundings. He was impressed with her skills, and how quickly she learned. He was beginning to see what Shade saw in this one. She had the basic skills and aptitude, now she just needed the experience and training to become a Medici warrior. As they kept watch over their grid, Aislynn loved the experience of being on the rooftops. She realized from this vantage point she could do a lot of damage with most any weapon.

She listened carefully and followed Raven's direction. She was discovering the fun-loving prankster she saw around the camp, was quite different from the serious and deadly warrior who was at her side when he was on duty.

Raven nudged her, and held his finger to his lips, a signal for her to be quiet. He pointed to the left, whispering to her, and giving her instructions. "Vamps in the area. I just pointed out their location in general. Tell me if you can see them."

Aislynn focused her attention, all her senses tuned to the activity on the ground. One club had a large crowd milling outside. She spotted their own Medici warriors immediately, mingling among the crowd. It took her a few seconds, but then she caught the scent of the intruders. "There are three of them, they were together, but now I can see them splitting up."

Raven punched her lightly on the arm. "Good eye! Watch their behavior. They seem pretty loud. If they were hunting, they'd not be this obnoxious. They don't seem to have a plan. It's usually easy to identify which mortal they've singled out as their prey, if they've chosen someone to feed from. But the behavior of these three seems pretty random, disorganized."

Aislynn kept a close eye on them. "They look like they've had too much Midnight. They're too loud, drawing attention to themselves instead of blending in."

As they watched, Raven lost track of one of the vamps and telepathically let one of the Medici warriors on the ground know. Then things started to happen quickly. Four more vamps appeared from inside the club, all of them way out of control and causing a scene.

Raven knew this had to be nipped in the bud before the mortals began to suspect something was wrong. And something *was* wrong, and he was pretty damn sure Aislynn had hit the nail on the head. They were drunk or on something even more volatile, and this could mean trouble. Thinking on his feet, he instructed the warriors to create a barricade between the vamps and the mortals.

The warriors on the ground slowly pushed the vamps to the outside perimeter of the crowd, getting them alone, and taking them out one on one. Working a mixed crowd was nearly impossible, but it was a scenario the Medici warriors were trained for, and they were expert at getting their targets isolated.

Aislynn and Raven watched from the roof as the warriors moved the vamps to the outside of the crowd without being noticed, taking them down. There was no use of weapons, and to any mortal bystander, it looked as if they were throwing their arms around a drunken friend's shoulders. The Medici warriors would walk them quickly into a dark recess or slip into an alley and snap their necks. But something was wrong. It was never this easy. The vamps were definitely on something.

Aislynn's eye caught one vamp that'd slipped free and was now following a small group of young mortal females. The Medici's had no issue with vamps feeding on mortals, as long as the deed was done in such a manner that didn't draw attention to the vamps or leave evidence of what had occurred. These vamps were reckless and irresponsible, risking exposure.

She nudged Raven and pointed them out. The females were taking a side street to another club and they were approaching an intersection. The mortals had wandered away from the crowd and if the vamp was going to make a move, this would be the place to do it. Aislynn knew if she was going to prove herself, it was now or never. "Let me take him."

Raven smiled at her. "Show me what you can do. We've got your back." He telepathically let his warrior know this one was on Aislynn, but stay close in case she had any problems.

Aislynn teleported into the alley between the vamp and the group of females. Slowly unzipping her top, she exposed a bit more cleavage for the vamp, attracting him closer to her. The rogue caught her scent and growled, signaling his sexual arousal. Aislynn lured him in.

"Those mortals won't give you what you need, but this immortal can. Hungry?"

Raven had tuned into her, so he could hear their conversation. He knew Fee used her feminine ways to lure an enemy in, but he'd never seen her in action. He watched as Aislynn pulled it off with ease. The vamp moved slowly up to Aislynn, his fangs punched through as he nuzzled into her neck.

The rogue whispered to her, his words slurred, "You want some good stuff to help you feel good first?"

Aislynn knew something had been off with their actions. Turns out, it wasn't Midnight but drugs. "Sure. What have you got?"

The vamp slipped his hand inside his jacket for the drugs when Aislynn stuck the knife straight into his heart. Raven dropped from the rooftop and put his arm around the vamp and dragged him off, the whole thing over in seconds.

Raven quickly gave orders to transport the bodies, getting them back to the Dead House to be disposed of in the enclosed courtyard to wait for the morning light.

"Aislynn, get back to the Dead House, now."

Aislynn didn't blink, but quickly teleported with Raven back to the Dead House. She felt nervous but invigorated and wasn't sure if she was going to get interrogated or praised.

As they entered the Dead House, Raven quickly gave orders for Theo to go out and help the crew get the dead vamps off the streets. He motioned for Aislynn to take a seat, as he sat in front of the computer and recorded the kills and the location, while it was fresh in his mind. He could feel her nervousness. Turning to her, he lit up a smoke and sat there looking at her.

Aislynn shrugged. "Speak, I can tell you have a lot to say. Just tell it like it is, just because I'm female don't go easy on me."

Raven laughed. "Oh, I had no intention of making anything easy, but you sure made that kill look easy."

Aislynn chose her words carefully. "Look, Raven, you told me to use all my skills. Using my femininity is one of them. It distracted him, he was high on drugs. It wasn't hard to do. Lure him in, take him down."

Raven listened. "What drugs was he on? Because I've seen vamps on drugs and they act the complete opposite of what I was seeing tonight."

Aislynn said she wasn't sure, but maybe they could get the bag off the vamp and have it analyzed. "It made them slow. That makes no sense to me, because clearly, it just makes them easier to take out."

Raven nodded at her. "You did great tonight. I'll talk to boss-man about it, fill him in and let him know how it went down. Those vamps were not warriors, for sure. No warrior would be that stupid. Easy targets."

Aislynn went off to clean her weapons and left Raven to his thoughts. She wanted to be recognized as a Medici warrior, to be the best, and to belong here. These males could teach her so much and she'd learned one thing tonight. They'd give her a chance, but she'd better make the best of it. She had her first kill. She just hoped it was good enough.

88

Shade woke to the sound of the blinds rolling up for the coming night. There were several messages on his cell, all from Raven. He showered, and watched as Kate took on her projects for the night before he settled into his study. He called for Raven to meet him in his office.

Shade grunted as Raven teleported inside the study, kid never uses the damn door. He nodded to the chair opposite his desk as Raven gave him a shit eating grin.

"You called, master?"

"Sometimes, I truly wonder what in the hell I ever saw in you."

Raven flopped down in the chair like he owned the place and grinned. "You saw style, character and speed, boss-man. Good eye, I might add."

Shade shook his head in wonder. "Well, how about your stylish ass gives me a rundown of what happened in D.C. last night. That might be a good place to start." Shade leaned back in his chair, steepling his fingers, his elbows propped on the arms of the chair.

Raven knew he meant business, so he settled in and went over the details, knowing the questions would follow, once he was done going over the play-by-play of events. Shade nodded and ran his fingers through his hair.

"So, you let Aislynn take the kill. That's good. You had enough backup if there was a problem. And you thought it was necessary to take out the other seven?"

Raven crossed one leg over the other and fiddled aimlessly with the shoelace on his boot. "They were causing a scene. You can't take out one and let the others live to tell the tale. Besides, they were drawing attention to themselves. They were all loaded up on street drugs. The dead were taken to the courtyard, laid out for the sun. No one will ever find them."

Shade sat forward in his chair. He knew there was more drug use among the rogues in the larger cities. Every metro area attracted rogue vampires because of the easy feeding grounds the cities provided, plus the access to drugs.

"We've seen the drugs before, but the only thing that concerns me is how many were together. Any ideas on that?"

Raven shrugged. "Friday night in D.C. and you have to ask me that? Maybe you need to roll with us a few nights. You've forgotten what the big city is like. I can work you in on the schedule."

Shade gave him a look. "One of these days, that smart-ass mouth of yours is going to get you in so deep your stylish bullshit will not work. I am just making a point that if we start seeing a huge influx beyond what is normal, we may have something more than a few gypsy rogues looking for a meal. I know it's fairly normal here, and we have seen all kinds wandering through. Let's make sure they keep on wandering. I approve of what you did, how you handled it. Just keep your wits about you and keep this as low profile as possible. I do not want to inform Alec we have another group moving in on his territory."

Raven shook out his long hair. "Look, boss-man, this was no pack, they belonged to no coven. I don't go around picking off vamps for no reason. We see enough of the scene to recognize a rogue. I'm telling you, these drugged-up vamps were drawing attention and heading for a conflict with the mortals. They needed to go down. I just did what you taught me to do. And besides, Master Alec likes me. He thinks I'm one of a kind!"

Shade threw back his head and laughed. "Oh, you are one of a kind, all right." Shade stood and poured himself a Midnight.

"Raven, I need you to do something for me. I hate to lose you for several nights at the Dead House, but I can't let Marcello go right now. The California house is being converted into an inn. Reynaldo and Luciano are running it for me, along with your queen. Mica was just hired as the manager out there. But we have no warriors or protection. This place is going to take off fast. It will be inhabited with mortals staying the night, like a hotel. They will tour the vineyards, buy the damn wine, eat and be merry. So, I need you to figure out how many warriors we need to keep the property under control, who we should send out there and if we have space for their accommodations, or if I need to provide another building. You will need to work with Mica closely and I can see that won't be a problem, I'm sure. You undressed him with your eyes when he was standing here."

Raven jumped out of his chair and began pacing the floor, his body coming alive at the mention of this opportunity. He couldn't believe it! He could spend time with Mica. And he'd be going where he'd always wanted to go, Cali-fucking-fornia! "Are you serious, or yanking my chain, boss-man?"

Shade sighed. "Do I look like I'm yanking any damn thing? This is serious and I need you on it like yesterday!"

Raven was ready to go this minute, fuck yeah, he was more than ready. "Then when can I leave?"

Shade shoved the file across the desk at him. "Details are in there. Arrange the schedule for the coming week at the Dead House, put someone in charge. And I do mean someone who knows what is going down. And then get your ass out there."

Raven picked up the file. "No problem, boss. I got this! Theo can handle the Dead House."

Shade nodded his approval. "Theo is a good choice. Now get your ass out of here and send Aislynn over to see me."

Raven was halfway out the door when he stopped and spun on his booted heels. "You aren't taking her down for this, are you? She took that bastard out without a thought."

Shade grinned. "Just do what I ask you, and we will be fine. You are doing a good job, so far. I'm adding a bit to your schedule, seeing what you can handle. And you let me worry about why I want to speak to Aislynn. Move!"

As Raven teleported out, Shade hoped to hell he was doing the right thing by letting Raven loose in California. He gulped down his Midnight and refilled his glass.

89

Shade could feel Aislynn the moment she teleported inside the house. He turned to see her standing uncertainly in the doorway to the study. "Aislynn, please come in, have a seat."

Aislynn felt her heart slamming inside her chest. If the master wished to see her, she knew she'd done something very wrong or very right. He rarely called the new warriors into his home. Sitting down, she tried to keep her nerves at bay. "I'm sorry I didn't come immediately, Raven was trying to explain where to land inside the house. I've never been inside before."

Shade smiled. "I am sure you have not. Please relax."

Suddenly, Shade felt *bel*, and her anxiety level shot up about ten notches. He recognized his mate was aware there was a female in the house and she was alone with her mate. He'd not really given a second thought about having Aislynn come here, besides, Kate needed to understand this was business and nothing more.

***

Kate was working upstairs with Theresa. They were modifying one of the guest bedrooms to permanently accommodate Theresa who'd move into the main house once the baby was born. Emma had already been selected to replace Theresa's old job as housekeeper once Theresa was promoted to the position of nanny, and Emma would be moving into Theresa's old room in the staff quarters.

As Kate and Theresa worked out the details of the move, Kate picked up on the presence of a female vamp inside the house. She stopped what she was doing and stood still, honing her senses to the presence. She could feel Shade and the young female warrior, but no one else.

Theresa looked up at her. "Is everything all right, my lady."

Kate shook her head, trying unsuccessfully to clear the image from her mind. She was trying to pick up on who the female was. She knew it wasn't Fiamma, but other than that, she couldn't get a read. The female was nervous, and Kate felt her energy.

"It's fine, Theresa... there's someone... Excuse me a moment."

She headed for the door. Despite her best intentions, she couldn't wipe the image of the female from her mind. She knew Shade's devotion to her. But as she neared the term of this pregnancy, she felt as big as a house, and it only exacerbated her insecurities.

He spent every night in the camp with the new warriors, including the females, young, strong, slender, and toned. They were all tall and beautiful and looked like they'd been poured into those leathers Cory crafted for them. It made Kate even more conscious of the changes in her own body.

Theresa sensed her tension and worry. "My lady, you know you have nothing to be concerned about. He worships you."

"I know he does, and he shows me every day. I wish I didn't feel this insecurity. It's my problem. I bring it on myself. He does nothing to deserve it. But I have to go downstairs."

Theresa shook her head as Kate left the room and walked down the stairs, heading toward the study. She could hear their voices, as she approached the door and hoped he wouldn't be mad at her intrusion. She stood in the doorway, seeing Aislynn, the tall brunette who wore her hair in the single braid down her back, seated across from Shade.

"Lover? May I join you?"

Aislynn's head snapped around when she heard her queen and she stood quickly, bowing to her. "Good evening, my lady."

Shade smiled, he felt Kate's insecurities, no matter how hard she tried. He feared nothing would ever get her past that fucking feeder incident Rissa had let loose on him. "*Mi amore*, please come in, you may always join me, you know this." Shade stood from behind the desk and moved to the sofa, making way for Kate to sit next to him. As Kate joined him, he nodded to Aislyn. "Please sit down."

Aislynn quickly sat down, her hands folded in her lap to keep them from shaking.

"*Bel*, I asked to see Aislynn because, last night, she had her first kill as a Medici. She was in D.C. with Raven, and I wanted to make sure she's okay. See how she was affected out there in a real situation."

Kate looked up at Aislynn with surprise. "Oh! Your first kill? I had no idea. Are you okay? I guess I assumed you'd killed many."

Aislynn bowed her head slightly. "Yes, my lady, I'm fine. I've killed before, but I'm assuming master is asking because it's my first kill as a Medici. It was nothing at all, really. I was well protected and had the backup of my brother warriors around me. Raven was teaching me some skills, working the rooftops. I learned some great tips. I'm hoping I'll be a part of the warriors selected to protect D.C. for Master Alec's wedding. I want to prove my worth here. I'm asking for no favors, no leniency."

Kate was surprised by her nonchalance in her admission she'd killed before and that it came easy. She couldn't imagine killing could ever come easy. She remembered being almost immobilized in her fear after killing Cuerpo. But she'd been mortal then. Would she feel different now? She hoped she'd never have to find out. But Aislynn's offhand comment reminded Kate that despite their domestic bliss, their home near the mountains, the stables filled with horses, and the rolling hills that produced the beautiful vineyards, Shade lived in a world of violence, as would her son, and she felt a shiver run through her. She turned to Shade, her hand lightly grazing his cheek. She felt shame over her insecurities. "You need to talk to Aislynn. Do you need privacy?"

Shade felt her concern, and it bothered him. "Not necessary, *mi amore*."

Moving his attention to Aislynn, he said, "I've spoken with Raven, you did well, Aislynn, I am pleased with the outcome. I have a few other questions I wish to speak to you about, but we can speak later at camp. I wish to have Fiamma in on that conversation as well, but I need nothing further tonight. Checking on your wellbeing is part of my job, understand that. I am responsible for all of my warriors and their actions, at all times. Go back to camp. I will be over after I've dealt with other business."

Standing, she nodded to Shade and then looked at her ladyship. "Thank you, master, my lady."

She teleported out. Shade was impressed with the new recruit. He knew she'd do well. He turned his attention to *bel.* "Talk to me. I know you felt uncomfortable having another female in the house. But I sense some fear and it has nothing to do with Aislynn."

Kate laid her head on his shoulder, fighting the urge to cry for no fucking reason. Her hormones were in overdrive. "Not fear, lover. Concern, maybe. You're home more now, and there's been no conflict in D.C. for some time. We live here in our own little world, and I'm able to block out the reality of some of the ugliness. I know the warriors are here to train, to learn to fight more efficiently and to kill, but I manage to block that out somehow. And our son." She squeezed her eyes shut, biting her lip, refusing to let the tears fall. "In my eyes, he's small and vulnerable. But I can see him as a man too, a warrior like his father. And the reality that I'll have both of you out there fighting just hit me."

Shade ran his hand through her hair, sighing deeply. She's so fearful for them both. He could feel her inner turmoil.

"I've hidden so much of my world from you, *bel*. In the beginning, I was fearful you would leave, have nothing to do with me. I couldn't have lived with that. I still can't live with that. I hoped once immortal you would perhaps understand this world better, but I see that being born a mortal, you can never really prepare for this, the death and the dangers are a constant. I'm a warrior, as was my *padre*. I have known nothing else and I apologize for being so insensitive to it. I've dealt with it since my birth. And as you can see, I am still here. Our son will be born into this world of warriors. He too will survive. He will have a purpose and reason to fight and return home. It's the same reason I return to you. I'll always come home to you. I may be broken, beaten and bleeding, but I will fight to my last breath to be in your arms. So will Lorenzo. Love gives you strength beyond anything I can teach or train. It's the most powerful weapon there is, *mi amore*."

She knew his words were true. She knew she'd fight through anything to get to him. Face any obstacle. Overcome any fear.

"I do know that, lover. I feel it in every cell of my being. Your warrior's blood runs in my veins as well. If anything were to threaten you, or our children, my attack would make Aegis look tame. I'm sorry. I'm afraid my emotions are on a rollercoaster right now."

He hugged her tighter as he kissed her. "More like a freight train out of control going full speed downhill and straight into the bowels of hell!"

As they both laughed she punched him lightly, he couldn't help but try to make her smile. "You know I'm teasing you, *mi amore*."

His hand slid along her cheek, gently taking her chin into his fingers and lifting her face to his as he stared at her. "You are so damn beautiful like this, pregnant with our son. Your skin glows, my lily-white, filled with a gift, a child born from our love. Even when you are tired, you still beam with happiness. You know I think you are fucking dead sexy, *si*?"

Kate laughed. "Seriously? Because sexy is the last thing I feel. I love this baby already with every fiber of my being, but I'll be happy when he's born!"

"*Si*, so will I. We will get through this together. We have not very long to wait, now. So, tell me, what can I do to help you? Love, feeding, presents, shoes?"

She sighed. "You already give me all those things. Patience, I just need your patience. And if you have any tricks that will encourage your son to get here a little quicker, now would be a good time to use them."

He chuckled. "You say that like I've done this *padre* thing before. I haven't. I have no tricks, the only trick I know is to love you for all eternity, and my *figlio* as well."

Kate smiled at him and those impossibly blue eyes. "And that is the best trick of all, lover."

90

Raven had prepared himself well, he'd be meeting Mica tonight and that was heavy on his mind. He was intrigued. He'd not been this excited to hang with another male, and he liked the fact Mica wasn't a warrior. Raven spent enough time around warriors. Most of them didn't understand him but accepted him.

But business was first and foremost, and he needed to check out the California property and decide exactly what he thought would be needed to provide adequate security there. He teleported around the property, saw the vast size of it, even larger than Bel Rosso. Boss-man was spending a lot of money here, and it looked like a goldmine in the making. The climate was a little milder here. It wasn't as humid as Virginia, and they weren't too far from the ocean, or from San Francisco. This was nothing like Virginia, and he knew instantly, this was the place for him.

Teleporting outside the front doors, he wasn't there but a few moments when Reynaldo opened the door and Raven grinned at him. "Feels like home, Reynaldo!"

Reynaldo grabbed him into an embrace and beat him on the back. Raven was always a favorite of his, always laughing and joking. He could tell Raven had done some growing up since he'd last seen him at Bel Rosso. He was moving up in the ranks of Medici and that pleased Reynaldo immensely.

"It was good to hear you were coming out here, Raven. How is my lady?"

Raven bobbed his head up and down. "She's huge with the baby. She walks a little like a penguin, but man is she awesome. I love her!"

Reynaldo laughed, some things never changed. "Well come inside. Mica is expecting you. I'll let him give you a tour and fill you in on the things that need to be taken care of. I'll feel more secure knowing we have Medici warriors here with us."

Raven followed Reynaldo in, and picked up Mica's scent. He closed his eyes and let the scent wash over him. Yeah, he belonged in California.

Mica sat in the expansive living room that would now function as living room and lobby area for receiving the new guests. Reynaldo had informed him Raven was arriving to assess their security needs and Mica was anxious to see the young warrior again. He wasn't usually drawn to the warriors. They were much too muscular for his taste, not to mention cocky. But Raven was tall and lanky. He seemed a little young, and the long hair threw him a little, but there was something about him that Mica was drawn to. He was curious to see if the sparks extended beyond their initial meeting. Mica needed to keep it professional, though. This job could be huge for him, and he didn't want to irritate the Medici.

He heard Reynaldo at the front door and their voices carried as the two of them entered. Mica wore light grey dress slacks and a blue cashmere V-neck sweater. Raven entered in jeans that emphasized his long, lean legs, a black turtleneck, heavy boots and rings on every finger. His long black hair swung behind him as he walked in, talking in an animated fashion with Reynaldo. Mica stood to greet him and their eyes instantly connected.

Raven took him in. He was dressed casually, conservatively, and that wasn't what he was usually drawn to. But Mica could be dressed like a clown and he'd still want this vampire's full attention. Raven approached him and his mind spun out of control, he had the worst time getting his mind to focus when Mica was around.

"We meet again Frenchman. Boss-man sure has a big place here. I checked out the boundaries when I teleported in."

Raven felt like he was rambling, and that wasn't like him. He flipped his hair back over his shoulder and smiled at Mica.

Mica could sense Raven's nervousness and he was amused. This warrior, used to killing at the drop of a hat, skilled in the use of every weapon known to mankind, stood before him somewhat tongue-tied. Mica smiled at him, their eyes never leaving each other.

Reynaldo looked from one to the other and chuckled. "I have plenty to do in the kitchen. I don't think you two need me for anything." Reynaldo took his leave as the two men barely noticed his absence.

Mica smiled. "Good to see you again, Raven. Can I get you a Midnight before we begin? I've been here a week now, and I have a few ideas already about what we may need."

"I'll pass...on second thought, hell yes, it's one long teleport out here. Midnight will be good." Raven walked around the room checking out the furniture and the layout of things. "So, the queen did all of this? She has good taste. Do you like her?"

Mica walked to the bar and poured them each a glass of Midnight. Returning to Raven he handed him a glass, making sure their hands touched. "I do like her, very much. It's clear to me the idea of turning this house into an inn was hers. I felt like your master was just indulging her." Mica chuckled. "I have a feeling he'd give her pretty much anything she wants. But I think your master will be surprised. We're already fully booked and have reservations through the Christmas holidays. This place is going to be a gold mine."

As their hands connected, Raven felt the same electricity he felt the first time and he wanted more of this vampire, a lot more. But he was here on important business for the boss. Taking a long drink of his Midnight, he looked sideways at Mica through his long hair.

"Master has a lot on his shoulders. He's been deep in the development of the new camp, plus they have the baby coming. He lets her do as she likes. Bel Rosso was nothing before she came along."

Raven looked around the room again. "And this gold mine means I have a purpose and a future. Give me your ideas. I don't really know anything about this type of business, so I'll need some idea about what you'll need."

Raven flopped down on the chaise and smiled up at Mica. *Cazzo, he's beautiful.*

Mica sat down on the foot of the chaise, as Raven shifted his long legs over to make a space for him.

"Well, it looks as if your queen decorated the place originally with the expectation they'd live here themselves, at least part of the time. There's a master suite upstairs that's locked and I understand it's theirs. Reynaldo had all the electronic blinds removed throughout the house except for their master suite. With an inn like this, the guest must have some freedom to come and go as they please, but at the same time, we're responsible for their safety while they're our guest. I think we need a way to secure the windows throughout the house. No bars, though. That sends the wrong impression. Maybe laser motion detectors? Or install some type of alarm that is triggered if the seal on the window or the glass is broken?"

Raven watched as Mica gave him a small smile. He wasn't sure how in hell he was going to get through this meeting. He wanted to grab him and kiss those lips, but he knew he couldn't make a move. He focused on the job at hand and got back to the security needs. Raven took a sip of the wine before answering. "Electronic sensors are easy to install on the windows. It's very high tech now. We can computerize everything, so if there's any type of breach, we're alerted. Once we have warriors on the grounds, they'll need to stay out of sight of the mortals. They'll need living quarters. We have our own barracks at Bel Rosso and all the other properties master owns. I've only seen Florence and Bel Rosso, and now, here. But they all have fully functional security systems and I can get Luca to help me get everything I need. That's not an issue. We can set up the system inside here, so it will be easy to monitor. I can teach you how it works once we set it up, if you think you can handle me teaching you."

Mica chuckled and ran his hand along Raven's leg. "The question, young warrior, is can you handle me teaching you?"

Raven never saw it coming, but he sure as hell felt it. The heat from Mica's hand traveled through his jeans and straight to his cock. His beast sat up, taking notice of the other male. Raven's breathing became ragged as he looked at those eyes for a second and knew he'd lose complete control if he responded. He quickly looked away. He wanted this man more than anything, but things were moving at a pace even Raven couldn't handle. The lump in his throat was huge. Mica's scent washed over him in waves and his closeness was going to kill him dead. He gulped the Midnight down.

"I might be young, but I've seen enough to know teaching goes both ways. Where do the workers in the vineyards stay? Do they have their own quarters?"

Mica smiled at his nervousness and found it endearing. "Currently, Luciano only uses mortal migrant farm workers. They come in when needed in the vineyards and leave at the end of the day. They're not housed here. Reynaldo lives inside the house, in the suite your queen designed for Luca, and I have an apartment over the garage where your master keeps all his expensive cars that never get driven. The housemaids are already staying in some apartments above the winery, which is not ideal. If we add security staff, your master will need to consider staff quarters that will accommodate everyone. Perhaps, you can connect the staff quarters to the main house by a tunnel, so the staff can move about unnoticed."

Raven nodded. "We have a tunnel system at Bel Rosso. I don't see why the same couldn't be done here."

Moving his booted foot slightly, he let it rub against Mica's side and they both made eye contact. Raven's breath caught in his throat. This was like fucking torture. "Once you show me around I can decide how many warriors we'll need here, and I can give master a recommendation on what he'll need for accommodations."

Mica felt him shift his foot until he made contact, as Mica gazed at him over the top of his glass of Midnight. "Your master can decide if he wants to build another building, or maybe sell those cars and convert the entire garage. It's big enough. In the meantime, the locks on all the doors need to be changed. The guest should only have a key to the front entrance, and the pool entrance, as well as to their individual room. Reynaldo had a company come out and install keyed locks on each of the bedroom suites, but right now, the guest can come and go through any of the exterior doors. We need everything locked down except the front door and the pool door. The only ones with access to the other doors should be staff."

Raven nodded. "I can manage that before I leave. A few phone calls and I can have services done. I'm assuming since my lady whipped all this up, everyone employed inside this mansion is immortal?"

Mica leaned in close enough for Raven to feel his breath on his face. "Are you going to protect me, young warrior?" He licked his lips before sitting up straight again. "And yes, all the work has been done by immortals. Your queen has quite a list of contacts for getting things done.

So, while you're at it, we're going to need camera surveillance, something that monitors the parking lot, and the front door, as well as all the other entrances. We'll need a camera out back that covers the pool and pool house. Do you have a pool at Bel Rosso warrior?"

Raven watched his tongue glide over those plump lips and he almost swooned. *Cazzo!* This vamp knew temptation, and he was definitely interested in him, and vice versa. Raven locked into his gaze. "I can protect you and that fine ass. Don't let my size deceive you. We don't have a pool at Bel Rosso, but there are other things there to entertain us."

Mica smiled at the warrior's attempts to seduce him.

Raven stood up from the chaise lounge and strolled around the room. "The security cameras can be hooked up with everything else and all of it will be computerized. You just need to find a place to set it up where you can view the monitors. Can you manage that?"

Mica followed him with his eyes. "Oh, I can manage it just fine. We have an office on the main floor which I suggest we use to install the security system computer and screens. The library, the dining room, and this living room are open for the guest to use, so we'll keep the security out of sight. Now tell me, are you going back right away? Or will you be staying over?"

Raven locked eyes with Mica. "That depends."

Mica held his gaze. "On what would that depend, my young warrior? Do you think I might be in need of a little protection?"

Raven shook his head, his black hair swinging. "Not from me. I do need to look around, see the space, inside and out. How the rooms are laid out. I'll also need to see the exterior, the entire landscape. So, do I get a room for free or do I have to pay?"

Mica stood. "Well, first things first. I'll gladly give you a full tour. The guests are out right now touring the vineyards and tasting wine in the winery. So, while they're out let's tour the interior first and you can see everything. All the rooms are booked. However, if you wish to stay for the night, my place is always open to you. The fee? Well, I think we can decide on something, don't you?"

Raven met his gaze. "*Si*, we can decide. So, lead the way." *Please, lead the way, before I can no longer breathe standing this close.*

Mica led him up the stairs, grabbing the master key so he could give Raven a quick tour of the bedroom/bathroom suites on the second floor. He walked him through each suite, showing him the number of windows in each room.

"Your queen has quite the imagination. The red bedroom and the black bedroom have been most popular. We have pictures of the rooms up on our website, and those rooms get booked first, especially among the newlyweds." Mica stood in the middle of the black bedroom, "Sexy huh?"

Raven took in the black bedroom. "Looks more like boss-man's taste. He was pretty wild in his day. I could see getting kinky in here. If you are going to do it, go balls to the wall!"

Mica laughed. "Is that your style, young warrior? You have no interest in the art of seduction? In taking it slow? Making it last?" Mica walked past him out the door, grazing his shoulder as he passed him.

Raven was offended. Who in hell did he think he was talking to him like that? Grabbing his arm, he spun Mica around. "You don't know anything about me. I'm more than what you see. There's more to me than this, a lot more. I'm a warrior first and foremost. But I know seduction, I just never found anyone worthy of the effort. So, before you judge me, get to know me."

Mica was startled by the flair of anger, but saw pain behind those eyes as well. He brushed Raven's hair back from his face. "I don't judge you, my young warrior. And I have every intention of getting to know you. As I hope you're interested in getting to know me. Let's see if we can alter history, shall we? And find you someone worth seducing."

The softness of his touch was kind, not given for any other reason than to soften the blow of the harsh words Raven threw at him. His eyes never left Mica, and there was so much sincerity in his face that Raven believed him. "I do want to get to know you. I'm sorry I blew up at you. Lead on."

Mica led him back down the stairs and through the main floor into the living room, a family room with a wide screen TV for the mortals, a library, and a large dining room.

"These are the rooms downstairs the mortals will have access to, if you follow me, this is the office area, and behind this bookcase is a hidden bunker full of weapons I'm sure your master had installed. Through here is the kitchen. This is Reynaldo's turf, so I stay out of his way."

Mica led him out the French doors to the large pool. "And this is the pool. It's lit at night for the guests. We'll be closing it soon for the winter, but it's been very popular."

Mica paused before turning to face Raven. "I apologize if my tone has seemed playful or mocking. I assure you I mean no disrespect. I'm very drawn to you, Raven. I don't want you to leave here thinking differently."

Raven's heart skipped a beat. They had a connection and they both felt it. And for once, he was going to work on making this happen.

"No need to apologize. I'm used to being teased by my brothers about my sexual preferences, my clothes, my jewelry, hell everything. I know I'm young, compared to you. I want to be with you Mica. I usually do hit and runs. I'm not into relationships, but I don't feel that with you. Something is pulling me on a deeper level. But I have a lot to prove to master, the queen, and my brothers. I'm young, but I've come a long damn way and worked hard to get where I am, and I won't lose that. I don't know how to be anything but a warrior. Master taught me. He pulled me from the streets to give me something more, so I owe him. I'm paying him back now with my service and loyalty. It's all I have. I know I come off flippant. That's just my way."

Mica sat down in a pool chair and motioned for Raven to do the same. "We all have our burdens to bear, young warrior. I was born in servitude. I'm part of Master Alec's coven, but he's more interested in mortal pursuits, so we've all been left to our own devices out here, trying to make it as best we can. So, you see, we both have something to prove. I understand your loyalty. The loyalty of the Medici coven to their master is known by all in the vampire community and envied by many, I might add. So, make no apologies for trying to live up to your master's expectations. I work hard as well, and I hope to be here a long time if your master will have me. I'm not usually drawn to warriors, and certainly never to one as young as you, but you have me intrigued. I can be patient, and I'll wait, because I think you're worth waiting for. So, do what you need to do. I'll be here when you're ready to settle down."

Covering his face with his hands, Raven tried not to lose his composure. His toughness and his humor created the mask he wore to hide his pain and vulnerability, but Mica had seen through it.

"No one has ever said that to me before. I can't leave Bel Rosso right now. I have to work my way to getting here. I want to be here. But my life is not my choice, it belongs to my master. He's the only person who ever gave me guidance and a chance to make something of myself. I think you'll be here for a long time, he's a fair master. Master Alec, well, he's just strange as fuck! I never met anyone like him. Who the hell leaves immortality to live like a mortal? He's getting married, in a mortal sense, to his mate. I have the biggest job of my life ahead of me making sure the entire city is secured during this shindig. Every warrior we have will be put to use and I'm in charge. I can do it. I just don't want to let anyone down. So, I need to work on this California gig fast and get it done."

Flopping back in the lounger he took a deep breath. "Growing up and having responsibilities sucks sometimes."

Mica chuckled. "If your master has entrusted you with such responsibility, then I have no doubt you're up for the challenge. No one doubts Shade Medici's authority. I've lived in service to master's, and they talk around us as if we're not there, like we're part of the furniture. I've heard them all discuss the Medici and his dynasty. Your master and his queen are quite different, they treat their coven like family, and I want you to take every opportunity he provides for you. Please him, young warrior, and he'll reward you. He has a lot of property here. Expensive property, and when the inn is in full swing and the vineyards are at full production, its value will triple. He'll need warriors here, and someone to manage them. Perhaps, that can be you. If not, I can manage a long distance relationship, if a relationship is what you're looking for. I'm not your one-night stand, Raven. That's not who I am. That's not what I'm offering."

Sitting up, Raven suddenly wanted more than anything in the world, for Mica to understand what he wanted and to know how serious he was. Reaching for his hand, he grasped it tight and kissed it softly, letting his lips linger, his scent intoxicating. Looking into his eyes, he'd never been more serious in his entire life. "I'm not looking, I found it."

Mica looked at him for a long time before standing and lifting Raven to his feet. They stood face to face, as Raven clung to his hand. Mica led him across the expansive grounds to the huge garage and up the stairs to his private quarters. He would make sure this was a night the young warrior would remember.

91

For once in a very long time, nothing needed his immediate attention. Shade was sitting in his study, thinking about the fact that, soon, his world would change dramatically. He was restless, and his mind was unsettled. He stood and paced, making his way to the back of the house and out onto the patio. Lighting up a smoke, he could hear the sound of the sword fights from the camp. At any other time, he'd relish that sound, but this night, it barely caught his attention.

The night breeze was cool and blew his hair across his face. It was Halloween night in the mortal world, and so many memories flashed through his mind. A year ago, he'd made love with her for the first time, his beautiful lily-white, his delicate *bel rosso* with the crimson hair. She was upstairs now, in their bed alone, sleeping, their son taking his toll on her small body, his arrival coming soon.

Shade began to walk aimlessly across the vast estate that was now his home. He found himself at the stables. Walking inside, he sought out Impavido, and the stallion pawed at the gate of his stall. Without thought, Shade saddled the huge black stallion and mounted him with ease. He took control of the reins and led Impavido outside, where they rode hard and fast across the open field.

One year, one short year, and his life had changed completely, in ways he could never have imagined 365 days ago. One year was like a day to an immortal, but he felt like he'd packed an entire lifetime into this past year. He'd met his mate and turned her into his immortal queen. They'd lost a son, who lay buried in the ground of Bel Rosso. He felt the stab of guilt race through him for that lost child, even though he knew another son was on his way.

His warrior camp in Florence still thrived under Marco's direction, full to the brim with new warriors aching to be Medici. He expanded his warrior camp in the States, letting everyone know the Medici was expanding his realm. Young recruits responded, as they sought to become part of his legacy. His new camp was thriving, and it was only in its first year. He'd built a feeder compound to accommodate the rising number of warriors he now ruled. The vineyards were successful, as was the property in California, and now Kate had turned the California property into an inn. They'd added the stables and brought over horses to breed.

And then there was their home. As his eyes roamed over what they'd built in a year, it looked like a small village carved into the rolling landscape. He could envision the fields that would soon bloom with lavender and whatever else his beautiful mate could come up with. They had the house in Paris, in addition to their vineyards in Italy, France, Greece, and now the States.

He'd subjected her to so much, the loss of the baby, the attack by Cuerpo, her turning, her initial rejection by those who felt she couldn't live up to what would be demanded of her. But she'd won them over, she'd won the hearts of his coven, and now she carried their son.

He brought the horse to a standstill and focused on his son. He felt Lorenzo turn within her belly, and her moan disrupted her sleep. His queen would give him another son, a warrior, a prince. Could he be everything she needed? How could he repay her for bringing his dreams to life, for giving him so much more than he'd ever expected? All of this was due to her. There would be no Bel Rosso without her.

Could he raise his son to be a warrior? His father had been so tough on him, and so distant. He'd made him a fierce warrior, but he wanted more than that for Lorenzo. His father showed no emotion, no tenderness. His *madre* filled that gap, as best his *padre* would allow her. Shade wanted his relationship with Lorenzo to be different. He wanted to show him a world different from the one he knew growing up. He wanted to raise their children together as a team, he and Kate, guiding their children in love. He wanted them to know the true meaning of Medici, the code of honor and integrity, and to be adaptable to an ever changing world.

Even the immortals felt the changes in a world the mortals had made, filled with ever growing terrorism and violence, making the immortal world more challenging as well. He knew Kate feared for him every moment, and she already feared for their unborn son. He only wished he could see the future more clearly, to know what lay ahead of him. He couldn't fail his son. He'd need to do more, be more, learn as he went. He felt like so much was out of his control. Having children felt like he had no control at times, he'd learned that already from Cory.

That was another great change in his life this past year, a son already roaming the earth, unbeknownst to him. His guilt in regard to that was huge and his emotions still raw from the discovery of a son he'd left to grow up in poverty, without guidance in a violent world where he'd had to fight to survive. A half-breed was like filth to the immortals. His sigh was as heavy as his heart. He'd tried to right the wrongs of his past, turn them into something positive. Cory was here with him now, his mother well taken care of. He could never go back and undo what was done. He could only strive to make amends.

Hearing the loud snort from Impavido, his attention was drawn back to the present and he became aware of the rising sun as it called him home. He looked at the estate in the early light, knowing he could never experience it during the bright light of day. It was his curse to live only in the dark of night. Standing in the stirrups, he took one last long view of rolling vineyards and open fields that spread as far as his eyes could see. He knew he'd fight every day to keep it, keep his *bel* and their *bambinos* safe.

Riding back to the stables, he knew one thing. He was loved, he was surrounded by those who loved him and would die protecting all he'd fought to attain. His life had changed, and his thinking had to change as well. He had to open his mind and heart to things around him. It would be up to him to guide them all to a future that kept them safe, happy, and well cared for. He *was* the Medici, and many relied on him, he'd not let them down, he'd not let Kate down, he couldn't let his children down. Their legacy lay on his shoulders.

92

Kate tossed and turned in the large bed alone. The night hours were usually time spent together, but Shade had insisted she stay quiet. She rolled on her side and tried to lie quietly, trying to quiet her mind and clear the long list of things to be done from her head. She felt Lorenzo shift his position and kick, and she smiled and placed her hand on her belly. "It won't be long now, my sweet boy."

She rubbed her hand over her belly, soothing him, when she heard a whisper in her head, *It's time.*

She sat up suddenly and swung her legs over the side of the bed, listening intently. She heard him whisper again, *It's time.*

Kate slid from the bed and stepped into a pair of ballet flats, as she scuffed to the closet. She pulled the nightgown over her head and put on a loose dress that draped around her frame. Grabbing a light jacket, she wandered downstairs, checking the study, but knowing already Shade wasn't there. She stood still and honed her senses, reaching out to him, and felt him in the stables. Stepping out into the chill of the early fall night, the wind caught her hair, blowing it around her face.

Brushing it away, she walked through the gardens, stepping around puddles from the earlier storm as she headed for the stables. She could hear Impavido, snorting and prancing about and knew he'd been out riding. Walking into the lighted stables, she saw Shade, leading Impavido back into the stall. "Lover, I think it's time to go to Florence."

He looked up when she entered and heard her speak. He shook his head for a moment, did she say Florence? "Are you in pain, because I do not feel it?"

"No. I don't feel anything. But Dr. Bonutti said we should go a few weeks before to be safe, and he said I'd know when the time came. Lorenzo just told me it was time."

He felt the grin spread across his face. Walking to her, he took her in his arms, kissing her with passion. "We shall go then. How soon can you be ready? I have the jet and Dante on standby. Everything has been prepared for our arrival at Castello. I have done all I can to be prepared for his arrival."

Kate placed her hands on both sides of his face. "I'm packed already. You had Theresa pack my things weeks ago, so I could be ready quickly. Theresa is ready as well."

"*Si*, Gi and Luca as well. I want my closest *familia* there to celebrate with me. Lorenzo has me in knots of doubt, *mi amore*, about my ability to be a good *padre*, but I want to scream from the highest mountains that he is coming. You must think I am completely out of my head lately."

Kate laughed. "Don't fall apart on me now. I'm going to need all the support I can get. Come. Let's get back to the house and figure out what we need to finish doing, before we leave for Florence."

Walking up the road with her, she held her hands over her belly.

As they walked into the house, Shade called out, "Gi! Now!"

Gi scurried to the door to see master with my lady. "Master! Is everything okay?"

"Our *figlio* is on his way. I need you to contact Castello, tell them we are coming. Contact Dante. We will fly at sunrise so I can take my death slumber on the plane. Have Kate's things loaded in the car and ready to go. Let Bonutti know we are heading to Florence. I want him to see Kate as soon as we arrive, just to make sure she is well. You and Theresa will fly with us, so get your things loaded as well. Go!"

He watched as Gi scurried off and Shade took her hand and led her up the stairs. "I need to shower, and then I will lay down for just a bit with you. I will sleep a few hours now, then complete my death slumber on the flight over. Do you think you will be all right? Theresa and Gi will be with you. I have made arrangements for everything here while we are gone. Raven will manage D.C., and Marcello will run the camp. Anything else I need to do?"

Kate laughed as he led her to the bed and encouraged her to lie down, handling her like a porcelain doll. "We have plenty of time, so the first thing you can do is slow down. And seriously, I hope you aren't planning to make me stay in bed until the baby comes. I should call Shannon and let her know we're leaving."

Pacing the floor, he ran his hands through his hair. Kicking his boots off, he slid out of his jeans and tossed them across the room.

"Shannon? Does she want to come with us to Italy? I need Luca with us so I can feed. I fucking knew I would forget something!"

Kate propped the pillows against the headboard and enjoyed the floor show, as he tossed his clothes around the room and worked himself into an agitated state.

"Go take your shower, I'll call Shannon. I'll see if she can join us, but I doubt she could stay the entire time since she still has a job, but she's welcome of course."

Stopping his pacing, he stood with his hands on his hips and looked at her lying casually on their bed as if nothing was happening. "Do you need anything? Any pain?"

"Uh..." Kate glanced at the clock by the bed. "No, no pain since the last time you inquired about fifteen minutes ago. Lover, the birth is still a week or two away. Dr. Bonutti said to go early, remember?"

He sat down on the side of the bed, looking at her, like it was the first time he'd ever laid eyes on her. He knew he needed to take control, she was depending on him and he took a deep breath, trying to get his mind settled. He kissed her gently before walking to the shower. Life was about to change dramatically for both of them.

Kate smiled at him in his effort to get his emotions under control. As he headed for the shower, she glanced at the clock again. Only 6:00 a.m. It might still be too early to call Shannon. She'd wait to let her friend know they were leaving. She heard a light tap on the door and Kate called out, "Enter."

Theresa came in, all smiles, to get the luggage from her closet. "I'll just grab your bags, my lady, and we'll have them loaded in the car. Dante will be here shortly. My bags are ready as well. Is there anything I can get for you?"

Kate shook her head. "I'm fine, Theresa. I'm just excited, happy, and very glad it won't be long now before we can hold this baby."

Theresa beamed at her. "It's been such a long time since we've had a birth in the Medici line. Shade's was the last. There were many that thought he'd never settle down, never find his mate, and the Medici dynasty would die out, just as so many of the great ancient covens have done. You must prepare yourself, my lady. If you think the coven was jubilant at seeing their new queen, it will be nothing compared to seeing the heir to the Medici crown being born."

Kate smiled and rubbed her belly. "Seems much will be expected of you, Lorenzo, and you aren't even here yet."

Theresa nodded. "Indeed that is so. He will carry the weight of inheriting the coven from the moment of his birth. He is born to greatness." Theresa gathered the luggage from the closet and carried it downstairs.

Shade emerged from the shower, towel wrapped around his waist, his hair still damp. "I feel better. Sleep with me now. When we wake, they will have everything loaded in the car, the plane ready and Dante will be downstairs to take us all to the hanger."

He walked to the bed, sliding beneath the blankets with her, the blinds already sealing out the day. He held her close as the slumber took him. "*Ti amo, mi amore*.

93

Rissa and Hyde spent the entire day attending to her busy schedule. She stopped at the house to take a quick shower, change her clothes, , and asked Hyde to wait for her. She wanted to teleport out to Bel Rosso to ride Biondo. She asked Hyde to ride with her this evening.

The riding had become a big part of her routine now, alternating her kick boxing and gym workout with the horses. She'd never felt better physically, plus it seemed to help her to mentally calm herself as well. Alec had been right, she needed to relax and have down time in an environment that was safe and secure, and allowed her to enjoy the beauty of nature.

Changing into her riding gear, she rejoined Hyde in the foyer and they teleported out to the stables. As always, Angelo had Biondo saddled up and ready for their ride. It was getting dark much earlier, now that November was here, the air was brisk, and as far as Rissa was concerned, this was the best time of year to ride.

Hyde mounted one of the other horses Angelo wanted exercised today as he joined her for the ride, a practice which had become quite common. He was an excellent rider and Rissa found him very compatible. He always helped her mount Biondo, and she never objected. In fact, she rather liked his gentlemanly attentions and his strong hands on her waist.

He had a firm grip. She felt it often, as he was always close to her throughout the work day. He easily led her through the crowds of press, his hand firmly placed on the small of her back. His voice was a constant reassurance in her ear piece, as he spoke to her about what he wanted her to watch out for, in his strong, commanding tone.

He'd been a great choice as her protector and every day that passed, they became closer. He looked at her, mounted his own horse and nodded, signaling her to move ahead. Rissa snapped the reins and kicked her heels into the horse, and Biondo took off. Rissa's hair flew behind her in a torrent of blonde waves as she laughed. "Let's ride!"

She took off through the pasture, riding hard and fast, pushing Biondo and freeing her mind. She could hear the hooves of the other horse following her and knew Hyde was close behind. As the fence line approached, she prepared to jump, leaning low over Biondo's outstretched neck, and lifting from the saddle as she jumped the fence with ease.

They were soon well away from the house and stables and out into the open fields near the mountain base. Hyde blasted past her, riding full out and she smiled, watching his fine ass in those tight jeans. He was so damn sexy, yet had all the qualities of a gentleman.

As he rode past her, he reached for her reins, slowing them both down. "There are some trails that lead up the mountainside. You interested?"

Rissa nodded as she patted Biondo. "Yes, we need a cool down. Lead on."

Following Hyde as he led the way up the trails, it was a perfect Fall night for a ride. After about thirty minutes of riding the curving uphill trails, they came to a clearing near a jagged rocky cliff. Hyde dismounted and helped her off Biondo, as they walked out onto the flattened, hard stone ledge.

Rissa walked as close to the edge as she felt comfortable. Her eyes scanned the incredible landscape that glistened in the moonlight. "This is a beautiful view!" Taking a deep breath, she inhaled the clean, cold air and felt the calming effect of being surrounded by nature.

Hyde stepped up next to her, sitting on the ledge, patting the space beside him for her to join him. "Come on, sit down, Rissa, and enjoy nature for a moment."

She carefully sat down next to him, as she scanned the valley below and absorbed the quietness of the night. It was so relaxing. She tried to clear her mind, but the ever present thoughts of the wedding pushed through. All the time and energy she'd spent to make it perfect, she only hoped it would come off as she'd so carefully planned.

Hyde pulled a flask of Midnight from his pocket and handed it to her with a smile. She quickly took a long, deep drink, feeling it sing through her system.

"Easy, there's only one flask full." Hyde could always tell when she needed to feed from Canton. She was easily agitated and tired more quickly.

Rissa handed him back the flask. "It tastes good, gives me some energy."

Hyde took a sip and let his eyes roam. "You need to feed more often, Rissa, your schedule is tough. You have a lot ahead of you. You need to be on your game. The press is all over us lately, and it will only get more intense."

Rissa could see through the now bare trees, the fiery glory of fall starting to fade from the branches. She could see the main house clearly from here. It was dark, and the house was usually well lit, but tonight, she saw nothing. She'd noticed little activity when she arrived and wondered what was going on. "I'm fine, Hyde. Alec is busy too." Her sigh seemed loud in the quiet. "I hardly ever see him lately. Both of us are too busy with our own endeavors to be bothered." She pointed to the main house at Bel

Rosso. “The house looks deserted. Usually, there are lights everywhere. Is something going on?"

Hyde looked down at the house. "Kate and Shade have gone to Florence. She’s ready to have the baby. It won’t be long before there’s an heir to Medici. Most of the household staff has gone with them, but the warriors and I have everything under control."

Rissa smiled. "That’s good. I hope by the time the wedding comes, Shade’s warriors have a plan in place. I’ll need you, Hyde. I don’t want one thing to go wrong! Do you understand me?"

Hyde turned to her. "Rissa, you need to stop worrying about things you can’t control. There’s so much security being planned it would make your head spin. There will be security inside and out."

She closed her eyes. “Will I have those long haired brutes roaming through my wedding guests? They’re so uncouth and look like a pack of street thugs."

Hyde couldn’t help the chuckle that escaped him. "Christ, Rissa, you make us sound like Neanderthals. Medici warriors clean up well, and Shade will select who’ll blend well among the mortals for the assignments on the inside. They’ll all be dressed formally. The rest will be stationed out of sight, outdoors. Washington will be well covered that night."

She lowered her head and looked at him. "You’ll be with me, though?"

He took her cold hand in his and squeezed it tight. "Of course, I’ll be with you the entire time, except when you take that walk down the aisle. Alec will be waiting. Why are you so worried?"

"I know I’m being ridiculous. I need for everything to be perfect. This is the biggest event I’ve ever organized, and it’s my own. It reflects on Alec. I do this for him."

Hyde let go of her hand as he returned her gaze. He saw a flash of fear and vulnerability, something she rarely showed. “I think you do this for you as well."

She looked away, trying to comprehend all that was ahead of her. She was excited and anxious, nervous with anticipation, and wishing it was over with already. Every eye would be on her, and any mistake would be on the front page, and Alec would punish her for it.

“He needs this to be perfect. His climb to the presidency is all he thinks about. I want him to get there without a hitch. I love him. I do wonder, sometimes, how different my life would be if we’d never met. Where I’d be now? Would I still be a mortal? Would I be married perhaps, with babies, living in the house with the white picket fence?"

She looked at the main house at Bel Rosso with longing in her heart. Why did Kate seem to have it all? She had the perfect mate, the money, the house, the babies, and this perfect little life. Not all of it was for Rissa, she knew that, but her mind still wandered there now more than ever. "I'm rambling. How pathetic I sound, and so middle class."

Hyde shook his head. "Rissa, your destiny is laid before you now, make the most of it. Be happy in what you have, others are not so fortunate."

She laughed softly. "Not from my viewpoint, at the moment."

Standing up, she stretched. "Let's get back, it's getting late and tomorrow will bring another busy day. The wedding is just weeks away. I'm as ready as I can be. I'll come out on top like I always do. The darling of G-town will rise to her element on that day. And everyone around me will be astounded at the perfection and beauty, the elegance and style of Mrs. Alec Canton, Senator Canton's beautiful, well-spoken wife. And eventually, I'll be the First Lady." She looked at him and smiled. "I can and will be fine. It's what I do!"

He grinned as he stood up. "I have no doubts in that, Rissa."

Giving a whistle, the horses came strolling back to the two of them. Hyde helped her mount and then mounted his steed as well. Taking the reins, he led the horses down the mountainside and back out into the open fields.

Once in the field, Rissa rode full out back to the stables, taking the fences like a pro. She knew she was the most prized catch in D.C, and nothing would stop her from having it all. She thought, *To hell with the 'Queen', and her happiness and her babies. I am Larissa Benneteau, and nothing will interfere with my destiny! Alec and I will rule this country together, two immortals rising to conquer it all. The world will bow at my feet someday, and I have no intention of letting anyone spoil my plans.*

94

Shade made his way to the barracks across the fields of the warrior camp. Being back in Florence a week now, he was still waiting for the arrival of his son, and it had him out of sorts. Everything was prepared. Kate was resting as much as possible, but the household at Castello, as well as the entire coven, was teeming with anticipation of the big event.

He needed to keep busy and Kate wanted him out of her hair. He hated leaving her side for one second, in case it was time. She was relaxed about the whole ordeal, and told him constantly to calm down. Heading straight to Marco's quarters, he'd not made a lot of time for his old friend except for the brief encounter when they'd first arrived. Rapping on the door with his fist, he knew the warriors would soon be at their duties and he intended to spend some time out here tonight with Marco. Besides, it was always good for the young Florence warriors to see their master on the field whenever he was here.

Marco recognized the knock on his door. He smiled to himself as he got off his bed and answered to his lifelong friend and master. "Glad you finally came to see me. Been a week already, brother. You sure your woman knows you're out?"

Shaking his head and laughing, it was like old times between them already. Their brotherhood went as far back as he could remember, and no one else would ever have the balls to talk to him in that manner and live to tell about it. "*Buonasera* to you too, old man. I have a pass card from my female to be out of the house, you need to stamp it or some shit, bro?" Flipping Marco the bird, he flopped down in Marco's sparse, all alpha male accommodations.

Marco burst out laughing, slapping his old friend on the back. "Maybe I should stamp it. You can take it back to the little woman; make sure she knows where you've been. You got a curfew or something? Wouldn't want to get her riled up or anything." Marco lit up a cigarette and tossed the pack to Shade before he flopped onto his bed.

Shade grabbed the pack in one hand and lit up, throwing his feet up on the table. He'd almost forgotten how simple and casual the barracks were, and what it felt like to be housed in these quarters, surrounded by males around the clock.

"You done yet? Let me know when you're finished." Taking a long drag, Shade stared at Marco. "If you'd settle your old ass down, you could have this life too, but you seem to have never finished sowing your wild oats. I prefer where I am now, to be honest, the love of a good female, feeding is pure and sweet, and my cock is never neglected. And now, I have *bambinos* on the way. Never thought I would be here, brother, but I am, and I like it."

Marco slapped his leg as he laughed. "Brother, your single life may be described in many ways, but your cock was never neglected. I'm surprised it still works. Or maybe that's the problem? You wore it out, so you had to settle down? Or you got some kind of extended warranty on that thing?"

Shade inhaled on the cigarettes. "I got more pussy than you could ever imagine, you always were jealous of how the females flocked around me. They didn't just go for my rugged good looks but the size of my dick! Don't lie. You know it's the truth. And I have a *figlio* coming, so we know it's not broken. It's working better than ever. You jealous of me or just like giving me shit for no good reason? Because I have news for you, my ass will be on that field tonight. So, if you want to test me, you will still lose like always!"

Shade dropped his feet to the floor and stood pacing, his hands instantly going through his mane of dark curls.

Marco sat forward, resting his arms on his knees, watching as Shade paced nervously. Marco knew he was eager for this baby to be born and waiting was never Shade's strong suit.

"Brother, when you die, that cock is going in the Vampire Hall of Fame. I imagine the women will still flock to it. We'll put it behind a glass display case. Sell tickets. Make a fortune. More money than you ever made on all that Midnight. Speaking of which, pour us a glass, old friend. And then, if you want me to beat your ass on the training field, I will gladly take the challenge."

Shade turned to look at him. "Yeah, well, no females will be getting anywhere near my tool. They will need to get through my queen first. *Cazzo*, brother, this waiting bullshit is killing me."

Walking over to the makeshift bar, there was no shortage of drink in Marco's place. Marco had laid heavy on the Midnight in his earlier days, more than Shade was comfortable with, but his brother never let him down.

Shade reminded him, "You forget, my ass has been training young warriors in the States. Damn, brother, I got this one female recruit, she is going to rival Fiamma at some point! Either my ass is getting old or they are getting a lot younger. They seem like babies to my eyes. They come to the camp and already have good skills with weapons and killing. I just need to teach them discipline and technique. My ass is getting a work out, but it's not like the streets. Kate is happier having me home and off the streets. I know I won't lose my skills...but fuck me."

Pouring Midnight into two glasses, Shade slapped the drink in his brother's hand. Downing the Midnight in one gulp, he poured himself another. "Just fucking look at me, five damn minutes with you and I am downing the Midnight like the old days!"

Marco chuckled. "Give me a whole week, and I will get you back to normal, brother. Heard you built a feeder compound inside your camp. Now you telling me you don't visit? Your woman must know every man needs a little variety in his diet, and you built a buffet. Surely, she can't begrudge you dessert as long as you always come back home for the main course."

Shade growled under his breath. "Watch it! You probably know more about that compound than I will ever know. She fucking hates feeders. *Cazzo*! Do you know who the matron is? How many times did we both tap that? Seriously, Kate is all I ever want. I don't crave anyone else, and I haven't had her blood in what seems like centuries. Makes me agitated and anxious, but it is worth it to hold my *figlio* in my arms."

Shade punched him hard on the shoulder. "So, I assume you are still whoring your ass around and not settled down yet by the comments that roll casually off your tongue. Don't you even think about it?"

Shade watched some of the humor leave Marco's face, and it was just as he thought. "Have you seen Theresa since we came back? Tit for tat, brother."

Marco looked at the floor. "Yeah, I've seen her. What the fuck, brother? She ditched the black and white uniform and took her hair out of that tight bun. She was in a pair of tight jeans, her hair hanging down. She added blonde highlights or something. Was wearing make-up. Does she have somebody in the States?"

Shade shook his head. "No one I'm aware of. She has changed, she will no longer be Kate's Lady in Waiting, but the nanny to my son. Are you regretting letting her go?"

Marco shrugged. "I will always miss Terri. But I'll never settle down, Shade, and to be honest, I never thought I'd see the day when you would. I knew you'd mate and produce an heir. That was expected of you to continue the Medici dynasty. I just never thought of you as a one-woman man, still having trouble buying it. I had heard how Kate hated the feeders. That is why I was so surprised when I heard you built the compound. And Matron leaving us? I have a feeling Gi had a hand in that selection. But Matron took some of our best young feeders with her to the States. So, what do you do when you need to feed now, just go from girl to girl, so you don't get attached? I'm pretty sure with the tight reins Kate keeps on you, she's not letting you hunt to feed."

Shade sat on the edge of the bed, his back to his brother. "The feeder compound is not an option. We found our own solution, one that she accepts. She struggled with it, but we have found peace. Close, convenient, and discreet. It's Luca. That is the reason I brought him along on this trip. He has a mortal female he is attached to in the States, but she was not able to join him. He has been teleporting back and forth to feed from her.

Shade waited. No one outside the Bel Rosso household knew of their arrangement. He wondered how the information would be received by Marco.

Marco let that sink in. "Wait, you're telling me you built a feeder compound right on your property, pulled the sweetest feeders Europe had to offer, and you lie with Luca?" Marco shook his head, slapping Shade on the back. "Brother, you got it bad. Never thought I'd see a woman that could tame Shade Medici. Remind me to bow down even lower the next time I see our queen."

Shade laughed. "And if you don't, I will push that stubborn ass of yours to the floor. So, take me out on the field, help me get rid of this fucking angst that is eating me alive. I fucking hate waiting!"

Shade stood and set his empty glass on the table. "One other thing I need to check out tonight. I need five warriors to come back with me to Bel Rosso, I will need them permanently assigned in California. Kate turned the estate into a working inn for mortals. I have housemaids out there and Reynaldo is running things at the moment. But we need protection, and now, I can't spare one warrior from my camp. Canton has this farce wedding coming up. So, I need them to get out there, once we have the living quarters settled, which won't be long. Raven has been overseeing things out there, setting things up. I need you to point out which ones you suggest."

Marco stood, draping his arm around Shade's shoulder. "Come on, brother. I'll point out a few I think you'll like. Good timing. All the new recruits came in the fall, time to assign some of the warriors who have been here a while, anyway. Barracks were getting crowded."

Marco led him out onto the well-lit training field where young warriors and new recruits were paired off, while older warriors trained them, challenging their skills and technique. They stood together on the field, listening to the familiar sound of the swords clanking, metal against metal.

Marco looked at his old friend. "That's the only music I want to hear. I will leave the sound of crying babies and lullabies to you, old man. Now pick out who you'd like to protect your assets...and your ass."

95

Marco headed to Castello. He'd made the final selection on the five warriors that were to return with Shade to the States, and he wanted to take him the list, see if there were any changes before he informed the warriors of the decision. He'd spoken to all of the candidates who'd been considered for the job. He'd informed them of what their duties would be and where they'd be located, if they were selected.

He walked through the long corridors of the castle. He rarely came inside, and it always made him feel uncomfortable, when he did. He could have sent Shade a message to come see him in the barracks, but secretly, Marco was hoping to run into Theresa. He'd seen her from a distance a few times since they'd arrived, and he'd made sure his presence was known.

She looked different, and he wanted to hear from her own lips if she'd found someone in the States. He'd let her go. It had been his choice to break the bond that kept them together. He didn't regret his choice. It was one he'd made for her. He wanted her to have a better life, and it was damn obvious she did. He needed to know she was well that she'd found her place in this life and was happy. He took to the upper floor where there was more activity, and tried to look casual and unobtrusive, as if he regularly strolled these halls on business.

***

Theresa packed away her black uniforms with the white aprons. She'd worn that uniform most of her adult life, as much a part of her as leathers were to the warriors. The uniform had identified her station. But now, as nanny to the children of her master, she'd dress in street clothes. She'd made several trips into Florence to buy a new wardrobe. She knew, in the beginning, the baby wouldn't be taken out much. The baby's need to feed, and not having restraint, would require he not be seen in the mortal world. Within a month, their feeding was more under control, and Lorenzo could be taken out for short periods of time, right after being fed.

She'd chosen a casual wardrobe of jeans and slacks, comfortable sweaters, a few dresses, and sensible shoes. She'd released her hair from the tight bun and allowed it to hang freely down her back. She had splurged and gotten some blonde highlights in her soft brown hair. My lady had recommended several make-up brands Theresa had been experimenting with, nothing too over the top, just a little blush and lipstick to add some color. Besides, once Lorenzo was born, she had a feeling neither she nor my lady would have a lot of time for primping. She ran the brush through her hair one final time, then picked up a bottle of expensive perfume. She examined the bottle closely, another suggestion from my lady. Kate said the fragrance suited her, so Theresa spritzed on the perfume. She gathered up the uniforms to take to Emma and headed out the door of her room, and straight into Marco. "Marco! I didn't expect to see you here. In the house, I mean." Theresa blushed.

"Terri." He gripped her arm to steady her. "I didn't mean to startle you. Just here to find Shade to inform him of some information on the warriors he needed."

He looked her up and down, she was so beautiful. Her hair was down and softer now, with blonde highlights that caught the light. She was wearing makeup. *Cazzo, she smells like a feeder ready to be ravaged. What the fuck has happened to her in the States?*

Theresa was keenly aware of how close he stood to her, and how ruggedly handsome he was. "Shade is with my lady. I can get him if you want."

His eyes never left her face. There was an ache inside him, he'd missed her, and he hated admitting that to himself. "No, not necessary, if he is with the queen, I will catch up with him later."

"You're looking well, Marco. How've you been? I thought you might contact me after the coronation, to just, you know, stay in touch."

"I apologize for not contacting you. I wasn't sure how you would respond. And I heard nothing from you. You look different. It seems to suit you, living in the States."

His hand trailed up and down her arm. He didn't think being this close to her would make him ache for the taste of her.

Theresa was aware of the light caress. "I thought you wanted a clean break. And when I didn't hear from you, I just assumed you'd moved on. I have a good life there, and I've been happy. But I'd be lying if I said I didn't miss you."

Marco lifted the strands of her hair, feeling their silkiness through his fingers. He stepped in closer, almost caging her in as her back went against the wall. "I miss you too. Is there...someone? Some other male who makes you happy?"

Marco stood so close she could feel his breath on her face, and the memories of their intimate times together flooded over her. "There's no one, Marco. I doubt you can say the same, though."

He leaned into her neck, his mouth watered with want for her. He felt like he was losing his mind! They'd not been together for so long. He missed the way she could calm him, satisfy everything inside him like no other. Kissing her neck gently, he whispered in her ear. "No one like you,

Terri, no one can take care of me like you did. Come to me tonight. Please, come be with me. I miss you, I need you."

Theresa turned her head away from him. "For tonight, Marco? Is that all you can offer me?"

Stepping back from her, taking her face in his hands, he wasn't sure what the hell he wanted. He just knew right now, he wanted her. "What is it you want, Terri? You are there and I am here. Nothing has changed. I can feel you, still. You want this as much as I do."

"I don't deny the attraction. We can both feel it. Why is your heart so hardened? Many vampires of our station are separated by duty. You could choose to commit to me. I'll be here often once the baby is born. Our master will want his coven to see this baby grow into a man. And there will be other babies that follow. Do you honestly think master would deny you? If you asked to visit me in the States, do you think he'd say no? I feed, but I have not chosen another male since leaving you."

Marco leaned his forehead against hers. He wanted her to be happy, and move on without him, but deep inside, he needed her more than he ever thought. Kissing her deeply, she didn't resist. He felt her heartbeat rise, her body warm, sweet in his embrace.

"I am still a warrior and that will never change. It is what I was born to do. Shade would deny me if he felt it necessary. He is like my brother, but he is business first. He would never let me leave here on a permanent basis like you have. Do you want this bonding between us? A commitment is what you seek?"

He stepped back and leaned against the wall. "You have not sought another since leaving here? Do I hold you back? Is it me you crave?"

She let the wall support her weight, as she looked back at him. "There are others I could go to Marco, but it's you I chose. You hold me back in that you still hold my heart. And yes, a commitment is what I want. I know what it means. I know we'll live on two separate continents and it will limit when we can be together. I can commit to you. Can you do the same?"

He looked at her. She wanted something from him he'd never given to anyone, not even her, but she'd held him longer than any other woman. Maybe Shade was right, maybe it was time he gave up his whoring ways and became more settled. She tempted him. She'd commit to him.

"I will not be able to feed often enough from you, Terri, you know that. Nor will you. I will have to use feeders. You can handle that? Trust me enough for that?"

"As long as you don't hunt, or give your heart to the feeder. I understand the demands of our bodies and what you must do. I don't want you to deny yourself, become weak because you're waiting for me. But can you limit yourself to feeders? And go only when your hunger demands it? Or must you continue in the tradition of the warriors, conquering every female because you can."

Marco sighed. "I didn't want to let you go. But I broke that bond because I wanted you to move on, move up in your station in life. Realize your full potential. Staying here would have held you back, and you would never have risen so high. Look at you now, nanny to the children of Medici. That would not have happened if I had asked you to stay here with me. I did it for you Terri, not me.

"Being a warrior is all I know. But I am finding out you can have the best of both worlds, or so Shade tells me. I am not a romantic, I don't know how to court you, but I know you love me. You always have."

Pushing himself from the wall, he captured her tight in his arms, holding her. "I have denied myself for you. But I thought you would move on and find someone that could give you what I could not. Not a warrior bound to a master and stuck here for all eternity. I love you, Terri. You have had my heart for a long time. I do not want it back."

"I never let it go, Marco." Theresa dropped the uniforms to the floor as he pulled her to him, letting him take her in his embrace. She slid her arms around him, inhaling the masculine scent of him. She'd only been with female feeders in the States. And while there were almost as many males at Bel Rosso now as there were at Castello, none would ever hold her heart like Marco.

Pulling her hair back from her neck, he nipped softly at the pulsing vein, not caring who saw them. It wasn't acceptable for the staff to behave this way inside the hallways at Castello, but right now, Marco could care less about the rules. He kissed her neck, then her lips, leaving her breathless and panting. "Then don't start now. Come to me tonight. Be with me, as it should be."

Kissing her hard and passionately, she melted into him. Breaking away, he took a step back and locked eyes with her. "You want a commitment, Terri. Here it is. You are mine."

Turning, he walked back the way he entered, a cocky grin on his face and his heart beating out of his chest.

96

Kate stood at the window in their bedroom at Castillo. She leaned her head against the cool glass and watched, as her warm breath created a frost on the window pane. She lifted her hand and drew a heart in the mist, sighing heavily. Looking out over the formal gardens, lit by the moonlight, she could see the lights of the warrior camp in the distance. It had been almost two weeks now, and she was growing weary of her beautifully appointed prison cell. She and Theresa had laughed at how overprotective Shade had been. He didn't allow her to lift anything heavier than a sock and hadn't wanted her to walk outside in case she'd fall. He insisted someone be with her on the stairs. She gently caressed her belly and whispered, "Anytime, Lorenzo."

She heard Theresa enter, followed by Emma. Theresa had been schooling Emma on her routine, since Emma would be coming back to the States and assuming Theresa's old duties. Kate turned from the window, smiling to greet them, when she was struck by a sharp pain, a spasm that started at her back and moved around to her belly. Kate took a sharp intake of breath, as she placed both hands on her belly, bending at the waist.

Kate looked up, making eye contact with Theresa as a sliver of fear ran through her. She'd waited for this moment, and now that it was here, she was hoping she had the strength to face what was ahead. There would be no drugs used, no epidurals. This baby must fight to be born. It was their tradition.

Theresa and Emma were at her side immediately. Theresa asked her to describe the pain, and Kate told her it was like a vice, squeezing her. Theresa nodded and told her to let Shade know. Kate straightened up, taking a deep breath as the pain subsided, and sent him a message. **"Lover, it's time."**

***

Pacing the field, he watched the warriors and their careful sword play. He and Marco had spent a lot of nights out here observing the warriors work. He'd suggested a few changes in technique for several of the new recruits, but otherwise was pleased with how this group was progressing.

Marco approached him and threw him a sword and grinned. "You ready to get your ass whipped, old man?" Marco raised his sword high in the air.

"Bring it, brother!"

They both went at it, the sound of the metal clanging was deafening, as the two most feared warriors in the world played at mock battle. Shade missed his mark and flipped over Marco's head to avoid the deadly point of his weapon, when her voice rang in his head. *It was time*.

He stood spellbound. The moment had come. He dropped his sword to the ground and stared at Marco.

Marco looked at him and laughed. "You are surrendering already, old man?"

Shade's face was emotionless, his heart slowed, and he stood tall. "It's time."

Marco nodded. "*Per sempre* Medici."

There was a loud roar from the warriors, but it was a sound Shade never heard. He'd already teleported inside Castello and landed inside the bed chamber. He found her cradling her stomach, Theresa and Emma beside her as they walked with her to a chair. "Kate!"

He crouched down before her, laying his hands on her stomach. "Emma, get Gi, have him summon Council and Dr. Bonutti. Have them escorted to the chamber the second they arrive. Theresa, go to the chamber, get prepared. I'll take her down. Go!"

As they scurried from the room, he tipped her chin up to him and smiled into her eyes. "I love you, it will be fine. I will be with you. Do you want to change into a fresh gown, anything you need before we go to the chamber?"

Kate heard him take control, delivering instructions to Theresa and Emma, who'd left to set things in motion. She was in the grips of another contraction, feeling the muscles contract around her middle. *Should they be coming this fast already?* She heard Shade ask if she wanted a fresh gown. It took a moment for her to process the question, as she looked down at the soft white gown that flowed to the floor, her bare feet peeking out beneath the hem.

She shook her head. "No, I think I'm fine. Theresa had just helped with my bath and put this gown on me."

Kate remembered the last ordeal in the chamber, and hoped this one wouldn't be as taxing, but her only references for women giving birth were the mortal images of starkly lit hospitals, and doctors behind masks, and she knew her experience would be nothing like that. They'd have their own protocol, secreted away, below ground in the chamber that lie beneath Castello. She gripped his hand as another wave of pain, circling her belly from back to front, washed over her.

He massaged her belly as the pain gripped her, he felt the intensity of it rip through him. "Breathe, *mi amore*, deep breaths, it helps the muscles release. Lorenzo is just making his way to us, *si*? I can teleport us down to the chamber."

Kate felt him lift her effortlessly, and she laid her head against his chest. In an instant, he had her below ground in the stone corridor, dimly lit by torch light as he carried her to the door of the chamber. Kate lifted her head from his chest to see Dr. Bonutti standing there already, and two members of Council. She couldn't remember their names, but they stood silently in their hooded robes, one in green and one in white. Gi was holding the Medici ledger that Shade had taken into the chamber when he'd turned her, and handed it to the doctor. He nodded to Shade.

"Theresa is already inside, master, and everything is ready. If there is nothing else, I will take my leave as we all wait for our new prince."

"*Si, grazie*, Gi."

Shade nodded to Ivor and Malachi as well as the doctor, and the three followed him inside the chamber. Shade had never witnessed a birth inside these walls. As far as he knew, he was the last person born here, and now he'd witness their son's birth.

The members of Council walked to the table that had been set up for them, Ivor placed his huge ledger down, opening it precisely to the bookmark he'd inserted earlier. Dr. Bonutti laid the Medici ledger beside it, the quill and ink already on the table.

Kate scanned the room as he carried her inside the chamber. Theresa had lit many candles, creating a soft glow throughout the craggy rock walls of the chamber. She'd draped the altar that sat atop the dais and placed many pillows there for Kate's comfort. Shade gently lowered her onto the altar, as Theresa encouraged her to shift her hips to the edge. There were no stirrups for her feet, so Kate laid back against the hard stone, not made much softer by the pile of pillows, as she bent her knees, her feet flat against the altar stone. She felt Theresa cover her with a clean white sheet, as she lifted her gown up around her waist. Kate looked at the ceiling, as things were set in motion around her. She must place herself in Theresa's hands to guide her through. Another spasm rocked her body and Kate lifted herself to her elbows, crying out softly, as the contraction took her breath away.

Shade felt helpless and knew his only duty was to keep her calm, and to help his son emerge with as little effort as possible. "Relax, *mi amore*, I am right here."

He closed his eyes tightly as her pain filled his own body, her soft cry echoing against the walls of the chamber. He felt at a loss as to how to comfort her, when he saw his mother and father standing to the side. Portia looked at Kate with worry. Shade caught her eye, and gave her a pleading look, to help him guide his mate through the pain that wracked her body. Shade knew they were visible only to Kate and him and Kate had yet to notice their presence. Portia moved toward him, letting her hand glide softly along his cheek.

"My *figlio*, make her comfortable, give her strength to bear the Prince of Medici. Do what your heart tells you to do, be a part of her, together as one, bring forth this *bambino*."

Without another word, he climbed onto the altar stone, propping the pillows to his back and slid in behind *bel*. As he straddled her from behind, he put his arms around her, cradling her to his chest, providing a place for her to rest her head, letting her body relax against his chest, as he took the weight and stress from her. Placing his hands over her stomach, he gently massaged the mound that was his son.

He lowered his lips to her ear, speaking softly, "Relax into me. Push against me, *mi amore*. We do this together, as in all things. *Ti amo*."

He saw his mother smile and move to the side of the altar, placing her hand on Kate's stomach. He knew *Madre* would calm her, help her as well. Shade looked to his father and nodded to him.

Kate knew he could feel her pain and would take it from her if he could. His strength, his presence, they comforted her, and she relaxed into him, letting her breathing fall into a more natural pattern. His voice was in her ear, soft and soothing as he calmed her. She felt the soft touch of another and opened her eyes to see Portia. Kate locked eyes with her as another wave of spasms overtook her, and she felt the warm gush of water flow from her, dripping to the floor, as the membrane encasing their son broke. Theresa pushed back the sheet and calmly told her everything was moving along as it should.

Shade looked to Theresa, who affirmed that all was well. He continued to rub her stomach, as he felt the tight contractions that pushed his son into this world. “That’s it, little warrior, find your path, fight your way out. Take it easy on your *madre*, I need her. We are waiting for you. Come out and meet us."

He could hear Dr. Bonutti chuckle and walk over to Theresa. "Let us have a look, my queen. I do believe this baby will not be long in arriving."

Shade watched as the doctor lifted the sheet and examined Kate, placing one hand on her belly. "He is moving into the birth canal, the pain may be more intense, my queen, but it won’t be much longer. I do believe this Medici will come much like his *padre* did, in his own way and on his own terms."

Kate heard the doctor chuckle as he prodded at her, telling her it wouldn’t be long, as she bared her fangs and growled at him. The doctor stepped back as Theresa stepped forward once more, seeing Kate's agitation with the doctor. She gently "shushed" Kate and watched as Kate's fangs retracted and she relaxed once more against Shade. Shade brushed her hair away from her face, as her hair clung to the perspiration. He spoke softly to her in a whisper, calming and soothing, as Kate prepared herself for the next wave of contractions.

Kate panted, her breath coming rapidly, as she fought not to hold her breath when the contractions overtook her, pushing their baby closer to this life. She was dimly aware of the two Council members who stood like silent sentinels against the chamber wall, observers of history, ready to record these events into the centuries old archives. Kate received a flash of memory from *Madre* as she saw Portia on this very altar, giving birth to Shade, and the birth of Shade's father, centuries before him. The next contraction was more intense, and Kate pushed her back against Shade for leverage, as she helped push their baby from her body.

Shade felt her pain more intensely. She had a beastly moment when the pain overcame her and he did all he could to calm her. He knew this was their process. Unlike mortals, she couldn't use drugs that would dull the pain, as the baby must enter the world in a pure form. Almost immediately, another pain screamed through her body and she pushed back against him. "That's it, *mi amore*. Do what you have to, help Lorenzo. You can do it. I'm right here, Kate."

Theresa dipped a cloth in cool water and wiped the sweat from Kate's face as she worked with each contraction to help Lorenzo. Her labor moved quickly, as was normal for their species, and within a few hours, the baby's head was crowning.

"He is ready, my lady. Your son is ready to come into this world."

Shade stroked the side of her face as he whispered to her, "Push, *mi amore*, push!"

Kate took a deep breath, as one contraction ended and another immediately began. Her gown was now clinging to her body, wet with perspiration. The muscles contracted with a power all their own, pushing this baby from her body. Kate tried to pant, to get her breath, but the pain overtook her and she cried out instead, grabbing Shade's hands, and gripping tightly as she pushed her back hard against his chest. She needed the pain to stop. To give her a break, if only for a minute, so she could catch her breath. Just as the contraction began to ease, she took another deep breath, and was slammed again with the intense pain of the next wave. Pushing harder, eyes closed tight, concentrating all her energy on that one small life that had been growing inside her, she felt him slip from her body, and into Theresa's waiting hands.

Theresa smiled as she saw their small prince emerge, raising one arm in the air, commanding attention already, a head of dark black hair, in matted wet curls. Theresa supported his head as his small torso followed. She guided his passage as his legs were freed, and he kicked at the air. Theresa wiped the blood and vernix from his face, inserting her finger into the baby's mouth, making sure it was clear. She lowered her mouth to his nose and sucked the blood and mucus away before spitting it to the floor, clearing his airway as Lorenzo took his first breath and responded with a strong, loud wail that echoed in the chamber.

Theresa heard Kate laugh through her tears, as she heard her baby for the first time. Theresa laid the baby on top of Kate's abdomen, she used two strips of thin hemp to tie off the umbilical cord, before lifting the baby and holding him up for Shade.

Shade's eyes never left Theresa's hands. His senses in overload, he watched the small baby emerged, his *figlio*. She administered to him quickly. He slid easily from behind *bel*, rearranging the pillows under her head. His fangs punched through as he bit through the umbilical cord, freeing his son from his mother. The blood squirted into his mouth and Shade let it slide down his throat, the bond between father and son established at the first moment of his birth.

Shade felt the blood flow through him, strong, fresh, and clean. He felt his son enter his body with a love and stronghold he'd never felt before, blood of his blood, true Medici. Theresa cleaned him off with gentle hands and wrapped him in a warm blanket. She walked to Shade and guided the bundle into his hands.

Looking down at his son, his breath caught in his throat and his heart pounded. He held in his hands the smallest creature he'd ever held, his tiny body was pink in color, his hair was curly and black as the raven's wings. Shade couldn't take his eyes from the miracle in his hands. His voice was soft, almost a whisper. "Lorenzo."

The infant's dark lashes fluttered and small eyes opened and locked with his, the most piercing pools of blue sapphire stared up at him.

"My *figlio*. You are handsome, *si*? Welcome to Medici."

A small coo escaped the tiny pink lips. Shade was aware of the presence of his mother and father as they saw their grandchild for the first time. *Padre* walked to him and Shade handed him the small bundle. His mother stroked the baby's cheek, as his father kissed his small forehead and Lorenzo cooed once again. Shade felt his father's hand on his head.

"He is strong, the Prince of a mighty King."

Shade took Lorenzo back into his hands and laid him gently in *bel's* arms. Kissing her damp forehead, he pushed her hair back from her face. "He is beautiful, *mi amore*. Like his *madre*. You have given me a son, my little warrior. *Ti amo*."

Shade looked at her, his beautiful *bel* as she held their child. A year ago, he couldn't have foreseen his life as it was now. But now he knew he'd secured another generation of Medici rule.

Kate accepted the baby into her arms, Shade knelt beside her. She looked at Lorenzo who returned her stare with those brilliant blue eyes. Kate ran her hand gently over his head, his dark black hair already falling in soft curls like a halo around his head. Just like Shade. She knew all along he'd look just like Shade. Kate spoke to him softly as Lorenzo stared at her, making a small cooing sound in return as he recognized her voice.

"My baby, my beautiful baby boy, we have waited for you."

Kate looked in amazement at his beauty, newborn yes, but more alert than a mortal newborn. This baby was already aware of his surroundings. She lifted the baby to her shoulder as he instinctively nuzzled into her neck. She gasped in shock as she felt the sharp sting of his fangs and Lorenzo began feeding immediately. Kate laid her head back, letting the baby draw life from her. She felt the bond between them strengthen, and knew she'd feel this child, wherever he traveled, for as long as she lived.

Kate whispered, "*Madre,*" and felt Portia step close to the altar. Portia caressed the baby's back, as she shared her thoughts with Kate. **"And now you know, my daughter, why I can never leave here, never leave this earthly plane to reside only in the spirit realm. I am bound to my son, as you are now bound to yours. We are forever connected, one generation to the next, by our blood bond."**

Shade felt his mother's joy and love abound for the three of them. Portia looked at him, her tears fresh on her face, a smile in her eyes. He felt her pride and he was overwhelmed with something for which he had no words. He watched his small prince feed from *bel* and his heart skipped a beat. Her face was angelic, her words soft and soothing as Lorenzo fed.

Once Lorenzo pulled away from her neck, Dr. Bonutti approached and took the baby from her arms. Laying him gently on her stomach, he unfolded the blanket and inspected him from head to foot. Wrapping him up gently, he placed Lorenzo back in Kate's arms. "He is healthy, strong and a fine specimen of Medici vampire. Congratulations to you, Medici, and to your coven."

Shade grinned. "*Grazie*. Thank you for your assistance." He looked up as Ivor and Malachi cleared their throats and Ivor stepped forward. "I must take Lorenzo from you now, for only a moment. We will not need to take his blood as we have witnessed his birth, but we must record the birth in the books."

Ivor accepted the small bundle that was the future Medici King. He carried him to their ancient ledger where Malachi used the quill pin to recorded his birth: Prince Lorenzo of Medici, son of King Shade and Queen Katherine of Medici. He recorded the date.

Malachi turned to Shade and nodded, as Shade stepped forward. Malachi lifted Shade's wrist and extended his hand, exposing the solid gold blood-letting ring on his finger. He sliced the ring across Medici's wrist and the blood flowed freely. Ivor unwrapped the infant and placed the tiny foot into his father's blood, before carefully positioning Lorenzo's foot over the ledger, and applying pressure against the ancient parchment, leaving the impression of the Prince's footprint.

Theresa stepped forward, wiping Lorenzo's foot clean, and wrapping the blanket back around the squirming baby. Shade lifted his wrist to his lips, licking the wound, and it healed quickly.

Taking the quill, Shade opened the ancient Medici ledger. The pages were worn and delicate, he carefully scrolled through them, coming to the births. The last recorded birth in the ledger was his. He recorded Lorenzo's birth as the Prince, born to Shade and Katherine, along with the date. Malachi then initialed the ledger as a witness.

He let the ink dry, as he turned to see Lorenzo once again in Kate's arms. "We wish to be alone now."

Dr. Bonutti took his hand, shaking it. "I will be in Florence if you need me. I'll come back in a few days to check on our queen and prince. If you need me, just call, I will come immediately."

As the doctor left the chamber, Ivor and Malachi offered their congratulations and informed him the news would be given to Council, and they looked forward to the reign of Medici for many centuries to come. Theresa stood to the side until the others had taken their leave before she approached him. Shade took her into his arms, hugging her tight.

"*Grazie*, Theresa, you have done well, I am pleased and can't thank you enough for your dedication and skills this night."

Theresa pulled back, tears in her eyes. "Congratulations to you and the Queen. Our Prince is strong and handsome."

She walked out, closing the chamber door behind her. Shade went to *bel* and climbed on the altar, pulling her into his arms, their newborn son in her arms between them. It was now their time alone, their beginning moments as a family.

Kate gently stroked the baby's face. "Lover, he's beautiful. I can't believe how beautiful he is."

He watched her with Lorenzo and let the image of the beauty of them together burn into his memory. "How do you feel? Do you need anything? This is our time now, *mi amore*, to be alone with Lorenzo. We can stay as long as we like. I want to be alone with you, be a family together before all hell breaks loose. They will celebrate for days on end. Tell me, is he all you thought he would be?"

Kate looked up at Shade, his skin golden in the candlelight. "I feel fine, and I have everything I need right here, you and Lorenzo. Look at him." Kate brushed her fingers across the silky fine hair on the baby's head as Lorenzo reached and grasped her fingers. "Lover, look at him. He's...perfect. His eyes follow me already. He knows my voice, he knows my blood."

Shade chuckled. "I love seeing you this happy. You are glowing, *mi amore*. You have given me such a gift, a Prince born of love. It is an historic event and it will change our world. You did well. I love you with heart and soul."

He looked down at the small bundle with his eyes open wide and staring back at him. Reaching over, he carefully removed the blanket and looked at his small frame. "He will be so strong, so brave."

Lorenzo reached out his small hand, grasping his finger. "My little warrior. Do you have any idea how much you are loved? You will rule this kingdom someday, and I will give you all the skills you'll need. I will protect you with my life. Nothing will take you from me. You are more precious to me than anything. I love you, Lorenzo."

Kate let the tears fall down her cheeks, overcome with emotion. She already felt such love for Shade, she didn't think it was possible to love him more. But now that she held in her arms this life they'd created together, this living, breathing symbol of their love for each other, her heart felt as if it would explode. Her body felt overly full of love as it spilled out of her. She leaned forward, resting her head against Shade as his arms encircled her. She felt his strength and protection for the both of them.

Kate closed her eyes, and saw Lorenzo's future flash before her. She saw his rise to manhood, his power as he stepped into the legacy of the Medici, leading the coven with honor and integrity. She opened her eyes and looked down at the small infant in her arms. She wanted to keep him like this, small and protected. But she knew he was warrior and would take his rightful place beside his father.

"Can you see him, lover? Can you see him as I see him? He can't wait to follow you, to be like you. He's so eager to begin. I want to cling to him and hold him close, and he wants to follow after you. He already feels the pull. He is warrior."

Tucking a strand of crimson behind her ear, he smiled. "*Si*, I have taken his blood, I feel him strong inside me already. He is warrior, *mi amore*. He will learn quickly. The task will be a huge one but one he takes on fully. He will be my shadow in all I do and say. But I also feel something else. I feel his heart soar when he looks at you. His love and devotion to you is overwhelming. You are his love and light as well, just as you are mine. He will be different from me. For one very simple reason, he has both of us to guide him, teach him, and love him. *Padre* was so damn difficult, I never felt good enough, always that ever present weight on my shoulders. Lorenzo will not feel that from me. Be with him as much as you can, *mi amore*, because he will grow to be a man before your very eyes. Cherish the moments you have with him. Ouch!"

Shade looked down and Lorenzo had sunk his fangs into his finger and he laughed out loud. "*Si*, this is my *figlio*!"

Kate laughed and gripped the baby tighter. "Oh, I'll not let him out of my sight. He'll never go unattended. Theresa or I will be with him at all times, until he's old enough to follow after you. Even then, I'm afraid I'll worry. Make him strong, Shade. Make him brave and fearless. Make him a powerful warrior who is feared by others, and maybe then, I'll not worry for him."

"Do not fret. You'll have two bad ass warriors to look after and attend to. What more could a queen want?"

Looking at her, he could tell she was tired, the birth taking its toll on her. "I would love to lock us in here for weeks, but I think it's much too uncomfortable and cold for such. I can teleport us into our bed chamber. Theresa can help you with a hot bath. Hell, I need a shower myself. And this little warrior can be with us the remainder of the night and through my death slumber. He will probably need to feed again soon as well. But first, you need to feed. Keep up your strength, *mi amore*. I still can't feed from you until Lorenzo is weaned, but I know one damn thing for sure, I can't wait to taste you again. I have missed you so deeply."

Kate's eyes felt heavy, and her body felt weak. The labor had moved quickly, and her body seemed to have healed, but it took a lot of her energy. Lorenzo took very little from her in his initial feeding, and Kate realized it was more of a bonding experience for both of them. He'd need to feed from her properly soon, so she'd need to feed from Shade.

"Take us back to our room, lover. You can hold our baby while Theresa helps me bathe, and then I will feed from you."

Standing, he lifted her into his arms. "Hold him tight, *mi amore*."

He teleported them out of the chamber and landed them softly in the bedchamber. Theresa was already waiting their arrival. As she went to run a hot bath, he took Lorenzo from *bel* and Theresa helped her into the bath. Shade held him firmly and walked with him around the room, his small body curled into his chest, when he heard the loud ringing of bells in the towers all over Florence. Walking to the window, he looked down at his son.

"Do you hear that, Lorenzo? They celebrate your coming. Their Prince has arrived. *Per sempre*, Medici."

Lorenzo looked up at him, his blue eyes clear and wide. Shade turned, so Lorenzo could see out the window. "All of this will be yours someday. So many have given their lives to make sure it remains Medici. I have spent my life building this for you. I will pass this to you, and you will wear the crown of King. It is a big job, *figlio*, but I will be right beside you all the way, and together, we will conquer."

97

Waking late, the sun long set, Shade sat straight up in bed, confused and shaking his head, trying to get his bearings. He cleared the cobwebs from his head as he recognized the surroundings of their bedroom at Castello, and quickly remembered *bel* and his baby. He looked to the windows where the blinds were up and knew his death slumber held him much longer than usual. The birth of his son, and feeding Kate, had taken its toll. He'd left her shortly after allowing her to feed, so he could seek out Luca, but he'd not taken his fill. His need to be close to his mate, and his son. It was a stronger pull than his hunger.

Kate sat in an ancient rocker and held Lorenzo in her arms. Her beautiful white silk gown draped softly around her body, her eyes glued to their son. Lorenzo cooed and Shade smiled at the soft sound.

"He is well, *mi amore*?"

Kate looked up at him and smiled. "He's well. Such a good baby. He fed several times, but quickly fell back to sleep. How are you? I'm the one who gave birth, but you slept like the dead. I don't think you even turned over while you slept."

"I apologize. I think the stress caught up with me. Did you get enough rest? I can have Theresa take him, if you need more sleep. I can watch him as well. We do have some obligations tonight. Do you think you are up for them?"

Kate gently rocked the chair, holding the baby against her breasts. Theresa had brought in a soft gown for him and wrapped him in a light fleece blanket. Lorenzo had slept soundly, warm and soft in Kate's arms. She sat staring at his long dark lashes, fanned out across his cheeks. His tiny hand was curled in a fist and held close to his mouth.

"I'm fine, lover. I slept well. And I can't stop looking at him. What are our obligations?"

Crawling from the bed, padding naked to her, he leaned over her shoulder, kissing her neck and then the top of his son's head. He walked to the armoire and grabbed a pair of jeans and slid them on.

"Outside these walls, there is not an inch of space to move, the entire coven is awaiting the sight of their new Prince. They know he has arrived but wait to see him. The warriors are out there, keeping the crowds calm as best they can. So, the sooner we get this done, the sooner the coven will get back to normal. We will need to go out on the balcony, show him to his legion of people. But first and foremost, he will be presented to the household staff. They are my *familia* and I don't know how much longer I can keep them at bay."

Kate leaned her head against the high back of the rocker and watched him. "Well, that I understand. Everyone will want to look at him. He's the most beautiful baby ever, I think. I knew he'd have your hair, your eyes. But look at him!" Her lips lightly grazed the dark curls on the baby's head.

"*Si*, he is handsome like his *padre!*" Shade laughed and walked over to her, crouching down, cocking his head to the side, he stared at his Lorenzo. "But he has your heart."

Laying his hand on Lorenzo's head, he felt his heart fill with love. How could something so small bring him to his knees?

"We will greet the staff on the main floor. It's also proper they bow and curtsy in his presence the first time introduced to him. It is tradition. Then we can come up to the balcony, *si*? We must wear our crowns, and I will present our son to our coven. They need to see their prince and know the Medici legacy is secured."

Kate watched his face as he looked at his son, felt the love roll through him as he explained the protocol. "I have no problems with sharing him with the staff. I know their devotion to you, and they'll feel that same devotion to Lorenzo. He'll rule here one day. I want the staff to bond with him, and he to them. I want him to grow up respecting them and loving them, not taking their adoration for granted. You plan to send him here to train, and I'll feel better knowing he's in loving hands. And of course, we can present him to the coven. And our prince should wear his crown."

Shade nodded. "I will inform Gi. He will gather the household, and Marco will let the crowd know our arrival will not be long in coming. Let us prepare to present Prince Medici to his people, *si*?"

"I need Theresa. I'll need to change out of my nightgown at least. And she can look after Lorenzo while I get dressed."

"I will send Theresa and Emma in to assist you and Lorenzo. I'm going to make the arrangements with Gi and Marco. I will be back in about an hour. I think that should work. I will have Gi bring the crowns here from the vault."

Pulling a shirt over his head, he went to the door and started calling out instructions before heading to the main floor to find Gi.

As Shade exited, Theresa and Emma entered. Theresa took the baby and informed Kate she'd have him dressed and ready to be presented. Emma led Kate to the bathroom where she ran a hot bath. She pinned up Kate's hair, and Kate sank into the hot water. Emma poured the rose scented bath salts into the bath, then laid out Kate's make-up and took the traditional red birthing gown from the closet. She hurried back in to help Kate from the tub and dry her off with the thick towels, rubbing her skin until it was pink. As Kate sat down at the vanity to do her make-up, Emma spritzed her with the rose scented perfume.

Kate smiled at her in the mirror. "Theresa has trained you well."

Emma nodded and beamed. "Thank you, my lady."

Emma led her back to the bedroom. "My lady, this is the traditional gown that is worn when presenting a new baby to the coven. You'll wear it after each birth."

Kate laughed. "Well, I better keep my figure then."

The gown was red, but simple in design, as Kate lifted her hands in the air, Emma slid it over her head. Theresa returned with Lorenzo who was wearing a long gown of the brightest white, his dark black hair in stark contrast.

"My lady, this isn't the same gown Shade wore when he was presented to the coven 500 years ago as the fabric has become too fragile, but it has been made to look identical to it. Your other babies will wear this same gown as well, and hopefully, it will be preserved and passed down to their children."

Theresa placed Lorenzo in her arms, his blue eyes wide open as he sought her out.

Emma opened the door to the hallway. "We're ready, my lady."

With the household finally assembled, Shade dressed and made his way back to their bedroom. He wore the ceremonial leathers. He entered to see *bel* holding their son. She was stunning in the red birthing gown, her hair falling softly around her shoulders, and she smelled of the sweetest rose.

Gi followed on his heels and carried the crowns. Shade took his queen's crown and placed it on her head and gave her a kiss. "You look so beautiful."

Taking the infant's crown, fashioned to look identical to his own crown, he placed it atop Lorenzo's head. "*Mi amore*, I am not sure how the hell this is supposed to stay on his small head. You may need to hold onto it, *si*?"

Gi assisted him with his own crown and then scurried ahead of them to join the staff in the grand foyer.

Shade turned to Kate. "Are we ready?"

Kate giggled at the sight of Lorenzo in the tiny crown, "Ready, lover."

"Don't get a fit of the giggles now!" Laughing, he latched her arm around his as they walked to the top of the staircase. "Just breathe, *mi amore*, they are our *familia*."

Kissing her cheek, they walked down the stairs and faced every servant that served the Medici household. Gi stepped forward, announcing their presence, his chest held in great pride.

“I present our King and Queen, and their son, our new Prince, Lorenzo Medici."

Gi stepped back into line with the other staff as Shade walked forward with Kate beside him and Lorenzo in her arms. Each male bowed low and each female curtsied to show their respect.

Shade addressed the staff, "It is with great pride and honor that I present to you our *figlio*, Prince of Medici. My queen has given me a handsome and healthy son. Welcome him into our home, as you always welcome us home."

Leading her down the line of servants, it wasn’t long before the females weren’t able to contain their excitement. They oohed and aahed over the baby. The males offered their strong handshakes and congratulations. Shade knew this was important to them. These honored members of his coven were the first to see the prince, and the future of Medici. It was a moment they’d share with their own children and grandchildren.

98

A good hour passed as the staff was enamored with Lorenzo, and Shade was getting antsy, although he knew this was how it must be. He was pleased his family adored this baby already. Marco approached, and Shade noticed his gait was more cocky than normal, if that was possible.

"Well, old man, now you have a mate and a son. But it's time. We need to move to the balcony before the crowds get out of control."

Marco gave him a brotherly hug but didn't go anywhere near the baby. Shade laughed to himself, not surprised, like babies were some disease he might catch. Shade made a move toward the crowd of female servants hovering around Kate.

"My queen, it's time."

The crowd dispersed from around her and Marco, Luca, and two other warriors, heavily armed and in ceremonial leathers, approached. He could see the worried look on Kate's face. Addressing the staff, Shade directed them, "We must present our son to the coven. Please retire this night to the ballroom. The queen and I have arranged a small party for all of you in celebration of our prince. *Grazie*, for your dedication and love."

Turning back to Kate, Shade took her elbow to lead her away. Kate looked to see Luca, Marco, and the two warriors carrying as many weapons as Shade did when he prepared for battle. "Lover, I don't understand. Why do we need the warriors? Is Lorenzo in danger?"

As they approached the balcony, he held up his hand to signal Marco and the warriors to step forward to the door. As the warriors positioned themselves at the door to the balcony, Shade walked her into a small alcove to speak with her. "*Mi amore*, listen carefully. I may be master of this coven, but there are many people outside. A crowd can always be dangerous, and I am simply taking precautions. The warriors will be right beside us. They will remain focused on the people. There are some who would wish us ill. We have done all we can to protect the city, but none of us have seen the likes of what is happening right now. There is a convergence of people, all here to be a part of history, the birth of the next in line for the Medici dynasty. I can take no chances, and yes, there are masters, right now, seething, and ready to take him out. You must know this. You must understand this. My warriors are on the ground among the crowd, but I kept my best on the balcony with us. You can't appear frightened. You must smile, but keep your eyes and ears open for anything unusual."

Kate's eyes widened as she pulled Lorenzo to her breasts, her hand protecting his head. The thought that someone would want to harm their child was inconceivable to her. "How can you be so calm? You want me to take him outside among the people, knowing there may be someone who wants to harm him?" Kate was backing away slowly, as she held the baby in a tight embrace. "How can you ask this of me?"

"Kate!" He could see the panic in her eyes as he felt her fear roll through him. "Listen to me. Our son will be their leader, their master. He is their prince, and one day, their king. He must be presented to them. Nothing is going to harm him. Do you think I would let anything happen?"

Kate leveled him with a stare. She looked to Marco and Luca, and then at the other two warriors, before looking back at Shade. She issued them a command, speaking firmly. "Nothing will happen to him. Nothing! Do you understand? You protect him with your life!"

Marco bowed to her, and then stared into her eyes. "My queen, we devote our life to Medici. Prince Lorenzo included. Come, we are here to protect him. I would give my life before seeing harm come to him."

Shade nodded to Marco and wondered how the hell he was ever going to get Lorenzo from her arms when, suddenly, his son began to squirm and scream. The baby felt Kate's fear and he became frightened himself, Lorenzo's fists shaking as he screamed. "Give him to me, *mi amore*."

Kate clung to the baby, turning her body away from him. "I'll hold him. You and the warriors need to pay attention to the crowd. You'll be distracted if you're holding him. I won't detect a threat as quickly as you, and I can't respond as fast. I want you to be able to protect him if it comes to that."

Shade closed his eyes, frustrated. He wanted this over with, it had to be done. Lorenzo was still screaming, refusing to stop, and his fear now out of control. "*Mi amore*, listen to our son. Feel him. He feels what you feel. You need to calm down, I am begging you. I know this is not easy, but this is our coven." As he tried to reason with her, he felt the presence of his *madre*.

Portia appeared, knowing her daughter was in trouble. "Listen to your master and your mate. He will let no harm come to you or Lorenzo. You must trust him. You now have two warriors in your life, sweet child, and it will take everything you have to handle the trials and victories that lie ahead. This is a simple one."

Portia laid her hand on Kate's arm and gave her a vision of when Shade was presented to the coven when he was an infant. "You see my face? I was frightened too, but my smile does not show such. It shows great pride in my son and my *familia*. You must share Lorenzo with his coven. Let the warriors do the job they were born to."

Kate listened to *Madre* and knew Shade and his warriors would allow no harm to come to Lorenzo. But she wouldn't give him up. She calmed herself, shushing Lorenzo, rocking him in her arms until his wailing stopped, and his tiny fists stop beating at the air. She took a deep breath and nodded at Shade. "I'm ready."

Shade sent out love to his mother and thanked her for her support, as she faded from view. "*Si,* I am proud of you, *mi amore*."

He laid his hand gently on his son. "My little warrior, your time has come. You must greet the coven that you will rule. My heart is so full. They welcome you to their hearts as well." Taking her elbow as she clutched the baby tight to her breasts, they walked to the doors.

Marco nodded to him. "We are ready, all the warriors are below. Your hand signal will tell them when you are ready to speak. The warriors all stand with their backs to the walls of Castello, and their eyes to your city. No harm will come."

Shade acknowledged Marco's instructions as Luca swung open the double doors. The air rushed over them and the sound of the crowd almost pushed them back from the doors. Shade gripped her elbow, hoping to hell she moved with him and didn't fight. "Come, my queen."

As they walked out on the balcony, the two warriors flanked each side of them. Marco and Luca were right behind them. Luca saw Kate start to back up and softly touched her back. "I am right behind you, my queen. You are safe."

The crowd was hysterically cheering, as the fireworks went off across the sky. The noise was deafening and Shade gave them time to settle and waited for the small fireworks show to end. Raising his hand in the air, he signaled for quiet from the crowd. The crowd became still, not wanting to miss one word he spoke.

Shade took a deep breath and his eyes scanned the largest crowd he'd even spoken to. His senses were on high alert, but it was clear this crowd was jubilant. This was his kingdom! "*Grazie* for joining us this night. Your master is well, as is your beautiful queen. Our legacy will continue with the birth of our son, your prince, Lorenzo Medici, born of true and ancient warrior blood. He brings us all a hope that is eternal for the future of our coven. He will uphold all the values of honor and integrity, respect and dignity for our coven, bringing protection with the power of his sword."

There was silence as the crowd looked upward, waiting. Shade turned to Kate, speaking softly to her, "*Mi amore*, he must be held up to be seen."

It was a leap of faith, and she knew she had to take it. She removed the blanket she'd wrapped around the small infant and passed him to his father. Lorenzo stared back at her, the small crown balanced on his head, as his eyes reflected brilliant blue even in the moonlight.

Shade took him in his arms and stared into his face. This was the proudest moment of his life, presenting his son. Shade laid him on his belly along the length of his arm, positioning his body, so he was comfortable. He held his fingers under the baby's chin, so he could support his head to hold him in the air to his coven. Raising him high, Lorenzo cooed loudly. "I present to you Prince Lorenzo of Medici. Warrior and future King to the Medici Coven."

The crowd instantly bowed their heads in respect. The seconds ticked by as he watched them all bow to his son. It was a defining moment in his life. "Rise, and salute your prince!"

The crowd rose up and shouted in unison, "*Per sempre* Medici!"

Shade lowered Lorenzo and cradled him to his chest. "*Ti amo, mi figlio.*" He turned to Kate. "I do not wish to stay out here any longer."

Giving her a kiss, the crowd roared. They both laughed against each other's lips, as Lorenzo cooed once again and squirmed in his arms. "*Si*, you want your *madre*."

Handing the infant to *bel*, he pulled her back a few steps and the two warriors stepped in front of them, facing the crowd.

He helped her get back inside the walls of Castello as the doors were closed, and still, the sound of the crowd vibrated the ancient castle. He stepped away from Kate and walked alone down the hallway, trying to compose his emotions, as they rolled through him. He stopped and covered his face with his hands. The King of Medici had fought and won many battles, the scars of those battles on body and soul, when suddenly he was overcome with something he'd never felt in his life. He felt completeness, wholeness, a feeling of coming full circle, and a feeling that the huge gap in his life had been filled to overflowing.

Kate saw him walk away and cover his face with his hands. She turned to a startled Marco who had stayed only a few paces behind her and handed him the baby. "Don't drop him."

Marco was stunned when she handed him the baby. "No, my queen... *Cazzo*!" He looked down, cringing as Lorenzo looked back at him. "Well, hell, you have that same damn look your *padre* does when he's waiting for me to fuck up."

Lorenzo cooed and Marco laughed, trying to juggle him in his arms. He sent a message to Theresa. "**Terri! Help me! I have the baby!**"

In an instant, Theresa appeared, and she was biting her lip not to laugh. As she took the baby, she looked toward Kate and Shade. Marco scoffed, "Old man is falling apart. He needed a moment. Handsome little thing, though, isn't he?"

Theresa slapped him on the arm and led him in the opposite direction, away from Kate and Shade.

As Kate approached Shade, she touched his arm gently. "Lover? Are you okay?"

Shade took her in his arms. "I am so overwhelmed. I don't deserve this, or you, Lorenzo, or my coven. It is like feeling the warmth of the sun."

Kate wrapped her arms around him, his head nestled against her. "I feel what you feel. The baby opens your heart to everything, making you feel things you didn't know were possible. But we deserve what we have fought for, and Lorenzo. We have struggled to get here, to find each other, to fight through the obstacles. We will face new challenges with Lorenzo, I'm sure. But never doubt you deserve this, my savage lover."

He locked eyes with her. She was all to him, forever his walking sin. She would always be his greatest strength and deadliest weakness. "My lily white, I need you. I am your humble master. I praise the love you give with such abundance. No greater love has been given, than the love I give to you."

Lifting her in his arms, he carried her to their bedchamber. His son was safe in the arms of his nanny, and the only warrior he knew who was as strong as himself. They needed this time to be alone, to ignite the fires that would forever burn in his heart.

99

They'd been in Florence almost a month, and Kate was anxious to get home. Lorenzo would have to learn what it felt like to sleep in his cradle, because with Theresa, Emma, and the massive staff at Castello, Lorenzo had been passed from the loving arms of one female to another. Nita, the wet feeder who'd been chosen for Lorenzo, had arrived and she'd be flying back to the States with them as well.

Kate wrapped Lorenzo in the soft blanket to ward off the chill. The old castle had been modernized with heat and plumbing, but its huge size made keeping it warm a challenge. Kate lifted Lorenzo to her shoulder and went in search of Theresa. They needed to finish packing everything, so their luggage could be taken to the plane. As she stepped into the hallway, she saw Theresa in an embrace with Marco. She stopped in her tracks, as she watched the intimate kiss exchanged between them before Marco turned and left.

Theresa turned around and spotted Kate, and turned bright red. "My lady!"

Kate gave her a sly smile. "Something I should know about, Theresa?"

Theresa approached, looking down at the marble floor. "We've decided to try again. I can't imagine my life without Marco, and apparently, he didn't seek out another female either, other than the feeders, of course. We both think we can manage a long-distance relationship. At least, we're going to try."

Kate beamed at her. "I think that's wonderful. You know how often we're here. And I know it's important to Shade that the coven is exposed to Lorenzo. He wanted them to see him grow up. So, I imagine we'll be here several times a year."

Theresa nodded. "We discussed that. We think we can make it work."

Kate reached out and took her hand. "I'm happy for you, for both of you."

"Were you looking for me?"

"I was. We need to finish packing everything, and I needed your help. Lorenzo frets when I lie him down. He's been so spoiled here. He thinks he's supposed to be held at all times."

Theresa laughed as she followed Kate back into the bedroom.

***

Finishing up the paperwork related to his businesses in Europe, Shade met with his lawyers and Luciano to address some of the expenses that needed his attention. Hauling his ass back to the bedchamber, he knew they'd be leaving Florence soon.

He walked into chaos in the bedroom as Theresa and Emma were both running around the room, helping *bel* pack. He shut the door quietly and watched. Kate was laughing as she teased Theresa about Marco. Did he miss something? Clearing his throat, it sounded like a hammer falling and everyone stopped and turned to stare at him, their faces red.

"Please ladies, resume your duties or whatever you want to call this. Where's my son? Which one of you has him?"

Kate carried Lorenzo to him, swaddled in his blanket, his eyes wide open, taking in all the activity around him. She slipped him into Shade's arms. "Your son is here, being spoiled as usual. He's going to have culture shock when we return home and I lay him in a cradle. Lover, have you spoken to Marco?"

Theresa shushed her from across the room, and Kate giggled.

Taking Lorenzo in his arms, he smiled down at his handsome face and ran his hand over his raven curls. "Marco? Why the hell would I want to speak to that old ass grouch? Is there something you wish for me to speak to him about?"

Kate laughed. "You mean other than being an old ass grouch? I don't know, maybe you should ask about his love life."

Theresa's eyes were wide open, as was her mouth. "My lady! I can't believe you said that."

"Seriously, Theresa? You don't think guys talk?"

He looked from one to the other. "Are you telling me what I think you are telling me? Oh, this calls for some major dressing down. I've taken more of his bullshit about mating and having *bambinos* in the past year to last me all of eternity.

So, tell me, Theresa, what torture tools did you use to make this happen? Give it up because I need all the ammo I can gather."

Theresa looked at the floor and shrugged. "No tools. We just really missed each other. I assumed he'd move on after we broke it off. And you know Marco, probably better than anyone. There's no shortage of females he could have chosen. But he only went to feeders. We've talked about it at length and we both decided to commit to each other. I hope you won't make him change his mind."

Shade turned serious. "Theresa, he loves you. But I feel conflicted. I need both of you in very separate parts of the world. We chose you as Lorenzo's nanny, no one else. I trust no one with him as I do you. And I need Marco here. If I ever lost an arm, he would give me one of his. Did you wish to remain here with Marco?"

Theresa shook her head. "No, master. My place is with Lorenzo, and the others that will follow. And Marco knows his place is here. Besides,

Marco can only be domesticated so much. He loves his life in the camp, surrounded by the warriors. We will be together when I come here."

"I never thank you enough for all the things you have done for us. We would have been lost without you, Theresa. I will keep him in line, I promise you. Just love him. The devil knows loving a Medici warrior is not an easy task. And you tell me if you need to return for a visit. If we can manage it, we will."

Theresa nodded. "Of course, master. Thank you."

Turning the baby over to Kate, he got ready to leave. "Now, I need to see my brother before I go. Finish packing and I will go see Marco."

He teleported out and landed at Marco's barrack's door. Pounding hard on the door, he called out to his friend, "Marco!"

Marco stood up slowly, grunting as he walked to the door, opening it to his oldest friend. "What's the matter, old man? You need a break from baby care already? Too much estrogen up there in Castello? You better get in here while you still have your balls."

Shade chuckled as he entered Marco's room, dropping into a chair. Marco admonished him. "You've been around the women too long, my friend. It has made your brain soft."

Shade punched him lightly. "I heard you were back with Theresa. Who has a leash around his cock now, brother?"

Marco stood with his hands on his hips, looking at Shade. He shook his head. "Life is not as easy for those of us not born with a crown on our head. You might do well to remember that. You have never known a life of servitude. You issue orders and they are done. You buy what you want. Take the women you want. Your life is your own. The rest of us? We find solace where we can. I let Terri go because I didn't want to hold her back. Doesn't mean I don't care. Or that it doesn't hurt."

Shade grabbed the half empty bottle of Midnight and swigged it down. He handed the bottle to Marco as he slid the back of his hand over his mouth. "I have a lot to lose and you know that, even more now, brother. Don't mess with her mind, or her heart. I will beat you ten feet under the ground. But, I feel it, you love her. Now you know what I feel inside, you need to come to the States for a visit soon. You need to see everything I have built there. It is for Lorenzo, and those that follow him. My purpose is different now, my whole life is different."

Marco tipped the bottle back, swallowing down large gulps. Drinking with Shade, just like the old days. "I know you have a lot to lose, because I've spent my life protecting it. You've been a good master. Now make sure you raise Lorenzo to follow in your footsteps. We don't need some whiny ass spoiled kid who thinks he's better than us just because he was born royal. And don't worry about Terri and me. We'll be fine. We both know our place in this world, and how to carve out time for us."

Shade grabbed the bottle and threw back his head, swallowing down the last drops. "*Cazzo*! You always have to empty the bottle."

He grabbed two more bottles as the two of them settled in on the floor. Shade looked at him. "If I stayed here all night, you think she would notice?"

They both laughed as Shade continued to talk. "She would rain hell down on this shack. You and I both would be delivered to the devil, our cocks shoved up our asses. *Cazzo*, brother, I love her! Lorenzo, he is so vulnerable. I fear for him. She keeps telling me I can be a good *padre*, but damn, I have never been more scared in my life. I want him to grow up differently than I did. I want him to understand he needs to be the best warrior, the best leader for Medici, but I also need to show him I love him. Fucking *Padre* would never give me points for any damn thing. I can't do that to Lorenzo, brother."

Marco took a long draw from the bottle. "I'll protect you from many things, brother. Lay down my life if I need to. But I'll not stand against that redhead for you. You're on your own there."

Marco swigged back the bottle, letting the wine slide down his throat. "Don't worry about Lorenzo. Well, yeah...worry about Lorenzo. He'll know he is loved. You're a different man than your father. Just don't be too soft. Lorenzo is warrior. He needs to be raised as a warrior. Like it or not, old friend, that is what your father did. You were his only son. It all rested on you. He had to make sure the Medici coven would survive. Look at how many of the old covens have not. We depend on you, and now we depend on you to make sure Lorenzo can handle all that will be required of him as well. Our queen will keep you in line, I think. She'll protect him. But she'll push him as well. And you."

Shade grunted. "She could push a mountain over if she had a mind to. You seem to have changed your mind about her since you first met her. You two were like oil and water. So, you are like my blood. If something happens..." Slamming his head back against the wall, closing his eyes. "Promise me you will help take care of Lorenzo, you and Theresa."

Marco shrugged. "I misjudged our queen. I will admit. I thought you were making a mistake by taking a mortal. She has proved me wrong. Don't get all maudlin on me. You two aren't going anywhere. But you have my word. If anything happens, you know Terri and I got your back. She will raise him like her own. And I will make him the best damn warrior this camp has ever seen."

"You fucking better or I will haunt your old leather ass for eternity!"

Standing up, Shade reached down and grabbed Marco's hand and helped him to his feet. He hugged his friend, pounding his back.

"We head out before sunrise. I hate flying! Talked to the lawyers and accountants today, huge raise for you, spend it on her, will you?"

Shade headed for the door, turning before he walked out. "He will grow up sooner than I can imagine, he will rule this place. When he does, you retire. That's the law. Cause I said so! We will be back soon, brother. I want Lorenzo to know this place, know those I love. Take care of our Theresa. Just let her in, brother, you just need to let her inside, she will give back more than you can imagine."

Leaving Marco behind, he decided to walk back to Castello. This was where it all began for him. And tomorrow, he'd show Lorenzo where it would begin for him.

100

Kate and Shade sat in the back of the car, Kate holding Lorenzo, as Dante drove them back to Bel Rosso. It had been a long flight, and the jet was full with Gi, Theresa, Emma, and Nita in tow. Luca had teleported home the day before, eager to be back with Shannon.

Their luggage was unloaded when they landed, and the staff headed back immediately in a separate car. Lorenzo was sleeping, and Kate laid her head on Shade's shoulder. She sighed, glad to be home. They'd been in Florence for almost a month and she'd missed Virginia. It was winter now as they moved into December, and the town of Charlottesville was lit in the festive lights for the Christmas holidays. It brought back memories of her life as a mortal. The vampires didn't celebrate the traditional holidays, and yet, they straddled both worlds.

"Shade, did you celebrate Christmas as a child?"

"No, *mi amore*, we never celebrate the mortal holidays. For most vampires whose lives intersect with the mortal world, we would, of course, appear to celebrate these activities so as not to arouse suspicion. Our children will need to understand the mortal culture. We have survived through the centuries because we have learned to adapt and integrate ourselves into the mortal world. We have learned to not draw attention to ourselves. It is why the rogues are such a threat to us, they risk exposing us all, and must be eliminated for the survival of our kind. So, it's not so much a celebration of mortal holidays as it is an education, although for a small child, it is hard to understand the distinction."

Shade laid his head back on the seat. "It is complicated, *mi amore*. There is much we still don't understand about our species. The Council keeps a record of all vampire births and deaths. Ivor records our genealogy, and we can see where we have roots in the family trees of the mortals, just as my family evolved from the mortal Medici's of Florence. We don't understand our origin, only that we are not the undead as portrayed in the mythology. The Council thinks we are a mutant form. Some aberration in our DNA that gives us an extended life, and demands we feed on the blood of others. Our records document there were immortals in the time of Christ. We are aware of your religions and beliefs. But your Jesus died for mortal man, not for the immortals. There is no heaven for us. We live until we are destroyed, sometimes for centuries, hundreds of centuries. But once our physical bodies are destroyed, our souls are forever earth-bound, like *Madre* and *Padre*.

"Our children will have a tutor, and will be educated in the customs and beliefs of both worlds. Lorenzo must know all things and understand all people, to be a great leader of the coven. Look at the changes I have faced in my five hundred years. I can't imagine what challenges lie ahead for him, but he must have a strong foundation to adapt to the demands of the future. We are his greatest teachers."

Dante turned the car down the long lane that led to Bel Rosso, and Shade sighed with a relieved heart. "We're home, *mi amore*. Welcome to your world, *figlio*. Wake up and see where you will grow up."

Kate leaned over and kissed him. "I'm glad to be home, and glad to bring Lorenzo home."

Dante exited the car and held the door open for them. Shade got out first, so he could help Kate from the car, as she clung to the warm bundle in her arms. The cold wind whipped down from the mountains, and caught her red hair, blowing it around her face. Shade slid his arm around her and hustled her indoors to the warm welcome of Luca and Shannon. "Damn that wind is cold! Next thing will be the snow."

Looking up, he saw Luca exit the door of his suite, and his grin was huge. "Welcome home!"

The two men hugged. Shade heard Shannon squeal with delight, as she ran to Kate and he rolled his eyes. *Here we go again with the oohing and aahing!*

Kate pulled the blanket away from Lorenzo's face. Lorenzo was awake, his big blue eyes staring back at Shannon as she squealed.

"Oh my god, look at him! He looks just like Shade. Can I hold him? Please?"

Kate laughed and shifted the baby into Shannon's arms. She rocked and bounced him. "Look at him, Luca. He's gorgeous!"

Luca walked over to her, sliding his arm around Shannon's waist. He rested his head against hers. Lorenzo stared back at them, his eyes moving from one to the other. Luca reached down and took the tiny hand, and Lorenzo gripped Luca's finger. "Nice strong grip there, warrior."

The words were barely spoken before Lorenzo lifted Luca's finger to his mouth and chomped down hard, drawing blood. Luca yelped and pulled his finger back. Shade laughed and Kate looked horrified.

She admonished the baby, "Lorenzo! You can't bite."

Shade held his sides laughing. "What the hell, Luca? My best warrior flinches when a tiny *bambino* nips his finger? *Cazzo*, that is priceless!" Shade glanced over at Shannon and her eyes were as big as saucers.

Shannon looked up at Kate. "He has teeth? He's only a few weeks old!"

Kate laughed. "He is vampire. How do you think he feeds?"

Shannon looked at her with wide eyes. "I never thought about it. But, how?"

Kate shook her head. "The same way Luca feeds from you. He just takes smaller amounts, and needs to be fed every few hours, just like a mortal baby. So, I guess you shouldn't put him near your neck."

Luca placed his lanced finger in his mouth and it quickly healed, then pulled out his finger and looked at it. "Fuck! Little bugger has sharp fangs. I definitely think you need to keep him away from mortals until he's old enough to understand the difference."

"*Mi amore*, remember when you were turned? Your hunger was intense, that's why I kept you hidden in the chamber for a while. But Lorenzo is different. He is too small to attack, but he will make no distinction between mortal and immortal. When did he feed last? I suspect his wee beastie is beating on his chest yelling for blood." He looked to Shannon and smiled. "Careful of your neck, he is my son, after all."

Shade slapped Luca on the back, as they walked to the bar and poured out Midnight. "So, what is her poison?"

Luca pointed to the mortal wine selection. "She prefers a white wine, if you have it."

"It was a good year for the Chardonnay in Florence. Greece produced a fruity variety as well."

Looking at the wine options, Luca selected the Italian wine.

Shade inquired, "Have you checked on the camp since your return? I am assuming the new warriors arrived and are housed up at the camp?"

Luca poured a glass of the white wine for Shannon, as he gave Shade an update. "Marcello has everything under control. He does a really good job, master. And the new warriors that were sent over from Florence arrived. He's been working with them, getting them ready to be sent to California. He and Raven have both spent time with them. Raven's been giving them a sense of the layout there, showing them the floor plans and the layout of the property. That new guy, what's his name? Mica something? He teleported in one evening to meet the new warriors, although, between you and me, I think he was really here to see Raven."

Luca chuckled. "Raven has things under control in D.C. He said nothing went down while we were gone. And no one got a call from Alec. Marcello has the new recruits on a tight schedule. They're looking good. Kate's wolf has been pacing ever since I got back home. She must have sensed she was arriving soon. All in all, pretty quiet."

Shade nodded as he downed one Midnight and poured another. Swallowing that one, he filled his glass a third time. Damn, fucking Marco had him drinking like the old days! "Sounds like Raven is taking his new responsibilities seriously. I wasn't sure when I gave him the spot, but Marcello assured me he would do well. Fiamma and Aislynn, how are they?"

Luca drank his glass of Midnight. "Fee is fine, she has a handle on the females, keeps a tight rein on them. Aislynn is definitely the strongest of the new recruits. She can hold her own against any of the new males. Very disciplined, no nonsense. All the warriors have adjusted to the feeder compound. They were a little over eager when we first opened it. Like kids in a candy store because the access was so easy, but they have all settled into their schedule. No issues. Matron runs a tight ship. But I think she was missing Gi. I noticed when he came in he made a beeline for the tunnels, so I'm pretty sure I can tell you where your man-servant is right now."

Shade almost choked on his Midnight. "Damn, all the males in this place are yanking for a meal!"

Slapping Luca on the back, he chuckled. "I'm assuming things are well with you and Shannon? I'm sorry you had to be away from her for so long, but she seems happy. I know this wasn't easy going through Kate's pregnancy. But you know you kept me alive...and sane. Well, it looks like the females are done inspecting my son from head to toe. We need to settle in. I have a few things I want to talk about with you and Shannon. But first, tell me, things are good between you two?"

Luca smiled back at him. "Couldn't be better. She understood why I had to go, and I came back to feed when I needed to."

"Good, I'm glad she understands, and it didn't create problems."

Walking back to the females, Shade set their drinks down, as they gathered around the fireplace. "Come sit down, Lorenzo isn't going anywhere and I have some things to discuss. I want us all to be comfortable."

Kate took Lorenzo back from Shannon. They all took a seat in the living room. She unwrapped the blanket and placed the baby over her shoulder, pulling her hair away from her neck so he could feed. The baby nuzzled into the warmth of her neck, his tiny hand flailing as he sought out her vein. He bit into her flesh, and the sound of his sucking could be heard around the room. Shannon was looking at her with her mouth hanging open, and Kate chuckled. "Get used to it, Aunty Shannon."

Shade watched his son feed. He couldn't get over the beauty of it, no matter how many times he saw them together. It was the most beautiful sight he'd ever witnessed. His love for them was overwhelming.

Knocking back his Midnight, he waited until he had everyone's attention. "Luca, as Kate's protector, it's custom for some covens to pronounce the protector of the mate to be protector to the *bambinos*. I wish for you to be Lorenzo's protector as well as Kate's. It will be daunting, but Lorenzo will be with one of us at all times. Do you accept this duty?"

Luca nodded. "I am humbled, master. But you know it's a duty I accept with great honor."

"You honor us, Luca. I want you and Shannon to look after Lorenzo, if anything happens to Kate and me. I do not foresee that coming, but I need to know someone will have his back, take the lead, and give him what he needs. Theresa and Marco will also have a hand in raising him. I know Kate wants this as well.

"It was a comfort for your *padre* when I promised him I would take care of you, Luca. I saw that in his eyes, he went to his death peacefully knowing I would take care of you."

Luca nodded. "When I took the pledge to our queen, I told you then I'd protect her, and all of your children. Nothing has changed for me. My life remains committed to you. Shannon knows where I stand. I think she struggles still to understand our culture, much as Kate did when she was still mortal, but in time, she too will understand. My loyalty to Medici remains steadfast, master."

Leaning forward, Shade laid his elbows on his knees, looking at Luca seriously. "You have always been special to me, Luca. Always. And you remain so. All my warriors mean a great deal to me, but you go above and beyond that. You have done well for yourself. You earned everything you have. And you will have more. Let's face it. I already know there will be more *bambinos* coming, two females."

Sitting back, he laid his head back on the couch, his dark curls falling away from his face. "I never thought this would happen, this happiness and peace inside me. I knew it existed, I just couldn't find it. Then this redheaded, walking sin strolled into my life and my world changed instantly. In one year, so much has changed for me. I could lose it all just as fast, I am no fool. But I will fight to my death protecting what sits in this very room. I know you will do the same. With that said, you will need to let him take your blood. You need to bond to him. It's vital."

Luca bowed his head. "It would be my honor, master." Luca chuckled. "Especially since he has already sampled mine."

"He is a Medici. What the hell did you expect?"

They all laughed and Shade nodded to Kate who placed Lorenzo in his arms. Taking his son, he held him across his chest, his small head nuzzled into his neck, rooting around in Shade's curls. "Little warrior, we need you to complete one more task for us before you begin to take your nap, so don't be getting yourself nestled in my hair."

Luca reached out and lifted the infant, placing him on his own shoulder. Lorenzo cooed, his tiny hand resting against Luca's face.

Kate stood beside Luca, prompting him. "Cradle him in your arms."

Luca shifted the baby in his arms and looked down at the bright blue eyes that stared back at him. He lifted his wrist to Lorenzo's mouth. Lorenzo turned his head, kicking his feet free of the gown. Kate shushed him, and placed her finger under his chin, turning his head back to Luca's wrist. She rubbed her thumb over the baby's lips until he opened his mouth, seeking a source, and Luca lowered his wrist to the wet, waiting lips of the infant. Lorenzo seemed startled, not used to the hard, firm skin of Luca's muscled arm, and started to turn his head again.

Kate spoke to him in a soft sing-song voice, "Drink, baby. Drink for mama." With her finger beneath his chin, she gently turned the baby's head back to Luca's wrist. "Drink for mama."

Lorenzo nuzzled against Luca's wrist before biting, and the loud, wet sucking sound filled the room.

Luca was startled by the baby's strength as he sucked at the wound, his small hands gripping his arm, the blue eyes locked on his. He felt the baby bond to him, and knew he'd be linked to him now, as he was linked to Kate and Shade for all time. Luca smiled at him as he showed no signs of stopping soon. Shannon stood and watched closely as the baby continued to suck at the wound. She'd seen much since making the decision to be with Luca, but nothing like this.

"Oh my god," she whispered. "He's just so...perfect."

Shade watched with such pride, Luca and his Lorenzo. He watched the baby make a little piglet of himself. Laying his hand on Lorenzo's dark head, his spoke quietly, "Lorenzo, enough. Luca needs to feed another this night."

Lorenzo's eyes quickly went to Shade, following the sound of his father's voice.

"That's my little warrior, come to *padre, si*?"

Lorenzo unlatched from Luca's wrist and cooed loudly and flailed his little arms. Shade grinned, picking him up, laying him on his chest, rubbing his back. Lorenzo nuzzled into his neck and sighed. Shade felt his small body relax as he walked around the room with him, rubbing his back. He laid his cheek against Lorenzo's.

Kate smiled at him. "I don't want to miss anything. I know he'll grow up so quickly. I want to enjoy every minute. He'll only be this small for such a short time. I can already see a big difference from the day he was born."

Shade returned to her, his smile soft and loving. Kissing her, they stood together. "It's our first night home, *mi amore*, with our *figlio*. It feels right. You had best take him and Shannon upstairs. I have a need to feed."

Kate looked at him, their eyes locked, their love exchanged in a glance. "Of course, lover." She took the baby and picked the blanket up from the sofa. "Come with me, Shannon. We'll go upstairs. You can help me introduce Lorenzo to the concept of a cradle." Kate laughed. "I don't think he's going to like it. He's been held by half of Florence, he doesn't know what it feels like to lay in a bed and not he held in someone's arms."

Shannon stood and looked about nervously. She knew Shade had been feeding from Luca throughout Kate's pregnancy, but she'd never been present when they were together. She had no illusions about what transpired, but she'd been able to put it out of her head. "Yeah, sure. Whatever you need."

Kate could feel her friend's nervousness and remembered it well. It wasn't that long ago she'd struggled with the same emotions. She reached out and took her friends hand. "Come on. I'll see if Emma can bring us some more wine."

Kate led her up the stairs and behind closed doors.

101

As the house settled back into their routine after the excitement of arriving back home, Kate stood at the nursery window, Lorenzo on her shoulder as she looked out over the garden at night. She was glad to be back at Bel Rosso. Shade had returned to their bedroom, and Shannon had gone back to Luca's suite. She'd just bathed and dressed Lorenzo after the long flight and had him in a clean gown. He had that sweet baby smell. The house was silent now, as she rocked gently from side to side as the baby cooed, one chubby hand wrapped in her hair. She stood quietly, lost in thought, when she felt Shade step up behind her, sliding his arms around her waist. Lorenzo responded to his father's presence, kicking his legs in excitement and Kate smiled.

As he wrapped his arms around her, he sensed a feeling of longing, a sadness that ached in her heart. He spoke softly to his son. "You look very content Lorenzo, and I think I may be a bit jealous of you, cuddling up to your *madre*." He kissed her neck. "If I make that sound Lorenzo makes, will you cuddle me as well?"

She didn't respond to his question. Something was definitely on her mind. "Talk to me, *mi amore*, what is in your heart?"

Kate leaned her head back against his chest, letting him support her. "Shade, we're so blessed with this baby. But I can't help but remember the lost one. He'd be a year old had he lived. Lorenzo's big brother. I try not to think of him. I know it would have been hard for him, a half-breed like Cory. But then I look at Cory, and how happy he is now. Our lost baby would have been loved. He wouldn't have had the hardships Cory had to suffer." Kate shook her head. "Sorry, I should focus on the here and now, not on what could have been. I know what happened was probably for the best. That baby wasn't strong enough to survive this world."

Shade closed his eyes at her pain, his guilt consuming him. He knew he'd caused this by switching out those damn pills. He'd made Gi take out the herbal supplements she needed, replacing them with a sugar mixture. But he'd do it all again. The pills were killing her, and he had to choose between her and the baby, and his choice was her.

"You were not strong enough either, *mi amore*. We can't go backward, only forward. It is the way of life. But we will always remember him, cherish and keep those we have lost in our hearts. What can I say, what can I do to make this better for you? Take this melancholy away from your heart. Can you not feel him with us always?"

She nodded her head, as a single tear escaped and ran down her cheek. "I still feel him. I'll always feel him. He's as much a part of us as Lorenzo is. My arms ache to hold him too. One baby doesn't replace the other in a mother's heart. I don't want us to ever forget him. I want our children to know him, to know there was one who didn't make it, but he's their brother nonetheless."

Shade watched as Lorenzo started to pick up on his mother's emotions, and he began to pout as if he, too, would cry. *Cazzo*! He needed to do something! "Come, I think our son needs to meet his brother. If he knows of him, you can always talk to him of our sleeping warrior, *si*? Perhaps, it will make you feel better. Let me grab a blanket."

He pulled a large blanket from the daybed and wrapped it around her shoulders with Lorenzo still kicking and issuing small hiccups of cries. Shade felt like he was failing at this *padre* business already.

As he wrapped the blanket around them, she turned herself over to his care. Kate allowed him to lead her down the stairs and out into the garden. The night was clear, and the air was crisp, their breath forming a mist in the cold. Kate pulled the blanket around Lorenzo's face as they walked down the footpath to the section she called 'The Baby's Garden'. The roses and lavender were dormant now as Shade led her to the garden bench, sitting her down as he slid in beside her, his arm protectively around her as she laid her head on his shoulder.

Kate gently lifted the blanket away from Lorenzo's face, as his bright eyes stared up at her. "Our sweet, precious baby. Before you came along, there was another. He wouldn't be warrior and he wouldn't be king, but he's your brother, and he would have loved you, Lorenzo."

Shade sat with her, knowing she needed to come to terms with this. Gliding his hand over Lorenzo's curls, he smiled down at him. "*Mi amore*, may I have him?"

As she gently handed Lorenzo over to his arms, he stood and crouched in front of the angelic grave marker.

"This garden was created for your brother. He sleeps and dreams here. I watch over him always, as does your *madre*. You have to watch over him too, inside your heart. He will fight beside you, guide you, and keep you safe."

Holding Lorenzo under the arms, he let the baby straddle his knee as he crouched in the garden. Lorenzo patted the small statue as he cooed.

"*Si*, your *fratello*. Your brother."

Kate watched as Lorenzo reached out, patting at the head of the small statue, and felt peace in her heart. She knew all their children would know of the baby that preceded them, this one small life that didn't survive, and yet, would live on through them. She sighed as she felt the energy of the lost one connect with Lorenzo.

Shade heard her sigh as something inside her was released. He turned his head to look at her, her red hair blowing in the chilly breeze.

"*Mi amore*?"

Kate lifted her head and looked at him, his blue eyes reflecting the moonlight. "Yes, lover?"

"Look at Lorenzo. Explain to me what just happened, something left you. It gives me a strange feeling, yet peaceful."

"I'm not sure, but I felt it too. And so did Lorenzo."

Squatting down beside him, she wrapped the blanket around the squirming baby and held him close to her breast. “'Let's go inside. We’re all one family again."

He threw his arm around her, kissing her cold cheek. "We will always be one family. Our lost one will never be forgotten or unloved. We are Medici."

102

Kate was already awake and sitting in the rocker, feeding Lorenzo. The day had been a long one for all three of them. Lorenzo didn't like being in the cradle and woke often on his first day home. Shade would immediately awaken from his death slumber, alert, adrenaline rushing, until he realized the reason for being jolted awake. It would take him some time to get accustomed to having a baby sleeping in their room.

He left their bed and began dressing. He planned on addressing the warriors and presenting his son to them when he felt Cory inside the house. Shade could feel his reluctance to come to them, and he needed to nip this in the bud. He and Kate had expected to see Cory when they'd arrived last night from Florence, but he was nowhere to be found.

Shade heard him on the stairs, going to his rooms on the third floor and called out to him loudly, "Cory, come join us, we are in the bedroom!" Turning to *bel*, he lowered his voice. "I want Cory to meet his new brother."

Kate shushed Lorenzo who startled at the sound of his father's loud voice. The baby settled and returned to feeding as Kate rocked him gently. "I did wonder where he was last night. But there was so much going on when we first got home, and Lorenzo demands so much of my time, I didn't have time to think about it. But he should come meet his brother."

Cory sighed heavily when he heard his dad shout for him. He knew they'd arrived last night, but he was so busy with the leathers and besides, he thought since it was their first night home, they might need time alone. Cory felt like a third wheel at times, so he just kept busy and tried to keep out of their way. Opening the door a crack, Cory stuck his head in. "Hey, welcome home."

Shade looked up as he finished lacing his boot. "Come on in."

Cory stepped inside, closing the door behind him and stood awkwardly, shifting his feet.

Shade motioned for him to come forward. "I want you to meet your new brother. Are you excited? You sure as hell don't look excited."

Cory nodded his head. "Yeah, I'm excited. But you just got back last night, and I was busy at the camp. I didn't want to intrude."

Shade looked back at his son. "Intrude? Cory, you are my son, and I have missed you." Shade opened his arms to him.

Cory shrugged and went to Shade, reluctantly giving him a hug. Shade felt something was different and knew this had to do with Lorenzo. He struggled with how to make Cory understand Lorenzo's birth changed nothing between them.

Kate watched the awkward exchange between father and son. Cory was still finding his way in the family, and Kate knew the new baby complicated things for him. She gently pulled Lorenzo away from her neck and wiped his mouth clean. He looked at her with wide blue eyes, as if to question her.

Kate laughed. "Lorenzo, you can't feed all the time!" Suddenly, the idea of wet-feeders was making a lot of sense. Kate realized this growing baby would demand much, and the help from Theresa and Nita would be necessary for her to return to any type of normal life and be able to allow Shade to feed from her again. "Cory, come sit down. You need to hold your new brother."

Cory looked at Kate with the new baby. "I don't think that's a good idea, he's really little and umm, well..." Shuffling his feet, he looked down and held his hands to his sides. "I don't know anything about babies! I've never been around them. I might hurt him."

Shade laughed. "Well hell, son, do you think I know what I am doing? He kept us up all day because he hates that cradle. You can learn with the rest of us. Once you get used to it, it will be easy."

Cory shrugged. "Yeah, I heard him a few times."

Kate smiled at him. "Cory, we're all just finding our way here. This is new for me too. But Lorenzo is strong. You can't hurt him. Come sit down, I'll place him in your lap."

Cory looked doubtful. Sitting down with a flop, he cringed. "You sure this is such a great idea?"

Before he could speak another word, Kate placed the baby in his arms. Looking down, the baby cocked his head to the side, staring at Cory. His eyes were wide open, and he seemed almost curious. In spite of himself, Cory grinned at him. Lorenzo grabbed a long strand of Cory's hair.

Kate laughed. "Oh, I forgot to warn you. He bites. Be careful he doesn't grab—" Before the finished words were out of her mouth, Cory had reached down to take Lorenzo's small hand and Lorenzo immediately put Cory's finger in his mouth, biting down.

"Ouch! Whoa little buddy, I'm a friendly here!"

Shade put his arm around Cory. "Yeah, you will learn real fast with that one!"

Cory stared at his finger and laughed. "I sure wasn't expecting that. But hey, he's a Medici—takes what he wants and asks questions later!"

Shade threw back his head laughing. "That's what I am talking about!"

Cory laughed and leaned his face down to Lorenzo. "Little buddy, I'm your brother, you aren't supposed to bite me. "

Lorenzo made a cooing sound then grabbed a fistful of Cory's long hair and yanked.

"I think he's trying to tell me he's the prince, and in control here. When he gets older, I think he's going to beat the shi...I mean the crap out of me."

Cory turned to Kate. "Are you feeling okay?"

"I feel fine, Cory. I think Lorenzo will look up to you as his older brother. He'll need some guidance. And there will be no fighting. Lorenzo may be a prince, but I'm still the queen. Theresa has moved into the house now and she'll begin to help feed Lorenzo and help care for him. I don't think she'll put up with much foolishness, either. Oh, he'll be spoiled. No doubt. But the prince won't always get his way. He's already learning that lesson when he was made to sleep in the cradle. He also has a wet-feeder who has moved into the staff quarters. Her name is Nita, and she'll take on his feeding in a few more weeks. Also, we brought a new housekeeper back with us from Florence, Emma. Do you remember Emma? You'll see her in the house now. One little baby sure did change things, didn't he?"

Cory nodded. "Yeah, I sort of remember Emma. She talks a lot, always looks nervous. Well, at least I don't feel like the only one making the changes happen around here. And I was joking about the fighting. I want to be his big brother. I never had any brothers or sisters."

Shade crouched down by the side of the chair.

"Cory, nothing has changed. My love for you is the same, if not more. I do not want you to feel this makes you any less in my eyes. I love you both. We learn together. Everyone here is our *familia*, and it will only grow. I will need you to be a good teacher and example to Lorenzo. He will look up to you. You will always be his older brother. Accept that we both love you."

Cory stared at the baby as his father talked. He knew it had been stupid of him to not come to the house last night, but he wasn't sure how he'd feel.

"I was worried about how you'd react once he was here, but I can see it doesn't change things. I'm sorry I didn't come in last night."

Shade kissed the top of Cory's head as he stood up. He ruffled his hand through Cory's hair before walking to *bel* and kissing her.

"In two hours, we need to head over to camp. I am having everyone assembled to meet Lorenzo. Luca is coming as well."

Looking over at Cory, he added, "Two hours son, your ass needs to be at camp. You stand with us as we introduce our newest son to the warriors."

103

Cory had already walked over to the camp with Luca. Shade led Kate, with Lorenzo bundled on her shoulder down the footpath in the moonlight. The air was brisk, and the wind swept down off the mountains. Shade walked taller, with pride beating in his chest. This was his home and now he had his heir, his Lorenzo. He couldn't wait for the day they'd walk together to the camp, and all the days ahead that would be filled with laughter, joy, and love.

As he opened the door into the meeting hall in the barracks, the room had been set up in preparation for this gathering. The warriors had already gathered, and a hush fell across the room as Shade entered. He guided Kate to the chairs that had been set in the front of the room for the family, as Cory made his way through the warriors to join them. Helping her to get settled with Lorenzo in her arms, Shade beckoned Cory to take his seat beside him, making sure everyone was present.

Shade turned to look at the warriors seated in the rows before him, all of them silent and waiting. He walked to the podium, pacing back and forth, looking out at his warriors.

"Your queen has given me a son, a warrior, our prince. He is born from love, a baby that holds the Medici name and already carries a great deal upon his small shoulders. The hardest job I will ever tackle lies before me, raising a warrior who can lead and make Medici proud. Prince Lorenzo Medici has come into our world, and your job is to protect him, as you do all of us, as you do each other.

"Luca has been named his protector, as well as for your queen. Theresa has been moved from her station as your Queen's Lady-in-Waiting to your Prince's nanny. We now have a new Lady-in-Waiting, Emma, from Florence. Your Prince's wet-feeder now resides in the staff quarters. So, there have been a lot of changes at Bel Rosso."

He kept walking back and forth, ticking off the things in his head he needed to go over with them.

"You will address him as Prince Lorenzo. I expect a good example set for him from all of you. He will need your guidance. This is a new beginning for the Medici reign. We have given the coven the next generation to ensure our protection and longevity. A year ago, I could never have foreseen this."

He turned to Kate and smiled. "Would you please come up beside me, so we can present our prince to his warriors?"

Kate stepped forward as she unwrapped the blanket that had covered Lorenzo and left it in her chair. Lorenzo perked up, looking around as the blanket that had shielded his view was removed, his blue eyes quizzical as he took in all that was around him.

Kate chuckled. "You know this is all about you, don't you?" As she stood next to Shade, she handed him the baby to be presented to the warriors who would protect him with their lives.

Shade watched his son take in everything around him, his eyes wide open. He nodded at Cory to join them. He cradled Lorenzo into the nook of his elbow, his little body in a sitting position facing the warriors. "I present to you Prince Lorenzo of Medici."

The warriors stood and lowered their heads in respect. Shade took in the moment and looked down at Lorenzo, whose eyes were wide as he stared out at the warriors he'd rule one day.

Shade called out, "Per semper!"

All heads were lifted as the warriors shouted in unison, "Medici!"

Shade smiled at them as he held his son. He was on top of the world right now. "Come, let us walk among our warriors so they may meet him, *si*?"

Kate hooked her arm around his. "Yes. Let the warriors meet him. He looks quite eager. He's not a shy baby, that's for sure."

Cory stood on the other side of his father, a family united.

"No son of a Medici is shy, only brave and honorable, *mi amore*. And now with your blood in the mix, I think our son is going to conquer the world!"

As they stepped into the crowd, many of the warriors came forward to meet Lorenzo, offering their words of congratulations. The evening turned into night and the warriors needed to get to their duties. Cory stayed behind and Shade teleported Kate and Lorenzo back to the house. He kissed his mate and his baby goodnight as he stood in the hallway at the foot of the stairs, watching Kate carry Lorenzo upstairs for the night.

He returned back to the camp, his night just beginning. The wedding was close at hand, and he needed to catch up on all the planning that had taken place in his absence.

104

Rissa stood looking in the mirror one last time. She was alone in the Folger Court, a large room inside the National Cathedral that had been set aside for her to dress. It was almost 8:00 p.m., and time for her to walk down the aisle. She'd not seen Alec the entire day. Alto had loaded everything she needed into the car and had driven her to the cathedral earlier that afternoon. She slid her hand over the Harry Winston diamond necklace, a gift she'd found in her packed things from Alec. She heard the soft knock on the door and knew it was Hyde. He'd been standing outside the door since she'd arrived.

***

Dressed in a tuxedo, his weapons secured and well hidden, Hyde had stood guard outside her door all evening. The small device in his ear gave him instant access to Shade, Raven, and Marcello. He looked like any other security that was out in force for this event.

It didn't help the wedding was scheduled near the holidays. D.C. was teeming with tourists. But so far, they'd had no problems.

He stood patiently at her dressing room door inside the massive cathedral. He'd watched as various personnel came and went. All the staff had been pre-cleared and given color-coded security badges, identifying the areas they were allowed to access. Anyone approaching the Folger Court had been prescreened before being allowed to enter. It was a short list of people that included her dress designer and stylist, her hairdresser, and a florist. She was well hidden from the hustle and bustle of the arriving wedding guests and dignitaries.

She'd been a bundle of energy and nerves preparing for today. He heard Marcello's voice on the speaker inside his ear, telling him all was secured, and it was time, code word for the event, "DIVA".

He tapped on the door lightly and heard Rissa bid him to enter. She'd been inside the room alone for almost an hour as the flow of people in and out had finally stopped. He'd take her downstairs and outside, so she could enter through the northwest door.

Hearing him enter, she had her back to him. Rissa picked up her bouquet and turned to face him. Hyde nodded with approval. She looked angelic, but he knew Rissa all too well, and she was no angel.

Her hair was down, lying in soft blonde curls down her back, her hair pulled back from her face and held by a diamond hair clip. He'd seen her many times in evening gowns, but this was different—she was breathtaking. She looked ethereal and airbrushed, classic and elegant.

"You look beautiful."

She smiled softly. "Thank you, Hyde. That means a great deal to me. If I can wow a warrior, Alec will definitely approve!"

Hyde chuckled, but he sensed her nervousness. He knew Rissa. Once she was in the spotlight, her inner actress would take over and this would be an Academy Award winning performance. Taking her hand, he offered her a few words of comfort. "Rissa, take a deep breath. You look regal. You've worked hard for this night, and everything is ready. Security is tight and everyone is in their place, all waiting your arrival. So, I suggest we get to the starting gates."

Speaking into the small microphone placed on his lapel beneath the boutonnière, his voice was strong. "DIVA on the prowl. Moving to point location."

Rissa gathered the train of her gown and draped it over her arm. They walked through the cathedral as the beautiful music from the choir and organ echoed off the old walls. She spotted a number of Shade's warriors along their walk, her safety the utmost objective of the day. She slowed her breathing and relaxed. She could feel Alec and knew he was calm and waiting for her, his game face on.

This was the fairytale she'd dreamt about as a little girl, but so much more. Hyde walked her through a side door that led outdoors, and took her to the main entrance, covered by the massive sculpture of Frederick Hart. Rissa looked up quickly at the sculpture, *The Creation of Day*, as it depicted the emergence of bodies from the primordial soup. She heard Hyde speak into his microphone again.

"DIVA in position. Green light."

Rissa smiled to herself as she looked down the long aisle into the nave of the cathedral to see her bridesmaids already in place. She was amused by the code name the warriors had selected for her. The nave was over one hundred feet tall, and the aisle was over four hundred feet long. Alec stood tall and handsome, waiting for her. The polished wooden pews were filled with everyone who was anyone. She dropped her train and Hyde quickly adjusted the gown so the lace trailed elegantly behind her.

She would take this walk alone, to her Alec. No one would escort her. Her parents and family long dead to her. She looked to Hyde and he nodded, as Pachelbel's "Canon in D" began to play.

"Just one step at a time, Rissa. I'll be near. Alec will take it from here. Smile, you look stunning."

Leaning in, he kissed her cheek so light and fast it shocked her. She wasn't expecting his display of affection, but it made her smile. Hyde disappeared behind her as the congregation stood to their feet, turning to face her entrance on cue of the music. She held her head high, walking with pride to Alec. He was her master, her lover, her friend, and he'd chosen her. This was their day, and she'd never been happier in her whole life.

105

After the ceremony, Shade and Kate stood with the rest of the congregation as Rissa and Alec exited, arm in arm, down the aisle, the paparazzi waiting at the entrance to the cathedral. Kate could see Shade speaking quietly into the small microphone hidden in the boutonniere on the lapel of his tux, issuing instructions to his warriors. Kate had never seen his warriors all dressed in tuxes, and Raven and Marcello both had their hair in stylish man-buns for the occasion.

Alec and Rissa were whisked away to the waiting limo by the warriors as they pushed their way through the crowd. Alto drove their limo, and Hyde took Raven, Marcello, and a few of the other warriors in a second limo. Kate knew there were others scattered through the crowd, and a number of them would remain on the rooftops, and invisible to the mortals.

"Lover, I'm glad you talked me into leaving Lorenzo at home. This crowd is much too large. He's much safer at home with Theresa, Luca, and Auntie Shannon."

Shade kept his hand on the small of her back as he guided her through the crowd, exiting the building where Dante was waiting to take them to the Old Post Office Pavilion for the reception.

Once in the car, Dante maneuvered through the traffic and Shade directed him through a few side streets to get them off the main route and away from the traffic. Once they arrived at the Old Post Office Pavilion, they waited in line as each car pulled up to the entrance, where valets were waiting to open the car doors and help the guests get out of the cars.

Shade remained in constant contact with his warriors. He heard that Alec and Rissa had already arrived and were doing press and photography in a pre-arranged room, as they waited for all the guests to arrive.

As they left the limo, Shade led *bel* inside, looking for their table. He remained alert at all times. The cathedral had been packed, and he was sure no one would skip this reception, as it was sure to be a party for the record books. This event would go on all damn night.

Once at their table, Shade pulled out the chair for Kate and took the seat beside her. They weren't positioned near the front of the reception hall, but much further back, at Shade's request. He could observe more from the rear and exit quickly if there were any problems.

Immediately, a waiter appeared with appetizers and Shade ordered two bottles of Midnight.

"What a show this is. This must have cost Alec more millions than he cared to spend. How are you feeling, *mi amore*?"

Kate pulled a cell phone from her evening bag. "I'm fine. But I'm going to call home really quick just to check on Lorenzo."

Kate hit dial and Luca answered almost immediately. "Now why am I not surprised to hear from you?"

Kate laughed. "I miss him already. Is he okay? Are you doing okay?"

Luca chuckled. "Trust me, Kate, between Theresa and Shannon, Lorenzo is being spoiled rotten. Don't worry about anything. Have a good time."

Kate ended the call and Shade just looked at her and smiled, shaking his head. "No one has put that boy down yet, have they?" He laughed. "You need to relax. I know it is not easy, but he is in good hands. Now have some Midnight and chill a bit."

Throwing his arm around the back of her chair, he nuzzled into her neck. "I am going to begin feeling neglected if you keep worrying about our son more than me!"

"Then you'll be happy to know that next week, Theresa and Nita take over all the feeding, and Lorenzo moves into the nursery. And I can have you all to myself again."

Kate stroked his cheek, his hair pulled back in a loose ponytail at the nape of his neck, exactly as it was the first night she had seen him. "Have I told you how incredibly sexy you look in this tuxedo?"

Shade smiled back at her. "Why do I get the feeling that even though you say I will have you all to myself, there will be a small *bambino* who can easily distract you?"

Impatiently, Shade looked around the room. "*Cazzo*, how long does it take for people to take damn pictures? I know we will be here a while tonight, but I am already tired of this business. I will be glad when our life gets back to normal."

Kate laughed as she sipped at the Midnight. "Normal? When exactly was our life ever normal?"

She saw a very tall man approaching, handsome in a very rugged way. His hair was long, and he wore a well-trimmed beard. He was clearly a vampire, and Kate was surprised she was able to recognize a vampire among mortals now. On his arm was a striking Asian beauty. He walked right up to their table and extended his hand to Shade.

"Shade Medici. It's been a long time. And this must be your beautiful mate, Katherine. I'd heard you were mated."

Shade had followed her eyes and saw Maximus. He wasn't on the damn guest list. What the fucking hell was he doing here? Shade stood as Max extended his hand and seemed in a friendly mood, but Shade was questioning the intentions of an uninvited master.

"It has been a long time, Maximus. This is my mate and queen, Katherine Medici. Kate, please meet Master Maximus. I do believe you know him by name but have never met him before."

Shade looked at the beauty by his side, recognizing her immediately and he couldn't believe he'd escorted her here. The whole fucking world just did a one hundred and eighty degree turn.

Kate nodded as Max extended his hand, palm up, to her. She placed her hand in his as he bowed his head and lightly kissed her hand. Kate responded with, "I've heard much about you. I'm pleased to finally meet you."

Max bowed his head to her. "And I you. It's a pleasure to meet the woman who finally captured the Medici. Most said it would never happen. But then, some said the same about me. May I introduce my mate? This is Lein. I'm sure you know her father, Shade. Fan Shen. He is Master of China, Thailand, and Malaysia, a very large and powerful territory."

Shade bowed his head slightly to Lein. "We meet again, Lein. I have known your father for centuries. He is a well-respected master. Please, sit and join us."

Shade's head was swimming, trying to put all the pieces together. Max mated to Lein! Her beauty was world renown and there had been much talk in his younger days he should mate her, and he'd rule half the world. Now Max had just upped his game with this mating, adding her father's territories and massive army of warriors to his own. Shade poured Midnight for all of them.

"My congratulations, Max, I had not heard of your mating. I have been a bit preoccupied with the birth of my son, Lorenzo. So, tell me, I have provided the security for this charade tonight, and I did not see your name on the guest list. Does Canton know you are here?"

Max sat with his arm draped over the back of Lein's chair as he lifted the glass to his lips. "No, actually. I'm afraid I must admit I'm a wedding crasher. I haven't been in the States for some time. I came back to check on my Virginia coven and heard the news of Alec and Rissa's wedding. I thought I'd stop in and give my best wishes to the newly married couple." Max chuckled. "I've never understood Canton's fascination with this mortal power grab, but to each his own."

Kate knew how carefully Shade guarded his properties. She knew Bel Rosso sat in the middle of Max's territory, and yet, this was the first time she'd seen him. She couldn't imagine Shade leaving a major territory unguarded for so long.

Kate nodded her head to him. "If I might inquire, what has kept you from Virginia for so long?"

Max sighed and tipped his glass in Kate's direction. "Ah, my darling, a broken heart. I'm afraid I was betrayed by a beautiful female. She made a fool of me, and I wanted nothing more than to be as far away from her as possible. I had a home in Thailand, so I went there to lick my wounds. I thought I was done with women for good, but I met my beautiful Lein, who showed me the path of true love and devotion. We've been living there but I realized I needed to get back in the game. I do have responsibilities to my coven here. So, I brought Lein to see my coven. I take her with me everywhere. I find I can't live without her." He looked at Shade. "And I sense you feel the same, do you not? I hear it in your voice, your pride for her and your new son."

"*Si*, Maximus. As you said, we both sowed our wild oats and no one could have imagined us here. But as they say, we both have saved the best for last. It is good to have you back in Virginia. I think you and Lein should come out to Bel Rosso, see what we have done with the place."

Shade nodded to Lein. She was raised in the traditional Asian culture, and she wouldn't speak until spoken to and so far, Max had given her no reason to address them.

Max smiled at Shade. "We'd love to see the property. I'd heard the house had been renovated. I must say, I never understood why Alec ever took that place. He let it sit dormant for years, letting everything fall apart while he played his little games in D.C., not that it mattered to me. But by all means, we accept your invitation." Max turned to Lein and kissed her cheek. "Won't we, my angel?"

Lein smiled demurely at him before casting her eyes downward.

Shade lifted his glass. "Fantastic, we look forward to your visit." Shade looked around the room and spied Rissa and Alec, making their way through the tables, speaking with everyone. He caught Alec's eyes and nodded. **"Yeah, I didn't know he was coming either, brother."** "Well, it looks like the happy couple is close by."

Alec caught Shade's eye, then saw Max at the table. He was a little confused by his presence, but perhaps Rissa had invited him. She'd kept making changes to the guest list. He slipped his hand around her waist and leaned down to whisper in her ear as she chatted happily with the guests at each table.

"Rissa, darling, let's head over to Shade's table, shall we? And don't forget to congratulate them on the new baby... Lawrence or something." Alec gently guided her in the direction of Shade's table.

Rissa sighed loudly. "Oh, the baby. I believe the yapping thing is named Lorenzo, not Lawrence. But I want Kate to see this dress up close."

Rissa had been in her glory all evening. Her plans had been perfectly executed. She felt like royalty with the press, photographers and guests all mooning over her dress, and the elegance of the whole wedding. She kissed both cheeks of the guests she greeted, and had a smile permanently plastered on her face. She let Alec guide her to their table. This was her day and she couldn't wait to see Kate's reaction. This wedding had made Kate's coronation look like a child's birthday party!

Shade stood as Alec and Rissa approached their table, extending his hand to Alec. "Congratulations, brother, on your marriage."

Kate smiled at Rissa. "You make a beautiful bride, Rissa. That gown is epic. You'll be on the front page of every newspaper and everyone will want that gown, not to mention your handsome catch."

"Thank you, Kate. It's a one of a kind piece of art, and my Alec looks so handsome. I'm so glad you could join us for this wonderful night."

She smiled at Kate and Shade and wrapped her arm through Alec's, leaning against his shoulder.

Max stood to extend his congratulations. Rissa had been so wrapped up in herself she hadn't even noticed him sitting there. Why should he be surprised? He'd learned the hard way the only person Rissa was in love with was Rissa.

"And please allow me to extend my congratulations as well. It's been a long time, Alec. I hope you don't mind that I decided to join the festivities when I heard."

Alec shook his hand. "No, of course not. What's one more in a crowd this size?"

Max smiled. "Well, two more, actually. I, too, have a mate. Allow me to introduce Lein. Angel? This is Senator Canton and his wife, Larissa."

Rissa felt her knees buckle. *Maximus! What in the hell is he doing here?* He could never get away with touching her here. Her heart raced and her mind was spinning. It was just like him to show up at her wedding! And then everything stopped as she heard him introducing his mate. Rissa felt her throat tighten as she unconsciously clutched at her neck. *Well, it didn't take him long to forget me and nail some foreign bitch*. She almost gasped as he called her 'angel'. *How dare he do this right in front of me!*

She felt her anger build as Max spoke to them. *Did he just call me Alec's wife? Oh, no you don't!* Her temper flared. "Correction, make that mate, not wife."

Max chuckled and bowed in her direction. "My apologies, Mrs. Canton. I thought we were playing mortal games here. Mate, of course. You're his loyal and *faithful* mate. Who'd ever doubt it?"

Rissa felt his eyes bore into her, his laugh cold. She wasn't going to let him get the upper hand. She gripped Alec's arm tightly and smiled, coyly cocking her head to the side.

"Apology accepted, Maximus. Yes, I'm his loyal and faithful Rissa for all eternity. Never forget it. Thank you for coming, and I'm sure Alec is quite honored to have you and your mate join us."

Alec felt her grip on his arm tighten and he wondered what had her so riled. The mortals had been referring to her as his wife all evening and Max was just playing the part. Alec nodded. "It's been a long time, Max, but I can see you've been busy. Your mate, she's the daughter of Fan Shen, is she not?" Alec looked at the demure Asian beauty on his arm.

Max nodded. "She is indeed. Her father has no sons and Lein is his only child. I met her in Bangkok last year after an unfortunate breakup with a cold-hearted bitch who played me. I left the country to mend and found my true mate. Her father was most pleased at our union, as it gave him someone to assume their dynasty and help take over his massive army of warriors."

Rissa was seething inside. He had no right to waltz in here, but she knew she couldn't do a thing about it without causing a scene, and so did he! She looked away so she could compose her face, pretending to look at the guests before returning her attention to him and responding, turning on the charm.

"Oh Max, I'm so sorry to hear that! What a hurtful thing for you to go through, but it looks as though you've recovered well. I'm glad you now have someone to look after you. I'm sure it's a dream come true, and it won't be long before you're announcing the arrival of little ones. How endearing!"

Shade sat watching the exchange, feeling the tension grow. Max had some balls walking in on this affair unannounced and now he seemed to have everyone on edge.

Max's power was now greater than Shade's, surpassing the size of his territory and the number of his warriors. If Max wanted to take over, he was well positioned to pull it off. Shade sat with his elbows on the table, his thumb and forefinger rubbing his chin slightly, his eyes focused in on Alec as they exchanged the look. They both knew this could mean serious trouble, especially with Shade's ass sitting dead center of Max's territory.

Rissa turned to Kate and smiled. "And you look much too beautiful to have just given birth weeks ago. Congratulations. I have a gift for Lorenzo, but the wedding has made it impossible for me to deliver it. I'll bring it along the next time I go riding."

Turning to Alec, she kissed him on the cheek and purred, "Please excuse me, my darling, but I must use the ladies' room."

She spun and looked at Kate. "Kate, would you join me? I need help with my dress." Reaching out, she grabbed Kate from her chair and pulled her through the crowd to the ladies' room.

Kate was surprised by the sudden gesture as she followed along behind Rissa, glancing over her shoulder at Shade who was engaged in a conversation with Max and Alec. She could feel the tension at the table. It was so thick you could cut it with a knife, and she had no idea what was going on.

They entered the ladies' room and Rissa was fuming as she fussed with her hair in the mirror. Kate was about to ask her what was going on when the door opened and Lein walked in. The quiet beauty who'd hardly spoken a word leveled a stare at Rissa that was deadly.

"I know all about you, Larissa. Max told me everything about the affair. How you tricked him, played with his heart. What kind of mate betrays her master, anyway? He's my mate now, and don't think for one minute I'd not set the forces of my father's army against you." Lein took a step forward. "If you go near him again, I'll kill you."

Kate backed against the wall, looking from Lein to Rissa. *What is she talking about? Rissa with Max? Rissa betrayed Alec?*

Rissa spun on her heels to face Lein. "Let me advise *you* of one thing—you can have him. He's useless to me, I have my mate well in hand and if you ever threaten me again, the fires of hell will rain down on you. And another thing, you know nothing about me. Max lies and fucks his way to whatever he wants, and if you think for one second you can hold on to his cock, think again! He mated you for one reason...the power your money and warriors bring to him. Nothing more. So be careful and watch your own back, you don't scare me. Master Canton is my mate and he taught me well how to hold onto what's mine. I suggest you do the same damn thing! Excuse us, I have wedding guests to attend to before you so rudely interrupted. So, waltz your ass back to Maximus, shut your mouth, and head on back to your shack on the slimy edges of wherever you crawled from. This is my master's territory, not yours!"

Grabbing Kate by the hand, Rissa stormed out the door. Speaking through her gritted teeth, she spat out her words to Kate. "Say nothing and smile. Act like you're my best friend and this is the best fucking day of your life. Nothing is ruining my plans tonight, not you or that backwater bitch in the bathroom."

Kate allowed herself to be dragged across the floor back to their table, too stunned to speak. On their way, Rissa was stopped by several people and no one would know by her gracious smile she'd just had a face-off in the bathroom. Kate broke free of the vice-like grip Rissa had on her hand and made her way back to Shade.

She slipped back into her chair, lacing her arm through Shade's and tried to control her shaking. *What the fuck did I just witness in there?* Her heart was pounding. She'd never seen a war between masters, but she'd heard the warriors speak of tales of past battles, and it was usually a fight to the death. Is that why Max was here? To challenge Alec?

Shade could feel her fear as she clung to him like he was her anchor. He wasn't sure what had gone down, but was certain Rissa was at the center of it. She had some damn balls, that one. "*Mi amore*, are you all right? We can leave if you wish?"

“I’m not feeling well. Maybe I’m just tired. I guess I didn't realize how much of my energy Lorenzo drains. Perhaps we should go."

"Of course, *mi amore*." Standing, he helped her from the chair. "Alec, we are heading home. Kate does not feel herself yet and she needs to attend to our son. Everything is in hand here. The warriors will remain on duty until the last guest leaves. Enjoy your night, brother. Call me if you need me."

Turning to Max, he nodded. "Good to see you again, Maximus. Let me know when you and Lein wish to visit."

He called telepathically for Dante to bring the car immediately and they exited the building. "Take us the hell home Dante, I am damn tired of this nonsense. Glad as fuck this is finally over with."

Alec excused himself from Max. "It was good to see you again, Max, and congratulations on finding your mate. But if you'll excuse me, I really need to mingle. We have a lot of guests here this evening."

Max nodded. "Of course. Please don't let me hold you up."

Lein returned to the table just as Alec was leaving. Alec nodded to her as he weaved his way through the crowd, reuniting with Rissa as they smiled and shook hands through the crowd. Rissa cast a final glance over her shoulder, just in time to see Max leave with Lein.

106

Kate sat in the back seat of the car next to Shade as Dante expertly navigated the D.C. traffic and got them on the highway heading back into Virginia. She'd been looking out the window, processing the information she'd heard exchanged between the two women in the bathroom. Shade had made mention, on a number of occasions, that Rissa and Alec had a 'different' kind of relationship, with implications of rough sex and the occasional extra partner for a three-way. Kate shuddered at the thought of it. She couldn't imagine sharing Shade, or him wanting to share her with someone else while he watched. If Rissa had a secret affair with Max while she was mated to Alec, she was certain that went beyond any boundaries of a 'different' relationship.

"Shade, while I was in the ladies' room with Rissa, Lein came in. She made some...accusations."

Taking her hand, he squeezed it. "I wondered what had you so worked up. What kind of accusations?"

Kate turned from the window and looked at him. "Lein implied Rissa and Max had been together. I don't mean before she was mated to Alec. I know Rissa was seeing Max back when we were all in college together. I didn't know he was a vampire then. This was more recent. And the remarks Max was making? The remarks he made about leaving the States because some bitch had played him? I think he was referring to Rissa. Lein was accusing her of being unfaithful to her mate, of being with Max while she was mated to Alec."

Shade stared at her and shook his head. "*Bel*, are you sure that's what she was implying? What was Rissa's reaction? You know there are a lot of...variations in Rissa and Alec's sex life." He turned his head, looking out the window. "As you found out at Castello."

"Oh, I'm sure. Lein said Max told her everything, how Rissa had played him. She asked Rissa how she could betray her mate. She said if Rissa ever came after him again, she'd send every warrior from her father's army after her. And Rissa didn't deny it. She practically threw it in Lein's face. She told Lein she could never...uh...hold onto Max's...uh..."

Kate looked to the front seat where Dante was driving. She knew the staff was discreet, but that didn't mean they didn't hear everything. "Well, you get the picture."

Turning in his seat, he needed to give Kate some insight. "I want you to listen to me. I have no idea what the hell went down with those two, but it explains now why there was so much tension at that table. Max and Rissa had a thing before Alec, I do not pay attention to that shit. I never have. I only notice when a master selects a mate, because who he selects can have a big impact on the balance of power. And Lein brings Max great power. Their mating makes me sit up and pay attention. Do not take this personally, but Rissa was a mortal, and she was nothing in the eyes of the vampire community. Meaning she brought nothing to Alec in the way of new territory, power, or money. His mating with her did not change his standing, nor did it advance his status. I don't care what the hell went down back there but be careful around Rissa. Don't let her pull you into this."

"I've learned to be cautious of Rissa. And I'm too busy at Bel Rosso, and now with Lorenzo, to get pulled into her world."

Shade lit a cigarette then lowered the window a crack. "Max's mating does concern me a great deal. We need to talk about that before they visit us. We sit in the fucking center of his territory."

Kate watched him fidget, clearly not comfortable with the idea of their visit. "This Lein, you knew her before tonight? Is she someone...from your past?"

He tossed the cigarette out the window and closed it. Turning to her, he kissed her softly. He had pledged there would be no more secrets going forward.

"Let me give you some details on her and her family. First, Lein. It was thought many years ago that we would make a good mating simply because her father is royal blood and a great warrior. It would have made me wealthy beyond description, and extremely powerful. I was not interested in settling down, but I was pressured a great deal by those closest to me, even Council. My parents were dead, and I was making it on my own, and there was a lot of pressure to produce an heir. So, I met with Fan Shen to discuss an arranged mating. I was invited to attend a few events where we could meet, and she was always accompanied by her *familia*, as is their tradition.

"We met several times, talked, but I felt nothing. I could not bring myself to commit to a mating that secured the future of Medici but left my heart feeling cold. I told Fan Shen his daughter was a great beauty, and she deserved to be mated to one who would love her. He dismissed my comments, telling me a warrior does not marry for love, but power. I left there, and never thought of her again, until tonight. But I am sure she got as much pressure to mate as I did. She is a huge prize to be won by any master. Fan Shen has no male heir; she holds all the cards. And now those cards have fallen into Max's hands. So, before I tell you of her *padre*, do you have any questions about Lein?"

Kate sighed. She was glad to hear Lein wasn't on his list of conquest. He'd spoken to her in the past about arranged marriages, and how the vampires had used them, just as the historical mortal royals did, to secure alliances and expand their power.

"No, I have no questions. What do I need to know of her father?"

"Fan Shen is the Master of China, Thailand, and Malaysia. My coven is nothing in comparison to the size of the territory Fan Shen controls. He has five times as many warriors, and they are equally skilled. They are an ancient coven and excel in sword and shuriken. They fight to the death. It is honorable to die fighting, to never surrender. His dynasty was handed down through generations and he took the reins with both hands, just as Lorenzo will do from me. My own *padre* was always concerned about Fan. The size of his territory alone made him a threat.

"And now we have Max in the picture. He is a warrior as well, with his own territories of Virginia, Maryland, and Delaware. We are in a very precarious place. Max and I need to work out an arrangement that allows him to feel safe with me sitting in the center of his Virginia territory. Max's warriors, combined with Lein's Eastern troops, Medici will be outmatched. I do not say this to scare you, *mi amore*, but I want you to understand. This is serious, deadly serious. Alec knows it as well. Max's mating just changed all the fucking rules."

Kate looked at him with concern. "But you've done nothing to Max. I mean, we mean him no harm. Do we? I understand Bel Rosso sits inside his territory, but he already knew Alec owned that land. He knew the land had been transferred to you. Surely, if he'd had an issue, he would have spoken up sooner."

"Think about this, *mi amore*. At the time, Bel Rosso was nothing. But that is no longer the case. It holds something that is a huge threat to him—the warrior camp. Think of what it looked like the first time you saw it.

"Now look at it. If he wants it, he will fight for it. I do not intend for that to happen. Max usually has a level head, so I am going to do all I can to talk this through first. But rest assured, I will fight to my death to save Bel Rosso. So, when they visit, and they will, we must be careful of our words, and careful of our actions. Max is a fox, a sly one. Lein was raised to keep her head down and her mouth shut, but she hears and sees all. Females like Lein look very meek and mild, but they are well trained to take it all in and report back. If you want to keep Bel Rosso, we may have to go to war. I hope to hell that does not happen, but if it does, be prepared, because I will win and take all of Virginia with it or die trying."

Kate felt his energy fill the car. Since she'd been with him, he'd never waged a battle for his own coven. She'd seen him and his warriors fight for Alec, and even that had ramifications for them when the rogues attacked Bel Rosso. But this was different. What he was describing was a turf war between masters. She'd heard him speak of them before, but for some reason she assumed it was something that occurred in the past. She assumed in these modern times, the masters had the territories defined and pretty much left each other alone. The idea of someone taking Bel Rosso made her fearful, but she found her anger overtook her fear. The idea that someone might attack their home, put Lorenzo's life at risk, brought out every maternal instinct she had and made the small hairs on the back of her neck stand up.

"I'll be careful, Shade. No one will take what we've worked to build."

Sliding his hand over hers, he felt such pride for her. "And that is why you are my queen. I need you to understand, I will let no one take what is mine. My *figlio* is born to reign and conquer, and I will see it through."

She curled up close to him. "I don't want a battle. But I'll not let anyone destroy what we've created. Please don't provoke Max, but if he challenges us—comes after us—I'll stand at your side."

He wrapped his arms around her as she laid her head on his chest. She had no idea of what lay ahead for them.

107

After Shade and Kate had left the reception, Alec went in search of Rissa. He saw her talking with other guests, her smile painted on, but he felt her anger. He had no idea what had gone down in the ladies' room, but it was enough to have all three women exit in turmoil. Rissa and Lein looked like they wanted to rip each other's heads off, and Kate had looked pale and shaken.

Stepping up behind her, Alec asked Rissa to dance and escorted her onto the dance floor. The floor cleared for them as the band played as he swayed with her. Every guest pulled out their cell phones to take a picture. The invited members of the press were also taking shots.

Alec held her close and whispered, "I have no idea what happened back there, but keep up appearances until we can get out of here. Too many cameras present to capture whatever is going on between you and Lein. So just smile, darling."

Rissa's nerves were rattled, and he felt it. They danced together beautifully, creating the perfect image for the photographers shooting them from every angle. She looked at him like any new bride—with complete love.

She smiled coyly. "Don't worry, this is our night and no one will take it from me. I love you, Alec."

They danced the evening away, mingled with the socially elite, cut the elaborate wedding cake, and watched as their mortal guests downed the expensive champagne. The crowd cheered as he knelt before her and slipped the garter from her leg. The men wolf whistled and howled as Alec tossed the garter into the crowd of eligible bachelors. As the evening came to a close, the women gathered in the center of the room to catch the huge bouquet of white lilies and roses.

Rissa scurried away, escorted by Hyde, back to the private room to change out of her wedding gown. She packed up her things that were to be delivered back to the house. She dressed in a tailored suit of winter white as she exited the dressing room and joined Alec. The crowd had moved outdoors to throw the traditional rice as the couple made a run for the limo. Alto ushered them inside the car and closed the door, heading to the airport and their private plane, where they'd be flown to Bora Bora for a week.

Rissa had hoped they'd stay longer, but Alec didn't want to be out of the public eye that long. He sighed as he settled into the seat, closing his eyes.

"So, my darling, what the hell went on in the ladies' room that had all three of you in such a state? Kate had to leave, for Christ's sake, so don't tell me it was nothing."

Rissa huffed. Not one word about the wedding or the reception. The first thing out of his mouth had nothing to do with the ceremony, how perfect it was, or how beautiful and stunning she was...but that fucking Asian bitch and Max. And now he's worried about Kate? She slowly turned her head to him and stared.

"Since when have you ever cared about Kate? She has that sniveling little brat now, even though we successfully rid her of the first one! Seriously, Alec, it wasn't anything, I handled it!"

Alec cast a sideways glance. "Calm down, please. Max is a rival. A very powerful one and the stakes have been raised significantly with this mating. We've always maintained a civil relationship, not through any bond of friendship or brotherhood, but because it was in both our interest to do so. I can't afford a confrontation with him right now. Very bad timing. I'm sure you handled it, but I need to know exactly what it is you handled."

Sliding off her shoes, she pulled out a gold cigarette case from her handbag and handed it to him. "I think we both deserve one of these, tonight. Alec, I promise you, I said absolutely nothing to provoke her. You were at the table, you heard every word. She walked in there and threatened me, told me if I messed with Max she'd take me down. I have no idea what the hell that was about. I've not had anything to do with him since I was in college. Apparently, Max must have told her about our relationship and she felt the need to claim her warrior. I made it perfectly clear to her that she had stepped into my master's territory and crashed our wedding, uninvited, I might add, and then approached me unprovoked to tell me to keep my hands off her man. Kate was scared out of her mind. She better learn where her claws are if she's going to be the Medici Queen. My God, she was like a little mouse shaking in the corner! Whatever it was, it's over and done with. Maybe she was jealous. Maybe she didn't want to come here in the first place, and Max insisted. Maybe she thinks he still feels something for me. Hell, I don't know, Alec, and I don't care."

Alec took the cigarette, lighting it and taking a deep drag. "So that's it then. You're telling me to drop it. There's nothing to worry about. I don't need to fix anything with Max."

"That's what I am telling you. I came from the bathroom and didn't return to the table right away, as I didn't want to stir up anything. I kept my distance for a reason. I surely didn't want the photographers to capture something."

Shrugging, she took the cigarette case, lit a cigarette, and laid her head back against the seat, taking a long, much needed drag. "She never acknowledged Kate, like she was invisible. Maybe Max was here for Shade. He's the one sitting in the middle of Max's territory. I'd not want to be in his shoes. But that does beg the questions. Why do you think Max was here? I know you don't tell me everything. He came here for something."

Alec shrugged. "I have no idea why he's here. I hadn't even heard he was mated. But I'm not feeling good about it. Somehow, I doubt his purpose in showing up was to spread good cheer." Alec put out the cigarette. "Anyway, nothing I can do about it now. I'll probably call Shade. Give him a heads up. Make sure he remembers Max wasn't on the guest list if he hasn't figured that out already. I gave him a copy so his warriors would know who was in attendance. But hell, no one is going to block a fucking master who shows up for our wedding, guest list or not. The warriors are all too smart for that. It would have created an altercation that would have just drawn attention to his presence there. The warriors did the right thing by letting him in and just keeping an eye on him. But enough about that, this is your wedding day, our wedding day, and a beautiful one at that. Don't you think it's about time we thought about consummating this union?"

Her laugh trickled throughout the limo. "Took you long enough!"

108

Kate was pleased that Lorenzo was adapting so quickly to his new routine. She and Theresa had been sharing the responsibility of feeding him and tonight, he'd fed for the first time from Nita. Lorenzo had been moved from their bedroom to the nursery, and Theresa slept in his room, for now, on the sofa-bed.

She stood at his crib as he cooed and responded to her voice. Turning to Theresa, Kate asked, "How will we know his gift? He doesn't sleep through the entire day. Does that mean he's a day-walker?"

Theresa shook her head. "Not necessarily, my lady. He wakes during the day because of his need to feed. We'll not know his gift until he's older. If it's essential, you can have Malachi taste his blood, but typically, families just wait until the gift presents itself."

Kate lifted him from the crib. He was dressed in a onesie now, and his chubby little body filled out the knit garment. Kate giggled at him with his full cheeks and his wide blue eyes, always inquisitive.

Gi came to the doorway of the nursery. "My lady?"

Kate turned to face him, holding the baby close. "What is it, Gi?"

"It is the wolf, my lady. Aegis. She's been more persistent than usual tonight, pawing at the back door. She and Night-Stalker have come to the door every night since you have returned from Florence."

Kate sighed. "I know. She wants to see the baby, but it's been so cold." She looked at Theresa. "Don't we have a little snowsuit we can bundle him in?"

Theresa nodded and ran to the baby's closet to retrieve it. Kate sent a message to Shade in the camp, asking if he could join them in the house.

***

Shade had been a bit on edge with the appearance of Max at the wedding. He'd informed the warriors of his possible visit with his new mate, and what it might mean for them. He was confident this could be resolved in a friendly manner. After all, Max had always been aware of his presence here. But either way, he knew his warriors were behind him. They'd fight and die for Medici, if it came to that.

Working with the new recruits, he heard Kate ask if he'd join them in the house and teleported to them immediately.

"Kate? What is wrong?"

"It's nothing. We're fine. You worry too much. I'm afraid if we don't take Lorenzo out to see Aegis and the other animals soon, we'll be replacing the back door. Aegis paws at it every evening. I thought you'd want to be with us. Do you have time?"

"Oh *si*, I always have time for my *figlio*."

Looking at Lorenzo, he scrunched up his face, put his hands on his hips, glaring at *bel*. "What the hell is that contraption he's wearing? How the hell do you expect him to move?"

Kate laughed at Lorenzo stuffed into the snowsuit, his little arms and legs held rigid and away from his body. "I don't think he's supposed to move. It's just to keep him warm."

She handed the baby to Shade and saw the light of recognition in Lorenzo's eyes as he stared at his father.

Shade shook his head. "I know, little warrior, I do not understand it either, but let's be compliant with *Madre*'s wishes, *si*?"

Lorenzo looked at him and smiled and Shade laughed. "Come, we must meet the beasties. Do not be frightened, *Padre* is here to protect you."

As they walked to the first floor, Shade carried the immobilized Lorenzo in his snowsuit and wondered what idiot mortal invented this thing. No warrior would ever be able to fight in this. "Are there pups, *mi amore*? I know Aegis was to have them. Have you seen them yet?"

Kate walked with him down the stairs. "There are pups. But they were born about two months before Lorenzo and I haven't seen them in a while. I imagine they're getting quite big by now."

They walked to the back of the house and out the back door onto the patio. Kate called out to Aegis and the wolf came bounding through the garden with Night-Stalker at her side and four smaller wolves following behind them. Kate knelt down to greet Aegis who licked at her face before moving to Shade and standing on her hind legs, trying to get a glimpse of the baby.

Shade admonished the wolf. "No! Down! *Cazzo, bel,* please you need to make her understand. She will scare the fuck out of him!"

He pulled Lorenzo tight against his chest and heard him begin to cry as he struggled to break free of Shade's grasp. "Lorenzo, it is fine, *Padre* has you."

Kate stood and took Lorenzo in her arms, shushing him. "Lorenzo, listen to me."

Lorenzo stopped crying and looked at Kate as if he understood her words.

"You have many warriors who will protect you. You have met daddy's warriors. Now you must meet mommy's warriors. This is Aegis, and her mate, Night Stalker. She guards us all and when you get older, she and her pups will play here outside with you. You have nothing to fear."

Kate squatted down and let the wolf approach as Lorenzo lifted his hand to the wolf's snout. Aegis licked the tiny hand. Night-Stalker cuffed one of the pups on the ear as they wrestled with each other, calming them down before joining his mate to look at the baby.

"See, Lorenzo? They are your warriors too."

Kate heard the low feral growl of the mountain lion as she stalked through the garden and entered the ring of light around the patio. Kate called to her, "Come on, Riparo. Come see the baby."

The mountain lion walked on silent feet as she approached slowly, nuzzling her head against Kate's arm before peering into Lorenzo's blue eyes, open in fascination, his tiny hand reaching for the whiskers of the large cat.

Shade tried to remain calm. He knew the animals listened to Kate, but his son was being held inches from the mouths of ferocious animals who could attack him if they so desired. He was still leery of her gift of animalism.

"*Mi amore*, be careful, please. I know you trust them, but they move so fast. Damn, this makes me nervous, I must admit. He seems to respond to them, though. He may have the same gift. I don't know."

Aegis walked in a circle and then sat down in front of Kate. Kate turned her head to the side, listening. "Aegis says he doesn't have the gift of animalism. But one other will. I guess that means another child? Yes. She says yes. Aegis says you need to trust her. She would fight to the death to defend what is hers, and all that is yours is also hers."

Kate heard the raucous cawing of the raven as Poe landed in a tree nearby. She shook her head. "Well, haven't heard from you in a while."

Shade pointed to Poe and grinned. "I like that damn bird, he hates Rissa!"

Night Stalker approached Shade and sat on his haunches beside him. Reaching down, Shade rubbed the wolf behind his ears. "Must be the old man's corner over here. You are one smart warrior, Night Stalker."

Kate chuckled as Shade adjusted to the intrusion of the animals. She was about to stand and go back inside when she heard the loud screech of the falcon and knew Danica had joined them. The bird of prey remained high in the trees, her silhouette clear against the night sky.

Kate chuckled. "Well, I didn't know it was going to be a party."

She was not sure if Lorenzo's vision was keen enough yet to see the large bird, but he definitely responded to the sound and looked skyward.

"Can you see him, Lorenzo?"

Kate caught movement out of her peripheral vision and looked down on the ground to see a large snake.

"Fuck!" She jumped up, stepping back quickly and clutching Lorenzo to her chest. Aegis danced around her, leaping up on her hind legs as Kate caught her breath.

"Are you sure, Aegis?"

The wolf chuffed at her and walked over to the snake. The snake was huge and looked like he could swallow Lorenzo whole, but Aegis was telling her the snake's name was Harley, and he was a member of the pack.

Shade reached out to her. "*Cazzo*! Give me Lorenzo, now!"

Taking his son in his arms, he too, was alarmed. "Damn it, Kate! A snake? What in the hell, this is like a zoo now! I am not keen on those reptiles and there is no way in hell I am letting Lorenzo near it. Just step away from it...please?"

Kate watched Aegis continued to step over and around the snake, until the snake curled up passively. Kate watched and listened to the wolf intently.

"Okay. Aegis knows Harley freaked us out, and she asked him to stop approaching."

She stood still for a second as she realized these animals were under her control as well, not just Aegis'. She approached the snake and acknowledged him. "I know you're here to protect, but it has me a little wigged out right now. If you don't mind, maybe you could visit another time?"

The snake raised his head as if to strike and Kate took a step back. His tongue flicked out as he turned and slithered back across the yard and into the dark.

"Well, that went well."

Kate was about to tell Shade they should take Lorenzo back inside when another large bird flew over. She looked up to see a large snow white owl land in the tree near Danica. "Seriously? What now?"

Aegis circled at her feet as Kate nodded her head. "Okay. I got it. His name is Wizard. Any more surprises?"

Aegis sat at her feet quietly. "No? Good. I think that's enough for one night."

She rubbed the wolf's head as she turned to Shade. "The animal parade is over. I think we can go back inside now."

He stood, cuddling Lorenzo, watching as her warriors arrived one at a time to make themselves known. Lorenzo cooed and tried like hell to reach to them, but his suit of puffy armor didn't allow much movement. His cheeks were rosy from the cold, but he was clearly enjoying the animals. "I think your son enjoys the parade, but I also think he is cold."

Shade held him up in the air and wiggled him back and forth above his head as Lorenzo cooed. Pulling him down, he went nose to nose with him. "*Padre* loves his little warrior, but I do believe it is time we went back inside where it is warm and we can snuggle with *Madre*, *si*? And if we are good warriors, she may let us both snuggle with her in the big bed!"

Cradling Lorenzo in his arms, he took *bel's* hand. "I think a roaring fire is in order!"

Kate slipped her hand in his as they walked back inside the house. She cast a glance over her shoulder as they went through the door to see the family of wolves, the mountain lion, and the birds of prey, all watching them closely.

109

Kate woke before him and lay across his broad chest, listening to his even breathing. She loved that her pre-baby shape was back, and they were now able to sleep as before with her arm and leg draped casually over him, her head on his shoulder. She felt him stir beneath her and knew he was awake, as the whir of the electronic blinds opened onto the darkening sky.

They were both sleeping better now that Lorenzo had been moved to the nursery, although Kate remained alert and knew every time Lorenzo woke during the day, and when he fed from Nita.

Shade slipped from the bed and started to dress in leathers as Kate watched him. "I've missed you, lover. We've both been so busy it seems. Stay with me tonight."

Shade ran his hands over his face, combing his fingers through his hair. "*Mi amore*, Marcello has scheduled trials today."

Kate scrunched up her face. "Trials?"

He continued dressing as he talked. "*Si*. For the new recruits. It is an exercise that has them moving quickly from one weapon to the next. They will fight mock battles, on the ground, on the rooftops. It is a means to see how they are advancing and where they need further work."

Kate pulled the blankets up over her shoulders and buried her face in the pillow. "Oh, okay." She couldn't hide her disappointment.

"*Bel*, are you all right?"

"I'm fine, really. I'll be busy with Lorenzo. You'd think with a nanny there'd be nothing to do, but somehow, he manages to keep us both busy."

Shade leaned over the bed and kissed her. "We need time alone, *si*?"

Kate looked up at him, his dark curls falling forward around his face. "Yes...alone time."

"Soon, *mi amore*. But right now, I need to be in the camp. Oh, the lawyers called. The seller accepted our offer on the land that adjoins our property. So, plant whatever you want."

Kate gave him a half smile. Is that what she wanted? Another project? She responded without much enthusiasm. "That's good news."

He kissed her again before leaving their room. She heard him stop in the nursery to check on Lorenzo before he left the house.

Kate closed her eyes and sighed. She didn't realize how much the baby would alter their lives. Even the pregnancy had dictated change. He'd continued to make love to her, almost until she delivered. But it was awkward and limiting. And he was so careful with her. She didn't realize how much she'd miss the intimacy of his feeding from her.

She knew each time he went to Luca, and although she was grateful for Luca's cooperation, she could feel their passion, and selfishly wished it was her.

Lorenzo was just over a month old now, and he fed almost exclusively from Nita. Kate had lost the baby weight and had her figure back. Now she wanted her mate back.

She climbed from bed and slipped on her jeans. She'd abandoned her jeans during the pregnancy in favor of dresses, so pulling them on and getting the zipper closed made her smile. She pulled a sweater over her head and slide on a pair of boots. She brushed out her hair before leaving the room and headed to the nursery.

As she opened the door of their bedroom, she could hear Cory clamoring down the stairs from his suite. He passed her in the hallway, waved and said, "I'm late!"

She waved back as he flew down the second set of stairs to the first floor and out the door.

Kate entered the nursery to find Theresa in the rocker, holding Lorenzo to her neck as he suckled. "Where's Nita?"

Theresa smiled. "She'll be here shortly. But he was hungry, and I hate to make him wait."

Kate shook her head. "Somehow, I think this baby is going to have a hard time understanding the concept of waiting for anything." She dragged a basket of clean clothes and linens and started folding them.

Theresa studied her. She'd spent more than a year now under the same roof with her and could read her moods. "Is something on your mind, my lady?"

Kate looked up at her surprised. "What? No. Nothing, it's nothing."

Theresa stared her down. "You're not very convincing, my lady."

Kate threw up her hands, tossing the laundry aside as she paced the room. "I feel so...restless...or something."

Theresa smiled at her. "Restless? Are you sure restless is what you feel?"

Kate flopped down on the sofa bed. "I don't know what I'm feeling. Confused? Frustrated? Agitated?"

Theresa chuckled. "My lady, Lorenzo has stopped feeding. Have you invited master to feed from you again?"

Kate looked at her skeptically. "Invited? What do you mean 'invited'? I sleep right next to him. He needs an invitation?"

Theresa laughed. "Well, yes, he does, actually. Not all masters would wait. Some would resume feeding whether their mate was ready or not.

But that was not how Shade was raised. Some females want a period of time after the baby stops feeding to regain their strength before their mate comes to them again. He needs to know you are ready."

Kate looked at her with a confused expression. "So, I just tell him?"

Theresa looked at her over Lorenzo's dark curls. "My lady, I don't think you need any direction from me on the art of seduction. I have lived under this roof as well, yes?"

Kate smiled at her. "Seduction. Oh, I understand seduction."

Theresa smiled back. "Indeed you do."

Kate stood and walked to the door. "Do you have everything under control here?"

Theresa gently rocked the baby as she answered, "Take all the time you need."

Kate returned to their bedroom to find Emma had already made their bed. She folded back the spread and blanket, and then stripped off the boots and jeans, tossing the sweater over the chair. She filled the room with soft candlelight before walking into the bathroom and filling the large tub with water, sprinkling in her rose-scented bath salts and tossing some rose petals on the surface. She lit candles in the bathroom, filling the room with a warm glow. She pinned her hair loosely on top of her head, letting tendrils fall around her face. Stepping into the large tub, she slid into the steaming hot water. Laying her head back against the tile, she took a deep breath then called to him. **"Lover? Can you join me please?"**

***

Shade and Marcello walked around the training field, observing the new recruits in action. Several of the newbies had been paired up with the experienced warriors to cover the outside security for the Canton wedding. It had been a small start to give them experience, even though the event went off without a hitch. Still, it gave Marcello an opportunity to observe how they'd handle themselves on a professional assignment.

Shade was feeling restless and sluggish. He should feed again, but didn't want to return to Luca. He knew *bel* had stopped feeding Lorenzo, and he was hoping he could wait it out. Luca's blood had sustained him, but it was her blood he craved.

Marcello was recording their observations about each recruit's performance during the trials when Shade heard her invitation in his head, and felt her desire wash over him.

Shade turned to Marcello. "You got this, brother? I think I'm needed in the main house."

Marcello looked up from his notes. "Sure, no problem."

Shade teleported to their bedroom, which was bathed in candlelight. He picked up the scent of roses. "*Mi amore*?"

"In here, lover."

He followed the sound of her voice into their bathroom, also lit by the flickering light of many candles. She had learned to will forth music, as Norah Jones seductively sang, "Turn Me On."

He pulled off the boots and stripped off the leathers as he looked at her. Her cheeks flushed pink from the heat of the water. The fine tendrils of her crimson locks clung to her face in the steam that rose from the bath. He walked to the tub and she slid forward, and he slipped in behind her. He lowered himself into the hot bath, his long legs straddling her, as she lay back against his chest.

"Lover, I've missed you."

His hands explored beneath the surface of the water, sliding over her hips and encircling her waist before moving up and cupping each breast in his hands. "*Mi amore*, are you ready?"

Kate lay her head back on his shoulder, exposing her neck to him, her lips slightly parted, her eyes closed. Her actions told him more than any words could speak. He bent his head to her, letting his tongue explore the pulsing vein in her neck, his cock growing hard, as the moan escaped her lips.

"Lover, it's been too long."

"*Si, mi amore*, much too long."

Her breasts filled his hands, her nipples hard against his palms as he slid his hands across those soft orbs. He lowered his lips to her neck, nipping first, breaking the skin, and letting a single drop of her deep red blood flow down her neck against her lily white skin. He heard her hiss as his fangs punched through, and he bit into that tender flesh, drawing deep. Her blood flowed over his tongue and he growled deep in his chest. He had missed the taste of her, the unique energy he got only from her. He swallowed, feeling her blood slide down his throat as every cell crackled with life. How had he managed to go five months without feeding fromher?

Kate felt the explosion of heat between her legs as his fangs penetrated her skin, and his lips closed around the wound, sucking and drawing her blood into his mouth. She cried out with the pleasure his feeding brought as her hands slide down his thighs, her nails gripping him tight. She could feel the heat from his steel-hard cock, throbbing against her ass. She pushed her hips hard against him. He drank from her like a dying man, thirsting in the desert, each swallow bringing both of them pleasure.

He unlatched, his eyes glowing red as he stood. Lifting her with him, he stepped from the tub. He carried her as he walked, glistening wet in the candlelight back to their bed. He sat her on the side of the bed and pulled the pins from her hair, letting her crimson fall around her shoulders as single red rose petals randomly clung to her body.

"My walking sin."

He removed the petals with his mouth, slowly, one by one, licking them away as they stuck to his tongue. As he held her hand in his, he dropped the petals into her palm. His breath hot against her skin, he watched the goose bumps that trailed behind the explorations of his tongue.

When he'd collected all the petals inside her palm, he looked at her, their eyes locked in a loving gaze. They needed no words to express what they both felt as their love washed over them.

"It seems as though we were like the petals of that rose, scattered, in disarray, yet still together. You hold my heart, *mi amore*. There will be times we struggle to be together, to be in sync with one another, but we are never without the other."

Kate sprinkled the petals across the sheets, and then lay down on their bed, pulling him with her.

"You've taken care of me, watched over me and Lorenzo, and we've both been pulled in a lot of directions. But I miss us. I want us."

He leaned over her, his weight supported on his elbow, as she ran her hands through his tangled locks, the tips of his hair still damp from the tub.

"*Si*. I did not want to rush you. Each female is different in their need after the birthing. I will not make demands, but I have such need, *mi amore*. With us, it is always a slow, simmering burn that erupts in fireworks."

Taking her in his arms, he willed the music of Lifehouse singing, "Falling In" to play softly in their room lit from the candles and the moon. He held her body, soft and naked against his bare skin, as he leaned down, kissing her neck before moving to her waiting lips. He rolled over, taking her with him as he stood and lifted her from the bed. His hands wrapped under her ass, lifting her to his waist. Her legs wrapped around his hips as she clung to him. He danced slowly around the room and watched as she leaned back, her crimson locks falling behind her. Leaning forward, he sucked a nipple into his mouth, letting his tongue tease until her nipple was a tight, sweet bud in his mouth.

Kate couldn't remember the last time they were playful. His mouth was hot and wet on her nipple, and it sent a chill down her spine. She rose up to meet him, kissing him slowly, biting at his lower lip and drawing it into her mouth before kissing him deeply.

"You keep kissing me like that, *mi amore,* there will be fireworks far too soon. Patience."

Her amber eyes stared back at him with such innocence, but he knew behind those eyes there was so much passion, reserved solely for him. Laying her on the bed, she slithered into a seductive pose and he growled.

As he walked to the nightstand he could feel her eyes on his every move. Rummaging in the drawer, his found the bottle of exotic rose massage oil. Walking to the foot of the bed, he poured a generous amount in his hands and rubbed them together, warming the oil in his hands as the fragrant scent wafted into the room. He stared into her eyes and a wicked grin slid across his face. "Turn over."

She slowly raised her arms above her head and rolled onto her stomach, arching her back, lifting her ass slightly. She looked over her shoulder at him through her tousled red hair. "Like this, lover?"

"*Si*, my brazen and wicked seductress."

Placing his warm oiled hands on her calves, he slid his hands slowly up her thighs and onto that beautiful ass. He massaged the oil into her cheeks, letting his fingers slip between her legs, teasing the swollen lips of her sex. He climbed onto the bed, straddling her, and clutching her hips, her body responding to his touch. His cock stood rigid, but he resisted the urge to take her.

As he leaned over her, she felt his cock sliding along her ass and across her back, coating his cock in the oil. She'd forgotten the sweet agony of the tease. She remembered all the times she'd tempt him, and how quickly he could turn the tables. She felt his hands, covered in the oil, slide beneath her and cup her breasts, her nipples erect and tingling at his touch. She buried her face in the pillow to stifle the moan that escaped from her as she lifted her ass, pressing hard against him.

Palming his cock, he moaned, his hand warm with the oil as the scent of roses surrounded them. Sliding the bulging tip inside her, she immediately responded, lifting her hips to receive him, but he held her steady, not fully penetrating her. He moved just a few inches of his steel slowly inside her, back and forth, teasing.

"Let me hear how much my beast calls to you, *mi amore*."

Kate gripped the sides of the pillow as she arched her neck and lifted her head. He teased her, penetrating slowly, and her fangs punched through, followed by a low growl deep in her throat. She raised her hips, shifting her weight to her knees to accommodate him.

He watched as she rose to his call and he slide inside her. She took him fully, and he groaned, his body aching for her. Sliding his hands slowly up her back, he gripped her shoulders and leaned over her, nipping at her neck as he buried his face into her crimson waves. His hips found her rhythm, they moving together as one.

Kate turned her head exposing her neck to him. Reaching up, she pulled her long hair aside as she waited to feel the sting of his fangs in her flesh.

He could see the vein pulsing in her neck and it called to him, and he sank his fangs deep. He felt her heat rise as his cock was gripped in a tight, hot, wet cocoon. As he fed from her, her blood across his tongue fueled his desire as he moved faster, deeper. Her blood whistled in his veins, filling him with love and passion and an erotic song only he could hear. Unlatching, he licked the wound and moaned as his balls tightened, aching to fill her. "Cum, *mi amore*, cum with me!"

The bolt of heat and desire that flashed through her when he fed pushed her to the edge, her hips moving faster to meet his rhythm, taking all of him with each thrust. His cock throbbed as he unlatched and begged her to cum. She felt her body ignite at its core, as the waves of pleasure extended out. He rode her hard, gripping her hips for leverage and she cried out, her hands clinging to the sheets. His body covered her, their skin sliding easily and seductively against each other with the warm oil.

Panting, he rolled off her onto his back. Before she could catch her breath, he reached over and pulled her on top of him. She straddled him as he gripped her hips and slid inside her once again. She threw her head back, her skin pale in the candlelight, her crimson tousled and swinging behind her. *Cazzo*, she drove him out of his mind! Reaching up, he pulled her to his chest, rubbing her back, his hands seeking her ass.

She slid her hands along the firm, hard muscles of his chest and lifted her face to him. His skin looked golden in the candlelight and glistened from the oil. His impossibly blue eyes stared back at her. Her love for him overwhelmed her and made her gasp. How could one person change everything, change her life, so drastically? There was no living without Shade now. She lowered her mouth to his, licking at his lips. She sucked at the tip of his tongue, nipping at him, before running her tongue over his fangs.

He felt her emotions take hold of her heart and he loved her so deeply. He felt her tongue slide over his fangs and he arched his head back on the pillow, his heart racing out of control. His body responded, his blood screaming, his cock rock hard inside her and her muscles gripped and pulled at him.

He closed his eyes and thrust his hips upward, gripping a handful of her hair. He was lost in the throes of passion when he heard Lorenzo cry out. He felt her pull away as she tried to escape him. He held her tight, not letting her go.

Kate was momentarily distracted when she heard Lorenzo cry, but his cry was quickly silenced. She had instinctively moved to go to him when she felt Shade pull her back.

"No, he is with Nita. Listen to him. He is fine, mi amore." He pulled her head to him and stared into her eyes. "No." His hips began to move and she responded, wanting more of him.

"That's it, *mi amore*, stay with your savage lover."

Kate willed the sounds of Enigma to fill the room, drowning out any distractions as "The Principles of Lust" played, its erotic beat creating the rhythm she matched as her hips rode his cock until she screamed his name and collapsed on his chest.

She felt him cum as he threw his head back, and she let go of her own orgasm at the same time. She bit into his neck, drawing his blood into her mouth as his cum filled her as well. She rode him hard, grinding against him as he thrust hard into her. She unlatched as the orgasm subsided and dropped her head on his shoulder. She felt his hands slide slowly up and down her back in a warm caress.

He lay with her, sexually sated and his blood lust satisfied. His hands caressed as their breathing returned to normal. She was a precious jewel he held with great care. He never thought he could love her more, but with the birth of Lorenzo, his love for her had doubled. The darkness that held him for so long was long gone and he smiled, his heart full.

"I have no words to tell you how much love I have for you, Kate. You have given me a son, and he is precious to us both. You have changed your life, given up much for me, for my warriors, and *familia*. I fell in love with this beautiful female with raving red hair. She did not respond well to my advances and made me work my ass off before I could have her. I knew you were the one. I could see this life together. Now it is here, unfolding for us, and I only want to share it with you."

He willed the music to play for her, as the sounds of The Script filled the room, and Kate listened to the lyrics of "I'm Yours". She clung to him, as they held each other in the warm afterglow of their love.

110

Shade looked at his cell phone after he hung up. Max was wrapping up his stay in the States and he wanted to visit Bel Rosso before he left. He would arrive the following evening with Lein in tow. He needed to speak with Kate about this visit. They'd need to be on the same page. Some things were never divulged or hinted at with another master, especially when Shade was sitting square in the middle of his territory.

Walking to the living room, he willed on a blazing fire, poured two Midnights and telepathically asked *bel* to join him. Nita and Theresa had Lorenzo well in hand already, but he knew she spent every spare moment of her time with him, as she should. But right now, he needed to speak to her before heading over to the camp for the night.

***

Kate had just finished giving Lorenzo a bath. She'd learned the hard way to strip down to bare essentials before bathing him, because Lorenzo loved nothing more than splashing. He'd slap his chubby little hands at the water surface, sending a spray of water in every direction, his laughter echoing off the walls.

She washed his dark hair and dipped him back under the flowing water to rinse away the suds. His blue eyes widened as he stared up at her, and Kate laughed at his expression of surprise as the water flowed over his head. Lifting him from the tub, she wrapped him in a towel, just as she heard Shade ask her to join him. She called Theresa and passed off the squirming baby as Kate dried herself off and tossed her wet undergarments in the hamper, putting on clean, dry clothes. She let Shade know she was on the way while she pulled a sweater over her head and stepped into her shoes.

Heading down the stairs, she could hear the crackle of the fire and turned in the direction of the living room to find Shade seated there, fire blazing, and a most welcome glass of Midnight waiting. Kate lifted the glass to her lips, sipping at the rich elixir before curling up next to him.

"Shade, I think as he gets older, we'll need to add a pool. Lorenzo loves the water. I'm drenched every time I bathe him and he hates it when I take him out of the water."

"A water baby. Well, we could have worse on our hands. I like the idea of a pool. Perhaps, you can expand the lower level and build an indoor pool as well as an outside pool, and the children can enjoy it year round, *si*?" He slipped his arm around her as he nuzzled into her neck, kissing her. "Mmm, what is that smell? It smells soft and clean."

Kate threw back her head and laughed. "That's baby shampoo. You know you're really a father when the scent of baby shampoo smells erotic. But let me get this one on his feet please before we have another."

Hugging her tight, he smiled. He knew she'd be a wonderful mother and he wanted her to have the time to enjoy each of them. "I agree we should wait a bit. Plus, I don't want you to feel overwhelmed. On a separate matter, I wish to speak with you about something before I go to camp. Can you sit with me a bit?"

"Lover, I can sit with you all night."

Chuckling, he took a sip of Midnight. "*Mi amore*, I wish I had all night, but after last night I think it wise for me to spend some time at camp, *si*? Max called and he and Lein will be arriving tomorrow. There is no protocol we need to follow, but the Midnight will flow freely. I want to show them our home, but the camp is off limits. I will not show him that, and I ask that you not discuss it with Lein, should she ask. We must be careful of what we reveal. I expect Lein will be quiet, so feel free to engage her in conversation, but keep to general topics like children or running the household. Do not discuss our business."

"I'll be careful around Lein. I've already seen two sides of her. At the table during the wedding reception, she barely spoke and kept her eyes downcast. In the ladies' room, if she'd had access to a knife, I swear she would have cut Rissa's throat. I'm not sure what's going on between those two, but I want no part of it. I can keep the conversation light."

"*Si*. That's what I mean. I expect no problems. But Max is not visiting to be social, I can guarantee you that. He is a powerful master in his own right. Add her into it, we need to have all senses on alert. Two other things. First, I wish for them to see our son. He is heir to the dynasty and is an important symbol in our culture. I do not think it is necessary to have him join us the entire time. Tell me your thoughts. Do you have concerns about this?"

His hand slide easily up and down her thigh as she sat curled soft and warm next to him. He had the life he'd always dreamed of, and he intended to keep it just like this.

"That's not a problem. I can bring Lorenzo down, let them see him, and then Theresa can take him back upstairs after a short visit. I'll ask Luca to stay close as well, in case he had plans to visit Shannon. With you here, as well as Luca and the warriors, I have no fear of letting them see Lorenzo."

He kissed her softly. "One more thing. I need for you to keep Aegis and the others out of sight. I do not want your gift revealed to Max. If he sees the creatures patrolling the perimeter, he may put two and two together and figure out it is your gift. Until we both understand your power, and you have learned to master it, it is better we not expose it."

Sighing heavily, he pushed the hair out of his face. "I need to have him here, feel him out, read his body language before I can judge where he stands on this matter. I need this territory thing settled and I intend to do it peacefully, if possible. I can't do that if I can't get a read on him and what he intends to do. Keep your warriors close, but out of sight. Can you relay that to them?"

"Of course. I'll tell Aegis to stay on guard but completely out of sight. I'll let her know we have guests, and they're expected. She'll listen, and she'll instruct and control the others. I know you don't completely understand this gift, nor do I, but I feel their intent, and it is clearly singular. They're here to protect all that is Medici, not just me. Aegis won't fail me."

He nodded. "Good. Together, we will learn how to leverage our power. I will take Max aside, see where his head is, and you keep Lein entertained. Now let me go, we both have warriors to attend to. And once you are done, there is a present in the armoire, just for you. I expect to see them tomorrow night, *si*!"

"A present? I love presents!" She stood as he prepared to leave, reluctantly letting him go. She kissed him as he easily lifted her into his embrace before setting her back down and heading to the camp. Kate watched him leave before returning upstairs and opening the armoire to find the gift he'd stashed there for her. She found a pair of shoes, beautiful dark brown suede heels with a mink ankle strap. "**Lover, you know the way to a girl's heart.**"

111

Max was in his Virginia mansion on the James River outside of Richmond as he finished tying his tie while Lein was putting the finishing touches on her make-up. He looked at her reflection in the mirror. She was a rare beauty, and she'd proved to be a powerful mate, expanding his territory a hundredfold. But it was a marriage of convenience, arranged between two masters, Max and Fan Shen. Fan had one child, a female, who was not born warrior and her only gift being the common one of day-walking. As much as Fan loved her, he knew she'd have trouble defending a coven the size of Fan's.

Lein's mother had died in childbirth. A very rare occurrence among vampires, and Lein had been a delicate child, born prematurely. She'd been raised in the traditional Asian culture and had learned to be submissive and demure. But Fan was no fool. He'd also taught his daughter that men rarely paid attention to the presence of women and she could learn much by keeping her ears open. Fan had attempted several times over the years to arrange matings for her. There were many who showed an interest, but not all would have made a good match for Lein, or for the coven. He'd always wanted her mated to a European or Western master.

Was it fate that brought them together? Max smirked. Lein was the only good thing that came from his obsession with that hateful bitch, Rissa. He shuddered every time he thought of her name.

He was back in the States to show Lein his coven when he'd heard about the Canton wedding. Invitation or not, he'd decided he'd be at that wedding. He'd eagerly anticipated the look on Rissa's face when he showed up mated, and her reaction didn't disappoint!

While he was here, he'd teleported over the property Shade had acquired. He was still in shock, although in hindsight, he realized he shouldn't be. He could handle the renovations to the house and the staff quarters, the expansion of the vineyards and the addition of the stables, but the warrior camp was a step too far.

He'd like a peaceful settlement with Shade. A battle between warriors was costly in lives lost, and most masters of modern day would go to all costs to avoid it. But Max couldn't ignore the blatant slap to his face of the warrior camp built right in the middle of his territory.

Max went to Lein, placing his hands on her shoulders as he leaned down and kissed her neck. "You look beautiful, my angel. Are you ready?"

Lein smiled at him and nodded, and Max took her hand.

"We'll teleport out. I want to take one more look at the warrior camp before we meet. Shade has built such high walls around it that it's not visible from the ground. The walls look old and covered in ivy. They look like they've been there for years, even though the camp is newly constructed. It's not visible from the main road, so it wouldn't draw the attention of mortals. And if a mortal were to wander down that drive, he has enough security to intercept them and make the mortal turn their car around, erasing their memory of anything that might have made them curious. Ingenious, really, hiding it in plain sight. I need you to do what you do best, my angel. See what information his mate is willing to share. She was a mortal, not born to our ways. She should be easy to manipulate."

Lein gave him a sly smile and bowed her head to him. "Of course, master. It will be as you wish."

Max slide his arm around her waist as they teleported out together. It wasn't a long teleport, and he took his time as he hovered over the Bel Rosso estate before landing at the front door. He straightened his tie and gave Lein a minute to straighten her dress before he knocked on the massive old wooden door.

***

Shade took his time dressing, his Italian made light wool suit was made for cold climate. His designer shoes gleamed. He brushed out his hair as he stood in front of the full length mirror, trying to tie his black curls back in a loose ponytail. He was struggling to gather the loose strands into a tidy ponytail and was cursing under his breath when he caught her reflection in the mirror.

As always, she left him speechless. She was beautiful when she dressed casually in her jeans and sweaters, but when she slid into a dress and heels, her hair and make-up perfected, he was always awestruck and remembered the first time he saw her across that crowded room. She had no competition.

Their eyes met in the mirror, his hands stopped fidgeting with his hair as they shared that moment, exchanging love in a glance.

"You look stunning, *mi amore*. And the shoes? Do you approve of your lover's gift?"

Kate was wearing a cashmere sweater dress in ivory that showcased her soft curves and red hair.

"The shoes?" She bent at the waist, tightening the ankle strap on the brown suede heels accented in mink. With her ass in the air, she looked up at him through the mass of red hair that fell forward around her face. "Love the shoes."

His eyes locked on the curve of her ass. He'd kill a million men for that ass. He chuckled. "Can you help me with this damn hair? You have a way with my hair. Even *Madre* could not handle this mop! Is my son ready?"

Kate laughed as she walked to him, pulling his hair back, then combed it with her fingers as she deftly tied the leather string. "Well, I don't know if your son is ready, but our son is."

Rolling his eyes, he sighed. "*Si*, I deserved that one. I am sorry, *mi amore*, a lot in my head right now. Then you stroll in here, tempt me with that sweet ass of yours. And well, my mind goes haywire."

She gave a sharp tug on his hair and he grunted. "Okay, okay, you made your point, woman!"

Chuckling, she kissed his neck. He felt Max's presence before he heard the knocker sounding loud.

"I do believe our company has arrived. I have asked Gi to show them into the living room. Shall we join them?"

Kate hooked her arm in his. "I'm ready. I'll have Theresa bring Lorenzo down after we're settled."

Taking her arm, they strolled down the hall and exited the stairs, entering the living room. Max stood with a glass of Midnight in his hand. His mate was already seated by the fire. Shade smiled and nodded to Lein and then shook Max's hand.

"Welcome to Bel Rosso. Please have a seat, Max, and make yourselves comfortable."

Leading *bel* to the couch, he sat her down before getting them both a drink.

"I am pleased you have come to visit, Max. It is good to be away from the throng of people, to be able to relax and talk. Can I get you a refill? Good year for the Midnight."

Max downed the glass and held it up for a refill. The ancient butler quickly complied, filling his glass.

"Don't mind if I do. The vampire world owes you much for the production of Midnight, Shade. Don't know what we'd do without it. There's a concoction they serve in the East that is similar to their saké. I can't say it quite hits the spot for me. Thank you for agreeing to see me, As I think there's much we need to discuss. But first, you're looking well, and your lovely mate. Life's been good to you, it seems. And my life has changed dramatically as well. A mate changes everything, does it not?"

"Oh *si*, most definitely, and all for the better, I might add. Wait until you have a child. I never imagined this future for myself, and I did not see my beautiful Kate coming, but when she did, I stopped existing and began living."

He took a sip of the wine then took a seat next to Kate as his free hand slid across the back of the couch, and around her shoulder, his fingers unconsciously playing in her crimson.

"I will be having a new brand of Midnight coming soon in celebration of my son's birth. I will make sure you get a case. Do you still have your mansion outside of Richmond? That place covered some ground if I remember correctly?"

Max smiled. "I'll gladly accept the gift. Yes, I still have the mansion. We're staying there now. It's not on as much land as you have here, but the house is quite grand. At last count there were one hundred and twenty-three rooms. Twenty-seven bedrooms, I think."

Max's chuckled as he sipped at the wine, looking at their cozy but humble home in comparison. He knew the Medici had chosen this place, as it appealed to the more pedestrian taste of his mortal mate. He'd seen the grand castle in Florence years ago and knew this was a big step down for Shade. Talking him out of it should be easy.

Shade didn't miss the dig, or the sly smile that spread across his face. "It sounds like Castello, but on a smaller scale. I rather like Bel Rosso, named after my queen, of course. I grew up in the luxury of a castle. We still go there and I have many memories there, but it can be cold as well. It does not provide the same comfort as here. I still have Castello, another home in Greece, France, and other places, but Virginia gives me what is important. This is where I find the simplicity of love, family, and a sense of home. Kate and I enjoy the nature of this place. It is very peaceful here, a nice change from the city, but it would be nothing without her. I am sure you have learned, being mated to Lein, that home is wherever your mate is." Smiling, he winked at *bel*. "Would you like to have our son join us? I do believe Max and Lein should meet the future of Medici."

Kate felt the gentle sparring that was going on between them. There didn't appear to be any animosity, but it was clearly a game of one-ups, men-ship going on. She remembered Shade warning her to tread softly. When he asked about Lorenzo, she smiled and spoke softly, "Of course."

Kate went to the foot of the stairs, calling for Theresa. The nanny appeared with the baby, dressed for the occasion in a blue outfit that brought out the color of his eyes. Lorenzo had been fed and was now wide awake. Theresa slipped Lorenzo into her arms and he immediately grabbed a handful of her red hair.

She laughed softly as she carried the baby back into the living room. "You are just like your father."

Shade stood as Kate entered with his son. Lorenzo took in the two strangers in his presence, then looked at his father and began kicking his legs and flinging his arms, cooing. Shade smiled down at him, taking him in his arms and laying him easily across his chest.

"May I introduce you to my son, Lorenzo, Prince of Medici, and heir to the throne? He is our pride and joy. You need to have a few of your own, Max. Changes how you see everything around you. Secure your legacy."

Max took in this little scene of domestic bliss, trying to decide if this was for show or for real. This was certainly not the Shade Medici he'd known from the past. He'd had only two pastimes—fighting and fucking. If this was his adversary, then his mate had tamed him but good. This battle might be much easier won than he'd thought.

"I am sure there will be babies in my future. Fan Shen will expect his daughter to produce an heir for the Shen dynasty. But I think we will wait a bit for that. We are newly mated as well. We have plenty of time to create a family, but a toast to you, my friend, and your good fortune."

"*Grazie*!"

Lorenzo shouted out as well and they all chuckled. Shade handed him back to *bel.* "Kate has done a good deal to Bel Rosso; it was just a shell when I acquired it from Alec. Perhaps, you'd care to have a cigar and take a walk outside? I am sure our beautiful mates would like some time to talk. I have some damn fine Cubans, if you care to smoke?"

Max nodded. "Of course. I'd never deny myself a good Cuban cigar."

He stood as he thought to himself he wouldn't have to go outside to smoke it either. Shade was looking like easier and easier prey as he handed the baby back to his mate. Max followed him through the house, small by comparison to where he lived, both in Virginia, and the Royal Palace in Thailand. But the house was well appointed and tastefully done. He took note of the original artwork and expensive antiques, all true to the Tuscan style as he followed Shade out onto a patio that was well lit, as were the landscaped gardens that surrounded the house, now dormant with the winter.

"I don't know about you, Max, but sometimes a damn good cigar is all you need after a glass of Midnight. I appreciate you coming here. We have to settle this situation between us. Neither of us wishes for this to become a problem. The land is simple here, the soil and the climate are perfect for the vineyards. It is vital in keeping the Midnight production for the States and that growing demand."

As they lit up, Shade began to walk, and Max followed.

"We added the stables. I wanted to breed some good horseflesh here; we have not started yet, but I do have some good Medici horses here now."

Max enjoyed the flavor of the Cuban cigar as they walked through the gardens down a path to the stables. The property definitely reflected a feminine touch as he tried to take in as much as possible. The camp wasn't visible from here, and he doubted Shade would bring it up.

"The land is beautiful, my friend. And you've done a lot to increase its value. So, I am wondering...what's your price?"

Shade chuckled. "Not for sale."

Max stopped and looked into the night sky, exhaling a large cloud of smoke. "Shade, let's not dance around the issue. We've known each other far too long to play such games. The warrior camp. I'm well aware of the open call, and the new camp. You found a mortal and have turned her, made her your mate, but surely you rule over her. You can live anywhere, and she'll follow. You can't expect me to do nothing with a rival master building a warrior camp in the middle of my territory, and I don't expect you to walk away without fair compensation. That's why I will ask again, what's your price?"

Shade knew it was coming, and he knew he'd die to keep Bel Rosso. He leaned his elbows over the fence railing, staring straight ahead at the mountains.

"Max, no sale. I could live anywhere, and my mate *would* follow, but this is where we chose to live. I won't play games. The camp is simply that, a camp. It is of no threat. I provide all of Alec's security, as well you know. I need to have a source of warriors here. D.C. is a fucking bevy of rogue activity and it draws vampires from all over. From one warrior to another, he could have easily asked you to provide his protection, but he asked me. I take that job very seriously. Alec gets exposed, we all do, and that threatens us all, so my camp serves all of us, Max, including you."

Max leaned against the fence rail. "I'm afraid I can't take that chance, old friend. Keep the property and move the camp. Move it anywhere, just get it out of my territory. You'd do the same if I built a camp in the middle of Florence. I'm sure you own more property than this in the States. And Alec still has his own coven in New England, and in California. If the camp is only here to serve his needs, then surely, he'd have no objections to you building a camp inside his territory."

Shade shrugged. "Well, that is easier said than done. I legally acquired Bel Rosso from Alec...how he acquired it from you is of no care to me. But I took it because it was a central locale for me. It provided me a home and was convenient to D.C. I can't house and train warriors inside his D.C. territory, it is too metropolitan, and, I can't keep a low enough profile in that environment. Warriors need to practice and train, and that makes noise. New England and California are too far away for a camp. Think about it, Max. This is a good locale. We are in the middle of nowhere. My warriors are disciplined, well cared for. You will not see trouble from them. I have nothing against you. We go back a long way, this can be easily settled between us."

Max looked skyward as he listened to Shade explain why he wouldn't leave. It wasn't the response Max wanted but wasn't unexpected.

"Oh, I've heard how you provide for the warriors, my friend. A feeder compound inside the camp? Very clever. I'm sure the warriors are most appreciative of your generosity, not to mention it provides a most convenient and diverse way to entertain yourself. Never have to leave home. I'm sure your mate appreciates that as well."

Shade lowered his head, laughing. Max was typical of masters who felt their position gave them the right to feed from whomever they found attractive, regardless if they were mated. It was accepted in their culture when the mate knew the rules, but Shade preferred to follow in his *padre*'s footsteps and remain faithful to his mate. He'd only feed from her, unless, of course, she was pregnant.

"No, I would lose my family jewels if that ever happened. I have never stepped foot inside that compound, nor do I have any idea of what it looks like or who is in there. Kate is not comfortable around the feeders. Her first experience was not a great one. A disaster actually, thanks to that bitch Rissa. So, feeders are completely off limits to me. She would feed my balls to the wolves if she ever found me even thinking about it! I feed exclusively from her. And I like it that way. She is all I will ever need."

Max snapped his head around, looking at Shade. "You can't be serious! You're a Master! You can feed from whomever you please. You let this mortal mate dictate to you?" Max shook his head. "I've heard many things in my lifetime, old friend, but this...I don't understand. You take nothing from her by feeding from others. She's still the only one who feeds from you. Her position in your life remains unchanged for all eternity. This I don't understand."

Shade stood straight and looked Max in the eyes. "Very easy to understand. I love her. She is everything to me. I've done my whoring and sowed my oats. I have no need for anything beyond her. Her blood is unique and made for me. I waited all my life for this one female who can walk beside me, rule at my side, and not stand in my shadow. I will not insult her by lying with another. She is mine, and I am hers. And until you find that, I don't expect you to understand. She wears the title of Queen of Medici for a reason, and she owns my heart and soul."

Shade turned and began to walk back to the house with Max beside him. "Max, I knew this would not be easy between us, but it seems as though we are not going to come to any reasonable conclusion that satisfies both of us. Will you agree to meet with Council over this matter and abide by their decision?"

Max walked in silence next to him, as he pondered his suggestion. "I think Council is the next step, my friend. I'd hoped to buy you out. You can live anywhere. But clearly, the solution won't be simple. Council it is."

Shade stopped in his tracks and they shook hands on the deal. "I will contact them and inform them we need a meeting. I'll have them contact you when they decide the night and time. It is the least I can do. Any argument with that?"

Max shook his head. "No argument. Now let's get back inside to the warmth of the fireplace and our mates, shall we?"

112

Max and Lein left Bel Rosso on good terms, but Shade knew this was just the beginning of the fight for what was his. Max would never give up, especially now that he knew of the warrior camp. Max was cordial, but Shade was no fool when it came to masters and their territory. He could think of no reason why the Council would deny his claim, but that didn't mean Max would accept their ruling. He knew it could get ugly.

He stood at the window looking out, playing back in his head the words they'd exchanged tonight. He was already thinking ahead as to where this could lead. He was quiet and lost in somber thought when he felt her arms slide around him from behind and her head lying softly against his back. She was always there for him.

"Are you all right, *mi amore*?"

"I'm fine. Is everything okay? You seem very quiet."

He pulled her in front of him, her back against his chest as they faced looking out over the beauty of Bel Rosso on this cold night. "Look out there, it is so peaceful and beautiful. And it is ours. Max offered me a few choices, I denied them all. No one is moving us from here. I worry this will not end peacefully."

"He wants us gone from here?"

Shade sighed heavily, his eyes never leaving the mountain range in front of him. "He offered to buy me out, for us to move on. I told him no. He is concerned about the camp. He would agree to let me stay if I moved the camp from Virginia into Alec's territory. Alec's territory is not practical for that purpose. It was a simple enough answer, but I knew he would not buy it. I have been through this before. We agreed to a meeting with Council and to let them decide the outcome."

Kate bit at her lip. "If you go to Council and they find in his favor, even though you own this land, we'd have to go?"

Shade squeezed her tight. Feeling her fear he gently turned her around to embrace her. "No, *mi amore*, we will fight. Go to war and win what is ours. Council will advise, and most masters take their word as law, but that will not stop two masters if they decide to disagree. This master and his queen would not be satisfied with that answer, but then, if the tables are turned, you must be prepared for Max not to settle either. He does not wish war, I know that. He may accept their decision if it is in our favor and be done with it. Or, he may reject it as well."

Rubbing her back, he laid his head on top of hers, feeling her breath on his neck as he slowly rocked back and forth.

She felt the strength of him as he held her and tried to console her. She said, "I don't want a war, lover. I hope it won't come to that. But I don't want to lose what we've built here. And if it means we must fight for it, you know I'll support you in that choice. Just make sure you're not the price I pay. Nothing we own is worth anything if I don't have you."

"Trust your warrior and master, *mi amore*. I fight for us, for our *familia*. I fight for Medici and its honor and integrity. You made this our home and it will stand as ours. So, tell me, how did things go with Lein?"

She took his hand, leading him back to the sofa. "She was very cordial. Not the viper I saw in the ladies' room at Rissa's reception. She seemed curious about the fact I'd been mortal."

Cuddling with her on the couch, he smiled. "Well, she would be. I doubt she has ever been exposed to many turned mortals, especially not one who becomes a queen. Tell me everything."

"She was more open than I expected. She shared their marriage had been arranged. She said it was common in her culture, and she grew up knowing her mate would be chosen for her by her father. I asked if she loved Max and she said love had nothing to do with it. She admitted she had a fondness for him, and he was a kind and good mate to her, but the whole point of the mating was to ensure the dynasty. To protect what generations of her family had built. That's why she couldn't understand our mating. She was pretty blunt about saying that as a mortal, I brought nothing to the table. I mean, I know it's true, and I know from my own experience there were many who objected to our mating, but I guess I've just never heard it spoken so bluntly before. She said to mate for love is a weakness. It allows your rival to use love as a weapon. I guess she's right. I mean, wasn't that the reason Cuerpo attacked me? To bring you down?"

He listened to her, knowing what Lein said had been meant to hurt her. "You listen to me. Love is not our weakness, but the most powerful weapon we hold! Lein and Max will never understand that because they never had it. A mortal is seen as weak. With most mortals, it is true, but you are not most mortals. So, do not take what she tells you to heart. I don't give a fuck what anyone thinks, including Council or even my own *familia*. I know in my heart what I believe and know to be true...we love like no other. Is that understood?"

Kate laid her head on his shoulder. "I know I'd let nothing come between us. I'll stand by you through all things. I think we're stronger when we're together. Would Lein stand by Max to the death if she didn't love him? If the answer is yes, then I truly don't understand her reasoning at all. You've said your parents' marriage was arranged, and yet, I know how deeply your mother loved your father. So, I know it's possible to have a great love in an arranged marriage. Still, I think it's a rare thing. I look at Rissa and Alec, and I wouldn't want their life, and yet I know Rissa loves him in as much as Rissa can love anyone. Now Max and Lein, they seem like business partners, not lovers." Kate shook her head. "Elana and Colin, I don't understand them either. The more masters I meet, the more I realize how rare our relationship is, and why they look at us so oddly. I hope you never grow tired of me. I know I think our life is filled with drama, but when I see the others I realize you've left a lot of that behind for what, to you, is a very quiet and simple life. I hope you won't grow tired of our life together."

"*Mi amore*..." He left the sentence unfinished as he gathered his thoughts. "Look at me. I am a shell of a man without you. I have conquered all I need. Lein brought much to the table for Max, and you think you brought nothing. But you seem to forget I need no riches, I need no warriors, I need no land. I have all that. What you brought to the table was a love that healed my heart, which makes me stronger. Lein's warriors are loyal to her *padre*, not her. They lay down their life because they are loyal to Fan Shen. But my warriors, they lay down their life because they love *you*. They are loyal, but their love for you is like nothing I have ever seen. I know warriors, and I choose them for more than their skill. I see beyond their exterior to their hearts and that's how I choose them. I have something I never had my whole life–love. It keeps me alive. It gives me light when there was only darkness for so long. You seem to think I had it all, that I had to give it up for you. The only thing I gave up was the aching loneliness that ate me alive. I should be the one asking you, if you would ever get bored with me, and leave me for another who could give you more."

Kate stroked his face and ran her hand through his thick hair, releasing the leather tie that held his dark locks in a loose ponytail at the nape of his neck.

"I don't seek riches or power. There's only one thing I want, and it's your love. I could never get tired of us, and the life we built together. So, push any thoughts of that from your mind. I'm yours, Shade Medici, for now and all time." She kissed his forehead.

"Don't ever leave me, *mi amore*, don't take this light from inside me. Do you think I would give up this? You are my world." Curling up with her, he covered her face in soft kisses. "I will fight for us. I will fight for Bel Rosso. Are you with me?"

"Am I with you?" Kate untied his tie and slowly slid it free from his collar. "Lover...I'm always with you."

113

Kate fell asleep in front of the fire, his arms tucked around her. He could feel his death slumber approaching. They'd spent the night together in front of the fire making love, being in love, and returning to something that was becoming harder for them to find; time alone to just enjoy being together.

He gathered her gently in his arms, careful not to wake her and carried her to their bedroom. He laid her gently on the bed and pulled the blankets around her. He wanted her to sleep. Their life had become hectic with the baby, and he worried about her no matter how much she rested.

Tucking her under the blankets he knew this woman would always be with him. He felt something stir inside him and heard Lorenzo. He teleported into the nursery, getting to Lorenzo before he could wake Kate. Lorenzo was crying softly, his little face scrunched up and his feet flailing about.

"Shh, little warrior, *Padre* is here."

Shade picked him up and settled him on his shoulder. Immediately, Lorenzo was rooting into his neck, looking for that life-giving vein. "Ahh, that's my *figlio*, wake the household for some nourishment."

He settled his large frame into the rocking chair and let Lorenzo feed. Shade remembered Dr. Bonutti's words that his son would seek him out, and he'd know when it was time. Lorenzo wouldn't feed from him often, but he'd need the bond of his father's blood from time to time. Nita and Theresa would keep him nourished, but he and Kate kept him Medici, and there was no blood more vital to him than Shade's own powerful and ancient blood.

Theresa rushed in through the door, her face flushed. "Master, I'm so sorry, I was helping Emma with some laundry and I felt him wake. Please, let me get Nita and you may return to my lady!"

Shade chuckled softly as Lorenzo suckled from him. "Theresa, it is fine. I like feeding him. It is not something I get to do often. I was awake and I did not mind. I need some time with my son all to myself. Go on. I will tuck him in."

Theresa hesitated for a moment, then nodded and left the nursery, closing the door behind her. Lorenzo unlatched and cooed, his fist unclenching from Shade's long curls. Shade pulled him from his shoulder and cradled him in his arms, staring down at this small life he and *bel* had created. Huge blue eyes stared up at him, his long black lashes dark as coal.

"Well, little warrior, here we sit, the Medici men, all fed, well-loved and waiting for the daylight to take us. But I have a feeling you will walk in the daylight, unlike your old *padre*. Never take that for granted, son, it is a gift that is useful to all vampires, especially warriors."

He watched as Lorenzo smiled up at him, as if completely understanding every word he'd said. Shade began to rock gently back and forth, admiring the bundle in his arms. He was perfect.

Lorenzo wrapped his fingers around Shade's thumb and his grip was strong. "You will have a good grip on your sword. Always remember to carry a weapon. I will show you how to use them all with precision. You will have so much to defend. Just like me. We will be warriors together. I will fight at your side."

Lorenzo cooed, and it was a sound so soft that Shade's heart flipped in his chest. He kept rocking and felt a small shiver run through Lorenzo. "You are cold? *Padre* will fix it, make it better."

Shade pulled the soft blue blanket that hung over the arm of the rocker, shook it open, and swaddled Lorenzo inside it, tucking him back into the crook of his arm.

As he rocked, he heard the sound of the electronic blinds and felt the death slumber closing in. Lorenzo's eyes fluttered, closing slowly, as he was lulled by the gentle motion of the rocker. "We both need our slumber, *si*?"

Standing up, he carried the baby to the crib and Lorenzo's eyes flew open as he gripped at Shade's hair with both hands. Shade looked at him and understood his son wasn't ready for his father to leave him just yet. "Don't worry, Lorenzo, I will always protect you."

Shade looked at the sofa-bed used by Theresa and decided he'd stay just a bit longer until Lorenzo fell into his slumber. Lying down on the bed, he turned on his side and curled his son into his chest. Adjusting the blanket around him, Shade watched his son's eyes close and his heartbeat settle, soothed by Shade's presence.

He pushed a stray curl from the baby's forehead, his arm protectively around his son as Shade waited for him to sleep, his own slumber now hitting him hard.

He heard the softest sigh escape his son. Closing his eyes, Shade let the death slumber take him.

***

Kate woke to the darkened room and was momentarily confused. She remembered falling asleep in front of the fire with Shade, but she was in their bed now, and without the warmth of his body next to her. She slid her hand across the sheets into the empty space beside her. Sitting up, she flipped on the lamp and looks about the room. "Shade?"

She was nude beneath the sheets and felt the chill in the room. Grabbing a robe as she slid out of the bed, she wrapped it around her. She looked at the clock. Shade would be in his death slumber now, and yet, he wasn't beside her. "Lover?"

Her heart beat a little faster. She knew he could only push back the pull of the death slumber for so long. She pushed down the panic and closed her eyes, letting herself seek him out. Their bond would draw her to him if she'd only let go. She stood quietly by the bed, feeling the pull and followed it, stepping outside their bedroom door and down the hall to Lorenzo's room, the windows protected from the sun, and lit by a tiny night light.

She saw his big, strong body curled around the tiny frame of his son. Kate smiled at him as she climbed onto the sofa-bed, curling up against his back, and pulling the blankets over both of them.

Shade felt her close and woke enough to feel his son in his arms and his mate at his back. He smiled as three of them in this bed left little room for movement, but he didn't mind. These were the rare moments he knew he'd cherish for all eternity.

Lorenzo stretched, cooing. Shade pulled him closer to his chest, but Lorenzo had no intentions of being held down as he kicked and squirmed. "What is it, little warrior? Feel your *madre*, do you? She is hard to resist, *si*?"

Kate kissed the hard muscles in his back as her arm slipped around him. No one would take this away from her, no one. "I love you more than Jimmy Choo shoes, Shade Medici. Now sleep."

Shade chuckled. "I feel honored, *mi amore*."

Feeling himself pulled into the death slumber once again, Lorenzo heard his mother's voice and settled down, his fist playfully pulling on his father's hair as he continued to coo. Shade paid no mind. They were happy, safe, and together. What more could he ask for?

114

Max teleported to Florence, landing outside the Council stronghold. The guards recognized him and confirmed his appointment, opening the massive gates onto the compound. Max looked about, shivering in the cold. He'd been living in Thailand for the past year in tropical heat and wasn't used to the cold winter weather. He hurried up the stone staircase where guards swung open the doors for him. He walked down the long corridor to the Council chamber. It had been a century or more since he was here, but he remembered the drill. He wouldn't be allowed to enter the chamber until summoned. He paced restlessly, eager to get this over with. He fumbled in his pocket and withdrew a pack of cigarettes, only to have one of the guards tell him there was no smoking allowed. Max mumbled under his breath as he replaced the pack in his pocket. He heard the echo of footsteps and looked up to see the Medici approaching. Max extended his hand. "Brother."

Shade greeted Max with a handshake. "Maximus, good to see you again. It has been a while since you have been here, *si*?" He had tucked the deed to Bel Rosso inside his jacket pocket. He knew he'd need proof that he and Alec had a legal transfer of the property. Alec was still on his honeymoon, so he wasn't sure Council could contact him for verification. If nothing else, Council did their homework long before the issues came before them.

Max nodded. "A century, perhaps. Since when did they ban smoking in here?"

"Quite some time ago. I have no idea why. Not like we are mortal or anything."

They were called forward and both Max and Shade entered the chamber and were presented to Council.

"The Prince of Shen Dynasty, Master Maximus, and King and High Master Medici."

As they walked to their appointed seats in front of Council, they remained standing until commanded to sit.

Malachi stood in his hooded green robe as the two masters took their seats before the Council. "Brothers, I wish I could say this meeting comes as a shock to me, but unfortunately, we all predicted this outcome. Before we get down to business, first things first, Master Maximus, on behalf of the Council, accept our sincere congratulations on your recent mating to Princess Lein Shen. It was an honor to witness your coronation. Your union with Princess Lein is the first recorded union in our records of a coven from Europe being merged with a coven from the East. I can't remember the last time we met with our brethren in the Eastern Council. This union could be a very positive one in bonding the two sides together. The Council wishes you much happiness, and may you produce a male heir to the dynasty."

Max nodded his head. "Thank you, Malachi. I will share your sentiments with my mate."

Malachi looked from one master to the other. "As we understand it, we are here today to settle a land dispute. Is that the case?"

Both Shade and Max nodded silently.

"Then without further ado, I will turn the proceedings over to Jasperion."

Malachi sat as Jasperion stood in his orange robe. "Brothers, I have researched the land in question, as a plot of land, 3,000 acres in scope, located in White Hall, Virginia, in the United States. My records indicate this land lies inside the territory of Master Maximus, and the land was deeded over to Master Alec in 1980 following a poker game between both masters, where the land was included as part of the wager. When Master Maximus lost the game, the land was transferred to Master Alec."

Max cleared his throat, remembering the foolish bet, made on a night when he'd had too much Midnight poured down his gullet. "That's correct."

Jasperion nodded, "So we are all in agreement then, as of 1980, the land passed free and clear to Master Alec. As we understand it, the land sat dormant and was not used by Master Alec, letting the house and the surrounding vineyards fall into ruin. Then, a year and a half ago, Master Alec assigned the property over to Master Shade as payment in exchange for the security services provided by Master Shade and the Medici warriors. We have recorded that transaction in our records. Master Shade, do you have a copy of your deed?"

Standing, Shade reached into his pocket and retrieved the deed. "*Si*, this is a copy of the original, and you may keep this. My lawyers have legally attested to this copy and it is signed and notarized."

He laid the copy on the table and an assistant retrieved it, carrying it to Jasperion. Shade took his seat once again and waited for Jasperion to look over the deed and verify its validity.

Jasperion took the deed and read through it, looking puzzled. "Master Shade, this deed has been transferred over to one Katherine Reese. It is no longer in your name."

Shade nodded. "Katherine Reese is now Katherine Medici, my queen. I deeded this property to her before our mating. As the Council can clearly attest, Katherine is my mate and queen now. What is hers is mine and vice versa. We rule Medici together as one."

Jasperion sighed and looked to Florian, in his purple robe. "Florian, can you give us a ruling please, based on our bylaws, given that Miss Reese was a mortal when the deed was transferred?"

Florian flipped open the huge ledger and read silently before standing. "Given that the mortal was subsequently turned and mated to the Medici and is now officially recognized by this Council as his rightful queen, all property owned by either party prior to their union becomes jointly owned property after their union. Therefore, the property deeded to Katherine Reese, the mortal, is now jointly owned property of both King and Queen Medici. The property is legally and rightfully theirs."

Max lifted his hand. "May I speak?"

Malachi nodded and Max stood. "I'm not here to contest ownership. I concede the land was deeded to Master Alec, and I was aware when Master Alec deeded the land to Master Shade. However, at the time, Shade seemed to take little interest in the property. I knew he stayed in the house on occasion and I figured he'd re-establish the vineyards. His presence there offered no threat to my coven. But it has come to my attention that Master Shade has established a warrior camp on the property. We're all aware of the Medici's history with training warriors, and the size and scope of the camp in Florence. The camp in Virginia is modest by comparison but its presence is a threat to my coven, nonetheless. I have most generously offered Master Shade to name his price. I'll pay him any price, double, triple the value of the property. Money is no object. He can relocate anywhere in the States, and he has refused the offer. His very refusal represents an act of hostility against my coven. I ask for the intervention of Council to ward off a land battle."

Malachi looked to Shade. "Master Shade, you own the property free and clear. But is it true you have denied his offer to buy you out?"

Shade was careful not to display any hostility toward Council or Max, but he wanted to make his position clear. Standing as Max returned to his seat, he responded to Malachi.

"Master Maximus did offer to buy me out. And yes, I make a part of my living as a warrior, training other warriors. Until recently, I worked exclusively in Europe. But I was hired to provide protection for Master Alec and his territory of Washington, D.C. In the course of providing that protection, my own house and property have come under attack, threatening the life of my mate. It takes many warriors to provide this service and I must have a space that provides privacy from the curious mortals. Alex's territory in D.C. would not accommodate a warrior camp, and his other territories in New England and California are too far from my work. The Virginia property is the perfect location for them, close yet far from the mortal eye. The farmland and vineyards provide the perfect cover and gives us adequate space to conduct our warrior training, without being discovered, which, as I am sure you will agree, is an issue for all of us. I have explained this to Master Maximus in detail. I am of no threat to Max. His warriors and mine both inhabit Virginia and have encountered each other from time to time. There have been no conflicts, nor do we interfere with each other. Master Maximus has never approached Master Alec or me in all this time. The only thing that brought him to plead for this territory is the establishment of a small camp where I train warriors."

Malachi nodded. "Thank you, Medici. You may be seated. Please give us a second while we confer."

Malachi, Jasperion, and Florian huddled together, talking in a low whisper for several minutes before retaking their seats. Malachi looked out at the two masters.

"The Council has reached a conclusion. Based on our bylaws, we can see no reason to request Master Medici to vacate the property. The land belongs to him free and clear. It is also his option to accept or reject the offer to sell the property back to Master Maximus. With that said, we find the property remains in the hands of the Medici, and the Council sincerely hopes the two of you will find a peaceful settlement. The Council would like to add we have issued warnings in the past about masters owning land that resides within another's territory for this very reason. It inevitably leads to a dispute. If there is no further business before us, we adjourn this session."

The Council members stood in unison and filed out of the room. Max stood, working hard to control his anger, as much at himself as at the Council and the Medici.

Shade nodded as the Council's decision was made, but he knew this was far from over. If Max decided he wanted him gone, he'd go to battle. He could feel Max's anger as he stood, not pleased with the results. As they were dismissed, Shade took the lead and walked out of the chamber with Max on his heels. He walked outside and away from the building, lighting up a cigarette. He watched as Max did the same.

"Listen Max, you have nothing to fear from my presence. I do not threaten your coven, nor do I want it. I have enough to control and rule. I want to stay where I am, that is all. Master to master, I am telling you, I am no threat to you, and never intend to be."

Max drew deep on the much needed cigarette as he paced. Shade didn't understand. Max must live up to the expectations of his new father-in-law and prove his rightful accession to rule as king of the largest coven on earth. How could he rule the East if he couldn't even rule Virginia? How could he prove his ability to protect all that Fan Shen had built, if he allowed another master to encroach on his own turf? He had known the

Medici for a very long time, and he wasn't fooled. He'd watched him expand from Italy, and into Greece and France. And now he had a foothold in the States. He was clever in his land grabs, and Max had to stop this before it got out of control. Unfortunately, he was out of ideas right now. Tossing the cigarette butt to the ground, he stomped it out before glaring at Shade as he teleported out.

"This is not over, my friend."

Shade knew in Max's eyes he was a threat. He watched Max teleport out, his words not gone unheeded. Max wouldn't take this lying down and now, Shade must wait for his next move. And unfortunately, he had no idea what that would be. He knew one thing for sure; this situation was going to get ugly.

Teleporting out, he kept his own thoughts under control as he landed outside of Bel Rosso. He took a deep breath. There was no place for anger. This was what he was born to do and had done for centuries, protect and fight for what he wanted. But this time he had a mate and son to protect, so the stakes were much higher and he was more than prepared to win.

115

Shade walked into the house, greeted by Cory who was on the way out. He'd stopped back at the house for something to eat and was running back out, munching on a slice of pizza. He threw his hand up in greeting as he headed out the door.

Walking to his study, Shade paced, processing his thoughts. He needed to have a meeting with his ranking warriors, including Marco. They would be advised of the outcome of the Council's decision, and Max's response to it. His properties and his coven needed to increase security until they knew what the hell Max would do.

Flopping down in the desk chair, he picked up his cell and was about to call Marco when he stopped. There was one person in his life that needed to know about this situation long before his warriors. He didn't want to scare her, but she needed to know what was at stake, and the potential for battle.

Kate was upstairs with Lorenzo when she felt the energy shift in the house and knew Shade had teleported back home from Florence. She could feel the level of agitation he fought to control and sighed. *Did Council rule against us?* "Theresa, take Lorenzo please."

Theresa took the baby. "Of course, my lady." Theresa had also felt her master's return. "Take all the time you need."

Kate left the nursery and headed down the stairs to his office. She found Shade at the desk. "Shade? Tell me what happened."

"The Council ruled in our favor. We are here to stay, but Max feels we are a threat to his coven by being here. He was pissed and his last words to me were, 'This is not over.' We must be alert now. I have no idea when or where he will strike. This is going to get ugly. Masters do not play mind games. We need to be prepared."

Kate climbed into his lap, brushing his hair back from his furrowed brow. "What does this mean? Are you telling me he'll battle for the property?"

"*Si*. Max now has access to his father-in-law's warriors in the East, and he has something to prove to Fan Shen. He could strike any of my properties, including my coven in Florence. Or he may only focus here. He could set fire to the vineyards, or any number of heinous acts before actually waging a battle. So, we must prepare and be on guard. His approach could be designed to tire us out and wear us down. I will meet with my warriors here, as well as Florence, Greece, and France. They will all be on alert."

Kate felt her maternal instincts kicking in. "The baby! Lorenzo! He wouldn't harm Lorenzo! We must tell Luca right away!"

"Lorenzo is safe in this house. Luca will protect both of you. But there are going to be some rules for you. I do not want you wandering around outside much, stay close to the house. If you need to go anywhere, Luca or I must be at your side. Lorenzo will not leave the house for any reason unless he is in my arms. I do not want to frighten you, but until we know what is happening we must take this seriously. I know you fear for him. That is normal, but you need to trust me, trust Luca, and those that serve me. I also need you to keep your own warriors alert and watchful. They have been helpful in guarding the property and they can warn us of what is coming even faster than my warriors at times. I will need their help as well."

Kate knew Luca and Theresa would both lay down their lives for Lorenzo, and she wouldn't stray far from him either until this was resolved. "I'll follow your command. I never leave without Luca anyway."

Luca was in his suite next to Shade's office when he felt Kate's wave of panic. He tossed down the paint brush onto the tarp on the floor beneath the easel and left the suite. He heard her voice inside Shade's office and walked to the door. He saw Kate secure in his arms, but her heart still beat rapidly.

"Master? Is everything okay?"

"No Luca, it is not. Come in. Max wants Bel Rosso. As you know, he visited with the intent of buying me out or getting me to move on. It has not been resolved peacefully between us. I have just returned from Council. They voted in our favor, but Max is not satisfied. You know what this means. We have to prepare for the worst. We are about to go into battle preparedness mode. I am going to rely on you heavily. This is no game; we now put to use all we have been taught. Maximus will not give up easily. And while I expect the warriors to defend Bel Rosso, my number one goal is to protect Kate and Lorenzo."

Luca nodded to him. "You know I'll go to my death to protect all that is Medici. I have one request. I feed solely from Shannon now. I hate to bring her into this, but it will be easier for me, and safer for all of us, if I don't have to leave to feed. I know I could use the feeder compound if you demand it of me, but I'm asking for this favor."

Shade nodded in agreement. "The easiest thing is to have Shannon come here and stay until this is over. I have no idea what the hell Max will pull out of his hat, so we need to have all bases covered, and that includes Shannon. You will need to make her understand she cannot leave until this is over. We will protect her, she is *familia* now. I know she has a job in the mortal world, so let her know if this drags on, I will compensate her for lost wages. Can you make her understand this?"

Luca nodded. "Of course, master. I need to know she can commit to this life. This will be a good test for her. A chance to know, when this is over if she wishes to stay or go, it will be her choice. But she loves Kate, and the baby. She wouldn't do anything that would put them at risk. She'll stay until the situation with Max is settled."

Shade nodded in agreement. "You will need to feed heavily to stay strong. That is a direct command! Make sure she knows if she does not want to be here, you feed elsewhere. I have no choice in the matter, Luca."

"Understood, master. May I go to her now? I'll bring her back to Bel Rosso with me."

Shade looked at him with a grin. "So, she is the one, is she? Get the hell out of here and bring back your female. Move!" He watched as Luca smiled and took off.

Shade's sigh was heavy and his head was spinning. "I never wanted this to happen, *mi amore*. I never wanted you to see us go to battle, but to be honest, it is a test of who we are together."

Kate looked at him. "A test of us? Lover, we've already passed all of the tests. There's no test of us. There's nothing that could come between us."

"I am proud you are my queen." He hugged her tightly, kissing her. "Now get that fine ass of yours upstairs to our son. Inform Theresa, Nita and Emma of our situation. Keep them as calm as you can. Theresa can help in that department. I will inform Gi. The old codger has seen a few battles in his time. I have a lot to do before I ever see my death slumber, and you may want to cue Theresa in that her male is coming in. That should make her happy. Where the fuck are we going to put him?"

Kate slipped from his lap to head up the stairs. "Oh, I think Theresa will make room for him in her bed. We can move Nita into the nursery until this is over, and Theresa can stay in her own bedroom with Marco when she's not with Lorenzo. Besides, that places you, Marco, and Luca in the house. I rather like those odds."

Shade chuckled at her. "Marco won't be staying, *mi amore*, just a night or two. I need him back in Florence. But we have a lot to plan. And don't be too excited about his visit. He makes a lot of noise; he is not house trained!"

Kate laughed as she headed up the stairs. "And you were?"

"I heard that, woman!" Shade chuckled and picked up his phone. It was time to get some warriors in line and a plan laid down.

116

Luca waited for Shannon in her condo. He'd sent her a text and told her he'd be waiting for her when she got home from work. He could hear her as she stepped off the elevator and hurried to the door. She flung herself at him, covering him in kisses.

"I don't know the reason for the unexpected visit, but I'm glad you're here."

He returned her kiss but not her smile.

"What's wrong, Luca?"

Luca held her in his embrace. "I'm here to ask a favor, *mia belleza*...more than a favor, actually. There's a conflict brewing, a potential battle between masters, between Shade and Master Maximus. Shade is preparing now. I need you at Bel Rosso."

Shannon nodded as the concern showed on her face. "Of course, I'll come to Bel Rosso."

Luca lifted her chin. "Let me restate that. You'll need to stay there until the battle is over, if there is a battle. I can't protect you here, and I can't leave to feed."

Shannon stepped back. "For how long? I have a job—"

Luca shook his head. "I don't know how long, Shan. It could be days, weeks, or months. Nothing may come of this. It's a territory dispute, and Maximus may accept the Council's ruling, but we doubt it. I can't protect your job. If you have time off, then take it, and hopefully this will be resolved quickly. If not, Shade will make sure all your expenses are met. Your bills will be paid so your home is secure."

"Wow, Luca...you ask a lot."

He nodded. "I know it's a lot to ask. I wouldn't ask if I thought there was another way."

Shannon looked around her condo. "So, when would I need to go?"

"Now, *mia belleza*. Tonight."

"Well, Luca, I have to say dating you is never boring." She turned and headed to her bedroom, pulling a suitcase from the closet.

"I'm sorry, Shan. But this is my life. You wish to be a part of it. You need to understand what that entails before we make anything irreversible."

Shannon pulled clothes from the closet and the dresser, folding them into the suitcase before heading to the bathroom to pack her toiletries.

"Oh, I'm in, Luca. Let me make a few phone calls. I'll take vacation, and if this drags on, maybe I can make up some kind of medical leave of absence or something. Wait, where will I be sleeping?"

Luca gave her a sly smile. "With me, *mia belleza*, always with me."

Shannon flashed her megawatt smile. "See, Luca, there's always a bright side."

117

The minute the blinds rolled up, letting in the soft glow of early dusk, Shade was up and moving. He'd been awake for some time, just lying there, restless, his head filled with the plans he'd need to put into action.

He dressed quickly and found Marco waiting for him with several of his Lieutenants and SIC's from his other territories. It was the first time Marco had been to Bel Rosso and unfortunately, this wasn't a social visit. Shade gave him the grand tour of the warrior camp and the property after which, they teleported across Virginia so he could show Marco Max's territory to give him an idea of the scope of what they were dealing with. He took Marco around D.C. as even though Shade didn't feel Alec's territory would be impacted, he wanted Marco to see his operation there and the setup at the Dead House, just in case.

As they returned to the camp he called forth his leaders and had them return with him to the house. They'd be meeting in his study and away from the listening ears of the other warriors. They'd settle what needed to be done and later, he'd return to camp to convey their final plan. Marco would relay the same plans, once back in Florence, to his other territories and warriors in Europe. He wanted the input of his key leaders, and their years of valuable experience in developing a plan to protect them all.

As they sat discussing details he watched with pride as Fiamma, Marcello, Raven, and Luca all joined in the discussion, sharing their ideas. Marco was encouraging and said he doubted they'd see any trouble in Europe but they'd be prepared for anything and if necessary, he could always send backup to Bel Rosso. They spent the best part of the night getting things in order.

As the meeting wrapped up, his group from Florence teleported back out, ready to implement their part of the plan immediately. Marco decided he'd stay behind for another night. Shade knew he and Theresa needed some time together and he knew Marco wouldn't be back until this issue was settled, and he had no idea how long that would be.

Shade could feel Shannon was in the house, so he knew Luca had brought her back and he was pretty sure she was already holed up with Kate upstairs. He'd requested that Kate not interrupt him unless there was an emergency. He needed to focus and make sure they overlooked nothing.

With the plans in place, he asked Marcello to start gathering the warriors in the camp. They still had some time before sunrise and he'd meet with most of his warriors, keeping a scab crew at the Dead House, leaving Theo in charge there so he could communicate to them what lay ahead. Raven could then fill in the warriors on duty at the Dead House when they returned to camp.

Grabbing a bottle of Midnight, Shade drank from it without the use of a glass. He propped his feet on the desk and Marco did the same. They exchanged a glance, both of them rehashing in their minds all that had happened this night. The Medici coven was at stake. Shade knew Max could strike anywhere, or everywhere, and none of them would know the time or place. Max was counting on that.

"It's been a long time, old friend, since we needed to be battle ready. This time, the battle is very different for me. I have never had so much at stake before. I need to make sure we win."

Marco grunted, taking another swig of Midnight. "You keep swilling that juice you won't be any damn good to anyone, including your mate. I've seen you so damn drunk on blood and Midnight you didn't know your own fucking name. So now you need to be responsible and warrior up. I do not envy your position as master with the responsibility for the coven, old man."

Shade laid his head back on his high-backed leather office chair, closing his eyes. "Marco, being a king is like being a *padre.* My coven are like my children. I feel responsible for them. Hell, we watched most of them grow from punks to men. We made them who they are. I cannot help but be proud of them, and I cannot do this without you. You know that, brother. If you were not with me, I would never be able to stay here, make my life here. I do not trust anyone else with Florence. But I know you have some damn good Lieutenants coming into the ranks. I like what I see so far. You have done a damn good job. I know sometimes I forget to tell you that."

Marco dropped his feet to the floor and sat forward in his chair, shaking his head. "I already know your ass would be dirt without me. But I got your back, brother. You go down, I go with you. Nothing has changed. We're tight, like brothers. Anything happens, she'll be taken care of. So will Lorenzo. You get your ass killed, you need to know that. You cannot let her, or the baby, become a distraction, Shade. You need to keep your head in the game. We could sit here all night pumping up each other's ego, but we have outgrown all those things. We are the ancient ones now, for Hell's sake. They will need to look to you for guidance. I don't doubt you and I know you won't be standing on the sidelines, shouting orders, but will be in the fucking thick of it. Just keep your head in the game, brother."

Shade stared at him and knew he spoke the truth. "I never ask my warriors to do what I will not do myself. I must be the first to enter the battle, to lead with pride and honor, if I expect them to follow. It is how it will be done. But heaven help me, I love her. I love Lorenzo. Her love encourages me, gives me strength, and makes me want to battle for them. I will die for them both and for this place we call home. There is nothing for me without them."

Shade sat up and set the bottle, now almost empty, onto his desk. "I guess we need to get our asses over there, it will be daylight soon. But I sure as hell do not feel like I need sleep."

Marco grinned. "It will come eventually, you know it will."

Standing up, stretching, Shade decided he needed one thing before he went before his warriors. "Have you seen Theresa yet?"

Marco laughed as he stood as well. "For about five fucking minutes!"

Shade slapped him on the back. "Grumpy in your old age! I have a mind to see my woman and my son before we head over. I will ask Theresa to come along as well."

Shade telepathically asked Kate to bring Lorenzo and Theresa to his study. He wanted to see her before he left for the meeting at camp.

Kate heard his message and excused herself from the conversation she was having with Shannon. Finding Theresa in the nursery with a sleeping Lorenzo, she shared Shade's request. Theresa headed down as Kate scooped Lorenzo up in her arms. Lorenzo made a face, showing his displeasure at having his sleep disrupted.

Kate laughed. "Where have I seen that expression before? Oh, my sweet boy, you are more like your father every day."

118

Max teleported into the Virginia mansion, smashing a large vase to the floor. Lein scurried into the room. She could feel his anger rolling off him and knew the meeting with Council hadn't gone well. She wished the matter could've been settled by the Eastern Council, where her father had more pull but the land, and the masters involved, fell under the domain of the European Council. His butler appeared with a glass of Midnight and Max angrily knocked the crystal glass from the tray, its contents spilling across the floor as the delicate glass shattered.

Max paced and muttered, "Even the drink that soothes me fills his coffers."

Lein cautiously approached him. "How can I be of help to you, master? Surely, there's a way."

The house staff responded immediately, cleaning up the broken glass and wiping away the wine. Lein asked the butler to bring him the sake blend with blood that was more popular in the East. When he returned, she took the glass and handed it to Max.

"Drink this please. It will calm you."

Max downed the hot wine and put the glass down on the table. He dropped into a chair and Lein knelt on the floor at his feet, slipping the shoes from his feet.

"Talk to me, master. I can't help you if I don't know the details."

Max grumbled, "What's to tell? The Council ruled in his favor. The land is his, free and clear. They wouldn't even restrict him from opening the warrior camp. I have no leverage over him."

Lein massaged his feet and ankles. "Master, there is always leverage. We have only to find it. You have looked at the obvious. Now it's time to look for the less obvious."

Max laid his head back on the chair. "Lein, I'm in no mood for your cryptic Eastern philosophy. If you have an idea, let's hear it."

Lein smiled at him. "You have approached the problem like a man. Now it's time to approach it like a woman. This Master Shade, he has made a fatal mistake. It is the reason my father forbade me to marry for love. He said marriage was a business deal, quite possibly the most important business deal of all. A master cannot afford the luxury of love. It makes him weak, vulnerable."

Max grunted. "If you're thinking about attacking Kate, think again. I tried that tactic once only to have it blow up in my face. Granted, it was

Cuerpo's ego that got the best of him. He never expected a mortal to fight back. And she's immortal now. He has a whole fucking army at Bel Rosso. I'd never even get close to her."

Lein smiled. "Master, you are still thinking like a man. I didn't say anything about attacking his mate. This love Master Shade has for her, and her for him. That is the weakness. It makes people do foolish things, makes them crazy with jealousy. Find a way to drive a wedge between them. Make one doubt the other. He fights for her, and without her, he crumbles."

Max let her words simmer in his brain. He knew only too well that love was a weakness. He remembered his pain after Rissa's betrayal and his own pledge to never give his heart again. He'd made stupid mistakes. He knew there was wisdom in Lein's words. Now he just had to come up with a plan.

119

Shade and Marco walked into the warrior camp. A great hush settled over the crowd and the tension was running high. Everyone knew the outcome of the Council meeting, and Marco's presence here emphasized the seriousness of the situation. With all of them assembled, the room was ripe with anticipation. He and Marco took their seats, and he looked up to see he had the warrior's full attention. Shade looked across the room at the warriors, some of them battle tested, others still green, before speaking.

"I ask that you hold any questions until we are done. Also, I want all my Lieutenants and SIC's up front...now."

Raven, Marcello, and Fiamma elbowed their way to the front and took their seats.

"We are officially on Yellow Battle Alert. For my new warriors, you'll find there is a yellow packet with your name on it. There is also a second packet labeled "Red Battle Alert", should it come to that. Inside, you will find the protocol that must be followed. It details the overall plan for defending Bel Rosso as well as my other territories and includes your individual assignment. Memorize that fucking packet! Don't ask another warrior, fucking learn it!"

Shade stood and paced in front of the warriors, never breaking eye contact with them.

"As most of you have heard, Maximus wanted me out of Bel Rosso. We went to Council, and Council found in my favor, but Max is not satisfied. He has issued a veiled threat, letting me know it is not over. I have no idea what his next move will be, but trust me when I tell you, he will do something. He has recently mated and now rules over Fan Shen's Eastern warriors. They can rival us in skill, knowledge, and training. Fighting against Fan Shen's army would be like facing an army of Medici. The yellow packet includes everything we know about Maximus, including his photo, and everything there is to know about his territories as well as the Shen Dynasty. Read and learn!"

Shade glanced at Marco who sat on the stool, his arms crossed over his chest and he nodded back at Shade.

"I have no idea where he will strike, what he will strike. For that reason, all of Medici is on yellow alert right now. I have met with my other SIC's and leaders from Europe. They are, as we speak, putting this same plan in place on all Medici owned territory. We expect Bel Rosso to be the target, but we must plan for the unexpected. We are covering all bases. You are expected to have a weapon on you at all times, which includes when you sleep. For my new warriors, this is where it gets real."

He scanned every face, looking for doubt or hesitation. He was proud when they all returned his stare with determination.

"I like our odds. We will continue our routine and perform as normal but be on guard for anything unusual. Keep your senses honed and alert. We roll as if there is no threat. As far as this camp goes, it is business as usual. The same goes for the Dead House. We are still obligated to protect Master Canton's territory. This situation has nothing to do with him."

He scanned the warriors as they sat in their seats, their attention not waning. This was what he needed.

"Florence and the other territories in Europe are well manned and ready to roll. If they are not attacked, Marco will keep the warriors in Europe on standby to respond to us. Marco will release those warriors as needed to teleport here. We are having a mass of weapons brought here and the weapon's bunker inside the camp and inside the main house will be battle ready. We will not run out of supplies. If you need armor, leathers, you need to see Cory. Cory will stop whatever he is working on to focus solely on getting us prepared. My household, your queen, your prince, and my son Cory will be protected above all. You will fight to your death to save them, leave me lay dead in my tracks if you can save them first. That is an order!"

He stopped his pacing and watched their faces, some of them a bit surprised. "You heard me right. My queen and my sons are my life. They can't fight or protect themselves as you can, so do your job. Luca will be in charge of the house. He is their primary protector and you will not see him on the battlefield. So, don't even think about contacting him. If you have a problem, you see anything suspicious, have concerns, you see Marcello. Marcello remains in charge as the SIC here at the camp. Raven is being sent to California to head up that territory. He will remain there in the event the California property is attacked, and he will lead my warriors there. In the event we go red, he will return to Bel Rosso. Theo and Skelk will rotate at the Dead House as SIC's while Raven is in California."

He looked at Raven who shook his head in acknowledgement, without a smile or a smartass remark, and that's when Shade knows they felt the seriousness of this threat.

"Fiamma will assist here with Marcello. If we go into battle, Aislynn will be in charge of the feeder compound because I will need Fiamma on the battlefield. Master Maximus knows the compound is here. But no one knows of the tunnels. Aislynn, your chief objective if we go red is to get everyone out of the feeder compound through the tunnels and into the barracks. Fast! Since the feeders are totally helpless, Aislynn will protect the feeders. If we go to battle, we will need the feeders for emergency feeding, there will be life-threatening injuries, and having immediate access could be the difference between life and death."

He smiled at her and she looked back at him and nodded. There was no fear in her eyes, and he knew he'd chosen well.

"For those of you who had permission to feed outside the compound, that changes now. You will remain inside this camp, and only use the feeders until further notice. You leave camp for assignments only, no roaming. When moving around Bel Rosso, you will only use the tunnels from now on. We will still use the training field, but the tunnels make our movement invisible to our enemy."

Shade looked to Marco. "Did I forget anything?"

Marco chuckled. "For right now, no, but damn, old man, if you have to ask me, you need a battle to refresh your memory!"

Shade slapped him across the back. "Marco is in charge of everything in Europe. And believe me, I would want no other but my brother."

They fist bumped each other. This was a routine they'd both faced together many times.

Shade looked to Raven. "Reynaldo and Mica have been notified, so have the warriors stationed in California. For now, just keep your ears and eyes peeled. If California is not attacked, and we go red, get your ass back here pronto!"

Raven nodded. "No problem, boss-man."

"I don't have to tell you what this means for all of us. We cannot lose anything that belongs to Medici. We fight until death for our coven. This is not just my home now, it is yours as well. This is where my *bambinos* will grow up, and if one fucking master thinks he will take it from me, he gets all of Medici full force. That is how we roll!"

A huge cheer rattled the windows as they all shouted, "*Per sempre* Medici!"

Shade nodded his head. They could do this, and they would. This was his home and his warriors. *Bring it, Max. I am more than ready to move your fucking ass right out of Virginia*. "Okay. We're done here. Move out!"

He watched the group as they all stood and took off, implementing their assignments. Shade looked at Marco and shook his head. "I hope to hell they get how fucking serious this is. Let's get our asses back to the house. I think the women are waiting."

Marco laughed. "No one gets any more serious than the Medici. They will be fine; you trained them the old way, so let them earn their keep now. Son of a bitch, I need to feed and have my female under me!"

Shade laughed as he threw his arm over Marco's shoulders and they headed back to the house. He'd done all he could for now. The next move was up to Max.

120

Shade and Marco returned to the house after the meeting and Marco took off to spend time with Theresa. Shade returned to the study and began going over all the details for battle preparation. He'd run them through his head over and over until he'd practically memorized them, making sure he hadn't missed anything.

He heard Luca return through the patio entrance. The electronic blinds would be closing within a half hour, yet he felt there was still much he needed to attend to. He walked outside, lit up a smoke and watched the sky lighten. This was as close to daylight as he'd ever get. He could feel the rays of the sun about to pop over the horizon, so he walked back inside as the blinds came down.

His mind was still working on what he'd need to do if Max decided to go to battle. He couldn't afford to miss anything. Not this time. He opened the packets for both yellow and red battle status and ran through the protocols again.

***

Kate had settled Lorenzo down for the day, leaving him to the care of Nita. She told Theresa to go join Marco, and to enjoy whatever time they had together before Marco returned to Florence. Luca had arrived with Shannon last night. They'd sat up and talked while the men were in the camp. But eventually, the hours grew too late for Shannon and she'd returned to Luca's suite to sleep.

The sun would be coming up soon, and Kate would spend those hours with Shade in his death slumber. She returned to their bedroom and took a hot shower, hoping Shade would join her but wasn't completely surprised when he didn't. He'd been meeting with the warriors, making plans to respond to Max. When she emerged from the shower, the electronic blinds were closing and still, there was no sign of him. Kate slipped a silk gown over her head as she stood still and focused her attention until she felt his energy in the study. She headed down the stairs to the open door of his study. He was alone, hair disheveled, looking tired and yet, filled with a nervous energy, as he shuffled through the mound of papers on his desk, glancing every few seconds at the images that flashed across the security monitors.

"Lover? It's daylight, and you look tired."

Shade was so preoccupied he hadn't heard her approach. "What? I apologize, *mi amore*, I did not feel you come in. I am a little busy, a lot to do. Go ahead and rest, I won't be long. Need to get some details in order. Go on. Go to bed. I need you to be rested for Lorenzo."

Looking back at the monitors, he spun around in his office chair, whipping open a file drawer. He pulled out a stack of file folders and began foraging through them.

Kate stood still for a moment. The house was quiet in the early dawn hours, Shannon still slept next to Luca and Theresa had crawled into bed with Marco.

"Shade, I know the pull of your death slumber and the toll it takes when you resist it. You need to be rested as well. Now come with me."

Shade ran his hand through his hair and closed his eyes. "*Mi amore*, I will only say this once more. Go to bed, I can handle this. I have done this more times than you know. Preparing for battle takes all of my time and energy. I must be ready. No one is going to take Bel Rosso from me. Just go, leave me in peace to do what is necessary. I will make it to my slumber soon enough, *si*?"

He glanced again at the monitors and saw Night Stalker and Aegis patrolling the perimeter, both relaxed, not picking up anything significant.

Kate looked hard at him. He'd only recently started to feed from her again, and not as frequently as he should. He knew Lorenzo still came to her on occasion, and he denied his own need. She saw the strain in his face, and knew he needed to give into the pull of his death slumber.

"It doesn't rest on your shoulders alone. Your key warriors are here, and they're all prepared. They stand guard even now. Aegis, Night Stalker, and Riparo, they all walk the grounds. Danica and Poe watch the skies. Nothing will get inside the perimeter without being seen well in advance. Please, don't fight me. You're a stronger warrior when you're rested."

Pushing back the chair, he stood and paced the room, his body tired but his mind overly alert. He took a deep breath, clenching his fists at his sides.

"Why is this bothering me? Why? I have done this so many times. Why now do I feel as though I am not prepared? Let them earn their keep, says Marco! How can I do that if I am not there at first strike? I must lead them and show them how it is done! So many are young and new to this, they have battle experience, but nothing like what we may be facing! *Cazzo*, Max! You will fucking rue the day you thought you could take what is mine!"

His anger spiked, his heart rate accelerated, and it only served to feed his nervous energy.

"I have weapons coming in tonight and I need to make sure it is enough, that they are distributed according to where I will need them. I need to make sure Marco's last orders from me are prepared and he knows them. *Cazzo*!"

Kate watched him becoming more agitated. She stepped away from the door and went to Luca's suite, tapping lightly. Luca answered quickly, wearing pajama bottoms only. Kate could see Shannon still curled under the covers, wearing the matching pajama top.

"Luca, I'm sorry to disturb you, but I need your help. The sun is up now and Shade's still awake, still insisting there's much to do. Please take over at the monitors and let me try to get him upstairs."

Luca was nodding, grabbing a shirt and sliding it on as she talked. "Of course, give me a second and I'll be right there."

Kate returned to the study and walked to him, taking the papers from his hand and laying them down on the desk. "Marco has fought many battles with you. He knows the drill. He knows what you expect, and he's a day-walker. Luca will be here in a moment. He'll keep an eye on the monitors. You worry because of me, because of Lorenzo. But you're no good to us if you're exhausted. You need to sleep, Shade. You know you'll wake if there's any danger. Now stop this and come with me."

Luca stepped into the room. "Master? Let me take over now. I've got this."

Shade's eyes were heavy with sleep, as he flashed a look from Kate to Luca. "I am fucking Master here! Since when do others dictate to me?"

He walked to the desk to sit down as he felt a wave of slumber roll across his body. He stopped and leaned on the desk. Taking a deep breath, his head down, he rolled his eyes up to *bel*. She was giving him that 'I told you so' look. "Don't say it! Just don't fucking say it! Medici blood can sustain me for longer than either of you!"

Kate felt a flash of anger at his stubborn refusal. She walked over to the desk and yanked the plug on the security cameras, the images immediately fading from view. "You forget, I'm a Medici too. You can't protect me in this state, nor can you protect Lorenzo. Now stop this before I call Marco down here and have him and Luca both haul your ass to bed."

Luca chuckled as Kate's anger flared. "I'd suggest, master, you follow her lead. She still has that crossbow tucked under the bed."

Shade sighed as he reluctantly gave in to the demands of his body. "Lead the way, woman. And if you have a mind to, feed me as well. Time to tuck your savage lover into bed; his demons are calling him home."

Kate shook her head as she linked arms with him and led him up the stairs, as Luca plugged the monitors back in.

"More like my stubborn lover. I will tuck you in, and you will feed. I need you strong...for me and for Lorenzo."

Kate led him to bed and slid in beside him as his weariness hung heavy in the room. She ran her hand through his hair and pulled his lips to her throat.

"Now feed."

121

Max had taken Lein's advice to heart. He too had noticed the love and devotion the Medici showed his mate. Besides, no one knew better than Max how love clouded the ability for clear thought. He'd let Rissa make a fool of him. He could have been exposed and lost everything in his pursuit of her. At the time, it wouldn't have stopped him. Winning Rissa back was all that had mattered. He paced the floor of the Virginia mansion, looking out across the great expanse of the lawn to the James River. The question remained as to how to exploit the situation. The Medici would not be lured to an underground club or tempted by the smorgasbord of sexual delights to be found there. He had a feeder compound on his property and managed to ignore those delights. Max dropped into a chair as he lit up a cigarette.

He inhaled deeply, dropping his head back on the chair as he exhaled the smoke into the air. He heard the soft shuffle of Lein's stocking feet as she approached and knelt beside him in his chair.

"Master, what troubles you? How can I be of help?"

Max shook his head. "I've thought about what you said, Lein, about creating a divide between Shade and his mate. I'm just not sure how to go about it. He'd decline an invitation to a club that didn't include his mate. And I doubt he'd partake of any of the sexual diversions offered. How do you tempt a man who doesn't want to be tempted?"

Lein laughed softly. "Master, men are simple creatures. My father taught me, long ago, they are ruled more by their desires than their brains. If you cannot lure this master to temptation, then you must trick him. The beast in him will respond. If the temptation is great enough, the beast will take over. The beast is more animal than man. In battle, does not the beast rule? Do you not step back and let him rule? The beast can be lured with passion and desire as well. The solution seems clear to me."

Max took another drag on the cigarette. He recalled Shade's conversation about the feeder compound and how his mate had made it off limits to him, and a plan began to formulate in his brain. He smirked as he looked at the porcelain beauty of Lein's face. "Simple creatures indeed, my angel."

Lein smiled. "You know, my father has a compound inside his palace. It is filled with virginal feeders and concubines. They're for his pleasure, but he also brings other masters there. He has found it to be a powerful tool when negotiating. I'm sure he'd provide you with unlimited access. Why don't you allow me to choose for you, master? I am well trained in the art of what males find irresistible."

Max laughed as she ran her hands along his thigh. "Oh, my angel, I'm well aware of your training. And by all means, please make the choices."

Within days, Lein had made her selection and the two feeders had been safely teleported to the Virginia mansion. The two young Asian feeders were both virginal, their blood like pure heroin to a vampire, making the scent of their blood irresistible, their pheromones undiluted. They'd been trained in the sexual arts by the concubines in her father's compound. Their delicate beauty alone was a powerful aphrodisiac. Lein had given them their instructions. They were to seduce, regardless of the resistance they received. She closed the door behind her and let Max know the feeders were ready. She kissed him lightly and smiled.

"Enjoy yourself, master. I doubt you will need my services tonight."

Max returned her kiss. There was a lot to be said for the arranged marriage. Who said you couldn't have your cake and eat it too? Max pulled the cell phone from his pocket and dialed up Shade.

***

Shade was in his office. They'd had several nights with the warriors on yellow alert, and nothing had happened. He wasn't sure if this was a good sign or a bad sign. Luca sat opposite him as they went over some weapons placement. The weapons cargo had arrived in several deliveries and it had taken some time to get them where they'd be most needed. He felt his phone buzz and looked at the number. It wasn't a number he recognized.

"Medici!"

"Shade. Max here. I've had time to think about the decision made by Council. I know I left angry, but I'd like to find a peaceful way to settle this. A war will not benefit either of us and will cost many lives. I visited you in your home. Now I'm asking that you visit me in mine, just the two of us. My mate is here, but she'll not intervene. Let us talk this through, my friend."

Shade stood up from his chair, walking around, his hand sliding through his hair. Max wanted to talk. He was leery and he wondered for a second if this was a trap. Perhaps, his warriors would ambush him, kill him, and then attack Bel Rosso. He dismissed the idea. Max was many things, but a master who settled a dispute in such a manner would never live to tell about it. He'd be given a death sentence by the Council, and a bounty placed on his head.

"I appreciate this opportunity. I feel the same. When do you want to meet?"

Max smiled. "No time like the present, brother. The sooner we get this resolved, the sooner I can take my mate and get back to Thailand. That's home for me now. I know you understand that."

"*Si*, we are on the same page, brother. I am on my way. Give me about twenty minutes."

Shade turned off his phone and stared out the window. It was close to midnight. Plenty of time to get to Max's, have their discussion, and get home before sunrise. Turning to Luca, he went back to his desk and flopped down.

"Block Kate, block her now. We need to talk."

Shade blocked Kate after instructing Luca to do the same so she'd sense nothing of their conversation. "Is Shannon with her? If she is, block her as well!"

Luca looked puzzled but complied. "Yeah, okay. It's done. What's going on?"

"Look, that was Max on the phone. He wants to talk, settle this. He's having second thoughts. He knows a battle between us brings mass destruction. He wants to get the hell back to Thailand with Lein. I'm going to his home, it's right outside of Richmond, on the James River."

He jotted down the coordinates and gave Luca the paper, just in case. "I am going alone. Don't worry, I got this. But I don't want anyone to know where I am, do you understand? That is a direct order! Max is not stupid. I don't think this is an ambush, but if anything happens, protect this house and get Marco on the battlefield."

"Master, are you sure? What if it's a trap? Let me go with you. I can stay out of sight. We can have the warriors on alert, ready to respond."

"No, Luca, if this is a trap, I need you to protect Kate and Lorenzo. I would not be going if I felt he meant me physical harm. You need to stay here, and I do not fucking care if you have to lie, you tell them nothing!"

Luca sighed. He knew better than to try to push past his master's stubbornness. "I'll do as you ask. But call me if you need me. I'll stay on high alert until you return. Leave the coordinates. If you haven't come back in a reasonable time, I can at least respond."

"*Si*, all I can ask of you, Luca. I need this kept quiet...if she knows, she will follow, try to stop me. I cannot take that risk."

He pulled out the top drawer and tucked the Glock into his leathers. "I'm out. I will be back before sunrise, if not, come after me. Let's hope whatever he wants in settlement is something I am willing to give. *Per sempre* Medici!"

Teleporting out immediately from where he stood, he followed the route of the James River and the mansion.

122

Shade made a few turns around Max's property, making sure he wasn't landing in some ambush. He detected no warriors, but seriously doubted Max would be that stupid. He didn't sense anything was amiss and decided to land outside the huge mansion. The house was massive and has three large wings. You needed a fucking map to find the front door.

He rang the bell and then banged the knocker loudly, waiting for a servant to answer. When there was no immediate response, the hairs on the back of his neck stood up. No servants?

Lein opened the door and bowed low. She was dressed in traditional Asian attire, her hair pinned up and secured by the long Chinese hairpins.

"Master Medici. You honor us with your presence. I apologize for the humble welcome. We don't live here full time and my master has decided against staffing the house around the clock. Please come in. May I get you something to drink?"

Nodding low as was custom, he responded, "Princess Lein, it is my pleasure to meet again so soon. I will pass on the drink, *grazie*. If you would graciously tell your master I have arrived, I think we are both most anxious for resolution."

Lein nodded. "My master has told me to expect your arrival. He asks that I bring you to his study, and I'm not to disturb him afterward. He says he has much to discuss with the Medici, and it is between the two masters to resolve."

Shade followed her as she walked silently through the massive house. "Your home is quite elegant, Princess. I can only imagine your Thailand home is even more beautiful. The East is full of treasures. *Si*?"

Lein nodded her head. "Yes, thank you. Perhaps you will visit us there sometime. I am sure my master will find a way through this problem between you."

"Max and I will decide this with great care. It will benefit us both, I assure you." He followed her through the long hallway. There was no sound, their voices almost echoed as they chatted.

He started to pick up a scent. It smelled incredible and got stronger the further they went. He thought, perhaps, it was her delicate perfume. Whatever it was, it was alluring.

Lein walked slightly ahead of him, leading the way to Max's study. As she reached the door, she placed her hand on the doorknob. She turned and waited for the Medici to step toward the door. Lein knew that once she opened the door, there was no turning back for him.

"My Master waits for you inside."

Shade smiled. "*Grazie*, Princess."

She flung open the door and the scent slammed into him hard. He almost went to his knees. He felt her small but strong hands push him forward into the room as the door slammed tight behind him.

Max lay on the huge bed with two Eastern feeders. He was feeding from one, fucking her deep and hard. The smell of the sexual activity would drop a vampire, and the blood was virginal. He couldn't think, let alone move, when suddenly the other feeder was on top of him. Her body shimmering from the sweat of hard sex, she smelled like a goddess dropped right into his lap. This was a fucking trap he'd never seen coming!

She ripped his leathers from him in one stroke, as his beast roared straight out of him. *No!* She gripped his cock with one hand and licked his vein with her tongue, soft and ready to fuck him where he stood. His eyes rolled back in his head, and his head spun, his senses in overload.

He lifted his hands to push her away from him when she slid down his body and sucked his cock deep in her throat in one swift move. His body fought to resist, but his beast was aroused and demanded to be satisfied. Shade inhaled the intoxicating scent of virginal blood as he tried to focus his eyes on Max.

Max stared back at him, his lips and chin covered in blood, as he grinned and growled at him. Shade swayed and slammed his back against the wall as the feeder worked her magic between his legs, stopping long enough to bite her own lip, releasing her own scent. He was paralyzed with desire. She climbed him like a tree and smeared her blood across his lips, kissing him, sliding her tongue into his mouth.

His beast was released, and Shade had lost this fight, his whole body shaking with need and hunger, like an addict on heroine. *I can't do this! No!* With the last of his willpower, he struggled to rein in the beast, but the beast snaked out his tongue and licked the blood from his lips, and he wanted more, needed more, demanded more. He was losing himself and he knew the beast would have what he wanted. He heard himself scream, "Nooooo!"

Lein slid the bolt into place and smiled at the sounds of the Medici as he tried to resist. She shook her head. "Foolish man. Foolish, foolish man. They always forget the power of the female." She walked away, knowing it would be a long evening for all of them.

Max watched as the nubile young feeder climbed all over him, his body responding against his will. He lifted his cell phone and started snapping photos.

"Smile for the camera, Shade. I'm sure your lovely mate will love seeing these...unless, of course, we can reach an understanding."

The feeder that clung to Max continued her ministrations to his large cock, riding him hard before lying down on his chest, and presenting her neck to him once more. Max responded by sinking his fangs deep into the tender flesh.

Shade's fangs punched through, dripping saliva, in need and hungry. His breathing was ragged, and his eyes flared a brilliant red. He saw a flash and heard Max's words scream through his head. His roar shook the windows, but his beast ignored him and took no more of his foolish resistance. Shade couldn't escape the agony of this hell. He was trapped in his own desires and the needs of his beast. He could no longer fight for his *bel*, and his promises to her.

His beast grabbed for the delicate dish that was naked and promising all he could imagine, and his hands slid into the raven silk that hung to her waist. He rubbed his hardened cock around her silk and spun her around and slammed into her full force, taking her from behind, fucking her hard.

His body felt pleasure wrapped in silken lips that gripped him tight and sweet. The beast grabbed her by the hair to fuck her until his body would spill his seed deep inside her. He felt his fangs sink deep, taking in her luscious, pure blood.

Shade broke, his heart shattered, his soul lifted him from his beast. He'd betrayed his mate. He mustered his soul to lift him from this hell. He could no longer watch his beast take pleasure and feed from another.

His dream-walking abilities lifted him from the physical cage of his own body. He left his beast behind. He was sickened and broken by the betrayal. He couldn't restrain the beast from taking what he wanted from this female. He was betrayed by the lure of virginal feeder blood, the blood that was designed to be irresistible, to ensure their survival, was now his downfall into hell and darkness. Leaving his body in a dream state, he floated above the earth, leaving his beast behind to ravage, rape, and feed until he was sated. He floated across the rippling oceans, letting his soul drift with the wind. His body now distant from all the things he loved. His beast left behind. He'd been beaten, and now betrayed...he'd lost it all.

***

Max watched from the bed as Shade's beast emerged, taking the pleasures offered. He felt Shade fight the pull of the feeder, losing the battle as his beast took his due. Max continued to photograph the graphic sex, as he felt the dream-walker take leave.

He chuckled to himself. "Suit yourself, old friend. Your beast will enjoy her just the same, and your mate won't know the difference when she sees the photos."

Max pushed the young feeder off his body and shoved her in the direction of the beast. The beast slavered and growled, taking them both, and Max continued to record the events. He'd already indulged in both feeders before Shade's arrival, sating his own desires, and making sure the air was filled with the scent of their irresistible pheromones.

He made sure Shade's face was clearly visible in the shots, his expression one of a beast lost in the throes of passion and pleasure. When the beast lay sated, drunk on the blood of the two virginal feeders, he called to Lein, who slid the bolt from the door. Max stepped over the beast as he lay on the floor, both feeders curled around him.

"You can leave anytime now, my friend. I have what I need. And perhaps, these photos will bring you to your senses. Let me know when you're ready to talk."

Max left the room, joined by Lein, as the sated beast lay sprawled on the floor.

123

Kate sat on the floor of the nursery with Shannon as they played with Lorenzo. Shannon was laughing out loud as the baby responded to her.

"I can't believe how much he's grown! He looks so much like Shade. Look at his eyes. He takes in everything!"

Lorenzo seemed to be awake as much during the night hours as he was during the day hours. Kate was still unsure if he'd be a day-walker, and Theresa had said he'd wake during the day for some time as he'd need to feed. Until they knew for sure, he'd be protected from the sun. Kate smiled at her friend.

"I know moving here has been an inconvenience for you, but I'm glad to have you here. I've missed you, Shannon."

Shannon smiled at her old friend. "I know. I've missed you too. Don't worry about me. I'll just use my vacation time. Whatever this is that's going on, I'm sure it will pass. I've been here a few days and nothing's happened. I'm sure Shade is just taking every precaution."

Kate nodded at Shannon, but she had started to feel a knot of tension in her gut. She stood up as the tension built. "Would you keep an eye on him for a minute? I need to see Shade."

Shannon nodded. "Of course! Take your time."

Kate made her way down the stairs to the study and entered to find Luca sitting at the security monitors. "Where is he?"

Luca looked up. He'd hoped Shade would return before Kate realized he'd even gone anywhere. "Uh, he went out, Kate. He'll be back soon."

Kate paced in the room, her breathing picking up, her anxiety level rising. "But where? Where did he go, Luca?"

Luca watched her, his brow furrowed. He tuned into Shade and didn't feel fear, but clearly, Kate was responding to something. "He had some errands. He'll be back shortly."

Kate's level of agitation increased, and she knew what she was feeling was his emotions, not hers. "Luca, something's wrong."

Luca shook his head. "Kate, I'd feel danger if his life were being threatened. There's no threat."

Kate paced and wrung her hands. She felt a pain like a knife being twisted in her gut. She cried out as she grabbed her mid-section and Luca leapt to his feet.

What the fuck is going on? He felt no physical threat to his master, and yet, Kate was picking up something. As he reached her, she dropped to her knees and screamed, "Noooooo!"

Luca dropped beside her. "Tell me what you feel, because I feel nothing."

Kate covered her face with her hands as she felt the heat of his passion rip through her. She felt his beast respond as he took his pleasure from another and tasted the blood across her tongue as he fed from another female. The tears streamed down her face as she cried out. "Stop! Why do you betray me?"

Luca grabbed her shoulders, shaking her. "Kate! Tell me what you feel! I can't help you otherwise!"

Kate sobbed, "He's with another. He lies with another, feeds from her."

Luca shook his head. "No, I know my master. And you know him as well. He'd never seek another female."

Kate sobbed inconsolably. Luca wondered if Max had laid a trap of a different nature and knew he must get Kate to push through if he was to help his master.

"Kate, he went to see Max. Push past your emotional pain and try to see him."

Kate cried out, "He went to see Max? He didn't tell me!"

Luca shook his head. "And he made me swear not to tell you. But I need you to focus now. Tune into him."

Kate closed her eyes, her heart ripped by pain as she pushed past the vile images in her head. She saw Max, laughing, taunting, and taking photos, and heard his mocking voice as he pushed the feeders on the beast, but Shade wasn't there.

She shook her head in confusion. Looking at Luca through her tears, she spit out the word through clenched teeth, "Feeders."

Luca knew immediately what Max had done. He only hoped Kate could get past her pain and anger to understand Shade had been manipulated and trapped.

"It was an ambush of a different kind, Kate. He was lured to the feeders. Where is he? Where is he now?"

Kate shook her head. "I don't know. He left. He left the beast behind. I can't feel him. I only feel the beast."

Luca looked at her. "Don't you see, Kate. Even when he was trapped he wouldn't betray you. He's a dream-walker. He used his gift to leave his body. When he couldn't control the beast, he left his body. It's the beast that satisfies his desires now. Not Shade. Find Shade, tell me where he is."

Kate went deep inside herself but felt nothing but a hollowed out shell. He was blocking her completely. She knew he was feeling the same pain of betrayal she felt.

"Nothing. I feel nothing. I can't see him anywhere. He's blocking me."

Luca sat down hard on the floor and ran both hands through his hair. "Fiamma. She has the gift of sight. Maybe she can see him. Remember the night you had the fight with Shade and he left? She was able to see where he was. It's her gift, which allows her to see through the eyes of another."

Luca telepathically called to Fiamma in the camp, asking her to join them in the study.

***

Fiamma and Aislynn were in the barracks and everyone was on edge. Fee was using the time to teach some mixed martial arts moves to Aislynn when Luca called her to the main house. She could hear the tension in Luca's voice.

"Aislynn, I need to go meet with Luca. Go back to your duties, or you can work out with Marcello, if you like. I won't be long."

She teleported directly inside the house and could hear Kate's sobs and immediately walked in to find them both on the floor. "What happened? Where is master?"

Luca looked at his sister-in-arms, hoping like hell she could help. "Our master was ambushed, but not in the way you might think. I think Max used feeders to lure him. Kate can't feel him now. He's blocking her. Tune into him, Fee. We need to find him."

Fee reached down and pushed Kate's hair from her face, gently wrapping her arms around her. "It is okay, Kate, we'll find him, relax for me. Hold my hand, sometimes it helps with the connection."

Kate looked at her with pleading eyes and Fiamma knew this wasn't good. Shade had completely blocked her. Concentrating, she closed her eyes, but she couldn't feel him at all.

"Okay, he is blocking heavily, but sometimes when a master has a weak moment, I can see. This might...wait, this isn't normal what I see."

Kate squeezed Fiamma's hand, almost choking on her tears. "What? What do you see?"

"Has he left his body?" She looked to Luca puzzled and astounded.

Luca nodded. "Kate says he left the beast behind when he could no longer control the beast."

Fiamma shook her head, knowing the pain and hell they were both going through. "Listen to me, Kate, I'll explain what I see, but I think it's already happened. I think I'm seeing a memory. Tell me if you know what this is? It is a gate? A chain link gate? It's covered in...locks, many of them. He grabbed a specific one, held it in his hands."

Kate looked at her confused. "A gate? A locked gate? That doesn't mean anything to me. A gate to a garden?"

Fiamma shook her head. "No, it looks like a gate, but I can see a river. There're a lot of locks on the gate. He picked one specific lock from among many. Think Kate, think! I have no idea what this is!"

Fiamma was confused and frustrated, what she saw had already happened, and she didn't know how long he'd stay in one place. She was frightened for both her master and Kate.

Kate gasped. "The Pont des Arts? The Lover's Bridge? In Paris? We went and placed a padlock there. Is that where he is?" She stood, ready to teleport to him.

Fiamma grabbed her hand and yanked hard. "No, Kate. Listen to me, this has already happened. My vision is affected by how much he's blocking you. The lock, he crushed it in his hands, it disintegrated. Hold on. I think I'm seeing where he is right now. Please, keep calm, it will come to me."

Kate felt as if he'd reached inside her chest and crushed her heart. He crushed their lock that would bind their love for all time?

Fiamma closed her eyes tight and spoke out loud. "Please master, please give me a vision. Let me help you." She stood dead still for minutes, and then her eyes flew open, "No Shade, no!"

Kate screamed at her, "Tell me! What do you see, Fiamma!"

Fiamma went to her knees, grasping for Kate. "Listen to me! You must know where this is. His life is in danger. I can see him somewhere up high, the sun is rising, and he's on a balcony. He's going to walk into the sun. Where is he, Kate?"

Kate knew exactly where he was. "The Paris house, he's at the house! Watch Lorenzo!"

She was gone in a second, leaving Luca and Fee staring at the vacant spot on the floor where she'd been. Kate teleported through the night, uncertain of her bearings. She was trying hard to remember everything he'd taught her, but the scope was much farther than she'd ever traveled alone before. No time. No time. She had to hurry.

Fiamma and Luca looked at one another, when Fiamma shouted, "Luca, go red, go red! Get Marco and tell him what's happened. He can take charge in Shade's absence. We must go red now!"

They both took off in different directions and Fiamma could only hope Kate made it to Shade in time. She'd never felt such an incredible broken spirit as she had in her master this night, but she dared not tell Kate that.

124

He dream-walked to escape the pain, but the pain followed him. Nothing would release him from this hell. He headed for Castello, where he could stay, far from her sight, knowing he'd betrayed her. How could he ever look her in the eye again? He was no different than the likes of all the other mortal men she'd been with. He was worse than the sniveling bastard Ethan he'd killed with such pleasure.

His beast rejoined him with his physical body in Castello, but he couldn't face all the people there. He didn't want to explain his presence. There were too many people to see his shame, his deceit and failure as her master, her lover and eternal mate.

He could think of one other place he could go to be alone, the empty house in Paris. He teleported over the Ponts de Arts and stared at their lock. They'd placed it there together and it would rust before their love ever died. He ripped it easily from its spot and held it in his hand, crushing it. He'd killed them both, killed their love. He should've been stronger, fought harder. He'd let her down. It was the one thing she'd asked of him from the beginning. Don't betray her. Don't break her heart. It was her inner most fear...his infidelity with another immortal.

He teleported inside the house. She was everywhere he looked, her hand had touched it all, creating this space for them, and his heart wept for the hell he'd put her through. He walked through the rooms and let his hands trail over the things she'd placed there. He was nothing without her.

His beast had responded to the primal demands when he'd entered the room where Max was already engaged in sex and feeding. He felt stupid for falling into the trap. He could stand against armies of trained warriors, but Max's feeders had been more than his beast could conquer.

He dropped his shredded clothes and showered, scrubbing his flesh raw to remove the stench of the females, making his stomach lurch as the vivid scenes of the sexual deeds played across his mind. He felt dead inside. Stepping from the shower, he grabbed the blanket from the bed they'd yet to even share and wrapped it around his shoulders. He could feel the sun was about to rise. He walked to the balcony and flung open the doors, Paris was already awake. He'd go to his eternal sleep and join his parents in the spirit realm. Kate would never come to terms with his betrayal, but she'd raise his son, and he'd rule Medici.

He sat just outside the balcony, the doors opened wide, as he waited for the rays of the sun. His heart was shattered, his soul broken. He saw images of their life together. How they'd slept together, how they'd loved, how they'd fought. All the things he wanted for her, the houses she'd made their home. The son she bore him. The pain he'd caused her. He couldn't even cry, he was so lost now.

He sat with his knees to his chest and closed his eyes. He could almost smell her, the scent of roses he loved, her lily white skin and the softness of her touch, her crimson mane that drove him insane with desire. Her lips and how they could make him want to never stop kissing her. How could he ever repair that delicate trust she'd had in him to protect and love her? He'd failed her.

***

Kate teleported blindly, tears streaming down her face, letting his energy and pain pull her. She saw the lights of Paris, their city of love. She found the house and attempted, for the first time, to teleport inside. She landed hard on the marble floor, landing on her hip and went into a slide, slamming against the wall. She stood and got her bearings, looking around to discover she'd landed in the first floor foyer. She rushed up the two flights of stairs, drawn by pain and hurt. She entered the bedroom she'd designed for them and saw his silhouette against the early light of day as he sat outside, waiting for the sun. Her heart pounded in her chest as she walked slowly toward the door, knowing he'd blocked her and didn't want to be found.

"Lover," she whispered.

He heard her voice and he groaned with pain. "Go home, Kate."

She stepped up to the open door, looking at him wrapped only in a blanket as the sky started to lighten.

"I am home, lover. I'm with you. You're my home. Now come inside."

His voice remained monotone. He couldn't look at her. "Go back the same way you came. I cannot be your home, I am not worthy of it."

He felt her hand as she reached out to touch him, and he moved away from her touch. "Do not touch me, you deserve better. Go home, take care of our son."

Tears flowed down her cheeks. "Did you hear what you said? Our son! Ours! He needs both of us. I need us. I know what happened. I felt it all. And I know you left your body, leaving the beast behind. Now come inside."

He sat still, staring at the sun as it was about to rise over the horizon and he knew it would bring her more pain if she watched him die in front of her. "He has Medici blood in his veins. All he needs." Standing, he let the blanket fall to the floor and could feel the heat building. "Go home, Kate."

Her panic spread but she wouldn't leave him like this. She screamed at him, *"What are you saying? That I'm not worth fighting for? You can walk away from me? You let him win?* If you leave me, you have let Max win!

And all I will remember is I wasn't enough. My love wasn't enough to keep you here. *Is that how it ends?"*

He felt his skin heat up, his blood hot as the sun peeped out, its first rays reaching into the sky. His death was calling. His body was lifted and hurled backward into the apartment, as if struck by a bolt of lightning, almost knocking her off her feet in the process. He lay on the floor on his back. His beast was snarling as he emerged and rose up on all fours, refusing to die, or to let Shade take him with him. His growl was deadly as the beast stared at her. "Go home. Leave me alone. Let me deal with my demons!"

Kate's anger flared as the beast appeared, and her own beast emerged. "*You!* You did this to him. You betrayed us both."

Her eyes glared red as her fangs punched through. She snarled, "You wouldn't fight for him. How could you give in? Max manipulated you, and you let him! I'll do what you wouldn't. I'll fight for him!"

Kate lashed out at the beast that betrayed her, clawing him across the face. The beast grabbed her off her feet, as she kicked and screamed, beating his chest as he yelled at her.

"Look at me! Can you say you still love me? Look at me, woman!"

Kate stopped pounding his chest and stared back at him. She relaxed in his arms, and answered in a soft whisper, her anger gone. "Of course, I still love you. I'll always love you. How could you even think otherwise?"

His beast spoke what he could not. The beast held her to his chest and snuggled into her neck. "Time. Give him time. Let him heal. Go home. He is broken but I will take care of him."

Kate laid her head on his shoulder and sobbed. "Don't let him die."

The beast held her. He knew Shade needed to mend his shattered soul before he could go back to her. His growl was deep, but he held her gently. "Luca comes for you now. Go home. I'll not let him die. I'll protect him, for you."

Pushing the hair from her face, he kissed her gently. Sitting her down on her feet, he walked away into another room, leaving her standing alone as the sunbeams stretched across the room from the balcony door, his beast protecting him from its rays.

***

Luca had landed in the Paris house only a few seconds behind her. He ran up the stairs and heard her in conversation with Shade. He leaned against the wall, letting his back slide down until he was seated on the floor. Whatever they had to work out, it would have to take place between them. He'd wait to see the outcome and make sure she was safe. He heard the raised voices between her beast and his, and then he heard his beast call. *Take her home*. Luca stood and walked into the room to find Kate, her face stained with tears.

"Come, Kate. Let me take you home. Give him space."

Kate reluctantly went to him. She knew Shade wouldn't return with her tonight. She looked around the empty room, trying to feel him, but he blocked her still. She yelled loudly to the beast. "This isn't over! You tell him! This isn't over!"

Luca slid his arm around her waist and gently lifted her and teleported them both back to Bel Rosso.

125

Raven lay curled into Mica, his mind spinning. Medici was on yellow alert and preparing for battle, which meant he may have to go back to Bel Rosso soon. He had the warriors in place here in California, and they were prepared for whatever might come. He felt like he belonged here, with Mica.

He'd been a street punk, and Shade had seen something in him, pulled him out of the mass of disenfranchised vamps who wandered, not associated with any coven. Shade had taught him discipline, and refined his skills, but Raven had built a wall around his heart, never allowing himself to commit or get too close. But this relationship with Mica was something new and unexpected. Mica was older, wiser, and his guidance and care of Raven made him wish he'd never spent so damn much time fucking off. He knew Mica cared for him, made him think seriously about so many things. And their time together was something Raven wouldn't trade for anything.

Raven looked at Mica as he slept. He was handsome, but it was more than that. Raven's attraction went beyond the physical. He didn't want this to end. He knew his assignment was temporary while they all waited to see what Max would do. If they went into battle in Virginia, then he'd have to leave Mica for who knew how long. Boss-man needed him, and so did Bel Rosso, and Raven would be there. It was what he'd trained to do, what he'd pledged his life to.

Mica felt Raven stir beside him and knew he was awake. They'd had a nice, few days here, despite the reason for the visit. Raven had secured the warriors for the inn and had drilled them on the protocol in the event of an attack. Reynaldo and Mica knew they'd have to get the mortals out of the inn under the pretext of their being some kind of plumbing emergency, or if necessary, they could keep them safe in an underground bunker. No one was expecting the attack to take place here, but it couldn't be ruled out either. Mica opened his eyes and wondered about the young warrior occupying his bed. He rolled over and pushed that long mop of black hair away from his face.

"So, tell me young Raven. What are your intentions here? I've been around a bit longer than you, by a few centuries, I'd say, so I can handle your choices. But I'd like to know where we stand. Am I just another notch on your bed post? Or do we have something serious here?"

Raven looked up at him and smiled, then gave him a quick kiss. "I'm very serious. I'm a warrior. It's all I know, and all I wanted. I love the freedom, but it's also a lonely life. I saw others finding mates, but never thought there'd ever be anyone out there for me, who understood me. Someone who could make me never want to be with another. I couldn't even let myself hope for it. I grew up on the streets. I'm used to disappointment. So, it's easier to have no expectations. But to find someone who offers a lifetime of knowing and caring, who loves me for just me. Yeah, I'm very serious."

Mica smiled at him. "I can be your lifetime, young warrior. I see your heart, your true heart. For all that bluster and bravado, I see the fragility inside. Save the fighting for your master, but save your heart for me. Is that too much to ask?"

Raven's heart went into overdrive, his breathing ragged. This couldn't be happening. This was what he'd wanted. If he could only open himself to Mica, trust him not to use him. Once Medici, Raven had become the user. It was a means of self-preservation and protecting his heart. There were older vampires who preyed on the younger, stupid ones with less experience. He knew that all too well. He'd lived it. Rolling over, Raven rested his head on Mica's chest.

"Mica, don't play with me. Just tell me you mean it because I'm tired of playing games."

Mica looked down at the vulnerable young warrior. "I'm not a player, Raven. I'm afraid I'm a romantic at heart. I've never jumped from bed to bed. I find my attraction to you quite surprising, and you, no doubt, are struggling as well. And yet, here we are. An unlikely match, but fate has brought us together. You're a warrior, and you live on the other side of the country. I know you must feed, and feed often. I accept the realities of that. So, think long and hard before you answer my next request. Can you stay out of the clubs? Can you avoid the temptation of male flesh and seek out only the feeders? Are you ready to commit to me, young warrior? Or am I moving too fast for you?"

Raven took a deep breath. "I can avoid a lot of things, for you. Commitment goes...both ways. So, can you promise me the same in return? I want that. I can do this because I want what we have together."

Sitting up, he heard Marcello in his head, telling him to get his ass back to Bel Rosso immediately. They had escalated to red alert. Shade had left and they thought he was in Paris and the queen had left to search for him. *What the fuck? Battle is about to be waged on Bel Rosso and their master goes to Paris? Something is not adding up here*. Jumping from bed, he rushed to get dressed, his mind already shifting into battle mode and on getting where he needed to be.

"I have to go back to Bel Rosso."

Mica sat up in the bed. "What's wrong?"

"We're on red alert. That means battle is about to start or something has happened to escalate the situation. I'm a bit confused at the moment. Marcello said Shade was in Paris. He said the queen went after him. Something doesn't add up, but it makes no difference, I need to go. We could be attacked. Here as well, you know the drill, so you need to really keep your ears and eyes open. Anything looks strange, the warriors will respond, and fast."

He slid on his leathers, pulled his hair up in a bun, knotting it like a pro, and pulled on his boots. He propped his foot on the bed and laced each boot with speed.

"Where the hell is my fucking sword?" Raven saw the sword propped in the corner and was working to strap it across his back.

Mica was filled with concern. He was no warrior, but he'd lived long enough to see masters battle, and it was always a brutal bloodbath. "I remember everything you've instructed. And Reynaldo says he's been with your master through many battles, so he knows the drill. But you...you be careful, my young warrior. I've just found you. I don't want to lose you over some stupid battle for land."

Raven stopped and looked at him. "Mica, this is not some stupid battle. This isn't about land. This is about Medici, and the coven; this is about all of us. This is my life. If we don't fight with all we have, we have nothing. I pledged my life to Medici. I'll fight to my death if it means saving Medici. He saved me, I'll save him. And don't worry, I'm small, but I'm like a speeding bullet."

Mica slid to the edge of the bed, swinging his legs over the side as he slid his hand between Raven's legs. "Not so small, warrior. And I admire your loyalty because I know your master reciprocates. But you're not invincible. So be careful. I'd like the chance to save you too, in my own way. I don't want to scare you away, but I'm afraid I love you already."

Raven dropped the sword and heard it clatter on the floor. No one had ever said those words to him. He hung his head, caught off guard by the declaration of love. He was warrior, he didn't show weakness. Suddenly, his emotions overwhelmed him.

"I...I need to go."

Mica reached out and took his hand. "Have I said too much? Am I moving too fast for you? Tell me what you need, Raven. Don't leave with words unspoken."

Raven wasn't sure what to say. Those words had never left his mouth before. Not those words. They meant commitment, and always forever. One blood tear slid down his face and he swiped it away quickly.

"I can take care of me, that's easy enough. But I have no idea when I'll see you again, how long this might take. Things will be chaos for a while, even after we kick their asses back to bum-fuck Thailand. Just tell me you'll still be here, waiting for me. I need to know before I go, because I never had anyone waiting for me, I never had someone to come back to, someone I wanted so much."

Mica stood and embraced him, stroking his hair. "Young warrior, I'm going nowhere, and I'll wait many lifetimes for you. Now just do me a favor and fight as hard to come back to me as you fight for your master's honor."

Raven nestled into his neck, taking in his scent, letting it give him courage to leave him behind. "I fight for us both. I'm good at what I do, taught by the best. And nothing will keep me from you. No warrior has that much power."

Raven kissed his neck softly, missing him already, whispering softly, "I love you."

Mica hugged him tightly to his chest, knowing, somehow, it was the first time those words had passed his lips. He'd love this fragile warrior, strong of body, but with the damaged, broken soul.

Raven felt his heart beat strong as his head lay on Mica's chest. He'd come back. He'd show Mica he was a true warrior and true to his word. Pulling back, he smiled. "I really have to go."

Yanking his hair from its loose bun and taking a strand in his hand, he picked the sword off the floor and sliced off several inches of his hair. Taking Mica's hand, he opened it, kissed his palm, and laid the thick strands of silky black hair into his palm and closed it. He secured the sword into the strap on his back.

"Don't forget about me."

Without another word, he disappeared, teleporting straight for Bel Rosso. He suddenly understood what boss-man had meant when he'd said there were more things to fight for than land and home. He understood now, he was fighting for love.

126

Luca clung to Kate as he teleported over Bel Rosso and Kate looked down over the estate. Every light was on in the house, the stables, and the camp. The warriors were everywhere. Shade's sudden absence had sparked the response to put all the warriors on high alert.

Luca landed with her back where he started, in the hallway outside of Shade's office. As soon as they touched down, Kate was limp in his arms, sobs racking her body. How could he not return with her? Through her tears, she saw Theresa and Marco emerge from the stairs that lead down to the wine cellar and the bunker.

Theresa was holding Lorenzo as he cried louder than Kate. Kate knew Marco must have insisted on taking Lorenzo to the bunker after both of them left. Shannon came running from Luca's suite, heading straight for her friend. She grabbed Kate, as Kate slowly sank to the floor.

"Kate. Are you all right?"

Kate looked up at Shannon and shook her head. "He wouldn't even talk. I couldn't get him to talk to me."

Shannon exchanged a glance with Luca, and he shook his head, mouthing to her they'd talk later. He'd had no time to explain things to her before he'd teleported out.

Luca knelt beside her. "Kate, give him time. He just needs time."

Kate looked at him and the pain in her eyes broke his heart. He knew both his master and his queen were broken, and he had no idea how to fix this one.

"How much time? I can't bear this, Luca. He's blocking me. I can't feel him. He's shut me out. He was ready to walk into the sun. How do I know he won't still?"

On hearing her words, Theresa gasped, and Marco dropped his head as Lorenzo kicked and screamed, feeling the emotional pain of both his mother and his father.

Luca shook his head. "Because the beast will take over, Kate. The beast works on instinct alone."

Kate spoke in anger. "The beast. The beast has already betrayed me. Who's to say what the beast will do?"

Marco approached. "My lady. The beast can only be what he is, a beast. He responds to our most base needs: to feed, to fight, to survive. The beast can't stop being what he is any more than you can stop your hunger for blood now. The beast will want to live even when a vampire is at his darkest. The beast will drag him from the sun."

Kate sat on the floor, her body exhausted from the tears, as she let herself go numb. "What if he doesn't come back to me?"

Marco and Luca locked eyes. They knew the beast would keep Shade alive, but the beast couldn't heal the pain. They both knew their master well and if he thought her life will be easier without him, he'd choose to stay away. Shade would know his warriors would protect Lorenzo, and her, as they had pledged. He had produced the heir to the Medici dynasty, secured the future of the coven, and if he thought he brought her less pain in his absence, then they both knew they might never see him again. He could choose to permanently block her and lock himself in his pain.

Luca soothed her. "He'll be back, Kate." He looked again at Marco.

Marco closed his eyes and tried to feel the one man he called brother, but he felt nothing. Marco shook his head.

Somewhere in the fog of her heartbreak, the wails of her son broke through and Kate called out, "Lorenzo!"

She lifted her arms to him, and Theresa moved to place him safely in her grasp. She held their son to her breasts, stroked his hair, fine as silk, and shushed his cries. Gradually, the baby quieted as he nuzzled into her neck, seeking comfort. Luca helped her up and Kate started up the stairs.

Shannon called after her, "Can I do anything? Tell me how to help you!"

Kate paused on the stairs and look backed at all of them. "Please, just leave me alone for a while."

She retreated to their bedroom where Emma had already pulled back the blankets on the bed. Kate kicked off her shoes and climbed fully clothed into their bed, holding Lorenzo close. The blinds were closed to the daylight as Kate turned out the bedside lamp, leaving the room pitch black.

She pulled the blankets over her, whispering to her son, "We must find him, Lorenzo. It's only us now." The emotional exhaustion took its toll on both mother and child as they slipped into a dark and unsettled sleep.

127

Shade slept like the dead. He felt dead, inside and out. His body was nourished from the feeder, but his soul felt hollow. His death slumber was long, an escape from reality. He could stay suspended here, in the black nothingness, feeling nothing, hearing nothing, seeing nothing. He'd shut out the world, all of it, including her. It was the only way he could survive right now.

He knew the betrayal belonged to his beast, and the beast had no care for the moral or emotional consequences of his actions. The behavior of the beast had never concerned him before. In his world of vampires, they all dealt with their beast. Shade knew the beast loved Kate, had even sought her out for him, helped him to identify her as his eternal mate, and yet, the beast had still inflicted this pain on them both.

How could she trust him now? She'd already had such insecurities before. How could he ever get her back? She'd sought him out, and his beast had held her. She'd said she still loved him, but Shade wondered if it was enough. He wondered if they could ever repair the damage that had been done. He wondered if it would ever be the same again.

He heard the blinds open in the Paris house, and he slowly woke, groaning with the pain in his aching head. He sat up, his face in his hands. What had happened? Max had set him up by throwing him into a situation he knew the beast could never refuse, no matter how hard he fought it.

He shook his head to rid his mind of the images of sexual abandon with the feeders, to have them replaced with something else; images of her, his *bel*. He was slammed with the pain of the betrayal and his heart was broken. He stood and walks aimlessly around the third floor of the house. He finally took a long, hot shower, trying to clear his head. Pulling on a pair of jeans from the dresser, he searched through the house, finding the bar stocked with Midnight. He drank straight from the bottle, cleansing his pallet of the taste of the feeders. He didn't kid himself, he couldn't go long without feeding, and he couldn't betray her further by feeding again from someone else. She'd also need to feed, and he knew she'd only feed from him. How long would she deny herself before she'd finally give in to the demands of her immortal body?

He grabbed a stool and dragged it to the balcony, opening the doors wide, and filling the room with cool refreshing night air. He sat there looking out, not seeing much of the Paris skyline, and oblivious to the noise rising up from the streets. His mind was consumed with all he'd lost and wasn't sure he'd ever regain again.

His body ached for her touch, her kiss, her hair on his chest when she slept. He missed his son. A small, tiny reflection of himself that he could never have imagined would change his life so drastically. He'd left them all behind, left everything behind to try to make himself whole again. Was that even possible? He grunted in agony, his mind tortured.

He had pledged to be the one who fixed everything for her, made it right. He'd turn the world upside down for her, and now, he had no idea how to fix this. She was in pain, he knew that. But so was he, more than she could ever imagine. But she was strong. She was a queen now and he knew his family would never let harm come to her or Lorenzo. She was better off without him. She'd find love again, love that she deserved and earned. He'd failed in the simplest thing. It was all she'd asked of him, and yet, he couldn't even give her that.

He drank throughout the night, his body becoming slack and his mind numb. The bottles lay empty around him. Trying to get off the stool, he fell over and onto the balcony floor in agony. He was drunk out of his head, and he couldn't remember the last time he drank like this.

His beast forced him back inside and he crawled slowly back into the room, kicking the door closed behind him. He emptied another bottle of Midnight down his throat as he slow crawled to the bed, but he never made it. He lay sprawled across the thick rug as the blinds closed and he felt his slumber pulling at him, the beast once again saving him from self-destruction. His last thought before plunging into the darkness was of her, his lily white, his walking sin. He called out her name in a voice wracked in pain and willed a rose to her bed. When she awakened, she'd know he missed her. He was still alive. But he wasn't ready to return.

128

Kate was losing track of time. She knew the electronic blinds had gone down twice, or was it three times? She'd not left the bedroom, or their bed. She felt Lorenzo wake and nuzzle into her neck and she let him feed. She vaguely remembered Theresa entering several times, trying to coax her from the room, but Kate would slip back into the oblivion of sleep. It was the only way to blunt the pain, and her growing hunger. She woke now to the sound of the blinds opening as she pulled the blanket over her head, blocking out the light, blocking out her life.

Lorenzo kicked at the blanket, his hands battling, and Kate lowered the blankets to look at him. His blue eyes stared back at her. He'd lain quietly with her, sleeping when she slept, for however long they'd been locked away in this room. She stroked his face, her love for this child healing her heart. She knew Lorenzo could heal Shade as well, if only he'd come home.

Kate rolled over to the side of the bed usually occupied by Shade and found a red rose on the pillow. She sat bolt upright in their bed. "Shade!"

She looked around the room, sliding out of the bed. "Lover? Where are you?"

She grabbed up Lorenzo and ran into the bathroom, but he wasn't there. She ran back in the bedroom and was about to run downstairs when she caught a reflection of herself in the mirror. Her hair was dirty and disheveled. Her face was still red and puffy. She was wearing the same clothes she'd climbed into bed wearing however many days ago it had been. If Shade was home, this wasn't how she wanted him to see her.

She called for Theresa, who responded so quickly Kate thought she must have been standing outside her door. "Take Lorenzo please. Bathe him and get him dressed in clean clothes. Hurry!"

Theresa was confused, but glad to see Kate up and moving, regardless of what sparked the change. She took Lorenzo and scurried away to the nursery. Kate returned to the bathroom, turning on the shower, and stepping beneath the steaming hot water. She washed her hair and scrubbed her body clean. Stepping from the shower, she dried her hair, brushing it to a high sheen, and spritzed on her rose scent. She pulled on a pair of jeans and a soft cashmere sweater in a soft shade of blush. She tore out of the room and down the stairs.

"Shade?"

Marco stepped from the study and Kate skidded to a stop. "Where is he?"

Luca heard her in the hallway as he left his suite, Shannon on his heels. Kate looked from one to the other. "Where is he?"

Marco responded, "Please, my lady, have you seen something? Heard from him? If you have, you must tell us everything so we can help you. We've heard nothing. He's still in Paris, we presume."

Kate looked at them all. "No! He's here. He's home! He left a rose in our bed. He must be here."

Marco took a deep breath and looked at Luca. Luca stepped forward to give Kate some comfort and hopefully explain. He recognized her fragile state and didn't want to send her back into hiding in their bedroom. "Kate, he wouldn't have to be here to leave you the rose."

She looked at him blankly. "What?"

Luca locked eyes with her, trying to keep her focused on the here and now. "He can will the rose from anywhere. Think hard. Did he send you a message?"

Kate felt her heart drop. Shade wasn't here. "No. No message. But the rose, it means something. The rose is a message, right?"

Luca nodded. "Of course. The rose is a message." Luca hoped the message wasn't good-bye.

Kate looked at Marco. "You've heard nothing?" She looked at Luca. "Nothing?"

Luca shook his head. "We've all been waiting. Just like you. Marco has taken over control of the camp, keeping the warriors on high alert in the event Max should decide to attack. There was a delivery from Max yesterday, addressed to Shade."

Kate looked at him with her brow furrowed. "What did it say?"

Luca shrugged. "We didn't open it, Kate. It was addressed to him, marked Personal and Confidential."

Kate looked from Marco to Luca, not believing her ears. "You didn't open it? It may tell us something! Where is it! Bring it now!"

Marco felt his anxiety rising. "My lady, this is between the two masters. I would have opened it if I thought it necessary. I keep hoping that hard-headed bastard comes to his senses and comes home." Throwing up his hands, he paced. "No, I don't think you should open it. No!"

Kate looked at him in disbelief. "Excuse me? I don't think I was asking your permission, warrior. This whole thing is Max's doing. He holds the key. And if the contents of this envelope might reveal Shade's whereabouts, or help us bring him home, then I'll read it. And if the contents of the envelope reveal Max's intent to fight, then we will fight. We'll defend what's ours and do whatever we must to ensure that Medici still rules. Is that clear? Now bring me the envelope!"

Marco stopped his pacing and blinked his eyes a few times as she put him in his place. Damn females! He lowered his head a bit and stared at her, holding back his growl, knowing she was the one in charge. He couldn't go against her wishes. In Shade's absence, she ruled the coven. *Fucking hell, old man, you did mate with one fiery vixen!*

Marco nodded his head. "As you wish, my queen. Please open it and instruct me as to what you wish your warriors to do."

Luca rushed to the console table in the living room where Gi sorted and stacked the mail, grabbing the large 8 x 11 brown envelope with its broad, handwritten scrawl addressed to Shade and Max's mark in the upper left hand corner. The envelope was heavy, and he carried it back to Kate. He had a knot in the pit of his stomach, fearing the hell enclosed inside a simple brown envelope. He handed it over to her.

Kate grabbed for the envelope, tearing at the seal. She slid the contents out into her hands when a folded note fell free and floated to the floor. Kate knelt down and picked up the note, flipping it open. It read, *"Give me what I want, and your precious mate will never see these photos."*

Kate sat down hard on the floor, aware now of what she held in her hands. Her anger flared as she flipped the photos over and looked at picture after picture of sexual depravity, the beast gorging himself on not one but two feeders. Kate felt the bile rise in the back of her throat, and she swallowed hard. She stood quickly, the photos spilling out across the floor. As she paced, the tears flowed, more in anger this time. Max had done this. He'd used their love as a wedge against them, and she vowed to bring him down. She screamed at the top of her lungs, "I will see him dead!"

She paced, walking over the photos, scattering them further, as her brain felt like it was on fire, her anger reaching a boiling point. "Who are they? Fiamma! I need to talk to Fiamma!"

Theresa saw the images on the floor and turned away, Shannon gasped at the savagery and debauchery. The vampire in the picture was beast, but clearly recognizable as Shade. Luca pushed Shannon back, not wanting her to see them in their basic rawness. He sent a message telepathically to Fiamma, "Your queen needs you."

Fiamma got the call and instantly teleported inside the hall and saw the pictures scattered on the floor. She looked at Kate's face and knew she had to step up. She'd die for either of them and right now, a calm head was needed. "My queen, tell me what you need, I'm at your service."

Kate paced as a plan formulated in her head. She walked over the photos, not looking down at them again. The images were seared in her brain. She needed no reminders.

"Fiamma, do you know them? Do you recognize them?"

Fiamma bent down, picking up the photos. The feeder's faces were fully exposed and displaying the pleasure they felt. Fiamma showed no emotion as she scanned the images.

"I don't know them, Kate. They're clearly Eastern, and our warriors wouldn't know them either. But you have a valuable resource sitting right here in camp. She knows them all, no matter where they hail from. These are virginal feeders, meaning they wouldn't have been with any warriors yet. They're always taken first by a master. Only few would know their breeding facility and one of them is right under your nose."

Kate stopped her pacing and looked at her. "Matron?"

"Yes, Matron would know of all the feeder covens. She must have resources to meet the demands for the variety of tastes that warriors need. If anyone would know them, she would. Do you wish to speak with her?"

Luca stepped forward. "Kate, I'm not sure Shade would want you to do this."

Kate snapped back at him, "Well, he isn't here, is he?" Turning back to Fiamma, Kate scooped up the photos and said, "Lead the way."

Fiamma and Kate walked to the warrior camp and entered the tunnels. As they approached the feeder compound, Fiamma unlocked the door with her fingerprint, and led Kate inside.

"I'll do whatever I can to help you, you need to know that. But as one female to another, this was an underhanded play and I hope you know he couldn't fight this, no matter how much he wanted to, and you know he tried."

"I understand that, Fee. I felt his fight, I felt the struggle. I know he was trapped, that Max tried to use our love against him. But I can't reach him now. He's been gone for days and he continues to block me. He wouldn't talk to me when I went to him. I don't know how to reach him."

As they entered the sitting area of the feeder compound, Fiamma laid her hand gently on her back. "You'll find a way. He loves you so deeply, he won't be able to let go."

Fiamma only prayed Shade wouldn't give up and hoped she'd not have to eat her words. As Matron entered, she nodded to them both, and Fiamma remained quiet, letting Kate take the reins.

"Matron, I need your help. I know that discretion is a big part of your code of conduct, but another master has used feeders to betray us. They're from an Eastern coven. Can you help me identify them? Tell me where I can find them?"

Matron had heard the gossip shared by the warriors. Their master had been tricked into feeding and was now nowhere to be found. She knew the feeders were pure, and not deceptive by nature, but they must also perform at the direction of the master. She didn't know what her queen would do with the information she provided, and Matron didn't ask. Matron accepted the photos and scanned them. The images saddened her.

"My lady, these two reside in a compound in Bangkok, Thailand. Every feeder bears a small mark of her coven. See here, on her shoulder? From the response of the beast, I can tell you they are both virginal, their blood is pure and untainted. Its pull on the beast would be undeniable, regardless of how hard he fought. The two in the photo are sisters, Malai and Suda."

Kate took the photos from her hand, burning the names into her memory. "Bangkok. Would they be there now?"

Matron nodded. "It is customary. The feeders only live within the confines of a compound. Once their assignment is complete, the master must return them to the compound. My lady, I beg you to be careful."

Kate nodded. "Thank you."

She took the photos back and turned to leave with Fiamma. In the privacy of the tunnels, Kate turned to Fee.

"I'm going to ask something of you I have no right to ask. I won't command you, I ask you, sister to sister."

Fiamma nodded. "Ask."

"As soon as we're out of the tunnel and walk out of the camp, I want you to teleport with me to Bangkok. If I go back inside the house, if I make my intent known, Luca or Marco will find a way to stop me. Please, I'm begging you. Ask me no questions, Fee. Just help me."

Fiamma couldn't believe what she was hearing, but she knew Kate wouldn't stand by and do nothing. She'd fight for Shade and do whatever she needed to do to bring him home.

"Well, you're right about that, Luca and Marco fight to keep you here. Everyone here is on edge. But be warned, I'm coming with you. You need protection, and Bangkok isn't a safe place for vampires from the West, and their feeder covens are nothing like what we have here." Fee looked hard at her, her skin more pale than usual, and realized it had been days since Kate had fed and yet she had continued to feed Lorenzo. "If we're going to go, then I have two demands. First, we go now, because if we're out here too long, Luca or Marco will come looking for you."

Kate nodded in agreement. "And the second demand?"

Fee pulled at the chain that hung around Kate's neck, holding the vial of blood Shade had given her the first time Kate had fed from him, pulling it free from under her sweater. "You haven't fed. You've already teleported to Paris, and you're feeding Lorenzo. You need to take this now."

Kate broke the sealed glass vial and quickly drank the thimble full of blood it contained, feeling Shade's power in her veins. As she dropped the broken vial to the floor she looked at Fee. "Ready?"

Fee locked eyes with her and shook her head no. "It'll help Kate, but it won't be enough. You'll need to feed. You can go to the feeders— "

"No! No feeders!"

Fee unzipped the bright red leather jacket, tossing back her hair. "Then me. Feed from me. I'm not leaving here until you feed. You'll never make it, and I'll not have your death on my hands. If you want my help, then feed."

Kate hesitated, feeling her heart break, but knowing she didn't have the strength or the knowledge to make this trip alone, and realized how much the feeding dictated their lives, how the feeding controlled them, allowed her to feel Shade's pain even more deeply.

Fee looked at the play of emotions across Kate's face. "You're not a mortal anymore. This is survival, not betrayal. Do what is necessary, my queen. I give my blood freely."

Kate closed her eyes, as a single blood tear fell down her cheek. She leaned into Fiamma's open arms and took what her body demanded. As the blood flowed across her tongue, the sexual pull was not as powerful as what she felt with Shade, and she remembered Theresa telling her that the females feeding from feeders didn't have the same level of sexual desire. Kate resisted the desire that rose up, unwanted. When she unlatched, she gently licked the wounds and watched them heal, then softly kissed Fiamma's cheek.

The two women locked eyes, and Fee hugged her tight. "Come quickly. We don't have time to waste." They headed for the doors that lead outside the camp.

Kate sent a telepathic message to Theresa to look after Lorenzo, and said she'd be home as soon as she could. She grabbed Fee's hand and let her lead the way, teleporting them into the dark underworld of Bangkok and the feeder compound located in the seedy Patpong district of the ancient city.

***

Luca saw the confusion cross Theresa's face at the exact moment he felt Kate exit. He knew she'd left the property. He felt the break in her energy, but he didn't know where she'd gone. Panic hit him square in the chest. Master would kill him if anything happens to her!

"Kate!" he called to her, but she didn't respond. She was blocking him. **"Fiamma, Kate is gone!"**

Fiamma heard Luca's panic. "I'm with her. Just take care of Lorenzo. I got this. And before you bust my ass, I'll take full responsibility. Chill out, brother."

Luca punched the wall. *Chill out? Is she fucking kidding?* Shannon stepped back at the uncharacteristic display of anger from Luca. Marco looked at him, and Luca responded.

"She's gone. Fee's with her, but I have no idea where they're going."

Marco stormed back into the office, slamming the door shut behind him. As if he didn't have enough fucking problems!

129

Fiamma returned with Kate, stunned by the turn of events in Bangkok as they teleported into Kate 's bedroom. She looked at Kate's disheveled appearance, her clothes covered in blood

"You need to shower before anyone sees you, and let Luca know you are home. Are you all right?"

Kate nodded, pushing the duffel bag under the bed. "I'm fine. And thank you, Fee."

Fee looked at her for a long, few seconds, reappraising her queen. "Of course."

Kate flashed her a look. "You speak of this to no one."

Fee nodded. "That's understood. Do you need anything else?"

Kate shook her head, and Fee told her she'd better get back to camp. She was already in enough trouble with Marco and Luca as it was.

Kate showered, watching the blood swirl in a vortex of water spinning around the drain. She stepped out and dried off, slipping a clean gown over her head. Tiptoeing down the hall, she opened the door of the nursery to see Theresa on the sofa-bed, and Nita feeding Lorenzo. Kate walked over and planted a soft kiss on the baby's head.

Theresa sighed. "So thankful you're home. Do you want to explain–"

"No, I don't want to explain anything." Kate said, cutting her off before she could finish the sentence. "Thank you for taking care of Lorenzo."

She turned and left the nursery, climbing into bed, exhausted. She let Luca know she was home and in bed and she'd see him tomorrow. She heard his grumbled response. Kate ignored him and turned on her side, stretching her hand across the expanse of the bed.

"Lover, how long will you make me wait?" She closed her eyes, the activities of the night having exhausted her. She slipped into a deep sleep.

Kate woke to the whir of the electronic blinds. She rolled over and stretched as the memory of Bangkok flashed through her head. She quickly blotted it out, rolled out of bed and rummaged through her closet. She pulled out a black dress and a pair of designer heels. She did her make-up, expertly applying the bright red lipstick. She picked up Shade's cell phone left sitting on his nightstand and scrolled through the contacts until she found what she was looking for and hit dial.

Max felt the soft vibration of the phone in his pocket. Pulling it out, he saw the caller ID. It was Shade. *Took him long enough. Now let's see if he's come to his senses.* Max answered, the smirk could be heard in his voice. “Hello, old friend. I've been waiting for your call."

Kate's palms were sweating, and she slid her hand against the sheets and transferred the phone to her other hand. She let her tears flow. "Max? This is Kate. I can't find Shade. Please help me."

Max was taken aback to hear Kate. "What do you mean you can't find him?"

Kate made certain he heard her sobs, but the tears came easily, as her pain was real. “We haven’t seen him since the night he met with you. He’s blocking me. Can I come over? You were the last person to see him. He might have said something. Maybe you can help me figure out where he is, please!"

Max was silent on the other end of the phone. *The envelope, what happened to the envelope?* "Kate, I mailed Shade a package."

Kate responded, "Yes, it’s here. Do you want me to open it?"

"No! No, don't open it. That was an offer I made to Shade for the land. He can consider it when he returns. Kate, I don't think I can offer any clues as to where he may be, but if it helps you, then by all means, feel free to come by. Do you want me to send a car?"

"Oh, that won't be necessary. I’m sure I can find it."

"Please, my angel. Come by anytime. I'll be waiting."

Kate ended the call and returned to the closet, finding a designer shopping bag. Standing on her toes, she reached onto the top shelf and pulled down a large hat box. She removed the hat and haphazardly tossed it back up onto the shelf. Exiting the closet, she carried the shopping bag and the empty box over to the bed. She dragged the duffel bag from under the bed and transferred the contents. Kate put the hat box into the shopping bag, then put on her coat and slipped the shopping bag over her arm and teleported out of the bedroom.

Luca felt her exit again and flew up the stairs, ripping open the bedroom door. "Kate!" Her bed was unmade, the wet towel cast across the chair, and the closet door open. **"Fee! Please tell me you are with Kate!"**

Fee responded to him that she’d brought Kate home before sunrise, and she’d not seen her since. Luca slammed the door shut behind him. “Fuck!"

***

Max informed Lein Shade's mate was on her way here, and he’d like for her to make herself scarce. Lein looked at him warily.

"Do not be deceived, Master."

Max laughed. “It seems Shade hasn’t been seen or heard from since his visit here and I need to console his lonely mate."

Lein shook her head. "Beware of a trap."

Max stroked her face. "She was mortal, only recently turned. He keeps her locked away. I think I can handle it."

Lein looked at him with skepticism. "Never underestimate the power of an angry woman."

Max smirked. "She's not angry, Lein, she's sad and heartbroken. I've got this under control. If Shade's gone, the estate is vulnerable. I need to see what she knows."

Lein would do as she was told, bowed to him, and left, but she had her doubts.

Kate arrived at the Virginia mansion that belonged to Max, landing outside his door. She rang the bell and waited for someone to respond, second guessing her decision to come here alone. She should have brought Luca, or at least Fee. When the door opened, she was face to face with Max.

"Hello, my angel. Please come in."

Kate steeled herself for what she was about to do. "Thank you so much for seeing me. I hope I'm not imposing. Is Lein here?"

Max smiled at her. "My lovely mate had business elsewhere. We're quite alone. Can I take your coat?"

Kate felt a chill run up her spine at the realization he'd sent Lein away. She set her shopping bag down as he helped her from her coat, letting his hand brush against her neck. He caught her scent of roses, and she could hear him inhale her as his lips were close to her ear. Kate stepped forward, releasing her arms from the coat and putting some distance between them.

Max directed her to a sitting room, and she picked up her shopping bag and followed him. He offered her a seat and poured her a Midnight. "This is a very good year, according to your Master."

Kate accepted the glass, needing both the alcohol and the blood. He sat down across from her as she sipped at the wine.

"Now tell me, my angel. How can I help you?"

Kate looked at him over the rim of her glass before setting the glass down on the table in front of her. "Help me to understand."

He tilted his head at her. "What exactly is it you need to understand, Kate?"

Kate looked about the room. "Was this the room?"

He looked at her, puzzled. "What room?"

She glared at him. "Is this the room where you tricked him? Where you trapped him? Did you honestly think you could break me? That I wouldn't feel his pain? His conflict?"

Max laughed. "My angel, from where I was sitting, I promise you, I saw no pain or conflict. I saw a beast unleashed, and enjoying all the delights in front of him, until he lay sated on the floor."

Kate glared back at him. "Oh you saw the beast, but my dream-walker was long gone." She stood up. "Did you think you could break us? You'll never have Bel Rosso. Not at any price. So, if it's a war you seek, then bring your best. The Medici don't negotiate." Kate stood and headed for the door. "The shopping bag is yours. My parting gift...my angel." Kate teleported out, moving as fast as she could back to Bel Rosso, but not fast enough to escape the sound of his roar.

Max lifted the hat box from the bag and opened the lid to discover the heads of the two feeders staring back at him with dead, glazed-over eyes, when he released a roar that shattered the glass in every room on the first floor of the mansion.

“You want a war, bitch! I will show you a war!"

130

He had no idea how much time had passed, but the sun had set once again, and his hunger was deepening. He walked the streets of Paris alone, watching the couples strolling past him, their embraces and soft kisses only making him miss her more. He ached for her arms around him, his face buried in that crimson silk. He had continued to block her so she couldn't feel him, but it also meant he couldn't feel her.

He kept walking in the soft rain. A mortal woman walked past him, bumping into him slightly. As he turned, she smiled at him. It was the kind of smile that was an open invitation. He knew he could feed from her and end his hunger, but he couldn't betray Kate again. He left the sidewalk and entered a garden, but there were lovers there too, and he felt he couldn't escape the pain.

He opened himself up. He couldn't take the loneliness, as it would surely kill him. He wanted to hear her voice, know she was all right. He stood in the park, staring up at the sky and closed his eyes, trying to sense her.

He felt her anxiety, and her nervousness. He could sense she was with someone, but he couldn't see who. He almost dropped to his knees, his body shaking. He shut down completely once again. He stood in the rain a long time, his face in his hands. Something deep inside cracked open and he felt as though a fire had ignited inside him, burning out of control. She was his and his alone! He was a fool to think he could ever be away from her and survive. If she loved him as he loved her, she'd forgive him.

He opened up to her again. She felt weak, exhausted, and barely able to feed their son. He teleported back to the empty house in Paris. He'd win her back and make her see no one could love her like he did. He'd do anything to have her back. He wasn't ready to return to Bel Rosso, but he wanted to see her, alone.

He showered in the steaming hot water, his body tired and his hunger gnawing at him, but his need for her giving him strength. He dressed in low slung jeans, a white dress shirt, unbuttoned that hung open off his broad shoulders. He walked through the house, finding every available vase and filling them with red roses. He willed red rose petals across the floors, filling the house with the scent.

When he was ready, he reached out and called to Luca. "**Luca, bring Kate to me in the Paris house. Now.**"

He waited for a response, praying she'd come to him. He wanted time alone with her. They needed to mend, to heal together. He paced, waiting for Luca to answer him.

***

Luca felt her as she teleported back into the house and he stormed up the stairs and threw the door open. She was standing in the middle of the bedroom, dressed in a black dress and heels.

"Kate! What the fuck do you think you're doing? You left here without me? Without Fiamma? Where have you been?"

Kate turned to face him, letting his anger wash over her. She was so tired, so very tired. She closed her eyes. "I went to Max."

Luca stood with his mouth open, unable to immediately respond, letting her words sink in. "You did what?"

She shook her head, despite her bravado in front of Max, and the challenge she threw in his face, the truth was she couldn't push much further without him. She kicked off the shoes and walked barefoot across the floor, lying across the bed. "You heard what I said."

Luca was fighting the urge to strangle her when he heard Shade in his head. He wanted her in Paris...now! Luca ran both hands through his hair. *Well, isn't this just perfect fucking timing*. He sat on the side of the bed. "Kate. Shade wants me to bring you to him in Paris. Now."

Kate sat up, looking at Luca's face. He looked as tired as she felt. "Luca. When? Did he call?"

Luca nodded, saying, "Just now, he spoke to me telepathically. Let's go."

Kate slid off the bed and grabbed her shoes, slipping them back on. "How did he sound? Was he angry? Or sad? How did he sound, Luca?"

She looked around for her coat and remembered she'd left it at Max's.

Luca responded, "I don't know, Kate. Tired? Insistent? He wants you in Paris with him. Isn't that enough?"

Kate grabbed another coat from the closet, the tears running down her cheeks. "Take me now, please."

Luca lifted her up, and despite his anger with her these past two days, he knew she was fighting to hold it together. He teleported her to the Paris house, landing in the foyer on the first floor. Setting her down, he looked at her before he left. "Will you call me if you need me?"

Kate looked at the hurt in his eyes and knew she had dragged him through hell these past few days as well. "Yes. I promise."

He teleported out, leaving her standing alone in the dimly lit foyer. She climbed the stairs, stopping on the first floor that contained the formal living and dining rooms to find them empty. "Shade?"

He didn't answer her as she climbed the stairs to the second floor that contained the bedrooms for Luca and Theresa, and family rooms for all of them to share. She started back up the stairs, catching the scent of roses as she approached the third floor that contained their master bedroom, and the rooms she'd created for their children. *How much does he know? Did he feel me feed? Does he know I took off to Bangkok? And Max? Did he feel me when I went to Max?* Her heart pounded in her chest as she reached the third floor and stood still at the top of the stairs. "Shade?"

He felt her come in and took a deep breath. He had to get this right. He had one shot and if he fucked it up, his life was over. He spoke softly to her. "Come, Kate. I am in here."

He stood as far from the door as possible. He wanted to see her enter the room and see her face when she saw him. He didn't know what the hell he'd do next. He just needed to see her face. He'd know when he saw her if she was willing to love him again. At least she'd come, and that was a start. He willed on the music and waited to see her come through the door.

The room was dimly lit and she saw him standing in the shadows. She stepped forward, moving slowly, her motion through the room making the candlelight flicker, keeping him in shadows. His face, she needed to see his face.

"Shade," she whispered. He had willed the music of Enigma to play, and she heard the refrain of the song, "Do You Love Me?"

"Until my dying day, lover." She sobbed as she felt all the heartbreak and pain of the last few days that she'd pushed down pour forth. "Until my dying day."

Her voice rolled over him like waves crashing on the shore. She stopped in the soft glow of the candlelight and he'd never in his life wanted anything more, even more than the first time he'd laid with her, or the first time he fed from her. This was his life standing before him. He had to reclaim it, make it solid once again. He slowly walked into the light, standing before her. He said nothing but took her hand in his and placed his other around her waist, dancing them slowly across the floor. The music surrounded them. Touching her was like a soothing balm to his soul. He wanted to be with her, to make her understand, he was nothing without her. He smelled the vampire on her; he didn't violate her, but he was so close he could have taken her, and he held down his beast and anger as he recognized Max's scent. He said nothing, just swayed with her, because this was what he needed right now.

Kate laid her head against his chest, listening to his heartbeat, feeling the rise and fall of his chest with each breath, feeling the warmth of him, and the protection of his arms. How she'd missed him! She let him lead her through the dance, as she gave herself up to him.

"I love you. Nothing changes that. Nothing will ever change that."

Shade stopped dancing. Dropping his arms, he stepped around her and unzipped her dress. He slowly lowered the dress past her hips, letting it drop to her ankles. She stepped from the dress as he took her hand, leading her to the bed, pushing her down gently. He knelt down and slid her heels from her feet, rolling the silk stockings down her legs one at a time. Taking her hand, he helped her stand and slowly pushed the bra straps from her shoulders. His lips brushed over the soft mounds of her breasts, kissing them gently. Reaching around her, he unhooked the bra and tossed it. Hooking his thumbs into her panties, he crouched in front of her, sliding them down the lily white skin of her hips.

She stood naked before him. He nuzzled gently into the soft patch of red curls between her legs and inhaled, his need for her overwhelming. He stood again, removing his shirt before taking her hand and began to sway to the music with her, as he held her to his bare chest. The music played over and over, looping the same song. She was his, and he was hers, her breath soft and warm against his skin. He felt her desire. She wanted him too.

His tongue sought out the vein in her neck, tasting her skin and feeling the soft beating of her heart. He nipped at her ear, sliding his tongue around the soft shell-like outline. Her hips swayed and brushed softly against his hard cock, still restrained by his jeans.

He stopped dancing with her and pushed her gently back from him. His eyes locked with hers as he unzipped his jeans and slid them down his hips. His cock was freed, hard and pulsing for her. He kicked the jeans aside and pulled her to his chest. He lifted her up until her legs wrapped around his waist and her arms clung to his neck.

His hands gripped her ass as he entered her slowly. Her head fell back as he penetrated her deep. His whole body screamed his need for her. She was so soft, and beautiful, and his.

She laid her head on his shoulder. She hadn't fed since the minimal feeding she'd taken from Fee, and she'd pushed her body far in these past few days. The nearness of his warm flesh and his male scent was more than she could bear. She licked along the pulsing vein in his neck and heard his moan. She sank her fangs deep, and drew his blood across her tongue, letting the fire spread through her veins, and hitting her at her core.

His body responded to the feel of her feeding from him, taking long, deep draws. His head spun at the feel of her, that she needed him so desperately. His need for her was the same, but he'd let her feed from him first. He felt her body respond as she swallowed his blood, her hips riding him, her sex gripping him with each passionate stroke.

He walked them to the wall and pushed her against it for support. His hands tangled in her hair as she fed. The music lifted them together. This was where they were supposed to be...how they were supposed to love.

"Cum, *mi amore*, cum for me."

She unlatched as she threw her head back and cried out with the power of the orgasm that shook her, riding him hard, her hands gripping his back, nails breaking his skin as the last waves of pleasure washed over her.

Her hands slid into his curls and gripped him hard as she pulled him to her neck. His fangs punched and he moaned. His body was aching to taste her. He'd held back too long and could barely breathe, his need for her so desperate.

"Feed from me, Lover. Take from me. Heal yourself. Heal us both."

She barely had the words out of her mouth when his fangs sank deep into her tender flesh, and he drew her sweet, hot blood into his mouth and across his tongue. As he swallowed, he felt it all come together. Her blood fed his very soul, and his cock, still buried inside her, hardened instantly. He walked with her to the bed, his fangs and cock buried deep, the urgency to cum inside her overwhelming.

Laying her down on the bed, he crawled on top of her, driving deep inside her, claiming her. Her blood ignited a fire in him. He threw back his head, roaring as he came inside her, letting her heal him.

He slumped over top of her, his weight on his elbows, his body renewed. Pulling her close, he rolled them across the bed onto his back and pulled her across his chest. He let the music roll again with their song, as Van Morrison sang, “Into the Mystic”.

They lie quietly together, catching their breath as he stroked her hair. He whispered softly. "What have you done, *mi amore*?"

Kate lay quietly in the aftermath of their lovemaking, listening to their song. She would keep nothing from him, she only hoped what she revealed didn't drive him away again. "You must promise me—"

"Just tell me."

He needed to know, because his mind was yet to settle, and before everything could be right between them again, they'd need to share it all. He'd love her no matter what. He knew now she never stopped loving him, even though his beast betrayed her.

She told him everything. How she hid away for days in their bedroom with Lorenzo, and how she'd found the rose and thought he was home. She told him about the envelope Max had sent along with his note, and the photos. She told him how the photos had ripped at her heart. She told him about seeking out Matron and learning where the feeders were, and who they were, and the revenge she planned. She told him she had taken his blood from the vial she wore around her neck, but it hadn't been enough, and she had fed from Fee. She told him how she'd left for Bangkok, and how she's killed and beheaded the feeders. She told him her need to take revenge on Max. How she went to his house, telling Max it was because Shade was lost to her, and how she'd left him with the severed heads of the feeders. She told him she had challenged Max, that he couldn't break them, that he couldn't take *Bel Rosso*, and if he wanted a war, then he'd have one. She talked without stopping, knowing if she paused—if she thought about her words—she'd stop. She wouldn't hide the truth from him. She wanted nothing hidden anymore. She'd love him through anything. Now she needed to know. Would he do the same?

***

He'd asked for details and she gave them to him. He lay there not moving, just listening. He didn't interrupt her. When she was done, she laid her head on his chest. He laid there a long time, absorbing the details, going over everything she'd told him. He was amazed and proud of her. She was both brazen and careless to go to such lengths without protection, and it only proved one thing to him—she'd fight and kill for Bel Rosso, for his coven, and for him.

He felt her fear that he'd now be angry and leave her once again. His hand glided along her back, tangling in her hair. He pulled her head up and stared into her eyes, deep and long, before kissing her hard. He kissed her with everything he had, his tongue seeking hers. He left her breathless and kept his grip on her hair as his eyes bored into hers.

"Then I believe the King and Queen of Medici should get home. We have a battle to win. I have a master to kill. We have a son to protect, and a coven to take care of."

Kate nodded at him, tears in her eyes. "Home. Yes, lover, home."

He held her tight to his chest, wrapping a blanket around them and teleporting back to Bel Rosso. As they landed in their bedroom, he set her down on her feet, taking her face into his hands. "Get our son."

As she grabbed a robe and scurried from the room, he called to Luca. **"Your master and his queen are home. Let us rest and when the night calls again, we prepare for the fight for Bel Rosso."**

Kate hurried to the nursery to find Lorenzo was asleep in his crib. Theresa heard her come in and sat up on the sofa-bed. "Is everything all right, my lady?"

Kate smiled at her. "We're fine, Theresa. But I'll take Lorenzo back to our bed tonight."

Theresa looked at her. "We? Is master home?"

Kate smiled at her as she lifted Lorenzo from the crib, and he grumbled at being disturbed in his sleep. Kate nodded to Theresa. "He's home."

Theresa got up from the bed. "Then if you don't mind, my lady, I'll return to my own bed. I have a rather grumpy warrior waiting."

Kate smiled. "Go to him, Theresa. I'm afraid I've tried everyone's patience these last few days."

Kate returned to their bedroom and slipped into bed beside Shade, laying Lorenzo in his arms.

Lorenzo cooed and Shade chuckled. "I think that is the most beautiful sound on this earth."

He pulled Kate close to his chest so they can hold him together. "This chain of love will not be broken, *mi amore*. I love you. I have never stopped loving you since the day you strolled into my life. All I need is right here in my arms. Always love me."

"I never stopped loving you, Shade. There's nothing or no one who can come between us."

He kissed the top of her head, as well as Lorenzo's, his arms enfolding them both. "Rest. We are home now."

131

Rissa and Alec returned from their short but restful honeymoon. Both of them quickly fell back into their daily routines. Santos had stacked all the mail for her, including the many cards and gifts that came pouring in, congratulating them on their nuptials.

It took Rissa several days to sort through everything and to get caught up with her schedule, but she was back at it, busy as ever and diving straight into work once again. She felt overjoyed with all the attention, as she was still the shining star of the social elite. She loved finding the paparazzi shots of the wedding, as well as some from their honeymoon still dominated the society pages of all the major newspapers and internet blog sites.

Santos had saved all the newspapers from the past week, and their wedding was given front page coverage on many of them. Not to mention, the photo of her and Alec, she in her gown and he in his tux, had made the cover of *People* magazine. Their wedding had been covered on the TV news as well as the celebrity news shows like *Entertainment Tonight*. Rissa couldn't be more thrilled. The publicity would be great for both of them.

Her voicemail and email were both filled with requests from new clients, and she started the process of returning the inquiries and seeing which she'd accept. Her day was jam-packed. She finally got home close to 7:00 p.m., with Hyde escorting her inside, as always. Alec had yet to return from his office; he'd been just as busy trying to catch up as she was.

As Hyde helped her off with her coat, she ran for the stairs. "Hyde, please wait for me. Give me a half hour to change. I want to go out to Bel Rosso and ride Biondo! I've missed her so much!"

Hyde took a deep breath. Rissa wasn't going anywhere near Bel Rosso and he needed to make sure she understood what was happening there. "Rissa, wait. There's something we need to discuss."

He saw her stop on the stairs as she swung her head in his direction, staring at him, her face already reflecting her agitation. She sensed he was about to tell her there'd be a change of plans.

She came back down the stairs with her arms crossed over her chest, taking a stand, her hip jutting out. "What could possibly keep me from riding? It's the safest place for me to be, remember? Is something wrong with Biondo?

"Relax, Biondo is fine. But right now, you can't go to Bel Rosso."

Rissa was puzzled. She headed for the sitting room as he followed behind her. Walking to the bar she poured them both a Midnight. Handing him a glass, she kicked off her heels and curled up in the chair. "Don't tell me you don't want a drink because you're on duty. Apparently, you're off duty as of now, so sit down and explain to me what the hell is going on."

He took the drink and sat down across from her, but not getting too comfortable. "Rissa, Bel Rosso is on battle alert. Everything's on lockdown. So, you need to forget about riding until this is resolved."

Rissa absorbed his message. "Who's at battle? And why?"

He could hear the trepidation in her voice as he tried to explain. "First of all, you're safe, so relax. Master Shade and Master Maximus are at odds with one another. He wants Shade off Bel Rosso and of course, Shade isn't leaving. Everyone's on alert now, waiting for whatever Maximus plans to do." Hyde shook his head. "Shade was right when he said Maximus had a damn good reason for showing up at your wedding, and it wasn't about wishing anyone well."

Rissa tried to calm her breathing. *Max!* Well at least he wasn't after *her* this time. Or was he? Her heart was racing and her fear returned.

"Hyde, you have to protect me! I can't be left alone. Max is a dangerous master. Tell me you aren't going back to Bel Rosso. I won't have it! I need you to protect me!"

She stood and began pacing in her stocking feet. Hyde was startled and confused by her fear.

"Rissa, it's fine. I'm your protector, I'll be with you. Nothing has changed. This isn't about you or Alec. Max wants Bel Rosso as it sits in his territory."

She kept pacing, her mind in a whirl. Damn Max! He could use this battle to kill her for sure. He'd never stop until she was fucking dead. "Does Alec know?"

Hyde watched her pace. He could tell her brain was in overdrive. What the hell did she have to fear from Maximus? "I very much doubt it. Shade's been busy, and the two of you were out of the country."

Rissa slammed her drink down on the table. "Well, if this isn't just one fine mess! Here we are supposedly protected by Medici warriors and now Shade has decided he wants to battle with Max and leave both of us unprotected in our own territory." Throwing up her hands, she looked at Hyde. "I'll not be happy if you have to leave me to go strap on a sword and cut off heads!"

Hyde sighed heavily, getting frustrated with her dramatics. He grabbed her arms to stop her pacing. "Rissa, you need to calm down. Medici has not stopped protecting Washington. My assignment hasn't changed. I'm here to protect you. The warriors assigned to the Dead House who cover D.C. carry on as normal. This battle, if there is a battle, will be managed by his other warriors and it has nothing to do with you or Alec. So, calm down. I'm not going anywhere."

She laid her head on his chest. He felt like ripped steel beneath that suit. He didn't wrap his arms around her, but she felt safe having him this near. "Thank you, Hyde. I just worry. Max isn't anyone to play with. Will you stay in the house until Alec comes home?"

She laid her hands on his chest and lifted her face to him, rolling her big blue eyes up to his. "Please?"

He looked down at her as she tried to use her beauty to manipulate him, but he knew her wicked game. "Yes, I'll stay until your master returns, so get on upstairs and take care of your business, I'll be right here."

Biting her lip, she smiled coyly. "Thank you, Hyde."

She walked out of the room, swaying her hips in an invitation she knew he'd never accept, but she'd love for him to try.

Hyde watched her walk out and shook his head. That one would never learn.

***

Alec arrived home later than usual. He felt like he'd spent the entire day returning calls. As soon as he entered the house, Santos was at the door, taking his coat, but Alec sensed Hyde's presence. That was odd. Hyde usually left as soon as he'd safely delivered Rissa home. Alec headed for the study and found Hyde seated near the fireplace. Alec gave him a questioning look as he poured himself a Midnight.

"Can I pour you a drink, Hyde? What's going on? You're usually long gone by now."

Hyde stood. "No thank you, Master Canton. Rissa requested I stay until you returned. I hope I didn't impose."

Alec looked at him, confused. "What's going on?"

"Bel Rosso is on red battle alert. There's no threat to you or Rissa. Master Maximus has decided he wants Shade out of his territory and Shade has refused."

Alec raised an eyebrow. "Max? Well, that explains his unexpected presence at the wedding. Thanks for staying, Hyde. You can go now."

Hyde took his leave as Alec dropped his briefcase and laptop on the desk, fishing his cellphone from his pocket. Downing the Midnight, he hit dial and settled in the chair behind the desk.

***

Shade was up and playing with Lorenzo on the bed. They'd just awakened from a long day of sleep following their journey back from Paris. He needed to get moving. He had to get some things done. He knew Marco had taken the reins while he was gone, but he needed to take back control and get to the camp. His cell phone buzzed on the nightstand. "Medici!"

"Shade, what's going on? Hyde just left here. He said you were on red battle alert."

"He told you right. Long story short, Max wants Bel Rosso, made me a money offer, and I refused. We went to Council and pleaded our case, where he lost. Max sabotaged me, my mate, and my future with a few virginal feeders from Thailand. I took off to Paris to get my head straight, and Kate delivered the heads of the feeders to Max in a box and now...I am waiting to see what the bastard does next. It won't be long."

Alec almost spit the Midnight across the room. What did he just say? He had to fight back his laughter. "Kate beheaded the feeders? Just because you fucked them? Oh, my friend, you're on a tighter leash than I thought." Alec shook his head. "And you think my life is fucked up. Seriously, do you honestly think Max is going to make a move on Bel Rosso?"

Shade growled, closing his eyes. "Yes, I do. And big news flash for you, brother, I will win, and when I do, I own Virginia."

Alec ran his finger across the top of the desk. "I need you to emerge the victor here. And you owning the Virginia territory would be a good thing for me. But be careful, Shade. He has his own warriors, plus the armies of Fan Shen. This is no small matter, and it won't be a small battle. Anything I can do to help?"

"Well, yes, there is something. I don't think it is safe for Rissa to ride until this is over. I have already moved some of the horses out. I did that to protect them. I left Impavido here, of course, and some other horses that are battle tested. I may need them. Hyde's assignment has not changed but if you feel it is necessary, I can assign him to be with Rissa 24/7 as a live-in. That is up to you. But whatever you decide, I would not leave Rissa alone. Max is a hot head and apparently, she and Lein had a few words at the reception. Let me know what you want to do with Hyde. We are still covering D.C., nothing has changed there. I pulled Raven back with me, but I have Theo taking on the role of SIC at the Dead House."

Alec ran his hand over his face. *Is Rissa at risk?* "I don't think Hyde needs to live here. Just keep the current arrangement where she's covered if she leaves the house. I'll call Alto in and keep him in the house 24/7. If you go to battle, Rissa's ass is grounded. I can't be sure Max's warriors will stay in his territory, especially when we're so close."

Shade nodded. "I will keep you informed, brother." Hanging up, he tossed his cell on the bed and picked up Lorenzo. "Little warrior, *Padre* needs to go to work—big things ahead of us!"

132

Heading into his study, Shade knew there'd be a lot to catch up on following his absence. His actions had left them all vulnerable and he needed to take control now. Marco had done a great job, but he needed Marco back in Florence. He felt restless. If they were going to battle, then he was ready to get on with it. A battle was something he knew he could handle. It was the waiting that wore on him.

Flopping down in his leather chair, there were papers strewn across the desk. A large envelope was tucked under a stack of papers on the corner of the desk. His brow scrunched up with curiosity as he picked it up, reaching inside, not prepared for what he held in his hand. They were the photos from Max, and he had to fight back the bile that was rising in his throat, as several of the pictures fluttered to the floor. He flipped through the photos, the images of his beast reveling in obscene pleasure, and the longer he looked, the more he wanted to kill Max.

The images were seared into his brain and his betrayal of Kate was lived out once again. He laid his head back with a soft thud against the high back leather chair and closed his eyes. His beast had feasted on sex and blood, taking both feeders, lying sprawled and spent in a tangled heap, his fangs dripping with blood and saliva.

He wanted to leap through the fucking glass window, teleport to Max's mansion and slice off the bastard's head, tear his cock off and shove it up his ass. He wanted Max's heart in his hands where he could squeeze it to fucking dust. But he knew that would be an even bigger mistake than the one that ended with these photos. His beast had done this. He'd left his body in a dream-state to avoid the hellish things he felt, but here it was, forever burned into photos for Max's amusement. And she'd seen them...all of them. It made him sick to think his beast could betray her so easily. How in the hell Kate could ever look at him again was beyond comprehension. There was evil and darkness deep inside him, and even she could never completely take that out of him, he hated his beast for doing this to them both.

***

Kate tucked Lorenzo into his crib. He'd fed from Nita and then Theresa helped her bathe him then slide his chubby little body into a fresh onesie. Kate giggled at his plumpness as she leaned down and softly kissed Lorenzo's round cheeks. "Sleep, my precious."

She turned to leave the nursery when she felt Shade's turmoil roll through her. Kate paused for a second, sorting out the emotion. They were all on high alert, waiting for some response from Max, but Kate didn't feel danger, just pain and anger. She hurried from the room and down the stairs, letting her senses draw her to his location in the study. She stepped through the open door to find him at the desk, the photos scattered before him, some on the floor at his feet.

"No!" Kate ran to him and started grabbing up the photos, tearing them into small pieces. "Don't look at them! Don't let him hurt us more than he has. They're nothing! They mean nothing! This isn't you."

He felt the hell roll through her, just like it did him and he was once again fucking helpless to stop the pain they both felt. "Kate, I can never apologize enough, and no, it was not me. Max betrayed us both. But I guarantee you one thing, that bastard will pay. I needed to see these. It fires my blood to lop that son of a bitch's head off and bring it to you on a silver platter!"

"Shade, I have no doubt you'll destroy Max. But there's only one thing I wanted Max to know. He can't break us. He can't separate us. We'll always be stronger together than we'll ever be apart. He can mate for power. He thinks he's invincible now with her father's armies, but his mating will never match the power of our love. They all doubt us still. They doubt me because I was mortal. They still don't understand."

Pulling her onto his lap, he leaned his forehead against hers, their red and raven hair falling together around their faces. "I love you so much. You are my ultimate strength in all that lies before me. They will always question your power because they do not understand and think you weak. But they are wrong, and that is our advantage. But fucking help me, you can't go out on that battlefield for any reason. I cannot lose you. You need to let me handle this. You need to trust me more than you ever have before. Because this is what I do, and I do this for you and Lorenzo. I can get through anything if I know you are waiting safely for me. Please, I am begging, *mi amore*, you must promise me you will stay inside with Luca during the battle."

Kate listened to his plea. "I'll stay here. I must stay for Lorenzo. I know Luca will guard us, but I'll guard Lorenzo as well. But you must understand one thing. There's nothing that we can't rebuild. Don't sacrifice your life for this land. Promise me. Promise me you'll come back to me."

Clutching her tight, he moved his hands up her back, fisting her hair. "No son of a bitch is taking you from me! I will fight and kill for you. I will win for you, *mi amore*." His voice sounded guttural and dark. His beast was speaking his oath to her. He could feel his fangs elongate. "What is mine remains mine." His growl was deep. Sinking his fangs into her neck, he drew deep, her blood easing his edginess, erasing the pain. He'd fought many battles for land, but this one, he fought for her.

His bite was sharp and unexpected as he held her in a tight grip and drank from her. She knew his beast was claiming her, letting her know that despite his betrayal, he still owned her and would destroy those who'd harm her. Kate gave herself up to him, letting him draw strength from her, knowing he'd need this and more to face what was ahead for both of them.

When his beast was done, his fangs retracted and he let go of the pain his actions had caused. He licked her wound gently, a lover who was sorrowful of his deeds. He stroked her hair and let his hands slide down her back. His lips were still at her neck, the taste of her still on his mouth.

"I am sorry, Kate, I did not mean to be so abrupt, you are so precious to me. Forgive your lover."

She ran her hands through his hair. She was immortal now, but she'd never know the depths of his darkness. She'd only seen what he'd allowed her to see, and she knew it was a deep cavern that she had only just seen around the edges.

"Shade, I know your beast. He takes what he wants. But I also know your beast will die for me. That is the beast I fear the most. I don't want you to die for me. I want you to live for me."

Kate covered his face with soft kisses, her lips brushing his closed eyes, his nose, his cheeks, before lingering on his lips. "There is nothing to forgive, lover. I know your heart."

"*Si*, you do, it belongs solely to you for all eternity." He kissed her with gentle passion. He was her savage lover, and she his walking sin.

133

Marco said his goodbyes to the warriors before leaving the camp and walking up to Bel Rosso. Since Shade had returned, they'd gone over everything, and it was time for him to return to Florence. Before he left, he wanted to see Terri one last time.

He hated to leave her, especially since this was most likely where the battle would be waged. He knew she'd be well protected, he just wished he was the one protecting her. He walked through the foyer and straight up the stairs. There wasn't much here that was off limits to him, not since Shade had lost his fucking mind and took off for Paris, leaving him in charge.

He knew exactly where he'd find her and headed for the nursery. Marco stood outside the baby's door, in the room where Terri often slept, and watched her and the queen fawning over Lorenzo. *Cazzo*, the prince would be turned to jelly and mush with all their damn pampering. He was warrior born, and Shade better be stepping in shortly or this baby would never be out from under any female's skirts.

Clearing his throat, he watched as they both turned their heads toward him. "Ladies, I'm taking my leave for Florence. Will you oblige me, my queen, and allow me to have a few moments alone with Terri?"

Kate smiled at his gruff voice. "Of course." Kate took Lorenzo from Theresa and nodded to her. "Go to him. Take your time. I'm fine here."

Theresa stood and joined him at the door, slipping her hand inside his, as she led him to her private bedroom in the house. Once inside, she closed the door behind them. "The time went by so quickly. I can't believe it's time for you to leave already."

Crushing her to his chest, he let out a deep sigh. "I don't want to leave you, but I have no damn choice in the matter. I want you to be careful, stay in the bunker. Shade and I have done all we can to make sure Bel Rosso is safe and well protected. The warriors won't let you down, but I still worry about you. I know you'll lay down your life to save her and the baby. It is your duty, as it is mine. That does not mean I like it."

"Marco, I fear more for you. I'll be fine. I'll be locked below ground in the bunker with Lorenzo. This house will be protected and Luca will remain on the inside. If the war comes to Florence, you'll be the one in the thick of it, leading the charge, no doubt. It's you I beg to be careful."

Smiling at her, he knew deep in his heart no other would have his love. "I am warrior, Medici at that. I have seen many battles and I'll come out on top. I really think the action will be here and not Florence, but there is something I beg you to do for me." He kissed her softly on the lips.

"If it is in my power to grant it, Marco, I will. What do you ask of me?"

He released her, pacing as he turned to look at her. "I know you'll be with the baby and Kate. Whatever you do, keep her the hell inside this house. She can be as hot-headed and stubborn as he is. We can't lose them both. If you can keep her calm, do it."

He knew Shade would fight to the death if it came to that, but the coven would need at least one of them to raise Lorenzo and make sure he was ready to assume his rightful place.

"You have healing skills, you know the old ways, Terri. They'll need you, just tell me you will be careful."

He lowered his head, locking eyes with her. He reached inside his leathers, removing a blood vial and placing it in her hands.

She felt him slip the vial in her hands. She didn't need to look at it to know what it was. His blood would sustain her for a while if she was injured, until someone could get to her.

"I understand your concern. My lady always had a temper, even before she was turned. She has as much warrior spirit as he does. My heart tells me she'll stay with Lorenzo. She understands she and Luca represent the last line of defense for the prince. I can't imagine she'd leave him. She'd lay down her life for Shade, but she also understands Lorenzo is the future of Medici and he must be protected at all cost. Our queen understands her obligations, Marco. But I'll do as you ask if it comes to that. Luca, Gi, we'll all work hard to convince her that her place is here."

Nodding, Marco embraced her, holding her close as he slid his tongue along her neck. "I love you, Terri. I don't know when I'll be able to return...when I'll see you again. This could take weeks, perhaps months, before it all ends and things get back to normal. But Shade promised me, once things settle down we'll be able to spend time together again. I need to go now."

His heart was heavy, but he was warrior and knew his duty would always come first. Lingering, he couldn't seem to let go. "I'll always remember this moment, right here, right now. Tell me what I need to hear. I can't move until you do."

She laid her head against his chest. "Stay safe for me, Marco. Stay safe for us. I love you. I've always loved you."

He laid his head atop hers and for the first time in his life, he felt pain in his heart, torn between duty and love. Never once in the past had he ever thought about what he was leaving behind, he fought for Medici and nothing more. But now, he'd given his heart to someone he must leave a world away, in what would surely be the epicenter of the battle, and he could do nothing to protect her.

Wrapping his hand in her hair, he burrowed deep and inhaled her scent to get him through whatever lay ahead. "*Ti amo*." Teleporting out, he headed home, leaving their future in the hands of fate.

Theresa stood alone in her bedroom. She walked to the window and looked out over Bel Rosso. It wasn't actually her bedroom, it was the bedroom given to her by her master. Just as Marco returned to Florence to protect what was master's. Neither of them was truly free to pursue any other path in this life. This was the path they were born to follow. It wasn't something Theresa allowed herself to think about often. She knew there were many in her position that had masters who were cruel, or uncaring. She knew she had been blessed in many ways to be included in this coven, which functioned as one large family. But still, it was the master's baby she held, not her own. She placed the vial around her neck and slipped it beneath her blouse before returning to the nursery.

134

The night was bitter cold and Shade felt as if it was a foreboding of sorts. He stood to look out the window and found it was snowing. "Fuck, snow. No damn wonder it is cold as a witch's tit in here tonight!"

The fireplace was blazing, the sound of the fire crackling, and the smell of the burning wood permeating the house. He heard rustling upstairs, and he sighed. Cory was up, and he needed to talk with him about what to expect. He'd been so caught up in the preparations for the war that he'd not taken the time to prepare his son. Plus, Cory had been busy, day and night, making leathers for the pending battle.

Shade made his way up the stairs to Cory's room and damn near got knocked ass over heels as Cory came barreling down the hall from his room. Shade grabbed his sleeve and whipped Cory around to face him. "Where do you think you are going?"

Cory looked up at his dad, surprised to encounter him here. "I have some things to wrap up in the shop, I won't be long."

Cory turned to leave, but Shade didn't let go of his sleeve. Cory sighed and rolled his eyes at him. "What?"

Shade almost laughed out loud at his eye rolling and exasperated sigh. He thought he'd better get used to it; he'd have more teenage attitudes to deal with in the future. "Watch your tongue. We need to talk."

Shade maneuvered him toward the door of his suite and led him inside. He looked around the rooms Kate had carefully designed for him and shook his head. There were clothes strewn everywhere, pizza boxes piled on the table in the living area, and the handsets for his video games on the sofa. Several skateboards were left on the floor and one in a chair.

Shade turned to him and Cory held up his hands in surrender. "Hey, I've been busy... I didn't have time to clean up."

Shade shook his head. "Close the door, son."

Cory closed the door and knew if his dad sought him out something must be wrong. Whatever it was, he hoped he didn't send his ass packing back to California for safety. He didn't want to go. He wanted to be here with everyone else.

Shade looked about the room. "I could assign the house staff to clean up after you, but I chose not to. These are your rooms, and your responsibility. So, first things first, get this suite cleaned up. You will have some time on your hands to do so."

Cory flopped down in an empty lounge chair. "Sure, but what do you mean, I'll have time?"

Shade paced around the room. "Cory, this battle is coming, and it could come at any moment. This is serious. I don't want you in the camp any longer. You are confined to the house for now. This is not a punishment. Your safety is vital to me, more so than I have words to tell you. You are my first-born son."

Cory stood up, his anger obvious, his pride injured. "I can defend myself, I'm not some kid. I'm vampire...maybe only a half breed, but you're my father, which means I'm Medici. I'm not helpless!"

Shade let him blow off steam before he responds. "Of course you are not helpless. But you are not a warrior. You will have a weapon, as will Kate. But you will stay inside with her and Lorenzo. You will listen to me, Cory. This is your life we are talking about! You have no idea what is facing this coven, but I do! I have just found you and I'll be damned if anyone is going to take you from me!"

Shade pulled him up from the chair and into his chest, hugging his son. "I love you, Cory. I can't lose you. I'm not banishing you to the bunker with the house staff. Kate and Luca will be inside this house and you will be with them. Lorenzo will be with Gi, Theresa, Nita, and Shannon, locked inside the bunker. But I am letting you stay out here with Kate and Luca. I know you can shoot. Marcello told me he and Fiamma have been giving you some lessons, and you are doing a great job with it."

Cory knew his dad would protect him, protect them all, but he wanted a chance to show he could be a part of this family too. "I *can* shoot, but I suck at swords, and shuriken's aren't my thing. But I can shoot. I want to help! Everyone here has a role, don't keep me out. It hurts."

Shade observed his struggle. "Cory, you do have a role, you clothe my warriors for battle. Marcello tells me you have a 50 caliber rifle and a new Glock handgun. Keep the Glock by your bed when you sleep and keep it on you at all times when you are awake. If we are under attack, Kate and Luca will come here to your suite. High ground. Luca can see everything from here, and he has a 360 degree view. My warriors will work hard to keep the battle away from the house, but if any of Max's warriors break through, it will be up to you and Luca to stop them. The 50 cal is long range. You can take them out long before they get in the house. Can you do that?"

Cory grinned. "Oh hell yeah!"

Shade chuckled. "The Glock is for closer range combat. You would not survive hand to hand combat with another warrior, so take those bastards out before they get to you, son. They're strong, but they're not immune to bullets."

Cory picked up the Glock, listening to the sound of the clip as he slid it in place and grinned. "I feel better now."

"Good, that's what I want. Now, you need to get this place cleaned up. *Cazzo*, you are worse than I ever was!"

Cory laughed. "I doubt it. I hear Kate mumbling about you leaving your shit everywhere! Wait! I have something for you!"

Cory jogged into his bedroom and pulled out the huge box, buried under his dirty clothes. Returning to the living room, he handed the box to Shade. "This is for you, Dad, for the battle."

Shade took the huge box and looked at him questioningly. He laid the box on the table and opened the lid. It held a full set of battle leathers. He felt the lump in his throat grow as his hand slid over the softest leather, the Medici crest hand-tooled on the chest plate. They were the most intricate and elaborate leathers he'd ever seen. Cory watched him and his pride grew along with the smile on his face. He'd spent every second of his free time crafting them specifically for his dad.

"I made them just for you. They're unique. No other warrior has anything like them. The leather I used is extremely supple, flexible, for ease of movement. I made you some arm guards as well. There's also heavier padding along the thigh area. The pants have a lot of places for you to sheath shuriken's and knives. And these straps are for your swords, so you can strap them to your back. I designed them just for you."

Shade held up the leathers but had no words. Cory went to him, hugging him tight. "It's okay, Dad, just wear them. I worry about you too."

Shade kissed the top of his shaggy head and held him tight. "Thank you, son. I will wear them with great pride. I love you, Cory."

Cory was filled with pride. "*Per sempre* Medici."

135

It was another bitter cold night. Kate stood at the window of the nursery holding Lorenzo on her shoulder as she swayed gently side to side, singing to him. It had snowed heavily, and the rolling hills shined bright under the full moon, the trees casting shadows against the white snow. She saw Aegis in the distance, anxiously pacing in the tree line. The wolf's behavior seemed odd, as she and Night Stalker had both stayed close to the house since they'd come back from Florence with Lorenzo. Nita had just finished feeding Lorenzo and was preparing to return to the staff quarters when Kate asked her to wait.

"Is everything all right, my lady?"

Kate continued to look out the window as Aegis took off, racing through the woods, and Night Stalker joined her. Kate furrowed her brow. "I'm not sure. Just...hang on a minute."

Theresa entered the nursery with clean sheets for Lorenzo's crib when she looked up, "What is it, my lady?"

Kate shook her head as she felt an anxious knot in her stomach. "Something's off with Aegis and Night Stalker. They're reacting to something. I can feel their fear."

As she stood at the window, she heard the mournful howl of the wolves, echoing through the night. She was about to step closer to the window, to see if she could see them when she was startled by a loud bang against the glass. Kate clung to Lorenzo and gasped, stepping back quickly as both Nita and Theresa emitted small cries of surprise. Kate was about to run from the room when she heard an incessant pecking at the glass and looked back to see Poe, frantically pecking and flapping his wings. The howling was far in the distance now but was nonstop. Kate slowly backed away from the window. They were warning her of danger. She saw the falcon swoop in close and land in a tree outside the window, her screech ear-piercingly loud. In a flash, Kate knew what this meant. It was what the warriors had been preparing for.

She screamed loudly, "Shade!"

Shade looked at Luca as they both heard the wolves howling in the distance, even here in the underground bunker. He heard her scream his name and he responded, instantly teleporting to her side with Luca right behind him, his dagger drawn, ready to protect her. Cory barreled into the room in his stocking feet, sliding into Nita as he tried to stop, the Glock raised in the air.

"*Cazzo, mi amore*, what is it? Tell me what you know!"

Lorenzo could sense their anxiety and began to cry, pulling on Kate's hair.

"Is it Lorenzo?"

Kate shook her head. "Not Lorenzo. He's responding to my fear. It's Max. His warriors. Aegis and Night Stalker have tracked them to the south and east. Danica and Riparo tracked them to the north. His warriors approach from three sides. There are many...lover, there are hundreds."

He wrapped his arms around her and the baby, holding them to his chest. "Luca, get everyone in their positions, now! Cory, get some fucking boots and leathers on. Move!"

He telepathically relayed to Marcello all the information Kate had told him and instructed him to gather the warriors and be ready to roll—the time had come. Shade turned to Theresa. "Give me a second with Kate. You and Nita stay right outside this room. I will want you to take Lorenzo in a moment, but first, I need to speak with Kate alone."

She nodded as the two females scurried outside the room. Shade clung to Kate as she held Lorenzo in her arms. He could feel her body shaking and her fear building.

"Listen to me. Calm down, you can't be upset, it only upsets Lorenzo. Go to the bunker with him, stay there. I will come for you when this is over. I will know you are safe inside with our son. Luca can stay outside of the bunker, nothing will get past him."

Kate shook her head. "That's not the plan. Lorenzo will be kept in the bunker, but the animals will give me information that will protect us all. I can't seal myself off from them. Let Theresa and Nita take Lorenzo, and go with Gi, Emma and Shannon to the bunker. That's what we planned. I'll stay here in the house, with Luca and Cory. I need to be able to feel Aegis. She'll warn me of anything in advance. It's our best way to protect Lorenzo."

He stared at her, his heart torn. It was what they'd discussed, but he'd never had so much to lose before. His hand slid down her cheek, and reluctantly, he nodded his acceptance.

He called for Theresa, holding Lorenzo against his chest then kissed him. He looked into Lorenzo's eyes as he handed him over to Theresa. "*Ti amo, mio figlio*."

He ordered Theresa to the bunker. She knew what to do. She'd been in this position before. Turning to Kate, he took her hand and led her to their bedroom. The leathers Cory had made were lying out across the chair. He dressed in minutes, loading all his weapons. He could feel her eyes boring into him. He sat down in the chair by the window, staring out into the night, the moon lighting the snow covered grounds he must now go out to defend. His voice was strong, as he remained calm when he spoke to her.

"Braid your warrior's hair. Make it tight and strong, like our love. I do this for us." He held up a strap of red leather. "Entwine this in my hair, I need you with me in spirit."

She took the leather strip from his hand, trying to hide the shaking in her own hands. Stepping behind the chair, she carefully braided his hair, keeping the red leather strip tight as she knotted the end. Leaning over, she kissed his neck, pausing there, inhaling his scent as she slid her hand down his chest. She would keep her worry to herself. With her lips at his ear, she whispered, "Fight for me, warrior. Fight for your son."

As her hand slid across his chest, resting on the Medici crest, he laid his hand over hers. "I know you are frightened, you cannot hide it. Before the sun rises, I will be back, and Bel Rosso will still be ours."

He felt her hair cascade along his neck as they took one moment to look out over the fields and mountains that were now home. He telepathically contacted Marco and Reynaldo, letting them know the battle was upon them. They both responded that all was calm so far, and in that, he found comfort.

Max was bringing the battle right where Shade wanted it, his own front yard. Marco was prepared to send in waves of warriors from Florence as needed. He'd not let Bel Rosso be taken from them. Pulling *bel* into his lap, he looked into her eyes. "I love you. I will come home, I promise you. You must remain inside this house, no matter what you feel or see. You are not to leave the house, Kate. Not even for me."

He leaned down and kissed her like it was the last kiss they'd ever share. He could feel what was to come, but he'd fight to his death, if necessary, and no one would stop him. This was what he'd been born to do, fight for his mate, his son, and all that was to come for Medici. It rested on his shoulders.

"How far away are they? Ask them, I need to know, *bel*."

Kate closed her eyes, honed her senses to find Aegis, then nodded her head. "She said they're still about five miles from our property line, although some are on the land adjacent to ours we just purchased."

Nodding, he pulled her head to his shoulder and inhaled deeply of her rose scent. "I need to feed from you, *mi amore*. It is one more weapon that will help me come home to you."

Kate pulled her hair back from her neck and moved close to his lips. "Take from me."

Kate clung to him as she felt the sweet sting of his fangs into her flesh. She fought the tears. He'd not want to see her cry. She wrapped both arms around him as he fed.

He savored the taste of her and felt his beast rise, ready to take on this battle. He felt the transformation of his body as he prepared for war. He felt powerful, and ready. He licked her wound, watching it heal and heard the sounds from outside as his army gathered, ready to carry out their birthright as warriors and use all the skills they'd been so expertly trained on.

He kissed her hard, her blood still on his lips. Moving her from his lap, he sat her back down on the chair and strapped the huge swords on his back. He stood before her, tall and proud, his muscles outlined in the leather, his breathing steady. His eyes blazed red.

"Put your leathers on, my queen. It is time to defend our kingdom, our throne, and our coven. *Per sempre* Medici."

Luca stepped inside the room, looking much the same, dressed for battle. They stared at each other, no words needed. Luca had checked the house and had everyone in the bunker. "Everything is secured, master."

Shade walked toward him, they bumped fists and Shade headed for the door. He turned slowly on his heels and looked back at Kate. She mouthed the words, 'I love you'. He winked at her and smiled before walking out the door, seeing Cory, dressed in leathers, his Glock in the waistband. He paused to look at his son before pulling him to his chest and kissing his forehead. "You know what to do."

Cory nodded and Shade continued on his way. He didn't need to say anything. This was his family and they knew what was about to happen, each of them had much at stake. His stride was strong as he headed down the stairs and out the door. He heard the loud roar of his warriors as he appeared in front of them.

"*Per sempre* Medici!"

He barked his orders and all warriors scattered to defend. They were split into three battalions, awaiting the arrival of the throng of Max's warriors. Marcello held Impavido's reins as Shade mounted the horse. Marcello took off, running to his designated post.

Shade kept watch as his warriors moved into position, as he constantly turned Impavido in a slow circle while keeping his senses open and alert. Impavido snorted and pawed. They were a team, and the horse was ready, just like his master.

Kate had watched him leave, her voice caught in her throat. She knew if she spoke her voice would crack with emotion.

Luca turned to her. "Where's your crossbow?"

She pointed to the closet.

Luca took charge, directing her. "Put on your leathers, Kate, and get the crossbow. We'll move to the third floor. Cory's rooms will give us the best visual advantage."

Kate ran to the closet and pulled down the leathers. It was only the second time she'd put them on. She dragged the crossbow from behind the door and stood quietly for a second. She took a deep breath before she stepped out of the closet. "Ready."

The three of them climbed the stairs to Cory's third floor suite. Luca armed with a number of weapons, Cory with the 50 cal rifle as well as the handgun, and Kate with the crossbow. Luca opened the windows slightly, despite the cold, so they could respond with weapons fire, if it came to that.

Kate saw Danica in the tree outside the window. She sent a message to Aegis to watch over them. She saw the she-wolf and her mate emerge from the tree line and approach the house, prancing around the perimeter. Riparo stalked on padded feet, as she also moved in closer to the house. Kate knew nothing was getting inside without getting past the animal guard.

***

Max had gathered his warriors from the Virginia coven. They only numbered fifty and were no match for the skills of the Medici, but he also had four hundred warriors from Fan Shen, and their skills would stand up well against Shade's army. They, too, were trained in the ancient art of warfare. Max had scoped out the lay of Shade's property and had decided to surround him on three sides, as his land backed up against the mountain range. Besides, the mountains belonged to the mortals, and Shade wouldn't want to take his warriors to that high ground. Max was mounted on a war horse and rode in front of his troops who marched on foot, moving into position. Max had heard the howling of wolves all evening as he had moved his warriors into position, stirred up no doubt by all the activity. He knew when he hit Shade's property line, whoever he had on patrol would see them, but he still had the element of surprise.

***

Shade felt the air stir, and Max's scent rolled through the fields. Impavido raised his head in the air, swinging his mane back and forth, and Shade patted him hard on the neck. "Good boy, let's get this bastard."

Shade kicked Impavido slightly in the sides and pulled the reins and faced him straight in Max's direction. He whipped out a sword strapped on his back and held it high in the air, signaling his warriors the enemy approached and to hold their position. All the warriors drew their weapons and stood their ground. Shade moved Impavido to the head of the line, his sword held high, the steel blade reflecting the light of the moon.

Max was confident as he led his warriors over the crest of the hill, but stopped short when he saw Shade, on horseback, with his army standing behind him. He held up his hand and stopped the forward motion. He'd been certain he had the element of surprise and expected to get well onto Bel Rosso property while the Medici scrambled to respond. Somehow, they were prepared and ready for him. Perhaps they'd had a scout. Max circled on his war horse, eyeing Shade across the field.

He spoke to him telepathically. **"So, it has come to this, old friend? A fight to the death?"**

Shade heard the words ring loud and clear inside his head and answered him. "**You cannot win. You challenge the Medici. Prepare to die."**

Sitting straight in his saddle, Impavido reared up on his hind legs, his front legs pawing the air high above the warriors' heads, signaling to the troops it was time to meet the challenge. His warriors crouched in a ready position, swords held high.

Max signaled to his troops as they stormed across the field, running head long into the Medici. Their swords were drawn, and they issued a loud war cry, prepared to win or die this night. The two armies encountered each other, and the night was filled with the sound of metal against metal as they fought with drawn swords. Max had lost the element of surprise, but he still had the advantage of numbers. His army was five times larger, and he knew even the Medici couldn't stand against those odds.

Shade watched as Max gave the signal and the enemy barreled toward them. He telepathically called to Kate. ***"Ti amo, mi amore."***

He lowered his sword and the Medici war cry rang loud, echoing off the mountains as his warriors swarmed around him and headed straight at Max and his army, much larger than his. He backed Impavido up slowly, as the warriors kept moving forward. He kept as close to the house as he could, watching the deployment of his warriors, led by his Lieutenants and SIC's.

He'd remain in contact with Marco, who'd release more troops from Florence in waves as needed. He kept his guard up. He needed to command, but he was also their target. If he went down, the battle was over. He rode around the perimeter, signaling to Marco for the next wave of warriors who teleported in, landing on the field with the other Medici warriors, and immediately throwing themselves into battle. The sounds of battle were tremendous and deafening, but all he heard in his head was the sound of her voice telling him she loved him. It was the most powerful motivation he'd ever felt.

Kate watched them all from the third floor window. Shade was easy to single out as he sat astride the massive black stallion in the white snow, the moonlight flashing off his sword. Her heart was pounding in her chest when she heard his message of love for her. **"Fight for me, lover."**

Raven led a platoon of warriors to the east, his troops made up of both experienced warriors from Florence as well as some of the new recruits. He was singled out by one of Max's Virginia warriors, who must be twice Raven's size. Raven laughed as he flipped quickly over the enemy's head, landing behind him and sliding the sword deep into his back. As his enemy dropped to his knees, Raven swung the sword and watched the head roll, blood spilling out on the white snow. He heard the footsteps behind him and spun around, swinging the sword in a large arc, and cutting his enemy in two. As usual, his enemies mistook his size as a weakness when his speed more than made up for it.

Fiamma waited for the signal to attack the enemy approaching from the south when she saw Shade blaze past her on Impavido, lowering his sword. She led her battalion into battle as she teleported over the first wave of Max's warriors and attacked them from the rear. The death toll was great on the Medici end as they'd been outnumbered, but she didn't let that distract her. She was born to be a warrior. She swooped down, flinging shurikens at Max's troops as they threatened Medici. She watched her warriors pairing off, one on one, as she pulled out the bow, providing backup to her battalion, shooting the enemy, and taking them down with her deadly accurate arrows. Medici warriors demonstrated their skill, picking off the enemy one at a time.

Shade unleashed Marcello and his wave of warriors from the north side. Shade watched as the snow becomes a slushy bath of red. Heads and limbs rolled under Impavido's hooves, and the night was filled with the screams of battle. Medici was taking a hellish hit but giving as good as they got.

He telepathically called for a second wave from Florence to reinforce his troops, and immediately divided them up to go in all three directions as Max drove closer to the house. The smell of death hung heavy in the air as he watched his young new recruits as they first struggled, then were felled, no match for the experienced warriors of Fan Shen.

Shade's beast was on his back, wanting loose like never before. He rode like the flames of hell straight into the throngs of battle, his sword swinging mightily from his arm. He rode like the devil himself, beheading anything in his path. His body was splattered in blood and he kept riding, having sent Marco the request for the final wave from Florence. They were badly outnumbered and must rely on their skill and experience to survive.

Bodies of fallen warriors, both Medici and enemy, were strewn over miles of Bel Rosso. The blood ran like a river through the white snow. Shade dismounted Impavido and smacked his haunches, the horse taking off for the mountains and out of sight. Shade drew his other sword from his back, and with a sword in each hand, went hand to hand with the enemy.

***

Kate watched the slaughter of both Medici and enemy warriors. Her hand was over her mouth, covering her silent scream. She followed the battle and could see Raven, his hair unbound, flew free. Fiamma was also easy to spot in red leathers and red hair. Marcello fought near Shade, and Kate gasped out loud when Shade dismounted and began to fight hand to hand with the enemy. She could see Skelk as he climbed a tree, using his skills with the crossbow to rapidly take down enemy after enemy. Her senses remained on high alert, and she felt Aegis and the others close by.

Although the number of bodies on the ground seemed equal between Medici and enemy, the Medici were still outnumbered and they were getting pushed back, closer to the house. Kate's heart was pounding out of her chest. She looked over her shoulder to see Cory with the rifle, standing guard at the window on the other side of the room. Luca was standing right behind her, watching the scene unfold as he looked over her shoulder. Kate looked at his face, emotionless, his face shows nothing.

"Is this...normal?"

Luca didn't answer her, but stared straight ahead at the massacre taking place below.

Shade battled on. His mind focused only on what was coming at him and come at him they did. He was their target, and he'd thrown down the gauntlet when he dismounted Impavido. His feet slipped and slid under him in the mush of snow and blood, but he kept going, taking on two, sometimes three, at a time. He focused on one thing, kill or be killed.

This was no ordinary army he faced, but rivals of equal ability and endurance. His arms ached, his body tired. It felt like they'd been at it for hours. He dared not look at the moon to see where she lay in the sky; he couldn't afford even that brief moment of inattention. He felt a shuriken breeze past his cheek and turned in that direction to face whatever was coming. Two of Max's warriors approached him. They were small and deadly, their speed amazing, he grounded his feet to face these opponents when two more dropped in behind him, and he was surrounded.

As he moved to spin and backflip over their heads, his feet slid in the mixture of blood and snow, slowing his motions only a second, but it was one second too many and he felt the blade strike him from behind. The blade struck deep and made him lurch forward as it wedged into his rib cage. His scream was a roar as he dropped to his knees in agonizing pain. He felt his blood gush out, running between his fingers as he clutched at the wound in his chest, feeling the heat of the blood running down his back and legs from the entry wound in his back. He gasped for air, his body shaking with the shocking blow of the deadly blade. He mustered his focus and strength to defend himself against the attempted fatal blow to his head, taking out that enemy by severing his arm with a swing of his sword. Shade felt like he could barely move, his body sluggish from the blood loss, making him dizzy, but he fought to keep his eyes and energy focused.

Marcello was close enough to hear Shade's roar and moved backward toward him to help as much as he could. Master was down! He took out the two remaining enemy, beheading them in a fast spin. He felt something whiz past his face and all he saw was black hair and realized it was Raven, also responding to his master.

Marcello felt the shurikens whizzing past him, as the enemy sensed their vulnerable position and moved to swarm them. He could barely see anything through the blood, as the mass of bodies piled up under his feet when he felt a shuriken lodge into his leg. Reaching down, he ripped it free, and used it to throw back at the enemy. He fought like never before, his only thought being to protect Shade.

***

Kate saw him the instant Shade was struck with the blade. She felt the stabbing pain in her chest and she too dropped to her knees as she let out a scream. "Shade!"

She jumped up and started to run from the room when Luca grabbed her. She kicked and clawed at him, fighting to get free.

"You can't go out there, Kate. Let the warriors help him!"

Kate struggled to get free, but his words rang in her head. *Let the warriors help him!* Why hadn't she thought of this before? She screamed at the top of her lungs. "*Aegis! Help him! Bring them all!*"

She broke free from Luca and was running back to the window when she heard Cory mutter, “Holy fuck!” Kate stopped and looked in his direction. "What's wrong?"

He looked over his shoulder. "They're everywhere!"

"Max’s warriors?" she asked.

He shook his head. "No. Animals. The animals."

Kate rushed to the window to see a wave of wolves and mountain lions coming over the crest of the hill, approaching Max's warriors from the rear. She saw others streaming around both sides of the house as they poured down from the mountain tops. The wolves and mountain lions tore into Max's army, ripping with teeth and claws, shaking and slinging the limp bodies in their massive jaws. The light of the moon was temporarily blocked out as the sky was filled with falcons and owls, who dive-bombed the warriors, the large birds of prey using their talons to rip at them. The sound of the large flock of raucous ravens was almost deafening as they flew into the faces of the enemy, using their long beaks to peck at their eyes, never letting up. As the enemy struggled to fight off the hoard of beasts, the Medici took control, and systematically slaughtered their opponents, beheading one after the other as fast as they could swing their swords.

***

Shade felt the rumble of the earth under his knees and had no fucking idea what was coming for them next. He heard the loud caw of the ravens and looked up to see the sky blacken with their swarm. He knew Marcello and Raven both responded to him and kept him from going down. But he was still bent over, trying to gather his focus before standing up. He heard the growls and ripping of flesh and lifted his head and couldn't believe what he saw. The animals had been summoned! His *bel* has called them!

Marcello stooped near him as Raven stood guard. "Stay still. We have this under control now. Feed from me. You need to heal before you try to stand. You took a good hit and lost a lot of blood. *Cazzo*, like some damn third world war with these animals. Just fucking glad I'm Medici tonight!"

Shade let out a grunt as Marcello shoved his wrist in front of his mouth and Shade felt his fangs punch through. His beast fed like he was starved, and he could feel his body begin to heal. His dizziness left him, but he didn't want to feed too heavily on Marcello. He, too, was drained and tired, as were all the warriors. Marcello helped him to stand and what he saw before him was unbelievable. The carnage on the field was unlike anything he'd seen, and almost nothing was left of Max's army, the animals had destroyed them.

***

Max felt the earth move under his feet and stared in disbelief as they were surrounded by wild beasts. The wolves and mountain lions were ripping his army apart, but they did not attack the Medici. *What the fuck is this?* He swung his sword, striking at a mountain lion that was prepared to leap on him. He heard footsteps behind him and turned to see a scrawny leather clad warrior with long black hair. Max almost laughed to himself. Did this runt realize he'd cornered the master? As Raven raised his sword, Max responded with a defensive move, blocking the blow. He spun and struck Raven's blade hard, knocking the scrawny warrior off balance. Max was about to behead him when Poe swooped down and pecked at his eyes. Max dropped one arm and threw it across his face. As he did, Raven kicked Max's legs out from under him and he hit the ground with a thud. Max went into a fast roll and jumped to his feet as Poe continued to torment him, striking endlessly at his face and eyes, blinding him to what was around him. He saw enough to know his army was falling by the hundreds. He called his war horse, who found him on the field of battle. Max leapt on the back of the horse and called for his army to retreat. Of the four hundred and fifty warriors he'd started with, he had maybe fifty remaining, and they all had injuries. He rode like all of Hell was behind him and away from the battlefield, as his warriors teleported out. Poe returned to Raven and landed on his shoulder. He issued a loud caw, only inches from Raven's ear. Raven knew he owed his life to the bird.

136

Shade felt his body sink, his heart sore from the loss of so many. He and his warriors watched Max's retreat, but Bel Rosso was covered in the blood of Medici and Maximus' warriors, shed for this land he now called home. The air was thick with the stench of death as the animals retreated to the edge of the woods. His body was tired, but he was still in one piece, his *bel* safely inside, as were his two sons.

They'd move into the future now, with this land and all of Virginia as part of his territory. He moved slowly, with the help of Marcello, through the snow soaked in blood, stepping in silence over the bodies and body parts of the fallen. There wasn't much time before sunrise and the rays of the sun would scorch the death from this land, and there was much yet to be done.

As he walked, he mustered his strength, now walking on his own without Marcello. He must still lead them. They'd taken a grave blow to their ranks this night. Both Florence and Bel Rosso warriors suffered losses. He telepathically let Marco know they'd been victorious, but their numbers had been severely diminished, and he needed help here for mass burial of the Medici bodies, or what remained of them. Within twenty minutes, Marco had sent him another battalion from Florence, and they worked with his warriors to gather the bodies of the fallen Medici, digging the shallow graves on the field of battle. The enemy dead would be left where they lay to be taken by the sun.

Shade assembled his top ranking warriors to give them orders, take stock of injuries, and coordinate with Aislynn to perform triage and get the warriors with the greatest blood loss in to feed first. He would need Theresa's skill with healing as well, as soon as the warriors had fed.

Raven joined him with Poe on his shoulder and Shade had no energy to even wonder what the hell that was about. Each of his ranking warriors gave him a head count of the fallen from their battalion. Marcello said he lost thirty, Raven said twenty-five. He scanned the crowd and didn't see her. Skelk stepped forward and said the count was fifteen. Shade gave him a quizzical look, still scanning the surviving troops. He looked back at Skelk who shook his head.

"She didn't make it."

Shade's heart lurched. He shook his head no, telling Skelk he must be mistaken. She was just missing in all this chaos. He closed his eyes and honed all his senses on Fiamma, but he felt nothing, and he knew. He almost fell to his knees. She was gone, his Fee.

His roar filled the night and all around him come to a halt. He looked at Marcello and watched his face as the agonizing reality of what had happened hit him. Marcello approached Shade, only to be brushed aside as Shade still struggled to accept the inevitable.

"No! I will find her!"

Shade used the last of his precious energy, energy he needed to heal himself, to teleport over the battlefield and spotted her red leathers and red hair, lying in the blood covered snow around her. He landed beside her body, sprawled out face up, her sword still in her outstretched hand. She'd been struck through in the heart, the enemy's sword still sticking from her dead body.

He knelt beside her, his heart slammed with grief. He'd seen hundreds of warriors perish in his lifetime, and he carried the burden of each of them, but this was different. She'd grown up in his camp, trained by him, and fought beside him for so long.

He let his hand slide through her hair. Her face was solemn and peaceful. She'd given her life for his. His body shook and he couldn't hold back the tears that spilled from his eyes. At least she'd died a warrior's true death.

He stood up and placing both hands around the hilt of the sword, then withdrew it from her body. He gently slid his hands under her and lifted her into his arms. Her red hair was cascading down, having come undone from the long braid she always wore in battle. He carried her limp body in his arms, walking the several acres in the cold back to the barracks as his memories of their past battles ran through his mind.

He'd not leave her body to be buried in the shallow grave with the rest, waiting for the burning rays of the sun to turn them to ash before they were covered. He'd take her back to the barracks and keep her underground, until they could have the memorial reserved for warriors of rank, and she'd remain forever a part of Bel Rosso, where she belonged.

He walked with his head held high, past the other warriors as they stood watching. He carried her down the road and into the camp. He saw nothing, heard nothing—consumed with loss.

***

Kate saw him slowly rise, unsteady on his feet, as Marcello helped him. She watched as Max's warriors, what was left of them, surrender the field, and she knew the Medici had been victorious. Shade would heal. He'd drink her blood again and he'd heal. She saw his warriors gathering as he took a count, knowing he'd suffered many loses tonight. She saw him looking around in a panic before he teleported across the field and out of sight.

"Where'd he go?"

Luca shook his head. "Not sure. Looking for someone, I think."

Kate strained her eyes, searching for him against the snow, now running red with the blood of the fallen. She saw movement in the distance, and a cry escaped her lips, "Nooooo!"

She saw Shade as he carried a body she recognized immediately, dressed in red leather. Luca staggered backward, as he whispered her name. "Fee."

Kate tore across the room and ripped open the door, running down the two flights of stairs and out the back door. "Lover?"

Her path crossed his as he approached the barracks. "Lover...is she okay? She'll be okay. She only needs to feed!"

He looked up to see Kate, but he had trouble focusing his mind, the shock of losing Fee, and his injury, diluting his ability to focus. Standing still, holding Fiamma in his arms, his voice sounded as dead as he felt, as he answered in a monotone. "She is gone."

He fell to his knees, weak from loss of blood, his body bent over hers.

Kate dropped down beside him. He must be wrong! She picked up Fiamma's limp hand and shook her shoulder, "Fee!" She scored her wrist with her teeth and placed it on Fee's lips, already cold and blue. "Just feed! Feed from me!"

Luca pulled Kate back, swallowing hard. "It's too late, Kate."

She shrugged free from his grip. "No. You can't give up. Why are you giving up? She just needs to feed!"

Kate looked at the faces of the other warriors who'd gathered around her, Marcello, Raven, and Skelk. She screamed at them. "Do something!"

Aegis approached, her muzzle covered in blood from the battle, she sniffed at Fee and backed away, whining. Luca lifted Kate to her feet.

"Kate, the sword pieced her heart. It's a fatal blow. She's gone. It's too late."

Kate stumbled backward and fell hard, sitting down on the ground, the tears streaming down her face as she looked at Shade, who was feeling as broken as she was. "Lover, the price is too high. I cannot bear this pain."

He felt her pain merge with his own at this heinous loss of someone they both cared for so much. His looked to Marcello as he crouched across from him and took Fiamma from his arms. Marcello couldn't speak, his heart was broken. He simply nodded to Shade and walked into the barracks, carrying the body of his fallen sister

Everyone around him was in such pain from the loss and carnage left behind. He felt the sun rising and cringed. Raven came to him quickly and helped him up.

"Come on, boss-man, you need to get inside. We can use the tunnel. Lean on me."

Shade pushed him back. "*Mi amore*...come!"

He stood on shaking legs. He'd leave this battle on his own steam. Luca helped Kate stand and Shade took her in his arms, cradling her to his chest, and with his last ounce of energy he teleported them inside the house, inside their private bath. He willed the shower on and stepped inside with her, stripping them both of the leathers, his injuries even more vivid on his naked flesh. He slid down the wall of the shower, taking her in his arms, cradling her. He knew he'd feed from her, and her blood would heal, and his death slumber would take him into darkness. He was home, with *bel*. He'd tackle whatever came when the moon rose again.

But now, he needed to be with her to be whole again.

137

Kate helped him clean himself up. He never spoke a word but let her wash his hair and body. He heard her gasp as she saw the huge wound in his back and chest. His pain was both physical and mental, and the loss had taken its toll. He knew he had to step up, direct the warriors now, get things underway, and get them healed.

So much to do, yet he couldn't concentrate. He kept seeing Fiamma's face as she lay dead in the snow. Kate draped his arm over her shoulder and helped him into the bed as he laid down moaning. He needed to feed but was dead tired. He knew the sun was already up without needing to look at the electronic blinds. He could instinctively feel it. He wanted to feed, start healing, and fall into his death slumber. He groaned and tried to roll over and roared with the pain.

Kate winced at his pain. She was pretty sure this battle was done, as he'd pulled all his warriors from the field, but she wasn't going to take any chances. She sent a message to Theresa for her and Gi to join them in the bedroom, but to leave Shannon, Emma, Nita, and Lorenzo sealed in the bunker for now.

"Shade, lie still. Let me look at this."

Kate examined the deep wound made by a sword that was through and through. She knew he fed briefly from Marcello on the battlefield, but that wouldn't be enough to heal him. Theresa and Gi appeared suddenly and Kate had Theresa examine him.

Kate started issuing instructions "Gi, run to the camp, find Marcello or Luca, and get a full report of what's going on. I know they must have their hands full with the injured, but if we don't give Shade a sense that things are under control, I won't be able to keep him in this bed."

Gi nodded and took off for the camp. Kate could feel Lorenzo and knew he was quiet for the moment. "Was Lorenzo okay during the battle?"

Theresa was examining her master's wound. Kate had already cleaned him up in the shower, and Theresa retrieved a salve from her bedroom that would help with the healing. She spread the foul smelling ointment on the wound. She looked up as she saw Kate wrinkle her nose at the smell. "Something from the old country. It will help him heal faster. He needs this salve, keeping quiet, and you feeding him. He'll need to feed often, small feedings, so don't let him gorge himself."

Kate climbed across the bed, pushing his wet hair away from his face. She'd never seen him this pale. His eyes were closed, and she knew his death slumber was pulling at him as well. "Shade, feed from me now."

She and Theresa rolled him onto his back, and Kate leaned over him, her neck at his lips and felt his fangs when they broke through her skin. He drank from her, but was too weak, and too tired to hold her. Kate remained in position for him until Theresa nodded that it was enough for now. Kate pulled away, and kissed his lips, watching him sink deeper into his slumber. Theresa told her he'd awaken throughout the day, just as Lorenzo did, because he'd need to feed.

Kate pulled the blankets over him and curled her body around him, trying to keep him warm. "You didn't answer me about Lorenzo."

Theresa was cleaning up the bandages and securing the lid on the salve, "Oh, I'm sorry, my lady. He did fine. He can feel the same fear you feel, that his father feels. He knows when there's danger and will instinctively stay quiet. It's a survival mechanism. Nita will feed him, and he'll sleep now. He's fine."

Gi returned, teleporting into the bedroom. "My lady, I am sorry to say it is chaos in the camp. Many are injured and need to get into the feeder compound. Marcello and Aislynn are trying to manage, but there's much that needs attending to."

Kate sat up in the bed, looking at Shade. He was in no condition to respond and yet the warriors needed direction. She had no idea how to help them, but she knew who would. She'd never tried to communicate with Marco before, but she reached out now, asking him to come. She heard a simple response, **"My queen."**

Marco appeared minutes later, and Theresa's sigh of relief was audible. He slid his arm around Theresa's waist and kissed the top of her head. "Tell me what you need, my queen." He looked at Shade, and knew from his appearance the injury was severe, but he'd heal.

"Marco, please take over the camp. I know Marcello is SIC here, but he's young and doesn't have your experience. Luca's helping him, and I know Shade would be there now if he were able. Do whatever needs to be done."

Marco simply nodded to her and said, "It is done," as he teleported out of the room and to the camp.

Kate looked at Gi and Theresa. "Is there anything else? Am I forgetting anything?"

Theresa shook her head. "We've done all we can, my lady. Now we just need time."

Kate sat for a second and thought. "Don't bring Lorenzo out of the bunker yet. I don't think Max will be back, but I can't take that chance."

Theresa nodded and started to leave the room.

"And Theresa?"

She looked back from the doorway.

"He'll be all right, won't he?"

Theresa smiled at her. "Yes, my lady. He will heal...if you can keep him in that bed."

***

Marco teleported over the grounds, looking at the battlefield covered with bodies and abandoned weapons. The warriors he'd sent earlier had dug the shallow graves and gathered the fallen Medici. The sun had risen above the horizon, and the bodies began to steam and dissipate almost instantly. Once they reverted to ash, the Medici would be buried on the ground they fought to defend, and the ashes of the enemy would blow away with the wind.

Sighing heavily, it was time to kick some ass into gear. Teleporting into the camp, the day-walkers were outside, some injured worse than others. The first order of business was for him to assess their condition, get them to the feeders and get them back on their feet. He didn't fear anything from Maximus, his ass was long gone, and he doubted he'd ever return to the States. Max wouldn't have won any favor with his new father-in-law with this fiasco. "Fucking bastards."

He sought out Marcello, who was also worn to the bone, a large injury in his calf from a shuriken, his hands cut and torn from sword battle. Marcello gave him a quick update on the number of injured. Marco ordered all the warriors inside, and then telepathically called on his warriors in Greece to come help out. He'd keep the Greek battalion on guard while some of the Florence battalion finished the cleanup in the field, and others to help with the wounded.

Marco spotted the tall, young female with the black hair. She'd obviously not seen the ravages of a battle this size before, but she remained un-rattled. He beckoned her forward. "Name?"

Aislynn told him her name and her assignment during the battle.

"So, you were in charge of the feeder compound? You did well, warrior. I'm Marco, SIC of all Medici warriors. Set up triage here, any warrior too weak to walk or already slipping into their death slumber will need to be carried to the feeders. They are to feed first. Then I need you to help those that can manage to walk into the feeder compound. They can rejoin us for other duties as I see fit. You will be temporarily promoted to the position of acting Lieutenant following the death of Fiamma. Your master is gravely injured, but he'll heal and be back on his feet shortly. Until then, you'll take on Fee's duties. Move out."

He watched her straighten her back as she moved quickly to implement his orders. He continued on his way, barking out directions, knowing the best way to keep Shade's ass in bed was to make sure everything was running smoothly in the camp.

Marco looked around, picked out Raven and called him over. "I need you to work with Aislynn, gather some Florence warriors, carry those that cannot manage to make it into the feeder compound. They'll need to be attended to immediately. Matron will help determine who needs to feed first once we get them in the compound."

***

Kate slept lightly beside him throughout the day. About once an hour, he stirred, becoming restless in his sleep, and Kate leaned over him, allowing him to feed. As the day progressed, he got stronger, and was able to roll toward her, pull her close as he fed from her. She'd kept a small light on in the room so she could see him, and she noticed his color improved with each feeding. Theresa had come and gone a few times throughout the day, checking the wound, and reapplying the ointment. Cory had remained close, coming into their bedroom on and off. He stood back at first, looking at his father from the door. Kate patted the bed, inviting him to join her. He slipped onto the bed next to his father, the fear evident in his eyes. Kate reassured him.

"He's going to be all right, Cory."

He looked back at her, fighting tears and only nodded his head.

"Where's your brother?"

Cory looked up at her. "Still in the bunker."

Kate stroked his face. "Why don't you go down, let them know it's okay to come out. Bring Lorenzo back here."

He looked at her with wide eyes. "Me? Bring Lorenzo?"

Kate nodded at him. "Yes. He needs his big brother."

Cory slipped off the bed and headed to the bunker.

***

Luca had retreated to the bunker after Marco arrived in the camp. After checking on Shade, Kate requested him to guard Lorenzo in the event there was a second attack. Nita, Emma, and Shannon were still inside from the night before, along with Lorenzo.

Cory unlocked the massive steel door and swung it open. Luca greeted him on the other side. "Kate thinks it's safe for everyone to come out now. She wants me to bring Lorenzo."

Luca inquired about Shade, and Cory shrugged and shook his head. "Kate said he's going to be fine, but he looks like hell warmed over to me."

Luca smiled at him. "If he survived the day, he'll be fine. But I'll go check on him."

He turned to Shannon. "Will you be all right for a few minutes? Why don't you grab something to eat, then you can take a quick shower in my suite. I know you slept on and off, but you're exhausted."

Shannon nodded, passing the baby off to Cory. "I'll be fine. Don't worry about me. You do what you need to do."

Luca teleported to Shade and Kate's bedroom, and made a quick inspection of Shade. He could see Kate watching his face as he inspected him. Luca gave her a soft smile. "Believe it or not, I've seen worse. He'll be fine, Kate. I'm going to go to the camp and see if I can help Marco."

Kate nodded as he teleported out.

Cory returned to their bedroom, cradling Lorenzo awkwardly in his arms. "I'm not sure I'm holding him right."

Kate chuckled at him. "You're doing fine. Come, bring him to me."

Cory handed her the baby, as she lay back down next to Shade, the baby curled up between them. "Join us, Cory. Lie next to him. He'll feel us. We'll heal him together."

Cory climbed back on the bed, lying on the other side of his father. Kate had Lorenzo lying on his chest as she lay with her head on his shoulder.

Cory slid his arm across his father, tucking his head next to Shade's. He whispered in his ear, "Dad."

Shade felt his sluggish body come awake, his brain thick with the fog of his deep death slumber. He remembered feeding from *bel*, and he could smell the acrid scent of the salve that was Theresa's homemade remedy, and knew she'd nursed his wounds.

He felt a weight on his chest and opened his senses to what was around him, and knew the weight was Lorenzo, sleeping on his chest. He felt *bel's* hair on his shoulder, and recognized Cory's scent.

His eyes remained closed. There was so much to face, yet he wanted a few more minutes of this peaceful bliss. They were here with him, all of them, safe.

Kate lifted her head as she felt him stir. "Lover? Do you need to feed? We're all here. Your family is safe, we're with you."

Cory rose up to his elbow. "I can hold Lorenzo if he needs to feed."

Shade's eyes fluttered open to see his family around him. He turned his head to his beautiful *bel.* He smiled and pulled her closer to him. "Kiss me and tell me you are fine."

She covered his face in soft kisses before landing on his lips. "We're all fine. Tell me what you need."

He tried to sit up and scrunched up his face in pain, slowly laying his head back down. "I need to get out of this bed and get to the camp. So much to be done."

Kate placed her hands on his shoulders. "You're going nowhere. Everything's under control. I called Marco, and he's here. I know Marcello is SIC, but there were so many injured and Marcello was tired as well. Marco took over, so you know the camp is in good hands. I kept Lorenzo in the bunker all day and had Luca stay there. I wasn't sure if Max would come back, but it's been quiet, so Luca's in the camp as well, helping Marco. Everything that can be done is being taken care of. Now I just need you to heal."

Lorenzo squirmed and began rooting around.

"Cory, can you take him to Nita please? He needs to feed again."

Cory jumped up, happy to have something to do, "Of course!" He kissed his dad on the cheek before lifting Lorenzo from his father's chest and leaving the room.

Shade's eyes followed Cory as he left the room with Lorenzo. Closing his eyes, he took a deep breath and pulled Kate to his chest. "*Bel,* I need to take care of things, I'm the damn master here. They need to see I am okay, that I can lead and take care of them. I am injured and let them down, I lost so damn many, I lost... "

His words caught in his throat. He felt his breath leave him. "I know if I just get up, I will feel better, I can get moving. I need to go to them. Marco may be there, but they need to see me."

Kate sighed. "Shade, I'm in no mood for your stubbornness. We're all tired here. The camp is fine. They'll see you when I say they'll see you. Marco can deliver any message you want. But you're not leaving this room."

He grinned as he pulled her close. "So, my queen has taken charge. May I remind you who is master in this house?" He ran his hand over her hips, looking deep into her eyes. "I am so proud of you. Are you all right? I know this cannot be an easy thing to witness."

She laid her head on his chest. "Lover, I'm fine. I was so afraid. I saw when you were injured. I saw you go down. I tried to run to you but Luca grabbed me and wouldn't let me go. That's when I called to Aegis. I told her to help you. I had no idea how she'd respond. I was thinking only about Night Stalker, Riparo, and the others. I had no idea she'd call so many."

He let his hands slide through her hair and down her back, comforting her, as she comforted him. They needed to heal together, physically and mentally. He closed his eyes as he remembered the scene. "I had no idea myself. Everything was fuzzy for me. I felt the damn earth move under me. I had to feed from Marcello to get off the field. But what I did see was something to behold. They will all know now, the gift you bring to our coven. You have solidified your legacy to Medici. No one here ever doubted you, you need to understand that. But others doubted what you could do for me and my *familia*. They will question it no longer."

Kate lay with her head on his chest, nestled under his chin. "I wondered what the point of my gift was. I envisioned it as better protection for the children, as they grew older and played outside. I never considered the animals for battle. What will be done with all the fallen warriors? I haven't looked outside since the blinds closed, but the number of warriors down...it was more than I could count."

"*Mi amore*, the Medici have all been buried on the grounds of Bel Rosso, where they fell in honor, true warriors to our coven. Fee is still whole because I carried her inside, but she won't stay in that condition too long. She is a warrior of rank, so she will have a different ceremony."

He felt his throat close just speaking of her. He wouldn't get over her death any time soon.

Kate bit her lip. Fiamma had been on her mind all day. Her friend gave her life so they could live theirs.

Shade heard the whir of the electronic blinds and knew the sun was going down now. "There is a special ceremony for warriors of rank who have proven they are valiant and brave. We will hold one for Fiamma inside the camp. She meant so much too so many. It is important to me that we do this for her."

He gingerly slid from the bed. "I need to get to the window. I need to see the grounds before the sun is completely gone."

She walked to his side of the bed, standing next to him as he stood for the first time.

Taking her hand, they walked to the window. He steadied himself on her shoulders as they stood looking out over the land that is theirs. The snow and blood seeped into the soil, the heat from the sun taking away all the visages of war. His warriors had cleared the field, removed the weapons, and seen to the proper burial of the Medici. Movement caught his eye and he noticed Aegis and Night Stalker as they prowled close to the house.

"Look, *bel*, your warriors. I owe them my life. I owe them so much. Without them, we would have been slaughtered. They came when you called them, their allegiance to Medici solid and strong. I saw Raven with Poe. What in the hell do you think that was about?"

Kate leaned her head against the glass, the memories of the carnage of the night before playing out in her mind. She shook her head. "I'm not sure. Whatever it is, Poe's drawn to him. I'll ask Poe next time I see him. So, what does this mean now? Is it over? Max retreated. How do you know he won't try again?"

"Max surrendered the field of battle. He withdrew. It is a master's prerogative to fight to the death or to retreat. However, to retreat from a battle means he forfeits the rights to the land he is fighting over. Fan Shen provided many warriors for him to fight this battle, and he will not be pleased that Max has lost Virginia to me. Max still has Maryland and Delaware, but most of his coven was here. He has very little left here. It all belongs to us now. Everything, including his mansion, and whatever remains of his Virginia coven, now belongs to Medici. I am now Master of Virginia. Fan Shen will punish him severely for such a grave loss. He has failed the Shen Dynasty."

Kate looked up at him in surprise. "What? You mean you have all of Virginia now as your coven? Not just Bel Rosso? The vampires that reside there will have to pledge to you?"

He was a bit surprised. He thought she understood the immensity of this battle went far beyond Bel Rosso. "Oh, *si*. Max challenged me for Bel Rosso, but by surrendering he loses it all. With Alec having D.C., and I Virginia, we are well protected now."

He stepped back from the window, sitting down in the large chair and pulling her to his lap. "Unfortunately, we will need to replenish the warriors I have lost. Many of my new recruits went down. I did not know Max would bring so damn many. The new recruits were not battle-hardened. Fan Shen's warriors are equal to my own in their skills. The carnage was proof of that. So, my lady, your warrior has secured for you the entire state and another mansion! I think I should be duly rewarded, *si*?"

Kate raised her eyebrows. "Another mansion? What am I going to do with another mansion? We already have more homes than we can visit. Maybe I'll open another inn."

He chuckled. "Whatever pleases you." He pulled her to his chest and kissed her when they heard Lorenzo. "Our son is restless as hell...giving Theresa a fit, I might add. I want to hold him in my arms, *mi amore*. I need to see him, look in his eyes."

"Of course, that we can do."

Kate called Theresa to bring the baby and she quickly responded, bringing the baby into their bedroom "I was just getting ready to bathe him, my lady. Nita has fed him, but he seems a little fussy."

Kate took Lorenzo and shushed him. "Come on, my beautiful boy."

She turned to Shade, thinking a dose of domesticity might be good for him. "Come. You can help me give him a bath. He loves to play in the water and it will calm him."

Kate laid Lorenzo down on their bed where she stripped him out of his onesie, and then wrapped the blanket around his chubby naked body, carrying him to the bathroom. She ran a little water in the tub and placed Lorenzo in, supporting his back so he was seated.

Shade gingerly squatted down beside her as the baby gleefully slapped his hands on the surface of the water, splashing both of them as he giggled with delight. This was what he'd fought for, this simple pleasure of being a family, at home with his mate and his son. Lorenzo splashed them both and laughed out loud. Huge blue eyes gazed into his, coal black lashes with small droplets of water blinked up at him. Wet dark curls surrounded his handsome innocent face.

Shade knew the time would go by quickly. Soon, he too, would be on a battlefield defending all he loved. Shade gently splashed Lorenzo as he giggled and sputtered, still slapping his hands on the surface of the water. Shade felt all the hell melt away from him. "I think we have a water baby, *mi amore*! Was he born under a water sign?"

Kate smiled at Lorenzo's joy in playing in the water and laughed. "Quite the opposite, lover. He is Sagittarius. A fire sign."

He watched as she put shampoo into her hands, massaging the baby's head, creating a rich foaming lather as she washed his thick curls. Lorenzo cooed at his mother in satisfaction.

Shade smiled. "I like when she does that to me as well. She is a good *madre, si*? She takes care of her warriors, and I am glad she is ours. Now, I do believe you need to get out of this water and come lay with us, *padre* is starving for your *madre*."

138

Shade was going over the details for Fiamma's memorial. It was a traditional ceremony, reserved for ranking warriors, and would be held the following night inside the warrior camp. Many of the warriors from Florence would attend, in addition to the warriors from Bel Rosso, those that were left. Marco would be present for certain. Marco had remained at Bel Rosso since Kate had called him, making sure everything ran smoothly, and giving Shade time to heal.

Shade had made it down to the camp, checking on each of the warriors personally, making sure they'd been cared for and their wounds were healing. He and Marco had reviewed how many warriors were lost, the toll the battle took on their forces and what their next steps should be. They'd need to reassign warriors in Florence and Greece, as well as some major recruiting for the Virginia camp in the spring. The recruits that survived this battle would continue on with their training.

He was healing quickly, but *bel* still worried and asked him to take it easy. She found him in his study, and he smiled at her. "What are you up to, *mi amore*?"

"Checking on you. How were things in the camp? Is there anything I can do for them?"

He shook his head. "No, I think I have everything ready for Fiamma's ceremony. It is something I dread, but I must do this for her."

The cell phone rang, interrupting their conversation and he picked it up. "Medici!"

"It's Jacks. I heard about Fee. I'm so sorry, Shade. I know you're having her memorial tomorrow. You know I loved her. We were like sisters. I know your mate has banned my presence. Is there any way you'd see fit to override that decision and let me attend? I wish to be there for Fee."

Shade listened and said nothing, just handed the phone to Kate. "It's for you."

Kate looked at him quizzically. Who'd be calling her on his cell phone? She took the phone and answered, "Hello?"

Jacks was taken aback, that bastard put his mate on the phone! She knew it was going to take a miracle to get his mate to ever let her step foot inside Virginia again.

"Kate? I'm sorry, this is Jacks. Please don't hang up. Look, I heard about Fiamma. I was calling to ask you to please allow me to come to her memorial. It's very important to me. She was my sister and my friend, and her loss is felt deep in my heart."

Kate was surprised to hear Jacks' voice and flashed a look in Shade's direction. She listened to her request, her back stiffening at the sound of her voice. She knew Fiamma considered Jacks her friend, and this ceremony was for Fee. "You may attend. Fee would want you here. Yes, you were her friend."

Jacks sighed in relief when she heard Kate's decision. "Thank you. I appreciate your letting me attend. Please give my regards to Shade, and I'll see you tomorrow. Fee was special, rare in her skills and leadership. She's one of the originals who forged the path for female warriors. You're very gracious."

Kate listened to Jacks express her appreciation but didn't want her to hang up with the wrong impression. "Just to be clear, nothing has changed between us. You're welcome here for the ceremony, and you'll be treated with respect. You may spend time in the camp with your friends after the service, but then, I expect you to leave. Understood?"

"I understand. I won't linger. I just want to pay my last respects. Thank you." Hanging up, Jacks pitched the phone down on the couch and wondered how that small little mortal snagged the most sought after master in the world.

Kate ended the call and handed the phone back to Shade without comment.

Taking the phone back, he sat down in his leather chair and stared at her. "I thank you for being so generous in your heart to allow Jacks to attend. She was close to Fee. It would have been important to her to have Jacks here. I am glad you understand that."

"I do understand that. I do this to honor Fiamma. Besides, I don't have to concern myself with the likes of Jacks, or flirtatious female warriors like Britt who show up at camp."

She climbed in Shade's lap and leaned her forehead against his. "I'm pretty sure I'm the only queen who has a pack of wolves at her disposal."

Chuckling, he issued a playful growl, kissing her mouth softly. "*Si*, and I am one of the wolves!" Picking her up, he winced a bit, his injury still healing as he carried her up the stairs. "I have a need to see my son. And perhaps, ravish his *madre* in the process!"

139

Shade found some solitude in the stables, attending to Impavido, checking him for any injuries and rubbing him down. Angelo gave him a wide berth, knowing he needed to be alone. The ceremony for Fiamma was later tonight, and he needed some time to get his head around what lay before him.

He heard Marco telepathically call to him, telling him all was ready. He finished up with Pavi, giving him a few carrots, before leaving the stables and walking down the long path to the camp. He let his *bel* know where he was and for her to get ready, have Lorenzo and Cory ready as well, as they'd all go to the ceremony together.

He walked slowly, his head down, his mind blank, but his heart saddened. This was his sister-in-arms. And for the first time in a very long time, he'd perform the simple ceremony to honor her death, and to celebrate her dedication and sacrifice to Medici.

The large gym inside the warrior camp had been set up to receive all that would attend. It was the largest indoor space to accommodate all the attendees. The large space was oddly quiet as it was normally filled with the sound of the warriors working out.

His warriors were suffering from the loss of so many, healing in their bodies and minds. Tonight, they'd let go of their grief, as they let go of Fee. He passed several warriors on his way to the gym, walking in silence.

This would be a private affair for Medici only, no outsiders would attend. Jacks would be the only warrior who was not a Medici, but she'd trained with them for a while and understood their legacy. As he walked past the warriors, no words were spoken. He gave them a simple nod of recognition. She'd been loved by so many.

As he approached the gym, the doors were closed and Marco stood outside, as if guarding her. He looked up at Shade and their eyes locked in a look that connected them as brothers. They hugged each other tight. Neither of them would find this night an easy process.

Marco's voice was soft in his ear. "She's ready, brother. Say your goodbyes now. No one is allowed inside until you come out. Take your time."

Marco opened the door and Shade stepped inside, Marco closing it behind him.

Shade stood inside the dimly lit room. His feet felt like they were encased in cement blocks, unable to move. Her body lay to the front of the room on a catafalque draped in black velvet. Huge white candles stood in candelabras at her head and feet. Candles were laid along the walls of the room, their light soft and flickering. Folding chairs had been lined in rows to seat the many who'd come this night, creating a center aisle that led from the door to where her body lay.

At Kate's request, they had placed a huge box of fresh, long stemmed red roses at the entrance. Their scent filled the room. He picked a single rose from the box and carried it slowly down the aisle to Fiamma. Each step felt like a mile.

He'd asked Marco to have the other female warriors prepare her body, washing her, fixing her hair, and dressing her in her ceremonial leathers. He and Marco had been through this many times, preparing the bodies of their fallen brothers, and it never got any easier.

As he stood before her, he looked down at her face. She lay solemn, her eyes closed, a soft black satin pillow cradling her head. Her hair was down, fixed the way she wore it when she was not in battle, long and loose in the back, and a single braid at each side of her face.

Her auburn lashes lay fanned out against her cheeks, now white and lifeless, her lips dead and cold. His eyes absorbed every detail. She lay on her back, her hands crossed over the hilt of her sword. His eyes traveled downward, and he saw her feet in their polished boots. She was ready.

The red shroud that would cover her was embroidered with the Medici crest and lay folded neatly at her feet. He walked all the way around her, inspecting her from all sides. He stopped at her head and broke the stem off the red rose, tucking the bloom gently behind her ear. His hand slid gently over her cold cheek.

"Thank you, my sister, for giving your life for me and mine. You always had my back. I will miss your laughter, your smile, and your smartass remarks. But remember, I will always love you, Fee. You are forever Medici."

He leaned down, kissing her forehead, his blood tears staining his cheeks. "There are so many people here that love you and wish to say their goodbyes. Hang on for a while longer, my beautiful girl. Soon, very soon, I will release you."

He stepped away, willing the music that would play throughout the night as the warriors come to pay their respects. Walking back toward the doors, he swiped away the tears that covered his face. He opened both doors wide, and he and Marco nodded. The warriors could come now, sit, and reflect on their sister and be together as family.

He walked back to the house with his head held high. It was time to let her go now.

140

Shade returned to the house, passing Theresa and Gi. He saw the grief on Theresa's face and stopped to give her a hug. "Go to Marco, be with him. He will need you during this. Everything is ready. Kate and I will be down shortly. Go on."

He watched as she and Gi headed for the camp. He was glad Marco was here for her. They'd need each other during times such as this. He rushed in the house and took the steps two at a time, barging into their bedroom. "*Mi amore*?"

He didn't hear her, but his senses told him she was nearby, probably in the nursery with Lorenzo. He stripped down and started getting into his ceremonial leathers. Once finished dressing, he threw his foot up on the chair and prepared to tie his boot when she walked in. He stopped as his eyes took her in.

***

Kate stood in the nursery, looking out the window toward the camp where she knew the warriors were gathering for the ceremony. Luca had told her the bodies of the other fallen Medici warriors had been gathered on the battlefield by their brothers. He explained that protocol dictated, as the victors, a shallow grave be dug before sunrise, and the bodies of the fallen laid to rest there, but not covered. Once the sun rose and they were reduced to ash, the grave was covered over. The bodies of their fallen enemies were left to lie on the ground, where the sun cremated them, and the wind scattered their ashes. That way, the victors remained on the soil they fought to defend, and the battle was named for the victors. He told her this battle would be known as the 'Battle of Bel Rosso'.

Since Fiamma was a ranking officer in their army, her body was retrieved and taken below ground, protected from the sun, so they could all honor her. Kate was still coming to grips with the fact they'd lost seventy warriors, and her friend Fee was among them. She'd asked Luca what she should wear. He told her the warriors all wore their ceremonial leathers, which happened to be black, and based on that, Shannon had decided to wear a black dress. Kate thought long and hard about her decision and hoped Shade would understand her choice for what she'd decided to wear.

She'd asked Cory to modify the leathers for her, and he'd quickly made the alterations. She could hear Cory's footsteps on the floor over her head as he finished dressing before joining them. Kate picked Lorenzo up from his crib. He had recently fed from Nita so he'd be calm during the service. She wrapped a warm blanket around him and carried him with her to their bedroom. She could hear Shade on the other side of their bedroom door, getting himself ready for the service. She opened the door and stood before him, dressed in red leathers.

He stopped tying the boot as he took her in. He smiled. "You look quite beautiful, my queen. Where did you acquire those, might I ask?"

"They belonged to Fee. Cory worked very hard to have them ready in time. I asked if it was too much to ask of him and he said not at all, he needed to stay busy. It was the best way I could think to honor her. Is it okay? I can change if it doesn't please you."

Finishing tying his boot, he went to her, taking her in his arms and hugging her tight. "No, I think Fiamma would love it, to be honest. She always wore red leathers when she was kicking warrior ass. She loved you, you know that, right? She admired you so damn much, Kate. I am going to miss her."

Kate relaxed into him, allowing herself to be enveloped in his embrace. "When we had the coronation in Florence, and the warriors pledged to me, it felt like, well...like ceremony. I couldn't imagine we'd actually go to battle, that warriors would give their lives. That Fee would give her life. This makes what we have so much more precious. We have an obligation to them, to all of them. I understand it all now, Castello, and Bel Rosso. These places must thrive because of the blood that was spilled. We owe them that. I understand Lorenzo's role, and why he's so important to his people. He carries the legacy of all those that came before him, that fought before him."

He rocked with her in his arms as she held Lorenzo. Cory tapped on the door and peeped in.

"Come in, Cory, we are about ready to go." Leaning down, he kissed *bel* softly, and smiled. "Sometimes, it takes loss to appreciate the gain, *mi amore*. It never gets easier." Turning, he faced Cory. "If we are ready, we should get to the camp. It will be quiet. It is a time for reflection, memories and honoring Fiamma. Music will be playing throughout. We sit together, as the *familia* she served. She devoted her life to the Medici, she died for the Medici. So, remember her with great respect."

He took Kate by the arm and led her down the long road to the camp. He was ready to let Fiamma go now. His strength was around him. As they walked inside, the candles provided a soft, flickering light to the many warriors. With the exception of the music playing low in the background, there was no sound.

He walked them through the open double doors, and just for a moment, let Kate and Cory take in what was before them. He knew it must be hard for them to witness Fiamma laid out before them in front of the large room. Leaning down, he whispered in Kate's ear. "Are you ready, *mi amore*?"

Kate felt a catch in her throat as she saw Fiamma, the sword held on her chest, the candles casting shadows as the music played. She felt her knees go weak as Shade steadied her, and Cory took Lorenzo from her arms. She steadied herself. She was their queen, and she must be strong for them. She owed them that. "I'm ready, lover."

He whispered softly, "Everyone here loved her very much, just as we did. The roses are just inside the door, as you requested. Take one if you wish to lay it atop her body."

Turning to Cory, he took Lorenzo in his arms. "Come on, little warrior, time to honor one of our own."

Looping his arm through Kate's, he paused as she selected a red rose, and he watched as Cory did the same. He walked them down the aisle to the three seats waiting for them in the front row, next to Marco and Theresa. Shade motioned for Cory to sit beside Marco. He got Kate in her seat as he took the aisle seat.

Luca and Shannon followed behind them. Luca gathered a rose but advised Shannon she'd not be allowed to approach the body and place a rose. Shannon nodded. She didn't know Fiamma well and felt honored and overwhelmed she'd even been allowed in their inner circle. She was the only mortal in attendance, and the only one, other than the baby, that was not dressed in leathers. She hooked her arm around Luca's as he led her to their seats behind Kate and Shade.

Shade sat staring straight ahead, as memories of Fee played out in his head; the battles, the laughs, the way she'd cock her head at him when she was teasing him. Her life had been full, and she was loved by many. He remembered the first time he saw her. She came to the camp in Florence, still a young girl, and he'd had no intentions of training her, her flaming hair like a target. She was quick to change his mind. She had what it took, and she worked twice as hard as the males to prove to him she could do this.

The warriors sat in silence, each with their own memories, when without any announcement, they began to come forward, carrying a single rose, and placing it on the catafalque around her body. He watched as Aislynn came forward, blood tears on her cheeks. Fiamma had been a great influence on this young warrior. She laid the rose across the sword and knelt down on one knee. She stayed kneeling for some time. When she rose, her body was shaking but she held her head up high and walked back to her seat. Shade sat motionless, nothing showing on his face. He was their master and today, they relied on him to be strong.

Kate watched as the warriors filed past them. Some she knew by name, some she only recognized their faces, and others, she'd never seen before.

They all knew Fiamma, fought beside her, shared centuries together, long before Kate had been born. She squeezed her eyes shut tight.

Shade felt Kate's pain vibrate through him, and he squeezed her hand. Marco stood and took Theresa's arm, leading her to Fiamma. They both stood arm in arm, their backs to Shade, and he saw Theresa tremble and heard her sob. Marco took her in his arms and comforted her. Theresa walked back to her seat and Marco knelt on one knee, placing his hand atop Fiamma's.

Shade sat quietly as he watched the warriors come and go. He felt a hand squeeze his shoulder and he looked up to see Jacks. She laid the rose atop Fiamma's body, standing a long time looking at her. Jacks held something in her hand, and Shade watched as she attached a brooch to Fiamma's leathers. She kissed her cheek and spoke softly to her sister-in-arms, but her voice carried in the quiet room. "Goodbye, sister. Fly with honor and glory. *Ti amo*."

Jacks didn't kneel but turned and stopped at Shade's seat before returning to her own and whispered to him, "*Grazie,* master."

Kate watched her return and nod to Shade, acknowledging him, but ignoring her. Kate huffed, some things never changed, and she'd always keep an eye on that one.

Shade sat and watched the procession of warriors, as Raven and Skelk paid their homage. Marcello was among the last to approach her. Shade saw him as he knelt before her. He knew Marcello was the closest to Fiamma. She'd been beside him since day one. When Marcello took his seat, he saw Marco turn to him and nod. It was time. The warriors had shown their respect. He nodded back, and Theresa stood and took Lorenzo from Kate.

Shade took Kate by the hand and nodded for Cory to follow him as well. Walking to the catafalque that held Fiamma, he whispered to his oldest son. "Cory, please pay your respects to Fiamma, then return to your seat."

Cory stepped forward and placed the rose on her body and knelt down on one knee for a moment or two. Shade was so proud of him. He honored her well and although Cory wasn't a warrior, he'd made himself invaluable to the warriors in his own way. Once Cory was seated, Shade turned to Kate. "It is your turn to say goodbye to our beloved Fee. Take as long as you wish, *mi amore*."

Kate knelt beside her, laying her head against the catafalque. She couldn't believe this lifeless body wouldn't rise up, laugh at them all, like it had been some prank she played. She fought back the tears. She felt the need to show strength to those that had come to honor her. She raised her head and looked upon Fiamma's pale face. Kate spoke to her, and in the unnaturally still silence of the room, her voice carried to all of them.

"Of all that kneel before you, I'm the one that has known you for the shortest time. And yet, it was for the life I lead that you sacrificed your own. My dear sister, with the generous heart, I make a pledge to you now, to be worthy of your sacrifice. My children will know your name. They will know the life they enjoy comes from you, and the others who fell before you." Kate stood and placed the rose across Fee's breast. "I am your humble servant, and the servant of all in the Medici coven. You have honored me, and I will not fail you."

Kate turned and faced the room of warriors. "I will not fail any of you. I pledge to you now, as you have pledged to me. None who die for Medici will ever die in vain. Shade will fight. I will fight. Our children will fight. And we will always prevail. *Per sempre* Medici."

The warriors repeated back to her in unison, "*Per sempre* Medici."

Shade felt the tears well in his eyes as his queen stepped forth, assuming the full mantel of her position. His pride was immense in spite of his sorrow, and he knew Fiamma felt her presence and her words in the spirit realm. He kissed her softly, whispering against her lips, "*Ti amo*, my queen."

He took her hand and led her back to her seat while Shade remained standing. Down the center aisle approached six warriors, all cloaked in black velvet robes, hoods over their heads. They approached the catafalque and stood to one side. The music stopped and the room was enveloped in silence. The hooded figures began a chant in their ancient language, which the warriors all recognized as "Immortal Memory."

Marco joined Shade as they each took their place on either side of the catafalque at Fiamma's feet.

As the warriors chanted, their voices echoing in the large space, Shade moved to her side. He gently removed each of her hands from her sword. He kissed her sword and held it high in the air, honoring her skills as a warrior. He looked directly at Marcello and locked eyes with him. Marcello stood and approached as Shade lowered the sword and placed it in his hands. "Guard this sword of our fallen sister."

Marcello knelt with the sword in his hands and repeated the same process of kissing the sword and raising it above his head before returning to his seat with Fiamma's sword clutched to his heart.

Shade returned to the foot of the catafalque where he and Marco each picked up the folded shroud that lay at her feet. Walking slowly to the head of the catafalque, the bright red shroud unfolded, covering Fiamma's body from head to toe. The Medici crest, hand embroidered on the shroud, lay over her chest.

Marco returned to his seat as Shade positioned himself behind the catafalque, so he now faced the congregation. The black robed warriors began a more traditional song in Latin, "Vide Cor Meum", and the sound was beautiful and haunting.

Shade pulled back the shroud from Fiamma's face and leaned down, kissing each cheek and then her forehead.

"*Addio mia sorella*. You have honored us greatly. Now fly free. Your mission is completed in this realm, but you are forever Medici."

Placing his hand on her forehead, he raised his eyes to the ceiling and summoned her spirit to be released. The candles flickered wildly, some of them blowing out, leaving the room dimly lit and quiet but for the voices singing.

He felt her spirit lift and release as her shroud covered body rose into the air. The shroud fell gently to the table, her body now gone, turned to ash. Shade lowered his head and dropped to one knee. She was gone.

141

As routines were restored and life was getting back to normal, Marco was preparing to return to Florence. He and Shade made a final inspection of the barracks. Shade would miss having his brother-in-arms around. It was good to see him here at Bel Rosso, but he knew Marco's home would always be Florence.

"So, I am guessing you are taking off for home tonight." Shade slapped him on the back. "Come on, let's walk outside, I need a smoke!"

As they stepped out onto the training field, things were still quiet. Many of the warriors were still healing, and he'd been rearranging the assignments for those able to resume their duties. The warriors that had been assigned to the Dead House with Theo the night of the battle were the only ones to remain unscathed.

Shade had assigned Raven back to California for a few weeks to give him time to finish up there. He was well aware of the budding relationship with Mica. Raven had served him well during the battle, and he deserved a little time to relax and rejoin his partner.

Shade lit up a cigarette before tossing the pack to Marco. He took a long deep drag and then coughed, holding his side and wincing. Marco caught the pack with one hand and lit up, but he didn't miss Shade's response to pain.

"You know, brother, I have no words to thank you for all you have done for me. Without you, I would have been fucked from here to hell. *Grazie*, for staying with Kate when I was in Paris." Shade looked down and scuffed the muddy ground with his boot. Marco stared back at him.

"Hell, you know I always have your back. But let's face it. Your queen saved our asses in this battle. There's no way we could have taken on Max's numbers without her. You feeling any better? You can't handle battle like you used too, you need to let the young punks take charge now, just lead them. You have a lot at stake. Little one needs your guidance. You are much like your old man, whether you want to admit it or not. He would never back away either."

Shade looked up at the moon and stretched, moaning a bit. "*Padre* would have never given up. Castello was all he had. But I have a lot more at stake, and I can't lead them if I don't show them. And you know as well as I do, this won't be the last battle we face together by any means."

Marco shook his head. "Fuck that, we better have one hell of a lot more slicing and dicing to come! This is one warrior who plans to go out with a sword in his hand."

Throwing his arm around Shade's neck, they walked the muddy path back to the main house.

"If you need reinforcements until spring comes and you get more recruits into camp, let me know. The Greek outpost needs a change-up. I want to move them around, let them see all that Medici owns."

Shade nodded. "Right now, we are fine. We are still functioning."

Marco grunted. "Well, you never know with Canton, he may piss off someone any day, and that means you will need more coverage."

As they approached the house, Shade saw Aegis patrolling close, and she appeared agitated. He wondered what the hell that was about. "Well one thing for sure, if Canton does this president thing, there will be much more coverage required."

Marco saw the wolf's eyes as they glowed back at him in the dark and he was grateful for the queen and her gift of animalism. He'd already heard from the warriors in Florence that the news of the battle was spreading like wildfire in the vampire community, and Marco knew the power of Medici warriors, combined with her gift, made the Medici something to contend with in their world.

"By the way, one of the original warriors who I sent over from Florence has requested to return. She came back to honor Fiamma, but she's asking to stay. I sent her to your office, told her to wait for you."

Shade looked over at him. "She?"

"It's Olivia. I know her performance was a little weak on her first rotation here. She knows it too. When she came back to Florence, she really threw herself into her training. She's made a lot of improvement. She wants a second chance. And let's face it, in the spring you will have new female recruits. You will need a few females here that already know the ropes."

"She was like a mouse when she was here before, Marco."

"I know, but listen to me. She's got great potential. Let her stay and work with the squad in the Dead House under Theo. She will benefit from the street experience. And besides, you need as many as you can get right now. I gave the temporary assignment as acting Lieutenant to Aislynn. You need to decide if you want to make that permanent. She worked really hard in the camp after the battle. She takes orders well, does what she is told. Give her a shot."

Shade shook his head as he headed into the house, knowing Kate would have detected the presence of another female under their roof. "Someday, brother, your ass is gonna burn for all the hell you cause in my life with my mate!"

They both entered the house laughing like hell.

142

Shade headed straight to his office, fist bumping Marco as he started up the stairs to see Theresa one last time before going back to Florence. He'd have the conversation with Olivia, and then he needed to talk to Aislynn and make a decision about both of them. Stepping into his office, he found Olivia waiting for him. She was tall but didn't appear as toned as the other female warriors. Olivia had always maintained a softness about her.

"Olivia. Good to see you again. Please, have a seat."

She bowed her head slightly to him as she greeted him. She had blue-grey eyes, and light brown hair that fell to her shoulders. Her complexion was peaches and cream, and she looked more like a feeder than a warrior. "Good evening, master."

He could already see the difference in her as she held his gaze. She stood taller, and no longer tried to blend into her surroundings, trying to go unnoticed. He sat down in his leather chair and crossed his arms. "Marco told me you wanted the opportunity to work at Bel Rosso again. Tell me where this is coming from?"

Olivia nodded. "I'm aware my performance wasn't adequate when I was here before. It was my first real assignment, and I let it overwhelm me. When I returned to Florence, Marco spoke with me at length about where I was lacking, and he assigned me to a number of different outposts to gain more experience. I worked harder in the camp as well. I'd appreciate if you'd give me a second chance, master. I wasn't ready before, but I am now. I want to work my way up in the ranks, prove myself to you and the other warriors. I know that Fiamma..."

She lowered her head and fidgeted with her hands as they lay in her lap, remembering what Fiamma had always told her. "Fiamma always told us that as females, we'd have to really put ourselves out there. We'd have to be outspoken, become our own advocates, and make sure people knew what our goals and objectives were. So, I'm asking. If you allow me to stay, I won't disappoint you this time. I know what you expect of me. I'll abide by your decision. If you send me back to Florence, I'll go and serve you proudly."

Shade hardly recognized this female before him. She was nothing like the Olivia that had been here only a year ago. Her confidence was greatly improved, and she had Marco's endorsement. "Your sister taught you well. Fiamma was a great warrior, a true leader. Marco informs me you have done well in Florence and have shown improvement. That does not mean you won't have a lot to prove to me. We didn't have the camp when you were here before. So, let me go over the rules. The camp is divided into male and female quarters. We have a feeder compound inside the camp, and no one leaves this camp unless I direct them to. There is no hunting without specific approval by me, and I grant it rarely. When you were here before, I was at the Dead House almost every night, and Tomas was my SIC. Tomas was a mercenary, hired by Alec, and he has moved on. Theo is in charge now, with backup from Skelk. If I assign you to the Dead House, you will take orders directly from them." He locked eyes with her and leaned back in his chair. "Any questions?"

Olivia pushed her long hair behind her ears and stared back at him. "No, master."

He held her gaze. "Fiamma was right about many things. She learned how to navigate in a man's world. I expect you to do the same, understood? I will cut you no slack because you are female. It does you no favors. You earn the respect of your brothers by fighting as hard and being as skilled. Show me that, Olivia, and I will let you stay. I will give you until Spring when we start the enrollment for the new recruits to prove yourself to me. Then we will talk again, *si*?"

Olivia smiled and nodded. "Yes, master. Thank you. I understand your conditions, and I won't disappoint you."

He stood and directed her to the door, "Then move your gear into the female barracks. See Aislynn for your work detail. Welcome back, Olivia."

She almost ran out the door, shouting over her shoulder, "Thank you, Master Shade. I won't let you down!"

He watched her scurry out the door and wondered how many warriors he'd trained through the centuries, and how many he'd lost. He was rarely aware of the passage of time, and the concept of age was a mortal construct, but sometimes, he felt his age, and this was one of those times.

143

Shade poured himself a Midnight and sat down in the leather chair, one down and one to go. Fiamma's loss had been great. She was his most experienced female warrior, and there were not nearly as many females as males in this profession. The females still struggled for recognition in a world where the ratio was about thirty to one. He didn't have anyone of Fee's caliber to take over leading the females. Aislynn worked hard, but she was still young. She'd caught his eye on her first day as well, standing out with her weapons skills, even among the males. He was glad to see his perceptions of her validated by Marco.

Aislynn was in the camp when Olivia returned and let her know she'd be staying. Aislynn assigned her a bed in the barracks and said she'd set up a meeting with Theo to get Olivia's assignments. She barely had Olivia settled in when she received a message to report to Shade in the main house.

She quickly left the camp and headed up the road. She knew her promotion had been a temporary one, made after the battle as a necessary means to keep things moving. She was pretty sure she was about to learn her fate. She kept her head up and went straight to his office, preparing herself to be demoted back to the rank of warrior. She walked in and Shade smiled and beckoned for her to take a seat across from his huge desk. She sat down, back stiff, and waited for him to speak.

"Thank you for coming so quickly, Aislynn. My office gives us more privacy than the camp, *si*? A few things I wish to speak with you about. First of all, you had a very important role during the battle, and you did it well. Never think I did not notice. You are a good warrior destined to be a great one, if you keep this up. Marco assigned you temporary status as Lieutenant, and you have displayed excellent leadership skills. You performed well under the pressure of battle and in the chaos that followed. I have decided to make your promotion to Lieutenant permanent. You will assume Fiamma's duties. I know we are light on females right now, but we will get more with the spring recruitment. What do you say to that?"

Aislynn felt her heart hammer in her chest. He'd noticed her! And he was giving her the position permanently. She held her head a little higher and pushed her shoulders back. This was the opportunity of a lifetime. She was a young warrior, and to be a ranking Medici was no small task. She'd put her nose to the grindstone and remember all the lessons Fee taught her.

"I'm ready and prepared to take on the responsibility and show you I can handle it, master. I'm honored you'd choose me. I had a great mentor in Fiamma. All of the warriors from Florence have taught me so much since I've been here, and I intend to be a great warrior under your guidance."

Shade nodded. "You earned it, Aislynn. I give nothing without it being earned. Remember that. I want you to move into Fiamma's room, as it is yours now. So, move your things out of the barracks into that room. I will speak to Marcello so he will know what is going on. You met Olivia, *si*? I just sent her down to camp. She and the other females will be under your command. Olivia is here on a contingency basis. I will re-evaluate her in the spring, so work with her, and be prepared to provide feedback. You are also in charge of the feeder compound. Meet with Matron, go over the schedules. She will help fill you in on how Fiamma managed things there. In the camp, you report to Marcello, and then to me. Any questions, warrior?"

Aislynn couldn't believe it! She'd be in charge of the females! "No questions, master. Thank you, I'll make you and Fiamma proud of me."

Shade saw the emotions play across her face and he knew how much this meant to her. She was hungry and eager for more responsibility. He loved to see his warriors stretching to their full potential. It was what made him a good leader. He gave her a curt nod. "Dismissed, warrior."

Aislynn backed out of the room. "Thank you again, Master Shade. I'll go move my things now."

She closed the door behind her before breaking into a dance. She sprinted back to the camp. She had her own room! She'd never had her own room before!

144

Aislynn returned to the camp, floating on air. She couldn't believe her good fortune. She started gathering her belongings from the open barracks shared with the other female warriors and headed straight for the room that had belonged to Fiamma. She entered the room with mixed feelings, excited over her promotion, but sad that it came at her friend's expense. She knew one thing, though, if Fee was here, no one would be cheering louder for her. Master had given her an opportunity to prove she could lead, help train the new warriors, and she was determined to show him she was up for the challenge. She wanted Fiamma to be proud of her, and she wanted her brothers to respect her.

She made several trips back and forth between the open barracks and her private room, finally dumping the last of her things on the floor and flopped down on the bed. She noticed a red envelope lying on the pillow of the perfectly made bed.

She picked up the envelope and looked at the name on the outside. It was handwritten in a beautiful script. 'Marcello'. She recognized Fee's handwriting as she flipped the envelope over to find it sealed. Aislynn felt caught off-guard. Was this something Fiamma had been planning to deliver to Marcello when she got back? Or was this a letter left for him in case she never saw him again?

She felt the thickness of the envelope, and knew it was a letter. Would Fiamma want him to have this now? Should she deliver it? Standing up, she made her decision, and headed for Marcello's private room. His door was open slightly as she tapped lightly. "Marcello, may I come in?"

Marcello looked up to see her standing in his door. He wasn't completely happy about the changes Marco and Shade had made. He knew Aislynn was a capable warrior, but Fee was not long dead, and they'd already replaced her. He understood the camp must move on, and there were jobs to be done, but he was finding Fee's loss harder to deal with than he'd expected. "Come in."

Marcello knew this was all new to her and he'd need patience. He was so used to working with Fee; they could read each other like a book, without ever speaking. "Is there a problem, Aislynn?"

Aislynn shook her head. "No. I don't mean to intrude, but I was moving my things into Fee's room and well...I found this." From behind her back, she held out the red envelope. Marcello looked at the envelope and then her. "What's in it? Why are you bringing it to me?"

She handed it to him, front side up so he could see his name.

"Where did you find this?"

Aislynn felt uncomfortable and doubted her decision to bring the letter to him. "It was lying on her pillow. I thought you'd wish to have it as soon as possible."

Marcello took the envelope and stared at it. "*Grazie*. Close the door on your way out please."

Aislynn left the room, turning to look at him one last time before walking out, closing the door behind her.

Marcello felt the lump in his throat and his stomach dropped. He lifted the envelope to his nose and sniffed. He could still smell her. He sat at his desk, resting his elbows on his knees and got lost in his memories of her. A red envelope; it was her signature color. He ran his fingers over his name before carefully opening the seal and pulling out the folded paper. They'd been friends for centuries, and he'd have a hard time thinking of a world without Fiamma in it. He started to read, and as he did, his already broken heart began to shatter.

Dear Marcello,

If you are reading this, then I didn't survive this battle. I can't leave this world with words unspoken. There are things in my heart I need to let go. We've fought together, trained together, and you were always there for me, the one person I could always trust. We were warriors first, but I'm also female, with a female's heart. We followed master's rule about fraternization, as we should, and I'm sure it saved us many times over in battle.

I remember the first day you walked into camp in Florence, so brave, so impatient, and so handsome. I have kept my feelings for you hidden all these years. But then our master found his mate, and for the first time, I felt I saw what real love is. How powerful it can be. It made me want to be loved in that manner. Marcello, I have loved you for so long. You never knew, or perhaps you did, and perhaps it wasn't our destiny to know such love. If I live through this battle, I've vowed to myself to let you know my true feelings. If I don't survive, you will know through this letter.

I will always love you, Marcello. I have given my life to Medici, and I'd never change that. It's who I am, who I was born to be. But know in my heart, had my life been different, it was you I craved to be mated to. My tears fall as I write this, hoping you'll survive the coming battle, and find true happiness and love. There's more to life, Marcello, than being a warrior.

I always had your back, and I always will. Never forget me, Marcello, or that I loved you.

Your forever love,

Fee

Marcello found it hard to see through his tears. They dropped onto the white stationery, marring her elegant handwriting. She loved him, she had always loved him. He'd thought many times of being with her but knew it would have led them down a path that was dangerous for them both. Warriors needed to fight without distraction.

He began to shake with emotion. He, too, had held back from being with her, from sharing with her how he felt. Now he felt guilt as well. While he couldn't deny the attraction to her, there was something inside that held him back. He knew in his heart she wasn't his eternal mate.

He roared in pain over the loss of her in his life and all the things they both left unsaid as he teleported out immediately. He had to get out of here, escape this emotion, this place with its smell of her, memories of her, and his guilt, knowing he couldn't save her. He'd not felt her go down. He didn't feel deserving of her adoration, and he felt he'd even failed her as a friend.

Aislynn heard his roar of pain and heard the footsteps of other warriors running toward Marcello's room. She jumped up quickly to join them, only to find him gone, the pages of the letter strewn on the floor.

She immediately summoned Master Shade. She picked up the letter and quickly shoved it back inside the envelope, preventing anyone else from reading Fiamma's last words to him. She spoke to the warriors who'd gathered there, holding up her hands. "Nothing to see here. I've summoned master. Please, return to your rooms."

The warriors slowly exited as Skelk came to her side, encouraging her to leave as well.

"Come on, master will figure it out."

145

Shade was wrapping up in his office for the night. Everything had been quiet and calm. He'd made his call to Council, informing them of the battle and the losses, knowing that news of the battle had reached them already. The battle would require another Council visit, as it involved a shift in territories, so the meeting was arranged. Besides, he had some unfinished business to attend to, and he'd take Kate and Lorenzo with him. They could use some time away after all that had happened.

He headed up the stairs in search of *bel* when he heard a beautiful voice, singing a sweet lullaby. He stopped and looked inside the nursery to see Nita rocking Lorenzo in her arms, singing him to sleep. He stood a moment, listening to her song, and was looking at his son when he felt two arms slip around his waist, and Kate's head leaning against his back. They listened to Nita sing to their son and he knew Lorenzo would always remember this. They'd made a good choice in Nita.

Without warning, he felt Marcello's pain wash over him. His body stiffened in fear for Marcello as he felt him leave the compound, followed by Aislynn's voice in his head, telling him what was going on. Shade spun quickly and kissed Kate. "I have to go. It's Marcello. I will be back as soon as possible."

He teleported inside the barracks where Aislynn filled him in as best she could. He didn't read the letter, but he knew one thing, Marcello was suffering greatly. He could relate to the warrior's pain. He followed his senses and teleported out, finding Marcello high in the mountains. He landed near the troubled warrior as he paced in the woods.

"If you were upset, you should have talked to me, Marcello. I know you are in pain over Fiamma. So, let's talk this out before you do something you regret. Your master is a perfect example of what not to do, *si*?"

Marcello spun on him, growling in anger. His voice was loud as he shouted at Shade. "I'm in pain over Fee! What did you expect? For me to just pretend it never happened? How can you act like none of it bothers you?"

He stood nose to nose with Shade, venting his anger, almost hoping for an altercation.

Shade let him spill his guts, ignoring the warrior's blatant disregard of his station. He understood this pain all too well and had a lot more years of experience dealing with it. "Take a deep breath warrior, and step back, because you do not want to test my beast."

Shade watched him turn his back on him and pace. "Marcello, I am hurting as well, we all are. I loved her too. What has you so upset, brother? Talk to me. I know there was a letter."

Marcello sighed heavily. "She was in love with me. I had a feeling about it, but it would have been disastrous if we'd been together and things didn't work out between us. It's what you taught us, and I knew that! She did too. But she never told me. Now I wonder if I should have just made the leap. The letter just stirred up a lot of feelings I've never addressed."

Shade lit up a smoke and sat down on a large downed tree. "If you didn't move on the relationship, deep inside, you knew there was a reason, way beyond both of you being warriors, Marcello. I have been in your shoes, except I did go there, twice, once with Adriana, and again with Sabine. Something told me the choice was wrong. My beast kept arguing with me, telling me these females were not my eternal mate. I assume you felt the same. So, you need to stop beating yourself up over that. The beast will know when she comes. He will recognize your mate, Marcello, and he knew Fee was not your mate."

Marcello kept pacing, listening to his master's words, but his mind was still churning. "*Cazzo*! I never felt her go down! I should have known she was in trouble! I never knew! How long did she lay there? What if I'd felt it? Could I have gotten to her, saved her somehow? Why the fuck did this happen? She was a damn good warrior. It's wrong, all wrong!"

Shade took a long drag on the cigarette, letting the wounded warrior vent his anger. This was good, he'd get this out of his system, and only then could he start to heal. "This battle was huge, brother. We were outnumbered, and there was way too much to tackle for any of us to feel the other. When Fee went down, I didn't feel her either and that bothers me as well. We are here, Marcello...we survived. and I can't question why. We continue on, keep our species alive. She died doing what she loved, something she was born to do. That's how I get through it. She died protecting Medici, our coven, and those she loved. And you know as well as I do, she knew she was loved. The letter was what was in her heart. And it's okay if she loved you. She just wanted you to know it, that's all. She wanted you to know how much she cared about you. Accept her love. You don't have to feel a passionate love for her in return to appreciate and acknowledge her love for you. Take it for what it was."

Marcello sat down beside him, taking a cigarette and lighting up. He knew he'd carry her inside him for the rest of his life. Fee wasn't just another warrior to him, she was his best friend. "I loved her like a sister. She was my sidekick. Hell, we spent so much time together. And what the hell, she isn't dead long, and you've got Aislynn taking her room and her position? It feels like everyone is just moving on, like nothing happened! It just fucking hurts!"

Shade threw his arm around his shoulder. "Marcello, I am master here, I take care of many. I need to keep all of us protected. I did not blow it off. How in the hell do you blow off that raving redhead? I never saw anything like her. I doubt we ever will again. That's what made her special. I will always keep her in my heart, but I can't leave positions unfilled. There are jobs to be done here. Give Aislynn a chance. She is a good warrior too. She trained with Fiamma and you know Fiamma would be the first to champion her. Fiamma lives in the spirit realm, Marcello, and she is legend now. And if I know Fiamma, she won't let either one of our sorry asses alone. Her spirit will probably haunt us both."

Marcello smiled at that remark. He couldn't help it, and it was the truth. "She knew how to keep our asses' inline, that's for sure. I'm sorry for blowing up. But I didn't know where to go with all this inside me. I never lost someone I loved and cared about so much."

Shade gave Marcello a hug. "No need for apologies. It hurts, it's supposed to hurt. I wish I could tell you she will be the last, but there will be more you love and care about that you lose. It's our life. We won't ever forget her. She is forever in our hearts. Now come on, let's get back home."

The two of them returned back to the camp. Shade knew Marcello would be okay with time. And Marcello would learn what every warrior was forced to learn—how to keep the lost ones in his heart, and how to be a better warrior for knowing them.

146

Walking back into the house, Shade looked down at his muddy boots and the trail of mud he'd left behind him. "Damn!"

He unlaced the boots and kicked them off. Running up the stairs in his stocking feet, he remembered how much he hated this cold weather. Going into the bedroom, he started rummaging for a sweater, anything to keep him warm, when he heard Kate come into the room. He stopped digging through the drawer as he smiled at her. "Lorenzo asleep?"

She looked at him with amusement. "He is. Can I help you find something? Where are your boots?"

"Boots? Oh, downstairs. They were muddy, I was up on the mountain with Marcello, and now I am cold! Is there a sweater someplace in this armoire?" Throwing his hands up in frustration, he grumbled, "You know I can never find any damn thing!"

She smiled and slipped in front of him, pulling a sweater from the drawer. "Wear this one...the blue brings out your eyes. Is Marcello okay?"

"Ah *si*, sweater!" Kissing her quickly, he shrugged out of his jacket and stripped off the tee shirt, slipping the sweater over his head, pulling it down over his washboard abs. He pulled her into his arms and sighed. "Marcello will be fine. He is better than he was a few hours ago, that is for sure. He has a lot on his mind right now, mainly Fiamma."

Kate laid her head against his chest. "Fee. I can't believe she's gone. She was larger than life. She was the first female vamp...the only female vamp who reached out to me. She helped me so much when you left for Paris, whether you'd approve or not. But I know she was close to the warriors. Their pain must be even greater than mine, though it's hard to imagine."

He took her hand and led her downstairs to the living room where he made a blazing fire and pulled her to sit next to him on the couch. "Fiamma left him a letter. She wrote to him before the battle in case anything should happen. Maybe she sensed something, I don't know, it bothers me a bit. But she told Marcello of her feelings for him. Did Fiamma ever speak to you of Marcello?"

Kate sat up, looking into his eyes. "She wrote him a letter? No, she never spoke of him. She referred to all the warriors as her brothers. I'd often see her with Marcello, but no, she never mentioned anything to me about him. Did you read the letter?"

He shook his head. "No. She left it in her room. Aislynn found it when she was moving in. The letter said she'd always loved him. It rattled him bad. It opened up a lot of things he'd been holding in since her death."

Kate stroked his face. "Oh Fiamma! She never told him? Did he know? Does he love her? Lover, this breaks my heart."

Caressing her, he rubbed her back. "Shh, do not upset yourself, I know you love happy endings. You want everyone to be in love like us, but that does not happen easily with warriors. You need to learn that. They dedicate their life to their craft and their masters. But no, he did not know of her feelings for him, and he loved her as a sister, as a warrior. Granted, they spent a lot of time together. Marcello said he felt an attraction, but he knew, deep inside, she was not the one."

Kate laid her head on his shoulder, allowing him to caress her back. "Then she never knew real love. We spoke about love often. I know it was something she wanted in her life, but she was also proud to be a warrior. She was so proud when she was promoted in rank. I know the other females looked up to her, aspired to be like her. She gave up everything for us. How do we ever repay that? How do we deserve that?"

"I don't know, *mi amore*. We have her sword. It is a tradition to give the sword to her *familia*. But Fee had no *familia*; we were her *familia*. She loved being a warrior. It was her true heart. I knew in the first five minutes of meeting her. Her sword is locked in the weapons bunker for safekeeping. Maybe we should do something with it. What do you think?"

Kate sat up straight. "Lover, yes. Her sword should be on display in the camp somehow. The warriors will see it and remember her and honor her sacrifice. But she wasn't the only one who sacrificed. Luca said the others were buried in a shallow grave together, the sun turning them to ash before they were covered. He said the battle would be known in vampire history as the Battle of Bel Rosso. We need a stone there, something that honors all of them, a large boulder, with a plague. Can we do that?"

He hugged her to his chest as the pain washed over him for the loss of so many. "We will place her sword in a glass case inside the barracks, a place where she will always reign. As for the others, we will never forget those that made the ultimate sacrifice for us. We will mark the battlefield where they were the victors, and now lie in peace in the ground they fought to defend."

Kate stroked his face, her voice a soft whisper. "Let me take care of it. The others fought. Let me do this."

He stood and took her hand, leading her to the rug in front of the fire where he lay down with her. She curled on her side to look at him. "Take care of it, *mi amore*. They all loved you."

He kissed her gently, a soft adoring kiss that was meant to show her how grateful he was for all she did for him. "I need to talk to you about something. There is something I need to make up to you."

She looked at him quizzically. "What do you need to make up to me? I can think of nothing."

He wrapped a tendril of her crimson around his finger before reaching into his jeans pocket to withdraw the padlock he'd asked the artisans of the coven to make for him. The lock was shaped like a heart, like the original one she'd found for them. On the front of the heart was etched their names, and on the back, the simple words, '*Ti amo*.' Keeping his hand tightly closed around the lock, he extended his closed hand to her. "Kiss my hand and I will reveal it to you."

She took his fist in her hands, kissing his closed fist. When he opened his hand, he held a padlock, similar to the one they'd locked onto the bridge in Paris.

"It's beautiful, lover. Is there someplace you have in mind for this one?"

"*Si*, the same place except this time, it won't be removed. There is something that goes with it." He pulled the small charm from his pocket engraved with Lorenzo's name and birthdate. He slipped the charm on the lock and dangled it in front of her.

She held the lock in her hand, their son's name attached. "Fiamma told me she saw your image on the bridge. She said you crushed our lock."

He sat up, and knew he had to explain to her what he'd done in Paris in his rage. "I was torn so deep, *mi amore*. When I was in Paris, I ripped the lock from the bridge. I crushed it to dust in my hand. I did not know how to fix us. I am so sorry, forgive me, please. I want us to begin again. Will you come with me to Paris? Bring Lorenzo with us. Let me make this up to you."

She clutched the padlock to her heart as she rolled away from him, and faced the fire, feeling the heat against her skin. She remembered the pain they'd both felt and remained silent, letting the thoughts run through her head. Closing her eyes, she sighed heavily. "Why do we do this? I'm always afraid you'll be tempted by another and leave me for a female born immortal. You always fear your actions will send me away, make me stop loving you. We hurt each other with our doubt."

She sat up and turned to him. "Promise me, we're through with the doubt. When we place this lock on the bridge, we both leave the doubt behind. Can you do that?"

He sat next to her, laying his head on his knees. "Kate, I know I keep hurting you, and it is the last thing I want. I can't explain why I do this. I wish I could. I only know I can never love you enough. You have stolen me, all of me. Sometimes, I think you deserve so much more, that it was selfish of me to bring you into this life. But I would change nothing."

She leaned her head against his shoulder. "So, we'll go back to Paris, with Lorenzo this time, and place the lock on the bridge. This lock must stay, and we'll add a charm to it with each new child. But this lock is missing a charm."

He slid his hand in his jeans pocket and withdrew the second charm that bore Cory's name. "*Mi amore*, I was not sure how you would feel. He is my son, and you have accepted him with open arms, but I feel like it is one more thing I have forced on you."

Kate took the charm from his hand and slipped it on the lock. "Family, our family, our sons. *Per sempre*...remember?"

He took her hand, letting his fingers slide over the diamond he gave her, the ring his *madre* had worn. He whispered, "*Per sempre*."

Lifting her hand, he kissed her ring before pulling her into him. "No one can love me like you do, my walking sin."

147

Kate was busy packing. Shade said they had to visit Council again to establish his new territory and the expansion of his coven to include Virginia, and then they'd stop in Paris on the way home. They'd placed Fee's sword behind glass and had it mounted in the main meeting room in the barracks. All of the warriors at Bel Rosso had attended, paying homage to their fallen sister. Kate had worked with a landscaper to find a massive boulder and had it moved to the field where the battle had been fought. They had forged a steel plague engraved simply, 'Bel Rosso' and the date of the battle. They could not make any reference to the battle in the event some mortal should wander onto the property. Each warrior had walked past the boulder, in single file, and struck the stone with their sword. It seemed too little, but Kate didn't know what else she could do to honor them, other than to make sure the dynasty stayed strong, so they hadn't given up their lives for nothing.

She called out to Theresa, "Do you have Lorenzo's things packed? How about you? Are you ready?"

She responded, "Yes, my lady. We have everything."

Kate sent a message to Shade in the camp, letting him know they were ready to leave.

Shade was going over last minutes instructions with Marcello, Theo and Aislynn, and stopped in Cory's shop to give him a final goodbye, letting them all know he could return on a moment's notice if they needed him.

He kept looking at his watch, waiting for *bel*. Finally, he heard her call to him, letting him know they were ready. Teleporting to the house, he saw the luggage piled at the door as Dante loaded up the car. Kate and Theresa walked down the stairs and he stood staring. "Is there going to be room in the car for me? Seriously, *mi amore*, what is all this stuff?"

Kate looked at him with exasperation. "Clearly, you've never traveled with a baby before. And we need Theresa."

He tried to corral them out the door. "I don't want to argue, but when will you learn you can have anything you need without dragging it to and fro?" He watched as Theresa hid a giggle. "Come on then, we are losing precious time!"

Kate continued toward the door, placing Lorenzo in his arms while she put her coat on. "Then make yourself useful."

Gi carried the remaining bags to the car where Dante was loading the trunk. Theresa was biting her lip not to laugh at Shade juggling the baby.

She looked at him over her shoulder as Shade dragged Kate to the car, Kate muttering under her breath. "I don't know why he hates flying so much. We schedule it to coordinate with his death slumber."

He followed her out the door in all the chaos. "I heard that, Katherine! Don't think I did not, and so did our son!"

Lorenzo wiggled in his arms like a worm, his head on a swivel trying to keep track of his mother. Shade addressed his son as Lorenzo looked back at him like he understood every word. "Learn a lesson, *figlio*, females never go anywhere without taking everything they own."

They finally got everything loaded into the car. Shade climbed into the back, holding Lorenzo on his lap as he fussed from the snowsuit Kate insisted on strapping him into. He looked so uncomfortable. Shade laid him across his lap and began to unzip and unbutton, trying to release his son from this contraption when Lorenzo began to wail. "I feel you son, totally!"

Kate leaned across the seat, soothing Lorenzo. "Shh, my beautiful boy."

He looked up at her, kicking his legs and flailing his arms, glad to be free from the constraints of the snowsuit, when he laughed the sweetest laugh. He melted her heart and eased the tension from the rush to get packed and on the road.

"Look at him, lover. Is he not the most beautiful baby?"

Turning his head, he kissed her and winked. "He is the best of us both, *mi amore*. What more could this *padre* ask for, *si*?"

Picking up Lorenzo, he ruffled his curls and smiled when Lorenzo snuggled into his neck, nestling and calm. As they arrived at the hanger, they quickly got settled inside the plane and were soon airborne for an uneventful flight to Florence.

Kate slept next to him on the flight, with Lorenzo between them. The baby woke once to feed from her and quickly fell back asleep. Landing in Florence, Dante quickly transferred their luggage to the waiting car and drove them to Castello. Antonio greeted them at the door, sending the staff out to collect their luggage.

Kate and Shade were barely inside the door before they were surrounded by the staff, all trying to get a look at the baby. Lorenzo was delighted with the attention, as each housekeeper took him briefly, cooing over him, before another one snatched him away. Lorenzo laughed, grabbing at the white caps they wore on their heads.

Kate could sense Shade's eagerness to get moving, so she apologized when she took Lorenzo away. "I'm so sorry, but we must get him ready for Council. I promise to turn him over to you when we return."

Kate turned him over to Theresa to get him changed as she changed into a dress, touched up her make-up, and brushed out her hair. "Okay, lover. Council it is."

Shade stood ready, having taken little time to prepare. He wondered if every time he came to Castello there'd be this overwhelming response from the staff to see his son. But it made him happy to know they had an heir, a boy they'd all watch grow into a strong male leader, who'd grow into his role of master.

"*Mi amore*, I didn't think about how much longer it would take to get through the staff with Lorenzo. They all want to hold him. For them, it is an honor to work here and be a part of the prince's life. Come, let us get to Council, *si*"

"I think your son rather enjoys the attention. I'm glad he's not shy around people." She looked at Lorenzo. "Do you like the attention?"

Lorenzo was blowing spit bubbles and laughed. Kate shook her head. "You are your father's son."

She clung to Shade as they teleported to Council, Shade holding her tight, as Kate held Lorenzo.

As they arrived at Council, they were led outside the meeting chamber to wait. Shade paced as he got some seriously intense scowls with Lorenzo in his arms. They better get used to it. His children would always attend Council. He wanted them to all grow up understanding their culture, but also understanding their own power.

They didn't wait long before they were bid to enter. Holding Lorenzo in his arms, the baby was wide awake and aware of his surroundings. Shade held Kate's hand as they made their way to their seats, the announcement of their arrival loud and clear within the chamber.

"The King and Queen Medici, with Prince Lorenzo."

Lorenzo realized his voice echoed in the large hall and started shouting out a loud 'BAH' sound, then laughing. The Council didn't look amused and Kate was trying hard to suppress her giggles. She took the baby, shushing him, but Lorenzo continued to shout 'BAH', followed by his giggles. Kate looked at Shade as she rocked him back and forth in her arms. She shrugged and whispered, "Better than crying, I guess."

Shade almost laughed along with Lorenzo, his giggles contagious. But decorum won over and he nodded to Council, hoping they'd just continue.

Malachi stood. "Medici, you honor us with a visit from the Prince. It is good to see...and hear...that he is doing so well. We have all heard by now of the Battle of Bel Rosso. On behalf of Council, I extend our deepest sympathies on the loss of so many of your coven. We are all now well aware of your queen's power as well. If there was any question about how she could use her gift to help secure the future of Medici, I think it has been answered. Ivor has recorded this incident as well, so we might establish for future generations, the power of the gift of animalism. It is possible one of your children could inherit this gift."

Shade nodded to him. "Thank you, Malachi. We are, as always, honored to be here. I do hope one of my *bambinos* inherits Kate's gift. It saved many of my warriors from their demise. But I am now Master of Virginia. Maximus surrendered the field of battle. He was not killed and his remaining warriors fled with him. I have met with his Virginia Coven, where some have chosen to follow Max and have left the territory. The remainder have pledged their honor and fealty to Medici. I have provided for your benefit the listing of the coven members who have pledged, so they may be recorded as my coven."

Jasperion stood in his orange robe. "Given that we have witnesses that have attested to Maximus's retreat from the battlefield, in effect, surrendering his position as master of that coven, I will transfer the ownership of that coven, the land, and any properties on that land, to the King and Queen Medici. Virginia will be transferred in its totality. However, Maryland and Delaware still remain under the control of Maximus."

He passed the document that Shade had presented to them containing the names of the vampires who'd chosen to pledge to Medici, down to Agathian. Agathian pushed back the hood of the blue robe and nodded to the King.

"We shall transfer the records of these new members of the coven in the census, along with the names of those that perished. It was a high price to pay. There were many lives sacrificed, from both your coven and Max's, but we do understand it could have been much worse had the queen not used her gift."

Shade nodded and slid his hand across the table to hold Kate's hand. "Both of us were determined to maintain our home. Maximus refused to accept Council's judgment, and he dealt the Medici a low blow. We stand before you as victors in that struggle. My mate has now, without doubt, proven she is well deserving of her role as queen of my coven. Her gift saved many lives in the battle, including my own. We work as a team. It makes us powerful and battle strong. We lead a large coven and it takes both of us to rule. My coven now understands her worth, her caring, and her ability to lead without reproach."

Malachi nodded. "If there was ever a question in anyone's mind about your queen's ability to rule, I think that has been settled once and for all. The word of the battle traveled quickly, as did the tales of the league of animals that responded to your queen's command."

As he spoke, Lorenzo picked up a wooden gavel that sat on the table before them and immediately put it in his mouth. Kate pushed the gavel away from his mouth, only to have Lorenzo slam the gavel down hard on the table, the sound echoing in the great hall.

Malachi suppressed a smile. "Well then. It seems the Prince has called this meeting to a close. If there is no further business, Medici?"

Shade put his hand over his mouth, trying not to laugh out loud, but he saw that Council had accepted his victory, his queen, and his son. "The Prince has spoken. We are done and have no further business."

Shade and Kate stood to leave, and Lorenzo bellowed once again, reaching for his father. Shade took him in his arms. "You have done well, little warrior, you have the Council in the palm of your hand already."

148

Kate woke when she heard Lorenzo crying. Shade was still deep in his death slumber when she slid from their bed and stepped into her slippers. The marble floors of Castello were unbearably cold in the winter. She grabbed her robe from the foot of their bed and slipped it over her shoulders as she walked to the room Theresa shared with Lorenzo. Theresa was already standing beside his crib when she entered.

Kate stood next to her at the crib, looking at Lorenzo as he continued to fuss. Theresa told her he'd just fed, so she wasn't sure why was he crying. Kate lifted the baby and placed him over her shoulder, swaying back and forth as she shushed him. "Lay back down, Theresa. I've got this."

Kate left the nursery, bouncing Lorenzo lightly in her arms. "What has you so stirred up, my beautiful boy? Hmmm?"

He quieted instantly at the sound of her voice and she chuckled. "You're so spoiled. What am I going to do with you?"

She walked with him through the long halls of the castle, letting him calm himself. She found herself in the Hall of Ancestors, talking to Lorenzo in a soft voice, pointing out the bust of the Medici's that came before them, both mortal and immortal, teaching him their long history. She stood in front of the massive oil painting of Shade, at age ten, standing with his mother and father. Kate turned Lorenzo so he could see the portrait.

"Look at this, Lorenzo. That's your father when he was just a boy, starting in the warrior camps. And that rather imposing looking gentleman is your grandfather. And that beautiful woman beside him is your grandmother. They would both be so proud of you. Goodness, you'd be even more spoiled than you are right now. Can you even imagine that?"

Portia watched her new daughter with her grandson, Lorenzo. How beautiful he was, his curls and eyes so much like Shade's. She remembered long ago, walking with Shade in these same halls, comforting him. She stayed in the shadows, watching Kate and how she spoke to him, teaching him the Medici history and she felt an overwhelming sense of pride. She knew Kate would be a great mother. There was never any doubt in her mind.

"He is a most handsome grandson, and I am already proud of both of you. My fingers itch to touch him, hold him in my arms."

Kate startled at the sound of Portia's voice, and turned to find her mother-in-law standing behind her. "Can you hold him? I never know if you are real?"

"I am sorry, daughter, I never meant to scare you, but *si*, I can most certainly hold him. Will you grant me this privilege?"

Kate looked at Lorenzo who could clearly see his grandmother. He was staring at her intently and was mesmerized by her voice. Kate smiled at her. "There's nothing I'd like more. Please, hold your grandson." She shifted Lorenzo into Portia's arms, and listened as Lorenzo cooed, delighted with the attention of one more admirer.

Portia took Lorenzo into her arms, cuddling him in the crook of her arm, and stared into his sapphire eyes. "He is so handsome, and he will be strong, like his father and grandfather. I knew you would give him a son, and he is perfect. He will be a great warrior *figlia*, maybe even greater than my own Shade. He looks so much like him." She slid a finger across his cheek and watched as the infant's eyes closed and then fluttered open. She looked at Kate. "Do you know his gifts yet?"

Kate shook her head. "No. Shade is hoping he's a day-walker. He wakes a lot during the day, like now, but Theresa said that's normal for all babies at this age and doesn't mean he'll be a day-walker."

"She is correct, but he may show you signs in a few years. Shade began having dreams, but he didn't know what to do with his gift. If you see signs, you must enhance them, never hold them back. The sooner they learn to master their gift the better. Speaking of which, I owe you much gratitude. I know of the battle, how you brought forth the animals to save Shade."

"*Madre*, you don't need to thank me. I'll always do whatever is in my power to protect what is mine...ours. I didn't realize the power of that gift. But you can be sure our children, your grandchildren, will all have the protection of my warriors. I can assure you, Aegis and the others already guard Lorenzo. Luca said after this last battle, it will take a lot for another master to attack. They all know it's a battle they can't win."

Portia smiled at Kate. Lorenzo flailed in her arms and she gently raised him to her shoulder, rubbing his back. She inhaled deeply, closing her eyes. "He smells of a rose musk; a little from you, a little from Shade, as it should be. He is Medici, for sure. As are you, my daughter. I have been through many battles, it is never easy. But you have a great advantage over me. Females in my time were housed inside, only to feel everything through our mates. I feared greatly at times. Christofano was such a great warrior. My pride in him got me through. In the end, he died trying to save me, but I would have it no other way. I could not have gone on without him. I wanted to die with him. To this day...I am sorry, I seem to be rattling on and on."

Kate dearly loved this woman. With every encounter, she saw why Shade held her so close to his heart. She wished Portia and Christofano could both be a part of raising Lorenzo. Kate sighed. "I'm afraid Christofano would find me quite brazen. I'd be much too outspoken for him. I can hear him now, giving Shade advice on how to tame his woman."

Portia laughed out loud and bumped shoulders with her. "Oh, he will do no such thing! Shade does not like you tame, he likes you just as you are...beautiful in heart and spirit, but as stubborn and headstrong as he is. You have a way of bringing him home, letting him rest from his duties. I know when he is with you, he forgets his burdens. A warrior needs a place to feel at peace. But I love that you have your own warriors. Jealous, as well. The things I could have accomplished."

Portia laughed and Lorenzo began to kick and make noises. "He is not one to stay still for long, is he? You are so much like your father if you but knew! Do not fret. Your mother is right here."

Portia handed Lorenzo back to Kate as she stared up at the portrait, looking at her son as a child. Her heart was both sad and yet overjoyed. "He has grown into a man of good heart and soul. He loves you. He loves his life. That is all I ever wanted for him."

Kate took the baby and turned to look at the portrait on the wall with the picture of young Shade. She saw so much of Lorenzo in his face. "*Madre*, you have no idea how much I love him. How much I love our life. There's no life for me now without him."

She turned to look back at her mother-in-law but found the hall empty, her spirit gone as quickly as it had come. Kate sighed and kissed the top of Lorenzo's head. "My beautiful boy, nothing will ever harm you. I promise you that."

About the Author

Emily Bex is an avid life-long reader, and a first time writer of the epic six book Medici Warrior Series. As she says, "Why start small?" She worked for over twenty years in marketing, developing ad campaigns, catalogs, product launches and promotional literature. She figured if she could write creatively about products, then surely she could write something about these characters that were rattling around inside her brain. She currently lives in Virginia, but has used her extensive love of travel, both foreign and domestic, to create the backdrop for her characters to play out their story.

View the Medici Warrior Series Here:

https://www.emilybex.com/books/

Make sure to stalk me!

Instagram:
https://bit.ly/3dAaO5k

Facebook:
http://bit.ly/3k5GHUC

Goodreads:
http://bit.ly/3ukYcVU

Twitter:
https://bit.ly/3s6m3GG

Bookbub:
http://bit.ly/2ZBJ9ZM

Website:
https://www.emilybex.com/

m

More From Foundations

www.FoundationsBooks.net

The Alyx Rayer Series: Book One, Vengeance Marked

by S.J. Pierce

Her Marked was more than just precious to her, he was precious in ways the world could only fathom. If she failed, she failed everyone.Alyx Rayer's existence in Atlanta, the eternally bustling capital of Georgia, is one of routine and blending in among the worker bees. But her 'normal' life is a facade for a higher calling. She's a three-hundred-year-old soul, sent from the darkness to capture her Marked when summoned by her superiors. Until then, she was to keep her distance. Except... something about him makes it hard to stay away.

While already trapped between honor and desire, a man in a black suit continually shows up when she least expects it, his presence evoking a strange response from the scar she was branded with at birth. Because her superiors never told her what this would mean, or much of anything except what to do when they summon, she can only conclude to try and keep her sanity-and her life-from completely shattering to pieces.This engaging first book of the series is a Paranormal Romance novel interlaced with twists, turns and thrilling suspense that is sure to satisfy readers of any genre.

May not be suitable for YA.

The Guardian League: Book One, Jasper

by TK Lawyer

Lauren was an assignment. He didn't expect to fall in love.

From her birth, Apollo watched Lauren mature, witnessing all her milestones with a strong sense of pride. Advising, protecting and whispering loving words to her, Lauren is strong and perfect. Unfortunately, she doesn't want to live.

A drastic decision one day sets Lauren face to face with her own Guardian Angel- a being she never knew existed. However, he won't leave her alone. He is relentless, encouraging her to better her life when he doesn't understand what it takes to survive on Earth. Despite this "flaw," she is drawn to him in ways she can't explain and Apollo soon becomes as necessary as the air she breathes. He asks for only one thing- to be his, forever.

Will she allow Apollo to love and care for her when many have failed?

Foundations Book Publishing
Copyright 2016 © Foundations Book Publications Licensing
Brandon, Mississippi 39047

10-9-8-7-6-5-4-3-2-1

The Medici Queen: Book Three of the Medici Warrior Series
Emily Bex

Made in the USA
Coppell, TX
04 August 2021

59944488R00402